PRAISE FOR

Floating Dragon

"Here is a novel guaranteed to double the national nightmare quotient, so watch out!"   —*Cosmopolitan*

"Buy it today. Anything by Straub is worth several thousand John Sauls and a million V. C. Andrewses."
                              —*The Philadelphia Inquirer*

"A deliciously imaginative story of hauntings and monsters."
                              —*San Francisco Chronicle*

"A book that positively bubbles with invention, jammed with characters, color, events, hackle-raising twists of fate, horrific monsters, terrifying nightmares, and a reality that shimmers and shifts as much as the noxious steam from a witch's cauldron."   —*Book World*

Berkley Books by Peter Straub

GHOST STORY
FLOATING DRAGON
SHADOWLAND

Floating Dragon

PETER STRAUB

BERKLEY
New York

BERKLEY

An imprint of Penguin Random House LLC
penguinrandomhouse.com

ISBN: 9780593335000

G. P. Putnam's Sons hardcover edition / February 1983
Berkley mass-market edition / March 1984
Berkley trade paperback edition / October 2021

Printed in the United States of America
1st Printing

FOR
EMMA SYDNEY VALLI STRAUB

CONTENTS

INTRODUCTION

After ten years in Dublin and London, my wife and I moved back to the United States with our our two-year-old son in the summer of 1979. We were so out of touch with American realities that to us Cape Cod, Long Island, and Connecticut's Fairfield County seemed within an hour or two drive of each other and more or less identical. That is, they all sounded like entertaining places to live. (We had no idea that New York City, specifically Manhattan, would be perfect for us, being the most reliably entertaining place in America.) Victor Temkin, the lively soul then president of Berkley Books, recommended Westport, Connecticut, for the excellence of its school system and its proximity to New York. So we arranged a long-distance rental, arrived in New York to spend a week at the dire, long-vanished Summit Hotel, known to us as The Abyss, then mushed north into Fairfield County, which, not very coincidentally, was the title of the book I intended to write after finishing my work-in-progress, *Shadowland*. Within a month, our real-estate agent, whom I will call Barbara Baxter, drove us to a terrific old house near Burying Hill Beach on Westport's Gold Coast, and by the end of the summer we had moved in, along with an army of carpenters headed by a twinkling, white-bearded giant named Ben Rohr.

While sawdust and the sound of hammering filled the air, I charged along through *Shadowland*, which I finished in the immense, beautiful new office Ben Rohr had created for me from a nest of maids' rooms and unfinished space on the third floor. Ah, what a place—just coming up off the narrow staircase and turning into the room made me want to get to work. The question was, what was *Fairfield County* going to be about?

Clearly, the book at least in part would be about the experience of moving *to* Fairfield County, a subject that occupied me daily, whether I liked it or not. Richard and Laura Allbee recapitulate most of the upsets and discoveries my wife and I encountered during the first year of our reentry into the country we had left a decade earlier. No one ever expects to get culture shock from their own country, but stay away long enough and you can't avoid it—America refuses to stand still. As we were, the Allbees are as amazed as rubes by the plenitude and abundance of goods in the local supermarket. As we did, they inwardly recoil from the astonishingly intimate confessions uttered by total strangers. (In front of the meat department in Waldbaum's stupendous grocery, a woman turned to me and said, "My first four abortions were absolute *murder*." "Ah," I said, backpedaling.) In England, everybody smoked and drank, what fun, but in Westport everybody jogged, and the only person choosing a pack from the drugstore's staggering cigarette cornucopia was me. People *assumed* intimacy; they actually hid behind a kind of *sincerity*, of all possible stances; they didn't know that conversation was supposed to be entertainment, a game, a giddy free-for-all, instead of deadly anecdotes punctuated with opinions about sports and politics, plus financial advice. All of this went into the book, as did some of the locals: Barbara Baxter became cheerful Ronnie Riggley, her cop boyfriend Bobo Farnsworth, Ben Rohr passed virtually unchanged into Ben Roehm, and the social columnist in the *Westport News* turned into the *Hampstead Gazette*'s Sarah Spry.

At first, I was vaguely planning to do something Scott Fitzgerald-ish, but the book snapped into clearer focus when the evening news reported that five workmen found mysteriously dead in a Stamford factory had been declared victims of carbon monoxide poisoning. A colorless, odorless gas had seeped into their chamber and before they had any idea of being in peril, killed them all with the efficiency of a machine gun. Suppose the gas were not carbon monoxide but something worse, something more complex and sinister; suppose it traveled like a thinking cloud northward above I-95 the twenty miles from Stamford to Westport and there settled to Earth, creating a bizarre, hallucinatory, generally corpse-strewn disorder? That would make half of the kind of book I wanted to write. The other half came from thinking about why such a colorful tragedy might descend upon charming little Westport/Hampstead.

Without ever admitting it to myself, I knew that this book

would be at least a temporary farewell to the supernatural material that had been my daily fare since I first began to butter my own bread by driving a succession of Staedtler Mars-Lumograph 100 B and Blackwing 602 pencils across hundreds of sheets of paper. Undead things in bandages, ancient curses, paranormal powers, the inanimate alarmingly animated, spontaneous combustion, visionary apprehensions, human beings uniting into ad hoc families to combat hideous literal evils, ghosts, ravening beasts, beckoning mirrors, vampiric entities, external horrors, that whole gaudy blaring blinding circus of metaphor made real—at a level just below consciousness, I had decided to take my leave of all this dear, goofy imagery by wrapping it all together in one gigantic package and then . . . blowing it up! Anything like restraint or good taste was verboten, the aesthetic was grounded in a single principle, that of excess.

As a narrative rooted in the principle of excess, *Floating Dragon* proceeds through a series of sustained, escalating set pieces toward a climactic moment of outright lunacy. Our band of illuminated heroes bursts into "Bye, Bye Blackbird"; a shotgun mutates into a glowing, outrageously phallic sword; a literal dragon explodes into a mountain of fire; an entire town more or less detonates. It is completely shameless. However, it is not without a measure of deliberate and conscious craft.

During the late seventies, I discovered the work of the English novelist Paul Scott, whose *Raj Quartet* seemed to me a master class in how to organize a great mass of complex material in a way that actually represented its complexity. Scott broke his material into a shifting continuum of third person accounts, quoted documents, and flashbacks in the form of stories told by the characters. The ongoing narrative was in constant motion, refracted through many different points of view. For sheer novelistic technique, I had never seen anything like it, and I went through the *Quartet*'s more than two thousand pages in a trance of awed delight. My whizbang, *Floating Dragon*, could never attain or even aspire to Scott's moral seriousness, but I could at least do my best to honor his method, which seemed the most promising way to stretch my canvas over dozens of different characters each intent on his or her own ends, and four or five separate eras in Hampstead's history.

I wrote the first third of the novel in my usual old way, by hand, in pencil, then typing up what I had written. At that point

Stephen King and I signed the contract for our first collaboration, *The Talisman*, and agreed to buy computers before we began the work. To accustom myself to a keyboard, I bought an IBM Selectric typewriter, which hummed and buzzed reassuringly through the middle section of *Floating Dragon*. Before beginning the final third, I bought an IBM Displaywriter, one of the first word processors—it was so expensive that for a couple of days two staff people from IBM headquarters in Stamford showed up to teach me how to use it. (King bought a machine he liked to call his "big Wang.") I wrote the final section in pencil across something like three hundred pages of lined journal, then typed the results up onto my brand-new monitor and printed them out. At the time, I thought that the epilogue was one of the best things I'd ever written, and I still do. It's full of the lovely, delicious agony of leave-taking.

I also thought that dedicated horror readers would love my exuberant valentine to their favorite genre, for it represented a kind of love letter to them. Instead, they scorned the book: I had forgotten that true believers dislike and distrust anyone who appears to be having fun with the object of their faith. Ordinary readers, on the other hand, practically vacuumed the book off the shelves, which was extremely reassuring.

—Peter Straub

Floating Dragon

Now time and the land
are identical,

Linked forever.
—John Ashbery, *Haunted Landscape*

The devil is a dumb spirit. All the
devil knows is what you tell him with
your own big fat mouth.
—Frederick K. Price

The Death of
Stony Friedgood

1

1962–1963

For Stony Baxter Friedgood, her infrequent adulteries were adventures—picking up a man who thought he was picking her up gave her life a sense of drama missing since she had been twenty and a student at Scripps-Claremont. Not only adventures, they were the salvation of her marriage. In college she had juggled four boyfriends, and only one of them, a mathematics graduate student named Leo Friedgood, had known of the existence of the others. Leo had seemed amused by her secretiveness, as he was amused by her private school nickname. Only after several months did Stony realize the extent to which amusement masked arousal.

She married him just after graduation—no graduate school for Stony, and no more for Leo, who shaved his beard and bought a suit and took a job with Telpro Corporation, which had an office in Santa Monica.

2

1969

Tabby Smithfield grew to the age of five in an enormous stone house in Hampstead, Connecticut, with four acres of well-tended ground and a burglar alarm on the front gates. The neighborhood, consisting of sixteen houses along Long Island Sound, was impressive enough to attract its own tourists; perhaps six cars a day trolled down Mount Avenue, the drivers and passengers leaning to glimpse the mansions behind the gates. Locally, Mount Avenue was "The Golden Mile," though it was twice longer than that; it was the original road between Hillhaven, the Victorian suburb of Patchin, and Hampstead. Mount Avenue, the site of the original farm settlements of Hampstead and Hillhaven, had once been the principal coaching road north to New Haven, but its hectic days were long past. Manufacturers with plants in Bridgeport or Woodville, a doctor, and the head of Patchin County's biggest legal practice lived in the impressive houses, along with others like them, older people who wished no excitement in their private lives. Tourists rubbernecking along the Golden Mile rarely saw them—there might be a visiting movie star taking the sea-laden air along the coastal road or a college president pausing for breath before he made his pitch for funds, but the owners of the houses were invisible.

Outside the gray stone house, however, those taking a fast peek through the opened gates in 1969 might have seen a tall dark-haired man in tennis whites playing with a small boy. Perhaps a uniformed nanny would have been hovering on the steps before the front door, her posture inexplicably tense. And perhaps the boy's posture too would have seemed awkward, inhabited by the same tension, as if little Tabby Smithfield were half-aware that he was not supposed to be playing with his father. They make an oddly static and incomplete scene, father and son and nanny. They are badly composed: one figure is missing.

3

1964

Stony Friedgood's first affair after her marriage was in 1964, with the husband of a friend, a neighbor in their neat row of tract houses: he was unlike Leo, being jovial and blond and easygoing, a very junior banker, and Leo invariably spoke of him with contempt. This affair endured only two months.

Stony's delicate face, which was sharp-featured and framed in shining brown hair, became familiar in galleries and art museums, in certain bars at certain times. Considered from a utilitarian point of view, one neither Stony's nor Leo's parents could have understood, the Friedgoods had a successful marriage. By the time Leo was promoted twice and transferred to Telpro's New York offices, their income had doubled and Stony weighed only a pound more than when she was a student at Scripps. She left behind her yoga classes, a half-completed gourmet-cooking course, four unused tickets to a concert series, the undigested and already vague memories of six or seven men. Leo left nothing at all behind—the company paid to ship east his sailboat and the eight cases he called his "cellar."

4
_____

1968

Monty Smithfield, his grandfather, was the great figure in Tabby's early childhood. It was Monty who kissed him first when he returned from nursery school, and Monty and his mother took him to his first haircut. Birthdays and Christmases Monty gave him stupefying presents, vast train sets and every possible sort of preschool vehicle from walkers to Big Wheels, even a dwarf pony stabled at a riding school. This was presented with much fanfare at Tabby's third birthday. August, 1968. Monty had provided a party for twenty children, a band playing Beatle songs and tunes from Disney movies, an ice sculpture of a brontosaurus—Tabby loved dinosaurs then, and only evolution kept Monty Smithfield from buying his grandson a baby monster. "Come on, Clark," called the jubilant old man as the gardener led out the shaggy little pony. "Mount your son on this great beast." But Clark Smithfield had gone inside to his bedroom and was at that moment whacking a tennis ball against the elaborate headboard with a well-worn Spaulding racket, trying to chip the paint off one of the wooden curlicues.

Like any child, Tabby had no idea of what his father did for a living, no idea that there was a living to be earned. Clark Smithfield was at home four or five days every week, playing his rock records in the living room of their wing of the big house, going out to tennis matches whenever he could. If at the age of three or four Tabby had been asked what his father did, he would have answered that he played games. Clark never took him to the company of which he was a nominal vice-president; his grandfather did, and showed him off to the secretaries, announcing that here was the future chairman of the board of Smithfield Systems, Inc. Before he showed Tabby the computer room, the old man opened a door and said, "For the record, this is your father's office." It was a small dusty room containing an almost bare desk and many photographs of Tabby's father winning college tennis tournaments; also a Richard Nixon dart board, as dusty as everything else. "Does my daddy work here?" Tabby asked with sweet innocence, and one of the secretaries snickered. "He *does*," Tabby insisted valiantly. "He *does* work here. Look! He plays tennis here!" A spasm of distaste passed over Monty Smithfield's tidy features, and the old man did not smile for the remainder of the tour.

Whenever his father and grandfather were in the same room—at the family dinners Clark could not avoid, at any occasion when Monty came into his son's living quarters—an almost visible atmosphere of dislike frosted the air. At these times Tabby saw his father shrink to a child only slightly older than himself. "Why don't you like Grandpa?" he asked his father once, when Clark was reading him a bedtime story. "Oh, it's too complicated for you," Clark sighed.

At times, more frequently as he grew closer to five, Tabby heard them fighting.

Clark and his father argued about the length of Clark's hair, about Clark's aspirations as a tennis player (which his father scorned), about Clark's attitude. Clark and Monty Smithfield normally kept a cool distance from each other, but when Monty decided to harangue his son, they shouted—in the dining room, in both living rooms, in the hallway, on the lawn. These arguments always ended with Clark storming away from his father.

"What are you going to do?" Monty called out to him after a wrangle Tabby witnessed. "Leave home? You can't *afford* to—you couldn't *get* another job."

Tabby's face went white—he didn't understand the words, but he heard the scorn in them. That day he did not speak until dinnertime.

Clark's wife and mother were the glue that held the two families in their uneasy harmony: Monty genuinely liked Jean, Tabby's mother, and Jean and her mother-in-law kept Clark in his job. Maybe if Clark Smithfield had been either a twenty-percent-better tennis player than he was, or a twenty-percent-worse one, the misery in the old house on Mount Avenue would have dissipated. Or if he had been less intransigent, his father less adamant. But Jean and her mother-in-law, thinking that the passage of time would reconcile Clark to his job and Monty to his son, kept the families together. And so they stayed, in their sometimes almost comfortable antagonism. Until the first truly terrible thing that happened to Tabby and his family.

5

1975

The Friedgoods, who appeared to be a model couple, moved to a builder's colonial in Hampstead in 1975, when Tabby Smithfield was ten years old and living with his father and stepmother in South Florida. As Leo Friedgood was on his way upward into the world he coveted, Clark Smithfield appeared to be running out his meager luck: he had a job as a bartender, quit that to take a job as salesman for Hollinsworth Vitreous, was fired from that when he got drunk on the yacht belonging to the president of the company and vomited on Robert Hollinsworth's carpet-weave slippers, did another stint tending bar, and took a job as a security guard. He worked nights and nipped from a bottle whenever his round took him back to the security station. Like his first wife, his mother was also dead—Agnes Smithfield had suffered a cerebral hemorrhage one warm May morning as she discussed the installation of a rock garden with the groundsman and her life had fled before her body struck the ground. Monty Smithfield had sold his big house on Mount Avenue and moved with the housekeeper and cook into a house called "Four Hearths" on Hermitage Road, five minutes inland. His end of Hermitage Road was only two wooded hilly blocks from the place the Friedgoods bought.

Leo was now a division vice-president for Telpro, making nearly fifty thousand dollars a year; he bought his suits at Tripler, grew a thick aggressive mustache and let his hair get long enough to be bushy. Always fleshy, he had put on twenty extra pounds despite a daily mile-long jog, and now— arrogant eyes, dark mustache and unrestrained hair—he had the faintly lawless, buccaneerlike appearance of many a corporate executive who sees himself as a predator in a jungle full of predators.

In 1975, the first year on Cannon Road in Hampstead, Stony joined New Neighbors, High Minds—a book discussion group—the League of Women Voters and a cooking class, the YMCA, and the library. She would have looked for a job, but Leo did not want her to work. She would have tried to get pregnant, but Leo, whose own childhood was an epic of maternal bullying, became irrational when she tried to discuss it. In the *Hampstead Gazette* she read an ad for a yoga class and quit the New Neighbors. Soon after, she left High Minds and the League too.

The *Hampstead Gazette* came twice weekly. The little tabloid was Stony's chief source of information about her new town. From it she learned of the Women's Art League, and joined that, thinking she would meet painters—one of the boys in California had been a painter. And because she wanted to, of course she did. Pat Dobbin was celebrated locally, neither especially good nor bad; he lived alone in a small house in the woods; he did illustrations—these much better than his paintings—to make a living. During one of Leo's business trips, she attended an Art League dinner with the painter: she was aware that the midge-sized red-haired woman carrying a notebook was Sarah Spry, author of the weekly social column "What Sarah Saw" in the *Gazette*, but was not prepared to see this item in the next week's column:

> *Sarah Saw:* Thistown's brilliant painter and illustrator PAT DOBBIN (can't say enough about the boy! Caught his stunning new abstract seascapes at PALMER GALLERY yet?) at the Women's Art League bash parading in elegant black tie and showing off a lovely mystery woman. Who's the unknown beauty, Pat? Fess up and tell Sarah.

When Leo returned from his trip, he read this paragraph and asked, "Did you enjoy the Art League thing Friday night? Too bad I couldn't have gone with you." His eyes were bright and ironic.

6

November 1970

Unlike her husband, Jean Smithfield was a careful driver. When she and Clark left their son with his grandparents for an evening, she always insisted on driving home if Clark went over his normal limit of two drinks before dinner and a couple of glasses of wine while they ate. On nights when Clark complained more than usually about his father or reminisced through ancient tennis matches, she drove home even if it meant listening to Clark railing about her relationship with his father. He would say, "You actually *like* that old buzzard! Do you know what that does to me? Christ, sometimes I think he turns you on—all those pinstripe suits get to you, don't they? You dig white hair. You don't have any more loyalty to me than to let the old man's phony charm get to you." If Clark were really bad, he'd pass out before they pulled through the gates. "He'll never get Tabby," he would mutter. "He'll never forget I existed and make Tabby into his son. One thing he'll never do." Jean did her best to ignore this ranting.

They usually ate at a French restaurant up toward Patchin on the Post Road. One night in late November in 1970, Jean took a dollar from her bag as they went outside and stationed herself where the valet could see her. "I can drive," Clark grumped. "Not tonight," she said, and gave the bill to the boy when he got out of their car. "We ought to have a goddamned Mercedes," Clark said as he let himself into the passenger seat. "All it takes is money," she informed him.

Jean pulled out across the oncoming lane and pointed the car toward Pigeon Lane, the next traffic light.

"He's at it again," Clark muttered. "He wants to send Tabby to the Academy—public school isn't good enough for his grandson."

"You went to the Academy," Jean said.

"Because my father could *afford* it!" Clark screamed. "Don't you get the point, dammit? I'm Tabby's father, dammit, and . . ."

Jean was looking at him and she saw his face go slack as the sentence died away. Clark no longer looked angry or drunk. He looked worried.

She snapped her head forward and saw a station wagon sliding across the dividing line, coming toward them. *Ice,* she thought, *a patch of . . .*

"Move it!" Clark shouted. And Jean twisted the wheel to the right. Another car which had pulled out of the restaurant just behind them struck her left-rear bumper so hard that Jean's hands flew off the steering wheel.

The station wagon, which had been going nearly fifty miles an hour before it struck the slick of ice, slammed straight into her door. Jean Smithfield tried to say "Tabby" before she died, but the door had crushed her chest and she did not have time.

In the mansion on Mount Avenue, her son woke up screaming.

The nineteen-year-old driver of the station wagon fell out of his car and tried to crawl away across the frozen road. He was bleeding from his scalp. Clark Smithfield, completely unharmed, took one look at his wife and threw up in his lap. Then he got out of the car and fell to his knees. Clark saw the boy who had killed his wife and yelled at him to stop. He struggled to his feet. The boy sat up twenty feet from his ruined car and was covered with snow and black mush that had been snow. Blood dripped from his nose and chin. Clark instantly recognized a fellow drunk. *"Animal!"* he screamed.

Tabby was rushing around his bedroom still yelling, feeling blindly for the light switch. He knew where nothing was; he was in an inside-out world. He caromed into his bed, slipped on a rag rug, and his screams went up an octave. Within seconds his grandfather and his nanny were at the door.

It took the Hampstead police ten minutes to reach the tangle of cars on the Post Road.

7

May 17, 1980

On May 17, 1980, the dragon came to Patchin County—no, did not come, for it had been there all along, but decided to show itself. Richard and Laura Allbee, after twelve years in London, had just arrived at their rented house on Fairytale Lane in Hampstead that noon: they were tired and confused, disoriented after two days in New York, more disoriented by suddenly finding themselves in the situation they had been projecting themselves into for months. Clark Smithfield had moved his wife and son into "Four Hearths," the old colonial on Hermitage Road, only two weeks earlier, and was already practicing the deception that would ruin his son's faith in him. A small, pretty woman named Patsy McCloud spent most of the day reading *War and Remembrance*. And what was Graham Williams, the mortal remains of a writer once notorious, doing? What he did every day in April and May of 1980. He had risen from an odoriferous bed at seven, put clothes on over his pajamas, splashed water in the direction of his face, and sat at his desk and put his head in his hands. When he heard the mailman's truck outside, he ignored it. Chances were that his mailbox had been cherry-bombed anyhow. After thirty minutes of silent prayer, ha ha, he wrote a sentence. Fifteen minutes later, he decided that it was banal and erased it. That was how Graham Williams customarily spent his waking hours.

The Allbees were pretending to be happier than they felt, old Williams was pretending to himself that his book could still catch fire, Patsy McCloud pretended that any minute she was going to get up and do something, Clark Smithfield's pretense was particularly elaborate. Leo Friedgood's deception was simpler than all of these, for he was not in New York at all, but twenty minutes down I-95 from Hampstead, at a Telpro plant in a small city called Woodville. And his wife had just decided to have another adventure.

Stony found a parking place in the station lot, went into a lively bar called Franco's, sat at a table near the bar and opened a book. It took less than fifteen minutes for a man to say, "Do you mind?" and sit down beside her. He was a man she knew, but even though this man was respected in Hampstead, none of the other men in the bar would have met him. His profession kept him from male company. Handsome in a weathered way, professionally discreet, this man was perfect for Stony. Very soon they left the bar, and Stony's leaf-colored Toyota led the way over the bridge across the Nowhatan River and down the green, already summery streets.

8

Christmas 1970

After Jean Smithfield's burial on the last day of November 1970, Clark stayed home with Tabby for a solid week, and for once his father did not insist on his going to the office. Neither did he blame Clark for getting too drunk to go to the funeral. "I should have been driving," Clark said more than once. "I wanted to drive—she wanted to protect me, can you bear it? She wanted to protect me." After the day of the funeral, he did not take a drink until Christmas.

For Tabby, the world had become as it was on the night of his mother's death; inside out, unknown, dark. His grandfather had taken him to the funeral home and let him touch the casket, and when he did, right there in front of Monty and the neighbors and all of his grown-up relatives, something happened to him. He *saw*. He saw blackness all around him. He knew he was in that box with his mommy. He let out a wail of blind terror and his grandfather snatched him up. "You're a good boy, sweet Tabby," his grandfather crooned, pressing him into the soft blue material of his suit. "You're going to be okay, darling." Tabby blinked and turned his head away from the coffin. He did not utter a sound during the burial service, and when they got home, he and Monty found Clark passed out on a chair before the television set. Tabby curled into his father's lap and would not speak or move.

After those first days Clark Smithfield went to work with his father five days a week until Christmas. He inhabited his office, he signed papers, he read reports. He issued memos and attended meetings. On Saturdays and Sundays he took Tabby downstairs and bounced tennis balls toward him on the concrete floor; Tabby tried to return them with his undersized racket. In the afternoons they took walks up and down the brisk cold length of Mount Avenue. "Mommy's *dead*," Tabby pronounced in his piping child's voice. "Mommy's dead, and she's never coming back because she's in heaven now." He pointed a mitten toward the sky. "She's up there, Daddy." Clark began to cry again, but this time for his son— for his brave small boy in his blue parka, standing with his mitten in the air and his Snoopy boots on the crusty snow.

On Christmas Day, Monty announced at dinner that he had another present for Tabby, the best present of all. Sitting at the head of the table, he looked gentle and refined, also proud of himself. "Nobody on earth can give better than a good education," he said. He sipped his burgundy. "And so I can take great pleasure in telling you all that Mr. Cathcart, the headmaster of Greenbank Academy, has agreed to let our Tabby switch to the kindergarten there as soon as school begins again in January."

His wife said, "Bravo." Clark started to say something but closed his mouth, and Tabby looked confused.

"You can go to school right across the street," Monty said. "Doesn't that sound good, son? And you'll be going to the same school your father and I both went to."

"Good," Tabby said, looking from his grandfather to his father.

"Well, I'm glad that's settled, anyhow," Clark's mother said.

"I don't want to step on your toes, Clark," said Monty. "We'll split the tuition right down the line. But I think I owe it to the boy to give him the best."

"You always do," Clark muttered. After dinner he made himself a drink for the first time since the day of his wife's funeral.

9

May 17, 1980

Stony waited on her driveway for the man to get out of his car. It was a minute before six, and if Leo had been home, he'd have been parked in front of the television set in the den, papers in his lap, a drink on the table beside him, all warmed for the local New York news.

The man left his car and glanced at the house. "Nice," he said. His hair lifted a bit in the mild breeze from the Sound. His eyes seemed kind and empty. He buttoned up his raincoat, though it was neither cold nor raining. "Nobody home," he said. He came toward Stony over the gravel drive and touched her hand. They kissed.

10

January 6, 1971

At eleven o'clock on January 6, 1971—the day before Tabby was to begin at his new school—Clark Smithfield drove his father's car through the gates and pulled up in front of the house instead of going around to the garage. He hurried into the house, glanced to both sides, and went up the stairs two at a time.

He could hear Tabby and the nanny talking in Tabby's room, and gently pushed the door open. His son gave him a broad hilarious smile. "Daddy, Daddy, Daddy!" he sang out. "A man and a lady were *kissing!*"

"What?" he asked the girl.

"I don't know, sir. He just said it."

"They were *kissing*, Daddy! Like this!" Tabby pursed his lips and moved his blond head from side to side. Then he burst into gleeful laughter.

"Yes," Clark said. "Emily, you can leave us for a while. I have to take Tabby out for a little bit."

"You want me to leave?" she asked, getting up from the toy-strewn floor.

"Yes, please, that's fine," Clark said. "We'll be gone a couple of hours. Don't worry about anything."

"I won't," the girl said. "Give Emily a good-bye kiss, Tabby." She bent toward him.

"Kissing, Daddy," Tabby shouted, and tilted his head to meet Emily's lips with his own.

When the nanny had gone, Clark pulled a green bookbag— Tabby's catch-all—from a shelf and began stuffing it with random toys and books.

"Hey, don't do that, Daddy!" Tabby said.

"We're just going to take a little trip," Clark said. "On an airplane. Would you like that? It's a surprise."

"A surprise for Grandpa?" Tabby shouted.

"A surprise for us." From Tabby's closet he pulled a small blue case and threw underwear, socks, shirts, and pants into it. "We'll need some clothes for you, and then we can go."

For ten minutes Tabby supervised the packing of his clothes, making sure that his father put his favorite T-shirts in the case. Tabby put on his own coat, mittens, and stocking hat. Clark took his own suitcase from under his bed. "All right, Tabby," he said, kneeling before his son. "Now, we're going to go right downstairs, out the door, and into the car. Just this once, we won't say good-bye to Emily. Do you understand?"

"I already said good-bye to Emily," Tabby said.

"Okay. Nice and quiet."

"Nice and *quiet*," Tabby called out, and they went down the stairs to the front door. The voices of Emily and the housekeeper drifted quietly from the kitchen.

Clark opened the door. Frigid January air cut into them. The ground was frosted with white, pocked here and there with the tracks of squirrels and raccoons. "Daddy," Tabby whispered. Clark looked once more back at the interior of the house, back at the marble hall, the thick rugs and plush furniture, the big paintings of ships. "Daddy."

"What?" He closed the door behind them.

"That man was bad."

"What man, Tabby?"

Tabby looked confused and lost for a moment—an expression on his son's face that Clark had come to know well. "It doesn't matter, Tabby," he said. "There aren't any bad men."

He threw the suitcases into the backseat and drove through the open gates.

When they turned west on the thruway, Tabby shouted out, "We're going to You Nork!"

"We're going to the airport, remember?"

"Oh, yeah, the airport. To ride on the airplane. For a surprise."

"Yeah," Clark said. And pushed the car up to seventy.

11

May 17, 1980

When Stony pushed open the bedroom door with her hip, she saw that the man was already in bed. He had propped himself up on two pillows. His skin was very white—against the pink sheets, his face and hairless chest were the color of cottage cheese. His whole face looked glazed. She said, "You don't waste any time."

"Time," the man said. "Never do."

"You're sure you're all right?" His clothes were thrown on the floor beside the bed. Stony held out his drink, but the man appeared not to notice—he was gazing at her glass-eyed—and she put the drink on the bedside table.

"I'm really all right."

Stony shrugged, sat down and took off her shoes.

"I was here before," the man said.

Stony pushed her skirt over her hips. "Do you mean in this house? Before we moved in? Did you know the Allenbys?"

He shook his head. "I was *here* before."

"Oh, we've all been *here* before," Stony said. "This is bigger than football."

12

May 17, 1980

You were dreaming for a long time and then you were not.
You were asleep in a place you did not know, and when you
awakened you were someone else. You had a drink in your
hand and a woman was looking at you and Dragon the world
was yours again.

13

January 6, 1971

"Airplane," Tabby said once in a voice full of wonder, and
then was silent as Monty Smithfield's car rolled down the
thruway past the lower end of Hampstead, past fields and
houses, past Norrington, past the office buildings and high-
rise motels of Woodville with their bright signs, under
bridges and past the crank of the window at toll booths, past
Kingsport, into Westchester County where the thruway grew
grimy and pitted, into Queens.

"What's the matter?" his father asked brusquely as they
took the interchange which led to Long Island. For some time
everything they passed looked bleakly threatening. From the
trim hills and sparkling landscapes of Patchin County they
had gone into the land of the alien. Tabby felt that here was
the world that had killed his mother. "Don't you want to take
a trip?"

"No."

His father cursed. Cars gray with filth complained about
them.

"I want to be home," Tabby said.

"From now on we're going to have a new home. Everything's going to be different, Tabby."

"Everything's different now."

"I don't have any choice, Tabs—I have a new job." The
first time he was to utter that lie; it would become habitual.

Clark left the car in the long-term parking garage. Gray concrete blocks mounted tomblike on all sides; the air too was
gray, smelling of dust and grease. When Tabby opened his
door and climbed out, he saw a wide stain on the concrete
beside him and thought it was a living thing. A hoarse shout

boomed from the level beneath. Portents of a world without love or grace.

"Move it, Tabby. I can't help it—I'm nervous."

Tabby moved it. He trotted beside his father all the way to the elevator and stood in the shelter of his legs.

The elevator lurched downward. Inspected by. Permit issued by. In case of emergency use telephone. "The emergency is getting to the airport," said a man in cowboy boots and a leather jacket. A woman with lion hair laughed, exposing feral lipstick-stained teeth. When she saw Tabby staring at her, she mussed his hair and said, "Cute."

"Stop daydreaming," Clark said, pushing his way into cold air. Doors whooshed open; they entered the terminal. Clark loaded the suitcase on the scale, produced a folder. "Nonsmoking," he said.

"Daddy," Tabby said. "Please, Daddy."

"What? What the hell is it now?"

"We didn't bring Spiderman."

"We'll get another one."

"I don't want—"

Clark grabbed his hand and jerked him toward the escalator. Tabby cried out in fear and despair, for in that second he saw the wide crowded terminal as filled with dead people—corpses flung here and there, one naked man covered with crawling white sores. It was only the vision of a moment, less than a second even, and when it passed his mouth was still making that noise. "Tabby," his father said more gently, "you'll get a new one."

"Uh huh," Tabby said, not knowing what had happened to him, but knowing that somewhere on the edges of what he had seen had been a boy with burning clothes, and that the boy had been the most important part of what he had seen. Because he was the boy. Bright red and yellow lights filled his vision, and he swayed on his feet. The little dots of light swarmed.

His father was kneeling beside him, holding him up. They were no longer on the escalator, and people were pushing past them. "Hey, Tabs," his father was saying. "Are you okay? You want some water?"

"No. Fine."

"Pretty soon we'll be on that old airplane. Then we have a nice ride, and then we'll be in Florida. It's nice and warm in Florida. There'll be sun and palm trees and places to swim.

And good tennis courts we can play on. Everything's going to be great.''

Tabby looked past his father's shoulder and saw a corridor endlessly long down which some half-ran, others rode on a moving belt. "Sure," he whispered.

"We need this, Tabby."

The boy nodded.

"Have you ever seen the tops of clouds? We'll be able to look down and see what's on top of the clouds."

Tabby looked up with a flicker of interest.

His father stood; they stepped on the moving belt. Tabby thought of the tops of clouds, of an upside-down world.

Then ahead of them was a wall of light—a curved wall of windows, blindingly bright with sun, before which huge numbers blazed: 43, 44, 45. People eaten by the sunlight lined at desks. Floppy suit bags claimed chairs in the bays before the windows. Animated uniforms strutted down a shadowed arch.

Tabby saw a familiar body, a flame of silver hair. *"Grandpa!"*

14

May 17, 1980

You carelessly put down the drink and it spilled to the floor. You watched the woman's face change and you took her not without tenderness by the wrist.

15

January 6, 1971

"I thought you'd try a dumb stunt like this," said the old man. "Did you actually think you'd get away with it?"

Tabby froze between the two men.

"You can come to me, Tabby," his grandfather said. He extended a hand. "We'll all go home again and forget about this."

"To hell with you," his father said. "Stay put, Tabby. No—go sit down on one of the chairs in there."

"Just stay there, Tabby," his grandfather said. "Clark, I pity you. There's no way in the world this crazy stunt could have worked."

"Quit calling it a stunt," Clark said.

The old man shrugged. "Call it what you like. The boy is staying here. You can do what you like."

"Sit down over there, Tabby," Clark ordered. Tabby was incapable of going anywhere. "How'd you know I was going to be here?"

"You talk like a child. Nothing could have been easier than to figure out what you were up to. All right, Clark? Are you ready to give up this ridiculous idea?"

"Go to hell. You're not going to get my son."

"Come to me, Tabby. We'll let your father decide how crazy he wants to be."

Tabby made his own decision; for that comforting voice, for the softness of the cashmere coat and suit with chalky stripes. In that way he thought he was deciding for both of them, for a present that was like the past. He expected no more than that.

He stepped toward Monty Smithfield, and heard his father scream, *"Tabby!"* His grandfather bent down and took his hand.

"Let go of my son!" his father screamed.

Tabby felt his world shredding—*"Get away from him, no-good!"* his grandfather yelled—and his soul, what seemed to be his soul, divided in two as if sliced by a cleaver. In such confusion, no reason. Monty's hand closed hard around his own, hard enough to make him cry out.

"Let go of my son," Clark growled, "you old bastard." He took Tabby's other hand and tried to pull the boy toward him.

For what seemed an endless time, neither of them let go. Tabby was too panicked and shocked to utter a sound. His father and grandfather hauled on his arms as if they wanted to pull him apart. He was only dimly aware of other people rushing toward them. "Let *go*," his grandfather barked in a voice not his. "You can't have him, you can't have him," his father said. In their voices he heard that they would indeed pull him apart.

"Daddy, I *see* something!" he screamed.

He did. He saw something that would not happen for nine years, four months, and eleven days.

16

May 17, 1980

For a moment you paused in your occupation; you had a witness.

From Stony Baxter Friedgood, the last of life bubbled out.

17

January 6, 1971

"I *see* something, Daddy!" Tabby wailed, unable to say any more.

He became aware that his grandfather had dropped his hand. When he opened his eyes he saw a tall man in a blue uniform grasping his grandfather's shoulder; he was on his knees in front of his father, looking up dazedly, seeing the angry pilot and his grandfather and the others behind them. His grandfather's face was very red.

"Are we going to settle this here or do we call the cops?" the pilot asked.

Tabby got slowly to his feet.

"I've had enough of you," his grandfather said. "You're totally irresponsible. Go. Get out of my sight."

"Just what I had in mind," his father said in a ragged voice.

"You'll deserve everything that happens to you. But my grandson will not. That's the terrible pity—he'll pay for your stupidity."

"At least there's one thing you won't pay for."

The old man shrugged himself away from the pilot. "If you think that's an answer, I'm sorry for you."

"Okay?" the pilot asked.

"No," said Monty Smithfield.

"If he leaves the terminal," said Clark, "yeah, sure." There was triumph in it.

Tabby backed away and leaned against a sand-filled ashtray. He watched his grandfather shake out his sleeves and turn away down the long corridor. "That bitch Emily called him," his father said.

Tabby's legs were trembling.

"What was all that about seeing something?" his father asked. Both of them were watching the old man march straight-backed down the corridor to the moving belt.

"I don't know."

They sat in the lounge twenty minutes, neither of them speaking. The animated uniforms glanced at them anxiously from time to time, as if suspecting that it might have been wiser after all to have called the police.

After the Eastern 727 took off, Clark Smithfield unbuckled his seat belt and turned grinning to his son. "From now on we're a couple of poor guys."

PART ONE

Entry

Were such things here as we do speak about?
—William Shakespeare, *Macbeth*

1

What Sarah Didn't See

1

May 17, 1980; a wonderful day, you would have said if you lived in Patchin County. No clouds, no moisture to spoil anybody's picnic on this Saturday—there would be a drought, but now the grass was still green and sappy. At Franco's, Pat Dobbin and his fellows had a few beers before lunch and looked out the front window at the train station and pitied the commuters so dogged that they went to work in New York on a Saturday like this (Dobbin left before Stony Friedgood came in—he had drawings for a children's book called *The Eagle-Bear Stories* he wanted to get back to). Bobby Fritz, the gardener for most of the big houses above Gravesend Beach, rolled back and forth on his giant lawnmower, already working on his summer's tan. Graham Williams erased a sentence, wrote it inside-out, and smiled. Patsy McCloud carried her Herman Wouk novel outside and sat in a lawn chair to read in the sun. When her husband, Les, jogged by in his red playsuit, she lowered her head and concentrated on the page; and when Les saw her perched on the chair, her neck bent like an awkward bird, he bellowed, "Lunch, girl! Lunch! Get busy!" Patsy read until the end of the chapter. Les would not make the swing back into Charleston Road for half an hour. Then she went inside, not to make the roast-beef-and-onion sandwich he would demand, but to write in her diary.

For we are in the company of diarists. Graham Williams kept a journal, Richard Allbee had done the same since he was a famous twelve-year-old boy, one of the stars of *Daddy's Here,* which was brought to several million American homes by the National Broadcasting Company, Ivory soap, Ipana toothpaste, and the Ford Motor Company. Richard did not make an entry until ten at night, Laura already in bed exhausted from packing, when he wrote: *Home.*

But this isn't home. May it become so. He paused a moment, looked out the window at enfolding night, and put down *Still it is beautiful here. Casa nueva, vida nueva.*

If, on that day which was Stony Friedgood's last and the All-bees' first day in Patchin County, we had an aerial view of Hampstead, Connecticut, we would first have noticed the pro-fusion of trees—Greenbank, where the Allbees would live, in particular looked forested. The Sound cradled the eastern edge of the town, and here are two strips of bright gold: Sawtell Beach, near the country club, is where most of the town goes to swim and sunbathe. Gravesend Beach is smaller and somewhat rockier. This is where the fishermen come at six in the morning, looking for bluefish from June to late September: it is Greenbank's local beach. Above it on a steep bluff perches the old Van Horne house. Along what should be the southern edge of town runs the Nowhatan River, fifty feet wide just before it narrows down at the parking lot beside Hampstead's business district. (In fact, the town extends a mile or two south of the river.) The Yacht Club, a vast as-semblage of moored boats, sits in the curve of the estuary across from the country club and its smaller marina—from the air all these boats are little fluttering stamps, brown, red, blue, and white. Hampstead itself, roughly trapezoidal, is di-vided by the Conrail tracks, highway I-95, and the Post Road. All three of these go through Hillhaven and Patchin, and through Norrington and Woodville as well on their way to New York: but from the look of this town, you would never know that New York existed. On Hampstead's northwestern edge lie placid little manmade lakes and reservoirs. The great bossy heads of the trees half-obscure the houses and roads beneath them, and obscure too the Mercedeses and Volvos, the Datsuns and Toyotas and Volkswagens which cruise along them. As the lights go on, you can see the massive white-columned front of the Congregational Church on the Post Road just before it dips into the business district—it is flanked, on either side of its extensive lawn, by a bank (which has copied its style), and a mansard-roofed shopping center with a record store, a theater, an ice-cream parlor, a health-food store, a craft shop (macrame holders for pots and giant effigies of Snoopy), and a store where you can buy down jackets and woolly hats for twice what they would cost in Norrington or Woodville.

And very late in the day, when Richard Allbee wrote *God help us both* in his unpretentious little book, you would have seen the streaming headlamps and flickering rooflights of two patrol cars speeding from the police station along the Post Road, then down leafy Sawtell Road, and up the Greenbank Road to the Friedgood house. Where every window poured light.

Seconds before they reached the Friedgood house, a light went out in the offices of the *Hampstead Gazette* on Main Street, just across from the bookstore. Sarah Spry finished her column for Wednesday's paper, and was going home. Once again, Hampstead's famous, near-famous, and obscure had been immortalized in the *Gazette*.

2

This is part of what Sarah wrote for that Wednesday's column:

WHAT SARAH SAW

Thistown presents a shifting kaleidoscope of moods and impressions. Thistown gives us memories and joys and ever-changing beauties. Our wonderful painters and writers and musicians give us spice . . . how many of you know that famed F. SCOTT FITZGERALD (the *Gatsby* man) and his family lived a stone's throw from Sawtell Beach, in the Mr. and Mrs. Irving Fisher house on Bluefish Hill, in the twenties? Or that EUGENE O'NEILL and JOHN BARRYMORE and GEORGE S. KAUFMAN too sojourned for a time here on the shores of Long Island Sound with us? If you ask Ada Hoff of that grand ol' institution, the Books 'n Bobs Bookstore right across Main Street from this great newspaper (chuckle), she might tell you of the day when poet W. H. AUDEN dropped in to buy a cookbook by Thistown's TOMMY BIGELOW—way to go, Tommy!

Just thought I'd mention it, dear ones. This is a week when my poor old brain wanders through the delights of Thistown, admiring our beautiful old Main Street, our grand old churches of all denominations, our precious shoreline, and our colonial past which is preserved in so many of our homes. Why, a week like this makes your tough old scribe feel positively Bi-Centennial!

And as that dashing young dragon-slaying lawyer
ULICK BYRNE said to Sarah the other day, Ain't it grand
to live somewhere where absolutely nothing happens at
least twice a week?

But you want to know what's going on, you say?

Sarah saw: That RICHARD ALLBEE, that darling boy
from *Daddy's Here* (catch a rerun on the late-nite tube
and see what a cutie he was), is moving in with his
bride, Laura—which is one of my alltime favorite
names! Will we be seeing you around the Playhouse,
Richard? (But rumor has it he acts no more, alas. . . .)

Sarah saw: a yummy long letter from former residents
BUNNY and THAXTER BAINBRIDGE in Los Claros, California, where they met Thistown's JIX and PETE PETERS, out
there visiting grandkids. . . .

A slow week for Sarah.

3

For Leo Friedgood, there would never be any slow weeks
ever again, though of this he was happily ignorant when he
took the telephone call at the Yacht Club that Saturday morning. He was puttering with his boat, as he did most warm
Saturdays. His eighteen-foot Lightning sloop, the *Juicy Lucy,*
had been in the water only a week, and he wanted to repaint
some of the interior trim. Bill Terry, whose Grand Banks boat
was docked at the next slip, answered the phone when it rang
on the dock and called out, "For you, Leo." Leo said,
"Shit," put down his paintbrush, and paddled down the
gently swaying slip. He was sweaty and his right arm was
sore. Despite his bushy bristling appearance, Leo was not at
heart a physical man. His ancient KEEP ON TRUCKIN' sweatshirt bulged over his belly, his jeans bore a constellation of
white specks. He wanted another bottle from the six-pack of
Coors on the sloop's deck. "Yeah," he said into the phone.
The mouthpiece stank of cigarettes.

"Mr. Friedgood?" came the anonymous female voice.

"Yeah."

"This is Mrs. Winthrop, General Haugejas' secretary," the
woman said, and Leo felt something icy stir in his gut. General Henry Haugejas—Leo had seen him only once, at a

Telpro general meeting, a gray-flannel slab of a man whose face was the color of cooling iron. The face was slablike too. He had been a hero in the Korean War and looked as though he took no more pleasure in that than in anything else; a willful tide of strength and propriety, of sternness and distaste emanated from the stiff red face and armor of gray flannel.

"Oh, yes," Leo said, regretting that he was not already out on the still-frigid water.

"General Haugejas has requested that you go to our Woodville plant immediately."

"We don't have a plant in Woodville," Leo said.

Mrs. Winthrop silkily answered, "We do if the General says so. I understand that it will be new to you. Here's how you get there." She gave him an exit number on I-95, and then a complicated set of directions that seemed designed as much to confuse as to elucidate. "The General wants you there in thirty minutes," she concluded.

"Hey, hold on," Leo wailed. "I can't make that. I'm on my boat. I'll have to change my clothes. I don't even have I.D. I can't get into some—"

"They'll have your name at the gate," she said, and Leo could have sworn he heard that she was smiling. "As soon as you check into things, the General wants you to call him at this number." She rattled off a 212 telephone number he did not recognize. He repeated it, and the secretary hung up.

In Woodville Leo got lost. Following the directions the secretary had given him, he had found himself in the city's extensive slums, driving past rotting houses, abandoned gas stations, and tiny bars where groups of black men congregated on the sidewalks. It seemed to Leo that all of them stared at him, a white man conspicuous in a shiny car. He drove in circles, the secretary's complex set of rights and lefts now a hopeless muddle in his mind. He began to sweat again, knowing that the thirty minutes the General had given him had passed. For a time, no matter where he turned, he seemed to swing back and forth between two poles, the thruway and the Red Devil Lounge with its crowd of lounging, already drunken men.

Going for the third time up a dingy street, he noticed the narrow track between two houses which he had previously taken for a driveway—this time he looked in and saw an iron gate before a slice of high gray wall. As he cruised past the little track, he glimpsed a guardhouse just inside the gate. Leo reversed his car and turned in between the houses, feeling like a trespasser.

For a second he thought he was wrong again, and frustrated rage burned in him. A sign on the gate read WOODVILLE SOL-VENT. A uniformed man jumped out of the guardhouse and pulled open the gate. When he approached the car, Leo lowered his window and said, "Hey, do you know where the Telpro plant—"

"Mr. Friedgood?" the guard asked, looking suspiciously at Leo's grubby clothes.

"Yeah," Leo said.

"They want you in Research. You're late."

"Where's Research?" Leo stifled the impulse to tell the man to go to hell.

The guard, moon-faced and moon-shaped, pointed across a vast, nearly empty parking lot. His belly wobbled as his arm rose. The only cars in the lot were near a windowless metal door in the high blank facade. "You go in there."

Leo sped across the lot and parked his Corvette diagonally across two spaces.

4

A white-coated man with sandy hair and rabbit teeth darted toward him as he reached the top of the iron stairs. "You're the Telpro man? Mr. Friedgood?"

Leo nodded. He glanced toward the little group of men and women the man addressing him had just left. They too wore white jackets, like doctors. His eyes snagged on a bank of television monitors. "Who are you?" he asked, not looking at the man.

"Ted Wise, the director of research here. Did anybody fill you in?"

Leo was self-conscious in his sweatshirt and paint-spotted jeans. One of the monitors before him showed his mop of hair, the back of his sweatshirt hoisted up above a roll of skin. His self-consciousness fed his anger at finding himself thrown into a plant Telpro had not trusted him to know about until there was a disaster. He yanked the shirt down over his belt. It had come to him that General Haugejas had sent him to the plant the same way he would send a first lieutenant over a hill—because he was expendable.

"Look, the General wants me to report back to him," Leo said. "Suppose you just stop worrying about what I do or do not know and fill me in fast." He was still taking in the room; white walls, black-and-white-checkerboard tiles on the floor. The television monitors were set above a desk on which sat a time sheet, a telephone, and a pen. A nervous-looking girl sat at the desk. She swallowed when he glared at her.

In fact the entire group assembled here at this second-floor foyer was as nervous as cats—more than nervous, Leo was realizing. Even as Ted Wise groped for words, the other three men and two women before him exuded a gloom of panic and fear. They were rigid as poles, restraining themselves because he had appeared. Not sensitive, Leo was an intelligent man, and he could see them holding in their twitches—if they let go, they'd roll across the floor like marbles.

At the moment that Wise nerved himself to ask Leo for some identification, Leo finally began to assess what sort of abyss might be before him.

"You want what?" he asked Wise aggressively.

"Just as a precaution, sir."

He was covering himself; as the General was covering himself by sending Leo Friedgood into this . . . mental hospital. For that was what the interior of the plant resembled. In disgust Leo took his wallet from his back pocket and showed Wise his driver's license. "The General got me off my boat," he said grandly. "He wanted me to take care of this thing as quickly as possible. Just show me the problem and then all you basket cases can take a Valium or whatever the hell it is you need."

"This way, Mr. Friedgood," Wise said, and the tense little group of five parted to let them pass through a door.

"We have been in this plant since 1978," Wise said. "After Woodville Solvent went under a couple of years before, the referee in the bankruptcy sold the buildings and the name to Telpro."

"Yeah, yeah," Leo said, as if he knew all about it.

"It took almost six months to make the necessary alterations. When we moved in, we sort of picked up where we left off in Wyoming. All of us—the bunch you see here—had been working out there in another Telpro facility. Until we had to shut down.''

"Something go wrong there too?'' Leo asked.

Wise was opening another door, and blinked at the question. ''We had been sited in a chemical factory, and the pipes in the drainage system were corroded. Some of the waste penetrated the aquifer to a very minor extent, two parts per million. It was not a serious problem. There was very little feedback.''

Leo peered into the room beyond the door. Sullen-looking monkeys peered back from cages. Zoo odors drifted through the open door. "Primate section," Wise said. "We have to go through it to get to the testing area.''

"Why don't you just tell me about your work," Leo said wearily.

Of course he had known that Telpro had certain Defense Department contracts. One of the divisions he oversaw, a plant in Trenton, manufactured the latching mechanism used in half-tracks; another factory in New Jersey put together circuitry panels that later formed a small part of the Minuteman missile. "But we're Special Weapons," Wise said as the seven of them stood in the room full of caged monkeys. Special Weapons was a separate endeavor which reported only to General Haugejas and his staff. They were two microbiologists, a physicist, a chemist, and a research assistant. Other research assistants and laboratory technicians were hired from the local pool. For eighteen months they had been working on a single project. "It's more complex physically and chemically than this, but for our purposes let's call it a gas," Wise said. "It's odorless and invisible, like carbon monoxide, and highly dispersible in water. It doesn't have a name yet, but the code is DRG. It's a . . . you'd have to call it a real wild card. We've been working to refine it down so we could increase the predictability factor.''

Predictability was the problem, Leo learned. The Pentagon and Defense Department had been excited about DRG since it had been first synthesized in the early fifties by a German biochemist at MIT named Otto Bruckner. Bruckner had not known what to do with his invention, and the government had happily taken it away from him. "For a long time the project was in limbo," Wise said. "The government had a lot of simpler concepts it tried to develop, mostly unsuccessfully. In the late seventies, interest in DRG revived again. From the point it came to us, Special Weapons—all of us here—had the job of localizing the effect of Bruckner's brainchild. We put it through a dozen changes—from ADG 1 and 2 all the way up to what we've got now. But it's still very random in effect. Some people are not affected at all, though only a very few. In some cases inhalation is immediately fatal. Lack of effect and termination are within acceptable parameters, from five to eight percent each. And as a sideline here, let me assure you that the agents in it which cause fatality are relatively short-lived. An exposed population is at immediate risk for no more than twenty-five minutes. It's with the mid-range that we're most concerned. You've heard of the Army's experiments with LSD?''

Leo nodded.

"Of course that was regrettable in the extreme. We have been at pains to avoid any taint of that sort of thing, and our brief does not extend that far in any case. DRG, originally ADG, is far more various in effect than LSD, and all we've been working on is the isolation of a strain which would consistently reproduce a single effect.'' Wise now seemed very nervous. "We had quite a range of choice. Some of the wilder effects take months to appear. Skin lesions, hallucinations, outright madness, flu, changes in pigmentation, even narcotization—some percentage of a treated population will simply be mildly tranquilized. There may even have been evidence of fugue state and telepathic ability . . . to tell you the truth, the stuff is so various that after a year and a half we're just beginning to get a handle on it.''

"Okay,'' Leo said. "Let's get to the good part. What happened?''

"Barbara,'' Wise said, and a tall dark-haired young woman with puffy eyes came past the wall of cages to open another door.

Leo saw a room within a room, the top half of the inner room lined with glass. Stepping in behind Barbara, he vaguely took in a clutter of laboratory tables, tissue slides, projectors, gas burners. His attention was focused on the three bodies in the glass enclosure. The two farthest from him lay sprawled a few feet apart on a black floor. Their eyes were open, their mouths yawned. They had clean innocent dead faces.

Wise coughed into his fist; his face was pink. "The people in there were preparing the chamber for an infusion of

DRG-16.'' He wiped his face, and his hands were shaking. ''The man nearest the wall is Frank Thorogood, and the man next to him is Harvey Washington. They were research technicians—Thorogood was a graduate student at Patchin University and Washington had no academic qualifications. He performed low-level tasks for all of us. One of them was supposed to connect a line from the storage facility to the vaporizer, which in turn is connected to the mask you see on the floor. Instead he plugged it accidentally into the vent line immediately below the vaporizer, and undiluted DRG flooded into the chamber. Washington and Thorogood died immediately.''

Leo was staring in horror at the third body in the glass chamber. It had bloated—at first Leo thought the body had burst. Lathery white scum coated the hands. The man's head, a white sponge, had seemed to leak toward a drain in the center of the chamber's floor. It took Leo a moment to realize that the lather that had once been skin was moving. As he watched—his eyes incapable of shifting away—the froth of the head crawled into the drain. ''The third man was Tom Gay, who was one of our best researchers, though he had been working with us only six months or so.''

The woman named Barbara began to cry. One of the men put his arm around her.

''You can see the effect of the lesions. He died only a few minutes before you arrived. We had to watch him go. He knew he couldn't open the chamber.''

''Jesus Christ,'' Leo said, shocked out of his pose. ''Look what happened to him.''

Wise said nothing.

''Is it safe to go in there now? Can you get rid of that stuff? I mean, I don't care what the hell mess you people get yourselves into, but *I'm* not going in there.'' Leo jammed his hands into his pockets. He saw wads of brown hair floating on the lather, and turned away from the glass, his stomach lurching.

''It will be safe in about fifteen minutes. As safe as we can make it, anyhow.''

''Then you go in.''

Wise abruptly turned an alarming scarlet. ''I'm afraid that isn't all. The circulators will more or less vacuum out the traces of DRG-16.''

''It's still your job, baby.''

"I was going to say, Harvey Washington would have replaced the filters on the exterior vents immediately after the chamber was empty. But Bill Pierce here switched on the circulators before we realized that the filters were still in their boxes."

"Why the hell don't you leave the filters in all the time?" Bill Pierce spoke up. He was taller than Leo, built like a football player, and the sole scientist to wear a beard. "We don't do that because they have a strong odor, which very quickly leaks back into the chamber. The smell prejudices the experiments. Our procedure was to seal the chamber, make our observations, and to have Harvey Washington install the filters while we dissected the subject. Then we switched on the circulators." He glared at Leo, full of guilt and challenge. "But when I saw Tom Gay going crazy in there, I just thought of getting the DRG out of the air. I was thinking that if I could change the air fast enough, I could save Tom anyhow—the other two just dropped where they were standing. And I guess I had our old procedure in the back of my mind."

"So where did that stuff go?" Leo asked. "Wait. Let me guess. The circulators circulated it right outside. That's the good part, isn't it? You dummies pumped a batch of this stuff straight into the air right after it zapped three guys in the monkey chamber here. So in about a second and a half we got a million dead *shwartzes* in Woodville. Right? *Right?*" Leo inhaled deeply. *"And!* Not only that, but we got a million lawsuits—*and* I'm supposed to get you jerks off the hook." Leo clapped his hands over his eyes.

"Mr. Friedgood," Wise said, "we've just lost three of our colleagues. Bill was acting in accordance with former procedure—for months we did keep the filters in place."

"You think that's a defense?" Leo bellowed. "You want me to feel sorry for you?"

"I'm sorry," Wise said around his rabbit teeth. "We are not quite in control of ourselves. Things may not be as bad as you imagine. Let me explain." The words were confident, but Ted Wise was still the most scared-looking man Leo had ever seen.

5

"I'll do better than write a statement," Leo was telling the General thirty minutes later. "I'll get us out of this whole mess. Telpro will never come into it. First of all, these geniuses that you have up here say that because this DRG was vented from the roof of the factory, it'll carry for miles before it settles. We've got a pretty good breeze going right now"— Leo was remembering the sloops, Marlins, and Lightnings, whipping along out on the Sound while he worked on his boat that morning—"and the stuff is going to *travel*. It could get to Rhode Island before it settles. Maybe it'll get all the way to Canada. No one in the world is ever going to connect it to Telpro—and if we're lucky, it'll blow out over the Sound and kill a few fish. And if we have a good rain anytime in the next week, the worst will never happen at all. Water dilutes the effect fantastically. Bottom line? Somewhere north of here could have a few deaths almost immediately. In a month or two, some citizens of Pawtucket or Stowe might start to go funny in the head—Wise says that the mental effects can take that long to show up. We've got no exposure, that's the bottom line."

He listened to the General's voice for a time.

"Months. That was what Wise said."

The General spoke again.

"He guarantees it, sir."

Leo heard the General out once more.

"That's right. Our problem now is to take care of the situation right here. That's what my idea is all about. One of these geniuses gave me the idea when he said that this DRG stuff is sort of like carbon monoxide. We'll rig it, is what we'll do. As far as anybody knows, this is Woodville Solvent. We'll keep it that way. And we'll give an anonymous phone call to the television stations in New York, we'll call the *Times*, we'll get all the agencies and public-health people out here, and we'll have the place all cleaned up and looking like a factory."

Pause.

Leo swept his eyes across the six people staring at him from the other side of the desk. "No, they won't say a word. We'll announce that the plant is closing while safety inspections are carried out, and you can move them somewhere else and start up all over again after everybody forgets about this. In the meantime, we can talk to this Bruckner guy in Boston and see if he can give us any help. He invented this crap, he ought to know if we can do anything about it.''

Pause.

''Thank you, sir.'' He hung up the phone and turned to the scientists. ''Let's go down and take a look at your furnace. We're going to hide this mess in plain sight. Some of you yo-yos are going to make the eleven-o'clock news.''

An hour and a half after his arrival at the plant, Leo Friedgood was seated on a wooden crate in the basement, watching Ted Wise and Bill Pierce work on the furnace. Two unmarked green trucks from an army base in New Jersey sat in the parking lot, and a team of soldiers was carrying out the monkey cages, canisters, crates of laboratory equipment, and boxes of records. What remained of the body of Thomas Gay had been scooped into a zippered bag and removed.

Two hours after that, Leo stood at a window and watched a CBS car pull into the lot just behind a police car. The temperature in the office was over eighty degrees. Everybody knew his lines. Leo turned back to the desk and called the Environmental Protection Agency. Then he called the Patchin County Health Department. At the start of both conversations he introduced himself as Theodore Wise. Turning back to the window, he saw the research director and Bill Pierce leaving the building to confront the police. A tall lean figure in a blue suit—the reporter—a technician and a man carrying a video camera and Portapak left the CBS car. The reporter drifted toward Wise and the policeman. When a sound truck came through the gates, Leo left the window to go downstairs.

Barbara, the research assistant, and two of the scientists stood by the desk in the foyer. Leo smiled at them, descended the stairs, and ambled out of the building.

The famous reporter from CBS stood next to Bill Pierce and held a microphone between them. ''Is there any proof to the rumor that this tragedy occurred because of carbon-monoxide poisoning?''

''To the best of my knowledge . . .'' Pierce began.

Thus, for several hours, it went. By the time the police had finished, calm still night had descended. And by the time he left to drive home, Leo Friedgood had almost forgotten about

the invisible, odorless cloud of something called DRG-16
which was floating high up in the air currents over Patchin
County.

6

Eventually, when Ted Wise and Bill Pierce broke their silence, they and a hundred newspapers would blame this almost thinking cloud for everything that befell Hampstead and
Patchin and Old Sarum, Witchley and Redhill and King
George, all these excellent towns between Norrington and
New Haven with their commuters and artists and country
clubs and granite hills and saltbox houses. There would be
investigations, there would be indictments, petitions, demon-
strations, lawsuits. There would be speeches, pompous, self-
serving, and well-meant. All of this would be proper, but
beside the point. For the blame for the months of coming
turmoil was not the sentient cloud's.

It was yours, you who lay on your bed now, dazed and
satisfied. You who had to begin discovering yourself once
more.

Your history, Hampstead's history. . . .

7

Two hundred years ago, there was no Hampstead, only
Greenbank, a collection of farms and a church above Gravesend Beach. The Beachside Trail (now Mount Avenue) connected Greenbank to Hillhaven and Patchin, of which it was
considered an adjunct. Thus when General Tryon sailed down
from New Haven to burn Patchin and landed on Kendall Point
in 1779, a small detachment of soldiers, only ten or eleven,
went down the Beachside Trail to burn Greenbank too.
Patchin's men took potshots over hedges and fences with their
Brown Besses, the women and children and animals took
shelter on Fairlie Hill or in Patchin Woods; and some lingered
in their town, boys and women. Reports said that one or two
male residents joined the destruction. The Reverend Eliot,
Patchin's vicar: "The burning parties carried on their business
with horrid alacrity, headed by one or two persons who were

born and bred in the neighboring towns.'' A boy (one of nine fatalities) was shot and killed, at such range that his clothes began to burn. The other eight murders are known to have been committed by Jaegers—German mercenaries—and British soldiers; this one, the murder of the boy, was unobserved and so remains a mystery.

This event, the killing of a thirteen-year-old boy in the midst of a general destruction, is the second stain on the land.

Ten years later, George Washington, the President of the thirteen United States, visited Patchin. His diary mentions that along his route—he took the Beachside Trail—he saw many chimneys standing in the ruins of burned houses.

For the next two hundred years, the same names recur in the parish records: Barr, Wakehouse, Jennings, Annabil, Williams, Winter, Allen, Kent, Moorman, Buddington, Smithfield, Sayre, Green, Tayler. The names go backward, too; the original four farmers on the Beachside Trail, settled in 1640, were named Williams, Smyth, Green, and Tayler. In 1645 they were joined by a landholder named Gideon Winter. (Monty Smithfield's manor on Mount Avenue was built on the site of Gideon Winter's farmhouse.)

And some of the names appear in Hampstead criminal records. In 1841, a traveling man who had camped himself like a Gypsy in the woods bordering Anthony Jennings' onion fields murdered two children named Sarah Allen and Thomas Moorman and roasted the bodies in a pit before he was captured by a posse of farmers led by Jennings. By torchlight they led him back to the Hampstead Common (now lost, cut in half by the Post Road), and under the eye of the town sheriff, put a rope around his neck and tried him on the spot. From his elegant house in Patchin, Judge Thaddeus Barr rode down the Beachside Trail on his bay gelding. He wore his robes and hanging hat and sentenced the man to death—he knew he could never have got the murderer to the county courthouse in Norrington. Under Barr's questioning, the murderer refused to give his name, saying only, ''I am one of your own, Judge.'' After his death, he was recognized by a man in the crowd as a feeble-witted cousin of the Tayler family who had been sent to the poor farm as a boy.

In 1898, Robertson Green—known as ''Prince'' to his friends—a twenty-two-year-old man who had dropped out of divinity school in New Haven and lived in separate quarters in his parents' big clapboard house on Gravesend Avenue,

was tried and convicted for the murder in the spring of that
year of a prostitute in Woodville. Details of Prince Green's
life emerged during the trial, and they were bizarre enough to
be taken up by the New York tabloids. His habits had altered
after his return from New Haven—he had insisted on sleeping
in an oaken coffin which he had ordered from Bornley and
Holland, the Hampstead undertakers. He never opened his
curtains; he invariably dressed in black; he was addicted to
laudanum, then readily available at any pharmacist's shop.
He had been visiting the Norrington and Woodville prostitutes
since his return from New Haven (Hampstead assumed), and
four of these women had been butchered by an unknown person from May to September 1897. Prince Green never confessed to these killings, but he was sentenced to be executed
as surely for their deaths as for that of the woman over whose
body he was discovered in a Woodville slum back street—
Redbone Alley. The New York *Journal American* quoted the
young man's father as stating that his son had been deranged
by excessive absorption in the verse of the decadent poets
Dowson and Swinburne. Early on, they had begun calling
Green "The Connecticut Ripper"; in some later editions he
was called "The Ripper-Poet." "There were days," his father said to the reporter, "when he behaved as though he did
not know his mother's name or mine."

In 1917, legalized murder occurred in France, and boys
named Barr and Moorman and Buddington were killed in the
trenches. Their names are on the World War I monument
erected on the Post Road, just opposite where the Lobster
House Restaurant is now.

The model for the soldier who appears on the monument, a
lean and handsome young man in puttees and campaign hat,
was Johnny Sayre, who in 1952 took his own life with a .45
automatic pistol on the grass leading down to the dock behind
the Sawtell Country Club. No one at the time understood
what made the fifty-three-year-old John Sayre, who had been
a lawyer and a power in town and much admired, decide to
end his life. He had canceled his appointments that morning;
his secretary told the police that Sayre had seemed distracted
and short-tempered for days. Bonnie Sayre told the police that
she had not wanted them to go to the club that evening, but
that John had insisted—they'd had a date with Graham Williams for two weeks, a premature birthday celebration for
John. On his actual birthday, they would be in London. The

secretary said that he had skipped lunch and stayed in his office; Bonnie Sayre reported that he had ordered only a salad for dinner. While the rest of them were having their drinks, John had excused himself. Then he had gone outside—he must have been carrying the gun in his belt all the time. They had heard the shot a few minutes later, but it had sounded like a car backfiring in the parking lot, like a door slamming in the rear of the club's restaurant. A waiter on his break had discovered the body.

Neither Bonnie nor the secretary thought it worthwhile to tell the police that John Sayre had written two names on the jotting pad beside his desk phone on the morning of his suicide: Prince Green and Bates Krell.

The secretary, who had lived in Hampstead only two years, did not know the names. Bonnie Sayre had only the dimmest memory of Prince Green's crimes. There had been a big house on Gravesend Avenue before which she and her sisters had been forbidden to linger: in it lived two old people who never came out. There was a shadowy memory of shame, of disgrace: of scandal. Bates Krell, now . . . When Bonnie Sayre saw the name deeply scratched into the telephone pad two days after her husband's death, some half-fledged feeling stirred in her, and it took her a moment to recognize it as unease. He had been of the generation immediately before hers, which is to say, the generation following Prince Green's. Bates Krell had owned a lobster boat, docked it on the Nowhatan River where the Spaulding Oil Company was now. He had been disreputable, perhaps threatening—a broad, filthy man, bearded and agate-eyed, who hired boys to assist him with his nets and beat them for the most minor infractions. One day he had vanished. His boat sat moored in the Nowhatan River until the state impounded and sold it. There was a story which went through Bonnie's school, a husband or a father ordering Bates Krell out of town, a story of wives or daughters out on the lobster boat at night . . . but why would her husband invoke this name before he killed himself?

Prince Green, Bates Krell. John Sayre's pen had nearly torn through the paper.

Now there are no lobster boats along the river, no fishermen at all where once there were many; now there are Spaulding Oil and the Riverside Building, which houses dentists and an insurance company; the Seagull Restaurant and the Blue Tern Bar, where teenagers drink; the Marina Restaurant; and the offices, in a little dingy section of warehouses, of the Scientology movement.

Now no one knows the old Hampstead names; now the hateful anti-Semitism of the twenties and thirties in Hampstead is gone, and the town is more than a quarter Jewish; now people move in from New York and Arizona and Texas; and move out to Washington and Virginia and California. The publisher who bought the green house does not know that eighty years ago well-brought-up girls were ordered by their parents to walk quickly past his six-bedroom brown clapboard house, nor that in his home office on the side of the house a dazed boy used to sleep in a coffin and dream of traveling through the sky on wings like a gull's, his mouth and hands stained red.

Now Hampstead has a trailer park (carefully hidden behind a screen of trees on the Post Road), two burglaries every hour, five movie theaters, two health-food stores, more than a dozen liquor stores, twenty-one trains a day to New York. Thirteen millionaires live at least a part of the year in Hampstead. There are five banks and three famous actors, a private psychiatric hospital with an active drug-rehabilitation program. In 1979, Hampstead had two rapes and no murders. Until 1980, murders were almost unknown here since the days of Robertson "Prince" Green, who had observed decorum by committing his crimes in Woodville.

The first murder of 1980 was discovered just after nine-forty-five at night on the seventeenth of May when the victim's husband entered his bedroom. It would be a long time before anyone thought to remember Prince Green and Bates Krell or even John Sayre, the statue of whom at seventeen everyone we shall be concerned with in this story drove past, seeing it or not, four or five times a week.

8

The thinking cloud, a thousand feet above Woodville and Norrington, preceded Leo Friedgood on his way toward Hampstead. It moved without haste, ultimately without direction. When a curl of air sent its wings sifting down, it brushed random lives.

A week-old infant lying asleep near an open window on this warm May night suddenly died—stiffened and ceased to breathe while her parents watched television in a downstairs room. Six blocks away (we are in Norrington now, in an area called Cumberland Acres), a fourteen-year-old boy cruising past a row of mailboxes on stakes pitched off his bike and lay still on a little mound of gravel, his bicycle sprawled a few feet beside him.

Joseph Ricci, the third of the Dragon's accidental victims, had been traveling home—much later than usual—to Stratford from a bar near the Kingsport offices of Loewen & Loewen, the accounting firm where he worked. It was a fifty-minute drive each way, but Joe Ricci had grown up in Stratford and could not yet afford a house in Kingsport, which because it was closest to New York was the most expensive of Patchin County's towns. Joe was twenty-eight; he and his wife, Mary Louise, had a three-year-old son who had his father's black hair and dark blue eyes.

Joe reached the first of the two toll stations he would have to pass through before he got home. This was at the southwestern edge of Hampstead; the next toll came just before his exit. Joe cranked down his window, held out the book of tickets, and the uniformed woman in the booth extracted the loose ticket from the pack. It was ten past eight—he'd told Mary Louise to expect him at eight, and he still had half an hour's drive before him. Joe Junior would be in bed already. It irritated Joe to miss his son's bedtime, especially for an unhappy reason like tonight's. His immediate superior, Tony Flippo, had asked him the day before to save Saturday night for him. They had to have an important talk. When Tony had asked him to come to Kingsport, Joe assumed that his boss and friend was going to go over some business ideas. They had talked in the past about starting their own office. But tonight Tony had not wanted to talk about Patchin County real estate, in which he fervently wished to invest, nor about the leasing company which was his other fantasy: he'd wanted to complain about his marriage. He wanted to hear himself rehearse his arguments for divorce. Tony was halfway to being in love with Michelle Sparks, one of the firm's typists.

It had been a pointless evening. Joe Ricci left his window down and gunned his car into the left lane. Two cars sped on before him; his mirror showed a phalanx of cars and a semi pushing on to the northeast. For no reason at all, he found himself reminiscing about his high-school girlfriend.

Then suddenly the almost empty scene before him changed. His first impression was that I-95 was crowded with wrecked cars, bleeding people stumbling toward him; he saw a huge truck canted over on the guardrail, the flashing lights of police cars and ambulances. This vision jumped into his eyes with the power of reality and for a moment he could not breathe or think.

He slammed on his brakes and cut his wheels to the side, realizing finally that he could swerve around the dreadful scene by using the shoulder. His head was buzzing oddly and painfully: for a fraction of a second he was conscious that the fillings in his teeth were vibrating. Yet in the midst of this buzzing pain, he knew that none of what he saw ahead could really be there. He took his foot off the brake and slammed it on the accelerator, wanting only to get past whatever it was on the highway, and the back end of his car fishtailed around.

When he saw his hands on the wheel, he bit through his tongue. Bit right through it—blood oozed over his lips. His hands were covered with white bugs. That was all he could make of the shifting, almost fluid white surface coating his fingers and the backs of his hands. Joe opened his mouth but could not scream. His car was moving toward a swarm of lights. Banshee noises, unearthly screeches, battered him.

The truck behind him, which had been blasting its air horn, crushed in the side of his car and slammed it into the guardrail. Another car struck the rear of the semi, shearing off its roof. It began to burn in a quiet, almost apologetic fashion beneath the truck. A green Ford rolled end over end like a flipping domino, and the car which had struck it piled into the side of the semi and the burning car wedged beneath it.

By the time they closed the Hampstead toll station, there were eight dead. Four cars, including Joe Ricci's, had incinerated. The state police and two officers from the Hampstead police force watched helplessly as the burning cars smoked and sparked. Twenty minutes later, a tow truck from the garage on that day's rota sheet began to separate the wrecks.

A Hampstead policeman named Bobo Farnsworth, who had responded to an assist call from the state police, peered in the shattered window of a demolished Le Baron and was amazed to see only charred upholstery and a sagging melted wheel—

no grisly mummy lay across the ruined seat. Bobo had seen enough burned-out wrecks to know that in *this* one a roasted body was inevitable—the hands should be fried to the chest, and the whole black thing no larger than the size of a big dog. He looked closer at the rubble within the car and saw the glint of a belt buckle resting on black liquid near an exposed spring. Mary Louise Ricci, still knowing none of this, fell asleep in the Riccis' most comfortable chair just as Butch Cassidy and the Sundance Kid blew up a train and picked themselves up from the Bolivian dust in a shower of paper money.

9

Leo sat in his car while the engine idled, pushing forward a foot every fifteen minutes. From the two out of five toll booths that were open, lines of stationary cars snaked backward halfway to Norrington and Exit 16. Outlaw cars cruised down the two left lanes, which had been officially closed, and tried to nose in farther ahead. Leo noticed with satisfaction that drivers were keeping almost bumper to bumper, refusing to let the outlaws improve their place in line. Ahead, on the other side of the Hampstead toll station, he from time to time saw flickers and flashes of red lights. So there had been a bad accident.

At nine o'clock, still fifty cars from the booth, he switched on his radio and turned to the Woodville station. The news reader described the latest confusion in Iran, and announced the number of days Americans had been hostaged there. He moved onto the fracas about property reassessment in Hampstead. Leo listened to all this with faint interest. Then the news reader pronounced the words "Woodville Solvent." Leo straightened in his seat and turned up the sound. "This bizarre tragedy resulted in the deaths of two men, Frank Thorogood of Patchin and Harvey Washington, a Woodville resident. Investigations conducted by the Public Health Department indicate that carbon-monoxide poisoning was the cause of death. The plant has been closed indefinitely so that safety-monitoring measures and repairs may be carried out." The nervous, straining sound of Ted Wise lying through his rabbity teeth cut in. "We became aware of the problem when . . . no one could feel a greater sense of loss than I . . .

possible that our owners may decide to terminate . . .'' That
was new to Leo—he must have been listening to Pierce when
Wise decided to be cute and refer to *our owners*. Of course he
had not decided to be cute: he had been too rattled to be
anything but stupid. But this was a lapse which only Leo
would notice. By the time the news reader had moved on to
the weather and the traffic report, Leo was almost smiling
with self-satisfaction.

All traffic funneled into one lane. An imperious policeman
waved a flashlight, flares burned, the bars of light on the tops
of police cars flashed blue and white and red. The wreckers
had towed away most of the crumpled automobiles, but the
sixteen-wheeler still sagged against the guardrail: a recumbent
elephant. The three lanes blocked off by conical orange markers were littered with broken glass, hubcaps and detached
tires, a fender dented in half like a huge silver V. The smell
of scorched metal and rubber hung over it all. As Leo inched
into his place in the single line of cars, he looked sideways
past the policeman with the flashlight and saw an unrecognizable car jammed beneath the undercarriage of the truck.
The entire top of the car was sliced off down to the door
handles. Inside that improbable cripple had been a human
being. *Stony,* Leo thought, and then recalled with terrible
clarity the two young dead men on their backs in the glass
room, eyes and mouths open: and again saw white froth sliding toward a drain. He pushed these visions backward into
some dark empty chamber in his mind and snapped his head
forward as the tall officer waved the flashlight past his
window.

Exit 18 was only three miles ahead. Now he was in a sweat
to get home. It seemed that a massive and cruel movement of
ill luck had touched him, brushing past with muscular haste;
or had not brushed past but clung to him as if he were its
epicenter. Darts of alarming light irradiated his mirror,
burned across his face. At a mule's pace he crawled the three
miles to his exit.

Rational, Leo knew that nothing had happened to his wife;
he understood that his fears were the product of his work at
the plant in Woodville and of the sudden reminder of mortality slipping behind him on the highway. He was not as
tough as he had been impelled to be in Woodville, and now
his mind was taking the toll for that callousness. You escaped

that, his mind was saying, but *this* you shall not so easily escape. And after all, were not the news items he had heard proof that his strategy had worked? His mind was punishing itself for that success.

All shall be well, all shall be well, and all manner of things shall be well.

Again he saw the two young men, Washington and Thorogood, on their backs in the glass room. He squirted out of the line of cars at his exit, gunned his Corvette up the ramp, and faked a pause at the stop sign.

Leo wound through the quiet Hampstead streets. Lights burned in the big frame houses, ordinary family life went on. A man walked a dog, a large woman in a sweatsuit thumped down Charleston Road. On his corner, a lost-looking teenage boy stood at the edge of the road, gazing at the sky as if for direction. For a second, for less than that, Leo thought he knew the boy, who was fair-haired, perhaps slightly undersized, and wore a striped rugby shirt with the sleeves pushed up on his thin arms. The headlights swept past him, the boy jerked away, and Leo swerved into Cannon Road

On their acre-and-a-half lots, the houses sedately marched uphill, pronouncing themselves good investments, not as grand as the houses on Hermitage Avenue up the hill, but shining forth from their lighted windows a solid affluence. In this world all children were blond, all refrigerators stocked with mineral water, expensive jogging shoes scuffed or virginal sat in every closet. Four houses up, Leo saw Stony's car parked in the driveway. Then he saw that all the windows were dark. The car left out of the garage, the black empty windows: Leo exhaled, seeing these first signs of disorder. The top of his head suddenly went cold. He turned into the driveway and pulled ahead of his wife's car.

On his way to the front door, he paused on the gravel drive and looked about him. The boy had vanished from the Charleston Road corner. The big trees loomed up into the darkness, where they coalesced into one tree. All was silence and growing dark. Mr. Leo Friedgood returns home on a Saturday evening from a noble day's work. Mr. Leo Friedgood surveys his estate. His chest felt tight. Leo turned around and went quickly to his front door.

It was unlocked. The house was darker than the outside, and he switched on the hall light. "Stony." No answer. "Stony?" He stepped forward, still thinking that there was a happy explanation—she had gone for a walk, she had stepped next door for a drink. But Stony never did either of those things, not at night. Leo turned on the dining-room lights and saw the empty table ringed with solid wooden chairs. "Stony?" The conviction that something terrible had taken place, which had begun in him when he had passed the wrecks on the highway, blossomed out urgently. He was afraid to go into the kitchen.

Okay. Let's get to the good part. What happened? They had stood beside a wall of gloomy monkeys in cages.

Leo pushed open the kitchen door.

A room within a room, a structure like a glass cube, a tile floor . . .

The mute presences of the range and refrigerator bulked in the dark kitchen. His own tile floor, red, was a shadowy sea. Leo flicked the light. He saw the Johnnie Walker bottle, the only thing out of place, upright beside the sink. His fingers gently found it. They pushed the bottle back into the corner where the draining board met the wall.

Slowly Leo left the kitchen and went back to the dining room. He glanced up the stairs and continued into the living room. Here were silvery couches and padded chairs, a murky glass table, their colors drained by moonlight streaming in through the window. A tall clock ticked resonantly from the corner. He had seen when he had come in that the room was empty. Still he turned on the nearest lamp, and the room sprang into life.

In a little alcove on a far side of the living room was a "den" with bookshelves and a desk. A previous tenant had outfitted this alcove with track lighting which Leo never used. He switched on the desk lamp. Framed diplomas stared down, as did a photograph taken at a Telpro institutional presentation of himself in the proximity of Red Buttons. Of course Stony was not in this little corner.

Irresolutely Leo wandered back to the entry. He looked up the stairs. He called out his wife's name. Leo went up three steps, peering into the darkness above him. He wiped his palms on the front of his sweatshirt. Then, grasping the handrail, he went up to the top and switched on the light. The door to his bedroom was closed.

Leo went down the hall to the door and put his hand on the brass knob. This is an empty room, he told himself. Nothing has happened, everything is just the same. When I open the door, I'll know that nothing's happened and that Stony will be back in a few minutes. He turned the knob and pushed open the door. As soon as he leaned forward and put his head into the room, he smelled the peaty aroma of whiskey. Stony's flat black shoes sat on the floor beside a neat pile of her clothes. Finally Leo caught the odor of blood, which in fact was very strong in the room. He glanced at what was on the bed, and then found himself back in the upstairs hall without any memory of having left the bedroom.

10

At ten minutes to ten the lights of two police cars streamed along the leafy streets toward Greenbank and the Sound; having finished her column, Sarah Spry finally left the *Gazette* building, unaware that the first page would have to be reset on Sunday afternoon. Richard Allbee put down his journal, undressed, got into the water bed in his rented house, touched Laura's shoulder and found that she was trembling. Graham Williams heard the sirens pass by on the street behind his house and rolled over in bed. Tabby Smithfield, still outside, watched the cars streak past him and stood riveted to the grass before an unknown house on Cannon Road, incapable of moving because a long-forgotten memory had nailed his feet to the ground.

Patsy McCloud did not hear the sirens or see the cars. As he did several times a year, her husband was hitting her upper arms and shoulders, every third or fourth blow slapping her face with his open palm, and she was making too much noise to hear anything but herself. The beating lasted until she ceased any signs of resistance and simply bowed her head into the protection of her raised forearms. Finally the blows were no more than a succession of taps. "You know you drive me crazy sometimes," Les McCloud said. "Go wash your face, for God's sake."

11

Leo Friedgood, still being questioned by the police, missed the eleven-o'clock news, which reported the apparent suicide, in Boston, of an MIT scientist named Otto Bruckner. Leo would not be left alone until past midnight, when he would take a room at the Colonial Motel on the Post Road and sleep in his clothes, so tranquilized by the police doctor that the noises from the discotheque in the motel's basement never disturbed him. But on the local news, Ted Wise spoke his piece, Pierce spoke his, and the famous reporter stood sleekly and elegantly upright as he announced that all the agencies had attributed the deaths of the two workers to carbon-monoxide fumes emanating from a faulty furnace. The famous reporter did not neglect to remind his audience of a similar incident in the Bronx four months earlier.

The Sunday edition of the *New York Times* carried a foot-long obituary of Dr. Otto Bruckner. There were anecdotes about his modesty and absentmindedness, a list of his awards, a reasonable assessment of his place in the development of modern biochemistry. In death Dr. Bruckner was treated fairly by the *Times*, which is to say he was accorded more stature than he would ever have ascribed to himself. His obituary did not mention his work on DRG.

Nor did the Sunday *Times* discuss the murder of Stony Baxter Friedgood. There would be only a short article in Monday's paper. But Stony was not to be forgotten in death. Her photograph would appear four times in the newspaper, the first in a row of black-bordered photographs. In thirteen weeks, over the rest of May, through June and July, six more people were to be murdered just as Stony was. After that the news which came from this section of Patchin County was spotty and unreliable.

2

The Allbees

1

For Richard Allbee, the first real shock of being back in his native country had come late at night in the hotel suite he and Laura had taken to wait out the availability of the house on Fairytale Lane. Moving house ranks just behind divorce and death of a spouse as cause for anguish, and Richard had been unable to sleep; he felt as though he had just made the mistake of his life. Nervously he had wandered into the living room, switched on the television and been confronted—in the most concrete possible way—with his own past.

Daddy's Here was showing on an independent station, as it did every night at twelve-thirty in New York. In almost every large American city, the old series surfaced once a day on one of the less distinguished channels, offering its spurious vision of family life to anyone so fixated that he watched television after midnight or before six in the morning. *Daddy's Here* was a staple, it was fodder for the softest programming hours, but Richard had not seen it since the days of its first airing.

In London, that the almost thirty-year-old series still had a life had been curious and funny, but no one in London had seen it—the program had been something to joke about at parties. *The ten-year-old me is still going strong, that's right. What's more, he's still getting paid. The ten-year-old me had an excellent lawyer.* This was truer than he had known at the time: along with Carter Oldfield, the only other principal actor still alive and the star of the series, Richard got a residual check every month of his life. The excellent lawyer, Phil Sawyer, had been Carter Oldfield's, and he had persuaded Richard's parents to accept a lower salary for the trade-off of an income even he had not expected to be lifelong. "Out here, nobody knows how long they're going to work, so make the program the boy's annuity," had been the persuasive sentence. *Annuity* was a magical word to Mrs. Mary All-bee. The other two chief cast members had turned down Sawyer's suggestion, but for Richard, beginning ten years after the program's cancellation, the residuals had begun to arrive. He had been twenty-four, and the unexpected money gave him a freedom he badly needed. There it was every month, enough to keep a young couple afloat as they moved happily into the early days of their marriage. Richard had gone to graduate school in architecture, worked for two years in an architect's office, moved to England and tried to write a novel, had finally found the work that satisfied him most. For three years the monthly checks had been invested, not spent—they had given the Allbees seven years of wandering without undue care, and after Richard and Laura had settled down in Kensington, the checks had been almost an embar-rassment, like a youthful habit not quite outgrown. Richard had his work, Laura was an editor for a women's magazine, and the green rectangle that meant *Daddy's Here* was going into its umpteenth year in Cleveland and Little Rock simply went into Lloyd's Bank and slowly multiplied itself.

Six years' worth of episodes, more than two hundred of them circling around the United States, showing the hard-working little Richard Allbee growing from eight to fourteen: growing through a youth utterly unlike his own real one. In the world of *Daddy's Here,* no problem existed that was not amusing and could not be solved by Ted Jameson—Carter Oldfield—in thirty minutes. There was no crime, no death or disease, no poverty, no alcoholism: the problems had to do with homework, girlfriends, buying birthday presents.

With a kind of fascinated dread, Richard sat down on the suite's stiff couch and watched himself move through his pro-fessional paces.

He had missed the first five or six minutes, and so had also missed *the line,* thank God. *The line,* the sentence which his character, Spunky Jameson, uttered in three programs out of five, which brought sacks full of cookies to the studio, had become a curse; at fourteen he had hoped never to hear it again, and he still hated cookies. The black-and-white images of his past would spare him that much, anyhow. The Jame-sons were seated around the table in their pine-and-Formica kitchen, and lovely Ruth Branden—Grace Jameson—was in a dither because she had dented a fender on the family car. She wanted to get it repaired before she told Ted. Flustered,

she put salt into Ted's coffee and sprinkled sugar on the roast.
Ted sampled his coffee, squinted, made a quizzical face.
"Hey, what's the matter, Pop?" asked David Jameson,
played by Billy Bentley.

"This coffee just doesn't taste right," said Carter Oldfield,
projecting kindliness and wisdom as well as momentary
puzzlement. "Switch brands, honey?"

Ten-year-old Richard Allbee giggled right on cue—he
knew about the bent fender.

That was how it had gone, more or less, for six years.

Richard could not help thinking of their fates, of what
had happened to the four of them. None of the other three had
found fame in movies that each, to different degrees, had
desired. Ruth Branden, that beautiful woman, the most professional actor on the set, had contracted breast cancer a year
after their cancellation; while working on the pilot for another
series, she had collapsed, and the doctors found that a new
cancer had spread throughout her internal organs. She was
dead in three months. Carter Oldfield was the only one of the
cast to still have a career in television—that aura of kindly
wisdom had been inextinguishable throughout Oldfield's
sieges of depression and boozing. Oldfield had moved from
Daddy's Here to another long-running series about a law
practice in a small Midwestern town. Now he appeared in
ubiquitous commercials for a brand of orange juice; "the
juice that wakes up your body." His hair had gone from dark
brown to silvery gray, but he still looked much the same. In
fact age had improved him—now he was like a hybrid of
James Stewart and Melvyn Douglas. Richard smiled, remembering in how many scenes Carter Oldfield had kept his hands
in his pockets because they were shakier than poplar leaves.
Still, he had survived, and Richard could now think of him
with affection. It was not the love with which he remembered
Ruth Branden, but the man was a better actor than anyone
credited him with being; he had only a one-octave keyboard,
but he played it beautifully.

But Billy Bentley . . . that was painful to remember, even
more painful than seeing Ruth Branden again. In the days of
Daddy's Here, Richard Allbee had been a boy without a father, without brothers or sisters—his father had apparently
vanished days after baby Richard's arrival home from the
hospital. Richard had idolized Billy Bentley. There was
something of James Dean in him, something sensitive and

rebellious. Ten years old to Richard's eight, fourteen to his twelve, he had looked five years older, with his dark broad face and fall of hair over his forehead. Billy had been a great, though an unschooled, dancer and had a small but real talent for music. Billy drank beer, smoked cigarettes, drove his own car around the studio lot, and shouted comic things at script girls. At twelve and fourteen, he had been innocently wild. Drugs had ruined him. And that had ruined *Daddy's Here.* On a street corner in West Los Angeles, he had tried to buy two nickle bags of heroin from a narcotics detective—he was seventeen and he looked at least twenty-five. The publicity had scuttled the series, scuttled Billy Bentley too.

Billy had disappeared into penal institutions for two years. In his absence he had been like a large unpaid bill, a nagging guilty center of awareness. He had written three times to his "brother." *You still gettin' high on Seven-Up, Spunky? Walkin' through "fields of flowers"? In here we got the whole elite of junior dope fiends and life ain't too bad, Spunks, not too bad. We ain't finished yet. We'll see the old red, red robin again someday.* In his sophomore year in college, Richard had read that Billy, now twenty-two, had been arrested again on a drug charge. He was still *Billy Bentley, actor and former child star of* Daddy's Here. Four years later, out again, he had called Richard in New York—he wanted to do a film about drug addiction, and he was looking for money. Richard had sent him a couple of thousand dollars against Laura's opposition. Chances were, it went straight into Billy's arm.

Richard had not cared—he felt he owed him at least that much. He had loved Billy, loved him just as if he had been a real brother. But he had refused to work with him.

That had come up first in Paris, where Richard and Laura were living for six months. Billy had called up in the middle of the night, full of an idea for his resurrection. "Hey man, there are all these dinner theaters out there now—all over the East Coast, man. We're naturals. They'd drop dead to get us. We just find the right play, and we're in. And we get on pretty good—hell, I practically *raised* you." Richard thought of the last time he had seen Billy: he had looked into the window of Horn and Hardart's on East Forty-second Street and seen him at a table, his face still broad and dark but all the innocence burned out of it. He wore the clothes of the hip urban poor, corduroy jeans and a Salvation Army suit jacket too large for him. His face was oddly pocked, full of small shadowy scars. Billy looked dangerous, sitting at the table in Horn and Hardart's; he looked like he did not belong in daylight. "Are you clean now?" Richard asked him.

"Hey, don't be a drag. I'm on the methadone program, I can get clean anytime I want. I'm ready for *work*, Spunks. Let's get something together. People want to see all that old stuff again."

Richard had said no and felt it like a betrayal. In the second year in London, there had been another midnight phone call—Billy was still thinking about dinner theater. "Billy," Richard had said, "I was an actor because my mother wanted to see my footprints outside the Chinese Theater. It was fun, but that's over for me. I'm sorry."

"I need you, man," Billy had told him. "Like you needed a dad in the red, red robin days."

"I'll send you some money," Richard had said. "That's the best I can do."

"Money ain't Spunks," Billy said, and hung up before Richard could ask for his address. Not long after, Richard read of his death in *Newsweek*. He had been shot to death in what the magazine called "an altercation over drugs."

Richard thought of all this while watching the innocuous twenty minutes of *Daddy's Here*. In the morning, he knew, Laura would listen sympathetically and then say, "Billy didn't belong to you, lunkhead. You didn't wreck his life, he did." That was true—but Laura had not heard Billy Bentley's half-whispered *I need you*, and responded with an offer of money. Sorry, Billy, I can't save your life right now, how about a nice fat check instead?

Welcome home, Richard.

He switched off the set as soon as "When The Red, Red Robin Goes Bob, Bob, Bobbin Along," the theme song, began to swing joyously beneath the credits.

2

It must have been because of the accident of unexpectedly seeing himself and Billy Bentley as the children they had been that Richard dreamed of being back in the series on his second night in Hampstead. Richard and Laura spent the Sunday unpacking their clothes—the summer clothes only, for all the rest could wait until they had their own place. The house on Fairytale Lane was theirs for two months only. Already they knew that this was a blessing. Hampstead was even now very humid, and the rented house was not air-conditioned: the attic fan cooled the bedroom floor, but it roared like a jet engine. The huge fireplace in the living room, though spotless, stank of ashes. The kitchen had only a few feet of counter space. What could have been a useful spot beneath some of the upper cabinetry was occupied by a microwave oven, the first one the Allbees had seen. The four bedrooms were small and dark, the stairs ominously steep. Whenever he rolled over on the hated water bed, the resulting wave threatened to knock Laura onto the floor. In the vest-pocket dining room, a large water stain announced that the ceiling would one day introduce itself to the table. All the wiring, to Richard's experienced eye, had been installed before the second war. A third of the window frames had rotted, leaving a papery, waferlike layer of paint. All in all, the house was a good candidate for Richard's professional services. He was a restorer of such rotting beauties.

He had worked on a dozen large houses in London, starting with his own, and had built a reputation based on care, exactness, and hard work. He took a deep satisfaction in bringing these abused Victorian and Edwardian structures back to life. What showed in his work was that the man behind it understood where the beauty in such houses lay and knew how to make it shine again. Richard had put himself to school to the buildings an earlier generation had dismissed as monstrosities, and in a short time, guided by an instinct he had not known was his, had learned their secrets. In a few years, he had even a small kind of fame—two magazines had done features about his houses, he was offered more work than he could accept. This would happen, he fervently hoped, in America too. Two couples, one in Rhode Island and the other in Hillhaven, had already contracted for his services. The commissions had given him the impetus to move back to America—that and the impending birth of his child. His son or daughter would be American, and would sound like one. Before he conceived a child, he had not imagined that to be important, but important it was. The child of Laura and himself would not have a Kensington accent—it would have the accent of Connecticut, where both his parents and Laura's had been born: where he and Laura too had been born, on the same day a year apart. Richard also felt easier about enrolling Lump—the only name they had yet—in a Patchin County school than sending her/him to a London comprehensive.

Her/him? Lump would be a girl, Richard secretly knew, and loved the knowledge.

Shortly before the packers had come, while the London house was still recognizable, Richard had dreamed that he was walking in Kensington Gardens. It was a day five or six years in the future. The sunshine which fell on the lovely broad lawn was sunlight still far out in space; the grass and flowers were the grandchildren of the grass and flowers he knew. The trees were slightly though noticeably taller. This atmosphere of futurity extended to Richard, who in the dream was slightly heavier than his actual hundred and sixty pounds. A child was tugging at his hand. He was taking this future child out to play in the future park, and all was well. Dream-Richard dared not look down at his child, for fear of weeping with joy. Lump was tugging him along toward the Round Pond, and he let Lump pull him, for the moment simply and quietly stunned with happiness. At last he did look down. She was a small, vibrant child with Laura's straight reddish-blond hair. She wore a little print dress and black childish shoes. Pride and love burst in his chest, and he sobbed, overwhelmed by the force of these emotions, and his bursting feeling woke him up. He had seen her, and she was perfect. The calm radiance of this dream had stayed with him for days.

He had never told Laura about seeing their child in the dream.

Neither did he tell her of the other dream. Husbands and wives divide psychic responsibilities, and Richard's duty was to represent the optimistic side of the wrenching move; it was Laura who could express their joint fears and doubts.

So it was Laura who asked, "Is this really going to work?" They were taking a walk, that first Sunday, plunging off into unknown territory. The Allbees had gone down to the steep end of Fairytale Lane and wandered across a bridge, gone past immense trees entangled with creeping vines, been

briefly joined by an amiable scurry of rotund dogs. All the
houses seemed huge, set at vast distances from each other. A
chain saw burped and spat from behind a screen of trees.

"Sure it is," he said. He put his arm around her shoulders.
"It might be a little tough at the start, but good things are
going to happen to us here. I already have two customers.
That's a good start."

"I'm in culture shock." Laura said.

"We grew up here," Richard pointed out.

"You grew up in Los Angeles. I grew up in Chicago. This
whole state looks like Lake Forest."

"Can't be bad." He caught the flash of her eye and said,
"Oh, I know what you mean."

They had been born here, but it was strange to them:
Laura's father had been transferred to Illinois and she had
grown up in a town house similar to their London house; he
had grown up in a series of apartments and small rented
houses. His first house had been the one he and Laura had
bought together. They were used to terraces—row houses—
and shops close enough to walk to, they were used to traffic
and pubs and parks. Hampstead, neither city nor country, had
a dissociated, unreal quality. The name conjured up pictures
of the Everyman Cinema and Holly Hill, Galsworthy's serene
white house and brick walks, for both of them.

"I think it will take a year or two," he said, "but we'll
adjust to this funny place."

"I'm not sure I want to adjust," Laura said, and he silently
applauded.

At that point a pack of men in short pants and sweat-
stained T-shirts burst from around a corner and pounded
toward them. "Hey!" shouted the leader, a Viking with flowing hair and a blond bouncing beard. Richard, who was wearing a tweed jacket and a necktie, suddenly felt overdressed
for this sunny May morning.

One of the things they had noticed already was that Patchin
County was resolutely healthy. Not only did joggers come
down Fairytale Lane at all hours, but the stupefyingly lavish
grocery stores were filled with people returning from or going
to tennis matches. The local drugstore was stocked with an
amazing array of cigarettes, but he had been the only person
buying them.

Of course there was a culture shock. When Laura went to

the grocery store where the customers all seemed to be modeling tennis clothes, she did not recognize the cuts of meat. Most of the breakfast cereals were pap coated with sugar. And strangers spoke to you with astounding directness. "My sister died," a woman said to Laura over the frozen yogurt. "She just fell over and died, and of course her husband never changed a diaper in his life." "What a shame," Laura replied, backpedaling. The men, like the Viking jogger, looked you in the eye and beamed, showing a million white teeth— they looked like talk-show hosts. There was an assumption of intimacy in that glad dopey gaze.

They would get used to all these things—which were finally unimportant—because they had to. And Richard knew that their first days in America were particularly strained because they were supposed to be at home with everything here. That was another expectation, one they had of themselves.

The Allbees went early to bed that night. While Richard read aloud from their current project, *Madame Bovary,* they from time to time stroked each other's thighs, caresses full of comfortable marital tenderness. Laura occasionally smiled to herself as the baby moved, which it had only lately begun to do. Tonight the baby was active, and she wanted Richard to feel it steeplechasing. He fell asleep with his hand on the rising loaf of her belly.

Sometime in the night, he dreamed of being back on the set of *Daddy's Here.*

He was not ten years old: he was his own thirty-six. He was saying *the line.* Billy Bentley, likewise adult, smirked from out of his shadowy, pitted face. "Not tonight, darling," Ruth Branden said, bustling onto the set through the door from the kitchen. "Don't you remember? There was an awful murder. There's something terrible outside. I couldn't make cookies with that on my mind."

"Oh, sure, Mom," he said. "I remember now. No, cookies sure would be a bad idea."

"Booga-booga-booga," Billy Bentley said. "There's a big bad killer and he's going to get *you.*"

An episode about a killer? Surely that was wrong. The sponsors would never have . . .

"He's gonna pounce on you outta the closet." Billy Bentley grinned at him. "The door is going to swi-i-i-ng open, and he's gonna crawl on out, coming to get you, babe."

"Now, David," said Ruth Branden. "That's not *nice.*"

"Dad's been looking a little weird lately," Billy said. "The old juicer needs a jolt. About time Dr. Feelgood gave him a happy pill. We'll be lucky if he makes it to the end of the season."

"I won't have you saying such things about your father," said Ruth Branden, still imperturbably in character.

They were not on the set, Richard finally noticed. They were eating in the vest-pocket dining room. There were no cameras and no crowds of stagehands and studio people looking on.

"Hey, Mom," he said.

"I want you to go to your bedroom now," Ruth said. "Lock your door. And make sure the windows are locked too."

"This isn't the—"

"Get upstairs," Ruth Branden shouted, and for a second her face was cronelike, raddled and drawn. "Get up there and lock your door!"

The room had four walls, but somewhere a camera was recording all this. "Scene Two," called a voice. "Places."

He was up in the bedroom: pajamas: night. Model airplanes covered the desk, a college pennant was tacked to the wall over the bed. APHOOLIE. (Arhoolie?) This was the set bedroom, and he was now truly Spunky Jameson, for he was in his ten-year-old body. A pair of skis leaned against the wall by the closet. A tennis racket in its zippered case; all the old boyish clutter. He touched his face, ran his hand over his crewcut. Yes. All was right.

He knew what the script called for. *SPUNKY walks to window, looks out anxiously, turns back to DAVID.* Richard went to the window. He remembered that view. The back wall of the studio, unused flats, dangling ropes. He looked out. What he saw was not the view of the studio, but a street, grass, a neighbor's picket fence. In moonlight, streetlamps marched down Maple Lane, a street which had never existed. A 1954 Chevy went by, its headlights making lines of tar in the road blackly shine.

He turned around, his mouth dry. "Hey," he said.

SPUNKY: Hey.

Laura lay asleep on the water bed, her hair spilling over the pillow. Billy Bentley, his face barely visible in the darkness, lay beside her, grinning at him. Richard knew that Billy was naked under the sheets.

"Booga-booga-booga," Billy said in an evil voice. "Bad stuff coming your way."

FRONT DOOR SLAMS.

The front door slammed.

DAVID: Guess it's here now, bro.

"Guess it's here now, bro," Billy said. "You sure you got the door locked?"

In shock, Richard gaped at the spectacle of Billy Bentley naked in bed with Laura. There was a definite atmosphere of postcoital ease. Laura breathed in and out through slack beautiful, blissfully unconscious lips. "Hell of a good woman you got there," Billy said, and Richard, in the midst of a searing blast of resentment, felt his powerlessness before Billy Bentley's adult body. "This is one woman who's got it all, you know what I mean?" Billy's spatulate hand, black in the dark room, rubbed Laura's sheeted rump. "But if you don't mind my saying so, you got yourself another little problem now, Spunks. I ain't too sure you locked that door after all."

"The door?"

"The bedroom door, Spunks. *Bad* ole thing a-comin'."

Richard could hear terrible noises coming from downstairs. A heavy object fell to the ground, accompanied by the sound of breaking glass and china. Ruth Branden screamed. A heavy vicious splintering sound, as of an ax repeatedly striking wood. Ruth screamed once more: there came a series of heavy thuds, and Ruth's screams abruptly stopped.

"Better get your ass in gear," Billy said.

Someone was shouting downstairs.

Richard went to the door and punched in the button on the knob.

"Kinda lost his cool when he saw that dent in the fender." Billy was still grinning at him, still rubbing Laura's rump.

BEDROOM DOOR RATTLES.

The door noisily shook against the lock. The person on the other side knocked once, then twice more. "Spunky? Hey, Spunky? Let me in, will you?" It was Carter Oldfield's expressive voice, but the voice sounded ragged and out of breath. "I paid for this house, I own it. Let me in, you little

creep.'' The voice also sounded drunk—Richard had heard
that dragging slur before.

"Go away,'' he said. And Billy Bentley chuckled from the
bed.

"Don't tell *me* to go away,'' roared Carter Oldfield. "I've
got some *business* to take care of with you.''

The ax began to strike the door with great thudding splintering blows.

Richard shuddered into wakefulness, his heart thundering
in his chest. The digital clock on the bedside table read 4:04.
Laura whiffled in her sleep, disturbed by the sloshing Richard
had created when he had awakened. Striped wallpaper he
would never have chosen shone for a moment on the walls,
picked out by the glowing scoops of a passing car's headlights.

3

On Monday morning the Allbees met the real-estate person,
Ronnie Riggley, at her office at one of the shopping centers
on the Post Road. Ronnie was a big brash transplanted Cal-
ifornian with an eager laugh and short shining platinum hair.
She had the physical grace and confidence that follows some
former athletes throughout their lives, and Richard supposed
that she had been a good high-school swimmer or diver back
in Marin County. When the Allbees had arrived the previous
spring to look at rentals, two innocent know-nothings, Ronnie
had taken them in hand. Despite its flaws, the Fairytale Lane
house had been the most suitable of all the houses they had
seen that spring. Ronnie had treated them fairly, had even
steered them away from rentals less suitable and more expensive. They liked her: she made the wearying business of
house-hunting more enjoyable than it would have been otherwise.

"Let's hit the trail.'' Ronnie held up a sheaf of listings.
"We'll look at three this morning, have a nice lunch somewhere, and then hit two more this afternoon. I want you to
get an idea of what's available in your price range.''

They got into her car, a blue Datsun with RONNI license
plates. "I hope you're sleeping all right,'' she said. "It can
be hard, in an unfamiliar place.''

"Not really," Laura said from the backseat. "The bed sloshes."

Ronnie whooped with laughter. "Oh, darn, I forgot—that house has a water bed! But don't you think you'll get used to it?"

"I'd rather not get used to it," Richard said. "Surfing is surfing and sleeping is sleeping, and never the twain shall meet."

He picked up the first of the listing sheets between himself and Ronnie. "Is this where we're going first?"

Ronnie nodded. "Say, I feel a little tacky, asking this, but I just have to do it. Could you . . . I mean, would you mind saying it for me? You know what I mean."

She wanted him to say *the line*. He glanced at Laura, who was grinning wickedly at him from the backseat.

"Or do you just hate it when people ask you to do that?"

"Nobody's asked me to say it in ten years at least. Okay. 'Hey, Mom, I want a *whole* plate of cookies!' "

Both women laughed.

"Well, my voice changed."

Laura said, "That wasn't so bad, was it, dear?"

"Not so bad? It was wonderful," Ronnie said. "I just had to ask—I can't believe that was you. I told my boyfriend—you know, Bobo, the guy who's a cop?—I was showing you houses, and Bobo said, ask him to say it. Sometimes when Bobo's on eight-to-twelve we watch your program after he gets back. It's on nearly every night, you know. I think it's just so *neat* that you're moving back to Hampstead."

"Of course, we hardly knew it," Richard said. "Both of us were practically babies when we left."

"Oh, you'll love it here—there's always something going on. When we had our big office party for our customers last Christmas, Jane Frobisher, she works with me, came up to some people I just sold a house to and she said, 'You just moved into Hampstead? You're so young to get divorced!'

"Oh, my gosh, listen, do you know about the murder yet?" Ronnie broke into their laughter. "Bobo told me about it. It happened Saturday night, and after Bobo got back to the station after that big accident on the thruway, everybody was talking about it. I hate to talk about the wages of sin and all that, but I guess the lady got turned into lamb patties by her Mr. Goodbar while her husband was out working."

That was how the Allbees first heard of Stony Friedgood.
"Madame Bovary in Patchin County," Laura said.
"So there's another house for sale in Hampstead," Richard
said.
"Oh, it's not for you," Ronnie said quickly. "I know that
house. It's strictly IBM. I Been Moved."

4

If, during lunch at the same French restaurant Clark and Jean
Smithfield had liked, Ronnie Riggley went into perhaps too
much detail about the circumstances of Stony Friedgood's
death; if these circumstances suddenly reminded Richard Allbee of his nightmare about a crazed Carter Oldfield battering
at a bedroom door with an ax; if none of the houses they had
seen were right—the affordable ones needed so much work
Richard would have had to neglect his clients—and if even
three houses tended to blur into each other after an ice-cold
martini and a glass of the excellent house white, still the three
of them began to experience the glow of a beginning friend-
ship. Richard even told a few well-worn anecdotes about Carter Oldfield's tantrums on the set of *Daddy's Here*. Laura
lovingly described the Kensington house (which gave Ronnie
some very specific ideas about what to show the Allbees).
Ronnie gave them hope that life in Patchin County could be
satisfying, interesting, and fun too: sitting across from them
with her smile, her swimmer's shoulders and shining helmet
of hair, she was a signpost toward a future where the things
that shadowed them could be weightless. She even offered the
hope of an infant social life by saying that they should all go
out to dinner with Bobo some night during the next week.
"Then you'll really get the lowdown on Hampstead," Ronnie
said. "Bobo knows it all. And he's a great guy besides. Well,
I would think so, I'm only in love with him."
    And she gave Laura the name of a good doctor. "Every-
body uses Dr. Van Horne," she said. "He's the best gynie
man in town. He's extremely sensitive, which you'd think
was pretty special if you had gone to some of the turkeys I
trusted with my life before I switched to him. He'll treat you
like a queen and recommend a good O.B. person too."

She smiled at Laura. "Lump. I think that's so cute. Lump Allbee, the healthiest kid in Stride-Rites."

Laura pulled a notebook from her bag and wrote down: Dr. Wren Van Horne, Gyn.

3

Graham

1

Instinct tells me that now is the time to emerge from the cover of the godlike narrator who knows what all his characters are thinking and doing at all times and who takes an impartial stance toward them. Already this pose has slipped, never more so than when I alluded to myself. This is me, Graham Williams, writing this account. Call me Graham. No, you damn well better not. Call me Mr. Williams, unless you happen to be within at least a decade of my age, which is seventy-six. I have outlived every doctor who had warned me that I was smoking and drinking myself into a premature grave, and I am a cranky old party. My views are fixed and my bowels are still good. I have twelve of my original teeth, which is pretty fair going, and a lot of expensive bridgework. I wrote thirteen novels, only three of them crappy, a self-consciously harrowing memoir of my years on the booze, and seven screenplays. At least one of these still sounds pretty perky when the movie shows up on the tube. This was *Glenda*, which starred Mary Astor as and Gary Cooper and James Cagney as lover and husband of. I am a failure and a coward. As a young man I learned to undermine my enemies by knocking myself before anybody else got the chance.

Of course these days I don't have any enemies left to speak of, which is a damn shame. All those battles turn into ancient history when your foes die off. Nobody cares about them anymore, and when you talk to a bunch of kids about the time you went head to head with some crass knucklebrained demigod of a studio boss, their eyes turn to stone. You might as well be talking about cave men and saber-toothed tigers. Even that sweaty weasel who bitched my life, the junior senator from Wisconsin, tail-gunner Joe, died a long time ago, and so

did most of his fellow weasels on HUAC. Sterling Hayden—
there's a man. Him I could talk to.

The reason for coming out of cover and talking directly like
this is that I lived through everything that happened in the
lower end of Patchin County, and the book I was writing
turned into this one. What I didn't know about, I had to make
up, but it all could have happened, and maybe did, just the
way I wrote it. I kept my eyes open, and I saw plenty. At the
end of it Richard Allbee said to me, "Why don't you sit
down and tell the whole story?" And that's how this book
will end, if you're one of those folks who has to turn to the
last page to see how it all comes out. My friends let me read
their diaries, and that's where a lot of this stuff comes from.

2

But a lot comes from what I saw and heard, as I said. Consider where I lived. My house was on Beach Trail in Greenbank, right across the street from the old Sayre house, which
the Allbees finally bought. "Four Hearths," where Tabby
went with his father and stepmother, is just two minutes up
the hill. Patsy and Les McCloud lived catty-corner across
from my backyard. Mount Avenue, the Golden Mile, runs up
toward Hillhaven just down the end of Beach Trail—I knew
Monty Smithfield, not well, and I met Stony Friedgood when
she was in that book group, High Minds. (If I stood on my
roof, I could chunk a rock right through the window of the
bedroom where they found Stony, at least I could have twenty
years ago.) High Minds was talking about one of my books
that week, *Twisted Hearts,* and Stony asked me if the husband in the novel understood that he was forcing his wife into
the affair with my hero. "Forcing her?" I asked. "They finally got a new paperback deal for *Twisted Hearts* because
some editor thought it was a feminist statement." "From the
neck down, no," Ms. Friedgood replied.

Gary Starbuck, the professional thief who played a minor
role in some of our lives and who will appear in these pages
soon, rented the roomy old Frazier Peters house only two
blocks away, and after his death I walked through the astonishing display of stolen silver, television sets, paintings,
and furniture with most of my neighbors before Bobo Farns-

worth and the other cops sealed the place. And I knew that
rascal Pat Dobbin, because I had seen him grow up: his father
was a friend of mine in the boozing days I wrote about in *Lost
Time*. I rescued myself, Dan Dobbin didn't, but he was a
better illustrator than his son.

But more important than all of that—or as important anyhow—I couldn't look at Mount Avenue without seeing the
Jaegers running down it with their torches in 1779, I couldn't
look at Monty Smithfield's big house without seeing the
wooden shack enigmatic Gideon Winter had put up on that
spot in 1645. I *knew* the area, my father knew it, and my
great-great-grandfather too. When I looked at some happy kid
named Moorman or Green, some kid in jeans and braces, I
saw in him the leathery old onion farmer or blacksmith who'd
had the same name and had given him a sixteenth of his
genes.

3

One thing is more important than my eccentric knowledge of
the genetic makeup of fifth-graders whose names were on the
oldest tombstones in Gravesend Cemetery. I was one of the
first to see the immediate effects of what I called the thinking
cloud after it settled down over us. Of course I made no more
sense of it than anyone else at the time, having no idea that
there was sense to be made.

4

Effects, I said. Two effects. I encountered the first of these,
the second ten minutes later, while I was taking a walk down
Beach Trail on Sunday morning, the eighteenth of May. On
most sunny mornings I limp down the street to Mount Avenue, turn right and walk past the gates of the Academy and
turn into the short public road to Gravesend Beach. I look at
the water and the people moving up and down on the beach. I
breathe in the salt air, which has kept me alive all this time.
No salt on your food, lots of good salt air in your lungs. If I
see them, I generally say hello to Harry and Babe Zimmer,
who materialize in their beat-up old Ford pickup around eight

or nine to fish off the breakwater. Harry and Babe are a couple of kids in their mid-sixties. They look like old jack o'lanterns left outside since last Halloween. Harry and Babe call me Mr. Williams. Then I crawl back. The whole exercise should take about ten minutes, but it takes me over half an hour.

That morning I never got as far as the beach. There had been a small interruption in the epic wander while I inspected the latest damage to my mailbox, several heavy bangs and dents I took as a homicide attempt. The mailbox killer had apparently switched from cherry bombs to blunt instruments. After the inspection, I resumed the death-defying journey.

I was just toiling past the immaculate lawn of the last house on my side of Beach Trail when I saw a body on the grass. The immaculate lawn was Bobby Fritz's work (Bobby knew every blade, every tree, every flower surrounding these houses, except for the poor stuff on my lawn), the body was Charlie Antolini's. Charlie appeared to be deader than my mailbox, and I scuttled up on the lawn to get a closer look.

Charlie was a toughie, about forty, the son of the family that owned the Lobster House and a couple of other restaurants in Patchin and Westchester counties. As a kid he had been a hustler—at nine or ten, back in the days before mailbox assassinations, he was my newsboy. Even then he was a nuts-and-bolts human being, jittery with the need to make more money, money, money. He had finally accumulated enough to put himself and his family into the big green clapboard on Mount Avenue. The wrong side, not the Sound side, but still Mount Avenue.

"Need any help, Charlie?" I asked. I had seen right away that he was not dead. He was very still, but his green eyes were open and he was smiling a little. This was not a typical Charlie Antolini smile. It was positively blissful. He was wearing pale blue silk pajamas. "Liable to get a nasty burn, Charlie," I said.

"Hi there, Mr. Williams," he said.

Charlie had not addressed me by name since about 1955. I thought he figured that a grubby old scribbler like me sort of lowered the tone of the neighborhood. "You sure you're all right?" I asked.

"Just fine, Mr. Williams," he said, giving me that smile his mother wouldn't recognize.

"Felt like taking the air, hey? It's a good idea, Charlie. Keeps the tubes clear. Why don't you come down to the beach with me, say hello to Harry and Babe?"

"Got up this morning and felt great," he said. "Just un-fucking-believable. Got outside. Felt even better. Felt too good to go to work."

"It's Sunday, Charlie," I said. "Nobody goes to work on Sunday." Then I remembered that he was probably due at the Lobster House to help out with the brunch crowd.

"Sunday," he said. "Oh, yeah."

I looked up at his house. His wife was semaphoring from the living-room window. "I think you ought to get off the lawn, Charlie," I said. "Florence looks pretty upset." Then I spotted his mailbox, formerly one of the apples of Charlie's eye. Metal like mine, but twice as large, it was painted the same shade of green as his house. Over the green Charlie'd had someone paint a pattern of flowers and vines trailing through a big red ANTOLINI. Now this contraption lay on the driveway, knocked right off its pole. The side was bashed in, and shiny aluminum shone through the paint. I said, "Say, the gang that killed my box got yours too. Yours is more of a case of outright decapitation."

"Just feel that sun," Charlie said.

Flo Antolini was waggling her arms behind the window, either telling me to clear off or to pick Charlie up and carry him inside. The latter was out of the question. Charlie must have weighed about two-forty. Under the blue silk and the flab, he still looked like the halfback he'd been on the J. S. Mill High School football team in 1959. I couldn't have lifted one of his legs. I shrugged to Flo, put my hands in my pockets, said, "Well, enjoy yourself" to Charlie and prepared to maneuver myself back onto the sidewalk.

I had just accomplished this when I heard a woman screaming Charlie's name. *"Mr. Antolini! Mr. Antolini!"*

"Better hustle inside, Charlie," I said, figuring that one of the neighbor ladies had taken offense at the sight of him beached out there on his beautiful lawn. This was Hampstead, after all, not Dogpatch.

Then I saw the woman from across the street barreling toward us. Evelyn Hughardt, Mrs. Dr. Hughardt. She was wearing a pink housecoat and had pink fuzzy things on her feet. She looked terrible.

"Mr. Antolini, *please*," she yelled, and ran across the

street without bothering to look both ways. When she got closer I saw how terrible she really looked. Normally she was a nice looking blond lady, almost as big and healthy as that real estate woman, Ronnie Riggley. Plenty of tennis keeps them that way.

She damn near knocked me over and knelt down on the grass beside Charlie. She grabbed one of his hands and tried to yank him sideways. "It's Dr. Hughardt, my husband," she said. "Oh, please. I don't know what to do, and he'd be so ashamed of me . . ."

"Hi there, Evvy," Charlie said, giving her that beautiful green-eyed smile.

"Come on, please, Mr. Antolini, please please help me."

"Gosh," Charlie said.

"Too much sun," I said. "Knocked him flat. Damn shame. Maybe I can give you a hand."

When she looked up at me I realized that she literally had not noticed me before. She blinked me away and went back to yanking on Charlie's paw.

"No help there, like I said," I offered. "He's just been born again. An uncle of mine did the same thing at a chautauqua on Fairlie Hill in 1913. Went down like an ox. But I'm pleased to offer my own services."

She gave an agonized pull at Charlie's hand once more and then looked up at me. "Please, Mr. Williams," she said. Her voice was all trembly. "Help me with the Doctor."

"Lead the way," I said, and followed her at a quarter of her pace across the street. She had the door open and was waving me in when I was only half way there.

5

Norm Hughardt was what I guess they call an internist today, now that G.P.'s are out of date, and he was a pretty good doctor and a very good snob. His dad used to be the same way. When I was some kind of a hotshot, old Dr. Hughardt was happy to see me and tell me to lose weight, change my habits, etc., but after I fell into disgrace he wasn't so happy about it any more. Norm went to J. S. Mill about ten years before Charlie Antolini did. After that he went to the University of Virginia and Yale Medical School. When he was about Charlie's age he returned to Virginia for some kind of semi-nar and met this big blond tennis player and brought her back here. He was in practice with his father, but after his father gave up on me (the old man died pretty soon after) he wouldn't take me as a patient because he thought I was a Communist, which was a lot of bilge. Still, he was supposed to be the second best doctor in Hampstead, the best one being Wren Van Horne, who shines up the plumbing of half the ladies in town. Wren and I went back a good ways, but he was no good to me as a doctor.

I guess Norm told his wife to always refer to him as Dr. Hughardt in front of other people. He had a pointy little beard and an impressive bald head. He couldn't be bothered with you unless you were famous or likely to be. He worked on all the actors and illustrators around town. When he thought of something funny, he called up Sarah Spry so she could put it in her column. He hadn't spoken to me in twenty years, I bet. Maybe twenty-five.

Evelyn was sort of hissing at me when I got to the front door. I could tell that even though she was too rattled to do anything herself, she wasn't easy about letting me in the house. I was Joe Stalin's nephew, or some similar nonsense. Besides that, I wasn't even dressed up to the pink housecoat and fuzzy footgear standard. I was wearing a pair of old black hightop basketball shoes, lumpy baggy tweed suit-pants, and a green turtleneck sweater with ragged holes at the elbows. Also, I had not shaved. I almost never shave under my chin anyhow. I don't want to cut my throat.

"Well, what is it, Evelyn?" I asked. The entry was papered with framed cartoons, and I recognized the styles of Hampstead's and Hillhaven's half-dozen famous cartoonists. The one signed *Hope this hurts you more than it does me, Best, Pat Dobbin* showed a little bald guy with a pointy beard sawing into the belly of a Dobbin lookalike while bills and coins spilled out of the wound. Pat Dobbin had made himself look the way he likely looked to himself in the medicine chest mirror, which is to say handsomer than he really was.

"Please," she said. "Come to the back, Mr. Williams. Dr. Hughardt was just going outside to check on the sprinkler system . . . and . . . I saw him fall and . . ." She was pulling on the ratty old turtleneck, trying to get me to increase my speed.

"He fell, did he?" I asked. "Tripped, maybe?"

She let out a sob.

"You just call the ambulance, Evelyn," I said. "They'll get here in a jiffy." I knew this from experience, and I told her the number. "Tell them Norm's unconscious and give them your address. I can find my own way to the back door. I've been in this house a hundred times."

Sure I had. About that, anyhow, back in the twenties. The kitchen had been enlarged into the butler's pantry and the range looked like a spaceship and a big copper hood floated in the middle of the room, but the back door was in the same place. It banged to and fro in the little breeze we had that morning. I heard Evelyn dialing the phone.

I got outside and stood there, breathing hard. The sun seemed a lot warmer than it had been while I inspected the damage to my mailbox. Norm Hughardt was lying down on the dry part of his lawn. Water from underground sprinklers sprayed up just beyond him, wetting most of the grass and the red brick wall at the back of his property. A hopeful little rainbow arched over one of the fountains. Three of the jets, the nearest ones, seemed to be out of whack. Norm's face was in the grass and the toes of his shoes pointed straight down. He didn't look anything like Charlie Antolini, or even like my Uncle Hobart, who collapsed on Fairlie Hill when he discovered Jesus.

I moved myself toward him. "Norm?" I said. "How you feelin'?"

Norm did not answer. Stroke? Heart attack? I knelt effortfully beside him. He was dressed in the vest and pants of a blue three-piece suit. His shirt was clean and starched. I bent over to look at his face and saw that his eyes were open and staring into Bobby Fritz's springy grass. "Oh, damnation," I said and pushed at his shoulder. His top half pitched over. Under the vest was a neat red and blue striped tie. I used both hands to push at his hip and rolled him over. Now he was staring straight up into the sky. "Norm, you stuffy bastard," I said. "Wake up." I wondered not for the first time why someone so right-wing would wear chin hair like Lenin's.

I put my head to his chest. Nothing moved in there. Then I put my face up against his mouth. No breath, just the smell of cologne and mouthwash. I pinched his nostrils and breathed into his mouth the way they do on TV. I was sweating. It was terrible, that someone so much younger than myself was dead. I repeated the breathing gimmick.

"What are you *doing?*" his wife screeched from the back door.

"My best, Evelyn," I said. "You called them?"

She gulped and nodded. Then she fluttered near Norm and me. "Mr. Williams," she breathed, "do you think he's . . . do you think he's . . . do you think . . ."

"Best to wait for the medics," I said.

"He looks so normal," she said. Which was pretty close to the truth.

"Help me up," I said. And stuck out my arm. She gaped at my outstretched hand as if it were holding a turd. "Give me a pull for God's sake, Evelyn," I said. And she grabbed hold and got me up on my feet. Both of us stood there looking down at Norm Hughardt lying face up on the grass.

"He is. He's dead," Evelyn said.

"Does sorta look that way," I allowed. "What a damn shame. Not a mark on him."

It could be that this was a tactless remark. Evelyn Hughardt stepped away from me, wrapped her arms around herself and went into the house. But maybe she had heard the bell, for after a few seconds she reappeared with my old acquaintances of the Emergency Services Medical team.

They froze when they saw me. "You again?" the big mustached one said, and the cop with them shook his head. This was a blowhard named Tommy "Turtle" Turk, the worst cop on the Hampstead force. He was only a couple of months away from retirement and had a belly the size of a half grown walrus, but he still liked to use his fists.

"Not me, Turtle," I said. "Open your eyes."

I sometimes call the paramedics when I get my bad chest pains.

By this time the boys were all over Norm Hughardt, hooking him up to the stuff I hope they never have to use on me. Turtle got tired with trying to slap me down with his eyes and went over to grill the widow. I watched the boys jolting Norm with one of those things that resemble truck batteries. Norm jerked, but not with anything like life.

"He's gone," said the big one with the mustache. Then he looked up at me and said, "This is the second one this morning for us, and the other crew had one of their own. What the hell's going on here?"

"Three heart attacks?"

"Who the hell knows?" he said, and sent one of the other

boys out to the ambulance for a stretcher and a blanket.

I wandered over to Turtle and Evelyn. Turtle was asking her if they'd had an argument before the Doctor went outside. He glared at me, then he glared back at Evelyn.

"No," she said.

"Okay, what are you doing here?" Turtle bellowed at me.

"This lady asked me to help. I rolled Norm over. I told her to call the medics. I was just walking by."

"You mean you were—" he stopped, and I wondered what word he had censored. Slinking? Oozing? Turtle hitched up his belly and grinned like an ape. "I scare you, don't I? I know I do, Williams."

"Mr. Williams," I said.

"And I know why. You're yellow. You're as yellow as they come. I know all about you, *Mr.* Williams."

"Nuts," I said. "Good-bye, Evelyn. I'm very sorry this happened. Call me if you need anything."

She blinked. I wanted to hug her. Turtle would probably have jugged me for attempted rape. I went slowly through the house and out the front door.

Charlie Antolini was still lying blissfully on his immaculate lawn. Flo Antolini squatted beside him, weeping but talking fast.

I crossed the street. "Norm Hughardt keeled over in his back yard," I said. "Damn shame. You want any help?" This was sheer bravado. I needed to lie down, bad.

"He won't get up, Mr. Williams," Flo said. "I can't make him come inside."

I craned over to look at Charlie. "How you feelin' Charlie?"

"Beautiful." *Beyoodiful.*

"It's time to go inside now. We might get a little rain soon."

"Okay," he said, and held out his arms like a child. I took one, Flo the other. He almost pulled us over, but Flo planted her legs and kept us steady.

"Jeez, that was nice," Charlie said. "I never did that before."

Flo thanked me and began to lead Charlie toward the house. He kept stopping to admire the grass and the daffodils, but finally she got him inside. The curtains closed with a silent crash.

Turtle blasted away from the curb with a big manly roar of

the patrol car. The paramedics were just bringing the stretcher out of Norm Hughardt's house.

I looked up and down Mount Avenue and mentally saw a crowd of Jaegers and lobsterbacks racing toward me, waving torches and muskets. I saw the storm, the bolts of lightning of that night. The big houses were burning. Rest was imperative. Among the German mercenaries and the British soldiers there was one other, the one the Reverend Andrew Eliot had mentioned. . . . *headed by one or two persons who were born and bred in the neighboring towns.* One person, I knew, born and bred in Greenbank. (Reverend Eliot, a decent man, had been protecting one of his own.) I could almost see his face. He looked a lot like me. Out there was a dead child—a real child, though I did not know it then. The ambulance zipped past me, blowing the illusion apart. I got myself turned around and went home.

6

Now suppose that the thinking cloud had been born in Hampstead instead of Woodville. Suppose also that Dr. Wise knew what he was talking about. We have about twenty-five thousand people in town. If the immediate death rate was from 5 to 8 percent, between twelve hundred fifty and two thousand people would have dropped dead Saturday night. The streets would have been full of bodies. Instead, only five people died in Hampstead over Saturday night and Sunday morning. The murder of Stony Friedgood stole everybody's attention, especially when it was followed by another murder like it, and we never got around to putting things together.

The oldest person to go was a guy my age, a retired boat dealer who lived on Gravesend Road. The youngest was a seven-year-old boy. That bites at me. No kid should die from something like that. It could have been Tabby, see, it could have been Tabby Smithfield. The kid's parents had only moved here eighteen months before.

Somewhere in between the boy and the boat dealer was a friend of mine. I heard about it when I got home. The phone was ringing. It was Harry Zimmer. Babe was dead, he said. She'd had a little emphysema, but that wasn't what killed her. She had just dropped dead as soon as she got out of the pickup—fell down, a goner, in the parking lot at Gravesend

Beach. Wasn't that a hell of a note? Harry was crying. "I just wanted you to know, Mr. Williams," he said. "Babe always said you were a real gentleman." I said the things you say. Hell and double hell. I can't write in my own voice anymore. Savage old Turtle was right, and I'm yellow. This is a screwball way to write a book anyhow.

So what I'm going to do is put down about the Allbees buying the house across the street and how they met Patsy McCloud. "Pasta is prologue," and that. Pretty soon we'll get back to Tabby, and then I'll tell you about Gary Starbuck, the thief, and the little gang Tabby almost got into, and the stories Pat Dobbin was illustrating. It all belongs here, believe me—or don't, you'll find out anyhow.

Then we'll get to the part I hate to write about. I loved Wren Van Horne, he was only eight years younger than I, and we grew up here together. But I loved Babe Zimmer too, that nice pumpkin-faced old lady who thought I was a real gentleman.

If I'd been like Tabby when I was a kid, I wouldn't have ended up this way.

4

Recognitions

1

"The husband didn't do it," Ronnie Riggley told the Allbees on Wednesday morning as she turned out of the shopping center. "There was something funny going on with that lady. I don't mean she was the town pickup or anything, but she definitely gave out her favors. Bobo thinks that her husband knew about it. On Saturday she came into Franco's and met some guy there. They didn't stay long, and none of the dummies at the bar recognized the man."

"From out of town," Laura suggested.

"Could be, but we always say that in Hampstead." Ronnie laughed. "If someone's house gets broken into, which happens all the time, people always say the burglar came from Norrington or Bridgeport. But what happened is that the guys at the bar looked at Stony and didn't even bother to look twice at the guy. Bobo says they have about five different descriptions of him. He could be a blond guy in his forties, or a white-haired guy in his sixties. The only thing they agreed on was that he wasn't a regular at Franco's. But I guess a few of the guys recognized Stony. I shouldn't be telling you this before you even move here, but I gather that some of our executive wives hang around Franco's. I don't know, what do they think they're going to find? Lumberjacks? I'm probably too straitlaced, but I think that's so dumb."

"It still could have been the husband," Laura said. "You said he knew about her affairs."

"Oh, he's got an alibi," Ronnie said. "Good old Leo Friedgood was in Woodville all afternoon. He works for some giant corporation, and not only could a couple of people vouch for him down there, he spoke to General Haugejas a couple of times on the phone."

"Henry Haugejas?" Richard said in surprise. "The one who was in Korea?"

"Is there another one?" Ronnie asked. "Iron Hank. One of the detectives talked to him personally. He told Bobo he felt like standing up the whole time he was on the phone."

"A real character, I guess," Richard said. "Still carries his guns around with him."

"He shot a mugger two years ago," Ronnie said. "Can you imagine that? It was in midtown New York." Ronnie laughed. "We're going to look at a four-bedroom house right on the Hampstead–Old Sarum border first. It has lots of character. And then we'll look at a house in Greenbank. I have a feeling about that one."

2

Ronnie was doing her best, Richard knew. Any real-estate agent is limited by the range of houses actually on the market. Besides that, house prices in Patchin County had tripled in the past ten years, mortgage rates were currently at their highest level in history, and many houses he and Laura would have liked were now far beyond their price range.

"Old Sarum is a lot more rural than Hampstead," Ronnie said—quite unnecessarily—after they had gone for nearly a mile without seeing a house of any sort. "A lot of people like that."

Laura made a noncommittal sound from the backseat.

"Unfortunately, the owner will be in the house while I'm showing it. Something happened, I guess. She really wanted to stay home. She's a widow."

Finally they reached an overgrown driveway. The house was a cottage to which rooms had been added by various owners. A glassed-in studio topped the modern garage. The whole thing had been built on the side of a densely wooded hill, and appeared to swarm over it, working its way toward the top like a bank of ivy.

Laura asked, "Can we really afford this one?"

"Mrs. Bamberger wants a quick sale," Ronnie said as they left the car. "She's going to Florida in a couple of weeks. I thought it was worth a look anyhow." She gave Laura and Richard a rueful look. "I'm afraid she'll talk your ears off."

Mrs. Bamberger, a wide old woman in a dark blue pant-suit, met them at the door. Gold eyeglasses dangled from a chain around her neck. "Hello, Mrs. Riggley," she said to Ronnie. "Mr. and Mrs. Allbee? Just come in and poke around. I'll stay out of your way."

But as Ronnie had predicted, she did not stay out of their way. Mrs. Bamberger accompanied them on their tour, describing the house and her possessions. These were uniformly eccentric. The rooms were so crowded with heavy antique furniture that Richard had to strain to get an idea of their true size. Some of the rooms were interconnected, so that going through them was like passing down a line of railroad cars. In some cases they had to go up a set of steps to enter the next chamber. Mrs. Bamberger talked and talked. That fire screen we bought in. All that Meissen was a gift from. Don't you love fireplaces. My children once. The ceilings in most of the house were only a few inches above Richard's and Ronnie's heads. Mrs. Bamberger kept up her commentary until they reached the studio over the garage, where she seemed to relax.

"This is the only part we added ourselves," she said. "It's a wonderful place to come to see the animals outside. The birds too. It's on a separate zone, so you can sit here in the cold season without spending your money on heating the rest of the house."

"That's nice," Richard said, thinking *and then you take a quarter-mile hike to get to the kitchen.*

"You'd probably like it if the rest of the house were like this," Mrs. Bamberger said. "Most young people feel that way. My husband and I just love the old cottage, low ceilings and all. It reminded us of Miss Marple."

Richard smiled: that was perfect. The original building needed only a thatched roof to make it an English country cottage in an Agatha Christie novel.

"Is there anything else you'd like to ask Mrs. Bamberger about the house?" Ronnie put in a little desperately.

The Allbees looked at each other. *Let's get out of here.*

"Of course I have too much imagination," Mrs. Bamberger said. "That's what my husband used to say. But I know something that's not imagination. You're Richard Allbee, aren't you?"

"Yes," Richard said. *Here it comes,* he thought.

"You were born in Hampstead at the end of the war? And you moved out to California before you went to school?"

Puzzled, Richard nodded.

"Then I knew your father," she said.

Richard's mouth fell open. "I never did," he managed to say. "I never knew him, I mean. Apparently he didn't care much for babies."

Mrs. Bamberger was fixing him with a very steady gaze. She suddenly reminded him of his fifth-grade teacher. "Never should have married, that's what. But he gave you your handsome face. He was shortish, like you. A very well-mannered man. But Michael Allbee was a butterfly. Could never stick to anything."

Richard felt as if the floor were swaying. He knew he would always remember these moments, they would be part of him forever: the fat old woman in a polyester pantsuit standing before a bookshelf in a room with a glass wall. *Then I knew your father.* Michael Allbee. He had never heard his father's first name before. "What else can you tell me?" he asked.

"He was good with his hands. Are you?"

"Yes. Yes, I am."

"And he was pure charm. He only lived down the road. Michael used to come here to help out with the repairs and the lawn. He worked on houses all over this town. After he met Mary Green he stopped coming here, and pretty darn near broke my husband's heart. We were going to help put him through college. But then he had the Green money to back him up, so he didn't need us anymore." She smiled at Richard. "Most ways, he was a good man. Nothing to be ashamed of. He didn't marry for money. Your father wasn't that sort."

"He worked on houses?" Richard asked, scarcely believing it.

"As much as he did anything, that was what he did. My husband always thought he could have been an architect. But he could have been a contractor, anything of that sort."

"Do you know if he's alive?"

She shook her head. "I don't know. He was one of those people who never spend a minute thinking about the future, so it could be he still has one. He'd be in his early sixties today."

Somewhere in the world a white-haired man with his face was buying a paper or cutting the grass. Living in a flophouse. Playing with children who would be Richard's own nieces and nephews. Standing on the deck of a cargo ship smoking a pipe. Asleep in a hut on a beach. Begging from strangers in Billy Bentley clothes.

"Is your mother still alive?" Mrs. Bamberger asked.

"No. She died six years ago."

"Mary was the strong one. I bet she made you work. She would have been afraid of that irresponsible streak."

"Yes. Yes, I worked."

"Well, you've come to the right place," the old woman said. "On your mother's side, you go right back to the earliest days in these parts. Your great-great-great- and a couple more greats grandfather settled this town in 1645. Josiah Green. One of the original Greenbank farmers. You've got pure Hampstead blood all through you. Greenbank blood. That's where we started."

"How do you know all this?" Richard asked.

"I know more about this town than anyone except old Graham Williams and Stanley Crane up at the library. And maybe I know almost as much as they do. I studied it, Mr. Allbee. I know all about those Greenbank farmers. A sharpie named Gideon Winter came in and got most of their land from them. I have a few ideas about him, but you wouldn't be interested in them. You're looking for a house, and you don't want to listen to an old woman talk all morning long."

"No," Richard said. "No, that's not true. I, uh, I . . ."

She squared her shoulders. "Are you going to buy my house?"

"Well, we have to talk about it, there are a lot of factors . . ."

She kept on looking into his eyes.

"No," he said.

"Then someone else will. I'll take you back to your car."

As she opened the door for them, she said to Richard, "Your father had a lot to offer. I hope you have as much, young man."

When they were safely in Ronnie's Ford, Laura asked, "How do you feel?"

"I don't know. I'm glad we came. I'm sort of stunned."

"Let's go back to town for lunch or coffee or something," Ronnie said. "You look like you could use it."

He nodded, and she backed out of the driveway. Just before she pulled out onto the street, Ronnie said, "Do you want to go up the other way? You could see where your father lived—there are only two other houses up this way. It has to be one of them."

"No," he said. "No, thanks. Let's just go back to town."

3

That was how the Allbees came to Greenbank and Beach Trail. They came in the afterglow of a revelation, and they bought the first house they saw.

"I think you'll like this one," Ronnie said as she took them down Sawtell Road. They turned right at the traffic light into Greenbank Road. "It belongs to another widow, Bonnie Sayre. Mrs. Sayre moved out last week, and the house has only been on the market a couple of days. We got the listing Monday. The Sayre house has four bedrooms, a living room, and a beautiful study Richard could use as an office. Both the living room and the study have fireplaces. There's a nice porch too. The house was built in the 1870's by the Sayre family, and it's never been on the market before. The Sayres' son is in Arizona, and his mother went there to live with him."

She went over the bridge which crossed I-95 and then the smaller, almost humpbacked railway bridge just beyond it. "And Greenbank is a special sort of area. It has its own zip code and post office, and it's the oldest part of Hampstead. Well, you know that. It might even have been named for one of your ancestors."

"My mother never talked about Hampstead much," Richard said. "All I knew was that we and my father were born here. Laura's parents too."

"Is that right?" Ronnie asked, delighted. "So this is a real homecoming. Oh, take a look to your right. That big house right on the Sound is Dr. Van Horne's. We're on Mount Avenue now. They call it the Golden Mile."

"How much would a place like that cost?" Richard asked. Dr. Van Horne's house, three stories of spotless white clapboard, was as long as a hotel. Its front looked directly over the last stretch of Gravesend Beach. A long drive wound through parklike grounds.

"Right now, I'd have to say nearly eight hundred thousand dollars. And that's without a tennis court or in-ground pool."

"We can't afford this neighborhood," Laura said matter-of-factly.

"The Sayre house is priced lower than the carriage house we were looking at," Ronnie said. "It has two drawbacks. Don't groan yet. The first is that it faces backward—you see the rear of the house as you drive up. There's a little hill, and the original Sayre, the one who built it, I guess wanted to look down into the forest that was there."

"What's the second reason?" Laura asked.

"Well, Mrs. Sayre lived alone for a long time, I guess. She took in a lot of cats. I guess she got a little crazy a few years after her husband died. In fact, she took in all the cats. She must have had a hundred of them. When I heard about her, people just called her the cat lady."

"Oh, no," Laura said.

"Well, they're not still there," Ronnie said. "But the memory does linger on. Be grateful! If it weren't for all those cats, the house would have been sold on Monday. There was an offer in for the asking price, but the prospect backed out when he got a whiff."

"It's really bad?" Laura asked.

"It's rank, just *rank*," Ronnie said, laughing.

"I know how to handle that," Richard said simply. "White wine, vinegar, and baking soda. Then a lot of soap and water."

The car turned up Beach Trail. Ronnie knew, but did not tell the Allbees, the reason why all the shades were drawn in the Hughardt home. Charlie Antolini, still too happy to go to work, waved from his porch swing. They went past an impoverished-looking party in black tennis shoes, Yankee cap, and baggy black sweatshirt. The old party was pushing himself home on the last leg of the daily constitutional, and his own last legs. They never noticed him, but being inquisitive, he noticed them.

I saw your mother, Lump. You would have been beautiful.

4

A second or two later the Allbees beheld their house for the first time.

5

From the journals of Richard Allbee:

We're house owners again, or will be as soon as I get a mortgage. We signed the papers and paid the first small check this afternoon in Ronnie's office. Does anybody know if he's doing the right thing when he buys a house? I can see myself waking up in the middle of the night tonight, wondering if the kitchen is even smaller and darker than I remember. Are *all* the sash cords broken? Will I find some way to run wires down through the house without knocking holes in the walls? (The wiring is ancient.) How much water got in past the deteriorated flashing on the roof? Rotted timbers? And will one of those chimneys have to come down? The list of these questions could go on forever. And there's the smell, of course. It's bad enough to cause brain damage. The whole house was one huge catbox.

But it's a beautiful house. When Laura and I walked in, we had one of those flashes of marital ESP and simultaneously said, "This is it." I think Laura will love it, and that makes everything else unimportant. It's a Second Empire house: mansard roof, rounded dormer windows, pillars beside the door, lots of good ornamentation. Very much the kind of house Laura and I hoped we'd find but were afraid we couldn't afford. The back, which faces the street, is very plain, but the front is stunning, and even the view into the gardens down the little hill is wonderful. I'm high on the place—I'm even pleased by its looking backward, which seems so appropriate to my work. And when I look into the future—our future, Laura's and mine—I think the old Sayre house will be a perfect place to raise our children. Big rooms, two acres of nice ground, an attic to make into a playroom—what fantastic, fantastic luck. I asked God to help us a couple of nights back, and I guess He did.

This day I acquired both a house and a father, and I cannot keep the latter out of my thoughts for long. Michael Allbee. I am sure he is still living. And I wonder if he might have worked on the old Sayre house while he lived in Hampstead. If he was a sort of free-lance carpenter, it's possible.

Maybe luck really has visited us and our troubles will begin to leave. Maybe, at least, I will stop dreaming of Billy Bentley.

This is such a happy entry that I don't want to mention last night's dream—but for the sake of having something to smile at years from now, I'll put it down. I was in the living room of a strange house. It was stripped bare. I was waiting for something. Outside was a streaming violent storm. I looked out the window and saw a figure pacing on the front lawn, and when I looked more closely I saw that it was Billy Bentley. In that instant he whirled around to face me directly. He scared me. That is the simple way to put it. He was grimacing at me fiercely. Rain had plastered his long hair to his skull. He was the embodiment of bad luck, of coming doom. The sky raged, and a ragged bolt of lightning sizzled into the ground behind him. Billy knew I wanted to keep him out of the house—that was suddenly the crucial element. He had to be *kept outside* in the storm. In agitation, I began to move around the empty room, and I woke up barely able to keep myself from going downstairs to make sure the doors were locked.

Enough of such stuff. As soon as we have the house tied up, I'll go to Rhode Island to locate a contractor for the work up there. I have a couple of leads. . . .

6

Telpro had given Leo Friedgood a week off, and he had requested another week, promising to be back in the office on Monday, the second of June. For seven days he had seen policemen almost every waking hour, either in his house or in a dingy little room of the cramped old Hampstead police station. During these sessions he had been forced to admit that his wife had been intimate with several other men, and that he had condoned, if not encouraged, her sexual activities. Admitting this had made Leo feel stripped bare. It was a humiliation deeper than any he had ever known. The police, at first sympathetic, had turned cold, almost contemptuous toward him. A massive old uniformed cop the others called Turtle smacked his lips at Leo the third or fourth time he went to the station. That this ravaged old brute, a failure even by police standards, might be expressing an attitude held by the other officers and detectives gnawed at Leo. He was a success, they were not. (By Leo's standards, no policeman could be a success.) He paid more in property taxes and mortgage payments than they made in a year. He was more powerful than they, more an engine in the world. His wristwatch was worth a third of their salary, his car three-fourths. But these things which meant so much to Leo seemed to count very little with the police who questioned him. Even when he was no longer even faintly a suspect, he had felt their contempt. "How many times a month did your wife go to Franco's? How many times in the past month? Didn't you ever ask her the names of the men she brought back? Did you ever take any pictures?"

The face of that fat old wreck called Turtle pushing out his meaty lips—bah! He was sure they laughed about him in those little rooms. This knowledge as much as his genuine mourning for Stony kept him home, incapable of working.

For the first time in his life, Leo drank at night. He warmed TV dinners or burned hamburgers under the grill, and invaded his cellar for good wines to waste on these terrible meals. Before dinner there would have been several whiskeys. With rubbery salt-heavy goulash in a tin tray he would drink a bottle of Brane-Cantenac 1972 Margaux while the television blared out soothing stupidities. When the uneaten half of the awful dinner went into the garbage, he began on malt whiskey or cognac until he passed out. One day he found an Israeli liqueur made of chocolate, and downed the entire bottle in two nights. He could not weep—as if the sight of Stony's mutilated body disarrayed on their bed had burned all the tears from him. Sometimes he put on a record and shuffled around the living room in a drunken lonely dance, his eyes closed, glass slopping in his fist, pretending he was a stranger dancing with his wife.

Doesn't your husband mind your doing this sort of thing? Mind? It's how he gets off.

He slept in the guest room. If he managed to get to bed before unconsciousness felled him, he took a glass with him. Two mornings, he woke up and caught an odor like that of death from a half-filled tumbler perfectly balanced on his chest.

The pale brown duvet bore a damp kidney-shaped stain that smelled equally of the distillery and the graveyard. The television set facing the bed showed crazed American couples leaping openmouthed before an oleaginous gent with a racetrack suit and dyed hair. A game show. "Oh, my God," Leo said. Head, mouth, stomach, all were in disorder. He was due at the police station in three hours. Maybe Turtle Turk would be there again, leering at him.

Hurriedly he got out of bed, switched off the television set, and went into the bathroom. His bowels released a ribbon of flame into the toilet. He dialed the shower up to an uncomfortable hotness and stepped in. The water boiled his hair and face. His hands found the soap. Leo lathered his chest, belly, balls. The stink of the night before sluiced toward the drain. He soaped himself again and more luxuriously, now feeling no worse than on the nine previous mornings. Leo let the water drum on his skin, needle against his tongue. For a moment he forgot about Turtle Turk, about Stony, about General Haugejas, about Woodville Solvent and DRG.

When he turned off the shower he noticed the specks on his hands.

He stared at them with incomprehension, dimly aware that the appearance of white spots on his hands meant something important to him but momentarily unaware of what they signified. Then he remembered what had happened to the body of Tom Gay.

"Hey," Leo said, grabbing for a towel. He dried himself quickly and inexpertly, all the while trying to keep his hands in view. Blue jeans, polo shirt, boat shoes. He licked at the spots and encountered slipperiness. He scrubbed the backs of his hands on his jeans. A few of the spots were now pink— like pitted little mouths. Leo watched in dread as the pinkness gradually filled in with white.

"Oh, my God," he said. His mind seemed frozen by the touch of an icy thread emanating from his belly. Panic recalled to him an irrelevant vision of a burning car wedged beneath a truck, the more pertinent memory of the three bodies in the glass room. "Oh, God. Oh, God."

The telephone rang four times behind him, then ceased.

Leo was staring at the backs of his hands, which were flattened on the rumpled duvet. How many spots were there? Ten altogether? On his left hand they described an irregular oval from the bottom of his thumb to the base of his little finger; on his right they fanned upward from his wrist. He prodded with his index: a trace of slipperiness came off. Leo shuddered. Still in the first stages of his panic, he began to pace aimlessly around the bedroom, holding his hands out before him.

Atop the dresser were strewn coins, books of matches, loose collar stays, rolled belts, a pair of suspenders, and a red Swiss Army knife Stony had given him years before. He seized the knife and sat on the bed.

Leo pulled out the smaller of the two blades and scraped at one of the specks. The white stuff gathered transparently on the blade and instantly began to replenish itself. He scraped again, to the same effect. More recklessly, he jabbed the point of the little blade into the speck at the base of his little finger and revolved it. A second's flash of minor pain: blood welled out from the cavity. When he dabbed at the spot with his handkerchief he saw that the bleeding had stopped. A tiny spot of white lay at the center of the red pit.

Leo ran into the bathroom to inspect his face in the mirror. Some dark webbing beneath his eyes, no white spots. He tore off his shirt and pushed down his jeans. One of the little specks rode just above the bone on his left shoulder, another rested in the fat part of his upper left arm. Below his waist there was nothing.

Again and with perfect clarity Leo saw the white lathery sponge which had been Tom Gay's head—saw it leaking into the drain.

But that had happened instantly. Maybe these few spots on his own body were unrelated to the fate of Tom Gay; maybe they were just some kind of infection? He experimentally squeezed the spot on the underside of his left arm. A trace of blood appeared through the whiteness, which told him nothing. Naked, Leo went back to the bedroom and took the matches off the dresser.

Seated at the desk, he lit a match and applied the flame to one of the spots on his left hand. The pain made him squirm. "Burn it out," he said to himself. He lit another match and touched it to three more of the spots. Sweating, he used another match to sear the last speck on his left hand. He smelled burned flesh. His left hand was now in agony. It looked like an illustration from a medical textbook. Grimacing, he went back into the bathroom and held his hand under the cold tap. When the pain had subsided, Leo wrapped the injured hand in a towel and sat on the edge of the tub. Cold porcelain on his buttocks. He closed his eyes, and his head was swimming. He tasted bile and a cottony afterwash of whiskey. Like his head, the floor too seemed to wobble.

At length he dared to unwrap the towel. The back of his

left hand looked appallingly unfamiliar. Blisters surmounted
blackened and reddened flesh from which clear fluid drained.
Leo closed his eyes again. He had seen no whiteness. After a
moment, he got up to bandage his hand and return to the
matches.

7

From the journals of Richard Allbee:

Today I heard from the bank—we have the mortgage we
wanted, at a rate that is almost reasonable for these days. We
called Ronnie, who was jubilant, and celebrated with a bottle
of champagne. So it is settled: we're in the land of our fathers
and grandfathers.

Unfortunately, I have not been able to shed what seems to
be my obsession with *Daddy's Here*. I know what it is now—
it's going back to where Michael Allbee lived and waking up
everything about him I buried inside me without even knowing it. Daddy's Here. Daddy's *here*. It's got to be that simple.
But knowing the reason does not keep me from having those
dreams about Carter Oldfield battering at the bedroom door
with an ax and poor Billy outside in the rain. Billy in bed
with Laura, Billy coming toward the window to break in. The
theme is the same: chaos, violence, disorder are out there and
I have to keep them from breaking in.

Stray thought: maybe it is *Laura* I fear for, not myself.
Pregnant and in a strange place . . . it is unsettling for her.

But I don't dream of Laura in danger.

Unless, another thought, Laura is the house in these
dreams. . . . I don't know where to take this idea. Restoring
our new house = restoring Laura to her old self? Saving the
house = saving Laura? I can see that she is close to tears
often, in a state where boredom and depression are very
close. When we talk, she says only that she misses London,
misses it in almost a physical way, wants to see Kensington
High Street and Holland Park, to walk down Ilchester Place.
She wants to go to the Standard Restaurant for an Indian
meal, take the tube into the West End for lunch, go back to
her office in Covent Garden. She knows the name of the hospital where our baby should be born—that big new hospital

on the Holland Road. That is where her thoughts went while we drank champagne to our new house.

I didn't want to put this down, but now I guess I have to. The other day Laura and I were in one of the shopping centers on the Post Road. Our arms were full of grocery bags. We were going up toward our car. We passed a sort of café— what I'm used to calling a *caff.* A diner. A counter in front, little tables in the back. I glanced in. Laura said, "What's the matter?" I shook my head. I followed her to the car. Nothing was the matter. But I didn't tell her that for a second, when I first looked in the window, I'd seen Carter Oldfield, Ruth Branden, and Billy sitting at one of the little tables in the rear—seen them very clearly. I could describe the clothes they were wearing. Billy was in his urban-waif clothes, a tweed cap on his head, and he was looking at me.

And the expression on his face . . . *triumph,* pure *triumph.*

As soon as I shook my head, my little family transformed themselves into the teenage boys they had been all along. One of them, the one not a monster, was staring at me, but after all, I had been staring at him, no doubt with a peculiar expression on my face. Our glances held, and I was sure that the boy, who was slight and fair-haired, knew me or thought he knew me—there was recognition in his face, but there was also pure fright. One of the twin monsters, the one with bib overalls, jabbed his hand with a fork, and the boy's eyes jerked away from mine.

No dreams tonight, I hope.

8

From the journals of Richard Allbee:

Nice days, terrible nights. My subconscious ignored my plea for relief from those absurd nightmares about Carter Oldfield and Billy Bentley. Evidently I'm still worried at some level about the effect of this move on Laura and me, about chaos vs. order, the legacy of Michael Allbee—who probably never spent a minute of his life worrying about such things. There have been two cases of chaos intruding on our little version of order here, one slight, one serious, but I'll get to those.

I met the famous Sarah Spry near the produce counter in

Greenblatt's grocery. She said, "Allbee. Richard Allbee. You look just the same. I've been meaning to call you. I hope you saw your name in my column." She's about fifty, very tiny and energetic, with owlish glasses and skinned-back hair redder than Laura's. She knew we were buying the old Sayre house. "John Sayre killed himself, you know," she said. "Lovely man. No wonder poor Bonnie went crackers afterward. When can you give me an interview? I'd like to do it as soon as you move in." She's not a woman you can fob off with vague excuses, so I'm being interviewed on the day we move. Half an hour, she said, nobody's life being so interesting that it should take more than thirty minutes of her time. What she didn't say was that in half an hour she'd wring anybody dry. But maybe the interview will drum up some new business.

On Sunday night we're invited to another house very near our new one, an evening Ronnie Riggley arranged. The people are named McCallum? McClaren? Ronnie sold them their house too. We'll finally meet Bobo, something I look forward to.

Now for the two intrusions. Our mailbox here on Fairytale Lane was pounded to a pulp last night. We heard the noise about ten o'clock, and it scared both of us. I went outside and saw a black car streaking off. Besides the mailbox, the vandals also broke a half-dozen pickets in the fence, just snapped them in half. They must have used a baseball bat or something similar. It's funny how even minor violence upsets you—as though it promises more to come, when of course it's just kids who roam the streets looking for something to break. But I'll have to repair the pickets and buy a new mailbox.

And to save the worst for last, there's been another murder. This happened yesterday, Friday the thirtieth. As before, a woman was killed in her house. Ronnie knew all the details, which were gory. Apparently there were no signs of a break-in; the body was in the kitchen, more or less eviscerated— Hester Goodall was her name, in her late forties, active in church work. This time there was no question of promiscuity. Her children were at school, the husband out of town. The Goodalls live out near the Country Club and Sawtell Beach, according to Ronnie.

Whoever he is, I hope they catch him fast.

9

From Mount Avenue the Allbees turned into Beach Trail, went past Cannon Road, looked speculatively and pridefully at their new house, turned into Charleston Road and found number 3 just where Ronnie had said it was—a long two-story house with brown shingles on a short lawn beside a stained split-rail fence. The blue Datsun with RONNI plates was already pulled around the side of the house, and Richard swung in beside it so that he too was parked facing the double garage doors. A magnolia beside the drive had dropped a carpeting of pink tear-shaped petals over the grass and the asphalt, and Richard and Laura walked over these as they left their car.

"Did Ronnie tell you anything about the McCallisters?"

"Their name is McCloud," Laura said. "Patsy and Les McCloud. Ronnie sold them their house, and she says they're 'a lot of fun,' whatever that means. I guess Les McCloud is some kind of executive, and they've moved around a lot."

"Real Patchin County people," Richard said, and rang the bell.

A giant opened the door. At least six-foot-six, he wore a tan corduroy jacket and a chocolate turtleneck over a massive chest. With his wide white smile, fuzzy mustache, and frothy curly hair, he looked no older than twenty-five. "Hey there," he said. "Come on in."

"Mr. McCloud?"

The giant laughed, gripping Richard's hand. "Jeez no, I'm just Bobo Farnsworth, the neighborhood cop. Les is up there in the kitchen and Patsy and my girlfriend are in the game room." He ushered them into the little entry. Now they were crowded into an area about three feet square, in fact a landing on a staircase that led up to the main part of the house and down to a family room that shared a wall with the garage. "You must be Richard, the famous actor guy. And I guess you're Laura." He beamed down at her. Richard saw that Bobo was well suited for Ronnie Riggley.

"If you're the neighborhood cop, I feel safer already," Richard said.

Bobo laughed again, motioning them toward the stairs. "I take tall pills."

Richard led the way up. As soon as he entered the living room—long modular sofa with zigzag purple and blue stripes and shiny black coffee table on a dark blue carpet, a framed

poster of a Steinberg *New Yorker* cover—he heard a voice
shouting, "Is that Dick Allbee? I'll be right out!"

A man six inches shorter than Bobo Farnsworth strode into
the room, holding out a damp hand. He had close-cut sandy
hair, a beefy face of the sort that always looks tan. "Patsy!"
he yelled. "Dick Allbee's here!"

The cold wet hand closed, and Les McCloud put his face
within three inches of Richard's as he pumped his arm. A
clear wave of alcohol, also of somehow possessive intimacy,
came from him. *"Loved* your show, just *loved* it—that was a
helluva good series, you know? *Patsy!"* (this over his shoulder.) "I gotta respect what you people can do, you know?
I'm Les McCloud, welcome, welcome. You met the fuzz
here? Good. And this must be your *Frau.* Nice to meet you.
Laura? Great. Patsy'll be here in a sec, and you can talk
woman talk. Hey, Dick, you got all dressed up."

Les was wearing a pink crewneck sweater and cuffed wash
pants. He looked like Dartmouth, vintage '59. "Get that tie
off, Dick. Or do they call you Dickie?"

"Richard."

"Whatever." McCloud finally let go of Richard's hand.
"Just putting ice cubes in glasses. What do you fancy? How
about you, Laura? I make the best martinis in the whole of
Connecticut."

"Nothing for me," Laura said, and "Just a beer," from
Richard.

"You want that nothing with olives or a twist? Are you in
the theater too, Laura?"

"No, I—"

"Two nondrinkers tonight. What do you people do to unwind? Do you sail or do you flail?" He was still staring directly into Richard's face with friendliness so aggressive it
was like hostility.

"Neither one," Richard said. "We don't have a boat, and
it's been a long time since we played tennis."

"What a relief," said Patsy McCloud, and both the Allbees turned to her. Standing next to Ronnie Riggley's large-
boned blond health, she looked fragile, with her thin exposed
shoulders and enormous brown eyes under lank, rather untidy
dark hair. Her face was very finely drawn. Nearly invisible
creases bracketed her mouth when she smiled. The smile exposed small white slightly irregular teeth. She looked like her
husband's appetizer. "Now please tell me that you don't jog

either. I'm Patsy McCloud. Welcome, Richard and Laura."
Her handshake was fleeting and graceful.

"I don't jog, and Laura can't," Richard said.

"Anybody can jog," Les asserted.

"Not pregnant women," Patsy said. "At least, I don't
think so. Do you have any other children?"

Laura's face relaxed at Patsy's intuitive remark. "No, it's
our first."

Les ducked away into the kitchen and Ronnie kissed both
Allbees. "I'm so happy you two are moving here."

"Thanks."

"Yes."

"Have you and your husband been here long?" Richard
asked.

"Two years. Before that, we were in Los Angeles for a
year. Before that, England. Les has been very successful."
This last seemed ambiguous to Richard, as if Patsy were dis-
tancing herself from her husband's travels as well as his
career.

"We were in Belgravia," Patsy went on. "Les hated it. He
couldn't wait to get back here. He absolutely detested England. I was in no condition to argue with him." She
wrapped long fingers around the chunky glass she carried.
"I'd just had a miscarriage."

Even Bobo Farnsworth seemed chastened for a moment,
and when Les came back in with Richard's beer, he said,
"What a dead bunch. Patsy must have said something. My
wife can murder cheerfulness like nobody's business. Happen
to tell these good folks something gloomy, little girl?" His
jaw colored: Richard finally saw that the man was already
drunk. The evening would be a torture. "Let's do it now,
honey. What do you say?"

Patsy nodded in a gloomy, distant manner.

Les McCloud looked up and beamed fiercely at Richard.
The class bully, grown up. "Hey, Dick, do us a favor, will
you? Say what you used to say. Say *Hey, Mom, I want a
whole plate of cookies.*"

"Hey, Mom, I want a whole plate of cookies," Richard
said. He was grateful for Ronnie Riggley's laugh.

"Gotcha," Les said, and ran back to the kitchen. He returned with a bowl filled with Oreos. "Go on, take one. I got
them for you."

Bobo Farnsworth: "Oh, no." But Les pushed the bowl toward Richard, who took one and slipped it into his pocket. Patsy McCloud, in evident desperation, asked, "Would you like the obligatory tour of the house?"

The evening toiled on. They toured the house, admired the pinball machines and jukebox in the game room, made the appropriate noises during dinner, which had a hasty, absent-minded quality. The fettuccine ("Pasta is prologue," Richard said, winning one of Patsy McCloud's best smiles) was over-cooked, and the lamb raw in the middle. Les McCloud drank unceasingly, refilling Patsy's glass only slightly less frequently than his own. Laura grew exhausted early, and Richard wanted only to get her home.

Bobo Farnsworth almost saved the evening. Unquenchably good-tempered, he drank Coke, ate hugely, and talked funnily about police work. Like Ronnie, he had taken to the Allbees on sight. Anecdotes poured from him. "Here I am in the patrol car, cruising down the Post Road behind this runaway horse, and I turned on my lights. Pull over, buddy, I said to the horse . . ." Bobo was doing his best to lighten the evening, and the Allbees were grateful for his presence. Patsy McCloud winced when Les, competing with Bobo, told an obscene joke.

"Okay, you don't like jokes," Les said. "I don't like the way you do police work. Why don't you catch that guy who's killing women? That's what you're paid for. You're not paid to sit here and eat my food, you're supposed to be out there catching creeps."

"And there are a lot of creeps out there, Les," Bobo said in a magnanimous tone. "We're working on it."

"Hey, why don't we all go sailing next weekend?" Les asked. "This is a great bunch. We'll go out on the boat, and my wife will do her party trick."

Patsy looked down at her plate.

"She won't tell you what it is. Hell, she doesn't even want me to tell you."

"I don't do any tricks." Patsy looked genuinely discomfited.

"Her trick is she's weird," Les said, and smiled as if he said something funny. "Dick, you and Patsy have something in common. Didn't Ronnie say that your family helped found this area? Well, Patsy's family did too. She was a Tayler. They moved in here even before the real estate had any value. But that's not why she's weird. Listen to this. When we were in college, Patsy used to be able to predict how I'd do on my exams to the exact number! A couple of times, she guessed the football scores, too." Les looked at all of them immobile in their chairs. "Does that run in your old swamp-Yankee families? You ever do anything like that, Dick?"

Patsy McCloud's discomfiture had multiplied itself into embarrassment. She looked pale, stricken. The enormous brown eyes in her grown-up child's face seemed to reach out to Richard, begging for help. He thought she might faint, or cry out—it was as though her husband had struck her.

He did strike her, Richard suddenly knew. That was the meaning of this scene. Les McCloud beat his wife, and poor trapped Patsy let him do it. And a second thought came to him: not a thought but an image. Patsy's horrified face called back to him the face of a teenage boy staring at him through the window of a Post Road diner.

"Silence means assent. Another weird swamp Yankee," Les McCloud shouted gleefully.

He would have to repair this rapidly. Laura too had grown more uneasy than anything in the situation called for. "Not exactly," he said. "Nothing like that, no."

"Well, what?"

"Just a couple of bad dreams," he said.

"You ought to see Patsy's shrink," Les told him. "Good old Dr. Lauterbach. Or get out on the golf course, take in some fresh air. You golf, don't you?"

"I'm sorry, but I'm very tired," Patsy said. She stood up. Her long fingers trembled. Her eyes met only Richard's, and this time too he understood their plea. *Don't judge us by this. We're not always this bad.* "I must apologize, but please stay on. You're all having so much fun." Then a bright brisk smile for everyone, and she left them. Les reached out for her, but Bobo intercepted his hand. "Got to run myself, Les—I'm on twelve to eight tonight." Then all of them were standing, smiling as falsely as Patsy, trying not to move too obviously toward the stairs.

"Let's do it again, huh? I guess I shouldn't have . . . you know. *In vino veritas* and all that. Come over anytime. We'll go out for a sail some weekend."

"Sure, anytime," Richard said. "As soon as our house is fixed up. Lots of busy weekends ahead."

Finally they got out the door. The four of them said nothing until they had reached their cars. Ronnie whispered,

"Gosh, I'm sorry I got you into this. They seemed so nice whenever I met them before. I don't know what got into Les. Honestly, he was just terrible."

Bobo said, "Let's the four of us get together later, okay? Hey, I never met the guy before. I didn't know he was a sadist."

"Yes," Richard said. "Yes, let's meet. And yes, he is a sadist. That poor woman."

"All she has to do is walk out," Laura said. "Let's get home. Please."

RONNI pulled out ahead of them, and Laura moved close to Richard on the front seat of their car. "I can't stand it, I can't stand it," she said. "That man, that fat carnivore. Are these the people we're going to have to live with? I *hate* this, Richard—I just hate it."

"I do too."

"I want to make love. Let's get back to that awful bed as fast as we can."

10

So on that mild night in Hampstead, Connecticut, at least two couples renewed themselves in the best way. While twenty-eight-year-old Bobo Farnsworth showered before going to work, Ronnie Riggley shed her clothes and popped her big luxuriant forty-one-year-old body next to his under the warm spray. She was giggling, and Bobo let out a great whoop of laughter. Together they rid themselves of the aftertaste of Les McCloud, and Bobo went to work jubilant. In the bedroom on Fairytale Lane, the Allbees undressed together, but on opposite sides of the bed, as married people do. And as married people do, they hung up their clothes.

"He beats her, doesn't he?"

"I think so."

"I saw a bruise on her arm when the top of that thing she was wearing slipped. He hits her on the arms so no one will know."

"Oh, maybe she likes it," he said, and felt it as treachery. Even then, he knew that this was untrue, and crudely so.

Laura stood like a tribal totem, her watercolor hair down, her breasts huge, her belly a soft pronounced bulge of taut skin and blue veins. Richard had not suspected how sexually beautiful women became when they were pregnant. Nature, having accomplished her aim, rewarded her servants in her own coin.

But Laura's face was almost as tense and drawn as Patsy McCloud's. She grasped his shoulders when they were on the rolling bed, gripped him hard enough to cut off his breath. "I don't want to lose you, Richard."

He extracted his throat from all of her flesh: she seemed exactly his size, her arms round and soft, her legs enfolding him. "You won't lose me, not unless you suffocate me."

"Do you really have to go to Providence?"

"Only for a day or two. Do you want to come along?"

"And sit in a hotel room while you talk about gesso and masonry with some contractor?"

"That's what I have to do."

"I'll stay here. But I'll miss you."

"Oh, my God," he groaned, at this moment unable to believe that he could part himself for longer than a breath from his wife. He kissed one of her nipples, rolling it on his tongue; licked the underside of the breast. A delicious sweetness exuded from her skin.

"You know I hate it here, don't you? I do. I do hate it. But I love you, Richard. I never want to lose you. But that man— it's so horrible here, and I want my friends back."

Throbbing, he held her. Her body was a furnace, a potbellied stove.

"I do love being in bed with you," she said. His fingers were brushing, rubbing, sliding. "Oh, yes." The amazing fullness of her belly pushed hard into him. "Sorry, baby."

He was still able to slide into her while they lay on their sides, facing each other, her hip up on his, knotted together in the closest embrace. They exhaled in unison, moving together gently. The bed comically yawned and pitched.

"Such a sweet man. You even said you'd go out on his boat."

"I'd rather be here in your boat."

Silence for a time. Intense, bursting pleasure: pleasure stretched so taut it imitated pain and made them gasp.

"Stop having nightmares," Laura breathed into his ear. "Don't stop this, just please stop having nightmares. They scare me."

Together, they brought themselves home.

Richard awakened hours later, feeling clean and refreshed

in spirit, aerated—as if his soul had been laundered. Gently he drew his arm from beneath Laura's shoulder. Kissed her back and tasted salt and cloves; eased back down into sleep. No nightmares: none of the old nightmares ever now, not at night.

11

Graham

My own journals remind me that I saw this Sunday night as peaceful, even dull, and so it was for me, at least until some short time after I made my constipated entry. I had read the book section of the *Times* in a complicated state yoking ire and disbelief, then written several pages. After dinner of a cheese sandwich and an orange, I napped at my desk with my pencil in my hand. I dreamed about my pages and understood that they would not do. In these pages, a woman had just met the man who would become her lover. The problem was to let us know how she first sees him. There had to be an erotic undercurrent, and this I had flubbed. My own experience of erotic undercurrents of any kind was sadly out-of-date. Yet I could remember meeting my first wife, also meeting my second. Both events took place in courtrooms. The emotions experienced were primarily boredom and lust. The rest came later.

Currents of another kind, not erotic, rolled through Hampstead. The bars were open until one, Tabby Smithfield was out wandering with his new friends, Bobo Farnsworth patrolled happily in his black-and-white and decided to do a good deed. Gary Starbuck had already robbed a house on Redcoat Lane and was preparing himself to rob another. Dr. Wren Van Horne, my fellow widower and old friend, sat up late at night in his conspicuous mansion and thought about buying a mirror for a spot he had just cleared on his living-room wall. Charlie Antolini lay in his hammock, smiling blissfully at the stars while his wife wept in the bedroom. On this night, birds began to fall dead and dying out of the sky. In my imagination, ghostly German mercenaries ran whooping down a Mount Avenue denuded of all its grand houses. Among these was a fellow to whom my mind gave the flat whiskery face of Bates Krell, the lobster fisherman who had decamped, as it seemed. He had not decamped. I had killed him with a sword, tra la la. And Joe Kletzka, the chief of police in those days, knew I did it. He didn't believe a word I said about it, not consciously he didn't, but he pretty well believed that Bates Krell had accounted for the disappearances of four women, and he saw the bloodstains on the lobster boat when I pointed them out to him.

One other person soon knew about me and Bates Krell. Tabby Smithfield. He knew because he saw it the way I see the burning of Greenbank by General Tryon's men, mentally. Tabby saw it the first time he met me, which was late that Sunday night. Put purely and simply, he recognized me, and that, tra la la, scared the living piss out of both of us. Wake up, wake up, indeed, you sleepyhead. *Sleepyhead.* Not Tabby—even though I could still smack him for keeping quiet about the Norman brothers the way he did.

5

The Smithfields and
the McClouds

1

Skippy Peters had gone crazy, that was the problem, though
to speak absolutely factually, he had always been a little bit
crazy. In the sixth grade he had shaved off his eyebrows and
replaced them with shoe polish—at the time he had been talking on the telephone with Dicky and Bruce Norman, the twins
from the large irregular family that lived in the trailer park
Mr. Norman managed, and he had tried to persuade them to
do the same. The next day, the Norman twins (who had
agreed to Skippy's suggestion) showed up at school with their
eyebrows intact on their bulbous heads, and screamed with
laughter when the teacher sent Skippy home. In the eighth
grade, when they were in the Middle School next to J. S.
Mill, Skippy Peters had been caught masturbating in the
shower room by the gym teacher, who had looked back in to
check why he was taking so long: a two-week suspension. On
their first day in high school, he had defined himself by falling down in Cancer Corner—the back corner of the parking
lot, where the older kids went to smoke—and pretending to
foam at the mouth. He had once tried to get himself tattooed
on his rump with the Marine Corps insignia, but the tattooist
had thrown him out of his shop.

The Norman twins valued Skippy especially for his willingness to do anything they suggested. By the time they were
fifteen and sophomores at J. S. Mill, the twins weighed two
hundred and ten pounds apiece and had long Indian-black hair
which fell to their shoulders. Their faces were round, fat-
cheeked, sallow. If it had not been for their eyes, which were
hooded and knowing, they would have looked retarded, with
these sallow, inhuman, otherwise monstrously dimpled and
innocent faces; but they looked like born malefactors. The

twins had been blamed, most often correctly, for every trouble which had occurred in their vicinity since they had outgrown Pampers. They lived on their own in an abandoned trailer down the weedy drive from the trailer where their parents and four sisters carried on their rackety disordered lives. They sometimes ate in their parents' trailer, most often at Burger King or Wendy's. At night they drove the rusty black Oldsmobile they had repaired over to Riverfront Avenue and the Blue Tern Bar and bullied college students into bringing six-packs out to them. The Blue Tern bouncers and bartenders all knew them and would not let them in. When Bobo Farnsworth or another Hampstead cop drove around the parking lots of the Blue Tern and the nearby warehouses, the twins sat in the Olds's backseat and grinned—they thought Bobo Farnsworth was a twink. All the Hampstead cops were twinks except for Turtle Turk, who had once actually scared Bruce Norman by lifting him off the ground and threatening to drop him off the overpass at Exit 18. They hated Turtle Turk.

Nobody trusted Dicky and Bruce, they attracted suspicion as fighters attract bruises, and so someone like Skip Peters was useful to them. The child of affluent, well-traveled, distant parents, Skippy was an outcast who at least looked normal. In grade school Dicky and Bruce had discovered that they could send Skip into Greenblatt's with a list of things to steal, and he would come out with twice what they asked for. Hostess cupcakes, bottles of Coke, steaks, whole chickens, Mars bars, jars of Planter's cashews: he was a walking shopping bag. Skip Peters looked so honest, also so nervous, that even if he were caught, shopkeepers felt sorry for him and sent him away with a warning.

But toward the end of May this eager erratic instrument of the Norman twins began to lose both his usefulness and his amusement value. One Tuesday during first-period geometry class, Skippy stood up from his seat in the last row and started shouting at Mr. Nord, the teacher. "You jerk! You dumb jerk! You're doing it wrong!"

Mr. Nord had turned around from the blackboard in a state between terror and rage. "Sit down, Peters. What am I doing wrong?"

"The problem, you dumb jerk. Don't you see that the angle is . . . is . . ." He burst into loud sobs. Mr. Nord had excused him from the class.

In the hallway between classes, Skip was waiting for the
Norman twins. "Hey, man," Bruce said. "What's hap-
penin'?"

Skippy was even paler than usual, his eyes red as a rabbit's. "You're a dumb pig, that's what's happening. Tell me
to multiply any two numbers."

"What?"

"Go on. Any two numbers."

"Four hundred sixty-eight and three thousand nine hundred
forty-two."

"One million, eight hundred and forty-four thousand, eight
hundred and fifty-six."

Bruce hit him just below the ear and knocked him into a
bank of lockers.

They must have talked together, the Norman twins; when
Jix and Pete Peters removed Skippy from J. S. Mill a day
later and shipped him off to a place like a resort hotel with a
golf course, a gymnasium and an indoor and outdoor pool,
the Norman twins must have lazed around their funky trailer
and talked about the new boy. They must, while pushing
chocolate cake into their mouths, while passing joints back
and forth, while drinking beer and watching *The Thing* on
their stolen television set, have measured his usefulness. They
had a plan.

On the Friday that a holidaying, already sunburned Chicago priest named Francis Leary walked into his sister's luxurious kitchen and in shock and terror dropped a heavy
grocery bag into what seemed a lake of her blood, Tabby
Smithfield looked up startled when a slopping cup of Pepsi
Cola encased in a grease-blackened fist thumped down before
him on the lunchroom table. "Hey, new kid," said a voice
from above him, "you thirsty?" Tabby looked up and was
unable to speak. The two most threatening people in his class
were grinning down at him from their monstrous faces. One
wore overalls over a T-shirt, the other a filthy sweatshirt
which still, though barely, read ROLL OVER. They put their
trays on the table and sat down on either side of him. "I'm
Bruce and he's Dicky," said the one in the sweatshirt. "Go
on, drink it, we got it for you. We're the Welcome Wagon
ladies."

By the time the Goodall lawn was filled with Goodall
neighbors, and Bobo Farnsworth was simultaneously trying to
keep Turtle Turk from popping a state cop in the jaw and lead

the two hysterical Goodall children to the house of whatever
Goodall neighbor could be coaxed away from the kitchen
windows, Tabby Smithfield was seated in the last row of his
world-history class. Dicky and Bruce Norman hulked beside
him like a pair of huge watchdogs. "Tell him about Skippy
and the eyebrows," Bruce whispered to Dicky. Both of the
brothers smelled—to Tabby, quite nostalgically—of beer.

2

Relations between Clark and Monty Smithfield had eased and
mellowed as the seventies came to their end. Tabby was the
reason for this. Though Monty had sworn to himself, after the
terrible embarrassment of the scene in the airport, that he
would live as though his son were dead, he was incapable of
pretending to himself that he no longer had a grandson. He
dreamed of Tabby, several times a month sat in Tabby's old
room and stared at the rows of toys his grandson had left
behind. And because they had led to the loss of Tabby, he
eventually came to regret the insults he had spoken to his son.
Maybe he should not have scoffed at Clark's tennis. Maybe he
should not have insisted that Clark join him in the company—
maybe he should have let Clark bum around out West, playing
tennis, as Clark had wanted to do after college. Maybe it had
been a mistake to give half the house over to Clark and Jean—
maybe that closeness had been the worst mistake of all. These
recriminations chased each other through his mind.

After a couple of months he looked up some of Clark's old
friends and classmates. He promised that he would not inter-
fere with his son's life, that he wanted only to send money
from time to time. An old man holding out his checkbook as
if it were his heart—two of Clark's friends took pity on him.
One of them had an address in Miami, the other a street number in Fort Lauderdale. Monty called Information in both cities, but Clark was not a telephone subscriber. On Tabby's
birthday he sent checks and notes to both addresses; two
weeks later he received a thank-you letter in Tabby's childish
writing from Fort Lauderdale.

On Clark's birthday Monty sent him a thousand dollars, but
the letter was returned unopened. Thereafter, Monty sent a
small check to Tabby every month and Tabby wrote him
whenever he and his father made one of their frequent moves.

On his eighth birthday he sent his grandfather a photograph of himself from Key West—a brown barefoot Tabby Smithfield standing on the end of a pier. Sun-bleached hair and puzzling eyes.

Shortly after Tabby's eleventh birthday—another photograph, Tabby in a peacock wicker rocker, sent from Orlando—Monty received an almost telegraphically brief note from Clark telling him that he had a new daughter-in-law. Her name was Sherri Stillwell Smithfield. Sherri and Clark had been married a month.

Monty, having learned his lesson, bided his time. He wrote a letter expressing congratulations and good wishes and sent it with a very generous check; this was not returned. Two weeks after the canceled check came back with his bank statement, Monty finally got a telephone call from his son. Monty told Clark, "I want you to know one thing. I'm leaving you this house when I go—it'll be yours free and clear. And if you want to bring Tabby and your wife back here to live in it, that's fine."

During all of these years, Tabby's life was odder than the Norman twins would ever have imagined.

He and his father had lived in single rooms, beer-fragrant apartments above roughhouse taverns, in transient hotels where they had to cook on a hot plate and swat roaches off tables; in a bad time they had spent a week living in Clark's old car. He had known many boys who promised to grow up just like the Norman twins—violence, stupidity, and craftiness were nothing new to Tabby. He had seen his father swim perilously into alcoholism and most of the way out; he had seen his father briefly go to jail, for what crime he never knew; by the time he was ten, he had finished only one year in the same school where he had begun it. Once he had seen his father come home flushed and triumphant and spread out on the kitchen table three thousand dollars he had won playing tennis. He had seen two men die, one knifed in a bar where Clark was working, one shot to death during a fight in the street. And once when he had opened the bathroom door without first knocking, he had seen a friend of his father's, a skinny ghostly Key West transvestite named Poche or Poach, sitting on the toilet and shooting heroin into his arm.

When he was fourteen he wrote down all the addresses he could remember of the places he and his father had lived, beginning with the house on Mount Avenue: without even hesitating, he listed nine addresses, including three places that called themselves hotels, one boardinghouse, and one foster home. After thinking for a few minutes, he was able to list three more.

Sherri Stillwell eventually changed all that. She was a hard-bitten loyal blond woman, half Cuban, five years younger than Clark. An earlier husband had walked out on her and she had become a regular at the bar, the No Name, where Clark worked in Key West. Sherri's father had been a Texas oil rigger, often away from home for long periods, and she had helped raise three smaller brothers: she liked children. There was still a lot of Texas in Sherri. When she moved in with Clark, she insisted that Tabby stay home with her at night and do his homework instead of messing around in the streets all night or sitting mascotlike in a corner of the bar. Sherri filled out Clark's tax returns, noisily got rid of worthless and criminal hangers-on like Poche, and made Clark promise that he would never lie to her.

"Honey, my first husband filled me so full of lies I thought the sky was red. Once is enough. If you fool around, you tell me who it is and I'll straighten it out fast. I want one thing, you being straight with me. Tell me one lie—one—and I cut out." With her peroxide hair and black eyes, Sherri looked like no one who had ever set foot in the house on Mount Avenue, but Monty Smithfield would have recognized her goals for her lover and his son. She encouraged Clark's occasional hustling because it could bring in immediate money, but she wanted him to stop tending bar and get into some business. She circled want ads. She made appointments for him. Finally it was because of Sherri that Clark got a job as a salesman. By this time they were in Orlando, in a little two-bedroom house with a scrubby sandy lawn, and they had begun to save some money. With the check Monty had sent them as a wedding present, they bought a new car and some furniture. It was Sherri who ultimately talked Clark around to telephoning his father.

During these years Tabby had successfully managed to repress nearly all the traces of the misfortunes which had preceded and accompanied his departure from Connecticut. He thought about his mother, but carefully avoided thinking about the vision of the interior of her coffin which had assaulted him just before her funeral; the odd visions he'd had

in the airport, part of a general and numbing panic, were
more difficult to suppress. Of his life in Connecticut he could
remember chiefly things so opulent they seemed invented—
the front of their house, his pony and a profusion of mechanical toys, the way his grandfather had looked and dressed. Just
when he was trembling on the edge of puberty, he was hit in
the head with a Louisville Slugger and knocked unconscious
while he played catcher in a school baseball game—coming
to on the coarse grass of the diamond with everybody bending
over him, he momentarily remembered seeing a man cutting
into a woman with a knife, a vision that had the taste of
nostalgia. A teacher kneeling beside him kept saying, *oh my
God, oh my God.* He did not recognize the teacher for a moment, nor any of the boys above him. Two naked people on a
bed, one of them thrashing in her own blood? In the middle
of his awesome headache, he saw the scene freshly again, as
if it had filled his mind while he was unconscious, and again
it seemed as though he had been there and watched it happen.

"Oh, my God," the teacher said again, and suddenly he
remembered her name. The odd and potent vision left him.
His eyes focused.

"How do you feel?" the teacher asked.

Tabby told her, "My dad said there are no bad men."

3

At only two other times during his life in Florida did Tabby
Smithfield demonstrate that he might be something other than
the quiet normal boy, the son of an itinerant bartender, that he
appeared to be.

The first occurred just after Clark had bought the little
house in Orlando. They had moved in that morning, and
Sherri was fussing from living room to kitchen and back
again, trying to pretend that she was not ecstatic. The U-Haul
trailer was still in the driveway, unhitched because Clark was
at work, and boxes full of dishes and clothes were all over the
floors. Sherri was waiting for the delivery truck from Sears—
a new bed was on the way. Tabby had found his Monopoly
game in one of the boxes, and was playing it by himself on
the bare floor of his new bedroom. There were four Tabbys,
and when one of them rolled the dice, the others hoped he'd

land on one of their hotels. Tabby II was winning so far, and
Tabby III had had nothing but penalties. Sherri had buzzed
into the room, seen what he was doing, said, "You're the
craziest kid, I swear," buzzed out again. Sounds of drawers
opening, boxes being ripped apart.

"Damn," Sherri shouted from the living room. "I can't
find it!"

He was Tabby IV then, a good cautious Tabby, not as
reckless as Tabby II or as unlucky as Tabby III, with a good
chance to overtake II and eventually win the game, and he
yelled out, "Can I help?"

"I can't *find* it!" Sherri squalled, pushed over the edge by
frustration. Tabby understood—moving house was hard on
the nerves. And then he—or, to be precise, the part of him
that was unlucky Tabby III—understood even more. Sherri
had misplaced her wallet, and she was going crazy because
she was afraid she'd have to tip the men bringing the bed and
would not have any money. He understood all this in an instant, and then, just as if Tabby III across the table with his
diminishing supply of funny money leaned over to whisper in
his ear, an instant later he *saw* it: he saw Sherri take the
wallet out of her oversized bag and absentmindedly put it on
top of the refrigerator.

Tabby never stopped to question this vision or to wonder
where it came from. He put down the dice and went into the
living room, where Sherri was pacing around with her hands
stuck in her hair. "Your wallet's on top of the 'frigerator,"
he said. "You kidding me?" Sherri said, and went off to the
kitchen at a trot. A moment later she returned, wallet in her
hand, with a grateful look on her face. "You're a genius,
kid," she said. "Now, tell me what happened to the charm
bracelet I lost when I was sixteen."

"Okay," Tabby said. "It fell down behind the backseat of
your cousin Hector's car. That was a '49 Dodge. It stayed
there a long time, but when Hector sold the car for junk the
guy in the junkyard found it after they took the seats out."
All this information was coming from Tabby III. "He gave it
to his little girl, but then she lost it at a party, and somehow it
went down a storm drain. . . ." He stopped because Tabby
III had just given him a very clear picture of Sherri, sixteen
years old, with her shirt and bra off. Her hair was as black as
her eyes.

Sherri was staring at him with her mouth open. "My cousin Hector? My sweet Jesus. Did I ever say anything about him to you?"

The bell rang. "They're here. Hey, thanks, Tabby. I was going nuts." She turned away, but not before giving him a puzzled, almost frightened look out of her black eyes.

The second event happened three years later, in March of 1980, just a month before they moved back to Hampstead. Monty Smithfield had died of a stroke, and his lawyer had written Clark that he was now owner of "Four Hearths." Clark wanted to leave immediately; Sherri did not want to leave at all, and they were fighting about it. Besides the house, there was an amount of money that seemed fabulous to them all, hundreds of thousands of dollars. "What about your job?" "They can stuff my job. I'll get another job there. Sherri, I won't even need a job for a long time." "I don't want to move up North." "You want to stay here? In this crackerbox?" "I won't know how to act. I won't fit in. I won't have any friends. I want to stay here where I belong."

Clark had now swung part of the way back into alcoholism, and he was drunk. As in the old days on Mount Avenue, he skipped work two days every week. Clark and Sherri had begun to fight about these matters. "Where you belong is wherever I take you," Clark yelled.

"So I am like something you pack in a suitcase?" Whenever Sherri got mad, her voice became much more Spanish.

Tabby slipped out the door, wanting only to get away from the sounds of their fight. He scuffed across the weedy lawn. Sherri's voice rose up like a flag from the house behind him. A glass shattered.

Then it happened again. He was somewhere else. For the first time he understood that he was seeing forward, seeing what would happen. It was night, a few degrees cooler than the actual night. The noises of the fight had vanished, and Tabby knew without looking back that his house had vanished too. Tall dark trees stood all about him: before him was a meeting of two roads. Light from a number of large houses shone steadily through and around the trees. He knew that this was not the countryside it appeared to be, but a rich neighborhood that imitated northern country. Once he had known this place. A bad thing had happened here. Lights from a car, set low to the ground, swept toward him. In a moment they were on him, dazzling his eyes.

4

So he stood there, in real time, six weeks later, on the night of May 17. His father claimed he had already found a job: when he got home at night he talked about the "accounts" he was getting, the commissions he was earning, all the while drinking steadily. Sherri had grown puffy with misery. She hated Connecticut. Tabby knew that Hampstead felt entirely snooty and unforgiving to her. He wandered the streets, looking for something. Twice he found himself in front of the gates on Mount Avenue, staring at his grandfather's old house. Still unaccustomed to the spaciousness of his new home, he could scarcely believe that he and his father had once lived in such a mansion. It was twice the size of "Four Hearths." Wondering, he turned away. A feeling of immanence drove him. Something, he knew not what, was due: some contract was to be sealed. He was silent and inconspicuous at school, half-thinking that his real life lay elsewhere, out on the quiet Greenbank streets at night where *it* was.

On that Saturday, Tabby was tormented by the certainty that *it* was about to happen. He still had no idea what *it* was, but it lay over Hampstead like a thundercloud. His anxiety kept him from eating his French toast at breakfast, would not permit him to read a book or watch *Spaced-Out Films* on Channel 9. Clark said, "Such a nice day, why don't we go out and play catch?" and Tabby's feeling of coming doom stripped half his skills from him. He dropped balls, threw them wildly. "Pay attention!" his father yelled, and finally gave up in anger and disgust. Tabby walked for miles—all the way down to Sawtell Beach, where he bought a chili dog at the concession stand and looked at the faces of the people lazing in the sun. Will it happen to *you?* Will *you* do it? He trudged back up Greenbank Road, looking at the faces in the cars that passed.

At one o'clock he sat on Gravesend Beach and fell asleep: vivid, clamorous dreams, filled with cries for help, chased themselves through his mind. When he awakened, he was looking at the Van Horne house, shining whitely up on its bluff above a concrete seawall. He groaned. It would come, and he would not be able to stop it. Seagulls wheeling over the little combers mocked the cries he had heard in his sleep.

He dragged himself home.

After dinner Tabby let himself out again. This time he turned not toward Mount Avenue, but into the little maze of streets inland from it. Charleston Road, Hermitage, Beach Trail, Gravesend Avenue, Cannon Road. He stared into windows and scrutinized faces. A patrol car passed him, then swung around for another look. A woman jogged past, and he managed to say hello. Imperceptibly the light died.

While he walked up Charleston Road for the third time, a wave of dizziness and nausea struck him. He smelled death, as clearly as if he stood over a body, and for a second remembered a scuffle in a Fort Myers tavern, one man punching a blade into another: *it* had happened, he knew, and then was swept by a series of images too rushed and incoherent to be understood. A sweatshirt that read KEEP ON TRUCKIN', a boy falling from a bicycle into a heap of gravel, a huge truck canted on its side. A woman screaming for help in a bird's voice.

It, it was going on or had gone on behind him. Tabby staggered, turned around, ran back down Charleston Road—and found himself on a corner in a stand of old oak trees with headlights set low to the ground reaching toward him. He looked sideways up Cannon Road. There was the house: its windows black: it had happened in there. The headlights of the car fixed him for a moment, and then the Corvette sped by around the corner. For a moment he saw the frozen, desperate look on the face of the man driving. He was where the sense of immanence had led him, in the place where he had seen himself weeks before.

Tabby could not move until the police cars roared past him. Then he recoiled backward as if stung, and ran between the trees and houses until he came out on the next street. He ran uphill to the far end of Hermitage Road; home. Once inside, he could hear his father and Sherri in their bedroom. They were noisily, frantically making love.

5

"Skippy used to stick his head in the mailboxes sometimes," Bruce Norman said. "To see if the cherry bombs were duds. Man, he liked to have blown his head off a couple of times. What a crazy dude."

Tabby Smithfield, lately an intimate of the Norman twins, was seated between them in the backseat of their rusted old car in the Blue Tern's parking lot. Dicky Norman had pushed bills into the hands of a suddenly nervous crewneck-sweatered college boy, placed his order, and now the three of them were mildly high, Tabby less so than the twins, on beer. It was ten-thirty on Sunday night, the thirty-first of May. Dicky and Bruce had scarcely let Tabby out of their sight since the previous Friday. At first a little frightened by them, Tabby had come to see that though the twins were obviously destined for inglorious ends, they were still just childish troublemakers. Their size and their menacing faces led the world to expect much worse. They shoplifted, vandalized, smoked dope, and loved heavy metal music. Tabby had known lots like them. He preferred the music of Ben Sidran and Steve Miller, but was not about to announce it.

"Anyhow, we gave up on cherry bombs," Bruce said. "Now we get 'em with the Devastator." He fondled the taped handle of a baseball bat. This had been lacquered black, but splintery white showed through all the nicks and dents. "Even makes a better sound, sort of a more honest sound. You cruise along, take a good swing with the Devastator, and the whole goddamned side of the box caves in. Ba-*joing!* How about going out on a run with us a little later, hey?"

"Okay," Tabby said. "I'll come along for the ride."

Dicky sat up, looked in the rearview mirror, and groaned. "Bobo the Clown." All three boys put their cans of beer on the floor behind their legs.

A moment later a police car pulled up beside them. A grinning Bobo got out and ambled over to their window. "Well, the Bobbsey Twins. Shouldn't you be home in bed?"

"Whatever you say, Officer Farnsworth."

"Who's your playmate? He looks too normal to be a friend of yours."

Tabby gave his name, and the officer looked him over with a friendly and distant regard.

"Well, kids, time for you to go. I'm going to check out the bar, and when I come back I don't want to see your car here. I'll tell you something. I'm sorry you guys ever turned sixteen."

"It's a bitch, getting old," Bruce said.

"I don't think you'll ever get that far, Brucie." Bobo slapped the top of their car and turned away.

As soon as Bobo had gone inside the Blue Tern, Bruce drained his beer and opened his door to get into the front seat. "That twink," he said as he turned the key. "Callin' me Brucie. Fuckhead clown." He loudly belched. "Let's drive around a little bit. Dicky, why don't you sort of set things up for Tabs?"

"You ever hear of a guy named Gary Starbuck?" Dicky asked.

6

It was barely possible that Clark Smithfield, if not Tabby, might have actually met Gary Starbuck in Key West in the early seventies. Gary Starbuck had been told by his father that the only way to keep out of jail was to keep moving—work a town for a while, then pick up and go at least five hundred miles away. Following his father's trade as Clark Smithfield had refused to do, Starbuck had lived off the pickings in Key West while Clark worked at the No Name Bar. In Key West, Starbuck was Delbert Tory; in Houston, Charles Beard; in Springfield, Illinois, Lawrence Ringler; in Cleveland, Keith Pepper. When he rented the Frazier Peters house on Beach Trail he called himself Nelson Sutter. From his father he had also learned to avoid meeting people; to sit alone in bars; to cultivate a professional politeness. This Starbuck was a squat youngish fellow, dark-haired and broad-shouldered, beardless. His face was solemn and large of nose, out of key with his top-heavy body. Off duty he wore pastel polo shirts and chinos; drove an anonymous gray van. When he worked he carried a pistol.

When he had first come to Hampstead, he had rented a trailer in the lot off the Post Road. The twins had seen his van parked beside the trailer day after day; sometimes it was gone on weekends, most often at night. Eventually—just about the time Starbuck found a house to rent—Bruce and Dicky decided to take a look inside both the trailer and the van.

Bruce got into the van one day while Starbuck must have been asleep. It was as clean inside as its owner kept the exterior: clean and empty. But Bruce looked into the glove compartment and saw that the California registration was in another name than the one under which the trailer had been rented.

"We got something here, Dicky," he told his brother. The next night they used one of their spare keys to enter the trailer.

And that was even better than they expected, filled with television sets, silverware, racks of suits—and half a dozen shoe boxes stacked with money. "Hey, this guy's the real thing," Bruce said, so impressed he looked poleaxed.

After school the next day they visited the trailer again. They rang the bell. The tenant came to the door and looked at them suspiciously. Bruce said, "Mr. Starbuck? Excuse me, I mean Mr. Sutter?"

When they left, they had a new television set and a Baggie full of good Mexican weed. Gary Starbuck had remembered more of his father's advice: "When you got partners, even partners you don't want, treat them right. A partner's a partner even when he's no good, and sooner or later a little grease will keep your ass out of the jug." He was sure he could find a use for the Norman twins.

7

Patsy McCloud lived with one big simple fear, and even on the night of her failed dinner party for the Allbees and Ronnie Riggley, it overshadowed all the other little fears. When she was seven her parents had taken her to the mental hospital where her Grandmother Tayler lived—her parents saw Grandmother Tayler two or three times a year, but this was Patsy's first visit. Her father had been grumpy on the long drive from Hampstead to Hartford, for he opposed allowing his daughter to meet his mother; but Patsy's mother, who had answered the old woman's increasingly frequent requests with uncomfortable evasions, had held firm.

They had been shown into a wide room painted in primary colors, like a nursery school. The nurses beamed at Patsy, who was already uneasy because of the tension between her parents and the odd, damaged people wandering through the ward. People whose heads were too large for their bodies, people whose tongues seemed too large for their heads. One man obsessively pacing off the length of a wall had a shovel-shaped dent two inches deep in his forehead. The locks and bars she had seen on the way up to this room made her feel she was a prisoner in the hospital. Maybe it was a trick, a trick to get her here, and her parents would leave her in this place! Though she was the only child in the room, it seemed appointed for children, with its desks covered with crayons and crude childish pictures taped to the wall.

Her grandmother appeared through a bright orange door. Two male nurses accompanied her. She was talking to herself. Patsy's first thought was that her grandmother was the oldest person she had ever seen; then that she belonged here. Her white hair was sparse and dull, her eyes glazed. White whiskers sprouted from her chin. She paid no attention to Patsy's parents but sat in the chair where the nurses put her and looked down at her lap and muttered.

"We brought Patsy," her mother said. "Remember that you were asking for her? We wanted you to meet her, Mother Tayler."

Her father made a disgusted noise and turned his back on them.

Patsy was looking into the old woman's vague, inward face.

"Don't you want to say hello to your granddaughter, Mother Tayler?"

"A man is hanging in his backyard," her grandmother startled Patsy by mumbling. "Just swinging on a rope. Too many bills, bills, bills. They'll find him next week, I guess. You brought Danny's girl?" The vague pale eyes lifted to meet Patsy's. "Poor girl," her grandmother said. "She's another one. Pretty thing. She doesn't like it here, does she? She thinks you'll leave her with me. Poor girl. Will they find him next week, little girl?"

The pale eyes lost a portion of their vagueness, and Patsy had seen the man hanging from the branch of a tree: through a window she saw a desk covered with paper. "I don't know," Patsy said, shocked.

"I'll love you, if you'll live with me," said Grandmother Tayler, and that had abruptly ended the interview. Her father scooped her up and carried her down to the car. Ten minutes later her mother joined them. Neither of them had ever suggested bringing Patsy to see Mother Tayler again.

Two days later she asked her father if they had found that man yet. Her father had not known what she meant. She understood that her father felt deep angry shame, both for himself and for her.

• • •

But she remembered Grandmother Tayler's acceptance. *Poor girl. She's another one.* When the old woman's eyes had finally met hers, she had felt as transparent as glass. In those eyes had been a matter-of-fact despair and an understanding beyond death. The only difference between Patsy and her grandmother was that Grandmother Tayler was better at it. Before she reached puberty, Patsy was able to move small objects across a table, to switch on lights and open doors, just by seeing these occurrences in her mind and surrounding them with a yellow glow of intention. This ability was her secret, her best secret. She had known instantly that Grandmother Tayler could do much more than that—that if she'd wanted, Grandmother Tayler could have brought down the hospital on all sides of her and walked away free and unharmed. But Grandmother Tayler didn't want. For Patsy, the old woman with her deliberately vague face and fractured mind was an inexorable image of her own future.

When she had her first period, the ability to shift objects at will left her. It simply was not there anymore: womanhood had taken it away and left cramps and blood in its place. For almost a year she was like every other girl she knew, and she was grateful.

Then a new girl had come into their class. Marilyn Foreman, a mousy creature with glasses, dull hair, and an implacable mouth. The minute Marilyn Foreman had appeared in the door, Patsy had known. And Marilyn had recognized her in the same way. The other girl had been an unavoidable fact: Marilyn was her destiny, as her grandmother had been. At recess, the other girl had come up to her and claimed her. "What do you do? I can see things, and they always happen." "Get away from me," Patsy said, but halfheartedly, and Marilyn stayed. Patsy was passive before her knowledge that Marilyn Foreman was to drive away all her other friends, and the two of them were to belong to each other. "It'll happen," Marilyn said in her grating, drawling voice. "It'll happen to you too. I know." Even without affection between them, for the other girl did not require affection, she and Marilyn became so close that they began to look alike, in a middle ground between Patsy's prettiness and Marilyn's plainness. Sometimes Patsy caught herself speaking in Marilyn's voice. The Taylers never understood why their popular, attractive daughter allowed herself to be so influenced by nondescript Marilyn Foreman.

Together they *traveled:* their word, Marilyn's idea. They
sat side by side, nights when they were supposed to be doing
homework, linked hands, and closed their eyes. Patsy invariably felt a sick thrill of fear, half-enjoyable, as their minds
seemed to join and float upward. Traveling, they saw strange
landscapes, hot molten colors—they never knew what they
would see. It might just be people eating in a restaurant, or a
boy in their class taking a walk along Sawtell Beach. Once
they saw two of their teachers, not married to each other,
making love on the floor of an empty room. Another time,
they saw a man they recognized as the shop teacher at J. S.
Mill deep in a green wood, lying naked over a boy who was
on the high-school football team. "That's filthy dirty," Marilyn said. But in general, Marilyn never cared what they saw
while they traveled. She was as happy watching strangers eat
a meal she could not taste in a restaurant she could not recognize as with their more colorful visions.

Another vision seemed to be located in the past, and would
have been unusual for that reason alone. The two girls saw a
street that was obviously Riverfront Avenue, but the oil company and office buildings were gone. Short chunky fishing
boats were docked at piers; snub-nosed old cars had been
pulled up on a grassy bank long since turned into parking lots.
On one of the boats a bearded man in a knit cap was pouring
wine into a coffee cup and a wineglass. A woman in a silk
dress lolled against the boat's railing. "This is wrong," Marilyn said. "I don't like this." She had tried to extricate her
hand, but Patsy gripped harder: this was for her, and Marilyn
Foreman was not going to take it from her even if it was
terrible. For it would be terrible, she knew. The bearded man
smiled at the woman and started his engines. The boat putted
out into the river and went slowly seaward. The man grasped
the woman and pretended to dance. He swayed, shuffled his
feet; the woman held to him and laughed. Patsy saw that the
fisherman was handsome as a bull is handsome, uncaringly.
"Nasty," Marilyn said. Smiling, the man stroked the woman's
neck with his blunt fingers. Then he closed his hands and
pressed into the soft flesh of her neck with his thumbs. His
eyes glittered. He leaned into the woman and toppled her to the
shiny deck. Their bodies struggled and rolled until the man
lifted the woman's head and battered it against the deck. All
his movements were concentrated and intent. Marilyn began to
shake. After the woman stopped moving, the man fetched a

roll of oilcloth from a locker and tied her into it. When he had thrown the wrapped, still-living body into the Nowhatan, he finished the wine. Patsy tingled with revulsion: as soon as the picture of the fisherman standing alone on his boat melted into that of another strange man, this one in a double-breasted suit and standing on what Patsy recognized as the country club beach, she dropped Marilyn's hand. She felt as if these scenes of death and violence would cynically unreel as long as she invited them.

Will they find him next week, little girl?

After the Foremans moved to Tulsa, Patsy never tried to travel on her own. She and Les both went to Connecticut State College: they watched the days-long drama of the Kennedy assassination on the television set in Les's fraternity house. Sometimes she would amaze Les by correctly predicting the grades he would earn on his exams. If she had prophetic dreams, she kept them to herself. Les was already calling her a "swamp Yankee." After they married in 1964, they lived in Hartford, New York City, Chicago, London, Los Angeles, and were transferred back to New York. They bought their house in Hampstead, and Les commuted to New York to, as he put it, "burn ass." Now they never spoke of anything personal. Les in fact rarely spoke to her at all. He had started to beat her in Chicago, after his first really significant promotion had followed the best efficiency reports of his life.

8

Les did not beat Patsy that Sunday night; he sourly and drunkenly told her that compared to Ronnie Riggley and Laura Allbee she was not a woman. He roamed around the house, finishing a bottle, while Patsy retreated to the bedroom. Now and then she heard him muttering about "pansy actors." When she heard him come up the stairs to go to bed, Patsy fled into the spare bedroom next to theirs, where she had set up some bookshelves, a desk, and a couch that folded out into a double bed. A black-and-white Sony with a six-inch screen sat on top of the bookshelf, and she switched it on to watch a movie until Les was safely asleep.

At twelve-thirty a noise of crashing and splintering from outside jolted her out of a doze. Les too had been awakened by the noises from the street, and she heard him thrashing around in the dark bedroom. The door banged. She called out his name, but instead of an answer heard the front door slam shut.

Patsy looked out the window of her hideaway. In the yellow glow from the security lights angling out from most of the houses, she saw a rusty black car speeding around the corner of Charleston Road. A second later she saw Les chasing after the car in his bathrobe and slippers. He was carrying a gun in his hand.

She knew Les well enough to know that if Richard Allbee and Bobo Farnsworth had not been in their house Les would have left the gun behind. But the youth and strength of one, and the fame, however meaningless, of the other, had provoked him. Patsy looked down the stairs to the landing, opened the door and ran down the street after her husband.

A dying sparrow fluttered pathetically on the grate of a storm drain beneath a lamp. Ordinarily she would have stopped, but she heard the crowing of a police siren around the corner ahead of her and ran toward it past the trembling sparrow.

At the corner where Charleston Road swung into Beach Trail stood a second streetlamp, and a child, a little girl with glasses and limp brown hair, stood directly beneath it, looking at her. Patsy at first thought that it was very late for a child to be outside, then that the child looked familiar. Her anxiety for Les kept her running until she was directly abreast of the streetlamp. She could see a patrol car nosed in toward a driveway on Beach Trail, that of the house which backed directly onto hers. A policeman stood beside a hunched old man and a slight teenage boy, and Les was crouched down before them, holding his pistol out in the firing position.

"Oh, my God," Patsy breathed. Les had gone crazy and was about to shoot someone, unless the policeman shot him first.

Then she realized that the child beneath the streetlamp was Marilyn Foreman. She involuntarily turned from the sight of her husband aiming his pistol at a policeman, and looked sideways at the child. Marilyn Foreman, with her ribbon bow tie and rolled white socks and pale indomitable face. Marilyn stood in the light and cast no shadow. "No," Patsy said. "It's not . . ." Marilyn opened her mouth and spoke, but no words issued from her mouth. Patsy heard the sound of a shot, very loud in the quiet street.

9

"Gary Starbuck is a pro," Dicky Norman told Tabby as they turned onto the Bridge Road and crossed the Nowhatan. "He's the real thing. Nobody even knows his real name besides us. Boy, does he have his shit together."

"What do you mean, a pro?"

Both brothers laughed. They were speeding up Greenbank Road, the Olds's rebuilt engine doing everything but shooting flames out the exhaust.

"He takes things," Bruce said. "Out of people's houses. Man, when he's done with a house, there's nothing left but termites. I bet Gary Starbuck makes more money in a year than anybody around here, I bet he's a fuckin' millionaire, man, the stuff he's got."

"Oh," Tabby said.

"And we're gonna hook up with him," Dicky crowed.

"That's not for me," Tabby quickly put in.

"Oh, not tonight. Tonight we're just going to exercise the Devastator. In Greenbank. We've got it all timed. We'll get in Greenbank just about ten minutes after that twink Bobo the Clown pulls out on his way toward the Post Road. We got that sucker *down,* man. We know *his every move.* And he's gonna look like a real asshole."

"Didn't you just get a few mailboxes in Greenbank?" asked Tabby, who had seen the evidence of the twins' enthusiasms.

"Yeah, but this is specially for Bobo," said Dicky, rapping the bat against the palm of his hand. "And afterward, maybe we can hook up with Gary Starbuck for a little talk. Unless you think you got to get home, little buddy."

"I think I do."

"We'll settle that later," Bruce said from the front seat.

"I don't steal from people's houses, and I don't want to meet anybody who does," Tabby said, his nervousness making him sound prissy. "I don't even especially want to cave in my neighbors' mailboxes."

Dicky patted him on the head. "Hey, man."

"It's my *neighborhood*."

"Hey, it's his neighborhood, man," Bruce said.

Dicky cranked his window down all the way and stuck out the bat just as they sped around a corner. A mailbox separated from its post with a crack like the breaking of a neck. Dicky shouted with glee, *"Got* that suckah!"

"Hey, we don't want you to do anything special," Bruce said. "We're just friends, okay?"

"Yeah."

"I don't know, you don't sound too friendly," Dicky said, slapping the bat against his palm again.

"Burglary's out of my league," Tabby said. "That's all I meant."

"Hey, but this guy takes all the risks," Bruce told him. "We ain't as dumb as we look."

Tabby said nothing.

"Here comes another one," Dicky said. They were driving near to the gates of Greenbank Academy. He stuck the bat out the window as Bruce slowed the car. One-handed, Dicky raised the bat and swung it hard toward the Academy mailbox. There was a loud flat crumpling sound, and Dicky whooped again as Bruce sped off.

When Bruce turned up Beach Trail, Tabby protested, "This is right where I live, you guys."

"Tabs, you're starting to piss me off," Dicky said.

Why am I here? Tabby suddenly wondered. Because these two lumps bought me a Whopper and a Coke? "This might sound crazy," he said, "but have you two guys ever thought about becoming cops? I bet you'd be a couple of great cops."

"Shit," Dicky said, and Bruce simultaneously. "Ain't no mon-*ee*, Tabs, no mon-*ee*. Hampstead cops all live in Norrington, man, you know that?"

"You get the next one, Tabs," Dicky said. They were circling aimlessly up Cannon Road, and did not see Bobo Farnsworth's patrol car, which was parked beside trees on Leo Friedgood's driveway. Leo had stopped turning on his yard lights.

"You know what I'd really like to do?" Bruce offered. "I'd like to off somebody really big someday—like the president, man, or John Denver. I'd like to be the first guy that actually tried to off John Denver."

Dicky pushed the bat into Tabby's chest. "Get on the other side of the road, Bruce."

"Not my own," Tabby said, seeing where Bruce was going. "I won't do it."

"Pisses me *off*."

"Hey, okay."

Bruce swung into Charleston Road and swerved across to the wrong side of the street. "You better do this one, Tabs."

In anger and despair Tabby thrust the bat out the window, holding the taped handle with both hands. He had never wanted to do anything less. The bat met the mailbox with what seemed terrific force, and almost jolted out of Tabby's hands. "All *right*," Bruce sighed. "You're blooded, man." Dicky pounded him on the back. His arms ached from the impact, which seemed to have traveled undiminished up the bat and registered in his biceps and shoulders.

Bruce accelerated. "One more for tonight—but lemme tell you about what we want to do. You know that parking lot in front of the diner, the one with the big sign that goes around?"

"Hey, some guy's running after us," Dicky called out, amused. "He thinks he's gonna get the license number. He's clean out of his gourd."

Tabby looked around and saw a man in pajamas pounding after their car.

"Bye-bye," Bruce said, and gunned the car around the Beach Trail corner. He reached in back, and Dicky placed the bat in his hand.

"Hey, I'm almost home," Tabby said hastily. "Why don't you—"

Bruce veered across the road and smacked a mailbox off its post.

As the mailbox sailed over the driveway, they heard the sound of a police siren coming down Cannon Road.

"Let me out," Tabby insisted.

"Jesus!" Dicky yelled. "Peel!"

"Hey, it's like with Skippy, man," Bruce calmly said to his brother. "Let's let him out."

Dicky quickly pushed Tabby toward the door.

"Dummy up," he hissed. "You'll be okay. Just dummy up."

Tabby opened the door and scrambled out thirty seconds before Bobo Farnsworth, siren going and lights flashing, turned into Beach Trail. Behind Bobo, Les McCloud ran up from Charleston Road, waving his gun and screaming obscenities.

10

In Greenbank, as in most of Hampstead, few lights burned from the houses. High-voltage yard and security lights lit up the lawns like stage sets. No one awake on the upper end of Charleston Road, though two second-story windows were alight in the McCloud house—Patsy and Les were in different rooms, Bobo Farnsworth deduced with no surprise. Sometime he would be called there to interrupt a fight, and find that tense pretty woman with a bulging eye and a broken jaw. And after Les spent a night in a cell, Patsy would take him back and come up with a story about falling off a ladder. No lights on in Beach Trail. He turned into Cannon Road, and saw from the corner that though the yard lights were off, the living- and dining-room windows in Leo Friedgood's house were ablaze with light. Insomnia. And he had forgotten to close his curtains. Unless Leo were stinking drunk, the odds were that he would welcome company.

Bobo pulled his car into the driveway and parked it next to a row of trees. No need to have a neighbor out for a midnight stroll get the idea that Hampstead's finest were still questioning Leo Friedgood. As he looked up toward the lighted windows he saw a shadow move across the living-room wall. Bobo went up the steps and rang the doorbell.

Friedgood did not answer, and Bobo rang the bell again.

"Who's there?" called a muffled voice from just on the other side of the door.

"It's Officer Farnsworth. I was on my patrol, and I thought I'd stop by and see if you needed anything."

Friedgood gave no reply.

"Maybe you just want to talk?"

"Get away from here," the voice said.

"You don't sound so good. Are you all right, Mr. Friedgood?"

The curtains on the windows to Bobo's left slid shut. Friedgood seemed to be uttering panicked, fretful sounds.

"Open the door, Mr. Friedgood. Let me help you."

"You think you can help? Open the door."

Bobo turned the knob and pushed open the door. Almost instantly he smelled the odor of burned meat. Friedgood was walking away from him into the living room to his left. Bobo saw with surprise that Friedgood was wearing a hat. Friedgood switched off the living-room lights before he turned around.

Bobo first saw that the man's eyes were covered with dark aviator-style glasses. The hat was pulled low on his forehead. His hands were gloved. Half of Friedgood's face seemed puffy, distorted; the other half, from under the rim of the glasses, and down into the collar of his shirt, was as red as raw steak. The bushy mustache was gone.

"Stay away," Friedgood said. His lips were white and looked lipsticked. "I've got something. Don't come any nearer."

"Who's your doctor?" Bobo got out. Friedgood lifted his right hand and drew it over the red side of his face. Even in the darkness, Bobo saw that the glove came away bloody. It looked as though Friedgood had the world's worst case of acne, and had tried to solve it by cutting off his skin. Or by burning it off.

"My doctor can't help," Friedgood backed farther into the gloom. "Satisfied? Now get out. I don't want your company."

Bobo peered at Friedgood hanging back in the dark—the left side of his face, the puffy side, was as white as his lips. The cheek on that side, either the bone or the pad of skin over it, appeared to be moving independently, like a mouse twitching in its sleep. "Take off your hat and glasses," Bobo said. "Jesus, I never saw anything like it."

He heard what sounded like an explosion from somewhere outside, and his heart nearly stopped.

Friedgood giggled. A car roared away.

"I'd better get going," Bobo said. "That's another one of those damned mailboxes. But if I can get anything, help anyhow . . ."

"Leave me alone," Friedgood said. "You can't do anything for me, just get out."

Bobo turned and half-ran out the door, his skin creeping. When he got to his car he saw that Friedgood had turned off all his lights. Bobo had a momentary image of the man in that big dark house, his ruined skin phosphorescently shining . . . and gunned his car into the street, scattering gravel.

He was looking for the speeding taillights of a car as he swung round the corner into Charleston Road, but noticed out of the side of his eye that Les McCloud's mailbox had been pounded in on one side. As he went by the house, the front door swung open, releasing a shaft of light—Les going out to inspect the damage. Bobo cruised by, looking quickly up and down the intersections for a flash of red light. The vandals could have circled around the little maze of streets in this section of Greenbank, or they could have turned down Beach Trail to get to Mount Avenue. That, he bet himself, was what they would have done.

Then he heard again the popping, banging sound of a mailbox being destroyed, and he switched on his siren and swung into Beach Trail.

A block down he saw movement, but no car. In front of a weathered old house a dented mailbox had rolled halfway across the street, and a boy was stooping to pick it up. When the boy heard the siren, he looked in Bobo's direction but did not run. He carried the box back toward its stump.

Bobo swung onto the side of the road, cut the lights and the siren, and got out of his car. "Hold it, son," he said to the boy. "You see any car going by—you see who did that?"

The boy shook his head, and Bobo stepped nearer. "Hey, I just saw you. You were with the Normans."

"Yes," Tabby said. "I live up on Hermitage Road. I saw this mailbox in the street."

"Don't even bother nailing the box to the stump anymore," came a resonant voice from up on the lawn. Both Tabby and Bobo turned their heads to see a bent old man in a gray sweatshirt and voluminous white trousers slowly making his way toward them through the darkness. "If I did, some harebrain would come along and make it even worse—see, they gave it a pretty good knock, last time they killed it they didn't even knock its head off."

Bobo saw the boy give the old man a wild, startled look of recognition: as if, Bobo thought, the old man was someone famous, some kind of movie star. Bobo looked at the old man more closely. He was no movie star. A silvery, gossamer fur clung to his neck and the underside of his chin. The face was deeply seamed, the cheeks sunken. Eyes bright under bristling, straggly eyebrows. White hair fell from the back of the man's bald, freckled crown and floated around his large ears. The face was withered but powerful. The old man was somebody, Bobo knew instantly, even if he didn't recognize him, and he altered the tone he would otherwise have taken.

The old man took in the boy's astonished stare, which seemed to Bobo to be widening out with every second, and then turned a humorous glance on Bobo. "The name is Graham Williams. I don't suppose this boy is the famous mailbox killer, do you? Are you, boy? You the Ramon Mercador of mailboxes?"

Neither Bobo nor Tabby recognized the name of Leon Trotsky's assassin, but Bobo's ear was caught by the old man's name. "Williams—I heard of you."

"Ask Turtle about me," the old man said. "He'll tell you a pack of lies. Thirty, forty years ago, I got into trouble with a couple of polecats named Nixon and McCarthy. A whole other bunch of polecats wanted me to testify before a committee. And I almost—"

Shouts from down the street stopped Bobo from saying that the only reason he recognized the man's name was that he had heard it from the Emergency Medical Services team.

All three of them looked toward the source of the shouting. A man in a flapping bathrobe was running toward them up the street. His bedroom slippers made a clapping noise on the surface of the road. "Hold it right there!" he yelled. "I gotcha now!"

Tabby's widening gaze went back to the old man. He whispered something Bobo did not catch, but which seemed to startle Williams.

The old man reared back and inspected the boy. "You're Monty Smithfield's grandson? The one they call Tabby?"

"On a boat," Tabby said.

"Hold it yourself, Les," said Bobo, who did not bother trying to make sense of this exchange. "There's nothing to get excited about." Then Bobo saw Les's pistol, and he held out his left hand to distract Les while he unclipped the strap on his holster with his right. "Did you see a car, Les?" Bobo asked quietly.

"Get out of the way and leave your gun in the holster," Les shouted. Now he was walking, puffing from his run.

"You're drunk, Les. Put that gun away."

"To hell with you," Les said, and braced himself in the firing position, both arms out straight and knees slightly bent. "That kid just destroyed my property."

"You got the wrong boy," Bobo said. Over Les's shoulder he could see Patsy rounding the corner from Charleston Road.

She seemed to be moving in a daze, and stopped to stare at a lamppost almost as raptly as the kid was staring at Graham Williams.

"And that's Patsy Tayler," the old man said. "She's got that bony Tayler face. Can't you get that man to drop his gun?"

"You're shielding a vandal!" Les screamed.

"Les," Bobo said quietly, "are you crazy? If you don't put that gun down, I'll have to drop you."

"Get out of the way!"

Graham Williams stepped in front of Tabby. "I suppose that's your wife back there," he said in a carrying voice.

The muzzle flashed, the pistol made a sound louder than a cough, softer than a thunderclap. Les whirled around after firing, and let the pistol dangle in his fingers. Patsy had begun to race toward him.

Bobo had his .44 in his hand, aiming it at Les McCloud's back. He realized with gratitude that this would not be the first time he had to fire his revolver on duty. Les McCloud was tottering like a man on stilts. "Don't! Don't!" Patsy was shouting as she ran. The pistol dropped from Les's hand and clattered on the ground. A second later Les sat down like an infant, his legs bowing out. Bobo heard old Williams exhaling, and quickly checked to see that he and the boy were unharmed. Williams had his arm around the boy's shoulders. "Stay there," he ordered, and walked toward Les and Patsy.

As he went he could hear Les sobbing with rage. Bobo bent and picked up the gun, which was a short-barreled .22.

"I aimed over your head, you bastard," Les told him. Then he turned his red, bloated face to his wife. "Get the hell out of here, Patsy. I don't want to see you."

"Jesus, I ought to take you in and lock you up," Bobo said. "What the hell do you think you're doing? You could be put away for this. What do you suppose you'd get for attempted murder? Fifteen years? Twenty?"

"I was protecting my property." He was still crying, and he clamped his eyes shut.

"You dumb ass," Bobo said. Then, to Patsy: "You going to be okay? You want me to take him in for tonight?"

Patsy shook her head. She looked stricken and half-dead with shock, but determined. *A good lady,* Bobo thought to himself, *too good for this jerk here.*

"I'll take him home, Bobo," she whispered. "Please."

"No, you won't," Les said, still sitting in the middle of the street with his legs out before him.

Patsy reached out to him, but he swatted her hand away.

"You're getting your tail home," Bobo said, and put his hands under Les's arms and lifted him to his feet. "You come around to the station in a couple of days for this twenty-two. And I want to see your permit."

"I got a permit," Les grumped.

"If I hadn't just eaten dinner with you, you'd be facing at least reckless use of a firearm. That's the *least*."

"I aimed over your head." Les reeled sideways, then straightened himself with the aplomb of a long-term drinker.

"With this shitty gun, that's more dangerous than aiming at me," Bobo said. "Get home."

Les took a few staggering steps up the street. When Patsy tried to take his arm to steady him, he batted at her.

"Let him go," Bobo said. "Jesus, that's the first time anybody took a shot at me, and I don't even get the satisfaction of an arrest." He looked at Patsy's drawn face. "How are you?"

"Not so good," Patsy said. "Do you have to ask?"

"Give him half an hour. Maybe you better sleep in the spare room tonight."

Patsy nodded. "Does anybody around here have a cup of coffee?"

6

Graham Again

1

"You killed a man," was what Tabby had whispered to me as crazy Les McCloud was yelling at us to *hold it*. Luckily, the big cop didn't catch the words, but even if he had, I don't suppose he would have run me in. I took my first good look at the kid. Up until then, I'd been thinking that he was just some kind of rich juvenile delinquent. He was old Monty's grandson, the one he had lost after having such hope for him. Losing him had been at least half Monty's fault, I knew— he'd always been too rough on Clark. All the old faces are dying out, they're all turning into the same round bland American potato-face, but in this kid I could see some Tabb, that's where he got the big wide eyes and fair hair, and a lot more Smithfield. Monty and Clark had once had the same sensible chin and generous forehead, but they had turned flinty in Monty and self-pitying in Clark.

"On a boat," the boy said.

And I knew.

He had the gift—that gift that never makes anybody happy, that bitches up lives right and left. The boy had seen me and Bates Krell out on the lobster boat that night in 1924, it had just unrolled behind his eyes like some kind of movie, and he was starting to shake. The last time I'd seen anybody with the gift so strong it was old Josephine Tayler, and she'd been shut away before she was forty.

Some people have the gift only for a minute or two, and then spend the rest of their lives wondering if it really happened—as I wondered after I met Bates Krell—and other people have it hung around their necks all their lives. I wouldn't want to be one of them. I can remember damn near everything that happened to me, but there are some things it makes me dizzy and short of breath to bring back. The first

time I saw Bates Krell, in pure fact everything that has to do
with Bates Krell, is in that category. And part of that package
is the afternoon on his boat. That this kid with the matter-of-
fact Smithfield chin could see it when he looked at me scared
me a lot worse than Les McCloud's pistol, which he started
waving around at about this point.

Right then I saw Patsy Tayler, Les's wife, kind of wandering toward us. At first I thought she was drunk, since her
husband was obviously stinko. But she was not drunk. I knew
that a second later. I knew that she was sober, and seeing
something the rest of us could not see. She was another like
the Smithfield boy. The gift had skipped a generation in the
Tayler family and gone straight from Josephine to her grand-
daughter. I'd seen this wispy girl grow up pretty near, not
counting the years I was in California and the three years I
spent abroad, and I'd never seen before that she'd inherited
something besides Josephine's endearing good looks.

And that rocked me too. Maybe if Tabby hadn't said what
he did about me killing a man on a boat, I would have gone
on thinking that the Tayler girl was just a drunk like her husband. But he *had* said it, you see, and that took me back into
the one time in my life when I was at least a little bit like
those two. I looked back at Tabby and then at Patsy again,
and they were alike. For a second it was like looking at two
photographic negatives, two people light where they should
have been dark and dark where they should have been light. I
felt pity and love and fear: fear because even then I knew that
the appearance of two such people—no, these two people—
in this one particular square mile of earth meant the coming
of awful things, that we were all going to be shaken up as if
by an earthquake, by a volcano, by an old-time Kansas
twister. I didn't have to know anything about Ted Wise and
DRG-16 to foresee that.

And then right on cue, the world told me I was right. None
of the others saw it, they were all looking at poor drunk Les
and his peashooter, but I looked up and saw a bird falling
right out of the sky. Dead. It landed on my lawn not far from
the stump where I set my mailbox, a little squashy puffball of
feathers.

"Get out of the way!" Les screamed, and I got myself
moving. I put myself right in front of Tabby. Because if
things were going to be so bad, I'd rather be dead myself, as
dead as the fallen bird, than live to see it. Certainly better me

than the Smithfield boy, who knew nothing of what I knew, or had known, or had suspected anyhow, since 1924. This act of mine was one of sheer cowardice and I make no bones about it. I even goaded Les by telling him his wife was there in back of him.

The gun went off but even I could see Les wasn't trying to hit anybody. He had that peashooter raised up at a forty-five-degree angle above our heads. Then what I was afraid of was that the big cop, Bobo, was going to plug Les out of sheer overexcitement, but Bobo stayed calm. His gun—a much more serious instrument than Les's—was out, but that was only right. Bobo was making sure that Les McCloud wouldn't try to do in his wife. Les anticlimactically collapsed onto his keester and started to bawl.

I had my arm around the boy's shoulders when Bobo went up to confab with the McClouds. The boy was shaking, as much because of me and what he'd seen as because of Les. "You're a special person, Tabby," I said. "We're all going to need you."

"I did get that mailbox," he said. "Not yours. His." He nodded toward the three of them in the middle of the street, Les swatting away the comfort Patsy wanted to give him.

"Just keep your lip buttoned about that," I advised. "About the other thing too. I'll tell you all about that, and you'll see why it had to happen."

"It *did* happen," Tabby said, as if he had not been sure. "On that boat, too." He separated himself from my arm, and looked up at me with that same trembling suspiciousness I would even then have sacrificed a limb to erase.

"Sure it happened. I just told you it had to."

Bobo and Patsy were coming up the street toward us and I had to shut up. I looked at the unassuming puff of feathers on my lawn and for some reason thought of Babe Zimmer, and Harry's voice choking up when he told me about her on the telephone.

Then Patsy Tayler and Tabby saw each other. Patsy had been saying something about a cup of coffee, she was being what they used to call "a game girl" when I was a kid, trying to act as if the sight of her pajamaed husband waving a gun on the street really wasn't much out of the ordinary. And she glanced up toward us and this act fell to pieces. She barely looked at me; her eyes locked on Tabby. She stopped moving. I knew that the boy was a part of whatever she had been looking at back there on the road when I thought she was drunk—he was the only thing on Beach Trail for her. Her grandmother had got that look now and then, when she walked into a shop and froze when she saw someone who was going to fall down dead of a coronary in a week or two. It was simple recognition, but horrifying because it was so simple. Tabby just stood and took it in. He had that strength.

Nothing is ever isolated, nothing is ever random, everything is connected, and I saw myself rolling over Norm Hughardt's body in his fussy little back garden—I saw Charlie Antolini giving me a smile full of innocent happiness. *Ah, shit,* I thought.

Bobo of course thought that Patsy was reacting to what had just happened and he began to push her along toward us, shepherding her with gentle nudges and pats. Now that nobody was going to get shot, he wanted to get her off his hands.

The physicists are right, there is uncertainty but no randomness.

"Could you help the lady out for half an hour or so?" Bobo asked. "I ought to be seeing if I can catch whoever whacked these . . ." He gestured toward my poor old mailbox.

"There's coffee on the stove," I said. "Good and strong. I'll see that the boy gets home, Officer."

Patsy was staring at the ground now, probably to make sure it wasn't going to cave in beneath her feet. "Tell Les to come down to the station with his permit," Bobo said, and she nodded. She glanced at Tabby again. I put my arms around both of them. Patsy was only an inch or two taller than the boy, and I fancied that I could almost feel the blood pounding along just beneath her skin. I towered over them like some ancient reptilian bird.

2

Five minutes later I was pottering around in my kitchen, pretending that I was an absentminded old slob who had trouble locating three clean cups. In truth I was an absentminded, etc., who had felt the shock waves of the meeting of Patsy Tayler McCloud and James Tabb Smithfield, and who could still virtually hear them booming through my kitchen. The dishes should have rattled on the shelf, the cups rotated on their hooks. The two of them, sitting silently and nervously on my kitchen chairs, set up reverberations so strong. Having seen so much in each other, they could not speak. They would not have known where to begin, the subject of their commonality was so vast.

It was as though they were two old lovers who decades ago had destroyed their marriages, abandoned their children, left an entire town flaming with outrage and rumor; or two generals who had once jointly directed a massacre. You see where I am going with these farfetched comparisons. Part of the immensity of the feeling that made me turn away from them was shame—guilt, too. They had learned to repress and hide their differences from other people. Now each was face to face with the one person who instantly saw through that disguise. They exposed each other. And this was much more difficult for Patsy than for the boy: she had lived longer with her disguise, and it was thinner than Tabby's.

At last I could stand it no longer. "We might as well speak," I said, and took three cups to the blackened pot on the range.

They stirred on their chairs, and pretended to be interested in the scars on the wooden table.

I set the coffee down before them. Tabby muttered his thanks, and Patsy sort of minimally nodded.

"The two of you know what you are," I said. "And if you don't want to talk about that in front of me, that's fine. I know a little bit about it anyhow—at least enough to recognize it when I see it." Tabby was looking at me alertly, Patsy concentrated on her cup. "And I knew your grandmother, Patsy. I remember what she was like and what she could do, though ninety percent of the people in this town just thought she was a good-looking woman who had a screw loose somewhere."

Patsy glanced up at me. "Was she attractive? I never knew her before she was . . . um . . . before."

"As attractive as you are yourself," I said. "And she chose to leave the world, to put it that way. Nobody committed her. She wanted to be there—I think she saw too many monstrosities on the outside—she didn't feel she could face them anymore."

I could not have selected a better noun. She had just used it herself in her diary.

"Monstrosities, yes," Patsy said, almost relaxing for the

first time. The dishes would have stopped rattling, the cups ceased to revolve. "I'm afraid I've become familiar with monstrosities."

She darted an inquisitive look at the boy, silently and shyly asking a question. I think it was the first time in twenty years that Patsy had ever, even so slightly, imagined that there might be this comfort in her talent, that it might be shared. But Tabby shook his head; and then he saved it for her. "I guess I have too. From when I was a little kid. One time. Maybe twice—I don't remember."

"Maybe three," I said. "Don't forget me and Bates Krell on his boat."

Tabby swallowed, and Patsy kept glancing at him as if he were about to burst into flame.

"Well, what have you seen?" I asked her.

Startled, she lifted her head. "You say you knew my grandmother. What did *she* see?"

"She knew when people were going to die," I told her flatly. "That's what I gathered, anyhow."

"I want to go home," Tabby said.

"Do you see people die?" Patsy half-whispered to him.

"How do you mean? Once I saw a guy get stabbed in a bar where my father worked."

"So Clark was a bartender. That must have given Monty the black-and-blue fits," I said. "But you know what she means, Tabby. Did you ever see it before it happened?"

Reluctantly he nodded. "Okay, if you have to know. I saw something when I was five. It was that woman, that Mrs. Friedgood, getting killed."

"Did you see who did it?" I asked, trying to stay calm. I was dog-tired, and my chest hurt: I was beginning to realize how much of the unthinkable was opening up before us.

"Sort of."

I kept looking at him, and he sipped at the coffee. "It was a long time ago." Then he glared at me with a fifteen-year-old's resentment. "What do you know about it, anyhow?" For a second I thought he would cry, he must have been thrust back into that moment with his father and grandfather in JFK airport, but he refused to show that weakness before us. I got the full blast of his resentment again. "Nothing's worse than that. You think it's fun to have stuff like that happen in your head?"

All during Tabby's speech, Patsy kept up a silent accompaniment of nods.

Mrs. Friedgood probably thought there was something worse, I almost said, but could not. The atmosphere in that room was extraordinary. Patsy and Tabby had united at last, even if it was against me. They had found each other; they could admit to themselves that they had found each other, with all that involved, and the release of emotion was like what you feel when you open the door of a blazing woodstove.

"He's right," Patsy said, reaching across the table to take Tabby's hand.

"To an extent."

"Is that what you think? Is that all you know? Do you know what it feels like to think—to know—that you're going crazy?"

"I did when I saw Bates Krell for the first time," I said. "And when I went out behind the Sawtell Country Club with John Sayre's wife and saw John dead on the grass with a pistol still in his hand." They could have made me weep then, with their beauty and their certainty. "I'll tell you all about that, because I'll have to. There are things you both have to learn."

"Why?" Tabby asked. Patsy's support made him almost belligerent.

"Why?" I echoed him mildly. "For one reason, because Johnny Sayre was a decent and brave man. His ghost deserves that you know what I think the real story of his suicide was. And for another, because the three of us are connected. Connected by history, which is something I know about, at least in this part of the world." I smiled at him. "I could tell you about it, but I'd rather show you."

"Show me?"

"Would you mind taking a short walk? You too, Patsy. It'll only take five minutes, even for me."

"I'm not going to that house," Tabby said. He blinked when he realized I didn't know what he meant. "The Friedgood house."

"No." I understood. He had been driven to look at it already. The day of the murder? *During* the murder? At that moment, I began to fear for him; for Patsy too; and for myself. I believed him, but I could have no guarantee that he would believe the crazy story I would tell him; the more so

since it was less a story than a messy assemblage of hints and
intuition. "I don't suppose you ever heard of the Dragon?"

Two blank looks met me.

"And I suppose you don't know that your name wasn't
always Smithfield," I said to Tabby.

He shook his head: disbelief was already setting in.

"I'll just get a flashlight," I said.

3

The English term for "flashlight" is "torch," Richard Allbee
reminded me when he looked at these pages, and my big
heavy-duty emergency flash certainly glowed like a torch as
we went down Beach Trail to Mount Avenue in the middle of
the night. I was thinking of those other torches that came
waving down this road, but the other two were not. They
impatiently went before me, trying to get me to speed up I
guess so they could get it over with and go home.

At the corner I could hear the sea hissing and slapping on
the stretch of private beaches up from Gravesend Beach. A
few forlorn streetlamps burned in the mist just beginning to
appear in the lower patches of Mount Avenue. Down by the
long drive to the Van Horne house, a tall looming tree picked
out by the light was skull-shaped, the point of the chin nearly
touching the ground and the great round crown far up in the
black sky. "Just a little way down," I said.

I suddenly felt rejuvenated—my chest stopped paining me,
my back straightened enough to remind me of what it was
like to be young. I'd need more of this, if everything I
thought was true.

"The Dragon had a name," I said, making the most of the
opportunity to be cryptic, and led them along the high stone
wall toward the Academy.

In a bank of dark green myrtle my "torch" found the low
marker, a bronze plate set in granite. THE BEACHSIDE TRAIL,
read the first line.

"Five, six years ago the Historical Society put this thing
here," I said. "Nobody ever stops to read it, of course.
Which might be okay, since it tells about a tenth of the real
story. But look at the names. Read them out loud."

Patsy silently read the stuff about this being the site of the
first settlement here, and when she got to the names of the

farmers, she read them out. "Ebenezer Williams, Roger Smyth, Josiah Green, and Benjamin Tayler."

"Okay," I said. "You're a Tayler, I'm a Williams, and Tabby is a Smyth. They changed their name around 1880 when a Smyth bought up all this land here—he thought Smithfield sounded grander than Smyth, I guess. His grandson sold the whole thing after the Civil War, and eventually the Vanderbilts bought it and put up the building the school uses now. But the name stayed."

"So what?"

"We're the last of these families, for one thing. That's important. Now I almost think that the last Green descendant has to be here somewhere in town—"

"Well, he is," Patsy said. "I had dinner with him and his wife tonight. Richard Allbee. He just bought the house across the street from you."

"Does he have children?"

"His wife is pregnant," Patsy said.

They were the people I had seen pulling into the driveway of the Sayre house.

"But there's another name," Tabby said, leaning over to read the raised lettering. "It's—"

"It's the Dragon," I said. "That's what they called him."

Tabby read the sentence out loud. "In 1645 a fifth farmer named Gideon Winter joined these men."

"I wonder if they used that wording on purpose," I said. "But that would be to presuppose that Gideon Winter wasn't a man, and I guess he must have been—a man in most senses, anyway. Born like others, more ambitious than most. Or just greedier. Well, not 'just.' I can't think he was 'just' anything."

And now the darkness around the area I was illuminating depressingly reminded me of everything I did not and would never know about Gideon Winter, and I switched off the big emergency flash. The sea rattled on the private beaches down the cliffs on the other side of the mansions.

"Two years after Gideon Winter's arrival," I told them, "most of the crops failed. There are no records of livestock sold, so I think most of the stock died." Patsy and Tabby were dimly back-lighted by the streetlamp at the entrance to Gravesend Beach. Because of the mist, the night was very slightly chilly. They still didn't get it. "In three years, most of the children were dead too. The first church was up the hill—Clapboard Hill in those days, but it doesn't have a name now—and that's where the children were buried. It would have been very near where your house is now, on Hermitage. Remember they had big families in those days. Five to eight children in a family was common. By 1648 our families were lucky to have one or two left. And Gideon Winter owned most of Greenbank. He had no children, at least none that were legitimate. All that is what they didn't put on the marker. And maybe it didn't happen. Maybe I just made it up out of sketchy old parish records. But Winter wound up with most of the land. And they did call him the Dragon. I can show it to you in the books." Now I felt exhausted again: my rejuvenation had been brief. I was breathing hard and I wanted to sit down.

"What happened to Gideon Winter?" Patsy asked.

"I think they finally killed him," I said. "I think they finally decided he was a devil instead of a man, and killed him." I didn't just want to sit down, I wanted to go to bed. Twenty-five years ago, I would have pulled a flask out of my pocket and had a couple belts of good cognac. "But that wasn't the crime, not the real crime. That was the response of a bunch of barely literate, superstitious farmers. The real crime was what their victim had done to them."

"But how could anybody do that—make crops and animals die? Make children die?" Tabby asked. He didn't sound shocked, but I heard in his voice that he had given up his belligerence and was almost interested enough to be believing me now.

"I hope we never have to find out," I said. "I don't even think we could. We're twentieth-century people. They were mid-seventeenth-century people, and for all practical purposes they lived on the edge of an endless forest. They believed in magic, in witches and demons."

I let them think for a second about what they believed in. "But here's one fact for you. Patsy, you and your husband moved here how long ago? Eight, nine months?" She nodded. "And, Tabby, your grandfather died about three months ago. So you've been in 'Four Hearths,' what, six weeks?" He too nodded. "And Mary Green's son moved back to Hampstead only days ago, I suppose. Williams, Smyth, Tayler, Green. Their descendants haven't all been together here since before World War II. The Taylers lived in New York. Tabby's grandfather lived in New York until he moved

Smithfield Systems to Woodville in 1950. No member of the
Green family has lived near Greenbank since 1944 or '45, I
forget which, when Mary went out to California. Williams,
Smyth, Tayler, Green. We're back. This place is ours, do
you see? *That's* magic, if you like."

"And if we're back, you're saying . . ." Patsy began.

"Yes. If we are, maybe he is too. Because it's not just that
you have come back, but come back so strong, if you see
what I mean."

Tabby said, "That's screwy."

"I'm on your side, kid," I said. "Just protect your flank.
When I first met Bates Krell, I had a damn funny experience.
I thought I was looking at a devil, and I'm an agnostic. I've
always thought politics was a hell of a lot more interesting
than theology."

We began to go back toward Beach Trail in the dark. I
didn't have the heart to turn on the torch again. It was
screwy, as Tabby said, but with the streetlamps way up on
Mount Avenue shining on the huge trees on both sides of the
road, I could almost feel myself back in the world I had tried
to resurrect for them, a world that was a few poor farms on
the crumbling edge of a great forest. Patsy and Tabby kept
trying to sneak looks at each other when the other wouldn't
notice. Huge black wings were unfolded over us all. I thought
so, I still hoped not.

That was the night the Norman twins met Gary Starbuck in
the parking lot of a Post Road diner and began to set up their
big score; three nights before a Hampstead policeman named
Royce Griffen shot himself in his car.

We stopped before my house. I sighed. The tasks, both
tasks, seemed impossible. "Will you meet with me once
more? Talk it over, do what you like, but I think we have to
see each other again. Tabby, maybe you could arrange to run
into this Richard Allbee. It might help convince you somehow, if it's like . . ." I nodded toward Patsy. "Another
meeting?"

Reluctantly they agreed. We went toward our separate
houses in the misty intermittent dark.

4

When you think about it, what *could* I have said to them? A being who killed animals and children three centuries ago is now murdering women in our little corner of Connecticut? And this same being was a lobsterman in 1924, when I looked at him from Rex Road across the Nowhatan and almost fainted because I knew I had seen the face of evil? And that someone we might even know, someone who moved freely through Hampstead, now wore that face?

Give me a break, Tabby could have said, and I would not have blamed him. Especially since what I had already told him and Patsy was that they and I and this Richard Allbee character had made him stronger just by being in Greenbank. And had meant that Gideon Winter was only a part of the madness hurtling toward us. *Wake up,* I really should have said, *sleepyhead wake up,* but I didn't know that then.

7

The Dragon and the Mirror

1

Not long after Graham Williams finally confessed his idea to Patsy McCloud and Tabby Smithfield—about the time that Dr. Van Horne was picking through the antique shops of Patchin County for the right mirror to hang on the space he had cleared on his wall—Pat Dobbin became concerned enough about the white spots which speckled his shoulders, chest, and arms to see his doctor. This was Tuesday, June 3. Dobbin still could not think that the spots meant that anything was seriously wrong with him. He certainly did not imagine that he had any sort of disease. He went to his doctor because he did not want the white spots to spread to his face.

In this regard, Dobbin's doctor was not very satisfactory. He did not produce a tube of salve (Dobbin's fantasy) and say, "Rub this on the area twice a day and your problem will disappear." Instead, he examined the spots carefully and asked a lot of questions about where they had begun and how quickly they had spread. He had leafed through a textbook on diseases of the skin and found nothing that quite corresponded to Dobbin's affliction. He had all but scratched his head. Instead of a salve, what the doctor produced was an appointment at the Yale Medical Center in New Haven.

Dobbin drove to the medical center two days later, still thinking that his congenial expensive doctor had overlooked some simple explanation. Parking his car, walking into the vast modern structure which was the medical center, he still felt a robustly healthy man. He knew he was booked in for three days, but he saw this time as a kind of eccentric vacation—he brought pencils and sketch pads, intending to continue his work.

The first morning his clothes were taken from him and he was swabbed, scratched, and stabbed thirty times for a series

142

of allergy tests; he was X-rayed and wired up to a variety of machines, only a few of which he recognized. Doctors came into his room in such number that he never got their names straight. They seemed to enjoy his skin condition far more than they did him. One doctor told him that every bite of food he took would have to be weighed and measured; another who looked as though he had just graduated from high school told him that all of his waste would have to be examined—he could not use the toilet in his room. The white stuff coating his lesions was scraped from his hands and shoulders by a man—a doctor?—with Coke-bottle glasses and stringy hair to his shoulders.

By Dobbin's second day, he no longer felt healthy. He learned that he was mildly allergic to certain pollens, certain kinds of pipe tobacco, cat hair, and starch. Even his un-affected skin was inflamed and bruised from the results of these tests. His blood pressure and cholesterol levels were high, his red count was low, he had a vitamin B_{12} shortage. One of the vertebrae in his lower back was a quarter-inch too close to the next vertebra, so he had an incipient back prob-lem, he had low-grade sinusitis and a very slight heart mur-mur and his liver was damaged. On top of everything else, one of the doctors informed him in passing that he could probably expect to develop gallstones sometime in the next five to ten years.

But none of this explained what was happening to his skin.

On the morning of his third day, the senior doctor assigned to him asked if he wouldn't mind staying in another four days.

He was popular for his sketches of the doctors and the day-shift nurses. He became so institutionalized that he watched television all day long. He ate and drank what they gave him and eliminated into Tupperware.

He answered what seemed to be several million questions about his life and habits. He listed every place he had been in the past decade, all of his living relatives, the liquor he drank, his sexual partners. The answers to this question created, he thought, a little stir on the fourth floor: New Haven was not so far from Hampstead.

On the fifth day Dobbin noticed the first of the lesions on his face, a tiny white speck at one corner of his mouth.

On the sixth, his next to last, day in the medical center, the senior doctor entered his room and sat in the chair by the bed.

By now of course Dobbin knew his name, Dr. Chaney; he had drawn half a dozen much-appreciated caricatures of his face, which was aloof and thin, underslung, like a giraffe's. Chaney smiled at Dobbin and perhaps absentmindedly began to take his pulse. "We've been looking very carefully at the material taken from your lesions, Mr. Dobbin," he said.

"Nice of you," Dobbin replied.

Chaney dropped his wrist and looked up from his watch. "It turned out to be a bit of a surprise for us. We found that it is a liquefied integument containing melanin, sebum, the cells of blood vessels and lymph channels, the characteristic material of nerve endings, epithelium cells, in short all the matter to be found in the dermis and epidermis."

"So it's skin," Dobbin said. He had recognized the last two nouns.

"Correct."

"That white stuff is skin."

"Correct again."

"Well . . ." Dobbin lolled handsomely back against his raised pillow. "I don't get it. What does it mean?"

"That your skin in a sense is becoming colloidal, not connected. And the function of skin is that it is connective—that is the meaning of integument." Dr. Chaney helpfully linked his fingers together to demonstrate. "Not many laymen think of it this way, but our skin is an organ, just as the heart and liver are organs. In your case, this organ is spontaneously losing the characteristics of a solid." He smiled again. "You're rather a rare bird, Mr. Dobbin. Your skin is liquefying."

Dobbin could not speak.

"Now, you're scheduled to go home tomorrow. And I think we will keep to that schedule. I shall want to see you back here in a week—"

Dobbin interrupted. "You mean I'm not allergic to anything? I don't have VD or cancer or what the hell, the mumps or even pimples? What are you guys going to do to stop me from turning into a puddle?"

"Well, you *do* have some allergies," the doctor said. "But that isn't the problem with your skin. That problem can only be a reaction to something you have encountered—like an infection, but in this case there is no virus and no bacterial cause. We are going to take some further samples of your skin, from both the affected and the unaffected areas, and we'll turn our computers loose on the problem. We will come up with some possibilities, Mr. Dobbin.''

"You mean you hope you will.''

"Our computers can assemble data faster than a roomful of researchers working twenty-four hours a day. We'll find out what sort of agent might cause a reaction such as yours. Then we will be able to halt the reaction. After that a few skin grafts will see you back to normal, should they be necessary.''

"Jesus.''

"There is nothing to worry about at this point,'' Chaney said. "Let's just leave it all to the computers, shall we?''

"Do we have a choice?''

Dobbin spent another day with the game shows, the soap operas, and made-for-television movies. His mind, protecting itself, chimed with commercial jingles for designer jeans and mouthwash. He ate three more hospital meals and slept with the aid of a powerful tranquilizer. Dr. Chaney did not appear again in his room, but the young doctor with cobweb hair came along to poke another needle in his hand, slice off an inch-long section of skin, and tape a thick bandage over the wound.

The hospital released his clothes, his car keys, and his money, and gave him an appointment card for his return. Half in a daze, he drove back down I-95 to Hampstead. This was the day of the third murder, though neither Dobbin nor anyone else in Hampstead would know it had happened until two days later.

When he turned into his driveway, his house looked smaller than he had remembered it. His mailbox was jammed with bills, magazines, and fliers with supermarket coupons.

Dobbin marked the date of his return to the medical center on his calendar. He wandered into his workroom and watered the plants. After he sat down at his draftsman's table, he looked through the drawings he had done—half of them he destroyed. Dobbin began again. This time he gave Baldur the Bad, the evil magician of *The Eagle-Bear Stories*, the face of Dr. Chaney.

2

While Pat Dobbin was in New Haven waiting to hear that he had contracted some new kind of super-herpes (for that had been his latest, and last, fantasy about the origin of his lesions), Hampstead suffered the visitation of an unseasonal flu. In the first week of May, there had been the usual wave of colds, brought on by the shift in the weather; but the flu was a winter affliction; it had no place in the first week of June.

For example, this was the last week of school at J. S. Mill, and the teachers were busy with year-end reports and grade computations. The students were supposed to be studying for their final exams. But the principal and four of his staff, too weak to get out of bed, missed the entire week. Tabby's class had a particularly large number of victims—forty of the one hundred and five sophomores missed at least three days of school.

Graham Williams spent three days moving, when he had to move, from his bed to his toilet and back again—he was too sick to think further about the subject he had brought up to Patsy McCloud and Tabby Smithfield.

Les McCloud felt a pain in his gut as he was driving home from the police station after showing his permit and getting a lecture from Bobo Farnsworth—his forehead began to drip perspiration, and he stopped his car on the stretch of Greenbank Road which paralleled the thruway and staggered out in time to vomit into a patch of wild chicory. Just as he was wiping his mouth, his bowels burst into agony and exploded. He lay down in the weeds and toed off his loafers. He thanked God he was not at his office in New York. Les unbuckled his belt and pushed off his trousers. Within view of several dozen cars proceeding up I-95, he gingerly removed his boxer shorts and tossed them aside. Then his stomach convulsed, and he threw up again. He felt like Job. Panting, he waited for his bowels to trumpet again, which they did. Then he wiped himself with weeds, slid his trousers on, and staggered back to his car. He drove the rest of the way home very slowly. As soon as he got inside the front door, he began yelling for Patsy.

At Greenblatt's checkout counter only two of the girls showed up for work all the first week of June. Bobo Farnsworth never got sick, and so he found himself filling in for those who did: he worked twelve-hour shifts for two weeks straight, twelve on and eight off, and when **Ronnie was** finally able to get out of bed she made him his favorite dinner at eight o'clock in the morning—southern-fried chicken and hash-browns. "What's it like out there these days?" she asked him. Ronnie herself could not eat the chicken; the smell of the oil turned her stomach. "Like a hospital," Bobo said. "I hope the killer's puking his guts out, damn him."

Hampstead's doctors saw their waiting rooms crowded with people they could not help. "It's a new strain," they told the victims. "There's no magic pill, just drink plenty of liquids and stay in bed."

The victims told each other: "The worst part is, you know it's not going to kill you." This was not completely accurate. Nobody who caught it actually wished to die, but several did. They were all male, and all over sixty. Graham Williams was lucky to have survived. Harry Zimmer followed Babe to Gravesend Cemetery only three weeks after her death. He felt a tickle in his throat while fishing off the breakwater Monday morning, and thought he must have caught a cold from Lee Wilcox, who had marched next to him, carrying the VFW flag, in the Memorial Day parade. By afternoon his nose was streaming, and his head ached. He disgusted one of the summer people, a chunky New York blond with sunglasses stuck in her hair, by sneezing all over her in the supermarket when he couldn't get his handkerchief out in time. The next day he nearly fainted when he tried to get out of bed. The freezer was full of frozen fish, but he was too weak to thaw and cook it. His only food for a day and a half was bourbon, peanut butter, and a yellowing lettuce he found in the crisper at the bottom of his refrigerator. He had a quart of milk, but it had turned bad—since Babe's death, Harry's housekeeping was erratic. He called his doctor twice, and both times the line was busy. He died in bed on the fifth night of the illness, never knowing that Lee Wilcox had died too. Harry's grandson discovered him a day later.

Four of the five older men who died were members of Hampstead's VFW post, and two were members of J. S. Mill's class of 1921, which meant that Graham Williams became the last surviving member of that class. "I'm a walking reunion," he told Tabby months later. "Now I owe it to my class to live forever." The fifth man, Dr. Harold Rubin, was a New York psychiatrist who came to Hampstead every summer and took a house on "Shrinks' Row," a series of pastel frame houses on a spit of land off the Millpond where cars were not allowed. Dr. Rubin caught a cold on his second day in Hampstead, took his sloop out anyhow, and two hours later thought he was seasick. His excellent lunch from the country club went overboard. He never made it to the cocktail party that evening given by his summer neighbor, Dr. Harvey Blau. He would have driven back to New York that night, but he did not think he could walk all the way to the parking lot at the end of the leafy mile-long spit of land. He died on the bathroom floor the next day, and his remains were not discovered until September. By that time, all his neighbors were dead too, though not from the flu.

Hampstead's only other fatality during these ten days was a seventy-year-old woman who died of a heart attack while eating lunch on the terrace of a French restaurant overlooking Main Street. Unlike Dr. Rubin, the elderly woman died in full view of fifteen to twenty citizens, Tabby Smithfield and Patsy McCloud among them.

For ten to fifteen days, Hampstead's doctors were under siege. The flu, which seemed to be local and spontaneous, doubled, tripled, quadrupled itself during this initial period. If, during this time, they saw patients with other complaints, they barely had time to properly attend to their symptoms: in any case, the few people who turned up complaining of the sudden appearance of ugly white spots on their hands or shoulders did not require immediate help. For a month after the initial wave of flu patients, the disease continued, though with less intensity, and the doctors still were not alarmed if the patients with the tiny skin lesions returned with a few more of them; in fact they paid no particular attention to these patients until another doctor sent a man to the Yale Medical Center and word came back about Pat Dobbin, who by mid-July was in full-time care. Soon after the second, and then the third, patient arrived at the medical center, Dr. Chaney had submitted a paper to *The Lancet,* the British medical journal, on the subject of what he called "Dobbin's Syndrome." By September Dr. Chaney could add a footnote to his article, alluding to the events of May 17 and the accidental exposure of Hampstead's citizens to DRG-16. He speculated that the missing researcher, Thomas Gay, was very likely the first victim of the syndrome he had identified but concluded with a defense of the name he had given it: "It may seem that

'Gay's Syndrome' should be adopted as the appellation for these symptoms, but for several medical reasons I hold to the original appellation. Patrick Dobbin was the first patient presenting these symptoms to the profession, and his surname is irresistibly literary *(Vanity Fair);* and I submit that this is in many of its 'unmedical' and 'spiritual' characteristics a prototypically literary and Victorian disease.''

Perhaps Dr. Chaney deserved what his patient had done to him in his illustrations.

3

On the Tuesday morning that Dobbin first went to see his doctor, Tabby Smithfield sat in the kitchen with his father, eating pancakes Sherri had made. "Come on, eat a couple anyhow," Clark said. "You're acting like the cook around here."

Sherri had perched herself on a stool before the range. "That's how you treat me, why shouldn't I act that way?"

Clark flushed, and swabbed up maple syrup with a section of pancake. "This is our home," he tried again. "I want you to eat with us. You're sitting there like a vulture."

"Come on, Dad," Tabby said.

"I don't feel good," Sherri admitted. "I couldn't eat nothing."

"You sick?" Clark looked again at Sherri, who did not in the least resemble a vulture. Her face was pale and doughy, her eyes puffy. Black roots were visible at the part in her hair.

"I want to go lie down. But I have to clean the kitchen first."

"Suit yourself," Clark said.

Clark was no longer the slim young man who had played ball with Tabby on the lawn before the Mount Avenue house. His body had thickened, a network of red veins had blossomed over his cheekbones. The petulance Graham Williams had noticed was now a permanent part of his features, and it spoiled what had been handsomeness. In fact, Tabby, who had finished his breakfast and was waiting to talk to his father, could see none of Clark's old attractiveness in the porcine face across the table. "Why don't you try to get some rest, Sherri?" he asked his stepmother.

"Let her do what she wants," Clark said. "When's the school bus come, anyhow?"

"About fifteen minutes."

"So read a book, do some homework. How's it going at school anyhow, Tabs?"

"Pretty fair."

Clark shrugged.

"How's your work going?" Tabby asked.

"How's my work going, he asks. Like work, that's how it's going. You'll find out."

"You going to see some accounts today?"

"That's what they pay me for, kid."

"What accounts?"

Clark put his napkin on the table and gave Tabby a flat glare. "You want to know what accounts I'm going to today? Okay. Bloomingdale's. That satisfy you? Caldor's. A couple others in Woodville. Then I get over to Mount Kisco and Pound Ridge. Satisfied?"

"He won't give a straight answer," Sherri said from her stool. "Don't even try."

"Hey, lay off, okay? What's it to you, anyway? I work, I come home. That's enough. I don't have to pass an exam on it."

"I was just interested, Dad."

"Okay. But do I pump you about school? Do I ask you who your friends are, what you do at night? Do I? Hell no. I got enough of that from my old man. You do what you want, that's fine with me."

"Did you know that our name wasn't always Smithfield?" Tabby asked quietly.

"I suppose it used to be Morales," Clark said, and Sherri got off her stool and left the room.

"She looks sick," Tabby said.

"She's sick of Hampstead, that's what she's sick of. You'd think she'd be grateful to be in a house like this. Don't worry about her, Tabs. She'll adjust."

"I sure hope so."

His father snorted; wiped his lips with a napkin. "What's that garbage about our name?"

"I heard it used to be Smyth. With a y."

"News to me. Where did you hear that?"

"A kid at school."

"Well, I don't know. Don't pay any attention about what those kids say. Just do your work, okay?"

"Okay."

"Anything else on your mind, Tabs?"

Tabby shook his head, and his father stood up. In a minute he would be gone; when he came home he would be drunk.

"Well, maybe," Tabby said.

Clark waited silently.

"Do you know anything about a fisherman being killed on his boat a long time ago, here in town? I know it sounds crazy."

"What the hell, Tabby. Go out to the bus stop." Clark pulled his suit jacket from a chair and turned toward the kitchen door.

"His name was Bates Krell."

"Never heard of him."

"Or did you hear of a farmer here named Gideon Winter?"

"Nobody's had a farm here for a hundred years," Clark said. "Get your ass in gear, Tabs. You'll miss your bus."

Tabby gathered up his books and papers and went outside to wait on the corner. His father drove past in his new red Mercedes and waved as he turned into Beach Trail.

When Tabby got near to J. S. Mill, he saw the Norman twins through the window of the bus. They were talking to a dark-haired man who looked muscular but not athletic. The three of them were across the street from the school's entrance, and the man was leaning against the side of a gray van.

4

"So you got another kid," Gary Starbuck said to Dicky and Bruce. "Does he know what he's supposed to do?"

"Hey, man," Bruce protested. "We don't even know what we're supposed to do yet."

"You know."

"What are we supposed to be, mind readers?"

Starbuck sighed. "Listen, it's a job, right? *That's* what you know. You're going in with me on a job, right? That's what you wanted, right?"

"Right," Bruce said.

"So you got this other kid."

"Well, yeah."

"Is he a big kid?"

Dicky and Bruce shook their heads.

"That's okay. He don't have to be big. He has to be smart, is important."

"He's smart," Bruce said. Tabby had somehow duped Bobo the Clown on Sunday night. Bruce had expected him to do it, but it at least proved his intelligence.

Starbuck sighed again. "I ought to have my head examined." He crossed his arms over his chest, and his biceps bulged. "Okay. You know that house just above the little beach there? A doctor's house?"

The twins nodded. "Van Horne," Dick said.

"You got it. We're going in next Saturday. I'll take the locks off, we go in nice and clean. There's no alarms on the house. Lotta goodies in that place. I even know a guy who'll take his piano. You guys can lift a piano, is my guess. I'll give you five hundred apiece, okay? Then we're straight, right? After Saturday, you never heard of me. You get your thousand, you're cool."

"You mean we all go in?" Dicky asked.

"No, I go in and you play checkers on the porch. What the hell do you mean? Sure you go in."

"What about Tabby?"

"The other kid? He's the lookout. He sits in the van with the radio. If he sees a cop, he tells us. He gets fifty bucks, plus whatever you guys give him."

"We get five hundred apiece," Bruce said.

"That's our deal."

Dicky and Bruce gave each other a look of perfect understanding. "We'll give him fifty apiece," Bruce said.

"Sure you will," Gary Starbuck said. "Just meet me in the Lobster House parking lot at eleven o'clock. This is an old guy here, he goes to bed at nine."

"But why not go in on a weekday?" Bruce asked. "I don't get this. He's a doctor, he goes out of the house all day."

"He's got a housekeeper and a cook, is why," Gary said. "The housekeeper's as old as he is and the cook drives in from Bridgeport. Eleven is the right time. We could do it later, but why should we waste the whole night?"

"One more thing," Bruce said. "You got a piece, right? When you go in, you're carrying."

"Just forget about that," Gary said. "I never used it yet. I do good clean work, just like my daddy taught me."

5

Dr. Wren Van Horne looked better than he had in years: his receptionist had told him, his colleagues at the Hampstead Clinic (in which he and they had substantial shares) had told him, even his patients were telling him that. Hilda du Plessy, who had been Wren Van Horne's patient for forty years and had adored him for each of them, had found something new to admire in Dr. Van Horne on her last visit. "You're getting younger!" she gasped. "Why, Dr. Van Horne! It's true. You look ten years younger."

"Well, then in a year or so I shall be passing you, Hilda," Dr. Van Horne purred at the old dear—who half an hour later as she piloted her ancient Bentley into the parking lot between the river and Main Street was still thinking about him. Her thoughts were generally of the kind widows are prone to have about the doctors with whom they are infatuated—the words *gentle* and *firm* never actually expressed, buzzed beneath her reverie—but also incorporated observations with the detail of more than half a lifetime's experience. Hilda du Plessy was right; Wren Van Horne did not just look better, he looked younger. His eyes were clearer, his back straighter. The crepe beneath his eyes was nearly gone. His hair looked somehow fuller: "Blow-drying," Hilda said to herself as she walked through the Waldenbooks store to emerge onto Main Street. "He's blow-drying his hair after all this time—why, I could have told him about that ages ago, if he'd paid any attention to me."

Hilda du Plessy passed right through Waldenbooks because she would never have bought a book there: Ada Hoff at Books 'n Bobs up the street knew what she wanted. Ada Hoff was a real book woman, Hilda considered, unlike the young people who worked at the big chain bookstores. Ada Hoff knew her customers by name and understood that some people had special tastes—there would be a nice little pile of new things waiting for Hilda behind the counter.

On the day each month that Hilda drove from her house on the Old Sarum border to her medical appointment, she gave herself a series of treats.

She pushed in the door of the rambling yellow colonial at the top of Main Street that was the Books 'n Bobs and went past the display counter of best-sellers without a glance. Ada Hoff was standing behind the front desk dabbing at her nose with a linen handkerchief the same daffodil shade of yellow as the bookstore—it was Ada's favorite color. "Feeling all right, Ada?" Hilda inquired.

"Rotten cold," Ada said. She was a large round-faced woman a few years younger than Hilda herself. Ada usually wore a blue blazer and a yellow shirt, or a yellow blazer and a blue shirt, as today. Her hair was elaborately black, somehow so mannered it looked painted. "We've all got it. Spence and Thom didn't even come to work today." Spence and Thom, two bachelors who lived together, were Ada's assistants. Spence did all the packing and unpacking and the bookkeeping, and Thom arranged the windows and spelled Ada behind the counter. Hilda considered Spence and Thom excellent company and could spend hours near the pottery and macrame sections gossiping with either one. The news that they were not in the store spoiled her day a little—Ada was too businesslike for gossip.

"Oh, what a shame," Hilda said. "Don't give it to me, please, Ada—I've just *come* from the doctor."

"Which reminds me. I have some new things to show you," Ada said, and searched under the counter for a time before placing in front of Hilda a stack of two hardbound and three paperback books. The hardbacks were *Nurse Thompson's Dilemma* by Janet Randall Minor and *The Hero in White* by Carrie Engelbart Hoskins; the paperbacks, *Love in a Ward, Dr. Batholomew and Dr. Dare,* and *Dr. Peachtree Makes His Rounds,* were all by Florence M. Hobart. Hilda gazed at them for a moment of unalloyed delight. Her addiction was hospital novels. And a new Janet Randall Minor on the same day as three rediscovered Florence M. Hobarts was almost miraculous for her. The little splash of disappointment of Spence and Thom's not being in the store burned to nothing in the blaze of Hilda's intense satisfaction.

"There are still five or six more of those Hobarts," Ada said. "Some are out of stock and some are reprinting, so they say. We'll have them in for you when they're available again."

"Oh, my goodness, thank you, but this is lovely," Hilda

gushed. "I'll take them all, of course. Charge them, please. I don't know how I'll ever decide which to read first."

Hilda signed the charge slip and left the bookstore to walk down Main Street, still virtually humming with delight. She heard a finch warbling in the branches of one of the dwarf fruit trees in oaken barrels strung out along the sidewalk, and tilted her head and whistled back at it. The heavy bag in her hand was full of treasure—soon she would be sorting through that treasure, sifting and weighing it. Hilda crossed the street, walked past the office of the *Hampstead Gazette,* and ascended the brick steps of a French restaurant called Framboise.

Here too one of the stages of her monthly ritual of treats began badly. The headwaiter was not posted by the lectern which supported a telephone and the reservation book. Hilda peered into the restaurant. Only two parties, a man and a woman at a table for two and a group of four men at a center table, were in the main dining room. The man and woman were conspicuously drunk. Another false note. Three waiters in dark blue waistcoats and black bow ties had congregated around a service trolley at the back. Hilda waited for the headwaiter to appear. One of the waiters glanced at her, then coughed rheumily into his fist. Hilda set her book bag on the floor beside the lectern and pointedly looked at the reservation book. There was her name, a version of it anyhow: DIPLESSI. She said "Ahem" in a clear loud voice. One of the waiters picked up a menu from the trolley and lounged toward her across the room.

"Where is François today?" Hilda asked.

"Home sick," the boy said.

"I am du Plessy, which you have misspelled in your reservations book. Will you please conduct me to my customary table?"

The boy in the blue waistcoat looked at Hilda blankly.

"Outside. On the corner of the terrace. More properly, the balcony. Which you are pleased to call the terrace. That is where I sit."

"This way, ma'am," the boy said, galvanized by Hilda's tone. Hilda picked up her bag of treasure and followed the boy through the restaurant and out onto the balcony, where four tables were lined up beneath a striped awning.

"Mine is the end table," Hilda said when he paused before

the middle table. At her table, she sat facing the street and
said, "I should like a drink, please. A brandy Manhattan,
please."

"Rocks?"

"Without ice, please. In one of those glasses with a
stem—you know." She sketched the shape of the glass with
her fingers.

The boy skulked away. Hilda lifted her bag to her lap
and extracted the books. Intense satisfaction: contemplation
of the jacket art, the familiar shapes of the authors' names,
the title pages, dedications, margins, bindings, whether or
not the authors' initials were stamped on the front covers
of the hardbacks. (They were not.) She examined the type-
face in the hardbacks, and then looked at the blurbs. These
were invariably nitwitted, and Hilda took little notice of
them.

Then she made her choice: *The Hero in White* by Carrie
Engelbart Hoskins. The Janet Randall Minor would be a de-
ferred pleasure.

Hilda delicately opened the chosen book. The loutish boy
put her drink down before her. With intense pleasure Hilda
glanced out at the sweep of Main Street before her, and
then—unable to wait a second longer—read the first sentence:

Edward Waterhouse was born to be of use.

Now that was the real thing.

*Others had said it often of him, he was even given to
admitting it himself in paraphrases such as: "I reckon
I'm happiest when I'm helping someone." From another
these remarks would have sought approval and approba-
tion; from Dr. Waterhouse they sought nothing. He was
speaking only the truth as he had come to know it over
the course of his forty-two years.*

Fairly purring with bliss, Hilda sipped her drink and read on.

*Forty-two: indeed that was Dr. Waterhouse's age, and
the years suited him well, having given him compassion-
ate lines at the corners of his eyes, and elegant streaks
of gray at his temples.*

Wren Van Horne in early middle age, Hilda thought, and I could not have described him better myself.

If his age was an advantage to him in many ways, it was a disadvantage perhaps only in one. Dr. Edward Waterhouse was at the far edge of those years in which a man must marry, if he is to marry at all.

All of which went to prove that Carrie Engelbart Hoskins was still under forty, Hilda thought. She looked up from the page, "a trifle irritated," Carrie E. Hoskins would have said, and surveyed Main Street once again. Across the street an intense young woman writing notes to herself and men in blue jeans and beards sat at the outside tables before Deli-icious. Hilda's eyes swept over the window of the Olden and Golden Antique Shop, the smaller window of Hampstead Pizza. A well-known actor left the hardware store on the other side of the delicatessen, and the bearded men frankly stared at him. Then Hilda's glance returned to the window of the antique shop. Couldn't she see, on the other side of the gilt lettering, the man she had just been thinking about?

She had become almost unpleasantly excited. Hilda bent forward and peered at the window. The owner, short and bald, was now visible beyond the gilt letters. Dr. Waterhouse had vanished from Hilda's mind, and she muttered, "Move— please *move*," flustering the waiter, who had returned to take her order. The boy and the shopowner moved simultaneously, and Hilda saw that the gray-haired man behind the window was indeed Wren Van Horne. Standing there gesturing, the doctor looked even younger than he had in his office an hour earlier.

"You want me to stand here?" the waiter disbelievingly asked from somewhere behind her; Hilda glanced upward as if asking for help, and saw another of the small orange-breasted finches just as it fell from a lower branch of the oak tree in front of the restaurant and plummeted lifelessly to the sidewalk.

6

You knew it was time for the mirror: did not know what it meant, but knew it was time.

• • •

Dr. Van Horne had canceled two of his afternoon appointments, and now was standing rather vaguely in the midst of the clutter of the Olden and Golden Antique Shop. "It must be special," he was saying to the owner, who did not know him but had clearly taken in his age and bearing, his white linen suit and panama hat and assigned him to the diminishing category of Old Hampstead Money. "Very special, if you see what I mean." He smiled, which did nothing to dissipate the impression of his vagueness. "I'll recognize *it*, you see, but what I mean is that it should recognize me as well."

"Well." Mr. Bundle was not sure where to begin answering a request so irrational. "There are some new things in—"

"Yes, of course. I've spent hours looking already—I went to Redhill two days ago, and before that I drove down to King George, many interesting antique shops down there, and all of them had mirrors, but none of them . . . They weren't right." He swept his arm around in a gesture of wholehearted negation. "Not at all. What I need—now, that's what we ought to be talking about, isn't it? I cleared a space on a wall in my house—at the time wasn't even sure what it was for. I just knew I had to get those paintings down because I needed the space. Then I knew. A mirror. Must be quite tall, and must be oval. Can't be new. New won't do at all."

Dr. Van Horne looked impishly at Mr. Bundle. "And today as I was sitting in my office, it came to me, just came to me, that you had precisely the mirror I needed. Isn't that extraordinary?"

"Well, it is extraordinary, because just this morning I took possession of some furniture I bought at an estate auction last week," Mr. Bundle said. "And there's a mirror very like what you describe."

"I knew it."

"Um. Yes. Extraordinary. Will you come back with me to see it?"

Dr. Van Horne nodded and followed Mr. Bundle to the rear of the shop. Here furniture was heaped and piled in crowded disarray, unpolished and untagged. Secretaries and sideboards, leather-topped desks and mahogany dining tables; the leaves for the tables were spread out on a canopied bed. "Now, I haven't properly priced these things yet, but I imagine we could come to some. . . ?" He cocked an eyebrow at the doctor.

"Oh yes. Oh yes." The doctor had stopped prowling through the dark clutter of furniture and was staring at the top, visible half of a large oval mirror in an elaborately carved gilt frame. "That's it. I used to own it."

"You owned it? It came from the auction I mentioned. The mirror's French and I date it roughly at 1790, but it may be even earlier. I think one of the Greens imported most of these things himself. They're all gone now, of course."

"I owned it," his customer said.

"Yes. I see, sir."

As they looked into the speckled surface of the mirror, something greasily dark seemed to move within it, a greasy shadow that made Mr. Bundle widen his eyes and bend forward to see more clearly. But then it was gone.

"Ah, there you are. It recognizes me."

"Needs a good cleaning," Mr. Bundle muttered.

7

Patsy pushed the bedroom door open with her hip and carried the tray to the bed where Les lay in a happy clutter of newspapers, boxes of tissues, magazines, and apple cores and peach pits in a bowl. Papers and reports from his office lay across his chest, atop a folded copy of *The Wall Street Journal*. He peered up at her with a thin and unshaven face. "What's that?"

"Your breakfast. Whole-wheat toast, cottage cheese, orange juice."

"You call that breakfast? Cottage cheese?"

Patsy set the tray beside Les. "Your stomach needs something mild."

"Oh yeah, I know, but Jesus . . . how about a poached egg or something?"

"Eat this and see how you feel. I have my appointment with Dr. Lauterbach in half an hour. If your stomach's okay when I get back, I'll poach an egg for you."

"I do feel pretty weak."

"You don't look good," Patsy said. She sat in the chair in the far end of the room, her feet flat on the floor, her knees apart, her chin cupped in her hand. "In fact, you look terrible."

"You don't look so good yourself." Les spoke almost reflexively, feeling himself under attack, but there was truth in what he said. Patsy looked worn and tired—forlorn, a more sensitive man than Les would have said.

"Why should I look good? I feel awful. And it's not the flu, Les. Maybe I should just say what I think and admit it's you."

"I can't help getting sick," Les said. "Half the town's got the flu."

"I don't mean the flu. I mean our marriage."

Les picked up a memo from the papers on his chest and expressionlessly scrutinized it.

"I suppose that's an example of what I mean. You won't even look at me now."

Les set the memo aside and turned wearily toward Patsy.

"The point is, I don't think we have a marriage at all."

"You don't."

"I have a husband who doesn't talk to me, who never wants to do anything with me, and who needs me only when he's so sick he craps in his pants. Does that sound like much of a marriage?"

"I don't accept your description."

"It doesn't look that way to you? You think that we share things? The closest we ever get is when you decide that you have to knock me around. You'd rather do that than make love. That's true, you know. You'd rather hit me than screw me."

"Jesus, you really like to blame it all on me. And your timing's great too—you clobber me with all this stuff when I'm so sick I can hardly get out of bed."

"The clobbering is all one-sided," Patsy said. Against her will, she had become very angry. "We don't have a marriage. I really don't see why we live together."

"Don't you love me?" Les asked.

"I don't know. I don't feel very loving toward you."

"Well, goddammit, I'm *sick*," Les wailed.

Patsy looked at her watch.

"Oh, I know—I get this now. Dr. Lauterbach. You go to this shrink, and you tell him about how miserable I am, and he tells you that you ought to leave me. He probably holds your hand while he's doing it."

"I have to go now," Patsy said. She stood.

"Remind this guy where the money comes from," Les

said, propping himself up on one elbow and letting the papers and the memos cascade onto the tray. "See how fast he decides that I'm pretty damn good after all."

"Good-bye," Patsy said, and moved toward the door.

"Good-bye? You mean, for good? You're just walking out?" He was smiling grimly.

"I don't *know*," Patsy screamed at him. "If I did, at least I wouldn't have to see you pointing guns at policemen!"

Les was going to shout back at her but he restrained himself. "You know why that happened."

"Better than you." Patsy closed the door and went swiftly down to the door. Les was calling something out but she ignored him and descended the steps to the family room and the garage. Fifteen minutes later she was going slowly down Main Street looking for a place to park.

In fact Patsy had seen Dr. Karl Lauterbach only once. His consulting room was in the Hampstead Clinic where Wren Van Horne had his offices, and on the day of her first appointment Patsy had walked up and down the concrete steps from the parking lot to the modernist huddle of low brick buildings three times. She had arrived half an hour early, and still was not sure she could go through with it. How much of her real life could she admit to this doctor? And how much could she conceal without falsifying her prospective analysis?

Patsy had seen herself on a dissecting table, her mind spread out like a clock under repair.

Finally she let herself into the building and looked at the nameplates on the broad oaken doors. She was still twenty minutes early. She found the door and admitted herself to a small dim waiting room. A receptionist behind a glass window smiled at her. She had spent what seemed an endless time looking at her hands folded in her lap.

Two minutes before the hour, a short bearded man with a stern, searching face had opened the consulting-room door and called her by name. He was no older than she—Patsy thought that despite the deep groove between his eyebrows, he might even have been younger. "Please," he said, motioning her in and toward the couch against one wall.

"I want to sit up," she said. "On a chair."

"Whatever you like. I'd rather you use the couch, however."

Patsy put herself in a chair before his desk.

"Why did you want to see me?" Dr. Lauterbach asked.

"I'm unhappy," she had blurted out.

"Everybody is unhappy," Dr. Lauterbach said, and Patsy knew that it was not going to work. How could this gruff and pessimistic man help her? "I'm unhappy that you want to start out by fighting me. We have a long way to go together, Mrs. McCloud, and we ought to begin with cooperation."

The analyst's deep somber eyes met Patsy's, and on the spot she burst into tears. He knew all about her already, she thought; he had simply opened up her brain with his eyes and seen everything—Les, Marilyn Foreman, her grandmother, everything. Patsy had not been able to stop crying. Dr. Lauterbach said nothing, and Patsy wept into her cupped hands. Not only exposed, she had felt humiliated.

Still weeping, she had stood up and left his office.

She had known that she would never return, and she never did. In a way that curiously paralleled Clark Smithfield's occupations, Patsy set off every day as if for her appointment but instead did things therapeutic in the simple sense that they made her feel better. She trailed through Hampstead art galleries or had coffee while reading a book at one of the tables in the deli; or walked along Sawtell Beach, feeling as light and irresponsible as a gull; or drove to Woodville and reveled in Bloomingdale's dress department. Normally Patsy resented shopping and the time spent on it; during Dr. Lauterbach's hour, she relished it.

But this was not a day for Bloomingdale's; nor did she feel like walking on the beach. The scene with Les, which had taken a direction she had not foreseen, still knotted her stomach. It was true, what she had said. She really did not know why she and Les were still married. That she loved him had always been the answer to that painful question, and now Patsy wondered if her "love" had been instead a means of never putting the painful question to herself. Since she had seen him pointing the gun at Bobo Farnsworth and the other two, what she had thought of as her love for her husband had somehow curdled. She had seen him as exposed as she had been herself in Dr. Lauterbach's office, and she could not now ever go back to seeing him in her old way. She realized, and the very realization was the knot in her stomach, that if she never went back to Les McCloud she would not miss him. Les was like someone who had died and was pretending life: no one had killed him, he had killed himself: he had murdered his feelings and intuitions and his generosity because he thought his company demanded it.

Thank you, Dr. Lauterbach, Patsy said to herself, entering the delicatessen.

When she emerged she carried a plastic cup of coffee to one of the outside tables. The men at the other tables momentarily inspected her legs, her breasts, her face. "Oink," Patsy said, loudly enough for the two men closest to hear, and then took her novel and her diary from her bag. She put the book to one side and began to write.

Men I could go to bed with, she wrote. *Richard Allbee. Bobo Farnsworth. Alan Alda.* Patsy was amusing herself. *John Updike. Ilie Nastase. Sam Shepard.* "And Rex, the Wonder Horse," she said to herself. Patsy closed the book on her pen, smiling, and looked at the potted trees bordering Main Street. Tabby Smithfield was walking toward her from the lower end of the street. Tabby did not see her, in fact he saw nothing; his face was averted, and he trudged as if he were kicking through leaves. Or wading in water ankle-deep. She hoped the boy would not glance up, would pass by, but when he drew up level with her he looked so wretched that she had to speak. "Hello, Tabby."

He snapped his head sideways and met her with a look of intense gratitude. So he had given her the option.

Tabby came shyly toward her. "Come sit down," she said, indicating the chair beside her. He sat. He looked at her again, not shyly, and Patsy knew: she said, "You just had another, ah, journey, didn't you?" and took his hand.

"That's a good word for it," Tabby said.

8

He had avoided the Normans as long as he could, knowing that the man they had been speaking to was the thief, but after the first class the twins loomed up beside him in the corridor outside the school library. Because of the unexpected shortage of teachers, Tabby's class had been divided into two study groups, and he and the Normans were in the group assigned to the library.

"Hey, Tabs," Bruce said, putting his arm around him, "you were cool. I don't know what you did, but you did it right."

"I didn't do anything," Tabby said. They stepped out of the line and let the others file into the library. A pungent odor from Bruce's body floated almost visibly about Tabby's head.

"That's always best," Bruce said, and began to pull Tabby down the corridor toward an exit. "Let's get out of this place. We got only one more class today anyway, last period. Why should we stick around? Nobody's going to do anything important, so many kids gone."

"I suppose," Tabby said. The Normans were always one step more daring than he would have been himself.

"Bobo didn't say anything about us?" Dicky asked.

"Hey, don't be stupid, man, Tabs was cool," Bruce said. "Let's just fade on out the door while nobody's looking, okay?" He drew Tabby along with him, and Tabby could not escape his odor, which was that of a bear. Bruce was excited, and the overpowering bear smell was the odor of violence. He rubbed his hands roughly on Tabby's back. "Bobo never mentioned our names, did he, Tabs? Nobody at all mentioned our names, did they?"

"No." Tabby separated himself from Bruce. "He thought I was just walking home."

Bruce punched his bicep. "My man." He pushed down the bar on the door, and the three of them went out onto a narrow asphalt path that ran the length of the rear of the school. The air was still and humid. "Pity about the flu," Bruce said, and Dicky laughed.

They circled the side of the building and began to walk across the parking lot.

"I don't suppose you would mind making fifty bucks," Bruce said.

"Nope," Tabby said. "Depends on what I'd have to do. But I'm not breaking into anybody's house."

"No way, Tabs," Bruce said. "No way at all. Want a ride downtown with us?"

"Okay. But I'm not having anything to do with a burglary."

Bruce winked at Dicky, and they all climbed into the black car. "We just want you to do some work Saturday night."

"It's with that guy," Tabby said. "He was here this morning, wasn't he? I saw you talking to him from the bus. I'm not doing it.''

"I'll tear your fucking ears off," Dicky said. "No shit."

"Tabby, you gotta see this is our big chance," said Bruce. "Dicky's all excited, and it's not even happening for four days."

Bruce drove out of the school lot and turned into a hilly suburban street. Colonials with basketball hoops over the garage doors; Volvo station wagons parked on the driveways; monstrous fleshy rhododendron hedges. "Just think about this, Tabby. Everybody here's got insurance, right? If they lose something, they get it right back again. Only the insurance companies lose, and they got millions—man, they got so much money they loan it to the *government*. And why do they get so much money? Because people like these pay it to them just in case they get robbed or lose something. So they might as well get robbed."

"I can't do it," Tabby said.

"Dicky and I'll give you another twenty-five apiece," Bruce said. "You'll go home with a hundred bucks in your pocket. Tabs, we need you. This deal won't work without you."

"I can't."

"Then I'll tear your fucking ears off," Dicky calmly repeated.

"He's an animal, he means it," Bruce said. "Look, we got four days. Thursday or Friday we'll see you at school, okay? All you have to do is sit in the van and see nobody comes up the drive. You got a radio, and if anybody comes, you tell us. But nobody's going to come. We can put the van under the trees and nobody'll see it."

"Where is this going to be?" Tabby asked.

"You'll find out Saturday. Get in the guy's van, get a hundred bucks."

"Or I'll maul you," Dicky said. "No shit, Tabs."

Bruce turned into Main Street. "You want a Coke or something, Tabs?"

Tabby shook his head. He did not see how he could escape Dicky and Bruce and avoid a terrible beating. Breaking mailboxes was bad enough; he had to avoid being made an accessory to burglary. Dicky was grinning at him: he had that bear smell too. Both the Normans would maul him, he knew.

They would probably take an ear apiece.

Then he saw his father's car parked on the street. It looked like a beacon, like a lighthouse. His father would be able to help him. "Let me out of here," he said.

"Sure, Tabs," Bruce said. "Whatever you say." He pulled over and stopped the car. "You going to hitch home?"

Tabby nodded, left the car, and felt almost safe again.

After Bruce had driven away, Tabby looked in the shop windows closest to the Mercedes. His father was not at the counter in the Camera Center, in Hampstead's Jewelers, or the Winery. Tabby crossed the street and looked in the windows there. Clark was not visible in the small market, Laura Ashley, or Enfants du Paradise, a store that sold children's clothing. Tabby walked up the street peering in the windows—County Trust, Rawhide (leather boots and jackets), Waldenbooks. Tabby crossed the street again and entered Anhalt's. Here were home computers and cameras, stationery and books, records and office supplies. Tabby even looked in the children's book department, but Clark was nowhere in the store.

And what was his father doing in Hampstead anyhow? Today he was supposed to be in Woodville, then Pound Ridge and Mount Kisco. Tabby hesitated on the canopied sidewalk before Anhalt's.

If he waited long enough, he'd eventually see his father. All he had to do was sit in the car, and before long his father would come out of one store or another. . . . Tabby suddenly knew that he would not wait in the car. There was one window he had not inspected. This was tinted so dark that it was mirrorlike for anyone on the street side, and red letters spread across it in the rise and fall of an arch: O'HALLIGAN'S. It was the only bar on Main Street.

Tabby dodged between the cars again and took up a position across the street and a few doors down from the bar. He stood in a brick alleyway which led from a parking lot to Main Street, and if he stepped close to the brick wall to his left, someone leaving O'Halligan's would be unable to see him.

He did not have to wait long. A few minutes after he had secreted himself in the narrow alleyway, O'Halligan's door opened and his father swayed out into the sunlight. He got across the sidewalk and stood over the curb, scowling down at the gutter. Then Clark turned around and stared moodily at O'Halligan's door.

"No, Dad," Tabby said.

A tall woman with black hair and electrically bright lipstick came out of the door after Clark. She wore a white sleeveless shirt and baggy tan shorts; she had, Tabby saw, beautiful legs. Then Tabby saw that she had heavy gold jewelry around her neck and both wrists. She made Sherri Stillwell look like a scrubwoman. This woman was not as drunk as Clark. She linked her arm through his and said something that looked conciliatory. Clark shrugged, then shook his head. The woman pretended to drag Clark back into the bar and Clark slapped at her hand on his arm. The woman gestured up Main Street, said something else; now Clark nodded. They began to move up the street. And where were they going? To Framboise, for a few more drinks and then a long lunch? And after that, to a Norrington motel?

Tabby watched them make their way up the sunny street. Now and then they paused so the black-haired woman could look into the shop windows—his father was used to this woman's company, Tabby understood. Of course. His father did not have a job at all. He just pretended to go to work. He had moved into "Four Hearths," bought the Mercedes he had yearned for, and settled down to the job of spending Monty Smithfield's money.

Tabby wanted to cry. He fled back down Main Street, his eyes hot. Had he actually thought that his father could help him with the Norman twins? His father's dishonesty was so vast that the betrayal it implied was too large for Tabby to contain: it spilled out of him, staining the sidewalk and the windows he saw. Dishonest, dishonest. Tabby saw his father as a ruined man; saw himself as ruined too.

He had reached the entrance of the big stone Hampstead library on the corner of the Post Road and Main Street, just before the bridge over the Nowhatan. He had to sit down; he had to think about himself and his father and Sherri. Tabby pulled the door open and entered the cool library.

He pushed through a turnstile and stood on a checked tile floor before a long desk. One of the two women at the desk looked curiously at Tabby, who frowned and darted past her. He would be able to hide himself in the midst of the tall magazine racks beyond the desk. Tabby felt as though everybody in the library—the old men reading newspapers at the tables, the women at the card file, even the small boy going upstairs to the children's library—were watching him, aware of his shame.

The library seemed to lengthen and widen, the black-and-white pattern of the floor to tremble and vibrate. A round schoolhouse clock behind the desk had ceased to move: the vividly black second hand hung between the two and three as if nailed to the face.

The magazine racks were swaying. No; rippling, Tabby decided, like seaweed growing underwater; like heat rising from a highway.

He stood in wonder more than fear in the altering library. His shame had gone. The walls seemed gently to be bowing out. At the same time that Tabby took in the warnings of the stopped clock and trembling floor, he was lulled by them.

Something was going to happen to him, he knew. The library seemed filled with a magical and transforming light.

His feet took him to the history section. Here were two long stacks with a narrow aisle between. Tabby stepped between the stacks and heard the broad room hum like a dynamo. His aisle was smokily dark: for a second, surrounded by the high wall of books, Tabby thought he saw puffs of brown dust rise between his feet.

Ah.

A fat, slow-moving bolt of lightning angled down out of a dark sky, lengthening itself like a telescope.

"So here is the boy," a voice said behind him.

The stacks and the library were gone, and he was outside, standing—hiding?—by the side of a wooden house. The night was full of noise—he could hear fire, loud curses, a dog furiously barking.

"You should have gone to Fairlie Hill, boy, with the others."

Hiding, yes. Tabby reached out and touched the smoothly planed wood of the house. His feet were caught in flowers.

"Master Smyth," the boy said. "Do you wish a ball in the back?"

Tabby turned around. He had been afraid that he would know the face, but he did not. It was long and arrogant and slightly crazed. The chin was wet with drool. The teeth were large and discolored; the tea-colored eyes, the worst part of the face because the least human, glittered as if they had been varnished.

"Your father is on a British prison ship, Master Smyth," the man said. "I believe he has not long to suffer. Nor shall you."

A long, weightless-looking musket swung up in the man's hand. When the barrel was six inches from Tabby's chest, the musket exploded.

Tabby sprawled backward into the flowers at the side of the house. There had been no pain, only that enormous blow. The tea-colored eyes gloated down over him. His shirt had been ignited in a dozen places by the flashing powder, and it was burning against his skin.

The reason that he could not feel his skin blistering was that he was dead. With a kind of impatience Tabby rose visibly out of the body in the flowers and saw that the boy's face was not his. Yet it was like his.

"Two of them this night," the man said, his chin gleaming with his drool. "Farmer Williams and the Smyth boy. They shall *not* go forward."

The spirit or soul which was Tabby rose above the men and the dead boy with burning clothes. The red of a hundred fires irradiated the sky.

Tabby saw a long white corridor before him, a pulsing incandescent light at its end. Radiations of bright color darted through the ball of light. The corridor and the light soothed and vivified him; he knew that in its midst would be the very sensations of heaven, which came to him as the touch of music against his skin, as cool and awakening as seawater. He began to move toward the pulsing light.

Then he was on his side, uncomfortable, on the floor between the stacks of books in the history section. One book lay open and face-down beside him. *History of Patchin*, by D. B. Bach.

"Son?" It was one of the women from behind the desk. "Are you all right?"

"Yes, thanks," Tabby said automatically. He got up on his knees, and his head swam. "Just a little weak. Don't know what happened."

The librarian bent over and, instead of taking his hand as he expected, removed the book from his grasp. "If you're a J. S. Mill boy, you're supposed to be in school," she said.

"No classes today," Tabby said, finally getting to his feet. "The flu."

"The flu is what you've got," the librarian said. "Go home and go to bed, young man. Don't stay here and infect the rest of us."

Clamping *History of Patchin* firmly under her elbow, she led him back to the turnstile and out the door.

Tabby stumbled as the sun struck him. He looked over his shoulder; the librarian was waving him away. Tabby went to the curb and sat, so that his head would stop swaying. His fingers found a long twig and dragged it through the loose dirt beneath the hedge.

Then he saw that the line he had drawn in the dirt was filling with red liquid: with blood: as if a lake of blood underlay the earth's surface. He drew another line in the dirt with his stick, and that too became a channel filled with blood. Sluggishly the red liquid reached the top of the grooves in the earth and overflowed to pool in the dust. In horror Tabby dropped the stick into the pooling blood.

Tabby's legs forced him upright. He turned the corner and went blindly up Main Street. When he reached the little pizza restaurant he saw Patsy McCloud sitting and writing at one of the little tables outside Deli-icious. If he turned around and walked away she would surely think he was snubbing her; but he did not want to force his company on her. She looked so ethereal, so much too good for Deli-icious . . . if she stamped one of her beautiful feet on the sidewalk, would blood darken just under the surface of the concrete?

Feeling as if every step were taking him deeper into exile by taking him farther from Patsy, Tabby walked past the front of the deli.

Then he heard her light, sailing voice, and could have fallen down out of gratitude. He looked shyly toward her: she was one of his own.

"Yes, I saw his face," he was telling Patsy five minutes later. "It was a crazy face—like a mean old dog. His eyes looked like someone was holding a match up behind them. He didn't even bother to think about shooting me, he just shot."

"And it wasn't a face you know."

"I never saw it before."

"And you think it might have been Gideon Winter?"

"Well, that's what he'd say, isn't it?"

"Yes," Patsy said. "I think he would."

They were silent for a moment; Tabby, who had no idea what he thought of the things that had happened to him that morning, also had no idea what Patsy was thinking. From the expression on her face, she could have been wondering if it was time to have her car serviced, or if she wanted new stockings.

"What was the book you were holding?" she eventually asked.

"A history book. *History of Patchin,* by someone named Bach."

"I think we ought to get a copy," Patsy said. "I'll do it." She smiled. "We don't want you to make a career of fainting in libraries."

He tried to return her smile.

"You see backward," Patsy said. "That's interesting. Did you ever see forward?"

"I guess," Tabby said, flushing. "Once. When I was five. You know—I saw Mrs. Friedgood." His flush deepened. "But mostly I saw backward."

"I've never seen backward," Patsy said. "Well, we make a dandy pair."

"I can't believe we're sitting out in front of Deli-icious talking about this," Tabby said. "In fact, I can hardly believe I'm talking about it at all." He shook his head. "There's another thing, too. After I left the library, I saw the ground bleed. I saw blood come out of the ground. I did."

Patsy looked questioningly at the concrete sidewalk, and Tabby remembered his fancy about her stamping there with her loafered foot. . . .

Both Patsy and he jerked their heads up in the following second, for a woman somewhere across the street had begun to scream. Everyone, the people passing by, the clerks from the hardware store, Mr. Bundle from the antique shop, the bearded men at the next table, was outside and standing up, looking across the street, trying to find the source of the screams.

Then a man was pointing, and then Patsy pointed, and then Tabby saw her too. A thin old woman in a loose black dress, standing beside one of the tables on the balcony of the French restaurant. Her hands were pressed to her eyes, and her mouth was open wide as a cave. More noise came from her than it seemed her body could produce: there was nothing left in her but the bellows which created that high ragged sound.

People from the restaurant burst out onto the balcony as Tabby and the others watched from below. His father was the third man to emerge from the interior, and seconds before his father could reach the woman, she collapsed.

Tabby knew that the old woman was dead: it was as if he knew that a person could not live after making such sounds because a person could not survive whatever had caused those sounds.

Tabby saw his father let the waiter kneel beside the old woman. Though the screams had finished, he could still hear them. Tabby watched his father wander past the kneeling man and the dead woman toward the railing—he was trying to see what had happened.

His father looked down at the sidewalk beneath the balcony; looked at the street; and then his father looked at the little crowd before the hardware store, the delicatessen, and the antique shop. And his father's eyes found him.

9

Hilda du Plessy watched in dismay and distress as the little finch struck the sidewalk. Her appetite had gone: she could not eat her lunch while a dead bird lay unnoticed on the pavement beneath her.

"Your order, lady?" the waiter said from behind her.

"Ah . . . nothing—just a salad," Hilda said.

"Just salad? What salad?"

"Any salad. Watercress. Tomato. Spinach. I don't care, you fool."

"House salad," the waiter said, and then mumbled something Hilda did not understand and which would have astounded her if she had.

In agitation Hilda sat at her table, *The Hero in White* forgotten beside her bread dish. She could no longer see Dr. Van Horne through the window of the antique shop. More than anything else at that moment, she longed to see his reassuring features—if he saw her on the terrace, he would smile and wave. Perhaps he would call out her name. Perhaps—if he were not busy—he would come to her table and join her for lunch. In the world of Florence M. Hobart, such things happened regularly.

In the novels of Florence M. Hobart, birds warbled, birds cooed and nested, birds printed their shapes against the sky at dawn, but birds assuredly did not fall dead from trees. Hilda glanced down at the sidewalk, hoping that the finch might have flown off while she spoke to the boy, but it was still there, an inert ungainly thing, with one fanlike wing extended.

She put her bag in her lap and nearly stood up to leave.

But there was Dr. Van Horne at the window of Olden and Golden: he had found something he liked, and was paying for it. Now, that was more in the key of things. That was more suitable for Hampstead in Patchin County on a fine sunny June morning. The town's best and most distinguished doctor buys some fine old thing . . . yes, that was proper, that was perfect in fact, as perfect as a moment in a myth. On such a moment, Florence M. Hobart or Carrie Engelbart Hoskins might have said, eternity could fairly put her seal.

Hilda relaxed back into her chair to wait for her salad.

Only a few seconds later Dr. Van Horne appeared at the door of Olden and Golden. The owner held the door for him, and out he came onto the sidewalk. He carried a large heavy mirror—his car was directly in front of the shop. In his white suit and white hat, the doctor resembled a hero from the movies, or some famous author or painter. Though large, the mirror seemed light in his grasp. Hilda waggled her fingers at the doctor, hoping breathlessly that he would look up.

Dr. Van Horne walked around to the street side of his car. He set the mirror on end and held it upright with one hand while he opened his passenger door with the other.

"Oh, Doctor!" Hilda tinkled.

He looked up. He did not know from where the sound came.

"Dr. Van Horne?" Hilda waggled her fingers again.

He saw her at her balcony table. But he did not smile. His features, his eyes, did not respond to her. Dr. Van Horne's mythic aspect crumbled at once. For an instant, he looked almost slow-witted to Hilda.

The mirror had turned black. It had been reflecting the potted trees, the steps up to the entrance of Framboise and the canopy, and then it had quite impossibly lost its light and filled with boiling smoke. Now it was black. The blackness seemed three-dimensional, like a corridor leading down from the oval door of the frame.

Hilda's fingers ceased to waggle. She was not even breathing.

Something was *happening* inside that mirror, she saw. A face flickered in the gloom of the long corridor. She saw a hand; eyes; teeth. Then she saw this little section of Main Street rotting and decayed, the buildings shattered, the canopies ripped into flags, garbage blowing onto the steps. She recoiled. Now from within this decaying scene Dr. Van Horne regarded her. His ears hung below his jaw, his eyebrows twisted into peaks, his nose was a curved beak. His teeth came to points. Hilda screamed without knowing that she was going to do it, and found she could not stop.

Some part of Hilda knew that she was attracting attention, that she was making a spectacle of herself, but still the screams insisted on tearing through her throat. They were runaway horses, dragging her after them.

10

When Clark Smithfield finally came home that Tuesday night, he was drunker than usual upon his return to "Four Hearths." His necktie hung untied over his belly, his suit was rumpled and creased. It was nine o'clock. Tabby and Sherri were sitting together on the living-room couch watching the ABC Tuesday Night Movie, *Magnum Force*, which had just begun. They had eaten hours before; Clark's dinner was keeping warm in the oven. Clark slammed the front door and Sherri jumped but did not look up from the television. Seconds later the door to the living room flew open.

"Cozy, aren't you?" Clark said, leaning against the jamb. "I suppose you two have me all wrung out and dried by now."

Sherri glanced at him, looked back at the screen.

"Oh, yeah," Clark said.

"Have a good day?" Sherri asked.

"Yeah, great. You fucking hypocrite. Don't pretend the kid didn't tell you all about it." Clark slouched into the room, tore off his jacket, and threw it onto a chair. He sat heavily in his rocker.

Sherri looked darkly at Tabby, then back at her husband.
"Get me a drink," Clark said.

"What do you mean?"

"Well, I *mean,* what I *mean,* is you should get off your
lazy ass and pour about three inches of Irish whiskey into a
glass with ice and then put the glass in my hand, or is that too
complex for you?"

"Excuse me," Tabby said. "I'm going to my room."

"Yeah, get out, fink," his father said. "You couldn't wait
to get home and tell her, could you?"

"Tell me what?"

"Well, her name is Berkeley, and she's about seven feet
tall and she's thirty years old, and she's got this great mouth
just like a fishhook, and the reason she's so tall is that her
legs start way up *here* and don't stop until they get to the
ground and . . ."

Tabby heard Sherri turning over the coffee table just as he
closed the door. They were shouting at each other by the time
he reached his bedroom.

Two hours later Sherri knocked at his door. He knew what
she was going to say, so he was trembling as he opened it for
her.

"Ah, you poor kid," Sherri said. Her hair hung wildly
about her head, her face was puffy and smeared with makeup.
As soon as the words were out of her mouth, she began to
cry.

"Oh no," Tabby said. "Please."

Sherri walked into the room and sat on his bed. "He never
even had a job here. That was a lie from the first day." Now
she was not crying, but angry. "He met that woman about a
month ago. All he wanted to do was party and spend the
money. I can't live with him anymore, Tabby."

"What are you going to do?" Tabby asked. He sat on the
floor and looked up at this raddled, severe Sherri, who
seemed to be speaking oraclelike through a badly drawn
mask.

"I already called the taxi," she said. "I'd take the car just
to spite him, but of course he's out driving around the bars
because I'm such a bitch." She managed to smile. "I'm taking the train to New York tonight. I'm going back to Florida.
I always hated it here, you know."

"I know."

"You can come with me if you want," Sherri said. "We

can always find something. I'm a worker, even if he isn't.''

Now Tabby was nearly crying.

"I love you," Sherri said. "I loved you since you were a skinny little kid in Key West.''

Tabby could not hold back the tears.

"You always looked so lost," Sherri said, and hugged him. They were both crying. Tabby was remembering the tough confident Sherri who had mothered him in Florida. He let his face rest on her shoulder as he wept for the loss of her.

"You *can* come with me," Sherri said into his ear.

"I can't," Tabby said. "But I love you too, Sherri.''

"You'd better." She put her hand on the back of his head. "I'll send you a postcard.. Write to me sometimes, Tabby. Like with your grandfather.''

"I will.''

"You'll have to take care of him. I tried, Tabby—I tried real hard, but if I stay here he'll kill me.''

"Do you have enough money?" Tabby's eyes were dry now, but he kept the side of his face resting on her shoulder.

"Enough for now. I can always get a job. I'm not worried about money.''

"I'll send you money.''

"Out of your allowance?''

"I'll have money to send you.''

"Worry about your father, not about me. Clark's going to need your help.''

They heard the doorbell ring, and Sherri hugged him more tightly. "He lied to me," she said to him. "It's not that woman, Tabby. You believe that—it's important.'' She kissed his forehead. "I'm going to miss you.''

He followed her out into the hall. She picked up a suitcase at the top of the stairs. Together they went down.

At the door he hugged her; then she went into the cab and was gone. He knew he would never see her again.

All this might have happened if Hilda du Plessy had not been sitting on the balcony of the Framboise; but that it happened on Tuesday night was a direct result of her presence there. The connections between Hilda du Plessy and what befell Richard Allbee the Wednesday following Hilda's death are less straightforward, but still clear. Again it is more a matter of timing than of the events themselves, which—and this too is clear—would have happened had Hilda been stillborn.

• • •

On Wednesday morning Richard had driven to the offices of Ulick Byrne, the Sayres' attorney in Hampstead, and picked up the keys. Along with the keys came a sour look and a lecture from the woolly-haired young Mr. Byrne. "This is really irregular, and in fact, Mr. Allbee, I've never before handed over the keys to a residence before the exchange of contracts. I advised against it. Very strongly. At least I am assured that you have your mortgage. All I can say is that being on television every night has some advantages. *But*"— he extended a thick index finger like a gun to Richard's chest—"the Sayres and I are holding you responsible for any damage to that property before we close. If you burn it down, you're buying what's left. And I advise you to be extremely grateful to Mrs. Sayre and her son, who insisted on giving you an opportunity the law usually does not accommodate." A snuffy atmosphere of illness still hung around the young lawyer; if he were stronger, Richard sensed, he would have fought the Sayres' kindly decision.

"Extremely grateful is just what I am," Richard truthfully said. "Mrs. Sayre's son must have been thinking about what it would be like to move into a house that smelled like an ammonia factory when he decided to let us have the keys early."

"When he priced the house, anyhow," the lawyer said. "Mr. Barbasch and I will be talking very shortly." John Barbasch was the Allbees' lawyer: he too was unhappy about the keys.

From Byrne's offices near Main Street they drove to Greenbank and Beach Trail. Richard had been itching to touch his new house, literally to get his hands on it—to test the sash cords and the smoothness of the windows, to get a good light into the attic and have another look at the beams. The inspection had answered most of his old questions, but had brought up new ones. Another week's wait would have been torture for him. Fairytale Lane seemed dingier and more depressing every day they spent in it.

This revulsion from Fairytale Lane was, he knew, the measure of his eagerness to begin their "real life" at number 32 Beach Trail, Greenbank. At that address was a truly bad atmosphere, but one wholly physical and feline in nature. As soon as the Allbees let themselves in, it struck them. "We need gas masks!" Laura said, rushing to the nearest window.

Soon all the windows on the ground floor and landing were wide open.

Richard began tugging at the stair carpet, yanking the tacks out of the wood. Like the living-room carpet, it had once been good—wool, light tan, with a Chinese pattern woven through it. These carpets had not been cleaned since the fifties, Richard thought—now they were composed as much of cat hairs as of wool. The stink came off them in waves, as if the carpets exhaled ancient urine. It was a shame to throw away carpeting that had once been beautiful, but Richard knew that even after a dozen cleanings, the cat ghosts would drift out on every damp afternoon.

Tread by tread, he pulled it up.

Sweating already, he rolled it into a fat tube at the bottom of the stairs and tugged it toward the door. The Greenbank garbage man was going to be earning a fortune in tips. When the stinking carpet was next to the driveway, he went back inside. Laura had a mop and a bucket and was wading through suds on the kitchen floor. Richard began taking up the carpet in the living room. Beneath it he was relieved to find a good oak floor, snugly joined and still smoothly polished. Some craftsman had done his best for this house, and Richard blessed him.

When he had half the living-room carpet rolled up, he sat on the smooth oaken floor and looked up at the intricate molding around the twelve-foot ceilings. *I'm going to love this place,* he thought. He could hear Laura humming to herself as she slopped water on the kitchen floor. *This is even better than the Kensington house.* He looked through the big dirty windows at the tops of maples and evergreens.

Together he and Laura got the heavy carpet out the door. "Can you help me move it to the driveway?" he asked. "Wait. Is there any strong cord or string in the house?"

Laura returned with a ball of twine left behind in a kitchen drawer; also with an odd look in her eye. Richard began looping the twine around the ends of the fat tube of carpeting, so that he could roll it to the side of the driveway.

"Do you believe in ghosts?" Laura unexpectedly asked him.

Richard wiped the sweat from his forehead and looked at her, expecting a joke. "Only on television."

"Well, you know how you say the smells in the house are the ghosts of cats?" He nodded. "Well, I just saw one."

"You saw the ghost of a cat." Richard raised his eyebrows.

"When I went in to get you the twine. I'm not kidding, Richard."

"Were you scared?"

"No. I was sort of charmed."

"How did you know it was a ghost? What did it look like?"

"It was sitting on the counter next to the sink. It was pale gray, very pretty really. A big gray tom. It had one paw lifted, as if it had been licking it. When I came in the kitchen, it looked at me—it looked pleased that I was there. Then . . ." Laura ducked her head, and her beautiful hair swung over her shoulders. "This is the part you won't believe. Then it vanished. *Poof*. It disappeared."

"You want me to believe this, don't you?" Richard leaned on the thick roll of carpeting and searched her face.

"Since it happened, I guess I do."

"How did you feel?"

Laura shrugged. "I guess it made me feel good, in a funny way. Like the house was welcoming me."

"So will the psychiatrists," Richard said, grinning openly now. Laura swung her fist playfully at him, he bent backward out of the way, and they both laughed.

"It *happened*," Laura said. "I saw it."

"Okay," Richard said. "But check the draining board for cat footprints."

"I did, smartass," she said, going back into the house.

Still smiling, Richard rolled the thick wad of smelly carpet over the back lawn to the driveway. When he had it lined up beside the stair carpeting, he swabbed at his forehead with his handkerchief. A nimbus of dirty cat hair seemed to be floating over the two rolls. Dingy ropes of hair clung to Richard's palms. Sweat dripped from his forehead and trickled behind his ears. He rubbed his damp palms on the rough exposed back of the larger roll, ridged with burlap and the knots of the design. Now he would help Laura wash floors until she'd had enough . . . then tomorrow they would finish the first washing, and he would mix up some of his formula to scrub into the floors and stairs.

He turned around, and his heart kicked. From across the driveway, in the shadow of a stucco wall overgrown with ivy, Billy Bentley was grinning at him. His arms were crossed

over his chest. A snap-brim hat rested on the back of his curly
head. Billy unfolded his arms, and a long knife blade shone
against the green of the ivy.

"No, no," Richard said. He barely knew why.

Billy's face was gleeful. He made a mock jab with the
knife. A large gray cat jumped from the edge of the wall and
twined through Billy's legs. Billy took a step forward out of
the shadow of the wall.

Richard had to keep Billy out of the house—hadn't that
been the message of his recurrent nightmare? Billy was not
there, but Billy had to be kept away from Laura even though
he was not there.

Richard turned his back for a moment on the specter of
Billy Bentley stalking him with a knife, jumped up on the
back porch, opened the door and punched the lock button.

He whirled around, breathing hard, and Billy was gone.
From the driveway a series of indentations marched across the
grass—four of them, as if Billy had taken as many steps.

The big gray tomcat padded into his vision, looked at him,
and gradually became transparent, fading away into the green
of the grass and the black of the driveway.

"Oh, my God," Richard breathed. "I'm going crazy.
Billy Bentley and the Cheshire Cat."

"What's that?" someone asked.

Up the drive came an old man in a Yankee cap, blue T-
shirt over large bony shoulders and concave chest, and tan
wash pants. His black basketball shoes scuffed on the asphalt.

"Just talking to myself," Richard said. The old man
looked familiar, but Richard could not think where he had
seen him before. He just wished he would go away.

"Better watch that," the old boy said, stopping to put his
hands on his hips, and wrenched his spine backward. "You'll
lower the tone of this ritzy neighborhood."

"You have a point." Richard's heart had ceased to bang;
he was decompressing, returning to normal.

The old man reverted to his habitual stoop and continued
on toward Richard. "Guess I'd better introduce myself," he
said. His voice was younger than he, clear and resonant.
"I'm Graham Williams. Live across the street." He waved
toward a colonial in need of paint which sat far back on a
lawn notable for its weeds.

"Oh, Graham Williams," Richard said. That was why the

old man had looked familiar. "You're the one who agreed to talk before the committee—right? And then didn't."

"And then didn't," Williams said. "Good memory you've got there. I hid out in England for a couple of years instead, wrote a bunch of crummy scripts under a pseudonym. Ancient history. Surprised you remember it." Williams' manner had begun to seem less friendly to Richard; his eyes glinted out from the shade of the cap's visor.

"I read your book about alcoholism. I thought it was very good."

"Now I shall fall down all atremble. Did you really? Product of another age, that book was. We all thought we had to kill ourselves with booze to prove that we were sensitive. Something like that. A lot of criminal nonsense."

"Like HUAC," Richard said. He still wanted the old man to leave, but he at least wanted Williams to know that he supported his decision.

"Most bartenders I knew were not in agreement." Williams nodded toward the back door. "There's a pregnant woman fighting your door there."

"Oh. It's locked." Richard turned away and went up the steps. Laura was twisting the knob from the inside; she rattled the door in frustration. The top half of the door was the original glass; imperfections made Laura's face swim and distort. "Turn the bolt," he said, and she clicked the lock open.

When she came outside onto the back porch, he said, "I just saw your cat. And this is our neighbor, Graham Williams. He lives across the street."

"I thought I'd invite you two over for a drink later in the week," Williams said. "Nice to meet you, Mrs. Allbee."

"And you, Mr. Williams," Laura said. "You saw it, Richard? The cat?"

"No cats left around here," Williams said. "Man from the pound cleared 'em all out a month ago."

"Well, we both saw it," Laura said. "Did Mrs. Sayre have a large gray tom?"

"She might have had twenty. I could never tell 'em apart. You know, I knew the Sayres most of my life. In fact, I was their guest at the club the night John Sayre shot himself."

Laura put one hand flat on her protruding belly.

"I didn't mean to upset you, Mrs. Allbee," the old man said. "All that happened nearly thirty years ago—1952. Even after Bonnie Sayre turned this place into a ranch for stray cats, you could tell that it was supposed to be beautiful. Of course, Bonnie Sayre's felines are long gone, all but the smell, I reckon.''

"Well, this feline is a ghost," Laura said—Richard understood that she was paying back Williams for the remark about John Sayre's suicide.

"Seeing ghosts and talking to yourself," Williams said. "What are we coming to?" This was offered lightly, but Richard saw that the old man had been affected by Laura's remark. His eyes had dimmed, and he was riffling the white scurf under his chin. "Saturday night, I was thinking. We can talk about ghosts, if you like. I thought your husband might be interested in hearing something about the history of the area, Mrs. Allbee."

"You mean because of his mother? Because of the Green family?"

"Yes. I'm glad you know about that already. I'm another one. And of course Patsy McCloud is too. Kind of interesting, our families being back here after all these years."

"Yes," Laura said. "Kind of."

"Well, there are some interesting chapters in our history," Williams said. "Come over after dinner if you like." He shook Laura's hand, then Richard's. "Maybe you want some . . . explanations? I don't know, does that sound mysterious?"

"I'll take all the explanations I can get," Richard said. "Did you know my parents, Mr. Williams?"

"I knew most people in Hampstead, back in the forties," Williams said. He was looking questioningly at Richard. "I knew Mary Green by sight—she was a nice little thing. Had a real sense of duty. I used to see your father, too. He was good with his hands. Michael used to do work around Greenbank. That was how he met Mary. Pleasant young fellow. Full of smiles.''

"Did he work on this house?" Richard almost held his breath.

"Don't believe so. But he left his mark on a lot of places in Greenbank. Come on over Saturday, and we'll talk about it."

"I'll have to see."

After Graham Williams had slowly walked back across the

street, Laura said, "I didn't like him, Richard. That old man gave me the creeps. I don't want to see him Saturday."

"I might learn something from him," Richard said. "You know, I really did see that gray cat." He wanted to turn the conversation, and Laura's mind, away from their new neighbor. Williams seemed almost to have been summoned up by the apparitions of Billy Bentley and the tomcat: for an instant, while his eye had dimmed and his hand searched his chin, his authority had left him and he had looked as though he also might fade away into invisibility. "I saw it disappear, too."

"So no more jokes about psychiatrists."

Richard knew, as he said *no* and shook his head, that Laura too was remembering Patsy McCloud.

"Didn't the cat sort of make you feel welcomed?" Laura asked.

"I'm not sure," Richard answered. "Maybe he wasn't so interested in welcoming me."

11

That night Richard Allbee dreamed that he was carrying a heavy sword through the old Sayre house. It was night, and rain spattered the roof. In the gloom the sword gathered into itself whatever light there was. Richard left the kitchen and went through the empty dining room. He had an impression of peeling walls, of something soft and rotten underfoot. A big cat incuriously watched him carry the sword into the derelict living room. Cracks zigzagged the plaster walls. He stepped over black holes in the floor. Richard opened the front door and stepped out onto the porch. The countryside greenly, wetly dripped. Richard stepped off the porch into the sweating rain and walked to the middle of the lawn. The sword seemed to weigh as much as he did. He got it up over his head. Then he swung it down with all his force. The sword hacked into the squashy ground. Blood foamed out from the wound, soaking his shoes and the bottoms of his trousers. A rivulet of blood ran down the hill and lapped against a tree at the end of the property. Richard pushed the sword deeper into the earth, and bright red blood, arterial blood, squirted so far up that it splashed the roof.

12

Years before, Officer Royce Griffen had been given a job he hated, but at least on the extra shift imposed by the flu he worked as he thought a cop should, driving a patrol car. Those eight hours were his dessert. The eight-to-four shift he endured as he would a bad dinner, knowing that when it was over he could get into a black-and-white and do real police work.

The trouble usually started in the locker room. If Turtle Turk was either coming on or going off shift, he would invariably try to amuse the other policemen. "Roycie Woycie," Turtle crooned when he saw him, "will you ring my doorbell today? Hey, Roycie, what do you say when some big old babe in a nightgown opens up? 'Officer Roycie Woycie Griffen, ma'am, at your service'? Do you show 'em your big gun, Roycie?"

Turtle usually waddled back and forth before his locker at this point, mincing and rolling his eyes. "Ooh, ma'am, I'm brave Roycie, and I'm here to tell you how to make sure no bad man ever comes in when you don't want him to. . . . No, ma'am, you see *entry* is one of the biggest problems a *bad* man has to overcome. . . ."

Unfortunately, Royce Griffen was only as tall as the official minimum for Hampstead officers, five-foot-six, and weighed only a hundred and forty pounds, or he would have attacked Turtle right in the locker room. But the other policemen knew by looking at Royce that he would jump on any man that laughed at Turtle's antics. His face went nearly as red as his hair.

"Oh madam, oh madam," Turtle crooned. "It's irregular, I know, but I wonder if you could accompany me to the special police showing of *The Choirboys* in a couple of weeks? I think I can promise you a thrilling time—it starts at midnight, you see, and all the boys in blue will be there, and, ma'am, I'm built like a jockey so's I can ride all night—"

"Can it," he said.

"Yes, Roycie," Turtle said, mincing away.

God, he hated that job. If he were still married, he could talk about it at home and explain how it demeaned him to spend his days soft-soaping housewives, how he had been picked because he was the smallest cop on the force, how the job was only a P.R. stunt dreamed up by the first select-woman. But his wife had left him after three years of trying to live on a cop's pay. Royce didn't blame her, he'd leave himself too, if he could.

The job had come about because of the steady rise in bur-glaries in the past three years; the murders of Stony Friedgood and Hester Goodall meant that Royce's frequent requests to be reassigned were doomed to go ignored for a long time to come. For two years he had been knocking on doors, intro-ducing himself, and counseling householders about burglary prevention. He inspected locks on doors, catches on win-dows, tested alarm systems, made recommendations—and all this drove him crazy. If a thief wanted to get into a house, he got in. That was all. You could make it harder for him, but he'd get in if you had dead bolts, savage mastiffs, and sonic beams that swept across the living-room floor at timed inter-vals. Alarm systems went off randomly, dogs slept, people forgot to lock their doors. His life was a waste. A girl scout could break into any of the houses he had inspected.

Two years before, he had divided the city into quadrants, and then each quadrant into quadrants. He was now in section three of the third quadrant, and if he could not get himself reassigned he would be knocking on doors like the Avon lady for another eighteen months.

Section three of quadrant three took in the lower end of Greenbank, including Mount Avenue, all the way to the Hill-haven border. Ordinarily Royce Griffen would have been pleased to get a peek at the interiors of these houses; but doing his hated job while he peeked made him feel like a servant; the big houses with their spotless interiors reminded him of everything he had sacrificed to become a police of-ficer. Since his divorce, Royce shared the top floor of a house near the trailer park with another divorced cop.

His second stop that morning was at a large white house overlooking Gravesend Beach which he had noticed for years without ever knowing who lived there. The mailbox was no help, bearing only the numeral five. Royce turned in between the gates. He had never before really taken in how much land surrounded the house. He could have been driving through a park. The drive angled off through trees, then returned toward the house on its bluff above the sea wall.

The lawn, unusually for such a place, had been permitted to get shaggy. Bobby Fritz must have been laid up with the flu, Royce imagined. Here and there he could see dandelions lolling against the green.

Royce pulled up before the front door, got out of the patrol car and rang the bell. He adjusted his holster, tugged his hat into the proper angle. He straightened his shoulders to make himself as tall as he could get. *Here we go again,* he thought unhappily.

An elderly woman in a white uniform opened the door. She looked both angry and distressed: as she glared at him, he saw that she had been crying.

"Good morning," he said. "I am Officer Griffen of the Hampstead Police. Is the lady of the house in?"

"Pah," she said, "there's no lady here."

"Well, then. I have been assigned to special duty in burglary prevention. May I take a little of your time and check out your locks, alarms, and so forth, and make recommendations for their improvement? Here in Hampstead, you know, we have an average of two burglaries every hour." All this was memorized, and Royce spoke it automatically. He was looking not at the cranky housekeeper or maid, whatever she was, but at the lock on the front door. A simple Yale.

"Doctor," the woman said, turning away from him, "a police officer."

Far back in the hall, a trim-looking man in a white suit came silently through a door. He was smiling; was almost hypnotically handsome. Royce stood even straighter. "Oh yes, Muriel," he said, coming nearer. "We must make the officer at home. Get him a cup of coffee, please."

"No, thank you, sir," Royce began, but the housekeeper interrupted him. "Don't I always get coffee for your guests, Doctor?"

"Of course you do, Muriel," the doctor said. He smilingly extended a hand to Royce. "Nice to meet you, Officer."

Muriel took herself away down the hall.

"Had to tell her I was letting her go," the doctor said confidentially to Royce. "I'm retiring soon. Have to do a lot of cutting back. Even had to let my yardman go." He touched Royce lightly on the elbow. "But that's not your concern, my boy. You've come to tell me how to keep the burglars away?"

"Yessir." Royce pointed to the Yale and gave his memorized speech about mortise locks and dead bolts. "A good

lock is your best protection," he said. "Could we look at
your windows and the other doors, sir?"

"Be my guest," said the doctor. He escorted Royce into
the dining room, where there were two windows with flimsy
catches, and on into the kitchen. The door onto a flagstone
patio had another simple lock. "I can tell just by what I've
seen already that you have a lot of tempting stuff," Royce
said. "Have you ever thought about changing the locks?"

"I've lived here all my life," the doctor said. "I know
everybody in town. Nobody would try to break into my
house, would they?" He was taking Royce back through the
house to the living room.

"Oh, this is beautiful," Royce said. The room was windowed on the sea side of the house from floor to ceiling.
Sailboats bobbed out on the water; Long Island floated hazily
on the other side of all that blueness. The room itself must
have been forty feet long. The biggest Oriental rug he had
ever seen underlay islands of furniture, a Bösendorfer piano,
plants and sculptures. Most of the sculptures were of women.
Royce bent to peer at the name cut into the base of a little
statue of a dancer: Degas. It sounded French, therefore expensive. On the opposite wall hung ranks of paintings and an
ornate mirror. "I think a lot of people would want to break in
here, yes. Don't you even have an alarm system?"

"Oh, I looked into it once," the doctor began, but Royce
suddenly was having trouble hearing him. Something was
wrong—he thought he must have caught the flu after all. The
doctor's voice seemed to be reaching him on a scratchy wavering radio band. The beautiful room looked to Royce as
though it had grown to the size of an aircraft hangar—it appeared to stretch on forever, to soar up hundreds of feet. The
light dimmed, then turned a lurid pinkish color. Suddenly
Royce had trouble standing up—the room was so immense it
threatened to squash him.

When Muriel appeared beside him with a cup of coffee he
wordlessly accepted it. The doctor was still talking, but
Royce could hear only beehive noises. The coffee stank like
sewage. He was looking at the wall hung with all those pictures of a sunny foreign countryside, and in their midst the
mirror seemed to be melting. *I looked into it once,* the doctor
repeated. Across the surface of the mirror appeared a jagged
bolt of lightning. *He* was in the mirror. He was a red-headed

dwarf. His mouth sneered, his eyes drooped. He was inexpressibly ugly—a sort of troll dressed up as a policeman.

"So you see, I never did anything about it in the end," the doctor said. "I've just relied on the goodwill of others, but I do lock the doors and turn on the yard lights at night."

"Yes," Royce said. He had to get out of this vast and terrible place. His troll self grimaced at him and slopped coffee out of a cup. The doctor took the cup from his hand and led him back toward the front door.

As soon as they were in the hall, Royce heard the murmur of a dozen voices behind the closed door, the buzzing of a million flies.

The doctor said, "I'm sure I'll consider your suggestions."

"Yeah," Royce said. He was frantic to get out. The doctor smiled and closed the front door.

Royce nearly drove into a tree on his way back down the drive.

From then on DRG—the thinking cloud—dipped him straight into insanity. His perceptions were wildly skewed—he heard music but the radio gave nothing but police calls, he smelled a gritty sour effluvium from his own armpits—his mood savage. He kept seeing himself as a ridiculously ugly troll.

His third stop went normally. Royce let his mouth say all the things it could say by itself (*Assigned to special duty, Missus, I advise such and so and this and that*) and got out of the house without experiencing anything more unusual than the beehive sounds he had heard in the doctor's house.

But in the fourth house he lost his composure. He was sitting at a metal outside table on a brick terrace, saying something about the French doors which led into another film-set living room. A slim pretty woman named Mrs. Clark was seated across the table from him, sipping iced tea. He knew it was iced tea, he had seen her pouring it from a pitcher in her refrigerator.

But reality gave a hiccup, everything turned yellow before him, and he was a troll again. The pretty woman's hair was filthy and matted. He could smell raw whiskey in her tumbler. His feet were on something damp and horrid—some dead animal? He saw that Mrs. Clark's arms were covered with thick dark hair like a pelt. "I'm sorry," he said, realizing that he had stopped talking in the middle of a sentence.

> Locks and bolts are my arms,
> Bolts and locks my legs,

Mrs. Clark sang in a cracked voice.

Royce cried out in panic and disgust: he had looked down and seen that the patio was covered with huge dead spiders, their bodies the size of puppies. Mrs. Clark stood up. Her back was humped, her lips curled over broken teeth.

> Kiss my bolts and stroke my locks
> And I shall marry you,

sang Mrs. Clark. She spilled whiskey on one of the spiders, and its fat body trembled. Brown slime dripped down the walls and over the French windows.

"I'm sorry," Royce repeated. "Not feeling well. Better go."

The huge black spider Mrs. Clark had anointed with whiskey twitched toward his foot. The walls of the massive brick house were mud, sliding downward. Mrs. Clark's face slipped toward her chin: she too was made of mud.

Royce ran away—if he stayed there he would be encased in the thick gray muck, he would never be able to leave. He sprinted around the side of the building. An invisible crowd laughed at his fear, his stature, his slow troll-shuffle . . . at last he found the patrol car and managed to get it started. He roared into Mount Avenue and turned left on Beach Trail.

In his panic he almost drove into a ditch as he turned toward the Post Road on Charleston. The air was bright yellow, and a yellow spider the size of a pickup truck lunged out of the ditch toward his car.

Royce screamed, twisted the wheel, and sped back toward the police station.

The cramped old station house was itself—nothing worse than Turtle's insults could happen to him there. He sat in the tiny squad room and typed fictitious reports about his morning calls. He filed the reports. To fill out the time, he went downstairs to the firing range and shot twenty dollars' worth of cartridges at a paper target.

At the change of shift, he went up to the locker room. "Hey, Royce!" Bobo shouted, coming in. "Meet any gorgeous women today?"

"All the time," Royce mumbled. He remembered Mrs. Clark's face oozing toward her chin.

"You don't look so hot," Bobo said. "You getting the flu?"

"Nah. I'm okay."

"Roycie Woycie," Turtle bellowed, entering the locker room with beer on his breath and tomato-sauce stains on his shirt. "Let me push your doorbell, lady. Let me set my finger on your button."

Royce stared at Turtle. What he saw was a corpse dead roughly three weeks. The body had been badly mutilated before or just after death, and the white shrunken skin puckered and bagged around the wounds. The eyes had turned dark brown. A flap of dead skin folded across Turtle's forehead, exposing colorless bone.

"Oh, God," Royce said. He stood up. No one else thought Turtle looked unusual in any way—his mind was going.

"Tell us about all the joy you had today, Roycie," uttered the horrible Turtle-thing.

"I'm getting out of here," Royce said, and went out to sit in his patrol car for fifteen minutes before he switched on the ignition. That night he avoided Greenbank; in fact he avoided patrolling altogether. He drove to an empty cul-de-sac in the woods off the Merritt Parkway and sat in the car with his eyes closed. He kept seeing Mrs. Clark; he kept remembering that oval mirror in the big white house on Mount Avenue.

13

The next morning Royce Griffen reported early to the station. He waited in the locker room for the others to appear. Turtle Turk, coming in with what was clearly a monstrous hangover, looked even worse than he had yesterday and smelled of death and cheap whiskey. One of his eyes had burst open. At morning call, when all of the officers reported to the ready room before going on shift, Royce looked around with horror—the captain and nearly all the policemen were dead too. Some had neat bullet holes through their uniform shirts, others like Turtle were battered and mutilated. After they were released, Royce drove to the wooded cul-de-sac and spent eight hours sitting trembling in his car.

At the change of shift he ran into the toilet in the station and locked himself into a stall. Something wanted to burst out of him; he barely got his trousers down in time. When he sat on the toilet, a clawing pain almost immediately canceled his relief. The pain tightened up, became more intense and tearing. His bowels had been ripped: he whimpered. To see what had caused him such agony, he peeked into the toilet as he wiped himself. Royce screamed. The bowl was filled with tiny spiders as red as his hair. A huge mass of them swam in the water, others already struggled up the sides. Royce hastily flushed the toilet, flushed it again. Now twenty or thirty scrambled over the seat; more small red bodies still spun in the bowl. He buckled his pants and left the men's room. He forced himself to walk slowly across the lobby to the door.

Inside his patrol car Royce locked all his doors. Then he unstrapped his Smith and Wesson. He had to hold the revolver with both of his shaking hands. He cocked it. "Dear God," he whispered. He pushed the barrel into his mouth and bit down on the front sight. Then he pulled the trigger and the back of his head exploded over the rear window and the top of the car.

14

On Friday morning the Normans appeared on either side of Tabby as he was taking books out of his locker. They had been out of school Wednesday and Thursday, and Tabby had been praying that Bruce had talked Dicky into releasing him from his role in the planned robbery. After all, Bruce had gotten him out of having to damage his own mailbox, hadn't he?

But the bear smell of violence was still on them, and Bruce's first words showed Tabby that the twins had not given up their plans for him. "You thinking about how you'll spend your hundred, Tabs?"

Tabby shook his head.

"Tabs . . ." Dicky breathed.

"We'll pick you up tomorrow night," Bruce said. "Around ten. Don't tell anybody where you're going or who you'll be with, okay?"

"I don't want to do it," Tabby said.

"Oh yes you do," Bruce said. "You know that grunts in Vietnam used to wear gook ears as necklaces?"

Dicky grinned.

"Help us out, Tabs," Bruce said. "We're friends."

"Yeah," Tabby said. "Ten o'clock." He would send the hundred dollars to Sherri. Then he would have nothing to do with the Norman twins ever again.

15

Six hours later that Friday Richard Allbee was tying new sash cord to a lead weight. He had opened the frame alongside one of the large windows in the living room of the old Sayre house, and two long painted strips of stop molding and a brownish, worn length of cord lay on the exposed oak floor. The smells of Mrs. Sayre's cats now were scarcely noticeable in the living room. One more good washing and repeated airings, now that the carpets were out of the house, would rid them of the cat ghosts.

Laura's footsteps came down the stairs; a moment later she opened the living-room door. "I'll work on one more floor," she said, "and then I'll have to quit. How are you doing with the windows?"

"One more to go in there. About forty-five minutes' work. When you're done, come in and keep me company."

"Well, I don't know. My last employer knocked me up."

"He remembers the occasion with gratitude," Richard said.

A few minutes later Laura poked her head around the door again. "Say Richard, I was thinking."

"Yes?" He looked up, letting the heavy weight swing on the white new cord.

"If you really want to go over to that old man's house tomorrow, I won't mind. Honest. I'll just go to bed early." She smiled at him. "Only because you were nice enough to pretend you saw that cat too."

"I wasn't pretending."

Laura withdrew her head from the doorframe, and Richard turned back to his job. He looped the cord over the pulley and tied the loose ends to the upper weight. He moved the sash up and down and saw that now it worked smoothly. Then he took up a handful of four-inch finish nails and used one to fix the stop molding in place. He moved the sash up and down again; it still worked smoothly. He carefully hammered in the other nails, checking the movement of the sash after each one.

Another window repaired, and only one more to go in this room. Three more days' work would see all the windows in working order. On Monday he and Laura would sign the papers in Ulick Byrne's office, and the lawyers could stop having heart attacks.

He deliberately was not thinking about Billy Bentley: that had not happened.

Then for a moment, not knowing where the vision came from, Richard saw a graveyard erupting on his front lawn: saw the graves splitting open, earth and headstones exploding into the air, then the bodies, the skeletons, the individual separate bones spewing up out of the ground: now saw the earth vomiting corpses and bones. The very earth was tearing at itself, destroying itself in a paroxysm of revulsion. Grass, clods of earth, broken pieces of headstones and broken pieces of bone went spiraling up. He shook his head. Oh, God. Billy Bentley, rest in peace.

He moved on to the next window. His hands were shaking.

PART TWO

Establishment

Ae fond kiss, and then we sever;
Ae fond kiss, and then for ever.
—Robert Burns

Replenishment

1

The First Threshold

1

For most of that week, Patsy and Les McCloud avoided each other, wrapped in their separate and very different conceptions of what had happened between them. Patsy did not want to fight with Les, so she was uncharacteristically happy that he had retreated; she wanted to sit quietly and chew on the new perception of herself and her husband she had come to before meeting Tabby at Deli-icious. Since that Tuesday, Les had been acting aggrieved and wounded, barely meeting her eye; he was pouting. He thought he could force her to apologize for the things she had said by putting on these infantine looks, and such tactics had been successful in the past. But Les looking stricken no longer infected Patsy with guilt, in fact she resented that once it had; as long as he was sick she would care for him, but she did not intend to bring in his tray, as it were, on her knees. When she looked at the pouting whiskery man on her marital bed she saw a patient, not a husband, and her mind led her through a series of propositions: if your man is supposed to be a tough masculine businessman, but if he is afraid that he can never be as tough and manly as he thinks he must be, then *you* are supposed to assure him that he already is; if his insecurities mean that he has to beat you several times a year just to make sure that your assurances were not lies, then *you* are supposed to take the beatings quietly; if he comes home with shit in his pants like a baby, then *you* can be certain that pretty soon reassurance time is going to roll around again.

By Saturday Les was out of bed, and Patsy retreated into the spare bedroom with the library's copy of D. B. Bach's *History of Patchin*. At eleven-thirty, Les looked in and said, "What about lunch?"

She said that she was not hungry.

"What about *my* lunch?"

"I'm sure there's food in the refrigerator."

"Jesus Christ." Les slammed the door.

Two hours later he came in the room again. He was glaring at her and his fists were balled. "You trying to get back at me or something?"

"I just want to be alone," Patsy said.

"Okay. I'm going to the golf course. Be alone, if you want to act like a spoiled kid."

Tabby and Clark Smithfield spent Saturday in a gloomy, but not a poisoned, silence. Clark tried to explain to his son that the fault for his charade had been Sherri's—that Sherri's unwillingness to adjust to Hampstead and Connecticut had driven him out of the house, and Tabby saw that his father believed this. "We'll get by, kid," Clark said. It was noon, and he was working on his second drink. "We're better off without her."

They watched television all afternoon. At six Clark drove to an Italian restaurant on the Post Road and came back with an enormous pizza. Wordlessly they watched the local news, the national news, *Solid Gold, Enos,* and the beginning of the Saturday Night Movie, *From Russia with Love.* Tabby kept looking at his watch as the light from the windows died and the nearly bookless "library" at "Four Hearths" darkened. "Dad," he said, "are you going to need a real job pretty soon?"

"I *have* a job," Clark said. He sipped at his Irish whiskey, looked sideways at Tabby. "I can get work anytime I need it."

"But you don't have a job," Tabby said. "You don't have a job now."

"I told you I did, didn't I?" Clark said, not looking at him.

Tabby stood up and left the room. Being with his father was like watching somebody drown. For a time he stood outside on the front steps. The trees of Greenbank and Hermitage Avenue inhaled on the short front lawn of "Four Hearths," exhaled farther down the quiet street. Above them the passive stars marched in order. Tabby went down the steps to sit on the grass and wait for the Norman twins.

2

Shortly after nine-thirty that night, Richard Allbee pulled into Graham Williams' driveway. When he got out of his car, he turned around to see how the old Sayre house looked from across the street. Already it looked improved, he thought—it looked inhabited. Like children and animals, houses too were civilized by the touch of informed love. That he had imagined seeing Billy Bentley there more than ever seemed a delusion; he was glad that he had told Laura, now in the hated water bed reading a Joyce Carol Oates novel and watching a James Bond movie, no more of it than that he had seen the cat.

Light footsteps came tapping toward him from the Charleston Road corner. Involuntarily Richard tensed his muscles. He braced himself to see a large gray tomcat padding silently into the circle of light just up from the corner.

Delusion, delusion.

A figure turned the corner. It was coming toward him. Then the figure emerged into the light of the streetlamp, and Richard saw that it was Patsy McCloud. She was carrying a thick book under one arm. Apart from the relief at the disappearance of his ridiculous fear, Richard felt a certain guilty pleasure in the sight of Patsy. He waved at her. She wore a pale blue shirt and white bib overalls which fit snugly at her waist and billowed around her legs. Patsy waved back when she recognized him.

"I should have known that you'd be here," he said.

"I thought you and Laura might both be here," Patsy said as she walked toward him over the lawn.

"Laura's in bed with James Bond."

"And Les has the flu. On the whole, Laura has the better bargain."

Richard asked her about the book she was carrying as they went toward the front door.

"Did Mr. Williams tell you anything about why he wanted to see us together? Did he show you the plaque on Mount Avenue?"

Richard shook his head and pushed the bell.

"Then I'd better wait for him to explain it."

"All Will Be Explained."

"All." She smiled at him.

Williams opened the door and peered out through the

screen. "Both of you! I'm very gratified." He opened the screen door and stepped out of the way, allowing them in. He was wearing his Yankee cap and a gray PAL T-shirt too small for him.

Patsy and Richard came into a hallway lined with book-shelves. Books leaned, books formed skyscrapers and towers on the top shelves, books were lined spine-up on the floor in front of the shelves. "Where do we go?" Patsy asked. The light bulb hanging from a cord in the middle of the hallway had burned out.

"First door on the left."

Patsy, then Richard, went into the living room. Here too the walls were covered with bookshelves, and books were stacked to waist height at intervals before the shelves. Framed graphics and posters for ancient films stood on the floor, propped either against the shelves or against the stacks of books. A dim overhead light burned, as did a standard lamp beside the shabby green couch, and a brass gooseneck lamp on the white pine table which held a typewriter—an old black manual—and several neat stacks of paper. The room smelled of must, age, books.

Williams hovered in the door. "Make yourselves comfort-able on the couch. Or on the chair." He nodded toward a brown leather library chair which seemed to dissolve back into the shelves of unjacketed books. The chair was so worn it looked as though it had been sanded—the dye had shredded away from the leather. A tall floor lamp and a heavy marble ashtray stood beside it. "Can I get you anything? A drink? Coffee?"

Both Patsy and Richard asked for coffee.

"Perking away. Be right back."

In seconds he was back with three cups; he set the tray on the coffee table before the green couch. Then he picked up one cup and pulled a metal chair from under the typing table and sat, facing the other two. Simultaneously they sipped the hot strong coffee. Richard was not sure why he had thought he ought to come. This would be a waste of time: Williams was a lonely old man. He had invited them for their com-pany, that was all. Richard rubbed his hand over the arm of the couch. The raised ornate pattern had been almost worn away.

"I suppose I ought to apologize," Williams said. He removed the Yankee cap and danced his fingers over his freckled bald crown. "This place deserves to be fixed up, and I never had the money to do it. Just got used to it instead. I put up all the bookshelves myself, forty years ago. Nowadays I couldn't even afford the lumber." His fingers still danced and drummed on the top of his head. The old man was nervous. Richard wondered how long it had been since another person had been in the house with Williams; how long it had been since a woman had been in this room.

Then the old man startled him by saying, "Patsy's a psychic, you know. Same as her grandmother, Josephine Tayler. There's a boy in the neighborhood who's another one. Tabby Smithfield. James Tabb Smithfield, that is. Up on Hermitage. Don't suppose you're one too, Allbee?"

"Me?" Richard said, swallowing too much coffee. "A psychic? No."

"I'm not either. Except for the one time I was, when I saw a man and knew . . . well, never mind what I knew. I'll save that for a time when young Tabby's with us. I gather you know about your family and all that? About the Greens?"

For a moment Richard had thought Williams had meant his father, and he was already shaking his head impatiently. "Oh. The Greens. I know a little."

"You ever see the plaque in front of the Academy?"

Richard glanced at Patsy and caught her staring at him. He shook his head again.

"Smyth, Tayler, Green, Williams," the old man said, mystifying Richard. "And Gideon Winter. Smyth, which became Smithfield; Tayler, who is our beautiful little friend sitting next to you; Green, who is you; and Williams, who is me. And Gideon Winter, who could be just about anybody. I guess I better explain."

3

"You're a smart little fuck, Tabs," Dicky Norman said, rubbing his knuckles painfully over the top of Tabby's head. They were jammed into the front seat of the old black Oldsmobile beside Bruce. The Normans were happier than Tabby had ever seen them. Both of them stank of excitement and beer, of marijuana too.

"Hey, I knew he'd come through," Bruce said, knocking Tabby's ribs with a huge elbow. "Our little buddy's a great guy. And you never made a sound about who you were going to be with, did you, little buddy?"

"Of course not," Tabby said. "But this is the last time I do anything like this. No more, after tonight. I want you guys to know that."

"After tonight, man, you're cool with us," Bruce said. "Ain't that right, Dicky? Tabs is cool with us."

Dicky responded by trying to play washboard on Tabby's head again. They had turned into Beach Trail and were going downhill toward Mount Avenue.

"Because I hate doing this," Tabby said. "I just want to keep my ears, that's all."

Both Normans responded with violent beery laughter. Bruce turned right on Mount Avenue and went past the front gates of Greenbank Academy.

At the thruway overpass Mount Avenue joined Greenbank Road; Bruce was driving south, toward town. Tabby asked, "Where are we going?"

"Parking lot," Bruce muttered. He went down Greenbank Road to the first light, then turned right toward the Post Road ón the Sayre Connector.

The man Tabby had seen across the street from school was standing beside his van in an empty corner of the Lobster House lot. Bruce drove up alongside the van, and the man watched them get out of the car. *He doesn't look like a burglar,* Tabby thought. Gary Starbuck had a pronounced nose— a perfume tester's nose—steady dark eyes, and a worried forehead. He was dressed entirely in dark blue. *He looks like an algebra teacher.*

The dark eyes rested on him for a moment. "Yeah, I see," Starbuck remarked, though no one had said anything. Then he spoke directly to Tabby. "You know what you're supposed to do?"

Tabby shook his head.

Starbuck reached into the window of his van and brought out a pair of small two-way radios. He handed one to Tabby. "Switch it on," he said. Tabby turned it over in his hands until he found a sliding button on the top. Both radios squealed loudly, and Tabby hurriedly slid the button back toward him. "They're too close now," Starbuck said softly, still looking straight into Tabby's eyes. "They have to be about fifty feet apart to really work right. But that's how we'll talk. You sit in the van. Front window, back window. You keep looking at the drive and the road. Simple?"

Tabby nodded.

"And if you see *anything,* you tell me about it. We'll be in that house maybe half an hour. That's a long time. Anybody stops and looks at the van, you tell me and describe who it is. What kind of car. Anything you see. If there's a cop, lie down on the floor of the van and call me *fast.* We'll come out and take care of him, but we'll have to get to him before he gets to his radio. You get your money afterward, as soon as we get away. Understand, kid?"

"I understand."

"I was beginning to think you couldn't talk," Starbuck said. "Here's one more thing for you to understand. If you ever talk about this with the cops, or if I even think you'll talk about this with the cops, I'll come back here and kill you." The sweetly, seriously worried expression on his face never altered as he said this. "I'm a businessman, see? I gotta stay in business."

The Normans were so impressed they looked as though they might levitate.

"And that goes for you two glandular cases too," Starbuck said.

"Hey, shit, man," Bruce said.

"Get in the van," Starbuck ordered, abruptly turning away. He got in the driver's seat, Bruce in the passenger's seat. Dick climbed in the back with Tabby, who was clutching his radio.

As Starbuck swung out of the lot across the Post Road to go back down the Sayre Connector, they passed the statue of John Sayre posing as a World War I soldier. Tabby noticed the statue for the first time: the young soldier's face seemed demonic to him, the creases in the bronze cheeks exaggerated by shadows.

Dicky leveled a forefinger at Tabby's chest and pretended to pump bullets into him.

"I never lived in a place like this before," Gary Starbuck said. "Not exactly like this, anyhow. What do they call this, anyhow? It's not suburbia, is it? Do they call this exurbia?"

"I dunno," Bruce said. "Who cares?"

Starbuck turned left on Greenbank Road. Tabby silently groaned. He should have known—they were going back to his neighborhood.

"Well, I been reading the local rag," Starbuck said, swinging the van around the curves on Greenbank Road. "You know what goes on in this town? You know how many drunken-driving arrests you get on the weekends? How many accidents? How many drug busts and stupid goddamned amateur break-ins by kids without any professional knowledge? Without any training? I say this isn't *sub*urbia, and it isn't *ex*-urbia. It's *dis*turbia."

4

Richard surveyed the bookshelves as Graham Williams spoke, randomly reading off names and titles to himself. Half of the longest wall seemed to be fiction, the other half history and biography. There was a long section of screenplays bound in black vinyl. The wall to his left held art books. Paperback mystery novels had been jammed in above the outsized art books—Williams was an addict of Raymond Chandler and John D. MacDonald, of Amanda Cross and Dorothy Sayers.

"All right," he said when Williams paused, "the descendants of the four original settler families are back in Hampstead—in fact, back in Greenbank. And our ancestors had some kind of trouble from a newcomer named Winter. But I'm afraid that I have to ask, so what?"

"The only reasonable question," Williams said. "You're right. Why should we care, really, unless we're historians? The only reason we should care is that whatever happened back then is still affecting us now. Isn't that always true of history? If the Normans had prevailed in England, we'd be speaking French today, or something like it. So let's look at our history here in Hampstead. I'm going to give you three names from three generations in Hampstead, from 1898 to 1952. Robertson Green—he would have been your great-great-uncle, Mr. Allbee—Bates Krell, and John Sayre. Robertson Green was executed by the state in 1898, Bates Krell disappeared from human ken in 1924, and John Sayre killed himself in 1952. I think Gideon Winter was reborn in each of these men, and that only John Sayre had the strength to fight him."

5

Les McCloud had snatched up his golf clubs as he steamed out of the house, thrown them into the trunk of his Mazda, and driven straight to the Sawtell Country Club after his fight with Patsy. Of course it had not been anything as satisfying as a fight: it had been Patsy needling, needling, needling him, provoking him as only someone who had lived with him for a decade and a half would know how to do. *I'm sure there's food in the refrigerator.* A rebellion against the proper order of things. Les did not actually feel much like playing golf, but he could not stand to be in the house a moment longer; golf was the best excuse for a long absence. He would spend four or five hours away, and come back and see if she had seen reason . . . or if she was still using the old needle, needle, needle. And if she was, then she was asking for what she knew she was going to get.

Once at the club, parked out in front of the long white columned building, Les had felt sweaty and dispirited. His forehead and hands paradoxically felt damply cold. He had decided that he could manage nine holes, if he could find some loser of a partner, so he got out of the car, shouldered his heavy bag, and doggedly marched past the front of the club toward the first tee and the pro shop.

"Hey, Les! You looking for a partner?" Ugly Archie Monaghan was smiling brightly at him from beside a display of golf balls. Archie, a second-rate mick lawyer, proved his point about losers. "Ulick Byrne was going to meet me here, and guess what? I just called his house, and he's down with the flu again. Poor bastard got it twice. I could use a partner, if you want to go around with me."

"Oh, I'll go around with you anytime, Archie," Les said. He smiled at Archie, taking in his red eager face, the yellow knit shirt bulging out over the watermelon belly, and the red-and-green-plaid pants, and said, "Today I'm really only up for nine holes, though. Just got over the flu myself. What do you say?"

"You'll go around with me anytime, hey," Archie said. "Nine is great with me, sure." And Les took in that this garish fool actually preferred to play only half the course with him.

Les opened the door, Archie shook his head and did a *No,*

you first gesture with his hand, and they hovered like that inside the door for a time until Archie grinned and surrendered and went outside before Les. "How's your wife these days, Les?" Archie asked. "She's such a pretty little lady."

"Patsy's fine." Les did not want to get into a discussion of his wife, especially not with Archie Monaghan, who had spent hours ogling her at a party last year. Archie, Les remembered, liked to talk about other men's wives.

"Patsy McCloud, Patsy *McCloud*," Archie said as he would lovingly pronounce the name of a movie star, and Les was so irritated that after he won the toss and teed up, his wrists were tight and the ball sliced deeply off the fairway.

"Bad luck, chief," Archie said. He rolled his belly up to his tee, flexed his arms, and punched the ball in a straight line more than two hundred yards toward the first green.

By the time they met again on the fifth green, Les had realized that Archie had deliberately thrown him off by saying his wife's name in that way, and he made himself stay loose and calm as he putted to stay three over par. Already he was having a bad day, but there was no need to make it worse. The only consolation was that Archie too was three over par, and likely to stay that way, unless he could make a thirty-foot putt. Archie seemed not to care. "I've been studying this a long time, Les, and I have come to the decision that there are two kinds of women. There's the kind that looks as though she enjoys it, and the kind that looks like they don't even know what it is. You know what I mean? In this town, at least eighty percent of the women are in the second category. They might have three kids, but to look at them they never broke sweat. Nice one." This was for Les, who had made his putt. Archie set his ball in place and waggled his club speculatively. "I was talking to Ulick about this once, and he named eight or nine right off the bat—you'd think the Women's Art League and their tennis game was the most important thing on earth. Lime-green skirts or those real baggy khaki shorts, right? You know the kind I'm talking about? Ultimate prep. Little bit of a drawl in their voice." Archie lined himself up, cocked the club back, and made his shot. The ball obeyed Les's silent prayers and rolled to a stop three feet short of the hole.

"Ho ho. I know, Les, you want to give me this one, but I insist on making the shot." Archie perkily strode up to the ball, paused, and stroked it neatly into the hole. He winked at Les. "You go out on the terrace of the club, you'll see about three hundred of them. Eating their salads and talking about their hairdressers. Is that what they talk about, do you suppose? Or do they talk about the same boring shit that we do?"

"What's your point, Archie?" Les hefted his heavy golf bag: he was sweating, but he felt chilly. His forehead had a block of ice strapped to it.

"My point is this. If the waitresses out there on the terrace are the only ones who look like they enjoy it, I'm glad I married a waitress. I said this to Ulick, see. And he said, Archie, your real theory is that all women are secret waitresses. Guess what? Around Ulick I gotta keep on my toes."

Les turned away toward the next tee. He understood two things, both of which were faintly surprising. Archie Monaghan liked him no more than he did Archie—that crack about "ultimate prep" had not been accidental. And Archie missed Ulick Byrne; Archie wished he were playing with the young lawyer instead of Les. Archie was in his fifties, Les was forty. Surely the two of them, whatever their feelings about each other, had more in common with one another than Archie could ever have with Byrne, who was still under thirty. "I guess Byrne is a sharp guy," he said.

"Sharp? Baby, if he was in a corporation, he'd already be vice-president and they'd be measuring him for the throne. How about we put a little money on the next hole, chief?"

"Hundred a stroke," Les said, but Archie did not wince. He grinned.

By the ninth hole, Les owed Archie three hundred dollars, and was about to go down a hundred more. The yellow shirt and hideous plaid trousers were a long way closer to the green. Down three hundred dollars to Archie Monaghan! Les had assumed that the size of the bet would rattle Archie, and now Archie was a chip shot from the green and he was sweating about three hundred dollars.

Les lined up his shot, pictured it in his mind, waggled the head of his wood beside the ball, and settled himself. He could not stop himself from thinking that if this ball went where he wanted it to go, the size of his debt would go down to two hundred dollars. The minute the head of the club met the ball, he knew that he had checked it: he had muffed the shot.

Then it was only a matter of watching it go wrong. The ball sailed up, looking like the best shot in the world, and kept on sailing; but where it should have soared between the trees, it dropped. Les watched as the treacherous ball fell like a stone into the pocket of trees.

"Wanna borrow my compass?" Archie called back to him.

Les fumed toward the trees, deliberately not looking at his partner. He did not want to see Archie grinning at him. If he could get any backswing, he could still match Archie on this hole: he'd been in those trees before, and they didn't have to hold you back. This was a par four, and if the lie gave him half a chance, he could still make it in four; and there was always the chance that Archie would lean too hard on his chip shot. Les stepped under a branch, and began to look around for his ball. He was breathing a little hard. Sweat dripped into his collar.

Archie was just lining up for his shot, and Les paused to watch him. Archie sighted down his line again, waggled his club and his rump. He brought the club back, then around . . . and hit the ball too hard. Les silently applauded. He knew what was going to happen. "Now make a joke about your fucking compass," Les said to himself.

He saw his ball almost instantly. The little flash of white sat about two feet from the mossy side of the largest oak. He was still in the match. Les moved toward the tree and heard a rustling in the bush on the other side of his ball. A squirrel. Les got around the oak and took a good look toward the green. Archie was standing in the bunker looking a lot less cheerful. Then from behind him Les heard the unmistakable sound of a child weeping. He whirled around and saw nothing. As he turned to face the ball, the sound came again. He turned and heard a scurrying in the bush. "Hey, get on out of there, kid," he said.

The child sobbed quietly.

Les propped his club against the oak and put his hands on his hips. "Everything's okay. Come on out."

The bush was still.

"Come on. I'm trying to play golf here. No one's going to hurt you. Get on out of the bush."

When nothing happened, Les picked up his club again. As if the child in the bush could see him and was afraid of being hit with the club, the bush rustled again—the boy was going deeper into it. It must have been a child of four or five, Les thought: a child any older would be too large to move around like that in the bush.

He could not make his shot with the bush rattling and rustling in that way. Then the quiet weeping started up again. Les put the club on the ground. "Do you want help, sonny?" There was no answer, and Les walked over toward the bush and bent down to peer through the dense leaves. "Come on out and I'll help you."

He heard a tiny voice say, "I'm lost."

"All right, I'll help you," he said a little abruptly, and parted the leaves of the bush with his hands. "How did you get here, anyhow? Did your daddy. . . ?" He took his hands away from the bush. A vise had gripped his head with astounding pressure. For a second his vision had gone black. He straightened up and blinked.

The tiny voice said, "I'm lost. I'm afraid."

"Okay, *okay*," Les said, and bent forward again. His hands went toward the bush. They stopped just short of touching the long pointed green leaves. Somehow a feeling of wrongness emanated from the bush, of the bush harboring a thing that could not come out into the light. Les thought he caught a curling odor of wet mud, of sewage, of stinking weeds.

The child wept again, but Les was afraid to touch the bush. *Wrongness.* There was something *wrong* in there. The ripe acrid odor curled toward him again.

He knew that if he touched the bush, the vise would close again around his head, his eyes would go black. The thing in the bush wept bitterly. Les peered into the leaves and saw only more leaves, leaves rustling against other leaves, leaves touched by sunlight and leaves shining greenly in the dark.

"Your ball lost that bad?" Les whirled around and saw Archie Monaghan's plaid pants and bulging yellow belly.

"I heard something," Les said, straightening up. "My ball's not lost, I heard something. There was a kid in this bush. He was crying."

Archie's eyebrows went up.

"He just stopped," Les said. "I can't see him anywhere in there."

"Let old Archie have a look," Archie said, and bent forward and parted the bush with his hands. Just for a second Les caught that odor of wet mud and sewage. He was aware of the perspiration standing on his forehead: his whole body felt so odd, so light, that he was afraid he would fall down. Archie Monaghan thrust his whole upper body into the bush, and Les was left staring at his wide plaid bottom.

"Well, guess what?" Archie said, pulling himself out of the bush. "Nobody's at home. You sure you heard a kid in there?"

"I heard him crying."

"Did you talk to him?"

"I talked to him. He said he was lost."

"Well, it's damn funny. There's nothing in there now. He must have run away." Archie scratched under his arms and looked vaguely at the trees. His face lightened. "Hey, there's your ball, and not too bad a lie. You can come out of this smelling like a rose."

Les put out of his mind everything having to do with lost children and bushes that could squeeze your head and blind you. He picked up his club from its bed of pine needles, straightened up before the ball, and smacked it home.

And that's how you get to be a vice-president in the corporate jungle, buster.

A little more than two and a half hours later, he was saying, "You might as well let me buy you a drink," to Archie Monaghan. He was feeling a curious mixture of bitterness and relief: relief because he had ended the match only one stroke behind Archie, bitterness because he had not smashed the fat little bog-trotter. He supposed it was the lingering effects of the flu that had spoiled some of his shots; but he still remembered the way that bush in the spot of rough had rustled, and how the child's voice had come from it. Before Archie had jammed his head and shoulders into the bush, Les had wanted to pull him back, yank him to the ground to keep him away from the bush . . . but of course, nothing had happened to Archie. There had been no lost child in the bush.

But he'd had an image . . . something with its jaws locked around Archie's trunk. Yet nothing had happened to Archie; he had put his head and chest in that *wrong* place and seen and felt nothing.

But there had been that smell. Rotting weeds, damp earth, and beneath these not necessarily unpleasant odors, another odor, headier, more biting.

Archie was accepting his offer of a drink and looking at him oddly. "Oh, I'm good for the debt," Les said. "Here, let me give it to you now." Archie started to smile and shake his head, but Les took his money clip out of his pocket and counted out two fifties. "There. Now you can take a trip to Dublin, Archie."

Archie pocketed the bills. "Actually, I just got back from Dublin last week."

Archie Monaghan led the way into the club's lounge. Old bugles and hunting horns shone from the walls, along with prints of red-coated men on horses. Archie bounced along the rows of booths, nodding and saying hello, going toward the bar. Les followed. Archie was now banging his palm against the back of a man on a barstool and laughing at some remark made by the man on his other side. When Les got closer, he recognized the foursome before himself and Archie. They seemed to be part of a group which included one or two executives like Les, a contractor he knew only by sight, and Archie's partner, Tom Flynn. Flynn was huge and jowly, about Les's age, and wore a madras jacket the size of an elephant's blanket. "You guys all know Les McCloud, don't you?" Archie asked.

"Nice to meet you, Les," the contractor said, and the others nodded and mumbled some kind of assent.

"I just lost a hundred clams to Monaghan here, let me set up a round," Les said. "The truth is, he played a terrible game. I just played a worse game." He took out his money clip and laid two twenties on the bar. "Hey, barkeep! Give these guys more of the same. And I'll have a martini. On the rocks, twist."

"Bottle of Bud for me," Archie said.

Les swallowed his drink and said, "Arch, what's your favorite pub in Dublin?"

Archie was talking to Tom Flynn and ignored him.

"There was a lost kid out by the ninth green," Les said. "He was hiding in a bush. You ever hear of anything like that before?"

"Les hears voices," Archie said. "The Joan of Arc of Sawtell C.C."

Les grinned hard through the laughter.

An hour and two martinis later, Les debated calling Patsy; the trouble was, he didn't want to leave the group. He was sure they would talk about him the second he left the room. To hell with Patsy, he decided.

He thought of his wife sitting in her little spare room with her book and her television. That was where she would be at this minute. She had probably eaten nothing. She was engrossed in a book or in her diary, and she had forgotten all about him.

Archie's name glinted at him from a plaque of former winners of the club trophy; the air conditioning seemed to freeze his sinuses. He touched his forehead, and it felt like wax. There was another brimming martini before him, and he lifted it and drank. "That kid out there was from another species," he said, and was gratified and surprised to hear laughter. "No kidding. I felt something really strange out there."

Archie whispered something to Flynn, and Flynn's eyes flashed at him.

Then he saw something he could not believe. A man sitting in the corner booth up at the top end of the bar was wearing raw steaks around his neck. The raw meat was a kind of necklace, the way it was spread out against the man's skin. "Hey," Les said (and "Hey," Flynn echoed).

Les stared in fascination at the necklace of raw meat until he saw that it was not a necklace at all. The raw meat was the man's chest and shoulders. His skin had been peeled back in big scallops. Les caught again the odor of wet earth and ripe sewage. The man in the booth was dead—he had been flayed, and now he was dead.

"Guess what?" Archie said. He muttered something, and the other men laughed.

Les stared at the dead man. That was what had happened out by the ninth green. The lost boy had been dead: he was dead, and he had been looking for Les McCloud. He felt the heavy martini glass slip out of his fingers.

When it hit the floor and shattered, all the laughter ceased. Archie and the other men were looking at him; he saw dislike in their eyes, and it was naked. Again he felt light-headed.

"I'm getting out of here," he said. Les kicked the broken glass aside and went toward the door.

6

"Reborn?" Richard asked. "You mean reincarnation? I can't believe in that. You can talk all you want, but you'll never convince me that this Winter person was born as three different men in three different decades, and all in the same town.''

"Not born in that way," Williams said. "I'm not talking about reincarnation in the strict sense—that's more a metaphor for what I mean. When your great-great-granduncle was born, Gideon Winter was nowhere in evidence. The Winterizing, to make a joke at your relative's expense, came later.''

"Well, if you're talking about possession, I'm not sure I believe in that either," Richard said.

"And that's fine with me," the old man said. "I'm not sure I do either. Not unless an entire stretch of seacoast can be possessed. Or can possess. A man named Gideon Winter arrived here roughly three hundred years ago, and various things happened. Bad things. Bad economically, bad in every way. You could use the word 'evil,' but I suppose you'll tell me that you don't believe in evil either.''

"I believe in evil," Richard said, and Patsy surprised them both by saying softly, "I do too.''

"All right," Williams said. He put his baseball cap back on. "Maybe it wasn't the man, but what happened to him here. Maybe it was something the place did to him. This is a fancy theory I have been working on for fifty years or so.''

"You mean since that man. Since Bates Krell," Patsy said.

Williams glanced appreciatively at her.

"Oh, I know about him," Patsy said. "I just didn't know his name until I heard you say it to Tabby. I saw him. I mean I *saw* him.'' She colored. "A long time ago. I saw him kill a woman.''

She colored even more deeply when Graham Williams picked up her hand and carried it to his lips. "Of course you did, and you don't know how good it makes me feel to hear you say so.''

"Shouldn't we talk about what it says in here?" Patsy said, touching the big blue library book. "About Winter?''

"Sure," Williams said. "If you like. You know what this is, though. Mrs. Bach was not a professional historian. She just assembled records. She didn't try to draw any conclusions from them. Her *History* is a sourcebook, but no more than a sourcebook.''

"Well, I thought it was kind of inconclusive," Patsy said.

Williams stood up and wandered off to a distant bookshelf; he returned with his own copy of the book. "Sure it's inconclusive." He dropped the book on the coffee table, then sat and picked it up and opened it in his lap. "Dorothy Bach expected other people to make the conclusions—all she wanted to do was gather as much data as she could. She just put together raw data." He flipped through the early pages of the fat blue book. "So you see what she was able to find. Land records. Stock transfers. Births and deaths, from the parish records on Clapboard Hill. Which got its name from the way of calling worshipers to service—they clapped two small boards together. Let's take a look at what she has for the year 1645."

"Gideon Winter's arrival," Patsy said. "Here it is. 'A landowner named Gidyon or Gideon Winter of Sussex purchased 8.5 acres of seacoast land from farmers Williams and Smyth.' And that's all it says about him on that page—until she says that his name did not appear in the parish records."

"Dorothy Bach was an old woman when I started to look into this," Williams said. "But I felt I had a compelling reason to bother her. I'd been brooding about Krell for two or three years."

"Hold on a second," Richard asked. "What *is* all this stuff about somebody named Krell? I keep hearing the name, but I don't know anything about him. Patsy, you say he killed someone? And you saw him do it?"

"Not really *saw,*" Patsy said. "I saw it with my mind once. I knew it was something from a long time ago. It was on the river, and the new buildings weren't there. There were more fishing boats. I saw him strangle a woman to death—or until she was unconscious, anyhow—and then wrap her in an oilcloth and drop her overboard."

"And you know that this was Krell."

"She knows," Williams said. "And I know—in part, *I* know because *she* knows so well. But what you don't know, Richard, is that I killed Bates Krell. I had to kill him. And doing it soured my life. It soured my life even though I always knew that he'd have killed me if I hadn't got him first—I even tried to turn myself in to Joey Kletzka, the chief of police here, but he wouldn't listen to me—it was like he knew more about it than I did . . . aaah. I'm getting worked up about this." He smiled at Richard. "You know, I can feel my heart pounding."

"I don't think I understand any of this," Richard said.

"Join the crowd. That's how I felt when I went to see old

Dorothy Bach. I say old, but she must have been six or seven years younger than I am now. She had given up on history by then, and spent all of her time in her garden. Oh, she gave talks to the ladies' groups now and then, because that was how she got started doing her research, but when she got too old to lift a parish record book she gave herself to her azaleas. She lived up at the top of Mount Avenue, right on the Hillhaven border. I'd looked into enough Hampstead history to know the right questions to ask her, so after she showed me into her drawing room—you see how long ago this was, people still had drawing rooms—I thanked her for agreeing to see me, and then I got right to it. I asked her if she had had more information about Gideon Winter than she had put in her book.''

He looked at Richard, then at Patsy. He had an eagle's face, Patsy thought, an old, old eagle's face. She had never been so conscious of Williams' age before, and she thought that she was so struck by it now because at this minute his eyes looked young.

Williams' mouth twitched. "She thought I was accusing her of doctoring the facts. I think she damn near threw me out of the house—Dorothy Bach was proud of that history book, a lot prouder than she'd ever be of her azaleas. 'Are you asking me if I suppressed information about one of the founders of Greenbank?' she asked me. I assured her that I knew she would never do anything of the sort, and that present and future historians of the area would forever be in her debt— she wanted to hear guff like that, but on the other hand it was true, and she deserved to hear it. 'I guess,' I told her, 'I'd be grateful if you could be more speculative than you could be in your book.' 'You want me to speculate about Gideon Winter, Mr. Williams? You want to know what I thought of the Dragon as I was doing my researches?' ''

7

"Yes, I would like to know just that," the young Graham Williams had said to the ancient lady on the brocade sofa. Her dress was at least ten years out-of-date, with its high black neck that came to just beneath her chin and its ruffled sleeves. Her face, as she set down her teacup without even glancing at it, was wrinkled, clever, considering. She had pushed her lips slightly forward, and the line at the top of the upper lip looked as sharp as a knife blade.

"What makes you think that I speculated at all about him?"

"Because of his mystery," Williams replied. "He came out of nowhere, he soon owned most of the land, catastrophe followed him, and he vanished. You don't name him in your compilation of burial records, so he wasn't buried. Not here, anyhow. I think you must have turned him over in your mind once or twice."

"Everything you have just said is in error, young man." The upper lip still jutted forward. "He came from the county of Sussex in England. Because the other farmers agreed to sell him no more land after a certain point—at least that was my conclusion, for they could certainly have used the money—he never owned more than just about half the land in Greenbank. And he was most certainly buried in Greenbank. But he was not buried in the church cemetery. No. When they buried the Dragon, they buried him on a beach."

"Gravesend Beach," Williams had said softly.

She shook her head. "Now you are the one who is speculating. No, not there. The name derives, I am almost certain, from the practice of burying anonymous shipwreck victims up the hill from the Sound at that point. Gideon Winter, and again I must say that I am *almost* certain, was laid to rest on the long spit of land that juts out into the Sound about a mile and a half west of the public beach. It was briefly called Point Winter. Since 1760 it has been known as Kendall Point. And it was where, as you may know . . ."

"Where General Tryon's troops landed to burn Patchin and Greenbank."

Her mouth relaxed. "So you know a little of local history, do you? Do you know what else happened at Kendall Point?"

He shook his head.

"It was once the most famous disaster in the state of Connecticut. And it still would be, if our memories were longer than they are. The entire congregation of the Greenbank Congregational Church attended a church social on Kendall Point in August of 1811. It was a beautiful spot, and considerably breezier than the church grounds, so on a hot August day it was much more comfortable. They could take their food and tables down to the Point on wagons, and only have to carry the tables the last thirty feet, at the end of the wagon track.

And once they were on the Point, they could see the traffic on
the Sound from both directions. Sailboats, merchant boats I
mean, steamers, even pleasure craft from Long Island and
down from New Haven—the Sound was even busier in those
days. Not to mention the fishboats.''

She was staring at him with pale eyes in which a hidden
joke lay sparkling. She picked up her teacup again, and Williams saw that her fingernails were black. He had blinked in
disbelief: in 1929, ladies, especially old ladies who were distinguished amateur historians living on the Golden Mile, did
not have dirty fingernails. Then the young Graham Williams
had remembered the azalea bushes crowding the side of the
house, and realized that Mrs. Bach did her own gardening.
But even so . . . wouldn't she have cleaned her nails before
greeting company? He glanced again at her blackened nails—
this time he saw brown earth smudges on her hands, and he
felt slightly sickened.

"Oh, they were going to have a beautiful time, a *beautiful*
time,'' Mrs. Bach had said. "Tables filled with roast pork
and homemade sausages, currant bread, potato salad, blood
pudding, preserves . . . it's in all the documents. They were
going to feast. The minister, Reverend Greenough, played the
violin, and after they had said their prayers and the children
had run off some of their nervous energy, the reverend intended to play some hymns for his flock. After the enormous
meal, there would be an hour or so of jollier music. Jigs.
There would have been many a man in that congregation who
could call a jig out of a fiddle or a banjo.'' Mrs. Bach knitted
her smudged hands together. "But there was no feast and
there were no hymns and there were no jigs. Instead, it
happened.''

"It?'' He thought. "Some sickness?''

"If you like—a fever, if you like. But it was Kendall Point
that was fevered. As they sat on either side of their three long
covered tables, the land split open underneath them. Great
fissures opened first on the inland side of the Point, and then
split seaward quick as you could wink. The first table fell in,
and the Reverend Greenough must have seen it. He was
standing up at the head of all three tables, saying a prayer.
The entire congregation was looking in his direction. Then
the land opened up and swallowed the most inland table before the people sitting around it could scream. You can't tell
me Reverend Greenough didn't see *that*. And if his responses

had been quicker, he could have saved himself and all the rest of them.

"But the Reverend Greenough did nothing, and the Reverend Greenough said nothing. The opening hole took the second table. And now there was plenty of screaming. The crew of a merchant vessel called the *Pequot* saw the second table go down and heard the screams. They anchored and sent a dory with eight sailors toward the Point. Well, of course, the people at the third table had scattered, and they too were screaming. The reverend had come out of his trance, and his voice was loudest among them. The sailors heard him invoking the name of the Almighty as he ran toward the water. On both sides of him, men and women were running in all directions . . . but they did not get far. Off the central fissure, smaller fissures opened up and took the people from the third table, took them one by one. And the last split in the earth took Reverend Greenough. They were all gone by the time the dory landed on the Point." Mrs. Bach nodded almost happily at the young Williams.

He had said, "You mean it was like the land had chased them? Hunted them down, one by one? Did they get out of the fissures?" But he had already known the answer to that.

"The sailors came up on the Point," Mrs. Bach said. "The sounds of the screaming hurt their ears. That's what the captain of the *Pequot* wrote in his log. *My men this day have had their ears punished by the screams of the Kendall Point dying.* They could see that wide crack in the earth, beginning thirty or forty feet back where the carts stood, dividing all of Kendall Point like the trunk of a tree from which the smaller fissures at the top branched off—zigging and zagging through the earth. And everywhere in this maze of fissures, people were trapped. The tables were upended, the food steamed all around them, they struggled to get free, but they could not." Mrs. Bach's eyes glinted. "And the sailors could not pull them free. And do you know why, young man?"

"Because the earth. . . ?"

"Yes. Because the earth was already closing on them again. Like a mouth when it is full of food. One of the *Pequot*'s sailors lost an arm and bled to death when he did not get away quickly enough. The stones sawed through his flesh and gristle, and took off his arm at the shoulder. The rest of them wept and prayed—they could see the faces of the adults, looking up in horror, and see the tops of the children's heads. It was as though the earth itself was screeching for help. For the screeches continued after the earth had closed itself up again. One of the reports I read held that the screams from beneath the surface of the earth continued all the rest of that day, but I suspect some old-fashioned fantastification there. I don't think the screams could have lasted so long, do you?''

"No. I don't think they could have."

"Thirty-six adults and fourteen children," the old woman said. "That's what else happened at Kendall Point."

"What year did you say that was in?"

For the first time, the old woman looked at him with real interest. "Eighteen-eleven."

"Eighteen-eleven. Thirty, thirty-five years after the burning of Patchin."

She was nodding vigorously. "Thirty-two years. You've seen the pattern, then, have you?"

"I hadn't gotten around to thinking of it as a pattern," Graham had said. "But of course I remembered Prince Green, and then about five years ago those four women disappeared . . ." He was deliberately keeping his face and his voice still, remembering Bates Krell and what had jumped out at him from clear across the Nowhatan River.

"Disappeared," the old woman snorted. "I don't suppose you ever heard of Sarah Allen and Thomas Moorman? Two children?"

Williams had shaken his head.

"They were skinned and roasted—in a pit in the ground, sonny. A half-wit Tayler did it, and they caught him in one of the Jenningses' fields and strung him up as soon as Judge Barr could get there. The Taylers are prone to go like that now and then; half-wit, I mean. And judging from the records, some of them are inclined to go another way too. But that poor half-witted Tayler killed those children in 1841. Exactly thirty years after the tragedy on Kendall Point."

"None of this is in your book," Williams protested.

"The death records are," she said.

He smiled. "You refused to speculate."

"That is correct. But didn't you come here to ask me about Gideon Winter? The man they secretly buried on the spit of land they named after him? Didn't you want to know what I thought of him as I was doing my research?" Her eyes shone vehemently out at him. "I'll tell you what I thought about him, young man. I thought that he would have gone far in this country if a handful of ignorant farmers hadn't stopped him. Oh, he took them, he took them all right, and that's why they called him the Dragon, he was smarter and stronger than they, and their women liked him—imagine this, young Williams, you're a hardscrabble farmwife with homespun clothes and the stink of pigs and tallow in your nostrils and up comes a fine gentleman from Sussex, clothed by a tailor and rich as a king, with a smile bright as the sun and a voice soft as velvet. Wouldn't this fine young man dazzle you?"

She was waiting, so he answered. "I suppose. Yes."

"You suppose. Well, think about this. In 1650 nearly all of the children were dead. But in 1651 there was a whole new crop of conceptions, because the parish records show a new crop of baptisms in 1652. There was a boy named 'Darkness' and a girl baptized 'Eventide.' Another girl was baptized 'Sorrow.' I think they would have baptized each of those children *Shame* if they could. I'm just *speculating,* mind you, but wouldn't you imagine that those children looked a bit alike?"

"So you think they killed him."

"Don't you?" she asked. "And don't you think he killed the first generation of children, or as many of them as he could?" She was cocking her head, and he could see a broad gray line of dirt at the side of her neck. "Remember, children were primarily economic power in those times—they weren't as sentimental as we."

"I think I can see how you feel about him," Williams said.

"Oh, women all love a dragon, Mr. Williams. I'm sure those four women who disappeared from town five years ago found a dragon to love."

He knew she was crazy then; he had only one more question to ask. "Something must have happened in 1870—in the early 1870's."

"Something did; of course something happened, you fool. Didn't I say there was a pattern? Look in my book! All the data are there." And then for an instant Graham Williams was like Royce Griffen on the patio of a splendid Mount Avenue home fifty-one years in the future: he thought he caught an evil smell when Mrs. Bach leaned forward and spilled her tea over her table and dampened the unfolded copy of the *Hampstead Gazette* lying there, he thought he saw something crawling down the walls . . . but it was only the convoluted pattern of the wallpaper. He pulled his handkerchief from his pocket and helped her mop up the tea.

8

"Anyhow, I was right about a couple of things," Graham said to Richard and Patsy. "Dorothy Bach was crazy, all right. She had fallen in love with the figure she thought she saw way back there in the past, and so she hid the facts about his behavior that most reveal it. She didn't suppress anything, she just *hid* it—behind her objectivity."

Patsy flipped the pages of *History of Patchin*. Suddenly she was tired. She thought of the story Mr. Williams had just told, of the sailors staring down in horror at the faces of those caught in the earth. . . .

History of Patchin shook in her hand. Graham Williams was saying, "One thing she let through her net is that Winter never attended the church services on Clapboard Hill—and imagine how that must have seemed to the others, who would have gone if they'd had to swim halfway across the Sound." Richard Allbee was drumming his fingers on his knee and looking puzzled, and the book by that crazy old woman Graham had met in 1929 trembled in Patsy's hand like a trapped sparrow. A second later it trembled even more violently.

Patsy dropped the book on the coffee table, gasping. The blue cover flew open and banged itself against the wood.

9

Gary Starbuck said, "I mean, I thought Key West was bad, but I sort of expected weirdness in Key West. Place is full of queers and transies, guys who think about two things only, dope and sex, and around here I thought I'd get your basic Norman Rockwell situation. But to tell you the truth, I think people are even screwier here than they are in Key West. And not just because they're richer. Their heads are fucked. They act like the real rules of life don't apply to them."

The Normans were rigid with attention, taking all this in as if it were Scripture, and Tabby was remembering Key West and skinny Poche sitting on the toilet seat with a needle drooping from the crook of his elbow. Poche had been wearing a ratty off-the-shoulder orange dress and high heels at the time. Poche had looked at him dreamily, his mascaraed lids just clearing his pupils, and said, "Beautiful eyes. Beautiful eyes." That was Poche-code for *Now I'm fine, man, now I'm as mellow as a monkey up a tree*. The real rules of life had applied to Poche, all right. A couple of months after Sherri had kicked him out of Clark's life, Poche had turned up dead in a cell in the sheriff's jail. The doctor certified that Poche had died of natural causes (overlooking various broken bones and bruises), and Tabby had wondered if Poche had been wearing his orange dress when he died.

Bruce Norman yelled, "Hey, what the fuck?"

Tabby's heart pounded. He pictured a police car turning on its siren, flashing its light bar, swinging in ahead of them. . . . Dicky too must have been nervous, for he shouted, *"What? What?"* Starbuck savagely cramped the wheel, and Tabby and Dicky pitched sideways in the rear of the van. Tabby grabbed the back of Bruce's seat and pulled himself forward so he could look out the windows. There was no police car ordering them to the side of the road. Tabby could see nothing but the black road, the headlights of the van streaming out, and a thick hedge on the side of the road. "Goddammit," Starbuck said, and twisted the wheel far to the left, swinging the van across the road.

Bruce was laughing.

"Shut the fuck up," Starbuck ordered; as he spoke, something thudded against the van.

"I never saw anything like it," Bruce said as Starbuck braked, shifted into the parking gear, and jumped out of the van. "I swear."

"What happened?" Dicky and Tabby asked together.

"A dog, a fucking dog," Bruce said. "It jumped right over the hedge and ran right into us. He tried to miss it, but . . ." Bruce stopped chuckling as Starbuck screamed *"Jesus Christ!"* from down on the side of the van.

Starbuck's face popped up in the side window. A thick vein stood out on his forehead; his deep eyes were now as flat and hard as a pair of black stones. He wrenched open the door and hurled himself into the seat. Then he clenched the wheel and straightened his arms. He looked as though the top of his head were going to lift off in a plume of smoke. "Did you see that?'' he said to no one in particular. "Can you believe that? That fucking mutt committed suicide! He ran into me deliberately!'' He rocked back and forth stiff-armed. ''And the son of a bitch dented my fender, God damn his mangy hide.'' Bruce was still restraining his desire to laugh out loud, and Starbuck nailed him to his seat with a glare. ''You two animals stink, you know that? You been stinking up my van since you got in. The way you fuckers reek is gonna wake the old fart up, I swear.'' Still fuming, Starbuck threw the van into gear and sped down Greenbank Avenue. Now and then he shook his head and muttered unintelligibly.

Almost as soon as they had passed the access road to Gravesend Beach, Starbuck twisted the wheel savagely and spun the van into an asphalt driveway between two pillars. In the back, Tabby and Dicky went sprawling. Starbuck cramped the wheel again and shot the van into a dark place beside a high thick wall of vegetation. He cut the lights, and for a moment they sat in darkness. Tabby was aware of the sour smell of Dicky Norman's exhalations. Then Starbuck flicked on a pocket flashlight and held it high up against his chest, making his face shadowy but visible.

''You. Kid. I hope you know how to drive this fucking van.''

He was still in a savage mood, and Tabby had sense enough to stretch the truth. ''I guess I do.''

''Okay. Remember, use the radio if you see anybody come in. Or if you see any lights go on. If a cop comes in and sees the van, you lie down on the floor and get us out right away. When I call you, you drive the van up to the entrance so we can load the stuff in. Got it?''

Tabby nodded.

Starbuck shook his head. ''I oughta have my head examined.''

Tabby watched Starbuck lead the Norman twins up toward the huge white house. A floodlight angling down from under the rain gutter dwarfed their bodies by pushing long shadows out behind them. They were fifty feet from the van, and still had a long way to go. *The radio!* Tabby suddenly remembered. He fumbled for it on the dark floor of the back of the van, found it jammed between a wheel cover and a metal wall, and switched it on. Gary Starbuck was just disappearing around a Japanese maple.

Tabby heard him breathing. Then beneath the breathing noises he heard their feet moving across the grass.

He looked anxiously toward the steering column and the gearshift, hoping that he would be able to figure out the van when Starbuck called for him. Clark had let him drive the red Mercedes once, but it had an automatic shift. Then there was a quick flashing illumination outside the windows, and Tabby stopped breathing. But it had been the sky, not the police.

"Didz whaz suppuf?" came Dicky Norman's voice over the radio.

"Shut the fuck up," Starbuck replied very clearly.

The sky flickered again: it was as if the veins and arteries in a body were suddenly illuminated.

Starbuck was now kneeling before the front door, and Tabby saw him look up. In the next instant the sky was black again, illuminated only around a cruising moon. Starbuck had been carrying a small satchel like a doctor's bag, and from it he took a tool which looked to Tabby like a slightly fatter bicycle pump. A rod extended from the tubular object. When Starbuck turned it on, a high-pitched electronic whine came to Tabby over the radio. As Starbuck inserted the rod into the lock, the whine changed pitch, became louder and more intense.

In less than a minute, Starbuck pulled the whole inner workings of the lock away from the door. "That's it," his voice said over the radio. "I don't want you assholes to make a single sound when we're inside. You just listen to me." Starbuck rose to his feet and quietly put his machine back in the pack. He pulled at the gutted doorknob, and the door swung open. Then he led the twins inside and closed the door after them.

Tabby thought of the dog deliberately diving at the van: he felt dizzy and light-headed.

"Kitchen," Starbuck's voice whispered over the two-way radio.

Then Tabby realized that he was all alone in the van. Starbuck and the Normans were already deep inside the house: they had forgotten him. He could open the door. He could climb out of the van and go home! They would never know until the job was done.

He hesitantly touched the door handle. From the radio came sounds of drawers opening. "Oh boy," he heard Starbuck sigh. The thief sounded happier than he had been all night. *If I even think you'll talk about this with the cops, I'll come back here and kill you.* What would Starbuck, who had said those words to him, think if he returned to an empty van? *I'm a businessman, see? I gotta stay in business.* Tabby took his fingers from the door handle. His head hurt. He craned his neck forward and stared toward the big white house.

<h1 style="text-align:center">10</h1>

Les McCloud sat in his car, staring at the front of the country club—it looked very much like the structure Tabby would be anxiously studying through a van window four hours later. Les wanted another drink: above all, he wanted to forget what he thought he had seen sitting in the end booth. His hands were trembling. From the outside, the Sawtell Country Club gave no signs that right beyond those big lounge windows there might be sitting a horror, a dead man with the skin peeled right back off his shoulder blades like an anatomy lesson.

But that was crazy. The whole thing was crazy. He'd been spooked, that was all, by the boy's voice coming out of that bush . . . by that feeling of pure and utter *wrongness*. Les swallowed. He turned his ignition key and then punched on the Sony digital radio that had been one of his last birthday presents to himself.

He wanted another drink. Where was he going to go?

The disc jockey said, "That was a request, friends. Johnnie Ray singing 'The Little White Cloud That Cried.' You've got to admit—"

Johnnie Ray. *Johnnie Ray.*

"—that he put a lot of emotion into that number. Now let's get back to our more usual material and—"

That was the voice from the bush. Not the singer Johnnie Ray, but a little boy who had showed up in the middle school on the first day of school in 1951, an undersized kid with protruding front teeth and blond hair so flat and lifeless it looked dead. His clothes were all wrong. All the boys in the seventh grade that year were wearing chino pants, plaid shirts, and brown tie oxfords that would have looked more at home on a British lord in knickerbockers. When the boy named Johnnie Ray showed up in Miss Larson's class, he was wearing a sweatshirt, boots, and blue jeans so new they hardly creased. Then they heard his name.

"—give a listen to Miss Ella Fitzgerald and Tommy Flanagan and his trio. 'How High the Moon.'"

The poor kid hadn't known what hit him. Suddenly the whole class had been laughing at him, laughing in that particularly jeering way that meant the whole class, all thirty-one of them, had found their scapegoat.

Les shook his head and backed his car out of the space to turn it toward the long drive and Sawtell Road. Johnnie Ray's voice. Even after the poor little shit had finally persuaded his parents that he needed a different wardrobe—they were from Texas, and Hampstead was the first northern place they had ever lived in—even after he made his parents take him to Sprigg & Son where the right chinos and shoes could be found, he couldn't do anything about his voice.

Les turned unseeingly out into Sawtell Road. Ella Fitzgerald was scatting crazily, pushing at an already relentless rhythm, but he barely heard it. The oncoming car he nearly struck honked angrily at him, and Les gave a distracted, half-hearted wave.

Johnnie Ray's Texas voice. A little husky, a lot slower than a Hampstead voice, dragging at the syllables. Not *I'm lost* so much as *Ahm loo-wust*. It had been the voice of that strange little Texas kid with the comic name. But that pathetic little kid from Texas had drowned the summer before they all went into the eighth grade. He had gone out with a boat from the sailing school—pathetically, he was trying to learn how to sail—and the sailboat had come back without him: tipped over, its mast shining under the water and the sail dragging like a shroud. August 1952. Hampstead police and the Coast Guard had dragged for Johnnie Ray's body and turned up only tree stumps and hubcaps and a splintered, rotting dory that had been sitting on the bottom for a year and a half. Two weeks later, the boy's body had rolled up on the beach at Sawtell Country Club at high tide, bloated and hairless and missing all its fingers and its nose and all but two toes. The fish had dined well on Johnnie Ray.

But his voice had spoken to Les from the bush.

Les screechingly stopped the Mazda as soon as he saw the red light at the Greenbank Road corner, and wound up jutting six or seven feet out into the intersection. He did not even think to back up.

August of 1952 had been a bad month for Sawtell Country Club. Four days after the Mexican ambassador to the United Nations, a guest at the club while he visited friends in Hampstead, found the body of the almost unrecognizable Johnnie Ray on the beach at seven in the morning, the respected lawyer John Sayre chose the same three square feet of beach as the arena for his suicide.

The light changed, and Les turned into Greenbank Road, unconsciously making the decision to go to Franco's.

He was driving fast on the final stretch of Greenbank Road before it crosses the tall iron bridge over the Nowhatan and ends at Riverfront Avenue. The dog which took off from under a porch, a black-and-white dog with a feathery tail and an almost girlish smile on its muzzle, did not penetrate Les McCloud's attention until it was nearly beside his window. He was aware only of a flash of color, of something moving quickly at his side, and he snapped his head over to see. The dog was smiling at him as it threw itself forward. Les slammed his foot down on the brake. His tires squealed and the Mazda's back end swung out, but not before Les had felt his rear tires thunk into something that gave them only a moment's resistance. *"Holy shit!"* Les yelled. He stopped the car on the shoulder of the road. He felt as though two conflicting orders of reality had just violently intersected: as though he had seen little Johnnie Ray's face on the grinning dog. Shaking, he got out of the car.

The crushed dog lay in the middle of the street. Blood moved slowly toward a drain. Les was grateful that the dog's back was facing him: he did not want to see that eerie smile on a dead animal. He wondered what in the world he was supposed to do now, and put his hands in his pockets and looked aimlessly around.

A tall man in well-faded jeans and a blue button-down shirt was striding toward him across a lawn. Behind him steamed a boy with the man's face in miniature, and a woman in tennis whites.

"Your dog, I guess," Les said when the man hit the sidewalk. As the man drew closer, Les had felt relieved; this was a being like himself. His face, though young, was smoothed out by the exercise of power; his shirt and his hair were crisp.

He all but had a sign pinned to his chest: HARVARD MBA, SIX FIGURES A YEAR, FUTURE CEO.

"You guess," the man said, and strode up until he was only a foot from Les. "And I guess you're the maniac who killed him."

"Wait a second," Les said. This was not going the right way. "You don't know what happened." The man's eyebrows knitted together. "Let me explain."

"Like hell I don't know what happened," the man said. "We were eating dinner in the dining room, and from there we get an excellent view of the road. You came along at twenty miles over the speed limit and killed my dog. I'm just damn lucky that wasn't my *kid* out there."

The boy standing next to the man opened his mouth and yelled, *"You killed Tapioca!"*

"I'm sure we can be reasonable about this," Les said. "If you asked your son to go inside for a moment, we could discuss—"

"Discuss? You think there's something to discuss?" the man said in a loud voice. "I *saw* it. You came barrel-assing down that road like there was no tomorrow."

"That dog ran straight into me! And when I finally did see him, he was jumping at my car."

"Jumping at your car," the man said. "Putting himself under your wheels."

"That's right. He jumped right at me."

"You're a liar. Or you're crazy. Either way, you ought to be talking to the police."

"Now, listen," Les said. "Your dog ran into *me.*"

"Because you were speeding."

"You killed Tapioca!" the boy suddenly screamed.

As Les and the man argued, the boy had stepped off to the side—obviously hoping that his father would deck this character—and now he suddenly dashed in toward Les and hit him soundly in the kidneys.

"You murdered my dog!" he yelled up at Les's face.

"God damn!" Les exploded. He stepped away from the kid before he belted him. "Look, you," he shouted at the man in the blue button-down shirt and exquisitely faded jeans. "I am a corporation vice-president! I don't have to stand around and take this shit anymore!" He took his money clip from his pocket. It was sadly depleted. He had one ten and two twenties folded together.

"What do you think you're doing?" the man asked.

Les took the folded twenties from the clip. He held out the forty dollars; when the man only stared at the money, Les dropped the two bills and he and the man watched them flutter down to the roadside grass.

"I don't believe you," the man said. "Forget that the dog cost about four times that. I just don't believe you. Get *away* from him, Van." The boy had been circling in for another assault on Les's kidneys.

"Sue me," Les said. His rage had evaporated from the front portion of his brain: for the first time in his life, Les experienced his own brain as a thing of layers and segments. The front upper part of his brain was floating in a crystalline calm; his anger still boiled, but it boiled down beneath this floating icy peace. He began to walk toward his car.

Les opened the door of his car and drove toward the bridge. When he looked in his rearview mirror he saw the man and his son standing in the middle of Greenbank Road, staring at him. The boy was waving his fist.

That cheered him up so much he was halfway across Riverfront Avenue and going straight toward the parking lot of Piggy Bindle's All-Beef Restaurant before he remembered that he had to turn left.

By the time he found a parking spot on Station Row and had swung in next to the curb, the entire top of his head felt frozen by some kind of tranquilizer. Up there, thoughts floated in an icy realm to which Les could retreat at any time he wished.

Beneath this icy paradise, his rage still burned. If Patsy were a normal wife, he would never have heard the pathetic voice coming from the bush, never have killed that wretched dog. The noises and the smells of a hundred and fifty people jammed into a small bar and grill jumped at him the instant he pushed open the door. It was just before sundown on a Saturday night in summer, and Franco's was the busiest place in Hampstead.

As soon as he got inside, some tall dude with blow-dried hair and a rugby shirt stepped backward and almost crushed Les's foot with his Dingos, but Les put his hands on the hips of the dude's designer jeans and pivoted him sideways. The dude spun around to glare, his beer glass slopping over onto the Dingos, but when he looked at Les's face he just nodded. Les pushed his way up toward the bar.

He floated up into the cold indifferent realm at the top of his head and grabbed the single empty stool at the bar before some clone of Bobo Farnsworth got it. "Double Glenlivet," he shouted in the direction of the bartender; when the curly-haired, mustached bartender cocked his head at him, Les shouted it again. "Double Glenlivet!"

"You got it," the barkeep said. "No need to shout."

"Hey librarian, listen to this," Les said when the bartender set down his drink. "You an animal lover? Well, you'll get a kick out of this. On my way over here, a dog ran into me. You get that? He ran into me. I didn't even see the little bugger until he was diving straight at me. I tried to turn away from him, but I didn't have time. Son-of-a-bitch mutt committed suicide."

"I heard of that," the bartender said, and turned away.

"You heard of that? What do you mean, you heard of that? I never heard of that."

"Never heard of lemmings?" The question was from a funny-looking dork one place away at the bar. The dork was definitely not one of the Bobo clones. His glasses were thick and smudgy; his thin hair did not curl, but frizzed. Deep lines crossed his thin forehead. "I've been sitting here thinking about the lemmings. Because of something that happened to me today—a lot like your story." The dork smiled ingratiatingly, and Les shrugged. He was way up inside the icehouse now, and even a pushy dork couldn't upset him.

"We got this cat," the dork said. "We call her McIntosh. She's a Persian, you know? *Beautiful* long silky hair. We've had her ten years—from even before we moved up here from the city. I loved that freaky cat. Well, today my wife was looking out one of the windows on the third floor and she saw McIntosh running across the lawn. She thought the old rascal was going to nail a bird—she's old, but she can still move when she wants. McIntosh used to get a couple of birds a week, and she'd leave the bloody corpses right on the doorstep where we'd see them first thing when we went out to get the paper."

The dork swallowed. "But that son of . . . that damned animal wasn't going after any bird. She was running toward the kids' wading pool. My wife saw McIntosh run straight up to the pool and dive in—*dive in!* A cat! McIntosh went right over the side of the wading pool and splashed into the water. My wife just stood there for a second, you know? She couldn't believe her eyes. She kept waiting for McIntosh to try to get out of the pool. But McIntosh didn't even try to get out. Her head never even came out of the water. She hit that pool like she meant business, man.'' He blinked behind the smudgy lenses. ''That's why I was sitting here thinking about lemmings.''

Les did his best to look clearly at the man who had told him this story. He saw that the man wanted him to say something to him, to speak more about the suicidal dog, to join him in the companionship of feeling beings, to talk about lemmings and what would lead an animal to suicide. He saw that at the most primitive level, the man with the thinning frizzy hair and the smudgy glasses wanted consolation: the consolations of alcohol and bar philosophy, perhaps, but more than that the consolation of emotions exchanged and understood. Les leaned forward, smiled, and said, ''Get stuffed.''

The dork recoiled. He spun rapidly forward on his stool and pointed his reddening face into his drink.

Les felt infinitely improved: his face did not move, but up at the top of his mind a smile cracked across his frozen paradise. Up there he felt almost warm.

He looked at his watch, and was pleasantly surprised. Somehow it had gotten to be nine-thirty at night. ''Get me another Glenlivet,'' he called out to the bartender. The short glass filled with ice cubes and dark fragrant liquid was set down on the oiled wood before him. He lifted it and took a sip of the malt whiskey. As he was appreciating its velvety smoothness, however, an uncomfortable thought penetrated his defenses. If he was such a success, why did he get such pleasure from telling a dork to get stuffed?

Also, if he was such a great success, what was he doing in a bar at nine-thirty while his wife sat alone at home?

He had the answer to that one. ''Stuff Patsy too,'' he muttered to himself, and put away half of the second Glenlivet.

But now some of that whiskey and the gin which had preceded it was clamoring to get out, and Les slid off his stool and pushed his way around the side of the bar and down the corridor past the telephone where a blond was necking with a beefy guy at the same time as she talked on the telephone. "I *know* the pot roast is in the oven," he heard her say. The pot roast in the oven and the boyfriend's hand on her tits.

He climbed back up into the cold region of peace, because his mind had just given him a picture of ridiculously named Johnnie Ray, his skin all blue and puffed out like the casing on a sausage, weeds caught in his hair, dark lines of damp sand trailing over the swollen chest, sitting in the last booth of the country-club lounge.

The entrance to the men's room was a few feet down the corridor past the telephone. One of the Bobo-clones was standing before the single urinal, and Les squeezed past him and pushed at the door of the stall. It was locked. Les shoved his hands in his pockets and looked at the floor, which was awash in piss. The small white tiles still bore muddy mop-stains from the morning, but they had been overprinted with the dirty ridged patterns of boot soles. The man at the urinal sighed and arched his back. Still spraying, he took a glass of beer from the top of the urinal and gulped. Les watched him with fastidious gloom. He could scarcely bear to breathe. The air seemed a mist of urine and antiseptic.

"You're in the barrel," the younger man at the urinal said, zipping up and stepping toward the door.

Les grunted. He gratefully unzipped, took himself out, and let go.

Whoever was in the toilet stall clunked something against the metal wall. Not metal: not the belt buckle Les had at first thought. Softer. As if the person in there had struck his hand against the side of the enclosure.

Then the hand slammed again at the side of the stall. Les glanced uneasily sideways.

"Help me," whoever was in there said.

Both sides of the stall banged, as if the person in there had thrown his fists out blindly.

"I'm lost," the voice said.

It was the voice of little Johnnie Ray.

Les stopped breathing.

"I'm afraid," the voice said. *Ahm affray-ud.*

Now Les heard fingernails scrabbling on the door of the stall.

He knew that if he looked sideways and down he would be able to see a few inches under the side of the stall. His flow of urine had dried up in the last few seconds, and his penis had shriveled back toward his trousers. If he looked under the side of the stall, he would see worn small sneakers, the cuff of jeans . . . Les pushed his shrunken penis back inside and zipped up.

"Help me," the small Texas voice whispered.

The fingernails slithered across the inside of the door.

Les dared to look down at the space between the wall of the toilet enclosure and the grubby, piss-puddled floor.

A fingerless hand attached to a thin bony wrist was probing up on Les's side of the gray enclosure. The stump of a hand and the bony wrist were encased in wet black mud.

Deeper inside the enclosure Les saw two black stumpy things that must have been feet.

Les's stomach moved upward, getting smaller as it went, so that by the time it climbed into his throat it was the size of one of his golf balls. Now he was conscious of the terrible smell in the toilet, the stink so bad it was like a loud noise, the sound of an explosion.

The mud-blackened thing in the stall fell to its knees.

Les backed toward the door, afraid to turn his face away from the stall. When he felt the aluminum handle strike the band of muscle beside his spine, he whirled around and tore open the door. He jumped through the opening and slammed the door.

His stomach was still tightly gathered in his throat. He thought he could hear a *slap-slap* from the other side of the door, the noise of something soft and damp striking a hard surface. Les's ears were roaring. He plunged past the bar into the thickest part of the crowd and stumbled toward the door. His second Glenlivet sat next to a ten-dollar bill on the bar, but he never noticed them.

11

Graham Williams was leaning forward on his elbows and saying, "Of course what I had to do was find out what had happened in 1873. And believe me, I had to dig for it. Dorothy Bach, who was fixated on what she thought she knew about the Dragon, wasn't going to say anything to me. And nobody else . . ."

The pages of the heavy blue-bound book were riffling, leafing themselves over so rapidly they seemed transparent. She felt herself invaded by a sensation she knew to be alien, but for some reason instantly familiar: as the smell of a specific cologne or perfume could evoke the feelings of a memory without revealing the memory itself.

The pages flew past. "No," Patsy said, and this time the two men looked at her.

Richard Allbee merely looked curious: he looked as if he were just working out that she probably had a headache and was wondering if Williams had any Bufferin in his medicine chest. But the old man looked more than politely concerned. He had opened his mouth and was gazing at her very intently. Neither one of them had noticed the book.

She looked back at the book and saw that the pages had stopped moving. "It . . ." she started to say to Graham Williams, who was boring into her with his eyes. Williams nodded. "It moved," she said. The old man's eyes, she noticed for the first time, were a fine blue. The right eye had a single fleck of gold near the iris. "Moved. In my hand." Then the eyes which were gently pressing her to go on, to say more, to let them know what was happening, were not the old man's anymore—they were Marilyn Foreman's eyes.

And the alien but familiar sensation was from all those years ago; it was the Marilyn-sensation. *This is why I saw her on the street,* Patsy thought. *They were going to take my will away and make me see things again.* She did not know who *they* were; *they* were an alignment of vast universal forces.

One more page flipped over in front of Patsy.

"I saw it happen," Richard said. "It happened." He sounded stunned.

Patsy felt just as she had before she'd had the vision of Bates Krell murdering the woman in the silk dress: a terrible thing was coming, but it was her terrible thing, and she could not stop it from unreeling before her. . . .

Something was moving within the open book. The white pages swirled with black. Black lines, lines where the pages were about to burst into flame, flew randomly over the lines of print. Grayish smoke curled just above them.

A green pointed thing broke through the surface of the page.

The green spike continued to rise. A malevolent black eye four inches across came up after it and immediately fixed on Patsy's eyes.

"What's wrong?" Patsy heard Richard say. She realized

that he could not see the dragon's head emerging from the pages of the book.

The dragon's eye seemed to be made of black stone shot with an iridescent wavering pattern of green. As the snout pushed up out of the book, the eye held her fast.

Then the long wrinkled snout was free, and the dragon swung its head sharply and hungrily toward Patsy. The long mouth opened, the malevolent pupilless eyes held hers.

"Patsy?" she heard Richard ask. "Are you all right?"

You're good, a good man, she thought at a level far too deep for ordinary rational process.

There was the head of a dragon; incredibly, there it was. The hard green spikes on its head were crusty with black and peeling skin. The black eyes were encased in circles of bone. It was a reptilian head, old and strong. Green-black scales lapped away from the eyes and marched down the length of the snout. The crude mouth hung like a gate on a hinge. Patsy's insides had turned to white powder, to something utterly insubstantial and weightless.

With a start, Patsy realized that through the head of the dragon she could still see Graham Williams. Behind the black eyes floated his sunken blue ones—she could even read his concern in them. Patsy watched as the ugly head retreated into invisibility. The air hissed at her ears. Those few feet of air before her had grown as hot as a glowing slab of iron.

12

"Kitchen," Gary Starbuck said.

He was playing his flash around the white entry Royce Griffen had stood in the day before his suicide. Finally the beam of the flash settled on the last door off the long corridor. Starbuck moved the light up and down, and after a momentary hesitation, Dicky and Bruce began to move toward the door.

Dicky pushed the door open, then stepped aside for Starbuck to enter. Nearly invisible in his blue clothes, the thief rapidly swept the flash over the counters. He glided through the dark kitchen and opened two drawers, then another. He flashed the light inside them, but took nothing. Bruce Norman saw him shake his head and begin to look around silently and certainly, shooting the light in different directions. Bruce thought he resembled an animal in a forest, a badger or a mole, sniffing out its way.

Starbuck began to move quickly toward a tall door on the far side of the kitchen. This had no knob or handle, and swung freely on its hinges. The three of them crowded into the tiny chamber on the other side of the door. Immediately opposite them was another swinging door—to the dining room, as Starbuck knew.

He played the light over the tall cabinet door in this narrow room. He chose one randomly, it seemed to Bruce. The flash picked out shelves stocked with bottles. On the shelf beneath were jars of nuts. Starbuck moved on to a lower cabinet.

He shone the light inside, and Bruce saw his shoulders hitch. Quickly Starbuck opened two more of the lower cabinet drawers. "Oh boy," he sighed happily.

Bruce leaned forward to peer into the opened cabinets. Starbuck had taken something from his bag and was pushing it into his hands. This was a green plastic bag—the kind Bobby Fritz used to stuff leaves into when he was clearing a lawn. "Get all of it," Starbuck said. The thief stood up and shone the light down on an array of silver utensils. The display of silver seemed at least six feet long to Bruce. Every piece was slotted into a kind of holster in a long soft cloth. Bruce and Dicky began sliding the silverware out of the felt pockets and dumping it in the bag. "Take out the whole thing," Starbuck hissed, and mimed pulling out the entire length of material. His face wore a furious grimace. Bruce tugged the whole heavy length of material out of the end drawer, and Dicky began folding it up on the pantry floor.

Once the silver was in the plastic bag, Starbuck led them out into the dining room. Here on a sideboard were several ornate silver trays, and these too went into the bag.

From the dining room Starbuck led them into the high-ceilinged living room. As soon as they noticed the wall of windows, the sky shattered: shafts of light ran across the deep blue and zigzagged through the clouds. The light flickered into the living room, and Bruce thought weirdly that he had seen right through his brother's body—that he had seen Dicky's heavy bones, and the individual cells of Dicky's blood sifting in his veins.

The house seemed to shift itself without moving: like an animal's dream of running.

"What?" Dicky said.

"The piano," Starbuck said, and flashed the light down to the far end of the room. But they could all see it anyhow, with the weak moonlight layering in through the window wall. The piano was fifteen feet long, every inch of it handmade and shaped; the body was built up of nearly twenty layers of wood bent and curved under precise degrees of tension; the shine on the surface looked as deep as a pool. It was nearly fifty years old. It was a special-order Bösendorfer grand, and Gary Starbuck had a customer in New York City who had wanted one like it for at least a decade. He would pay Gary twenty thousand dollars for it, which was about a fifth of its real value.

"Can we get that monster in the van?" Bruce whispered.

"Just," Starbuck said. "For now, you two get it out on the patio." He strode across the room and unlocked the windowed doors in the long wall.

Dicky put his hands under the keyboard and experimentally tried to lift the front of the piano. His upper arms bulged; his jaws worked. He managed to pick it up perhaps half an inch.

"For Christ's sake, not that way," Starbuck whispered. "You want to get a hernia? You want to rack yourself up? Get under it. Get your backs under it and lift it with your legs."

Again the house made its mysterious moveless tremor.

"What?" Dicky said.

"Do I have to repeat myself?" Starbuck asked.

His flashlight found the mirror where it stood on the wall among the Impressionist paintings.

Then for a second or less, another oddity occurred in that house, something that really only Dicky Norman would notice, but which would haunt Bruce Norman's mind in the weeks after his brother's awful death. Dicky had said, "What?" again, and sounded so stupid Bruce wanted to brain him, but Bruce had turned like Dicky in the direction of the flash. And he had *almost* seen, or he had *thought* he had seen, that the mirror did not reflect the light, but took it in and swallowed it. The beam of light (this, he thought, was what had made Dicky speak) fell into the ornate mirror like a stone into a well: as if the mirror were sucking the light out of the flashlight, and would take it all, would drain the batteries dry . . . but then there was a bursting dazzle on the mirror's surface, and a beam from within the depths of the mirror came up to meet their own.

13

As soon as Les McCloud had closed the door of the bar behind him, cutting off the rumble and chatter of the patrons and the *bing-bing* of the cash register (which had just rung up no sale on the last bill Les would ever fold into his money clip), he inhaled hugely. His stomach had gradually crept back down to its proper place in his body. The alcohol he had taken during the day now was burning like a lump of charcoal somewhere in his gut. Les gulped more air. He did not want to think about what he had just escaped in the men's room at the back of Franco's, he wanted only to get home . . . but in his mind he saw that stumpy hand come probing from under the partition, and his stomach tightened and shrank again.

He wanted to get home, yes. And if Patsy were in the spare bedroom, he would straighten her out. Come to think of it, no matter where she was, he was going to straighten her out.

Everything came back to Patsy. When he got home he'd back Patsy into a corner of the bedroom and raise a few big purple bruises on her shoulders, then on her sides (and she'd be screeching by then, the big tears would be rolling down her nose), and then he'd pop her one in the gut. . . . Les almost smiled.

He stepped down onto the sidewalk on Station Row and turned up toward his car. A small black shape dipped out of the sky and twittered past his head.

Les swung his hand at it, thinking that a bird was attacking him. The shape darted crazily off into the streetlight's illumination, and he saw that it was a bat at the same time he saw two more bats fluttering toward him over the top of the streetlamp.

One of the bats swung right at his face. A fishhooklike claw on one of its feet sliced his cheek, and Les screamed with pain and disgust as he hit out at it. A blow like a stone struck his chest. Les opened his eyes, for the first time aware that he had closed them, and saw the second bat clinging to his jacket. Its wings were folded like creaky robes, the little head turned up to his. He furiously swept at it with his hands, but the bat tightened its grip and chattered up at him. He saw loathing in its tiny black eyes. He plucked at the leathery body but its claws were dug far into the fabric of his jacket.

When he looked up he saw the sky full of chattering particles. Bats swooped over the streetlight and fluttered past the front of the station. Another came diving in toward the side of his head, and Les ducked just in time to see its clawlike toes, the tiny head like a ball of dried snot staring at him. A shimmering flag of bats wheeled toward him.

Les bolted toward his car. The bat sticking to his jacket bounced as he ran, thudding softly against Les's chest. One of the oncoming bats thudded against his head; another flapped straight into his face before it fell away. Les put his hands over his face. He felt a sudden sharp pain bloom in his right ear, and a moment later he felt blood dripping down his neck.

When he at last reached his car, he seemed to be in a cloud of bats, a world of bats. He yanked at the Mazda's handle.

The door was locked. One of the bats tangled itself in Les's hair, and he grunted in disgust as he slapped it away. Another bat fastened on his sleeve, and he slammed its body against the outside of the window. The bat dropped to the road.

Another of them whapped into the side of his head, and he staggered sideways. They were boiling around his head, and Les clamped his eyes shut after a set of needling claws brushed his forehead.

Les swirled his hands up in the air and connected with his left, brushing one of the small bodies away. He had to get his car keys out of his pocket, and he hunched his back and turned away from the majority of the bats while he waved his left hand in front of his face and dug in his pants pocket with his right.

A bat settled on the waving hand and extended its wings. He could feel the needle claws settling into his skin. *As long as they don't bite,* went through his mind. His fingers found his car keys.

The bat on his head sank its teeth into his skin; the face, half a baby's, half a dog's, swiveled toward him.

Les bellowed and flapped his hand, dislodging the bat, which hovered two feet before his face and looked at him with implacable hatred. Les wanted to kill this bat—he wanted to toss it to the ground and jump on it, cracking its ribs and shredding its filthy wings. The other bats momentarily separated before him, and he saw the one that had bitten him skitter six inches up into the light from the station lamp. Les jumped forward and swung, but the bat skittered away again. The bat still clinging to his jacket bumped against his chest when he landed. Les swung out again at the bat that had bitten him, and saw that the back of his right hand was bloody. He could feel the blood dripping down his forehead and soaking into his eyebrow, and now his collar was wet with it. Les groaned and trotted back to his car.

He twisted the key in the lock, cracked the door, and slid quickly in, banging his head on the frame. He slammed the door shut after him.

A small clutching body stirred near his heart.

Les uttered an inarticulate roar of panic and disgust. He looked down at the bat still clinging to his jacket, and the bat's eyes locked on his.

"Uh . . . uh . . . uh," Les grunted, tearing at his jacket. The bat continued to fix him with its small eyes. At last Les got one arm out of its sleeve and whipped the jacket around the back of his head, almost weeping with disgust and fury. In a second the jacket was a ball of material before him on his lap, the sleeves dangling from either side of the ball like elephants' trunks. Les threw it on the dash and began battering it with both fists. He felt the animal inside the jacket struggle and tremble, fighting to claw its way out, but he banged it and banged it with his fists until it was still. Les was drooling. Blood and sweat plastered his hair to his head. He raised both fists and battered the limp thing in the jacket again. He lifted his fists and dropped them weakly on the pulpy remains. "Got you," he breathed.

Then he saw that his windshield was blanketed with small furry bodies.

Les gunned his car forward and almost instantly caromed off the steering wheel as the Mazda slammed into the car in front. His mouth wide open but no sounds coming from it, he backed hard into the car behind him, then hauled at the wheel and shot out of his parking spot. A section of bats near the edge of his side of the windshield tumbled away.

As he turned right at the end of the block, he remembered to turn on his lights; one of them seemed to work.

Les turned left at the next corner, blasting through as the

light changed from amber to red. From what he could see through the corner of the windshield where he had visibility, his was the only car on the road. He twisted the Mazda into the ramp for the east-bound side of I-95.

Here there were no toll stations until Stratford, twenty minutes up the road. Les floored the accelerator, and saw the bats flatten out against the windshield: two or three at the farthest edges flipped into the airstream.

He rocked the car sharply to the left, then to the right, and back again. He never heard them, but other drivers blasted their horns behind him.

His maneuvers had cleared the windshield of all but half a dozen bats. Their red eyes glared in at him, their tiny mouths worked, and he knew they were screeching at him. Les could see their mouths working in an almost human way. Whatever they were saying slipped backward in the breeze.

Les looked at his speedometer and saw that he was going just under ninety miles an hour. Another one of the bats flapped upward and peeled off the windshield like a black leaf.

Les emitted a trembling, high-pitched giggle and for the first time felt his shoulders loosen. He lifted his foot from the accelerator. The lights flowing by on the west-bound lane seemed reassuringly ordinary: people going somewhere.

Then Les became aware of another presence in the car. Some small dark shape was in the other bucket seat. Les unconsciously said, "Hey," and looked toward it. What looked like a nine- or ten-year-old boy made completely of mud slumped against the black fabric of the seat. Water dripped from the mud-boy and pooled on the cushion.

A lung-searing blast of foulness struck Les, the odor he had caught on the golf course magnified a hundred times. The odor formed a hot brick in Les's chest. The boy opened his eyes.

"I'm lost," he croaked. "I'm afraid."

Les came down on his accelerator with all his weight. He was screaming, but he did not know it. He was traveling at just over a hundred and fifteen miles an hour when he rammed into the side of another car a quarter-mile up I-95, a Toyota Celica belonging to Mr. Harvey Pilbrow of West Haven, Connecticut, and killed Mr. Pilbrow's eighteen-year-old son, Daniel, and his girlfriend, Molly Witt, also eighteen

and of West Haven. Les McCloud died only an instant after
the two young people; their cars sent up a plume of flame fifty
feet high.

14

Patsy opened her eyes. "Something's happened," she said,
then realized that she was lying down on the couch in Graham
Williams' living room.

"How do you feel?" the old man asked.

"Something happened," she repeated.

"You're right, something happened," Richard Allbee said,
coming into her field of vision. He took her hand, and
warmth seemed to spread out from his touch. "You passed
out after the book stopped moving."

"Oh," Patsy said. "The book."

"Are you all right?" Williams asked.

"Help me sit up," she said, and Richard pulled her upright
on the couch while she swung her legs down. Her head was
as light as if it held only bubbles. She realized that she could
not stand. "I'll be okay pretty soon."

"Remember the book?" Richard asked. He was still holding her hand, and knelt on the floor before her, looking into
her eyes with an expression of total concern.

"I do, but that's not what I mean," she said. Richard let
her hand go, and went back a few feet to hear her out.

Patsy did not know how much she could say. Already she
feared to sound crazy, even to these people, who knew so
much about her. She had had a fit of some kind, she supposed; she remembered the Marilyn-sensation, and the head
of the dragon rising up from the book—that much she would
tell. But the fit made her feel guilty and ashamed for her lack
of control. It also made her feel dirty. That she'd passed out
in the midst of it somehow connected itself in her mind with
her husband, with Les; with her failed marriage.

And that was the part she could not discuss with these men,
as much as she already cared for them. Before she had awakened, she had seen a column of fire and had understood that
her marriage was being cleansed in that fire. Real destruction,
real cleansing. In this was a danger as present as that intended
by the dragon. What had gone through her mind in the instant

before she had awakened was that Tabby Smithfield was very near to death.

But did that mean that Tabby was in the column of fire? And if he was in that pyre or going toward it, then . . .

"Just relax, Patsy," Graham Williams was saying.

. . . how did that connect to her marriage? She did not see how it was possible, but what was happening to Tabby was going to echo through her future with Les McCloud, whatever that was to be. She wished the boy were there before her now, so that she could hug him with all her strength. She looked straight into Richard Allbee and thought, *I'd like to hug you too.*

"Oh, I don't know what I mean," she said, and saw a line of worry furrow between Richard's eyebrows. "But I guess the two of you didn't see it, did you? The dragon's head?"— it was such an extraordinary sentence to utter.

The line between his eyebrows grew deeper.

"It came up out of the book. It was looking at me."

She remembered that black eye shot with the wandering pattern of bright green—like a stone.

"We didn't see it," Graham said. He looked as shaken as she by what she had said. "But I believe that you saw it, Patsy. And you know what it means, don't you? It means . . ."

"He was warning us," Richard said.

"Gideon Winter was turning his attention to us," Williams said. "That's what it means. In that sense, it's a warning." He snatched up the book, and then looked at Patsy with wide eyes. "It's *hot.*"

Richard reached over to touch the book; he glanced again at Patsy after his fingers had rested on the page. He nodded.

"I don't want to touch it," Patsy said.

"No, but I want you to look at the page," Williams said, and held up the book with the pages spread out before her. She saw the black lines burned into the paper. There were more of them than she had remembered. A few of the burn marks were just dark squiggles over the lines of print. These reminded her suddenly of bats, and just as that occurred to her, she thought she saw one of the bat-squiggles move, one of the wings flap in a broken and unhealthy way. *Les,* she thought, and a second later: *Tabby.*

"I saw the burn marks before," she said. "They came just before . . . just before *it* did."

"I don't mean the burn marks," Williams said. "Look at the dates on the tops of the pages."

Patsy looked. At the tops of the pages were a pair of dates, the same for both of the facing pages. 1873–1875. She shook her head. Williams held the book toward Richard and let him see the dates.

"1873–1875," Richard said. "Don't tell me. More roasted children."

"Not quite," Williams said. "But you're on the right track. It's the next date in the cycle. In 1811, the entire congregation of the Greenbank Congregational Church was killed by a freak accident on Kendall Point. By the way, and this is important, there were two Williamses among those who fell into the fissures, and two Taylers, a father and daughter, and four Greens. And an old man named Smyth. Mrs. Bach didn't tell me that—she didn't want to tell me that—but I looked it up in the newspapers. The Kendall Point accident nearly wiped out all our families. After that, all our families weren't in Greenbank proper for a long time. My relatives lived in Patchin, as did the surviving Greens. They were members of the Patchin Congregational Church, and so they survived the day. In 1841, Rustum Tayler went crazy, went crazy all the way instead of the half-crazy he'd been all his life, and killed those two children and ate most of them before Anthony Jennings led a posse that found him sitting at the top of his roasting pit."

"Ate them," Patsy said. She closed her eyes and caught a dimming afterimage of the column of flame. *Tabby.* Where was he?

"Ate them. Mrs. Bach didn't feel that the last days of a half-wit Tayler were worthy of being in her book, but she read the same newspapers I did, and she knew about it. And she had walked through that old Greenbank Cemetery on the Greenbank Road, about two miles from here, and she had seen the headstones for the children Rustum Tayler killed. The headstones are still there. *Sarah Allen, 1835–1841. Taken Cruelly from Us.* And *Thomas Kirby McCauley Moorman, 1834–1841. 'Little Tom.'*" Graham Williams put down the book. "It's cooling down now. Yes, she knew about those children all right, but she didn't write about their deaths any more than she wanted to write about what happened in 1873, and for the same reason. I'm not even sure she was conscious of it, but she wanted to hide Gideon Winter behind the most day-to-day view of things."

Williams looked sharply at Patsy. "Do you want to rest, Patsy?"

"I'm going to be fine," Patsy said in a faraway voice.

"Well, what did happen in 1873?" Richard asked.

"One person from each of our families died in a fire at a mill," Williams said. "But so did forty-one other people. July and August of 1873 were called 'The Black Summer' for two decades—it was more than a year before strangers began coming through Hampstead again. Oh, they came through on the coaches, but they came through fast and they didn't stop, they just rolled on until they got to Hillhaven. The reason I know that is that in 1874 a new coach inn called the Halfway House was put up in Hillhaven. There had always been a Halfway House in Hampstead, right on the Greenbank Road in fact, but after 1873 it just seems to have fallen in on itself . . . it went out of business and slipped right out of the records. After the Black Summer people seemed to avoid Hampstead. I've looked at the logs of ships that docked in Hampstead harbor—now that's where the yacht club is—for years, right on up from the 1860's, and seen that starting in 1873, they went the couple miles farther up the coast to the Hillhaven harbor. After about 1875, they came back here again. But I'll tell you something Dorothy Bach didn't keep out of her book. Before the Black Summer, the town population of Hampstead was 1,045. Two years later, in 1875, the Town Council held its own census. The population of Hampstead was 537."

"Half of them died?" Richard asked incredulously. "I thought you said only forty-five people died that summer."

"Well, a lot of them probably moved out," Williams said. "They could have gone just up the road into Hillhaven or Patchin, or as far as they had to go in order to think they were safe, and I think a couple hundred of them probably did just that. They were betting that later they could come back and find their houses pretty much the way they'd left them. You find a real flurry of livestock transfers during and just after the Black Summer. People selling up and getting out."

"But that still leaves a couple *hundred*," Richard said.

"Yep," Williams said. "That it does. You know, before you people came here, I wasn't too sure about all this stuff.

And I would have read about Mrs. Friedgood and Mrs. Goodall and just wondered about it. But when I saw Patsy and Tabby on that Sunday night, I knew. *He* was on his way back. And he was getting stronger, too—maybe as strong as he must have been in the Black Summer and the months after it.''

"What makes you think that?" Richard asked.

"The Black Summer of 1873 started just the way this one did. A woman was found cut to pieces in her farmhouse. A week later, another woman was found behind the row of shops along Main Street. She was in the same condition. There were two others, one of them a little Smyth girl. And all of that was *before* the deaths at the old cotton mill.''

Richard asked another question, and Patsy heard his voice as if it came from a hole deep in the earth or from a telephone receiver left lying unattended on a table. "What made the Black Summer so much worse than the summer of 1841?''

"Oh, we were all back by then, you see," Williams said, and Patsy sluggishly thought *all back, isn't that nice, just like a reunion.* . . . "Williams, Smyth—Smithfield by then, of course—Tayler, Green. All back. The Greenbank Congregational Church had been revived too—by 1873, something that had happened all the way back in 1811 seemed like a fairytale to them.''

"Those children with the terrible first names," Richard said. "'Darkness' and 'Eventide' and 'Sorrow.' They had our last names, didn't they?''

"You're thinking well, Richard," the old man said. "Sorrow's full name was Sorrow Tayler, and she married Joseph Williams. Darkness was Darkness Smyth, and Eventide's last name was Green. And there was a 'Shame' too, as Dorothy Bach knew very well. A little girl named Shame Williams was born in 1652, and died before she could be baptized.''

"Sorrow Tayler," Patsy murmured. The name seemed very beautiful to her.

"Most of them were girls," Williams said. "And in time they all had children themselves. Williamses married Taylers, and Smyths married Greens, and then Williamses married Smyths.''

To Patsy it seemed like a beautiful formal dance, all these marriages and couplings going on so long ago in the past. . . . Her fingers twitched, and her lips were numb. A Williams took a Tayler, and a Smyth took a Green, and then a Williams took a Smyth . . . it was all a circle, and for a second she saw the circle in her mind, glowing gold like a wedding band. Something smoky, something not right, flickered in the middle of the golden circle, and Patsy shook her head.

But then Marilyn Foreman's hand clamped down hard over hers, and Patsy saw what was in the middle of the circle.

She did not hear it herself, but she emitted a low terrified moan, and both Richard and Graham realized that Patsy had fallen back into the couch. As she moaned, she slipped down, already unconscious, and her head fell to the cushions. Before they could reach her, Patsy's hands began to twitch, and then her whole body shook violently enough to rattle the couch against the floor.

Richard grabbed her hand, not knowing how to stop her convulsions. Finally he stepped next to her and put his arms around her and held her tightly against him, taking the shock of her movements into his own body.

15

"Get that piano outside," Starbuck said, "and put it down easy. Then come back in and get this mirror."

No, Bruce thought, and knew that Dicky was thinking the same thing, *let's just leave that mirror where it is, we don't want to mess with that thing, no sir, no way.* Just before he had seen the light from Starbuck's flashlight burst on the surface of the mirror the way it must have done right away, he thought he had seen something in there, something touched by the swallowed light (which of course had never been), something like a worm or a leech—flinching back from the light.

Like hell. That was a crazy thought. That was something to tell freaked-out Skippy Peters, and then watch his Adam's apple bob around in his skinny neck.

"If you shake your fucking head at me once more, I'll tear it off your fucking neck," Starbuck whispered at him. "Get moving on that piano." The light burned in Bruce's eyes. "I swear, I'll shoot your balls off if you don't get moving."

"I was just thinking," Bruce whispered back, and he felt Dicky quiver beside him.

"Thinking, *shit,*" Starbuck hissed at him.

"We could put the mirror in the piano, make only one trip," Bruce improvised.

"Yeah?" The light swung toward the mirror again. "Yeah, okay. It'll go under the top of the case. Just don't chip the frame."

Dicky and Bruce edged around the piano and began to thread their way across the room. Starbuck played the flash idly on the sculptures, and as idly picked up the one nearest him. It was a small statue of a dancer, and he was surprised by its weight. He turned it over and saw the name scratched into the base: Degas. "Hold it," he said, and the boys froze. "No, not you, assholes," he said, and excitedly shot the flash toward the next small sculpture. It looked just like the one he cradled in his palm. When he shot the light down the length of the room, he saw two more of the little sculptures of dancers.

Starbuck pulled the radio out of his pocket and spoke into it. "Hey, kid? You there."

"*What?*" came Tabby's frightened voice.

"Get the van up here right now. We're gonna split in a couple of minutes."

"You want us to . . . ?" Dicky and Bruce had frozen half-way to the wall where the mirror hung.

"Fuck, you're dumb," Starbuck said. "Get the mirror. Get it inside the piano. Push the piano outside. Then you can get *yourselves* back in here and take all those pictures off the wall. You understand all that?"

As the shaken Norman twins continued toward the wall, Starbuck went for the second Degas sculpture.

He was speculating, in the last few seconds of his life, that the things in this room represented at least two years' worth of the good life, even at ten cents on the dollar, which is what he knew he could get for them. With the silver, the piano, the sculptures, and the paintings, he would be able to fade out of the Beach Trail house months before any of the dozy local cops began to look for him, and take his time getting to a new place. He was thinking of going back to the Midwest, territory he had not seen for a long time; to Grosse Pointe or Lake Forest, some town so rich that when you inhaled, your bank account got fatter.

Then he dimly saw an old man with a gun in his hand coming through the living-room door, thought, *no, he's young, he's just a kid,* and then he heard Dicky Norman screech in pain and terror. After that the room seemed to explode, and the explosion cut him off forever from the interesting spectacle of Dicky Norman spouting blood all over a painting he would have sworn was a Manet. His own pistol was in his hand by then, but first his fingers would not work and then he was wondering if you could still sell a Manet that had Dicky Norman's blood all over it, and then he was gone.

16

Tabby tossed the radio onto the passenger seat and then climbed into the driver's seat. Static-laden conversation erupted from the radio, and he jerked his hand out for it before he realized that he was picking up Starbuck's orders to the twins. The thief sounded angry. Tabby twisted the key in the ignition and then put his foot down on the accelerator.

The engine caught. Tabby had now exhausted everything he knew about driving the van. He looked in dismay at the gearshift, which was four feet long, and angled like the shift on a truck. Above the knob at the end of the shift was a red button. Tabby grabbed the shift, pressed the button, and yanked the shift down. He did not depress the clutch, since he did not know it was there.

The van growled: it sounded as though it was eating itself, devouring its own wheels and gears.

Tabby let go of the shift, then grabbed it again and wrenched it sideways at the same time as he floored the accelerator.

The van trembled like a dog in a seizure. From the sounds it was making, soon it would begin to defecate its own parts out the exhaust pipe. This was hopeless.

Tabby threw open the door and began to run up the drive. Then he remembered the radio, and sprinted back for it. He was running past the Japanese maple and about thirty-five feet from the house when he realized that since he was going to be seeing Starbuck in seconds, he would not need the radio. The security light angling down from beneath the rain gutter dazzled and fixed him—he saw himself exposed before a pitiless judgment.

He would have to confess to Starbuck that he could not make the van go, that was all. The thief or one of the Normans could go back down to the gates and bring the van up. All Tabby had to do was go inside and tell Gary Starbuck that he could not get the van to move.

Fearful Tabby closed his eyes and *saw*. A column of flame rose fifty feet into the air; then it lifted from the ground and was in the shape of a huge bat with its wings extended, a giant bat made of fire.

Tabby stopped running. His mouth had gone cottony, and his heart was pounding.

He took a tentative step forward. Something was going to happen inside that house; all the atmosphere seemed charged with that weird electricity which had flickered earlier through the sky. Tabby saw something glowing in one of the downstairs windows.

The radio, forgotten in his hand, emitted a long wavering screech of agony.

Tabby took another step forward. Whatever was glowing in the downstairs window was urging him forward. Part of him knew that whatever was going on in that house was too much for him, that it was like that still very dim memory of a future event he had *seen* when his father and his grandfather had tried to pull him into twin halves at gate 44 in JFK airport—that dim, shocking memory of a man opening up a woman's skin with a long red weapon—but the rest of Tabby Smithfield heard a silent voice from within the big imposing house which softly and insistently invited him inside.

It's nice in here, Tabby, just come up to the door, it doesn't matter that you can't drive the van, nothing like that matters anymore, just come in and join us. . . .

Dazed, and with the two images—the fire-bat and the man opening up the dying woman's skin—rolling down through a receding corridor in his mind, Tabby took another step toward the house.

Then he heard a shot coming from the same room where the inviting shape had glowed through a large window.

17

Richard's arms ached: Patsy thrashed against his restraint like a bull in a pen. "I don't know if I can hold her much longer," he said desperately to Graham Williams.

"I'll get her legs," Williams said, and went as quickly as

he could around the coffee table. He grasped one of her ankles with his right hand, and she kicked out strongly enough
to throw him off-balance. He sat heavily on the flimsy table,
and both men heard it crack. Williams grimly leaned forward,
pursing his mouth with effort, and caught her flying leg under
his arm. As he pinned it down with his elbow, he reached out
and grasped her other leg with his free hand. Patsy's hips
whipsawed. Williams felt a sudden pain in his chest.

Richard saw Graham's face go white: it was as if the sharp
crack from the table had come from within the old man. Patsy
thrashed against his arms again, and screamed a single word.
"Run!"

Richard shook his head at the old man, telling him to let
go, that he could handle Patsy's convulsions, but Williams
strengthened his grip, and Patsy's movements became tighter
and more easily controlled.

"Run!" she screamed. Then she let out a long wail that
made Richard almost drop her.

Richard heard a loud cracking noise behind him.

He ducked his head, imagining that a window had exploded in, and then saw the glass front of a framed film poster
beside Williams' desk shatter and crumble to the floor in a
glittery jigsaw puzzle.

"Aaaah!" Patsy screamed.

The paperback detective novels jammed on top of the art
books were snapping out of the bookcase, sailing into the air
and then swirling upward. Richard heard the frame of the
poster behind him crack apart like kindling. He watched the
books on the top row of the bookshelves across the room
cannon off the shelf and sail across Williams' desk.

The typewriter rocked on its pad, then rolled right over and
thunked against the floor. *Bing!* rang the carriage return.

Books flew randomly off the shelves: Richard and Graham
watched two of them ascend straight up to the ceiling, where
they clung for a moment like flies before dropping to the
floor.

Another of the framed posters (*Glenda,* Richard saw, a
tinted drawing of Mary Astor in Gary Cooper's arms) flopped
straight over on its face and jittered like a dying cat as the
glass tinkled into a thousand bright sections.

18

Come on in, Tabs, we need you now, said the silent voice in his mind, and he stepped forward again. For a moment he saw dozens of people lined up at the big windows; then they broke apart, turned to one another or turned away. *Why, it's a party,* Tabby thought, *how can there be a party?* He lifted the radio to his mouth and said, "Hey, what . . ."

"Come on in," the radio said to him. "Get in here, Tabby."

He could not see the people very clearly, but the Norman twins were not among them.

"Get in here," the voice on the radio said again.

The people parted, and Tabby saw that what had been glowing was a mirror far across the room. Now its center was a delicate rose-pink that pulsed and glowed. Tabby began to move again.

But then Bruce Norman burst through the front door. He had his arm around Dicky's chest, and seemed to be pulling at him. Dicky's face was marble-white. He was moving very slowly. *"Where's the van?"* Bruce shouted.

Bruce was red with blood: blood plastered his shirt to his thick chest. Dicky too had splashes of blood on his face, and his entire side was stained so deeply that the colors of his clothes were not visible.

Tabby pointed down the long lawn. He had seen that all that blood was Dicky Norman's.

Then he saw a knob of white appear in the midst of the soupy redness where Bruce was holding up his brother. Dicky's arm was gone, and the knob of white was his shoulder. He rushed to help Bruce support his brother, and his mind cleared: he seemed to himself to have been moving in slow motion since the column of flame had bloomed in his mind.

Tabby firmly clamped his arm around Dicky's back and felt Dicky's heaviness, his slowness. Dicky was going to die, he knew. Together he and Bruce half-carried, half-pushed Dicky all the way to the van. Tabby moved to open the rear door, but Bruce screeched at Tabby, *"Not in the back! In the front! On the seat!"* Bruce's eyes seemed to take up most of his face. Tabby helped get Dicky in the passenger seat, and then Bruce ran around the front of the van to climb in the driver's seat.

Tabby jumped in the back and slammed the door shut just as Bruce slammed the van backward into a tree. Dicky slumped toward the floor. "Pull him up, for Chrissake!" Bruce screeched, ground the gears, and shot out from under the trees in a shower of scattered earth.

Tabby bent over the passenger seat and tried to haul Dicky back upright. His left hand slipped on the sheet of blood covering Dicky's left side, and Dicky waveringly rolled sideways. The white knob of bone slid along the fabric of the seat.

"Get him *uuup!*" Bruce yelled. He spun out onto Mount Avenue and turned in the direction of the Sayre Connector.

Tabby hauled at Dicky's right arm, and then Dicky got his legs under himself and helped push himself back onto the seat. Leaning over, Tabby looked into his eyes. They were looking straight ahead, focused on something a long way off. Dicky's eyes were unearthly. Tabby thought that Dicky Norman looked more intelligent than at any other time in his life, but he was glad he couldn't see what Dicky was looking at so intently. "Hold on, Dicky," he said, and patted his good shoulder. Dicky did not even blink.

"Where's the guy?" Tabby asked. "Starbuck—where's Starbuck?"

"Fucker's dead," Bruce said.

"Dead? I just talked to him on the radio."

"Fucker's dead. The old guy shot him."

Bruce sped straight through a stop sign.

"How did . . . I mean, what happened to Dicky?"

"*I don't know!*" Bruce screamed. He wiped a hand over his jowls, and left a bloody smear. "We were supposed to pick up this fancy mirror and put it inside this big black asshole of a piano. We were just gonna get the mirror when the old guy comes in with his gun. He doesn't even say, 'Stick 'em up,' or nothin', he just shoots. And he got Starbuck—he blew that fuckhead away. Then Dicky gives out this gawdawful yell, and I look over at Dicky, and he's shootin' blood all over the wall and his goddamn arm is gone and he's just standin' there lookin' up, and I thought the old guy was gonna blast us both." He shook his head. "I thought the old guy shot him too, until I seen that his whole fuckin' arm is gone. So I just got him out."

"I saw other people in there," Tabby said.

"Tabs, the old guy was the only other one in that room.

You gotta get out now. I'm taking Dicky down to Norrington General, and you gotta get outta this van."

Bruce pulled up at the traffic light on the Sayre Connector. "Out, Tabs. Fast."

Tabby jumped down onto the road and slammed the door. "Good luck," he said, but the van had pulled ahead through the red light and was speeding toward the on ramp to the thruway.

Fourteen minutes later, at eleven-fifty-six, Bruce Norman made it to the emergency room of Norrington General Hospital, a feat he accomplished by keeping the accelerator floored and the engine in the overdrive Gary Starbuck had constructed. When he came to the toll station he did not even think of slowing down. He hit the barrier at better than a hundred and ten miles an hour and split it into half a dozen flying saw-toothed sections. The nurses in the emergency room peeled his brother off him as soon as they came through the door, strapped Dicky to a cot and slid an IV in his arm. Dicky's eyes never lost the intelligent faraway stare Tabby Smithfield had seen. An intern named Patel, who had been born in Uttar Pradesh and had a medical degree from the University of Wisconsin, began doing what he could to Dicky's shoulder. But Dicky died while Dr. Patel was still putting little metal clamps on the severed arteries. It was three minutes past twelve.

Dr. Patel stood up, looked at the clock, and then at Bruce Norman, who was sitting in a chair at the side of the emergency room, watching him with slitted and dangerous eyes.

Dr. Patel picked up Dicky's remaining hand and felt for a pulse; but his hands had been in Dicky's wound at the moment of his death, and he knew there would be no pulse. He gently lowered Dicky's hand to his chest.

Bruce stood up. He stank of blood, and blood had soaked and smeared over his shoes, his jeans, and his shirt. The blood on his face was like war paint.

"This is a dead boy," said Dr. Patel, whose accent and diction were still those of India. "Can you tell me please how this wound was inflicted?"

Bruce walked up to the small brown-skinned doctor and hit him squarely in the side of the head, knocking out two of the doctor's teeth and sending him flying into Dicky's IV stand. The doctor fell to the floor in a pool of dark liquid, and Bruce picked up his brother and carried him back outside to the van.

At that moment, the nurses were all either in the emergency patients' cubicles or around the corner at the nursing station, and none of them saw what had happened until Jake Rems, an alcoholic with a black eye and a broken nose, began squalling that a monster boy had killed his doctor.

Dicky was back on his seat; Bruce was calmer. He drove down the highway to Woodville and the next hospital, St. Hilda's, and there he accepted the news that his brother was dead.

It was now twelve-thirty-one on Sunday morning, the eighth of June, and Patchin County was beginning its twenty-fifth day without rain.

19

Just after a quarter to one, Tabby had turned into Beach Trail and was trudging slowly up toward Hermitage and "Four Hearths." He was too tired to think about everything that had happened. He wanted only to get inside his house, go up to his room, lock his door, and crawl into bed. In his mind he saw the fire-bat widening its red wings . . . the wings were as red as Dicky Norman's left side, where Dicky had looked as though a crazy painter had slapped him with brushful after brushful of bright red paint.

The fire-bat's eyes were black holes, and clouds shone palely through.

Tabby looked ahead up the road and saw the houses march one by one on either side of the black street, the streetlamps throwing circles of light on the ground, and thought that all of it, right up the hill to his house, looked like a setting in a dream, and that soon these houses would begin to swell and bloat, blood and foul yellow liquid would pour from the windows, the street would crack and turn over and bruised white hands would thrust up through the exposed earth . . . and the fire-bat would soar overhead, setting the bursting houses alight and crooning, *Master Smyth. Do you wish a ball in the back?*

He groaned, lifted his hands to wipe his face, and saw for the first time since the Normans had come through the front door of the doctor's house that he was still carrying Gary Starbuck's two-way radio.

It crackled in his face. *"Tabby! Tabby Smithfield! You get back here! You get your tail back here right now or I'll kill you!"* The voice leaped out of the radio on a cascade of static, but it was strong and clear. It was the same voice he had heard speaking to him while he stood on the doctor's lawn—Gary Starbuck's voice. Starbuck was not dead, he was back there in a fuming rage because Tabby and the Normans had run out on him.

Tabby stared down at the radio, not knowing what to believe. Bruce Norman had seen the doctor shoot Starbuck. But he himself had seen people at those windows, people Bruce had told him were not there. *"Aaagh,"* the radio whimpered.

Radio signals, Tabby thought. It was picking up some kind of radio signals, and pretty soon Dr. Demento would come on, announcing that the next number would be "Surfin' Bird" by the immortal Trashmen.

But he knew that these were not radio signals. He was never going to hear "Steve Miller's Midnight Tango" or "Song for a Sucker Like You" on this radio, and Starbuck, he was certain, was dead. And Dicky Norman too would be dead by now, his arm savagely ripped off by . . .

. . . by a delicate rose-pink light that glowed at the center of an antique mirror?

The lump of black metal and plastic in his hand grew suddenly warm. With an almost exhausted curiosity Tabby lifted it nearer to his face: an acrid electronic stink. Then the thing in his hand was unbearably hot. Smoke poured from the grille. The top edge drooped and grinned. A strip of metal sizzled against his palm, and he jerked his hand, sending the radio flying onto a lawn.

It burst into flame while it was still in the air. Something within it went *pop!* and when it struck the lawn, a small specific cloud of blue gas emerged from its diminishing surface. Many of the pieces still burned, it cracked down the center, and as the plastic melted, small burning elements from inside the radio twisted and moved across the grass.

One fiery piece seemed to have tiny legs and a shiny back like a beetle's. It staggered some inches from the melting body of the radio, then turned crisp and transparent and died.

A few tiny flames began to feed on the dry stalks of grass.

Tabby realized that the entire lawn could catch fire, and he jumped onto the lawn and began stamping on the tiny flames.

"Tabby? Is that you?" a woman called, and when he

looked up he saw Patsy McCloud standing on the front step—
then he recognized Graham Williams' house. He had been too
bone-weary to identify it earlier.

"It's me," he said, and she jumped off the porch already
running. Graham Williams poked his head around the front
door, and Tabby waved. Williams grinned and waved back,
rubbing his chest with his other hand. He stepped outside and
pushed his hands into his pockets.

Patsy ran into Tabby and almost knocked him down before
she hugged him. "Are you all right?"

He nodded.

"What were you doing?"

"I was holding a radio, and it sort of exploded," he said,
feeling a little light-headed now that he was circled by her
arms. A metal catch on her white overalls dug into his neck.
Patsy smelled pleasantly of perfume and fresh perspiration.

"I was so worried . . . I passed out, actually I guess I had
a kind of *fit,* and I dreamed you were in terrible danger." She
straightened up and took her arms from around him. "You
were in danger, weren't you?"

"Well, I burned my hand," he said, and showed her the
fat strip of burned flesh across the palm of his hand.

"We'll soak that in cold water, but that's not what I mean.
Where were you tonight? What were you doing?"

He could not answer that question. If he had to, he could
explain, and Patsy would believe him, but the explanations
would take too long, and he was too tired.

"Why, you've got blood on your shirt," Patsy said.

He looked down. It was blood, all right—Dicky Norman's.
That was where he had wiped his hand after trying to pull
Dicky back up on the van's seat.

Patsy's face had gone even whiter. "I'm all right," he
said. "I'm not hurt. I was just out with some people." *And
two of them are dead now.*

Patsy's head jerked back as though she had intercepted this
thought. Her wide dark eyes caught his.

Then the image of the fire-bat, its wings extended and
clouds drifting past its empty eyes, slammed into his mind,
along with

I saw this
oh no
I saw this I saw this I saw this and it was going to kill you
we can't do this nobody can do this

tell it to the Marines, buster, because we're doing it.

The words had flown between them as the dreadful image of the fire-bat had faded, and at the conclusion Patsy's mouth actually twitched in a smile. "We are," Tabby said. He tried

I saw that too, Patsy

or it slipped into his mind and he felt it instantly transfer to hers.

we can't
no can't
tell
can't can't tell
anyone
anyone else
even Richard
(Richard?)
yesss

A complicated series of emotions involving warmth, guilt, and deep physicality blew into him along with the sibilant *yes,* and he backed away mentally, knowing that this was too private for him.

"Richard Allbee," he said out loud.

Patsy nodded, and then Graham Williams was on them, saying, "Come on in for a second, Tabby, you have to meet our fourth member, you look like you could use a rest anyhow, I guess we all could." He realized that he was looking directly into Patsy's face: she was exactly his height.

this scares me, he thought

and two of them are dead now? Patsy thought.

later

the fire-thing?

later

the fire-thing, damn you?

I don't know

it was going to kill you, Patsy thought in Tabby's brain, and he knew that she was telling him no more than the truth. The joyousness of what he and Patsy McCloud had discovered they could do went black and cold.

"Are you all right?" the old man was asking him. "What the hell happened to you? What's all that blood?"

"I'm fine, really," Tabby said.

"Where were you, son?"

"I can't tell you," Tabby said. "I can't tell anybody—not now, anyhow. But I'm not hurt."

Williams glowered at the boy. "I get the feeling I'm missing something. There's something going on here, and I'm missing it. Did he tell you what he was up to, Patsy?"

Patsy shook her head.

"Well, I suppose you'd better come on up and meet Richard Allbee," Graham said. Then he shot another dark glance at Tabby. "You're not in trouble with the police, are you? Were you out on another mailbox massacre?"

"Something like that," Tabby said, and could not look at Patsy. His face reddened.

"Well, anybody your age has a license to be stupid," Williams said. "But don't overdo it."

The three of them were walking across the overgrown weedy lawn back toward the house, and a fourth figure, a slender well-knit man in his mid-thirties, came out to stand on the porch. He was only two or three inches taller than Patsy and Tabby, and his longish dark hair was combed straight back. The man looked sleek and capable to Tabby. Then he was close enough to see the man's face in detail, and something in his chest jumped, whether in fear or in confirmation, he did not know.

Richard Allbee, the fourth descendant of the original Greenbank settlers, was the man he had seen through the window of the Gryphon Diner in the Post Mall shopping center.

The Normans had been bragging about a kid named Skip Peters, how he had done everything they wanted him to do, even the craziest things. In the midst of the Norman stories, Tabby had seen Spunky Jameson staring in at him through the window.

Then he had seen that this was an adult; it could not possibly be Spunky Jameson, Spunky was a ten-year-old kid . . .

. . . and he had suddenly had the feeling that this person knew him, that they had met, and that events both terrible and wonderful would flow from that meeting . . . he had felt himself slipping into a panicky dream, and then Dicky Norman pushed the tines of his fork into Tabby's hand and broke the feeling apart. . . .

"I should have known that you'd turn out to be Tabby Smithfield," the man said.

"You met each other before?" Graham Williams asked with evident surprise.

"We *looked at* each other," Tabby said.

"Mysteriouser and mysteriouser."

The four of them stood outside a moment longer, not speaking, aware that it was the first time that all of them had been together.

Graham Williams knew that what was "mysteriouser and mysteriouser" was their meat and drink now, and that knowledge filled him with dread—he knew that what was to come would make Patsy's fit only a footnote to their story. Tabby had none of these premonitions, at least not while they all stood in the darkness outside Graham's house. During that moment when currents of emotion jumped between them all, he first had felt unreasonably secure, as if nothing could hurt him now. Then he realized he was with an old man, and a younger man and woman: it was the structure of the household on Mount Avenue just before that household blew apart with the death of his mother.

"Well, let's get inside for a bit," Williams said. "Tabby, there's something you have to hear about. Patsy saw the Dragon tonight."

Richard Allbee opened the door, looking down at Tabby with an expression of kindly puzzlement, and Tabby remembered how Les McCloud's gun had looked, how enormous it had been when its barrel was pointing right at his chest. That moment now seemed to have taken place centuries ago. He looked uneasily back to the place on the lawn where the melted, broken pieces of the radio lay.

Graham Williams put his arm across his shoulder. Tabby went up the steps to follow Patsy into the book-lined corridor.

20

At three-fifteen that night, two small boys could have been seen walking down the newly paved access road to Gravesend Beach. The smaller of the two, four-year-old Martin O'Hara, was limping slightly. He wore dark blue shorts and a light blue T-shirt with a shiny portrait of Yoda on the front. His nine-year-old brother, Thomas, was wearing a new pair of Keds, straight-leg jeans and a dark green T-shirt with short yellow sleeves. Thomas had scaled up the waist-high chain-link fence across the public road at the entrance to the beach, swung his leg over, and then swung the other leg over and jumped down. Then he had reached down and lifted Martin over the fence. Now Martin was struggling to keep up with Thomas.

"Hurry up," Thomas called to his brother. He did not look back.

"My *feet* hurt, Tommy," Martin said.

"We're almost there."

"Oh, thank God," Martin said in an eerie echo of his mother's voice.

A second later Thomas said, "You're going too slow again."

"But I don't *want* to be slow."

"You're stupid."

"I'm *not* stupid, Tommy!" Martin wailed.

In minutes they had reached the wide part at the end of the access road. Ahead and to one side of them was the gray empty beach, to their right the long length of the breakwater from which Harry and Babe Zimmer had liked to fish. The Sound was at low tide, a long black shelf of barely moving water with silver glints of light on its small rolling waves.

"This is it," Thomas said.

"Yeah, this is it," Martin repeated.

Thomas jumped on top of the concrete retaining wall at the edge of this parking area, and helped Martin to get up on top of the two-foot wall beside him. Then Thomas jumped down onto the sand. "Come on, Martin," he said. "Jump down."

"Carry me," Martin said. "I can't jump. It's too high for me."

Sighing, Thomas came back and lifted Martin down onto the sand.

"Now we have to take our clothes off," Thomas said.

"We have to?"

"Sure we have to," Thomas said, and sat down calmly and began to untie his shoes.

Martin sat down on the sand only inches from Thomas and yanked at his own laces. A few seconds later he furiously yelled, "Tommy, I can't! I can't get my shoes off!" His brother, naked except for his shirt, knelt before him and tugged off the sneakers without bothering to untie the snarled laces. As Thomas pulled his shirt off over his head, Martin pushed down his shorts and red cotton underpants and stepped out of them. Then he sat and grabbed the toe of his right sock with his left hand, grunted, and pulled the sock off. He repeated the technique with his left sock.

"Come on, come on," Thomas said. He was standing up in the darkness, and to Martin he looked as tall and powerful as an adult. "Get your shirt off."

"I want to wear my Yoda shirt," Martin said.

"You have to take it off," Thomas said.

"I want to wear my Yoda shirt!" Martin said, his face working.

"Jesus," Thomas said.

"You're not supposed to say that!" Martin exploded.

"All right, come on. You can wear your shirt." Thomas led the way across the beach.

A fat, nearly continuous strip of seaweed marked the high-tide waterline. The boys stepped over it and cautiously marched down the drying strand. They didn't want to step on any of the sharp rocks or on the broken crab shells that litter the beach.

"Horseshoe crab!" Martin screamed. "Look! Horseshoe crab!"

"It's dead, it's yucky," Thomas told him. "Come on, Martin."

Martin scampered ahead and reached the water first.

"Brrr!"

"The water's okay. It's just a little cold," Thomas said loftily. He strode into the water after his brother and repeated, "Just a little cold," though in fact it seemed much colder than that to him. "It'll get better."

They had to walk out nearly to the end of the breakwater before the water was even waist-high for Thomas. Martin was bobbing grimly along, holding his head up. "It's still cold," Martin said.

"Just go as far as you can," Thomas said. "It doesn't have to be far."

"Don't go away," Martin said, his shirt billowing out around him in the black water.

"I have to," Thomas said. "You know I have to, Martin." Then he looked down at his brother's intent small face. "Give me a kiss, Martin," he said on impulse, and bent to touch his brother's cold lips with his own. Then he threw himself forward into the water.

Martin struggled to stay on his feet, and bounced forward another step. The water was up to his chin. He lifted his feet from the stony floor and paddled his arms. That was all the swimming he knew how to do. *"Tommy!"* he yelled when he realized that his feet could no longer touch the bottom. His brother paid no attention, but continued swimming toward the buoys. Martin paddled a few feet farther out. His shirt felt heavy, heavy. His head went under, and he desperately inhaled half a pint of burning seawater. Spluttering as his head surfaced again, he windmilled his arms, taking himself farther out past the end of the breakwater. Then his head went under again. A huge black shape opened its mouth and darted toward him.

Thomas kept swimming until his arms were too heavy and slow to lift—he had gotten more than fifty feet past the buoys. His body felt warm and tired. He let his head slip under the water, jerked it up when water splashed into his nose, did another overhand stroke, and then slid backward into the water as if something on the bottom were sucking him down.

Half an hour after the first Bloody Mary was poured at brunch in the Sawtell Country Club, a woman named Rae Nestico-Bell carried her beach chair down to the far end of Gravesend Beach to get away from the noise of a volleyball game eight teenage boys had set up near her original place. Besides the shouts and the flying sand, what drove her away were the leers and stares the boys directed her way whenever they thought she might be looking at them. Mrs. Nestico-Bell had reached the first of the boundaries that mark off the private beaches, and she was just putting down her chair at the edge of the seawall below the Van Horne house when she saw two oddly shaped bundles of sand and weed rolling in the waves directly before her. She dropped her chair and took a step forward. From one of the bundles a white foot extended. She clenched her hands in front of her mouth and began to call for help, at first so quietly that the boys playing volleyball did not hear her.

These images, the screaming of a woman in a bikini and the happy pounding of eight teenage boys down a stony beach, marked the true ending of the events of Saturday, the seventh of June, in the year 1980. The first threshold had been crossed.

2

Naked Swimmers

1

By Monday, the ninth of June, word had spread through town that the killer of Stony Friedgood and Hester Goodall had been shot to death while committing a burglary on the Golden Mile; no one in the police department had expressed this view publicly, but off-duty Hampstead officers in bars on the Post Road and Riverfront Avenue talked about the way a gutsy little doctor named Wren Van Horne walked into his living room with a pistol and shot down an armed housebreaker—who had his gun out, ready to kill the owner! That was the deciding point. "You wait," these officers breathed into the receptive ears around them, "there aren't going to be any more killings in Hampstead for a long time. We're done with that guy." The bartenders and the other customers went home and told their wives and husbands and parents that Hampstead was safe again, and the wives and husbands and parents went out to their grocery stores and bowling alleys and Nautilus exercise rooms and dance classes and told their clerks and instructors and partners that Hampstead had nothing to worry about anymore. The monster who had savaged Mrs. Friedgood and Mrs. Goodall was dead. "Of course we'll never be able to prove it," the policemen had said in the bars, and "Of course they'll never be able to prove it," the wives said to their hairdressers and vendors of *baguettes,* "but he had to be the man. Why, he wasn't even from around here! I heard he was from Florida . . . from New York . . . from Illinois."

Sarah Spry answered the phone at her desk on Monday morning and heard Martha Gable, one of her oldest friends, babble for ten minutes about somebody getting shot and somebody having a bagful of antique silver and somebody not being a problem anymore, and finally had to say, "Martha, I think you'd better slow down and spoon-feed me. I can't make head or tail out of this." When she finally got the story out of Martha, she cursed herself for not checking in with the desk officers at the police station as soon as she arrived—she usually did, but this morning her editor had hit her with the news about the O'Hara boys and suggested that before she met Richard Allbee for his interview, she might swing over to the O'Hara house and talk to the boys' mother.

"And what would be the good of that?" she had snapped, still trying to see around the deaths of those two kids—kids she had seen about once a month since they had been born.

"You're a friend of the O'Haras, aren't you?" Stan Brockett asked her.

"So *what?*" she nearly yelled. "You want me to ask Mikki O'Hara how it feels to have her children drown? Do you want me to ask her how the death of her children will affect her *work?*"

Mikki Zaber O'Hara was one of Hampstead's many semi-professional painters. She had shows and openings in local galleries; her husband, a gem appraiser with an office on Gramercy Park and another in Palm Springs, had had a studio built for her in their attic, but she sold paintings almost entirely to her family and her friends.

"No," Stan Brockett had said. "Her work never was anything but deep-dyed shit, and you know it. I want you to ask her what her kids were doing out on the beach around three in the morning."

"What do you mean, three in the morning? Mikki O'Hara would never have let her kids play outside at that hour."

"The coroner says that they must have entered the water around then. So ask her about it."

"I'll do it," Sarah had agreed, "but only because I know you're wrong. And her paintings are beautiful. I've got one hanging in my living room."

"Then you'd better keep reviewing her openings," Stan Brockett said. "Try to set it up for around two, two-thirty, okay? I want to see both pieces by six tonight."

And that gave her about an hour and a half to write each piece, which would not be a problem for her; and she still had the whole morning to do the "What Sarah Saw" column and her review of the White Barn Players' production of *Hot l Baltimore*. She was assembling the information for her column when the telephone rang; she picked it up to hear Martha Gable incoherently trying to tell her that the killer of the two women had been shot by Dr. Wren Van Horne in a burglary attempt.

"I heard it from Mr. Pascal at Everything Bread, and he said that he had heard it from a customer who had heard it from a policeman," Martha Gable said. "So I wanted to call you and see if it was really true. But, Sarah—the policeman said it *was* true. He said we'd never have to worry about that man again."

As soon as she could get Martha off the phone, Sarah called Dave Marks at the police station. Dave Marks was the desk officer on duty when Sarah came to work most mornings, and over the years they had worked out a mutually satisfying relationship. Dave Marks gave Sarah any important information from the previous night, and she got his picture into the *Hampstead Gazette* whenever she could. When the *Gazette* ran its pictures of the Memorial Day parade, there was Officer Dave Marks striding prominently along with his fellow officers; when the *Gazette* ran a piece on teenage drinking late at night on Sawtell Beach, there was a picture of Officer Dave Marks leaning on the guardrail at the beach parking lot, looking youthful and authoritative. Sarah got her information before any of her competitors at the *Norrington Highlife* or the *Patchin Advocate*, and Dave Marks got a lot of attention from female police buffs who thought he was a celebrity.

"This guy was Gary Starbuck, and he was a biggie," Dave Marks told Sarah. "He's been breaking into houses all his life, traveling all over the country. I betcha this Starbuck guy had about six, seven hundred thousand scattered here and there in various accounts. We're going to open his house up so the folks can walk through and identify their property—we think he's done at least twenty burglaries in Hampstead since he arrived. You oughta see his place, Sarah. It's like some kind of a cave, all that stuff he's got in there. I guess he just ran out of luck. Dr. Van Horne shot him once, and that was all it took."

"Will Wren Van Horne have to answer any charges?" Sarah asked.

"Hell, no," Officer Marks said. "He shot Starbuck in the commission of an armed robbery. The son of a bitch had his weapon right in his hand. Van Horne'll be lucky if the chief doesn't bring him down to the station, declare a press conference, and give him a medal. Cops all over the country have been looking for this guy for at least fifteen years. It's funny—he was just like his father. This guy's old man lived just the same way. Work a town, fence all the stuff, move out fast, rent a house somewhere else. He was caught *once*, over a forty-year career, and did fourteen months in jail. The old man dies two years ago, in a nursing home in Palm Beach, he leaves his kid a pile of money, and the kid carries on where he left off. Like it's the family business, you know?''

"Did Starbuck do the murders?" Sarah asked bluntly. "I hate to say it, but he sure doesn't sound like the type."

Dave Marks was quiet for a long time. Then he sighed. "I had three calls about that already this morning. People wanna believe what makes them happy, you know? *We* never related Starbuck to the murders, and we never will. There might be a couple of our guys who think he was the one, but you know what that is, Sarah? It's hard for a cop to face that a guy like that is actually running around free. Every day he isn't caught is like another insult, see?"

"Yes, I see," Sarah said. "I was afraid of that. But a lot of people are going to believe that they don't have to worry about a stranger showing up at the door anymore."

"If it's a stranger," Dave Marks said. "Well, let's get off that subject. You want the rest of the stuff or do you want to wait for the file?"

"Anything big?"

"A traffic fatality. A Leslie McCloud of Charleston Road. McCloud was going about the speed of light up I-95 and killed a couple of kids from West Haven coming home from New York."

"Was he drunk?"

"There was enough booze in him to float a navy," Dave Marks said.

"I'll wait for the file."

"He was some kind of big shot."

"I'll still wait for the file."

2

Patsy had heard nothing of Gary Starbuck's sudden end, nor that the murders were now supposed to be solved. She had not been to a hairdresser, to an exercise room or a dance class or even a grocery store since Saturday night. She had returned home from Graham Williams' house not long after one-thirty, seen with no surprise that Les was not home, and went to bed in the spare room. She had noticed that his clubs were gone: Les would play golf all day, then eat at the club and sit in the lounge until closing time. He would be getting angrier and drunker, drunker and angrier. Tomorrow he would boil over, and begin beating her again.

This time she would fight back, Patsy vowed. This time, she would not go into a defenseless crouch. She would kick him—this time she would kick him in the balls, if he gave her half a chance. At Graham Williams' house, she had gone through an extraordinary array of emotions, from terror to humiliation to love, and what was most extraordinary to her was that the other three were not threatened or disgusted by all that had happened to her. They were simply calmly wonderfully *there:* they accepted her. If she had shown so much of herself in front of Les, he would have ordered her out of the room. Somehow, that she'd had a fit (setting the cause aside, for the moment), that she had then passed out and afterward experienced unhesitating love for the two men who had made sure she wouldn't concuss herself or swallow her tongue, that then she had apparently found that she had a telepathic link with a teenage boy—somehow Les would have seen all this as primarily a threat to his job.

That was not at all how the wife of a corporate vice-president was supposed to spend her Saturday night. Even through her deep exhaustion, Patsy felt rage—Les had put her into a straitjacket, her marriage had walled her up within iron conventions. She now remembered all the discussions Les and she had had soon after their marriage. −You can't act like that, Patsy, Les had said. −Like what? −Like you were acting with *Johnson* (or *Young,* or *Olson,* or *Gold*). −I wasn't acting any special way at all. −I know, but it looked like you were *flirting* with them. And if enough people think you were flirting with *Johnson* (or *Young,* or *Olson,* or *Gold,* or any of the twenty other young executives Les had climbed so expertly past), then we'll never get the Chicago posting.

Les had got the Chicago posting, rising so far above Johnson and the others that he could see the molt in their hairlines, they had moved to an apartment twice the size of their New York apartment, Les could afford to buy five new suits and a fistful of new striped neckties, he had his name on the door and a Bigelow on the floor . . . and he had started hitting her.

He had four drinks instead of one when he came home from the office. He stopped talking to her; he had stopped even listening to her. He worked nine-hour days, ten-hour days, then twelve-hour days. On the weekends he played golf with clients, with accounts, never with people; Les had stopped knowing people.

Because of one client, he took up skeet shooting. Because of another, he started going to the Bears games in the fall. Another got him into the Athletic Club. Les McCloud was ambitious and successful and admired. When he came home at night to the woman who had known him when he was only ambitious, he had his four drinks, grumbled about her plans for dinner, and started to short-circuit. Then she could see the Les driven desperate and half-loony by the twelve-hour days, the constant pressure of reports and decisions and responsibility. And then he started to hit her.

If he tries that again, Patsy swore to herself, I won't just kick him in the balls, I'll go after him with a knife. He can't come in loaded after playing golf all day and decide that it's time to show little Patsy who's the boss. I'll stick a knife in his arm if he tries that again.

It was as if the entire history of her marriage since Les had objected to the way she spoke to Teddy Johnson gave license to that image—herself jabbing a long carving knife into her husband's arm. She fell asleep with that picture in her mind, where it simmered in an angry glow of moral satisfaction.

Just past four o'clock in the morning, Bobo Farnsworth, still working double shifts, woke Patsy up to tell her that her husband had died in a fatal accident in the east-bound lanes of highway I-95.

Patsy knew that once Les had been good, as good anyhow as his world and character permitted, and that his goodness had been starved to death on what his career fed it. His onetime shyness had turned into social bullying, as on the night of the horrible dinner party with the Allbees, Ronnie, and Bobo; his sunniness had turned to calculated heartlessness; his humor had turned to acid; and his unaffected love for her had turned to grumpy jealous possessiveness. She mourned what there was to mourn. She had felt a moment of shocked guilt that around the time Les had immolated himself in his Mazda she was imagining pushing a knife into his arm, but that guilt lasted only long enough to be recognized. In some sense Les had stopped being her husband the day she had refused to make lunch for him—the day she had met Tabby Smithfield during Dr. Lauterbach's hour—and that momentary guilt had not earned enough to pay its way. It was for some other woman, not for her. If she felt guilt, it was for the teenagers Les had killed.

On that Monday, Patsy had the morning to fill before going to the funeral home to consult with Mr. Holland. She did not look forward to the meeting. Mr. Holland was a fussy little man who had been so well trained to his profession by his father and grandfather that he never betrayed any human feeling whatsoever—he was a propriety machine, and if he had ever had any idiosyncrasies they had been ground to dust many years before. Mr. Holland knew the McClouds, and he was not going to be happy with the idea of cremation. Not only would he want to sell her an expensive coffin, he would want to avoid a scene with Les's parents.

Patsy opened Les's closet, a cedar-lined walk-in a few steps from the bed. He had claimed it for his own immediately after they had moved, giving her the darker, less convenient closet next to the bathroom door. Here hung his twenty suits, his ten jackets, here were his fifteen pairs of shoes in a neat row, each stuffed with a wooden shoe tree. In wooden cubicles his shirts and sweaters made neat stacks. From a hook beside the ranks of suits dangled four pairs of suspenders, one with a pattern of death's-heads. Drawers concealed stacks of starched pocket handkerchiefs and ironed socks.

I will cremate him, Patsy said to herself. *I will.*

She brushed her fingers against the sleeve of a dark blue cashmere jacket, and then jerked her hand back. The soft material felt like a rebuke.

What could she do with all these clothes? Give them to his parents? Goodwill? She had to select the suit to give the undertaker.

She did not want to touch his clothes, and she did not want to go to Bornley & Holland to see Mr. Holland, she did not want to put up his parents and listen to them going through the inevitable cycle of criticism and mollification. *(I don't like to say this, Patsy, but is your house always so messy? Of course, I know you young women see things differently now.)*

If I had any character, Patsy thought, I'd give the clothes to Goodwill and put Bill and Dee in a motel. Laura Allbee would have been capable of such a gesture.

Patsy wandered back down the hall to the spare bedroom. It was here that she was most comfortable. She supposed that when Bill and Dee came, she'd have to give them this room and move back into that other room, so redolent of Les and her marriage. She ripped the sheets off the bed she had been using, and put on her newest, prettiest ones.

Patsy was walking toward the living room when the phone began to ring.

When she lifted the receiver, she heard a man's voice saying, "Patsy? Patsy McCloud? This is Archie Monaghan."

"Oh, yes. Hello." The name was barely familiar.

"I just heard about Les, Patsy. Jesus, what a damn shame."

Years of living with Les McCloud had trained her to hear the falsity in men's voices, so she said only, "Yes."

"A terrible thing. I was with him nearly all day that Saturday, you know. On the course."

And in the bar, Patsy thought. "I didn't know that."

"Oh, yeah. We played eighteen holes. He had a good time, Patsy. I thought you ought to know that."

"Thank you, Archie."

"So how are you making out? How are you holding up?" She suddenly remembered what he looked like. A short paunchy red-faced man in garish clothes. Bright clever blue eyes.

"I'm just trying to get through the morning, Archie. When it's twelve, I'll try to get through the afternoon. I couldn't tell you how I was holding up."

"Well, I'd be happy to come over anytime and help out. I'm a lawyer, I've seen a lot of things, Patsy. Any help you need—getting the estate in order, just talking things through. I make a great shoulder to cry on, Patsy."

Patsy said nothing at all.

"And if you want to get out of the house, I'd be real happy to take you out for a bite anytime, Patsy. What about tonight? I bet there's a lot of stuff you want to talk about, things you have to say, things you're afraid you'll never be able to say. I can help you, and I'm betting that you need a little old-fashioned help. Should I just come by for you around seven?"

"What did you have in mind, Archie?" she asked. "Candlelight and wine? Does that strike you as appropriate for the young widow?"

"I think the young widow should have anything she wants."

"Oh, good. Then I'll tell you what I want, Archie. I want you to go into the bathroom."

"Huh?"

"Into the bathroom. Then I want you to switch on the light. You have to be able to see yourself very well. Then I want you to take off your pants. Then I want you to take off your underpants. I want you to stand over the sink and think about me. I'm five-five, Archie. I weigh a hundred and sixteen pounds. I'm actually pretty skinny, Archie. I want you to put your hand on yourself."

"Hey, what the hell is this, Patsy?"

"Well, it's what you're going to do anyway, isn't it, Archie? So I might as well want you to do it. Because you're not going to do anything else."

"Jesus, you're sick." Archie hung up hastily.

Patsy smiled—a little wearily, a little bitterly, but she smiled.

3

When Mikki O'Hara opened the door of her long white clapboard house on Hampstead's hilly north side, Sarah Spry said, "Oh, Mikki," and held out her arms and embraced her. Mikki O'Hara was eight inches taller than Sarah, and had to stoop down. Sarah kissed her temple, leaving a little streak of lipstick, and briskly patted her back. "Oh, Mikki," she repeated. "I'm so sorry." She clung to the taller woman for several seconds before releasing her.

When they parted, Sarah saw her original impression of the dead children's mother confirmed. Mikki's face had sunken in—she looked twenty years older. Her eyes burned from far back in her head, her cheeks were shadowed. "Honest," Sarah said, "if you don't feel like talking to me, I'll go right back to my car and go on my merry way. Stan Brockett can take a running jump for all I care. I'd understand perfectly."

"Don't be dumb," Mikki O'Hara said. "I'm glad for the company. For some reason, I seem to be all alone."

"Alone?" Sarah was shocked. "Where's Des?"

"Des went to Australia with a client. They're doing something way out in the outback, someplace called Coober Pedy, and I couldn't even get through to him until last night. He's coming back, but he won't be here until tomorrow."

A faint though biting odor of whiskey accompanied this speech. Sarah thought that was understandable. Mikki O'Hara had identified her children's swollen bodies, spoken to the police, and then spent a day and a night alone. Probably tranquilizers had seen her through the night, but Sarah didn't think that she had had more than an hour's sleep.

"Come on in, will you?" Mikki asked. "Don't just stand around on my doorstep, you'll make me nervous."

"Do you want company for tonight?" Sarah asked. "You shouldn't be alone."

"Oh, my sister's coming in from Toledo, but thanks, Sarah. You want a drink?"

They were going into the living room, which had been decorated with long high-backed Italian furniture of pale brown leather, glass-topped tables, and track lights pointing down toward Mikki's bright watery abstractions. The drinks trolley had been rolled up to the edge of the long couch.

Sarah's mouth was already forming *no,* but she looked at the eight or nine bottles on the trolley, at the ice melting in the silver bucket, and pity made her say, "Yes, just a small one of whatever you're having."

Mikki wobbled toward the couch in her long brocaded caftan, saying, "Great, great, great." She sat down heavily, reached down to get a clean glass from the trolley's bottom shelf, and then looked across at Sarah, who had seated herself in the massive chair which faced the couch. Mikki's face looked blowtorched—the decorative caftan and the pale furniture in the bright room, even her own harmless and pretty paintings, conspired against that painful face. There was no room here for grief, no provisions had been made for it. "So Brockett thinks I'm of public interest, does he?"

Sarah took her notebook and pen out of her bag. "I'll just sit here and have a drink, if you'd like. I mean it."

"Oh, Sarah, you always mean everything you say. Have some Scotch." Mikki poured half an inch of whiskey into Sarah's glass, dug a few swimming cubes out of the ice bucket with her fingers, and then held the glass out toward Sarah. "Come and get it."

Sarah stood up and took the glass from Mikki's fingers.

"Really," Mikki said. "I don't mind talking about it. Really I don't." She picked up her own glass from the trolley and sipped what looked like straight Scotch. "It's all I think about, why shouldn't I talk about it? The only thing is, you have to promise not to be embarrassed if I cry. Just take a little snort and wait until it blows over."

"Fine, Mikki," Sarah said.

"You know what the funny thing is?" Mikki O'Hara asked. "Those kids never went out at night, especially not by themselves. Never. They just never did it. *And* they never went to the beach without permission. I don't think Tommy especially liked the beach anyhow. He liked sailing, remember? Tommy was crazy about sailing. We were going to get him a little Sunfish for his tenth birthday—he would have loved that." Mikki O'Hara's face worked, and her mouth trembled. She slugged back a huge mouthful of the whiskey. "But I'll tell you what I really don't get. You know what I don't get, Sarah? How those kids got all the way to Gravesend Beach. That's four miles away. *Four miles.* You know—they didn't walk all that way by themselves. Someone picked them up. Someone took them there. Some total creep picked up my kids and . . ." Mikki ducked her head and sobbed while Sarah sat stiff with self-contempt.

"Ah, shit," Mikki said finally. "I can't even say it without crying, but I think that's what happened. They wouldn't walk all that way by themselves. Little Martin was still using a baby bottle. I used to think he'd end up carrying the trusty old Evenflo off to college with him."

"But they left the house by themselves," Sarah said. "At least, I didn't hear that anyone was considering the possibility of kidnapping."

"It was Tommy," Mikki said. "It had to have been Tommy. He must have egged Martin into it. He must have gotten him out of his bed and put his clothes on him and told him some crazy story . . . and then gone out with him." Mikki flashed her sunken eyes, and for a second looked to Sarah like some crazy old woman you'd see on the streets in New York, an old woman with no teeth and a bulging sack filled with torn-up papers and all her clothes. "Honestly, if Tommy walked in the door right this minute, I'd hit the little bastard so hard I'd probably kill him."

The terrible eyes clamped shut again, and the shoulders shook under the brocaded caftan. Mikki was making a kittenish mewing sound. Sarah was trying not to feel like a grave robber: she could not imagine why Stan Brockett had sent her here.

Sarah stood up, walked around the coffee table, and sat down beside Mikki. She put her thin arm across Mikki's broad back. Then she pulled the other woman toward her.

Mikki's sobs eventually ticked down to a ragged trembling. "Oh, my poor babies," she got out, and a fresh line of tears jetted out from the corners of her eyes and spilled down her cheeks to her jawline. "Martin was so impatient with himself. He wanted to be a great big boy just like his brother. And Tommy called him stupid and all the normal abusive things boys say to their brothers, but secretly he was bursting with pride that Martin idolized him so much." Mikki slowly straightened up, and drained what was left in her glass. "I want them to get the guy who took my children to the beach and killed them. I want them to stake the son of a bitch to an anthill. I want them to peel his skin off while he's still living." Her eyes were those of the crazy toothless bag lady again. "I want to see him suffer as much as anybody can suffer and still live. And then I want to kill him myself."

Then Mikki surprised Sarah by hitting her hand on the reporter's knee and leaning close to her as if she were going to confide a secret. "You know, I did something. I had this dream." She leaned back again and smiled at Sarah from the burned-out eyes. "Remember when I told you that if Tommy came in I'd knock his block off?"

Sarah nodded.

"Well, I dreamed that Tommy *did* come in. Into my bedroom. He was so cold his teeth were chattering. I held out my hand, and he took it. He was all wet. I could smell the water on him, you know how you can do that? He was freezing. *Freezing.* So I pulled him toward me, and I lifted up the sheet, and I just pulled him into bed with me. Then I tried to warm him up by hugging him and hugging him."

Sarah put her arms around her friend again. Now, how, she wondered, would Stan Brockett want me to put that into my story?

4

On Monday morning Richard had a phone call from a man who said, "Hey, this is Baumeister Trucking and I'm on the Post Road, how do I get to this Beach Trail anyhow?"

"Who was that?" Laura asked, coming into the kitchen carrying a container of Ajax and a wet rag.

"Our stuff will be here soon. That was the truck driver."

"We get our furniture back at last?"

"Yeah," he agreed.

"I have a surprise for you," Laura said. "I've been saving it for today."

"I have a surprise for you too. When I was at the supermarket this morning, I heard the two women in front of me discussing the death of that man who killed the two women here in town."

"Did you really? Oh, thank God." Laura's hands had flown to her mouth, where they knitted together in an unconscious reference to prayer. "Thank God. Oh, I'm so glad. I mean, I'm not happy that he's dead, but I'm happy that he's not still walking around. It's such a relief, with you going off to Providence tomorrow."

"I thought you'd like to know," Richard said. "But I didn't know you were worried about me going away. Sweetie, I'll only be gone a couple of days."

"I know, but I was nervous anyhow. I didn't want to talk about it because I didn't want to make you feel defensive about going."

"I'm *already* defensive about going," Richard said. "This house is going to be such a mess."

"Just you wait. We'll have everything unpacked by tonight and the furniture all set out and the dishes all put away. The mess won't be so bad. Lump and I will survive if you're gone for a couple of days. At least we'll have our own bed back again."

"Farewell to Surf City," Richard said, and embraced her.

"You really heard those women say that, didn't you?" Laura asked.

"Sure I did. You think I made it up?"

"How did that man die?" She had her arms around him, and her head lay against his chest.

"I guess it happened just down on Mount Avenue. The man broke into a house, and the owner was there with a gun. The man got shot."

"I'm glad that's over," Laura said.

Richard saw a brown truck pull into the driveway. "Here's the rest of our life," he said to Laura.

A bulletlike man with a cigar stuck in his jaws eased down out of the cab and began to move slowly toward the back door. The rear doors of the truck swung open, and two muscular black teenagers jumped out.

"Do they have the right address?" Laura asked.

"It's their famous continuity of service," Richard said. "They try to bring most of the same furniture they took away from you in the first place."

Sarah Spry pulled into the driveway as the two teenagers were teetering down the planks between the ground and the back of the truck. Between them was a massive Victorian sofa. The driver sat enthroned in his cab, too grand to help the boys. Boxes that were full, half-full, and empty—the same gray and yellow boxes they had first seen in London—covered the kitchen and living-room floors. Two of the chairs that matched the sofa sat in puddles of crinkly brown paper on either side of the fireplace.

Richard held the door open for her, and she came in and put her hands on her hips and tilted her head back and looked around appreciatively. "You're a whiz," she said. "That awful smell is completely gone. And you've started to fix up the old place already."

"Well, we wanted to get as much done as we could before the furniture arrived," Richard explained. Sarah Spry's manner was just what he had remembered, but her face looked odd . . . her eyes were puffy and rimmed with red, as if she had some kind of eye infection.

"I know I look funny," the reporter said. "I've been crying. I had to do something pretty miserable before I could come here. Have you heard about the two children who drowned themselves at the beach just down the road? Happened Saturday night. I had to see their mother, and she's an old friend of mine. Hello, you must be Laura," she said to Laura, who was standing rather gloomily just inside the door to the kitchen. "Isn't your hair a beautiful color? Mine's as red as an old fireplug, but yours, my dear, you look like a fairytale princess. So anyhow, we cried us a river, as Julie London used to say."

The two teenage boys were now coming awkwardly through the door, their biceps bulging like weightlifters'. Richard knew that the sofa must have weighed three hundred pounds. "Facing the fireplace," Laura said, and they staggered toward the living room.

"What a terrible thing," Richard said, and Laura nodded and said, "Is she all right?"

"She's getting drunk," Sarah said. "Her husband is in some backwater in Australia, and that's the kind of thing you get in Patchin County. Husbands hop all over the world like bugs."

"Would you like some coffee?" Laura asked. "I just discovered a kettle and our old cups. We brought some instant from our other house."

"You not only look like an angel, you have the temperament of one. What a splendid idea, coffee. Instant is dandy with me, by the by. It's practically all I ever drink. Who has time these days for all that other stuff?"

Laura disappeared back into the kitchen.

"Two children drowned themselves?" Richard asked, remembering how she had phrased it. "You mean they killed themselves? Two brothers?"

"I didn't mean to make it sound worse than it was. They must have gone in swimming very late that night—around three in the morning. It looks like they just swam out until they couldn't swim any farther. Or maybe one got into trouble and the other died trying to save him. That's probably what happened."

"They were teenagers?"

"Nine and four."

"Oh, my God," Richard said.

Sarah Spry nodded grimly. "It's one of those terrible things. Hampstead has had its share of them, over the years. Why, do you know that one of my first jobs as a reporter was to go out to the country club and see the body of the man who owned this house? John Sayre? Well, it was. And he was a suicide, let me tell you."

"Yes, I know," Richard said.

"You talk to your neighbor across the street, he'll fill you in. Old Graham Williams. He was there that night. He was one of the last people to see John Sayre alive.''

"Graham is a friend of mine," he said.

"Then you've got better taste than most of the people in this town." They had gone into the big living room and Sarah put herself down on the huge sofa. She opened her bag and took her notebook and pen from it.

"Talk about yourself," she said, opening her notebook. "What was it like, being on *Daddy's Here?* What do you think about it now? Do you ever plan to go back to acting?"

So he talked about *Daddy's Here.* He described his respect for Carter Oldfield, his love for Ruth Branden. He did not mention Billy Bentley's name—he wanted not to think about Billy Bentley.

"Well, that sounds good, anyhow," Sarah Spry told him. Laura had come in with three cups of coffee, and she sat on the sofa with the reporter.

Richard could tell that she was furious with Mrs. Spry for staying, furious for implying that he had just lied to her. He knew she was furious because she sat very still and did not blink for long periods. Laura wanted everybody out of the house.

"As for what I'm doing now," he said, "I guess I'm trying to bring the past to life." And that was an unfortunate choice of words, he thought, considering what he and Williams and Patsy had been talking about; but he went on to describe their house in London and the business that had grown from it.

"I'm sorry," Sarah Spry said. "I'm losing track somehow. Could you repeat what you just said?"

Laura swung her foot up and down, up and down, burning with impatience only Richard could see.

"Sure," Richard said, "and then I guess we'll have to break it off. Laura and I have tons of things to do . . ." He paused, seeing that the reporter was staring at her pad, flushing.

"I'm sorry," Sarah Spry repeated. "I seem to be . . . I seem to be having . . ."

The telephone rang in the kitchen.

5

There, in the middle of her notebook, was what had caused her to lose the thread of the interview. Sarah knew she was blushing, but she could not help it any more now than she had been able to back in her blushing days, when any boy with a crack about fire-engine hair could bring the blood burning into her cheeks. She stared at the sentences, but they would not unwrite themselves. *I guess I'm trying to bring the past back to life. Naked swimmers. I believe in the structures of these older houses, I believe in the values they express, and I . . .*

Then, farther down the page, in her neat small writing, was the second wrong thing. *I was trained as an architect, but I didn't really begin doing the kind of work I truly loved until we bought our first house in London. I'm lost. That first house was my real university. I'm afraid. My business took off when a few people . . .*

Sarah dropped her pen on the floor.

Naked swimmers.

I'm lost.

I'm afraid.

It was as if those two poor lost children, Martin and Tommy O'Hara, had spoken to her straight through her pen. She had not heard Richard Allbee say those words, she had not consciously written them: there had been a moment when it was as if a gear had slipped, or the picture had gone fuzzy on the television tube, and in that moment of mental fuzz the unspoken words had expressed themselves through the pen and onto the paper. *Lost. Afraid.* She bent to retrieve the pen, her head seeming to detach itself from her body and view her awkward groping for the pen with cold indifference.

"I'm sorry," she said. She heard herself say it and saw her fingers close around the pen. "I seem to be *(having some trouble)* . . . I seem to be having *(a little difficulty keeping myself in order)* . . ."

When the telephone rang she could have fallen on the floor with gratitude.

6

"Patsy's in trouble," Richard heard Graham say. "I don't know what kind of trouble, but she needs us, Richard. Believe me, I wouldn't call you on a day like this if I didn't think it was serious."

"Trouble like Saturday night?" Richard asked, imagining Patsy trembling and convulsing somewhere on a strange floor.

"I don't know. I don't think so, no. It didn't sound like that. But she needs our help, Richard."

"Where is she?"

"At the funeral home just off the Post Road on Rex Road—around the corner from the Tack Room. Bornley and Holland."

"I'll try to get away," Richard said.

When he came back into the living room, Laura had left the couch and was standing in the back door with the two teenage boys. "Everything's out of the truck, Richard," she said. "One of the dining-room chairs has a broken leg, but that's the only damage I can see."

He looked toward Sarah Spry, who was clutching her pen and leaning forward over her knees like a third-grader who has to go to the bathroom. The flush was gone from her cheeks, and her entire wizened face looked inward and withdrawn.

"Okay," he said. "If we see anything else, we'll write to the company. You guys did a good job." He gave each of them ten dollars.

"Mister, is that lady all right?" one of the boys asked.

"I think so. Here's five for the driver, but it's five more than he deserves."

The boys left, and he turned to the reporter.

"I'm afraid that the interview must be over," he said. "I have to go down into town. Do you have everything you need?"

She nodded, put her hands on her knees, and dipped a little when she pushed herself up. "Yes. I have plenty."

"Would you like to rest here for a bit before you go? Can I get you anything?"

She smiled. "No, thank you."

"I just thought you seemed . . ." He paused, for he did not want to say "disturbed"; then he realized that a more accurate word was "frightened."

"Oh, I seemed, did I?" she said. Sarah was still smiling. "I think that conversation this morning caught up with me. That was not nearly as pleasant as this one was. No, I'll be fine, Mr. Allbee. I'll just be on my way. The story should be in Friday's *Gazette*."

He walked her to the back door. The moving truck was gone, and a mountain of brown paper and devastated packing cartons reared up beside the driveway. Beside the yellow-and-brown mountain smoldered two cigar butts the size of dog turds.

He waved as she got into her car, and then turned back to Laura. She was standing a few feet away and had her arms crossed over her chest. A black smear of dust bisected her forehead. "I can't believe that woman came here to interview you on our moving day. She'd better be good to you in her article or I'll go over to her office and burn her desk."

"Well, it's over with," Richard said. He patted his pockets to locate his car keys. "The timing for this is terrible, but Patsy McCloud apparently is in some kind of difficulty. That was Graham Williams on the phone. Patsy's down at a funeral home on Rex Road. I really ought to go, and I'd like you to come with me."

"Graham Williams can't handle it himself?" Laura inspected the palms of her hands, then wiped them free of dust on her jeans. "You and Graham are the Patsy McCloud Appreciation Society, it looks like. You spend all Saturday night with her, and now you have to rush off to help her bury her husband."

"I know it looks funny, I know it sounds funny and probably smells funny too, but she needs help. That's all I know. I wish you'd come along."

"I wouldn't dream of missing it," Laura said. "But the real reason I'm annoyed with you is that you forgot all about your present, and I spent about a week picking it out."

"My present?" he said stupidly. "Oh, my God. You got me a present. I did forget. The movers came, and then Sarah What's-her-name, and then Graham called . . . Oh, Laura, I'm sorry. I really am sorry."

"You ought to be, buster," she said. "I hid it in a kitchen cabinet. Do you have time to see it now, or do we have to rush off to your precious Patsy right away?"

"Let's go see it," he said, and put his arm around her as they went back into the kitchen.

Laura bent over and opened one of the bottom cabinet doors. She took out a silver-gray box about a foot high. "I sure hope you like this," she said, standing up and offering it to him. "It's a house present. I never spent so much on anything before in my life."

He took the box and set it on a counter. The box weighed less than he had for some reason expected. He lifted the top, and then looked sideways at Laura. She was still miffed, but far more than that, she was eager for his response.

"Whatever you do, don't drop it," she said.

He lifted the paper covering the top of whatever was in the box, and then put his hands in. It was cool porcelain with a smoky yellow glaze. His finger found a square bottom. This was hollow, which accounted for the lightness of the object. He hooked his fingers into the base and picked it up out of the box.

His expectant smile froze on his face. He was holding the grinning yellow head of a dragon. Two horns pricked up from its flat forehead; a thick wing like a frozen wave rose up just behind the head.

"It's Chinese," Laura said. "A roof dragon—an ornamental tile. The color means that it was on an imperial palace. I thought it would be good luck for us."

"Yes," he said, scarcely able to breathe.

"I see your enthusiasm is unbounded. Put it back in the box and I'll take it back as soon as we get our stuff unpacked."

"No," he said. "I want to keep it. I think it's beautiful."

"Do you really?"

"I do. I love it. I was just surprised. Honest. I love it."

"You look funny."

"I remembered something Graham Williams told me—there used to be a man here who was called the Dragon." And that was all he could tell Laura about Saturday night.

"Did your father know him?"

That made him smile. "No, it was a long time ago—back at the start of Greenbank."

"Well, now there's another one," Laura said. "Let's find a place for it."

Richard carried the dragon's head into the living room and set it on top of the mantel. Then he hugged Laura. Part of him felt that now the chaos had been admitted, had been allowed inside, that the door in his dream had opened and Billy

Bentley had come storming in with his hair plastered to his forehead and his clothes dripping from the storm.

"You do like it, don't you?" Laura asked. "You're not just saying it?"

He felt between them the cushion that was Lump Allbee, the modest darling of his dream. "I love it," he said. "Of course I do."

7

When Patsy opened the massive front door to the funeral parlor, she tried to dismiss the memories of the previous night. Mr. Holland had been waiting for her, and his narrow face as he came oozing across the carpet was a rebuke to fancy of any sort. He was actually a kind and nervous man, Patsy knew, but nature or heredity had given Franz Holland the face and structure of a Dickensian villain. His eyebrows twisted and twirled, his nose pointed, his shoulders hunched. He always wore expensive suits on his lanky frame. His lips were slightly too red for his pallid face. He wanted to be thought "civilized" and "superior" and so he aped those mannerisms he thought represented distinction. He was fond of laying one finger slantwise across his upper lip, of standing with his hips cocked and one foot slightly forward; of walking with his hands behind his back. When he walked toward Patsy across his thick carpet, he actually combined two of these gestures, and held his left index finger slantwise across his upper lip and his right hand behind his back. Patsy thought he looked like some pompous bird begging for silence.

As he neared her, the left hand languidly dropped, the right languidly met it, and Mr. Holland very slightly bowed. "Mrs. McCloud, thank you for coming to us," he said in a pleasant baritone voice. "Just remember that we are here to make this process as easy and painless for you as it can possibly be. As I said to you on the telephone yesterday, Mrs. McCloud, the last ceremony we give our loved ones can be as much a thing of beauty as the others—as beautiful as a christening or a wedding. Now, you have a suit for me?"

Patsy had been assured yesterday by Mr. Holland that although Les had been too burned in the fire that followed the accident for an open coffin, there was certainly enough of Les left to be dressed in his favorite suit. "Which we really do prefer, Mrs. McCloud, don't we? We want to think of our loved ones as attired in the raiment of glory, my father used to say, which often as not is provided by Brooks Brothers. So if you'll bring along some suit, shirt, and tie Mr. McCloud particularly liked . . . ?"

Mr. McCloud's favorite shoes were not required.

Patsy passed over the small brown paper bag she had been carrying. Franz Holland hitched it up under his arm as easily as if it contained his lunch.

"Mr. McCloud's parents will be arriving today, will they?"

"Yes," Patsy said. "They're taking the Connecticut limousine from Kennedy."

"Ah," Mr. Holland said, bowing forward and clasping his hands behind his back. "Of course I remember the senior McClouds very well. They came to us when your husband's grandfather passed away, and I think they were very pleased with what we did for them. Which brings me to an important question. Have you thought about the casket you would like to provide for your husband's remains?" He guided her, without actually touching her elbow, around a corner into a large room filled with reclining coffins.

"I think you can see that we offer a wide range of choice, Mrs. McCloud," he said, very nearly gesturing at the rows of yawning coffins. "And I'm sure you would agree with us that in this most personal of matters, choice is essential. And if I may . . . Madame is a Tayler, is she not?"

It took Patsy a second to realize that Mr. Holland meant her.

"Yes."

"My father and myself conducted the funeral for Madame's grandfather. Bornley and Holland have worked with many generations of Taylers, Mrs. McCloud."

"But not Josephine Tayler," Patsy said.

"Pardon?"

"You didn't work with Josephine Tayler, did you? My grandmother. Tayler was her maiden name too; she and my grandfather were distant cousins. You worked on her husband, but not on her. You put him in one of your boxes, but not her."

"Madame's grandmother fell ill, did she not?" Mr. Holland inquired, stepping one pace back. "It was a very sad story. Madame's grandmother was a lovely person. I believe other arrangements were made."

Patsy could not have said why she felt so hostile. "Yes, they certainly were. Madame's grandmother was the town crazy lady, and so her fine husband let her be put away in an asylum for most of her life."

Now the finger was back at its post across the upper lip. "It is a tragic history, Mrs. McCloud. And no doubt the circumstances bring it back to you. But if there is something to be learned from that history, madame, it is that we ought provide as well as we can for our loved ones when they are no longer able to provide for themselves."

"I want my husband cremated," Patsy said. "He was almost cremated anyhow, wasn't he? I want to finish the job. Just sell me the simplest damn coffin you have, and cremate him inside it."

Franz Holland visibly drew back. "Of course there are other family members to consider . . ."

She flashed out: "I don't want to cremate any other family members, at least not yet, I only want to cremate my husband! And if you won't do it, I'll take him somewhere where they will!"

"Mrs. McCloud," Holland said wretchedly, and in that instant—the instant before control left her altogether—she pitied him, who was after all a sensitive man and talked that way because his father had taught him to do it. "Mrs. McCloud, as the wife of the loved one your wishes are supreme, and we will do whatever will make you most comfortable. But we do have *your* comfort in mind, and I want to ask you to consider . . ."

Patsy nearly fainted. Mr. Franz Holland was dead. That pleasant, modulated baritone voice was coming out of a cracked, discolored mouth. The upper lip had split all the way into the nose, and she saw sunken gums and the roots of teeth standing out like distended veins. His tongue had blackened. Mr. Holland's skin was dry and parchmentlike, very slightly brownish in color. In places it seemed to have exploded open, leaving ragged holes into a sagging horror of ropy purple organs. Patsy finally saw that the creature before her wore only a dickey and a necktie. The skin on its hips had sunk in around the bones, and the penis had shrunk almost completely away.

Patsy screamed, having found her throat.

The creature jumped, and then held out a hand toward her. The nails were purplish-black and several inches long.

"Don't touch me!" Patsy screamed.

The creature backed away, hushing its dead bare feet across the thick carpet.

This was what her grandmother had seen. Josephine Tayler had gone on as long as she could, seeing her friends and strangers suddenly presented in rotting bodies when they were going to die soon, and then she could take it no more and she had had herself subtracted from the world. Mr. Holland was going to die within a month, and eventually this is what he would look like.

Only no one was supposed to see him when he looked like this.

"Mr. Holland," Patsy said in a shaking voice. She was looking down at the carpet. "I am sorry for screaming. I am having a difficult time. Please do not come near me. I apologize for making a scene. I am afraid that I am not quite myself."

"Of course, Mrs. McCloud," came the low voice, and Patsy shuddered.

"I wonder if I might use your telephone. I must call a friend to help me. No, please, do *not* come near me, Mr. Holland. Just show me where your telephone is."

The skeletal, shriveled feet hushed backward, and Patsy saw one of the claws pointing back out into the hall. "That's fine," she said. "I'll find it."

"At the desk in the alcove beside the Chapel of Rest," the thing said, and Patsy bolted past him, looking the other way.

"Have I done anything?" she heard him ask. "Have I offended you so terribly?" He sounded almost tearful. "If you do wish to cremate your husband, then of course . . ."

"Yes," she called backward. "Stay in that room, please, Mr. Holland." She saw the alcove half-hidden behind a red velvet drape. There was the desk and the telephone. The book was in the top-right-hand drawer, and she quickly looked up Graham Williams' number and begged him to come as quickly as he could.

"Yes, Richard too," she said. "Both of you. Come get me out of here."

8

What happened after the other three arrived at the funeral parlor was anticlimactic and can be reported in only a few sentences. Laura Allbee, who knew so much less than the other two about Patsy, seemed to comprehend the situation inside Bornley & Holland much better than her husband and Graham Williams—Laura immediately went to Patsy and put her arms around her. Richard and Graham huddled foolishly behind Patsy's back, patting her shoulder and glancing uncertainly toward Franz Holland, who seemed uncertain whether he could now emerge from the casket showroom. Eventually Richard went over to speak to him, but Laura called out to the funeral director, "There's no problem about a cremation, is there?"

"Not if Mrs. McCloud wishes one," Holland said. "I will make all the arrangements."

"That's settled, then," Laura said. She stood, and Patsy stood with her, still holding on to her. "We can all go home again."

Graham took Patsy back to Charleston Road, agreeing to drive her back for her car later that afternoon. "I had a touch of the Josephines," Patsy told him. "Still, at least I know that all of you are going to have a long life."

"Josephine Tayler could never tell when her family or her friends were going to die," Graham told her. "Only strangers and people she did not know well. But thanks anyhow."

Richard drove up to Rhode Island for his first appointment with Morris Stryker the following morning. He and Laura had parted with a long embrace after their first night in their new house; and with a promise to see Patsy McCloud after he returned.

9

Two nights later, while Richard Allbee was beginning to admit that he could not stand his client and that Morris Stryker very likely had little affection for his restorationist, Bobby Fritz was still agonizing to Bobo Farnsworth and Ronnie Riggley about the loss of his best customer. The three of them sat in the side booth just past the bar in the Pennywhistle Café, and two empty pitchers joined handles in the middle of the wet table. Ronnie kept drawing circles in the spilled beer, and Bobby knew—as he had known or suspected many times in the past—that Ronnie was bored by him: she thought he was immature or stupid, she thought he was a hick, not good enough to be a friend of Bobo's. Bobo had not come into the Pennywhistle, Bobby's favorite bar in Hampstead and at one time Bobo's, more than three or four times since he had gotten serious about Ronnie. And two of those times had been while Bobo was on duty.

"He fired me, man," he said, even though he knew he had said it not five minutes before.

"Do you think you could ask him to give you the job back?" Ronnie asked, still drawing circles in the puddled beer.

Ronnie Riggley, he considered, was one of the best-looking women he had ever seen. If not an outright 10, she was at least a good solid 8½. It didn't matter a damn that she was about a decade older than Bobo and himself. It didn't even matter that Ronnie did not particularly try to look young. She did not have to. Even when she looked kind of tired and draggy, the way she did tonight, Bobby wanted to get his hands on her; the more beer he drank, the more he wanted it. He was afraid that she would laugh right in his face if he ever tried anything.

"I can't beg, Ronnie, the man fired me," he explained. "But I just hate to go by there in my truck and see what's happening to his lawn. All the weeds are getting in there, he's got timothy and wild grass all over the place, and pretty soon he's gonna get that broom grass from outta the marsh. . . . I don't even want to think about what's happening to his garden."

"I think Ronnie's right," Bobo said, putting his arm around her and causing Bobby exquisite pain. "Just go up and ring his bell. Tell him how much you care about it. Maybe you can work out some kind of deal."

"Deal, huh," Bobby said. "If I walked up to his house he'd probably shoot me stone dead. Jesus. He must be pretty good with that gun, huh? He shot that Starbuck guy with the gun right in his hand, didn't he?"

"That's how we found him," Bobo said. "The gun right in his hand." In fact, though Bobo did not want to say this,

Dr. Van Horne had become a minor celebrity around the Hampstead police headquarters; Turtle Turk ragged younger men by telling them they should take shooting lessons from Van Horne.

"But those murders are over now, aren't they?" Bobby said.

Ronnie was nodding her head; but Bobo said, "Starbuck was a housebreaker, he wasn't a maniac. Too many people think we're out of the woods. There'll be another murder one of these days. Wait and see."

"You say," Bobby said. "*I* say they're done. That's part of the reason the other cops are so fucking happy, right?" He slapped his hand against his forehead. "I'm sorry, Ronnie, I should watch my mouth. I just don't feel right tonight."

"You did have a lot of beer," Ronnie said. "I'm not blaming you, but you drank most of those pitchers by yourself, and now you're working on a third one."

"Hell, I'm not drunk." He sounded belligerent to himself; he saw himself through what he thought were Ronnie Riggley's eyes. Immature, none too bright, drunk on beer.

"Well, I'll tell you what," Bobby said. "If I ever see him, I mean Dr. Van Horne, I'll talk to him real nice" (Ronnie was smiling at him, and Bobby suddenly felt this was possible, that he could put things back together again) "and I'll bullshit a little bit and all that, and then I'll tell him that I'll do his lawn free. Twice a month. Free lawn service. Because I can't *stand* to see it go to hell that way. And then what do you bet he takes me back? That's what he'll do. He'll take me back."

"You're blasted, you dope," Bobo said, reaching across the table to pat Bobby's head. "Ronnie and I will drive you home."

"I'll do it for free. Don't you see how totally *brilliant* that is? Then he'll have to hire me back!"

"Come on," Bobo said.

"Only if I get to sit in front next to Ronnie," Bobby said. "How'd you ever get a woman like this, anyhow?"

The look on Bobo's face told him that maybe he was drunk, after all.

The little house where Bobby lived with his parents was on Poor Fox Road, which one long-ago selectman had called "Hampstead's Appalachia." The road ambled along the bank of a tidal estuary and gave up just before it would have butted into the Greenbank railroad station. Who the Poor Fox was and what had happened to him, human or canine, had been forgotten long ago, but the name still had its former appropriateness. Poor Fox Road was the only street in Greenbank to be hidden, since to get to it you had to take an unlikely narrow road off Mount Avenue across the street from the entrance to Gravesend Beach, and then follow along the estuary until you came to a series of crumbling frame houses. Once these had been faculty houses for Greenbank Academy, but the school had sold them after World War II. Now a cranky and reclusive painter lived in one, a young man who worked at a body shop on Riverfront Avenue rented another, one particularly sinister house had been empty for at least fifty years, and the last belonged to the Fritz family.

As they turned onto Greenbank Road, Bobby found himself thinking more and more obsessively about putting his hand on Ronnie's thigh. He could not stop himself from imagining what it would be like to fondle Ronnie Riggley, what she would feel like. And if he gave in to this powerful yearning, he knew, two things would happen: Ronnie would have her most demeaning vision of him confirmed; and Bobo would throw him out of the car and never speak to him again.

So he said, "Hey, Bobo, just let me out where you'd turn, okay?"

"You want the exercise, Bobby?" Bobo asked him.

"Yeah, I want to clear my head before I get home."

"Good idea," Bobo said, and pulled Ronnie's car over to the side of the road as soon as he entered Mount Avenue. "That's where it happened," he said, nodding toward the lights of the Van Horne house, which were visible through the trees.

"Good for him," Bobby said. "I mean it. Good for him." He got out of the car and waved as Bobo drove off up Mount Avenue.

Bobby realized how drunk he was as soon as he started walking. The edges of Poor Fox Road seemed to tangle and twine, and within a few feet of the entrance he was up to his knees in weeds. "Oh, lonesome me," he said, and backed out onto the road's surface again. His feet took him all the way to the other side of the road, and then he straightened up and made himself go in a more or less straight line toward his house. For a moment he saw two moons overhead, two roads before him, but he squinted and brought the images together. Two and a half pitchers of beer hummed in his blood, two and a half pitchers of beer muffled his head.

With terrific suddenness he had to urinate. "Lordy, lordy, lordy," he sang, and turned into the weeds along the side of the road, unzipped himself, and barely got himself out in time. His piss splattered in a wide arc across weeds and tree trunks. On his right leg he felt a spreading damp spot. "Shitzky." Finished, he zipped up again and faced Poor Fox Road.

The moon seemed twice as large as it should have been. It was a bloated, rotting sphere leaning down toward him. Chill light streamed toward him from this enormous moon: he felt the stain on his right leg turn freezing cold.

The moonlight seemed to crackle against his skin. Poor Fox Road was supernaturally bright. Bobby saw the perpendicular shadows thrown by pebbles on the road. Then he saw that there was a face in the moon. The face was sneering and coarse, inhumanly cruel. Bobby threw out his hands, as if they could protect him from the terror this awful face promised, and saw that in the light they looked covered with silver fur.

The moon leaned right up to his own face and whispered, *Look down.*

Bobby looked down; screamed. Blood was flowing down the road in a sluggish tide, lapping over his shoes. Its smell enveloped him—the road stank like a butcher's shop. Because the cynical moon was so close now, the slow-moving tide of blood was black.

Look up, the moon whispered in the black-and-white world, and Bobby jerked his head up. He saw silvery trees, black leaves, a silver-and-black bend in the road.

He's coming, the moon blew toward him on a foul wind, and opened its bloated mouth and grinned.

Bobby heard footsteps splashing through the tide of blood. He tried to step backward, and a blood-soaked creeper whipped out of the side of the road and grasped his ankle and dumped him into the cold, slow-moving tide.

Coming, the moon whispered into the back of his neck, and Bobby struggled back up on his feet. His hands were black with blood; his jeans adhered to his legs.

He could not move in this black-and-white, this silvery

world. The crazy idea that all this blood on the road was really his own jumped into his mind—he was dead, it just hadn't happened yet.

He knew that something awful was coming toward him, and he stepped toward it, raising his fists.

He was almost disappointed when nothing more frightening than a man came around the silvery corner. The moon rode hugely behind him, and Bobby could not see his face.

"Stay away," Bobby said. His voice sounded small and high.

A familiar voice said, "You're all right, boy. Why, you've just had too much fun."

The black figure stepped forward again, and Bobby saw that there was no river of blood washing down the road. His own urine stuck his jeans to his leg. In the moonlight, his hands were once again painted with silver, not black. The man advancing toward him was someone he trusted.

"Had a lot of beer tonight, didn't you, Bobby?" the man asked, and then he lifted his head and Bobby saw the white hair and civilized face of Dr. Wren Van Horne.

"Oh, I was just talking about you, Doctor," Bobby sang out, his relief making his voice louder than it needed to be. "No kidding—I was! You know what I said about you? Good for him, that's what I said, good for him, and I meant it too."

"Thank you." The doctor came slowly toward Bobby in the streaming moonlight.

"No birds," Bobby said. "You notice? No bird sounds. Usually if you come down here at night, you hear an owl or two."

"Oh, the owls are dead now," Dr. Van Horne said as he came toward Bobby weaving in the middle of the narrow moonlit road.

"No shit. I see a lot of dead birds on my lawns, you know? A couple more every day—I hate to run the big mower over 'em, you know? It makes a terrible noise." Then a connection formed itself in Bobby's mind, and he said, "Now, that reminds me of what I was gonna say to you. Dr. Van Horne, I just can't *stand* seeing your lawn go to rack and ruin the way it is. What I want to do is, you let me come work on it for free for a little while."

Now Dr. Van Horne was standing only a foot or two in

front of Bobby on the narrow road. Bobby could see an au-
reole of silvery hair standing out against the still-enormous
sphere of the moon, but the doctor's face was again a sheet of
black in which floated denser patches of black.

"What do you say?" he asked, and then recoiled, for the
foul stink of sewage and rot had opened around him, and it
was worse than that, it was the smell of something that has
died in a cover of weeds and weeks later is struck by the
shovel, and spills out this almost liquid smell.

"You want to work for me?" Dr. Van Horne asked him.

Bobby stepped backward, and felt the tide of blood lapping
at his ankles. Dr. Van Horne held out his hand, and in it was
a small curved blade. Before Bobby could react, the blade
slipped through the air and punched into his neck just below
his left ear. The doctor drew the blade quickly down and
across, and a huge bubble of blood burst from Bobby's neck.

Bobby fell to his knees. He felt no pain at all—all he could
feel was the warmth and wetness of the blood rushing down
his neck and chest. All that life, rushing to get out of him!
Dr. Van Horne swung down at him again, and this time there
was a great flare of pain, for the doctor had sliced off most of
his left ear. Bobby held up his hand, almost not believing that
all of this was happening to him, and the little curved scalpel
came down between his second and third fingers and split
open his hand. The little scalpel went away again, and
Bobby's heart obediently pumped out another gout of blood,
and he lost consciousness just before Dr. Van Horne sliced
off his left cheek.

Bobby Fritz, Greenbank's excellent gardener, toppled forward into a vast blackness; Dr. Van Horne rolled his body
over, sliced off his shirt, and then began to rearrange what
was beneath it. He cut through Bobby's chest, exposed the
ribs and snapped them back, sliced away the matter surrounding the heart, and lifted it out. He set the heart in the hand he
had split open. Then he opened Bobby's belt, unsnapped his
jeans, and pulled them down. After that he sliced off the
penis and testicles and put them in Bobby's right hand.

All of this was similar to what he had done twice before,
and would do three times more. They would not go forward,
his victims.

He dragged Bobby's scarcely recognizable body into the
weedy ditch beside Poor Fox Road. When it was out of sight
he took a sheet of paper from his hip pocket and put it inside

Bobby's chest. The sheet of paper, and the poem lettered on it in writing so anonymous it might have come from a computer's printing station, were not discovered until several hours after the body was found. This was two days later, on the thirteenth of June.

10

It was a mailman who found Bobby Fritz. Roger Slyke drove a blue-and-white mail van over most of Greenbank every morning, and then spent most of the afternoons back in the central Hampstead postal station sorting mail. For two or three days Roger had been feeling oddly disoriented—his teeth hurt, and there was a more or less constant noise in his ears, and sometimes he caught himself at the point of putting someone's mail in the wrong box. He wondered how many times he had done it, in these past two days, without noticing. On Wednesday morning, when he should have been turning into Charleston Road, he had found himself way off his route, all the way over to the Old Sarum Road, without any idea of how he had got there.

At noon on Friday, the thirteenth of June, Roger Slyke had driven all the way up to the end of Poor Fox Road just to deliver a letter from the Bush-for-President campaign to Harold Fritz, who was a lifelong Democrat and would never get out of bed to vote again anyhow. On the way back, his head had started to swim, and he had gotten a bad feeling, a really bad feeling in his heart, of being sick scared wrong, as he sometimes did when he looked at that empty house between the Fritz house and that place where the boy had all those wrecked cars. Roger had let the mail van coast to a halt. He had caught an awful smell. For a second Roger Slyke was certain he had seen the daytime moon leaning up toward him and grinning at him; then he stopped the van and jumped out and held his head, which felt as though it wanted to explode.

Roger had not set the brake on the mail van, and while he was holding his thundering head, the van slid forward a few inches and then rolled on into the ditch. It promptly pitched onto its side and dumped hundreds of letters into the weeds.

Roger looked up with bloodshot eyes and said, "Nah." He walked over to the ditch and looked down, shaking his head. He stepped into the ditch after making sure it was not filled with poison ivy—Roger was wearing short pants. He made it to the van and pushed at it. With the help of one more man, he could get it upright. Roger knelt down to begin picking up the letters and magazines scattered through the weeds. Suddenly that smell of a smashed possum was stronger than ever, and then Roger found himself looking through a green tangle of vines and straight at Bobby Fritz's grinning face. Roger Slyke let out a whoop and backpedaled up the side of the ditch and ran all the way to the entrance to Gravesend Beach. There was a phone in the guardhouse. When the police found the block-lettered poem in Bobby Fritz's chest, they found that several of Roger's letters had slipped down in beside it. The letters stank too, but Roger Slyke delivered them the next day.

The state police did not recognize the poem, nor did anyone on the Hampstead force.

Rich men, trust not in wealth,
Gold cannot buy you health;
Physic himself must fade;
All things to end are made;
The plague full swift goes by;
I am sick, I must die—
Lord have mercy on us!

Beauty is but a flower
Which wrinkles will devour;
Brightness falls from the air;
Queens have died young and fair;
Dust hath closed Helen's eye;
I am sick, I must die—
Lord have mercy on us!

Strength stoops unto the grave,
Worms feed on Hector brave;
Swords may not fight with fate;
Earth still holds ope her gate;
Come, come! the bells do cry;
I am sick, I must die—
Lord, have mercy on us!

Nobody could identify this poem until Bobo Farnsworth thought to call his former English teacher, Miss Threadgill, who was now the head of the English department at J. S. Mill. "Are you developing an interest in English poetry, Bobo?" she asked him.

"Only in this poem, Miss Threadgill," he said.

"What you read to me were the second, third, and fourth verses of a famous poem by Thomas Nashe called 'In Time of Pestilence.' Nashe was generally a rather feverish, violent writer, the greatest of the Elizabethan pamphleteers. He was given to the grotesque."

" 'In Time of Pestilence,' by Thomas Nashe," Bobo said. "Thank you, Miss Threadgill."

"What in the world are you people doing over there in the police station?" Miss Threadgill asked, and Bobo told her that she would be reading about it in the papers.

11

The stanzas from the Thomas Nashe poem were printed on the front page of the *Hampstead Gazette* the following Monday; but even before that, they appeared in a *New York Times* Metropolitan Section article headlined "The Connecticut Ripper?" In a box beside the article were photographs of Stony Friedgood, Hester Goodall, and Bobby Fritz.

In a long conversation he had with Patsy McCloud on Tuesday night, Graham said, "It's poetry, do you see? That's the link. He's deliberately referring to Robertson 'Prince' Green. Young Green's father claimed he had been corrupted by poetry. And there was a newspaper article about the 'Ripper-Poet.' He wants us to know, Patsy. He wants us to know who he is." All through this conversation, Graham Williams heard the whicker of the dragon's wings: he heard them while Patsy told him about her marriage; he heard them in the title of the Nashe poem, which lay printed out before them on the front page of the *Gazette;* he heard it especially in a list of children's names which were given in another *Gazette* article.

On the night of the thirteenth—Friday the thirteenth, the day Roger Slyke accidentally found Bobby Fritz's body— Richard Allbee called Laura from Providence; he said that he was having more problems than he had expected with the job, and would have to stay in Rhode Island four or five more days, maybe as long as another week. Laura told him not to worry about her: she said she would be fine, that she was sorry he was having difficulties but knew he could sort them out. She told Richard that things were quiet in Hampstead.

Laura could not have told him about Bobby Fritz, for she did not hear about the discovery of the killer's third victim until the next morning, when Ronnie Riggley called her up with the news. Yet she could have said, and did not say, to Richard that five more children had followed the example of Thomas and Martin O'Hara and drowned themselves. This had happened on the night of the eleventh, the same night Bobby Fritz was hacked to death, mutilated, and concealed in a ditch on Poor Fox Road; and Laura did not tell Richard about the five children because she knew he would worry about it, would worry about *her*, and she did not want to add to his troubles. Laura had seen the first article about the five children in Friday's *Gazette;* their names were given again in the following Monday's paper, which Graham Williams and Patsy McCloud had open on the table before them.

Within what is known there is a deep layer of the unknown. No one on the staff of the *Gazette* ever said it in print, but the town had gone into shock: the nightmare of the random killings was not over after all, and an even worse cycle seemed to have been visited upon them. No one on the *Gazette* wanted to do more than report the facts, to print what was known: that was all there was, they imagined.

And here is what was known. On the night of the eleventh of June or early on Thursday morning, the twelfth, these events took place: a twelve-year-old boy named Dylan Steinberg walked into the water at Sawtell Beach after leaving his clothes neatly stacked beneath his shoes on the sand and swam out until he became too tired to swim any farther, went under the water, and drowned; in separate incidents, three children named Carl Blockett, Monty Sherbourne (the son of the principal of J. S. Mill's middle school) and Annette Crowley (the child of a travel writer on the staff of the *Times),* who were six, seven and thirteen respectively, drowned themselves with the same crazy deliberation off Gravesend Beach; and a five-year-old boy in Redhill named Hank Hawthorne (the son of an insurance executive and grandnephew of a noble old lawyer in Milburn, New York) left his bed in the middle of the night, stripped off his pajamas and threw them on his bed, then went downstairs, unlocked the door, and drowned himself in the wading pool on his front lawn. This is what the police and *Gazette* reporters knew; they would truthfully have said that there was no need to report the effect of this information on the town of Hampstead. That seemed obvious enough—it was not printed in the newspaper, but on the faces of those who were shopping for spaghetti sauce and romaine lettuce at Greenblatt's, the faces of those buying typing paper or just looking at the big-screen-projection television at Anhalt's on Main Street.

But even here there was a profound layer of the unknown. Those people buying groceries at Greenblatt's or stationery at Anhalt's would have known that the mothers and fathers of the dead children were distraught, in emotional shock, traumatized; Hampstead was a sophisticated town, and the shoppers would have predicted that some of the parents would find their way into psychotherapy and others into the divorce courts. Because they were verbal and sophisticated people, they could have described the guilt the parents of the dead children must be suffering; they would have speculated about cults and phases of the moon and sunspots (much as Sarah Spry was soon to do); might have gone on to mention other cases of childish mass hysteria, which this did seem to be, after all, and if you had kids you ought to be locking them in their rooms at night or taking them back to the city, where they'd be safe. But probably no one except Mikki Zaber O'Hara—and possibly Sarah Spry—would have guessed that Mrs. Sherbourne and Mrs. Crowley and Wendy Hawthorne in Redhill dreamed on the night their children were killing themselves that they were comforting cold wet sons and daughters—taking their frozen bodies into their beds and holding them tightly against their breasts while they chafed their backs and brushed sand from their chests.

12

When Richard spoke to Laura on Friday night, he did not have to say that the source of the problems that would keep him in Providence was his client, for when there were problems it was usually the client who caused them. Laura would have known that, and Laura had seen her husband cope successfully with clients who could not make up their minds, who changed their minds in the middle of the job, who thought that they could do the job better themselves. Richard had not made friends with all of his clients, but he had at least been friendly with all of them. Laura knew these things, but

Laura had not met Morris Stryker. Morris Stryker defeated most of Richard's expectations, and Richard had begun to fear by Friday night that Stryker would defeat him too.

They had begun badly, and maybe the beginning underlay all the subsequent troubles. Richard's first impression of Morris Stryker was that he was a great deal like the truck driver who had left a mountain of rubble in the middle of his driveway. Stryker was large and flabby and nursed a cigar with his lips; Stryker was a bully who had terrorized his secretary and cowed the contractor on the job, Mike Hagen, into agreeing with everything he said. And for his part, Stryker thought he was a fraud—Stryker had expected him to be English.

Richard had discovered that three days before, when he had driven up to the job for the first time. He had come into Providence on I-95, checked into his hotel, washed and changed his clothes, and driven to College Street. Stryker and Mike Hagen were already there, sitting in the backseat of Stryker's Cadillac. When Richard left his car and walked across the street, his eyes on the lovely but dilapidated eighteenth-century mansion he was supposed to restore, Stryker and Hagen emerged from the Cadillac to meet him. He had immediately known which of them was the contractor and which the client, for Stryker wore a powder-blue suit, a navy-blue shirt, white shoes, and a gold chain around his neck. Contractors, in Richard's experience, usually dressed in a way that made them look at home in their pickup trucks.

"Allbee?" the massive Stryker said. "Mr. Allbee?"

"Yes, nice to meet you, Mr. Stryker," Richard said. "This is a lovely Georgian house we have to work on."

"I want it to look like the most expensive house on the block," Stryker said, and looked at him a little oddly. "This is Mike Hagen, he's doing the work. Mike and I went to school together, right here in Providence."

"Hiya," Hagen said. He stood in back of Stryker, hands in his pockets.

"Well, Mr. Stryker," Richard had said, "this is going to be an interesting project. I can see plenty of opportunities to use contemporary techniques, for example in the paints." Richard was revving up, thinking about the pigments he could use to get the brightness and clarity of an eighteenth-century interior.

"Hey, you're not English," Stryker unexpectedly said. "You're supposed to be English, aren't you?"

"I was born in Connecticut," Richard said. "My wife and I lived in London for about twelve years, and that was where I started doing restoration work. That's probably where you got the impression I was English."

"Toby," Stryker shouted, turning back to the Cadillac. "Toby, get out here right now."

A colorless blond man opened the front passenger door and stood up nervously beside the car.

"He's not an Englishman, Toby," Stryker said in a lowering voice.

"He's not?" Toby squeaked. "I thought he was. I mean . . . he's from London, isn't he?"

"Mr. Allbee just worked there, Toby. He is from Connecticut, which you should have found out about, don't you think, Toby?"

"Yessir," Toby said.

Mike Hagen just stood with his hands in his pockets, not looking at anybody or anything. He'd had a long experience of Morris Stryker.

Stryker shook his head, then leaned over and spat out his cigar. "You worked in England though, huh?" he asked Richard.

"Until now all of my work was in England."

Stryker shook his head again. "Well, we might as well go inside." He glared at Richard. "I thought, you know, you were English, and you just came over to Connecticut so you could work in this country. I wanted somebody English."

"We can make the house look as English as you like," Richard had said, and that had been a mistake.

13

This was Saturday, the fourteenth of June, a week after the attempted burglary at the Van Horne house, and Tabby Smithfield awoke in the middle of the night confused and feeling somehow that time was escaping him. He had to hurry, he had to rush, he did not know where. Gasping, he got out of bed and felt for his clothes. He was late for school . . . he was late for an appointment with his grandfather. He slid into his jeans and pulled the day's shirt over his head. In the dark he laced his running shoes. He knew that he could not make any noise—his father was in the room downstairs with Berkeley Woodhouse, and he would be furious if Tabby disturbed him.

Berkeley Woodhouse was the woman Tabby had seen with his father just before he'd had the series of visions in the library. Clark had invited her to "Four Hearths" for dinner, and she had given Tabby a kiss that left lipstick on his cheek. Clark and Berkeley were drunk when they had arrived back at the house, and got drunker during dinner. She talked about her divorced husband, he talked about Sherri. Berkeley had kept reaching across the table to grasp Tabby's hand. Immediately after dinner Clark had switched on the television set and taken Berkeley upstairs. The orders were clear.

But now Tabby had to get out of the house, he had to get on his way. His grandfather was waiting, and Dicky Norman was waiting, and Gary Starbuck too.

Tabby eased out his bedroom door, aware that something was wrong with these thoughts, but in too much of a hurry and still too fogged with sleep to know what it was. He went quickly down the stairs. The house was completely dark. He opened the front door and walked out into the brightest moonlight he had ever seen in his life.

His grandfather was waiting. No, someone else was waiting.

He looked back up at the place where the moon should have been and saw the face of Gary Starbuck looming down toward him. *Run!* Starbuck ordered him, pushing his great white face through millions of miles of empty air. *Run!* Starbuck's face was dead—dead as moon rocks, the color of white cheese.

Tabby ran from the moon with Starbuck's face in it.

He pounded out of Hermitage Road and turned the corner into the long descending slope of Beach Trail. Momentum carried him forward, and for a heart-stopping few seconds he seemed to be traveling above the ground as if he had shot off a ski jump. Then his feet found the surface of the road again and held to it, and he was racing down Beach Trail. It seemed to go straight down, and be made not of asphalt but of slick mud. When one of his feet struck the road, it slid crazily along and he had to fight for his balance until he could get the other foot out in front of him, and the whole process began all over again.

As he sped toward Graham Williams' house, he saw it enveloped by a red glow. He raced forward and down, the hill much steeper than he knew it was. There was an enormous scorched circle on the lawn where he had thrown Starbuck's two-way radio seven days before, and from the black circle a line of singed and burning grass led straight to the front door. Tabby drew closer and closer to the old man's house, unable to stop or get off Beach Trail, and saw the glow surrounding the house flicker redly.

Behind him the Starbuck-moon blew toward him and almost knocked him over with its breath.

Now he could see right into the glowing house, he could see every room. Books were circling lazily as sparrow hawks in the living room, and a comic-book devil was strangling Graham Williams in the upstairs bedroom. As Tabby sped by, truly unable to stop, the devil, who was red and horned and had a thick saurian tail, tightened his grip on Graham's neck and turned sideways to face Tabby. He was grinning. His face was enormous, and a flickering tongue the size of a baseball bat curled and danced out of his mouth. His massive penis was split into two erect twitching forks. The devil twisted Graham's head and then lifted the body to show Tabby how limp it was.

Tabby screamed, but the scream slipped out behind him and he was careening into Mount Avenue, struggling to stay on his feet. The dead breath of the moon slammed into his back and lifted him along down Mount Avenue.

When he sped past the historical marker before the walls of Greenbank Academy, it swung up from the ground like a gravestone on hinges and the fire-bat flapped up out of the ground. The fire-bat circled over speeding Tabby Smithfield, looked down at him with its empty eyes, and then lifted up. Tabby saw it move quickly away, even its fire whitened by the frozen silver light streaming from the moon. The fire-bat dipped its wings at the Van Horne house and then sailed over the water. Tabby watched it flying toward the Millpond.

Of course he could not see the Millpond: that was a mile away, and trees and houses intervened: but as Tabby jumped or was blown over the fence across the short road to Gravesend Beach, he was aware of two areas which glowed as if they burned. These areas were roughly equidistant from him, and neither one was normally visible. Far off to his right, the fire-bat was settling down on the spit of land known as "Shrinks' Row," and far off to his right, jutting out into the Sound like Shrinks' Row, Kendall Point shone red too. Tabby looked right and saw the bat's wings brush the tops of the pretty frame houses, saw flames spring up under the eaves; looked left and saw all of Kendall Point glowing a poker's angry red.

Then he was walking down the road to the beach in ordinary moonlight. The sky showed a trace of red over the tops of the trees to his right, but he could see no flames.

It seemed to him that he had been moving for the past ten minutes in a crazy dream. He looked uneasily up at the moon, which looked nothing like Gary Starbuck. He stopped still on the narrow road to the beach. The air around him stopped too. The ground was solid. The redness over the tops of the trees between him and Shrinks' Row could have been from a police car, he thought.

He did not believe that those houses were burning any more than he believed that an enormous bat made of fire had climbed up out of the ground beneath that slab of a monument.

Tabby looked once more at the redness, daring it to show him an actual flame, and then continued up the road to the beach. *Wait a second,* he thought. *Why am I going this way? Why not just go home?*

"Do you really think you could sleep?" he asked himself out loud. *Not for about a week, no. Besides I have to . . .*

Have to what?

. . . go up to the water.

What for?

To see it.

He had to walk up to the Sound and look into the water. Simple, really, wasn't it? And all the rest of what had happened, Gary Starbuck and the devil and Graham Williams and the fire-bat, had been the little sideshows and inducements to bring him this far, so that he had only another twenty yards to go before he could walk out on the sand and take a good look at the sea.

From where he stood he could see a long black line of water. He did not want to get any closer to it.

Please.

The wind pushed him forward, scurrying at his back.

Please.

Please yourself.

A part of him did want to see what was going to happen up there; part of him wanted to find out what would be the last act of the night's performance.

He stepped forward, and the wind teased his hair, fluttered his shirt. His stomach ground in upon itself, and he was afraid for a second that he would throw up. He stepped forward again, then determinedly strode all the way up to the retaining wall at the end of the parking lot, jumped over the wall, and landed on the sand with both feet. Now he was on the Dragon's territory.

Tabby looked up. The moon had retreated and the world was safe. Away to his right, the sky above the trees showed a persistent tinge of red. To his left was the curve of the beach, then the series of little private beaches, each marked off by a row of upended slabs like headstones. The last of these, sweeping out into the water beneath a wooded hill, was the beach which had once been his grandfather's. Small dark waves spattered into froth at the edge of the sand.

The only noise he heard was the hissing of the waves. The breeze gently pushed at his back; the hissing of the waves called him forward. Tabby walked across the sand toward the shingle, the stripe of seaweed-encrusted pebbles at the high-tide mark.

"Show me," he said.

The froth of the waves turned red as it bubbled toward his feet. When he looked out at the seething water, he saw it too was now red—a deep sluggish red that went black in the troughs between the rising waves. The air reeked of blood, and then the first flies appeared.

They had been awakened by the smell of so much blood, and in seconds it seemed to Tabby that every fly in Hampstead had come to feed at Gravesend Beach. The silence had become a single great buzzing. Tabby frantically waved his hands before his face, trying to keep the flies from his eyes and mouth. Now the shingle and the entire stretch of the beach were a black glistening carpet of flies. He felt them shifting over his feet, weighing on his shoes. Their buzzing grew louder and louder, more rhythmic as hundreds and thousands more of them clustered on the blood-soaked sand.

"Show me!" Tabby yelled.

He disgustedly spat out the flies which had entered his mouth and watched a giant red wave swell up in the moonlight. The wave bulged out, layering and layering as it moved toward the shoreline, and growing—Tabby thought—ten feet high. He stepped backward, and felt the flies crushing beneath his feet. They buzzed furiously about his head. Half a dozen or more crawled down his collar inside his shirt. The towering wave arched above Tabby, and he saw his father and Berkeley Woodhouse tossed within it. They were naked and dead, tumbled together inside the wave, and when the red wave shattered on the beach it sent them rolling. Immediately a thousand flies descended. When the next wave rolled them back, the flies' monotone buzzing scream grew louder and more hypnotic.

"Show me!" Tabby yelled, and saw another wave far out in the Sound begin to speed toward him, growing more massive with every foot it traveled. The wave rose up fifteen feet into the air and was still growing when it crested at the shoreline. Tabby ran backward over the surging flies, looking up into the arching wave.

First he saw Graham Williams, his thin arms and legs splayed as he was borne up by the water; then Richard Allbee's body, not only naked but hacked and mutilated, spun into sight; and then Patsy's dead nude body revolved as the powerful weight of the wave buffeted her past Richard's corpse.

The wave of blood towered up over Tabby, almost seeming to walk up on the sand, and the flies attacked it.

When it fell, tumbling the bodies of his friends into the sand, it knocked Tabby over. Every inch of him was instantly drenched with the thick heavy fluid. Tabby was carried down the sand as the blood withdrew. For a horrible moment he was looking into the dead eyes of Richard Allbee, whose body swept past his. Tabby dug his fingers into the soaked sand, and scrambled with his legs. He felt dampness cover his hands again, and then saw that where his fingers had clawed into the beach, blood welled out. Richard Allbee's body slid back into the Sound. He could not see the other bodies. Tabby pulled his hands from the bleeding sand and got to his feet. The wet flies struggled in the pools of blood dotting the sand; thousands of others found Tabby.

They landed on his eyelids, in his hair, burrowed into his ears. Flies blanketed his hands.

Tabby slapped his hands against his wet shirt, scattering hundreds of them and killing as many. He wiped at his eyes.

"Show me!" he screamed. *"It's just water and the flies aren't even here! Show me what you can really do!"*

For an instant, for a moment so brief it was almost gone before he realized what it meant, Tabby was standing in dry clothes on an ordinary Gravesend Beach; there were no flies.

Then the world gave a hitch and he was slimed with blood once again, the air stank, and battalions of flies lifted and fell around his head.

He groaned and staggered back. Then he realized what had happened, and he laughed. He had stopped it for a second; he had startled the Dragon and made the merry-go-round come to a halt, however temporarily. He laughed, and the flies crawled in his mouth, and he kept laughing. Then he shouted again.

"I won! I won!"

The flies lifted off him in a buzzing mass and circled out over the shingle, making for some new target. Tabby stood in his blood-soaked shoes, breathing hard. Wherever he looked on the red sand, flies clustered in greedy buzzing knots. "They're not dead," he said softly. "My friends aren't dead."

Not yet, hissed the red froth on the shingle.

The flies which had left him lighted on another body cast up on the red shingle. Their sound intensified and reached that rhythmic food-frenzy he had heard before. At first Tabby thought it was Patsy's body they were swarming upon, and he squashed across the sand to drive them away.

But the body seemed too large to be Patsy's as he got closer to it, and then he noticed that it had been hacked and cut as Richard's had been . . . yet it was a woman's body. Tabby froze a few feet from the body. He had seen that the belly was savagely cut open, and a small lump of flesh that must have been an unborn child rested beside the woman's body. On the fetus too the flies lifted and crawled. Tabby saw its unbelievably tiny fingers clenched in a fist. Then he knew who the dead woman was. She was Laura Allbee, Richard's wife. He began to shake—after all he had been through, it was the sight of the unborn child's clenched fingers that affected him most.

The red water began to hiss louder and louder, and a viscous wave slapped down on Laura and the fetus. Tabby began to walk backward, unable to take his eyes off the linked bodies. He heard the water beginning to slap and roar, as it did during a storm.

Clouds scudded together, blotting the moon. Off to the right, the redness in the night air was unmistakable—houses were burning. Tabby could smell smoke now, as well as another, graver odor underlying the pervasive stench of blood. The waves were pounding toward the shore, whipped by the wind across the water. Red foam boiled on each successive series of waves and was tossed into the air like bloody rags.

Another body washed up on the shingle. Laura Allbee and the tiny fetus were gone, sucked back into the bloody Sound, and a more massive body now lay half-submerged in the rolling, violent waves. The flies streamed between it and Tabby in a buzzing knotty veil. The bulky body surged forward on a large incoming wave, and then it reached forward and elbowed itself out of the water.

A bolt of lightning cracked down out of the sky and screwed itself visibly into the sand to Tabby's left.

The body at the edge of the water was getting to its knees. One shoulder looked like an auto wreck—a red-stained bone protruded from ragged flesh.

Tabby backed away toward the retaining wall and the parking lot at the end of the drive. The body was trying to stand, but it had difficulty rising from its crouch. Tabby saw Dicky Norman's face above the body. Another brilliant stroke of lightning sizzled above the Sound. Dicky finally got to his feet. Long neat autopsy scars divided his forehead and his chest. His mouth sagged open, and blood from the Sound leaked down over his chin. Dicky started moving toward Tabby.

Now the wind, which had pushed Tabby here, pushed him back toward the beach. From the direction of the fire, sparks rose and floated in the twisting currents of air.

"No, Dicky," Tabby said.

Dicky Norman gnashed his teeth at the sound of Tabby's voice.

"You're not real," Tabby said, hitting the concrete retaining wall with the back of his thighs.

The wind tore the words away and broke them into nonsense syllables. Dicky was now halfway across the beach, clawing forward with his one arm, leaning into the wind. Blood-soaked sand flew and scattered. A white McDonald's bag spun out of the parking lot, struck the sand in a series of skittering hops that stained it irregularly red, and went sailing into the seething water.

"Dicky, go back," Tabby said noiselessly.

Dicky's jaw worked; more red fluid drooled from the corner of his mouth. To Tabby it looked almost as if Dicky Norman's torn corpse had muttered *I'm tired*.

For no reason other than it was an instinctive grasping for safety, Tabby let his mind say *Patsy? Patsy?*

Dicky Norman took another step into the bruising wind. Tabby felt his mind groping for Patsy's and in a growing panic failing to find her. For a moment Tabby felt his mind falling toward a great vacuum, some psychic black hole, and Dicky canted his head over toward his shredded shoulder and beamed at him as if he had just told a joke.

Patsy!

He felt a circling fuzzy response, as faint as the signal of a Tennessee Bible station on a car radio.

Patsy! Trouble!

Patsy was asleep. Dicky took another step toward him, still gleaming at him. The warm response he'd had was dwindling to a pinpoint. *Patsy! Help me!*

(oh, dear Tabby, what . . . ? Tabby . . . ?)

It was not much, no more than a moment of dim contact, but Dicky Norman fell to his knees six feet from Tabby. Tabby groped again for Patsy with his mind, but found only a dwindling spot of warmth. Dicky was struggling to turn around, flat on his stomach on the bloody sand. The wind had died, and the flies returned, first to Dicky's shoulder, then to the puddles in the sand, then to Tabby. He waved them away from his face. Now Dicky's torn shoulder was black with them. Dicky's feet dug into the sand and pushed, his hips shifted from side to side. Freshets of oozing blood opened where Dicky's feet scratched beneath the surface. Like a damaged tractor Dicky toiled back toward the Sound.

Tabby had not won, he knew, but at least it had been a draw. Because of Patsy McCloud's almost unconscious help, he had done that much. Now Tabby could clearly smell the fires burning along the side of the Millpond.

Dicky Norman reached the shingle and crawled into the shallow water. As Tabby watched, the Sound lost several degrees of redness, declining to a dusky pink, then altered to violet, and then became inky blue once more.

He was dry. There were no flies, no bloodstains on his clothes or the sand. On the shingle the meek waves deposited a white froth. Tabby ran up the steps to the changing rooms and the public telephone.

14

Very late that Saturday night, three events of varying importance took place which were related to the fears of Richard Allbee and Tabby Smithfield, and which pointed the direction things would go now the threshold had been breached. On that Saturday night, Hampstead was irrevocably into the second stage of its destruction.

The first of these events was that Richard Allbee telephoned Laura at eleven-thirty, just about the time that Tabby Smithfield awoke in the grip of an inexplicable urgency. He was out of sorts after a long evening of listening to Morris Stryker destroy his initial plans for the College Street house—Stryker, incredibly, wanted a Bauhaus interior—and he was drunk enough to be slurring his words. Stryker had insisted on putting a bottle of fifty-year-old cognac on the table and having Toby Chambers pour out for all of them. Chambers himself was excused from drinking, but Stryker made it clear that Hagen and Richard had to have as much of the cognac as he did.

Laura answered the phone on the eighth ring, and he suddenly felt much better. "Oh, thank God," he said. "I know it's late to be calling, but I was worried."

"Worried about what?" Laura said.

"About . . . you know what. The client just told me that there'd been another murder in Hampstead. He read about it in the paper. I think the client's a mobster. He thought it was a barrel of laughs."

"Are you drunk?" Laura asked.

"Of course I'm drunk. I've been out with Morris Stryker, and the penalty of not getting drunk is being roasted over a slow fire. I couldn't risk it. Really, Stryker's a mobster. Every night, men rush up to him in restaurants and give him padded envelopes."

"Oh, dear," Laura said. "You're not having a very good time, are you?"

"I'm having a terrible time. Being roasted might be a ball, compared to this. But tell me what happened. Who was killed?"

"Nobody we know. The gardener who works around here. I think I've seen him a couple of times."

"Sure you've seen him. He's always working. *That's* who was killed? Where? When?"

"I'm not sure. The body was only found yesterday. He'd been dead a couple of days, I gather. Richard, I'm very tired. You woke me up, and I don't want to talk about this now. I just want you to come home."

"I wish I could," he said. "I'm going to have to redo a lot of my work, so I'll probably have to be here another couple of days. Please be safe."

"I'll be safe," she said. "Next time, call at a regular hour. I'm going back to bed."

Richard said, "I'll call tomorrow, whenever I can get away from Ivan the Terrible."

"Love you."

"And I love you. Why aren't you here with me?"

"You went away," she said.

Some short time after that, Patsy McCloud stirred in her sleep. Her in-laws had just left that evening to return to Phoenix, and Patsy had not been able to keep her eyes open past ten o'clock.

A second later, something penetrated her dream with the force of a blow, and she shook her head, still not really awake. She saw Tabby Smithfield before her, a Tabby who needed her in some pressing but unspecified way—it was as though Tabby were her child, and the fact of maternity had told her that he needed her. She saw him not wounded but in some awful and potential danger, as if she were to see him drink half a fifth of gin and then get behind the wheel of a fast car—and she sent out to this troubled Tabby as much fragmented concern as she could call up. For a second her eyes fluttered. Through her open window she smelled smoke. Then Patsy's body relaxed, and the odor melted into a dream-picture of herself as a witch on the edge of a forest boiling something in a huge black pot, and then this image too melted into a ceaseless flow.

The Hampstead fire department had already received two calls about the fire on Mill Lane (the official name of Shrinks' Row) by the time Tabby Smithfield telephoned them from the pay phone above Gravesend Beach. Two trucks had gone out from the Riverfront Avenue fire station, then two more had followed from the central station in back of Main Street. When the extent of the damage was reported by the first men to arrive, Hampstead requested two trucks from Old Sarum to augment the other four.

Mill Lane could be reached only by traversing a narrow bridge across the Millpond, and of course the trucks could not get across the bridge. The first two trucks arrived at the Millpond parking lot at the same time as the deputy chief, Harry Yochen, pulled up in his car. While Harry went across the bridge to see how many of the houses were going up, the two Main Street trucks pulled into the lot; a minute later, the fire chief, Tony Archer, followed the trucks in. Archer jumped out of his car and started ordering the men to link up their hoses—he could feel the heat blasting at him from all the way over across the bridge and up the path, and he fatalistically knew that most of the little houses would be lost. Harry Yochen came panting back across the bridge a moment later, and he confirmed it: all of the houses were burning.

"All?" Archer asked. "How the hell could they *all* be going so soon?"

"And here's something else," Yochen said, wiping at his face: Chief Archer knew then what Yochen was going to say, and knew why he was hesitating. His deputy was sure that an arsonist had set the fires. Yochen blinked. "There's a uniform burn rate."

"On all eight houses?"

Yochen nodded. "All the houses started up at the same time."

"You talk to anybody?" The crews were now pounding across the bridge with their hoses.

Yochen shook his head. "They're inside. All of them."

"Jesus wept," Archer said, and then began bellowing orders as he and the deputy chief ran across the bridge with the second crew.

As soon as he was on the little path on the other side of the bridge, Chief Archer saw what had made Yochen suspicious. The flames, which had started on the roofs of the frame buildings, had reached a parallel point in all eight houses, just above the doorframes. Someone had ignited these houses. And that person had killed the people inside them. In these houses, the bedrooms were on the second floor, just under the roofs. The smoke would have gotten them first; then the fire had taken them as they lay unconscious in their beds. As smoke poured from the dying buildings, the crews were playing their hoses on the two nearest houses.

Archer and Yochen and all the firemen squinted against the searing, blasting heat. The lawns began to burn, and a maple tree across the path from the yellow house Dr. Harvey Blau had rented suddenly shot into flame. Archer directed the Old Sarum crews to the far end of the path, to keep the fire from spreading into the wooded parkland which separated the Millpond from Gravesend Beach. He could smell the stink of burning fabric and baking greenery, and the roaring snapping elementally destructive noises of the fire—sucking in air like an animal crouching to spring—filled his ears.

They're all dead, he thought, thinking of the people who had been asleep in those upstairs rooms. *Who would do a thing like this?* Hampstead, Chief Archer's home for the past twenty years, seemed to have dipped into savagery and lunacy this summer, to have turned dark and crazy. Children drowning themselves . . . he had known the little Sherbourne boy, and what had happened to him just didn't make *sense,* no more than someone spilling liquid paraffin along the roofs of seven houses and then setting them alight . . . more than ever the fires sounded to him like living things.

He looked up at the smoke pouring from the roofs of the burning houses. A line of flame was dripping down the roofline, letting small orbs of fire fall to the grass like drops of water. The drops of flame hit the ground and split apart. For a moment the chief reflected that these moving flames seemed almost alive, the way they moved so rapidly across the dry grass. The mass of black smoke also seemed live, twisting and writhing upward.

Then Chief Archer thought he saw something moving in the smoke. Within the blackness, darker shadows darted and flickered. Just before he moved to join the first crew, Archer peered into the writhing, ascending column of smoke. Coming from all eight houses, it braided together twenty feet in the air and rose into the darkness. *Birds,* he thought, *some damn birds got caught in the smoke* . . . then he saw the shape of a wing and thought they were bats.

"Chief?" Yochen asked him.

Archer saw their necks and their open furious mouths; he saw them hovering in the smoke as bats would never do. Thousands of baby dragons were floating in the smoke, swirling upward, spinning away.

The first crew of firemen exploded into flame twenty feet from him. The hoses they carried blew apart, and several tons of water instantly flashed into steam. The crew next to them dropped their hoses and ran to the other side of the path, getting away from the scalding steam. Their own hoses must then have turned hot in their hands, because they dropped them an instant before they too blew apart. Now men were screaming, and eight men were outlined in flame, some of them rolling in the baking weeds and setting them alight, some of them crazily running straight into the larger fires. Liquid drops of fire streamed from all the houses and pooled between them.

"Get those hoses on the *men!*" Archer screeched at Yochen, and saw the thousands of little dragons spinning out of the smoke over Yochen's head. As the deputy chief turned to obey him, his arms suddenly flew out to his sides. For an instant Chief Archer saw smoke leaking from Yochen's sleeves. Then Deputy Chief Yochen's uniform shirt burst into flame; a fraction of a second later his gray hair frizzed and crisped off his head. His trousers smoked and burned. Archer struggled out of his jacket, in order to wrap Yochen in it and stifle the flames, but the jacket was still hanging from one of his wrists when Harry Yochen uttered a muted, bubbling scream and fell to the ground, completely encased in flame. His skin blackened and shriveled as Archer continued meaninglessly to struggle with his jacket.

Tony Archer stood there in the midst of the pandemonium with his golf jacket hanging from one wrist, hearing the rushing sound of fire and wondering how things had gone so wrong so fast when white dripping fire flowed out from between the houses and blistered his face, then seared his lungs, and took his life even before his clothes began to burn.

The fire on Mill Lane burned itself out before it spread into the park, but by dawn the houses of Shrinks' Row were only eight smoking foundations. The inhabitants were identified by the location of their bones, as were the firemen, all of whom perished in the furnace Mill Lane had become for a few minutes that night.

One of the fire trucks, the one closest to the bridge, had exploded because of the heat, but the real measure of the temperatures on Mill Lane that Saturday night, said the Wednesday *Gazette,* was that on Kendall Point, which faced the farthest extremity of the lane across Gravesend Beach and nearly half a mile of water, the ground was still warm the next day and the bark on many of the trees still smoked.

15

Richard Allbee had promised himself that he would call Laura that Sunday. He was going to wait until just after breakfast, when she would be sure to be at home; but at eight o'clock he sat down with his drafting paper at the desk in his hotel room and forgot all about food. At noon he ordered a sandwich and a beer from room service, and kept working—he had thought of a way to compromise with Stryker and incorporate a contemporary feeling into the Georgian shapes and dimensions of the rooms. Stryker could have his white walls and even his track lighting, if he insisted, and Richard would smuggle in his period detail. Once he saw how the details would augment the total design, the project came back to life for him again.

At six o'clock he realized that he was starving, and went down to the hotel's restaurant for grilled scallops, asparagus, a half-bottle of chilled Puligny-Montrachet, and two cups of coffee; during dinner he made notes, and when he was finished with his coffee he tipped hugely and returned immediately to his room.

It was eleven-thirty before he thought again of calling home. It was too late—he could not wake her two nights running. Richard gloated momentarily over the amount of work he had accomplished, then took off his clothes and went to bed.

On Monday he called home at ten in the morning, and got no answer. Laura was probably at Greenblatt's, he thought. He promised himself to call her before dinner, even if he had to make a collect call from one of Stryker's terrible restaurants. Richard spent all Monday afternoon at the College Street house, ironing out his plans and making sure of his measurements, and then went back to the hotel before the ritual dinner with Stryker. He called Laura from his room at five-thirty, but again there was no answer. He rang down to the desk, but there was no message for him.

Stryker called him at six and gave him directions to a restaurant named Pickman's. The restaurant turned out to be twenty minutes away, on the city's north side; almost in the country. It was a converted Victorian house, easily the handsomest of all the restaurants Stryker had chosen. The valet took Richard's car, he went inside to a series of rooms as handsome as the exterior. Red leather chairs, vibrant flowers, sparkling glasses and shining silver: Richard put his plans under his elbow and felt better than he had since his first meeting with his client.

Stryker, Mike Hagen and Toby Chambers appeared fifteen minutes late. Stryker barely nodded at Richard before he called the headwaiter over and began complaining about the table. It was too central, there was too much traffic around it, didn't anybody here remember what Morris Stryker liked in a table? In the middle of his tirade, Stryker lit a huge cigar and exhaled smoke over the rejected table. The headwaiter made suggestions; Stryker settled on a table in the end room, in a far corner. "Don't give us lousy service there, just because we're outta the way," he said.

Amid much fussing, they were seated at the back table. Stryker himself sat facing out, his back to the wall. "Ah, this place is so full of crap, it gives me a headache to come here," he complained to Richard.

"Then why do you come here?"

"A change, it's a change. Toby likes this kind of shit." Stryker puffed at his cigar, then leaned over and said to Toby, "Why don't you get that little weasel out here so I can talk to him, that banjo player? Hey? Call him up and get him out here." Toby scurried off to find the telephone. Mike Hagen smiled at the ceiling.

"Do you ever go out with your wife, Morris?" Richard asked, and Mike Hagen's eyes drifted away from the ceiling toward Richard.

"What the hell is it to you?" Stryker asked loudly. "Dinner is part of work with me—part work, part relaxation. Get it?"

The waiter brought their drinks. Stryker, a water buffalo, leaned massively forward. "So what you been doing?" he asked Richard. "You were at the house today? Yeah? Great. What you do Sunday? I was gonna call you, take you out to the golf course, but something came up. This banjo player, that's what came up. We're gonna straighten his head out for him."

"I worked all Sunday," Richard said, taking up the sheaf of papers from beside him. "I really think I came up with something we can use. I want to show you how we can handle the downstairs rooms."

"Save it," Stryker said. "I don't want that kind of stuff now. I just don't want it."

"Well, I really would like your opinion on it," Richard said. "I've put in a lot of time, and I have to get back to Connecticut soon."

"I *told* you to can it, didn't I?" Stryker bellowed. "Don't you have ears? I don't give a damn about how hard you worked, I don't give a rat's ass about how soon you have to get home, I don't want that kind of crap tonight. Just sit here and lap up the goodies. That's all you have to do tonight."

At that moment Richard came as close to quitting as he could without actually doing it. If he had been five years younger, if Laura had not been pregnant, he would have done so immediately; but he was still thinking about it when Toby Chambers' skinny form slid back into his chair. "Nine-thirty," Chambers said.

Stryker grunted. He rolled his eyes and puffed out a cloud of reeking gray smoke. "Call him back. That's too soon, I don't want to see his greasy face when I'm supposed to be having fun. Tell him eleven. We'll still be here."

Chambers uncoiled from his chair and streaked off again.

I need this job, Richard told himself. *Morris Stryker isn't just a crude bully, he's ten thousand dollars closer to being about to put Lump through college.* He swallowed half of his drink, and then unclenched his left hand.

"Have another one," Stryker said. "That's what you're here for, right? The goodies."

That night Richard did not get back to his hotel until ten minutes past twelve. He called home, and heard a busy signal. Richard dialed his number five more times between midnight and one o'clock, and heard the busy signal each time. He spoke to the operator, who suggested that the party had left her telephone off the hook.

On Tuesday morning Richard tried to call home as soon as he had showered: with the towel around his waist and his hair dripping, he sat on the bed and dialed his number. He endured a long delay during which he first knew that there would be another busy signal, then that the phone would ring. Neither of these happened. The delay stretched on until Richard was ready to hang up and dial again, then the line clicked twice and the dial tone buzzed in his ear. Richard tried again, with the same result. A long pause, two clicks, the dial tone. He dialed the operator and asked her to try his number. When the operator could not get the number, she conferred with a Connecticut operator and came back to say, "I'm sorry, Mr. Allbee, but that number has a fault on the line and is temporarily out of service."

"But that's my number!" Richard said.

"It is temporarily out of service, but the fault has been reported," the operator said. "Try again later."

Richard hung up, dried his hair with a towel, dressed. He ordered breakfast from room service, then canceled it five minutes later. He could not stay in his room, he was too restless for that. A fault on the line? What did that mean?

In minutes he was outside on the sidewalk, aimlessly moving. He was due to meet Stryker and Hagen at the College Street house at eleven-thirty; that gave him three hours to kill. The air was warm and clear, huge with the sounds of construction. Near Richard's hotel an old building had been demolished, clearing an entire block of the city; now a scaffolding rose like a gallows over a pitted wasteland. Through smoke and dust Richard could see men stripped to the waist, goggles shielding their eyes. Sparks jumped in the boiling dust, hammers rang against metal. Dimly Richard heard a foreman swearing rhythmically and passionlessly.

For minutes Richard stared into the construction site as if he had been hypnotized. A man lifted and dropped a sledgehammer, lifted it and swung it down, lifted it again; another worked a heavy drill, the muscles jumping in his arms. Periodically a cloud of dust enveloped them. Behind them a yellow crane swung lazily about, performing some invisible function.

Richard felt his mouth go dry, and did not know why. He was shaking, and he did not know why. The little fires flared in the boiling smoke and dust. It was a look into a small hell.

He looked up at the crane and saw Billy Bentley running along the machine's long arm, running up slick yellow metal at a forty-degree angle. LORAINE, read the black lettering Billy scampered over. Billy ran up to the end of the crane, ignorant of gravity, and waved at Richard far below him.

Richard astounded himself—he threw up. His stomach had flipped inside out almost before he had known it was going to happen, and now he was left with a sharp but diminishing pain in his gut and a pink spatter on the dirty sidewalk. He stepped away from it, looked up, and saw Billy Bentley climbing hand over hand down the cable attached to the crane.

He turned and ran. Hell stank and snarled behind, and from it Billy Bentley pursued him. Richard turned into the next corner and pounded down the street.

Gritty Providence spread out around him. At his back he still could hear the banging and pounding from the construction site. Billy Bentley waved to him from a doorway across the street, and pretended to be counting out money. The smell of death and rot drifted in the sunny air.

Richard turned around and crossed the street in the opposite direction. Horns blared, a man yelled. The traffic light had not changed, and cars sped by him. Richard feared that he would fall over from dizziness in the middle of the street and be killed beneath the wheels of a truck.

He made it to the other side of the street. Brown University hugged the hill above him. The city seemed full of sunlight, dust, and smoke. Old-fashioned streetlamps marched up the hill toward the university. Behind them eighteenth-century houses kept their own counsel in the high clear air.

Billy had climbed out of hell on LORAINE the crane and now hell was everywhere—Richard had to return to Hampstead, to Greenbank and Beach Trail.

He turned back to his hotel. He saw Beach Trail, saw the old Sayre house with its lights blazing, saw Laura opening the door . . . "I'm going to be checking out in about fifteen minutes," Richard told the desk clerk. "Please have my bill ready."

Richard dumped his things in his suitcase, closed it, walked out of his room and pushed the button for the elevator. He waited in the dark plum-colored hallway and listened to the humming of the wires behind the big metal doors. Then the light over the doors flashed, a bell dinged, and the doors opened onto a roomy coffin. A smell with the weight of a truck rolled out and nearly knocked Richard over. Billy Bentley sat in a corner of the elevator cross-legged, a guitar on his lap. He gave Richard a bright consoling smile. Now the flesh seemed to be sliding off his bones, but Billy's expression was so animated that his corpse looked particularly gallant, sitting cross-legged on the elevator's carpeted floor.

Richard could not get in that traveling coffin. Once the doors closed, the smell alone would be fatal. He lifted his bag and waited for the doors to close again, which they obediently did. Then he went to the staircase and opened the door. He carried his suitcase down ten floors to the lobby.

At eleven-thirty he was sitting in his car on College Street, as he had been for twenty minutes. The doors were locked and the windows were up. The radio pumped out Rickie Lee Jones. Stryker was not in the house and the Cadillac was nowhere in sight. From one of the upstairs windows Billy Bentley looked down, leaning on his elbows. At twelve o'clock Richard and Billy were still in their places, but the college radio station was playing Phoebe Snow's "Poetry Man."

By one o'clock Richard was starving and half-crazy with frustration; he had to drive back to Connecticut, but he could not—he could not allow himself to do it—leave without speaking to Morris Stryker. He glanced up at the window, and Billy shook his head at him.

At one-thirty the Cadillac rolled up across the street and Toby Chambers jumped out of the passenger seat to run around the back and open the door for Stryker. Stryker was wearing black sunglasses, shiny black boots, a gray suit of some exquisitely soft material, and a dark gray shirt with a rolled collar. For once he did not have a cigar in his mouth. Looking relaxed and expansive—Richard realized that he'd just had lunch—Stryker pushed his belly across the street toward him. "Got hung up," Stryker said. "I got time for your plans now. Let's get inside and take a look at what you got, okay?"

"I've been here better than two hours," Richard said. "Is 'Got hung up' all you're going to say to me about it?"

Stryker cocked his head and looked at him coldly. "I got hung up. I was gonna have one appointment in the restaurant, instead I had five or six. It goes like that sometimes. You want me to kiss your hand?"

"I want you to kiss my ass, Morris," Richard said. "I can't spend any more time in Providence. I'm quitting this job as of right now. I'm giving up and going home. You wouldn't understand why, so I won't bore you with explanations." Richard opened the door of his car, and Stryker said, "You're outta your mind or something. Toby! *Toby!*"

Toby Chambers sprinted across the street from where he had been talking with Mike Hagen. Stryker ambled away into the middle of the street and stood looking up with a bored expression on his face.

"I'm quitting, Toby," Richard said. "I'm worried about my wife, and I have to get back to Connecticut. Besides that, I can't take my client anymore. He's one of the worst human beings I've ever met, and as much as I wish I could, I just can't work for him. I couldn't take another week of sitting in those restaurants and inhaling his cigar smoke. Good-bye."

"Mr. Stryker can see that you never get another job," Toby said, speaking very slowly. "Mr. Stryker might even decide that you need to be disciplined. Look. I'm trying to help you, Mr. Allbee."

"I'm a lot more disciplined than Mr. Stryker," Richard said. "Now, get out of my way, Toby."

Richard got into his car and closed the door. Stryker spat on the ground and ambled toward the sidewalk—finally. Richard saw that the client was giving him the finger.

It was Tuesday, the seventeenth of June, and Richard Allbee found his way back to the interstate highway shortly after two o'clock.

16

Late that evening, Patsy McCloud was seated on the worn leather chair in Graham Williams' living room. She held a tall glass half-filled with a watery drink on the top of which floated three slivers of melting ice. Graham Williams, in his PAL T-shirt and Yankee cap, sat on the couch. Like Patsy, he too was sweating lightly. On the table between them a bottle of Bombay gin stood next to a half-full six-pack of eight-ounce bottles of tonic and a plastic ice bucket one-quarter filled with cold water. Patsy did not know it, but she was mourning Les, and mourning him more satisfactorily than she had ever done alone or with his parents.

"I never told his parents that he used to hit me," she said. "There I was, with my one big fat last chance, and I couldn't do it—no matter how nasty Dee got with me about the cremation, I couldn't tell her. Why do you think that was?"

"Because you're a decent person," Williams said. He sipped at his own drink. "Maybe because it wouldn't have made any difference anyhow. His mother would have thought that you were lying, or if he did beat you, that you deserved it. Anyhow, at a certain point it isn't appropriate anymore for parents to know such things about their children. They prefer the myth they know.''

"It wouldn't have made any difference, you're right," Patsy said. "She never understood what Les was—I mean she never understood what happened to him after he left home. She didn't grasp his success, and she couldn't ever see what his success did to his personality. Did you ever have any children, Graham?"

"Never," he said. He smiled.

"Why are you smiling like that? Oh, I know. It's because I forgot. You told me before. You told all of us. We're the last of our families. At least until Richard's baby is born."

Patsy looked around the room. "Don't you have a record player or anything, Graham? I'd sure like to hear some music. Don't you like listening to music?"

"I have a radio," he said, and stood up to go across the room and turn it on. He found a station playing dance music, big bands breathing out standard songs like "Rose Room" and "There's a Small Hotel," and let it play softly.

"Oh, that's nice," Patsy said. She tapped her stockinged foot. "Pretty soon I'll ask you to dance, Graham. You'd better be ready."

"I'll be honored."

"You know when I decided that you were one of the good guys? It was on that terrible night when Les was waving his gun around. I saw you step in front of Tabby. God, I thought that was wonderful. You could have been killed."

"Most people would do it." Graham leaned forward and tipped more gin, then more tonic, into her glass. He dipped his hand into the ice bucket and retrieved three half-melted cubes and dropped them into Patsy's glass.

"That's what you think, buster," Patsy said. "You're dead wrong there, and you think that way because you're one of the good guys. You know what I thought later? I thought, there were three men there, and mine was the worst. Honest to God."

"He was certainly the drunkest," Graham said.

"Let's face facts, Graham old buddy, he was the worst. But I was remembering some little things about him when his parents were around, and you know, sometimes I wish we could have another chance at things, you know?"

Patsy went on to speak about Les in an emotional and thoroughly confused and contradictory way, sometimes with resentment and sometimes affectionately. She continued to drink, waggling her glass at the Bombay bottle when she wanted Graham to pour her a refill, and once or twice she seemed to be close to tears. Graham Williams minded none of this, in fact he cherished it. He wanted her to say anything that came into her head. He would listen to everything with the same seriousness and good humor. He understood that it was often difficult for any woman, but a woman like Patsy especially, to be taken seriously, and that maybe this was the greatest flaw in her marriage: Les McCloud had taken himself so seriously that there was no seriousness left over for his wife.

3

Civilization
and Its Discontents

1

Six weeks after DRG-16 had been vented from the secret Telpro plant in Woodville, the town of Hampstead, Connecticut, had altered from what it had been before May 17—the changes were not as great as they would yet become, but nothing now was quite the same. In the imagery of Richard Allbee's dream, Billy Bentley was inside the house: he had broken a couple of windows and was going to smash up some of the furniture before he moved on to bigger things. Things were different in Hampstead. The tides still came in on Gravesend and Sawtell beaches, the tennis matches still grunted and sweated along on the private courts and at the Racket Club, men still squeezed into the parking spots at Riverfront Station and took the 7:54 and the 8:24 to New York; at eleven o'clock on Sunday morning, Hampstead people still sat on the deck of the Sawtell Country Club and drank their complimentary Bloody Marys and watched the sailboats far out, the windsurfers rolling and tipping in the nearby surf, before the Sunday brunch. But many parents now locked their children in their rooms at night—in the five days since Richard Allbee had returned from Providence, a fourteen-year-old boy from Hampstead, a seven-year-old boy from Hillhaven, and a twelve-year-old girl from Old Sarum had drowned themselves in Long Island Sound.

And by now there had been four murders: one more since Bobby Fritz. Women alone at home had become careful about answering their doors, and the UPS drivers and Bloomingdale's deliverymen often did not bother ringing doorbells in Hampstead anymore; they slipped the packages inside the screen door, knocked hard, and left. No one ever jogged alone now, but only in pairs or groups of three. Sometimes in

the middle of Main Street you might see a slender, pros-
perous-looking woman suddenly choke up and burst into
tears; and you would not know if she were in the midst of a
divorce or if one of her children had gone out for a one-way
swim—or if Hampstead's troubles had just become too much
for her.

Yes, there were tennis matches and parties of six at the
country-club Sunday brunch; and people went into Greenblatt's and Grand Union and bought beer and spareribs and
charcoal briquets, just as if it were an ordinary summer. But
now the conversations on the tennis courts and the sparkling
deck of the country club were as much about death and suicide as about Wimbledon and the bond market and the colleges their kids were applying to, come autumn. Now the
conversations were apt to be about how quickly you could get
out of Hampstead and if you could still sell your sixty-five-
year-old Federal colonial with three wooded acres and twenty
more years to go on the mortgage. And sometimes the conversations would slip into muddy waters, into areas no one
understood or even wanted to understand—Archie Monaghan
tried to hint to Tom Flynn, his law and golfing partner, that
not long after Les McCloud's messy crack-up on I-95 he had
imagined hearing and smelling something odd coming from
that same bush Les had been so excited about.

Ronnie Riggley could have answered the questions about
selling those desirable colonials on three wooded acres—if
she had felt like being utterly honest, she would have said
that if it was in Hampstead, you couldn't give it away for free
with the purchase of a box of Cracker Jack; and that if it were
in Hillhaven or Old Sarum, you had about a fifty-fifty chance
of being able to give it away for free. What you couldn't do
was sell it. You couldn't even lease it, not since the discovery
of the fourth body and the suicides of all those children.

Graham Williams saw a For Sale sign on Evelyn Hughardt's lawn, but never saw Ronnie or any other salesperson
showing prospects around the Hughardt house; instead he one
day saw a moving van parked down at the bottom of Beach
Trail, and Evelyn Hughardt supervising the men carrying her
furniture out of her house. "You find a buyer, Evvy?" he
asked.

She shook her head. "But I'm going back to Virginia anyhow. Hampstead doesn't *feel* right to me anymore." She
looked back at her house, where she and Graham saw a man

inside the front door packing up the framed cartoons. "Does that make sense to you, Mr. Williams?"

"Perfect sense," Graham agreed.

She was not alone, he knew. As in the Black Summer of 1873, many people were simply moving out. They decided to take their vacations early, or they suddenly remembered that they had always wanted their kids to see the Smoky Mountains or that these same kids hadn't seen their grandparents in a year and a half. Now there was a vacant house every couple of blocks, most of the time with a realtor's sign before it, but sometimes not; Graham bet himself that by August there'd be two or three vacant houses on every block. And that by then people wouldn't care if they sold their houses or not—they'd just want to get away.

Evelyn Hughardt looked at him sharply, and he saw a pallor beneath her honey-colored tan, and some indefinable expression at the back of her eyes: an expression that should have been no part of a handsome woman like Evelyn Hughardt. "I wonder what you know," she said.

He shook his head. "I think there's only one killer," he said, pretending that this was what she had been alluding to. There were people in Hampstead who claimed that Gary Starbuck had killed the first two victims and a "copycat killer" the second two.

"That's not what I mean, Mr. Williams. Have you noticed that you never see birds anymore in Hampstead, not live ones anyhow? They're all like *that*." She pointed her foot at a bundle of feathers rolled into the gutter across the street; ten feet from it was another dead bird. "And you know what else you never see in this town anymore? Pets. There are no more pets. The dogs all ran away or got run over, the cats just vanished . . . maybe they all got run over too. What do you think?"

"It's a mystery, Evvy. I'd guess they just took off, being cats."

"And it makes perfect sense to you that I'm leaving the only house I have. I'll say it again. I wonder what you know."

"One thing I know is that this happened once before—about a hundred years ago, the town's population dropped by half."

"A hundred years ago," she said, sounding disgusted with

him. "A hundred years ago, did people hear things they shouldn't?" He beetled his eyebrows, wondering what she was getting to, and she said, "Or see things they shouldn't? Let me fill you in, Mr. Williams. There are people in this town who have sophisticated electronic equipment. This equipment can be used to record voices, and then play them back by remote control. The equipment can *project* voices and make them sound like they are right in the next room, Mr. Williams. And I think they can do this with pictures too, Mr. Williams—not just voices, but pictures! *Moving* pictures. Projected right into your own bedroom! Doesn't that sound like something our friends in Moscow would use on us, Mr. Williams?"

So Evvy Hughardt had absorbed her husband's politics and his view of the Scribe of Beach Trail.

"I heard Dr. Hughardt talking to me," she said. "They're testing that machinery on me, aren't they? I'm the guinea pig for their fancy equipment. It sends out rays. Or beams, whatever you call them. Are you one of their colonels? That's what they usually are, aren't they, the high-ranking ones?"

Evelyn Hughardt had heard something, had thought that she had seen something, and since then her mind had been chasing itself in obsessive circles.

"You should have left the pets alone," she said, and turned and ran toward her front door.

MASS MURDER IN CONNECTICUT, ran the headline in the *New York Post* after the fourth murder, and the *New York Times* asked, HAMPSTEAD: THE CURSE OF AFFLUENCE?

It was this second article which Ted Wise and Bill Pierce, now far out in the deep country at a Telpro installation in Montana, read on their computer screens—Telpro paid for their access to the *Times* and to the wire services, in order to sweeten their isolation. "We have to tell," Pierce said; and Wise agreed, but asked for more time—he didn't understand the *Times* paragraph about the children who had drowned themselves, for that seemed totally unrelated to the action of DRG-16.

Hampstead did feel cursed, and not just because its expensive real estate had lost its value; what was happening to the town seemed to some like an almost biblical set of afflictions. The unease in Hampstead went beyond the fear for safety or the paranoid suspiciousness of strangers people began to exhibit; it became an unease of soul. The town seemed to be punishing *itself*, as if the madman who had killed and butchered four people had been somehow created by Hampstead's deepest, most secret impulses—as a judgment on its values. Values, yes. The punishment was for wrong and distorted *values:* and if the comfortably potbellied middle-aged men in the town's pulpits played this wrinkled old card in the sermons on that Sunday, they could look for justification no farther than the excellent, sometimes great *New York Times.*

Residents of Hampstead not in the churches on Sunday, the twenty-second of June, might have seen a camera crew rolling slowly up the middle of Sawtell Road, relaying the memorized words of a CBS correspondent to a studio in New York. Hampstead and its bizarre set of problems was the cover story on Charles Kuralt's *Sunday Morning.* The correspondent, who wore thick eyeglasses and an expression combining soulfulness and fret, came out onto Sawtell Beach and looked soulfully, fretfully (and in fact mistakenly) over his shoulder at the bright water. "This," he said, "is where it ended for Thomas and Martin O'Hara and nine other children—here on this gentle beach in this exclusive community. And up Bluefish Hill, in a three-hundred-thousand-dollar house only a hundred yards from where I stand, is where it ended for Hester Goodall, the second victim of this community's mass murderer. Death is no respecter of persons, nor of the place they hold in the world. And here in Hampstead, Connecticut, they are wondering where it all went wrong: where the dream went sour." Another glance out at the gently lapping water. "Back to you, Charles."

2

The day after the CBS reporter implied that Hampstead somehow deserved its problems because it was rich, Sarah Spry was still in her office at six o'clock, trying to write a *Gazette* article. Sarah would have called this article a "think piece," and she intended it to show that she had indeed been thinking hard. She had seen *Sunday Morning*—a program she normally respected. Unfortunately, Sarah was having troubles in bettering its hackneyed efforts—she had ideas of her own she wanted to get down on paper, but the usual effortless connection between Sarah's mind and her typewriter was failing her now.

When she thought of a phrase—and it took more concentration than phrase-making usually did—she rattled the keys of her typewriter and a few minutes later saw that most of the words had sailed in from some lunatic's mind: they were not at all what she had imagined she had been typing. Her first paragraph read:

> Have we nayamgam this Oregon ourselves? Such is thamm wisney of thup medstar and checkout girls. Many will hack and hout about a plague, quotinga the pometry flacked in the booty of gardenmaker Robert Fritz. Hazzenwits redoubt and doubt again.

Sarah stared at these lines, at one moment seeing in them the sentences she thought she had written, in the next seeing only the dreadful macaroni she actually had typed. Sarah shook her head—it was as if her eyes were cloudy. She tried again, and her fingers pounded out *Now we must swim against the currents of guilt which* . . . Sarah peered at the page.

> Naked swimmers nakt swim gainst, say which

She jerked her fingers off the keys.

Sarah Henderson Spry had never thought of becoming a gossip columnist, and although that was how most people would identify her, "What Sarah Saw" was only a small portion of her duties at the *Gazette*. She edited and did most of the layout for the paper's second section, she reviewed art openings and all the plays at the Hampstead Playhouse and the Theater in the Glen; and she still did some of the basic reporting which had been her first job at the paper, back when Sarah Henderson had been completing her second and last year at Patchin University. Reporting then was all she had wanted to do, it had stirred her blood—finding out how things worked. The *Gazette* had become her home, and she had never wanted any more than it gave her.

Of course one of the things it gave her was her introduction to tragedy. She had been twenty-five and still the youngest person on the staff in 1952 when she had been ordered out to Sawtell Country Club to cover John Sayre's suicide. She took a camera and a notepad, and when she got out onto the beach behind the club building, Mr. Sayre's body was still there. Sarah had photographed the policemen, the waiter who found the body, Bonnie Sayre and Graham Williams, and then finally she had the stomach to photograph the dead lawyer. Joey Kletzka, once known as "Nails" because for twenty years he'd worked as much as a carpenter as a policeman, stood a short way down the beach with his hands on his big front porch of a belly and talked about some boy named John Ray, a boy who had been washed up dead on this same spot four days earlier. . . . Chief Kletzka was sixty-three then, in two years he would be retired; in three, himself a suicide. John Sayre's brains had been blown out the back of his head, and his face was black with powder burns. Sarah took the picture because her editor demanded it, but she didn't ever want to look at it. She went around the body to talk to Bonnie Sayre, who instead folded into the arms of Graham Williams. It had been a hot moist night. Under Williams' sleeves had been large scoops of perspiration. "Not now, Sarah," he had said gently, winning her respect. Then he had won her affection by saying, "Tomorrow we'll probably be going to John's office. Maybe you could meet us there. Bonnie is in no condition to say anything now." And so she had gone to the office, and she too had seen those names scratched into the telephone pad. *Prince Green, Bates Krell.*

As her job on the newspaper had grown, so had her role in Patchin County—Sarah was single-minded, but serially single-minded about many tasks. When her job at the *Gazette* was done, she had no qualms about chairing meetings of professional women, about organizing groups and seminars for women in newspaper and magazine work, about buzzing off to fund-raising parties and charity balls . . . in fact, nearly thirty years after she had tried to photograph John Sayre's body without really looking at it, Sarah was a nearly indispensable part of social and professional life in Patchin County.

Sarah pushed herself away from the typewriter, squinted again at the gibberish she had written, and shuddered. *Naked swimmers*—those words again, typed out as if by themselves. She saw the little O'Hara boys as she had known them,

Thomas smiling and baby Martin scowling, being serious about some *Star Wars* invention, and quickly went to another desk in the *Gazette* office. She pulled out a legal pad and a pencil from the top drawer.

"Good night now, Mrs. Spry," said Larry, the pressman, as he walked by. Larry rattled his bundle of keys at her. "You're the last one, now—be sure you lock up."

"I won't forget, Larry," she said. "Good night."

Larry went out the front door onto Main Street and Sarah faced the empty office and tapped the pencil against the strange desk. Something had happened to her—something had happened to the whole town, but the disability which had visited her could be the instrument that led her to define what had actually hit Hampstead. *Muddled writing,* she wrote on the pad, or hoped she did. *Like dyslexia. What could cause it? Other symptoms: stuffy sensations in head, ringing in ears—one spell of double vision. Tiredness. A disease common to entire town, causing brain disorders?*

Sunspots?

Nuclear waste—radiation sickness?

Chemical dumping?

A chemical spill, perhaps result of road accident?

She looked over the list she had made on the legal pad, nodded her head, drew two thick lines beneath it, and started another column.

What about earlier history—history of town.

Previous mass murders. Any?

Previous child suicides—any?

Need conjunctions. Items that provide context for m.m. or c.s.

Sarah held the legal pad up close to her face and scrutinized every word she had written. For "mass murders" she had put down "mace murders." She corrected the phrase. All the rest was what she thought she had written: which seemed to prove that writing by hand and writing more slowly for the most part bypassed the problem.

She decided to spend some time investigating her second set of ideas, and this was characteristic of her: if something upsetting had happened to her writing, she would concentrate on something else until the writing settled down again. She would take a closer look at things: that was the motto of her life. And tonight she was lucky, for the newspaper that employed her had been publishing in Hampstead since 1875—before that there had been a two-page folder, and before that a one-page broadside. (For two years, 1873 and 1874, there had been no newspaper of any kind in Hampstead, though Sarah did not know this.) The earliest issues up through the issue for January 3, 1965, had been put on microfilm, and in 1968 an old compositor named Bill Bixbee had made it his private project to create a giant handwritten index for every issue of the *Gazette*. Bixbee had worked nights, weekends, and holidays, and probably the project had lengthened his life—after he had retired as compositor, he had still come into the office every day to work on his index. He had taken enormous pride in what he was creating: Sarah could remember him saying that there was more of Hampstead in his index than she or Stan Brockett would ever know, in fact there was more of Hampstead in the index than there had been in the *Gazette* itself.

Now there were two copies of Bixbee's index, one up in Hillhaven at the Patchin Historical Society, and the other back in the newspaper's records room, on a shelf above the microfilm viewer.

The index was known as "Bixbee" in the office. If a reporter doing research for an article on marshland preservation wanted to know how the town's attitude toward its wetlands had evolved, Brockett would tell him to "look it up in 'Bixbee.'" The old compositor had earned his justification.

Sarah went into the records office at the back of the building, switched on the light, and took heavy "Bixbee" off its shelf. She lowered it to the counter beside the viewer and flipped it open, and then paged through until she got to M. Then she turned several more pages, looking down the headings column for "Murder."

When she found the heading column, she looked under it at the entry column. This at first seemed longer than she had expected, but then Sarah noticed that most of the articles were grouped around a series of three dates. The first of these was in 1898, the second burst of articles was from the autumn of 1924, and the third set of articles was grouped in September of 1952.

Well, that must have been one of Bill Bixbee's famous "contributions" to the town, for there had been no murders in Hampstead in 1952. Sometimes the old compositor had used his index to draw conclusions that the newspaper never had. If you looked under "Funds, misappropriation of," for example, one of the entries directed you to an otherwise straightforward article about the widening of Highway 7 and the huge sum of money this construction was costing the town. Another entry took you to a factual piece of reportage about the construction of the bleachers on the softball field on Rex Road. The same contractor's name appears in both articles, along with a mention of his being the cousin of a prominent selectman. Another entry points you toward a story about the selectman's recent purchase of a three-hundred-thousand-dollar house. It was in this indirect sort of comment that "Bixbee" contained more of Hampstead than the newspaper itself.

Sarah took out the first spool of microfilm and threaded it into the viewer. She wound it up until she saw the first page of the first issue of the *Hampstead Gazette,* tightened down the focus so she could read the dates without squinting, and turned the pages past the viewer until she came to 1898.

HAMPSTEAD MAN CHARGED WITH WOODVILLE DEATH, she read in the issue specified in "Bixbee." Three issues later, SECRET LIFE OF GREEN: DISSIPATION AFTER SEMINARY. Six months later, GREEN CONVICTED. The implication running through these articles was that Robertson Green had committed all the murders of prostitutes in Norrington and Woodville.

The next article concerned a farmer on the Old Sarum border who had killed his wife with an ax. Sarah did not make notes about this case, but switched spools of microfilm and ran the new spool past the viewer. Now she was in the summer of 1924, and the *Gazette* had become larger and easier to read. There were still advertisements on the front page, but there were graphics too.

In the issues Bixbee had indexed, the first pages of the *Gazette* showed photographs and drawings of women—three women, each of them found dead in the marshland on the west side of the Nowhatan River in the first weeks of that summer. WAVE OF DEATH CONTINUES, read the tall black headline for the issue of June 21, 1924. ANOTHER VICTIM? inquired the headline for July 10—beneath was a photograph of a woman named as Mrs. Dell Claybrook. Mrs. Claybrook had vanished from her home sometime during the evening of July 8. AND YET ANOTHER? asked the *Gazette* on July 21, over a drawing of the pert, snub-nosed face of Mrs. Arthur

Fletcher, who had disappeared from her home while her husband tended to his bond business in New York. THE SIXTH VICTIM? the *Gazette* asked its readers on August 9. Mrs. Claybrook and Mrs. Fletcher were still missing, and a Mr. Horace West had returned home from a business trip to the mills in Fall River to find his wife, Daisy, inexplicably missing. Two days later, Daisy West still absent, Mr. West had gone himself to the police station and confronted Chief Kletzka. Chief Kletzka had found it necessary to use physical restraints on the agitated Mr. West. Neither man had sworn out a complaint against the other.

Another entry was utterly puzzling, for it had nothing at all to do with murder. It was a small item on page sixteen about the impounding of a fishing boat belonging to a Mr. Bates Krell. Mr. Krell had apparently left Hampstead abruptly: before his creditors could have him jailed, the article seemed to imply.

Bates Krell? Sarah thought. *Now, where . . . ?*

Was Bixbee implying that Krell had been the last victim of the unidentified 1924 murderer? Sarah thought he was, but she still could not have said why the fisherman's name seemed familiar to her.

When Sarah turned the next spool of microfilm to the issues Bixbee specified for 1952, she found herself looking at the first important story she had ever written for the *Gazette.* JOHN SAYRE TAKES OWN LIFE. Here were two of the photographs she had taken on that wretched day: Bonnie Sayre crying into the gloved palm of her hand, the rear of the country club and its little stretch of well-mannered beach.

Yes, but murder? No doubt under "Suicide" Bixbee had a long set of entries—why did he list this obvious case under "Murder"? No one had ever suggested that anyone but John Sayre had taken his life. On impulse, she leafed through Bixbee to "Suicide" and checked the date—yes, there it properly was.

Sarah looked at her notes. On the far left side of the yellow page, separate from her more detailed observations, she had written:

> 1898, R. Green
> 1924, second mass killings
> (B. Krell vanishes)

Now she added:

1952, J. Sayre (?)

And beneath it put:

1980, Friedgood, Goodall, et al.

And looking at these jottings, she remembered: she remembered standing in John Sayre's office while his wife and his secretary wept with their arms around each other; remembered going to the lawyer's desk with Graham Williams and seeing with him the two names scratched in the notepad. *Prince Green, Bates Krell.* Had she told old Bixbee, and asked him about the names? Sarah could not remember—but Bixbee had put them all together in his index. A killer of prostitutes, a fisherman who had run out of town (or been killed), a respected lawyer. What could possibly be the link between them? And between them and what was going on in Hampstead in 1980?

Sarah drew circles around the names and dates, then sat up straight in her chair before the microfilm viewer. She had seen that there was roughly thirty years between each of these incidents. With the exception of the period 1950–52, there had been a series of murders in Hampstead every thirty years. No, she caught herself—Robertson Green's killings had been done in Norrington. Killings, then, in or *around* Hampstead, once in every generation. . . .

The *Gazette* office suddenly seemed dark and cold to Sarah. She switched off the viewer. Already she knew that if she looked back into the records she would find the pattern repeating and repeating itself, going back as far as the records themselves went . . . and before that, in a time when man did not inhabit the Connecticut coast, did the animals insanely attack and kill one another, bear against bear and wolf against wolf, every thirty years?

Sarah wanted to hide: that was her first, instinctive response to what she thought she had discovered. She felt like turning off all the lights and crouching in a corner until it was safe to come out again. Being Sarah, instead of that she reached for the telephone.

3

At the same time that Sarah Spry was reaching for her telephone—just after seven o'clock—a man unseasonably dressed in an overcoat and tweed hat ducked out of a porno theater on West Forty-second Street in New York. The man looked both ways and then continued east on the street, going toward the Avenue of the Americas. His hands were thrust deep in the pockets of the overcoat, but a flash of white from beneath a rucked-up sleeve showed that his hands and arms were bandaged, as was his face. When he thought that one of the street's regulars—one of the threatening men who spend all day on Forty-second Street—seemed to be paying too much attention to him, he slipped past a teenage girl with peroxided hair and tight satin shorts who whispered, "Wanna go out? Wanna go out?" and entered another building that had once been a movie theater.

In most towns or cities, a gentleman bandaged up like Claude Rains in *The Invisible Man* and wearing an overcoat and hat in the middle of June might reasonably attract a sort of following; in most towns and cities, there would be stares and questions, there would be gasps and pointing fingers. This, however, was Forty-second Street, and most of those who saw Leo Friedgood in pursuit of sexual satisfaction assumed that he was just another lunatic. A man named Grover Spelvin leaning against a marquee saw Leo dart into the converted theater and nudged the nodding man next to him, saying, "Hey, Junior, you just missed the Mummy, man."

"Fuh," Junior commented.

Leo, who was now what people in Patchin County would learn to call a "leaker," knew that his foray into the sleaziest neighborhood in New York was dangerous, but had correctly assumed that if he looked weird and confident, he would be reasonably safe; to look weird and weak would be to invite attack. Of course he was still in danger—anything that split his web of bandages would kill him—and that made him more furtive than he would have been otherwise, but Leo's arrogance was still his best armor. He assumed here especially that if you could pay for what you wanted, it was yours.

But besides all that, he simply could not stay away. Leo

Friedgood had always been a voyeur. For the most intense sexual pleasure, Leo had to see or imagine other people making love: when he made love to Stony, he had fantasized about the other men he had encouraged her to meet. The encouragement had been subtle—Leo had never directly spoken to Stony about the other men—but it had been pervasive. After Stony's death, Leo had imagined that his sexual life was dead too. He could still feel the humiliation that Turtle Turk had caused him, and that humiliation seemed the tombstone set upon his sex life. The discovery of the white spots on his body and their slow but inexorable growth should also have contributed to the end of Leo's desire—but oddly, perversely, the more the white spots covered of his body, the more obsessively he thought about sex. He could not perform anymore, but performance had always been of secondary importance to Leo. Leo had cut himself off from Telpro and General Haugejas—no one at Telpro knew what had happened to him—but in the end it had become impossible for him to cut himself away from his deepest fantasies. And these had led him back to Forty-second Street.

Leo went unnoticed past a row of booths showing reels of pornographic films for a quarter every two-minute segment, shoved a five-dollar bill at a bald man in a cage who did a double-take at Leo's bandages but pushed across five dollars in quarters. Then Leo ducked into a cubicle and spent a dollar watching four high-school girls rape a skinny dark-haired man with a pronounced curve in his penis. Then he left the booth and went to the back of the old theater and beneath an arch reading NAKED LIVE GIRLS 25¢. A row of doors like lockers stood closed in a hemisphere. Leo opened a door above which there was no red light, stepped into blackness, and inserted a quarter into a slot before him. A window in the front of his cubicle was gradually revealed as a black metal plate ascended.

Leo was looking into a round well-lighted space with a fake tiger rug on the floor and a ripped plastic-covered sofa at the far right end. Across from him was a series of windows like his, about half of them exposed by the raising of their own metal plates. Visible in these exposed windows were men's faces as vivid as portraits from hell—tinted sizzling red—all turned to the body of the woman dancing to a Bruce Springsteen tape in the middle of the round space. She was a beautiful little Puerto Rican girl, Leo saw when she gyrated around and lifted her bush toward his window, no more than seventeen. A black man in a window across from Leo's grinned crazily and waggled his tongue at the naked girl. The girl looked in Leo's window and did not miss a hitch of her hips after noticing his bandages; her reflective, almost pouting face did not alter in the least. Not a furrow appeared in her sweet forehead, not a trace of interest in her huge quiet eyes. Her right shoulder rolled back, the right hand rose, a small brown breast rolled back too, and a molded hip revolved and spun the perfect little body around. Leo feasted on her lithe back, earthy bottom, and the graceful backs of her thighs. When the metal plate began to descend over his window, he quickly put another quarter in the slot.

The girl was moving lazily around the circle of windows, bending backward as if she were trying to limbo beneath a bar. Leo was breathing slowly, half in a trance: he was imagining this girl, obviously a hooker and probably a junkie, beneath a succession of men, twining and untwining, pumping that round little bottom, locking those molded legs around one man after another. Leo could take this only for the duration of another quarter, and by then the little Puerto Rican teenager was putting on a robe and a tall Dust Bowl redhead with stretch marks had begun to snap her fingers and move before the windows. Leo pulled his hat farther down on his bandages, turned up the collar of his overcoat, and went back out past the rows of booths.

"Sex show, sex show," a black man whispered to him as he left the building and turned west.

Well, that was just what he had in mind, but the real thing, not a hasty facsimile. Leo hurried down the street, now and then hearing a black voice behind him calling out *Mummy, hey Mummy babes.* He was going to a club he knew just up from Seventh Avenue. This "club" was a place he had discovered in 1975, the year the Friedgoods had moved east—it consisted chiefly of two rooms with a pane of one-way glass between them, and it catered to people who shared Leo's tastes.

"Shit, he ain't no Mummy," Junior Bangs said to Grover Spelvin as they watched Leo's form disappear up a stairway just inside a door next to a theater showing horror pictures twenty-four hours a day. "That mother's goin' up to the Look-Show. Fuh. He ain't no Mummy—ain't no *real* Mummy."

"We'll see him when he drags his dick downstairs, Junior," said Grover, putting his hands in the pockets of his frayed jeans and preparing to wait.

Leo was at the top of the stairs. He opened a door marked EZ STUDIOS, and a black girl with a blond wig smiled at him and said, "Have you been to our club before?"

Leo nodded.

"You get burned?" the girl asked. "I mean, I had a friend, and she got *all* messed up. Wore them bandages for two months straight. Uh, that's thirty-five dollars."

Leo extracted bills from his coat pocket and counted the money onto the desk.

"Fine," the girl said. She showed him an acre of gleaming pink gum, stood up and led him through a door where half a dozen middle-aged men, some in jeans and sweatshirts and others in suits, sat on metal chairs in front of a six-foot-square window. Rock music was piped in, but all the men seemed to be consciously ignoring it. On the other side of the window was a smaller room where a rumpled bed stood on a bare floor. The girl pressed a button in the wall and said, "The performance is beginning, gentlemen. Each performance lasts fifteen minutes. If you stay through to the next performance, a second payment will be collected. If you stay, you must pay."

A young white woman and a large black man padded into the room. They immediately climbed on the bed, and Leo felt disappointed: when he had come here five years before, the couple—both white—had fondled and kissed each other for a long time before getting into bed. The man in the bedroom now seemed bored and angry. He squeezed the girl's ass, rolled her on top of him. She moved up and down on his massive body, pretending to get excited. The man never even obtained an erection—he was too bored and hostile even to take the minimal steps required to conceal his flopping penis.

A few minutes later, the girl pretended an orgasm. She immediately left the bed and went out of the frame of the window, to wait, Leo thought, for the next ringing of the buzzer. After a few seconds the man also left the bed.

Leo was seething—five years before, the act had been real, not feigned. He felt as though his money had been stolen.

A little ratlike man next to him in a pinched felt hat was looking at him oddly—fearfully, because of the bandages, but almost sympathetically too. "I know," this little man said to Leo. "It ain't real no more—they got busted a couple times and now this stuff is all they do. But if you wanna see the real thing, I can set it up for you. A hundred." He was bending close to Leo, and when the black girl with the enormous gums and the blond wig came in again, he whispered, "Follow me. You got the hundred?"

Leo nodded, and the man darted ahead of him down the stairs. When Leo reached the street, the man was jittering on the sidewalk, a flattened cigarette stuck to his lip. He was in his sixties, a decayed little entrepreneur in his thin plaid shirt and felt hat. "Eighth Avenue," the man said around his cigarette, and began jerkily to move down the street.

"The Mummy is movin'," Grover Spelvin said to Junior Bangs, and they began to amble westward after Leo and the entrepreneur.

"Yeah, but he's movin' *with* Cockroach Al," Junior said. "He ain't no Mummy. Cockroach Al gonna take him to that shrimpy little Mona Minnesota and that crazy fucker Dog. I ain't gonna mess with that fucker."

"Mummy goin' come out again too," Grover pointed out.

"Come out a poor man," Junior said.

Ahead of them, Cockroach Al led Leo Friedgood across Eighth Avenue and then into the lobby of a great gray pile of bricks called the Hotel Spellman. A clerk deliberately looked away, and Al took Leo up the dark stairs to the third floor. "The money," he said, jittering outside a door.

Leo counted out a hundred dollars from the overcoat pocket and placed the money in the man's shaking hands. "Okay, okay. I'll knock, we'll both go in, I'll leave, right? This is the real thing. You'll get what you want, mister. Straight up." The man darted a quick, nervous look at Leo's bandaged face, then knocked twice on the door.

A man with bulging bicep muscles covered with vivid tattoos opened the door. He wore only white cotton underpants, and as he stepped back to let them into the tiny, foul-smelling room, prominent muscles jumped and subsided in his calves and thighs. He was nodding, as if to music only he could hear. The man's blond hair was almost shaved off in places, in others was about an inch long; he had cut it himself without a mirror. "You get paid, Al?" he said in a slow Midwestern voice.

"Sure, Dog," Al said, his head bobbing.

Dog looked Leo over and grinned. "Jeesus H. Christ. Lookit this guy. He's real different."

Leo edged away from Dog and saw a thin drowsy-looking girl staring listlessly up at him from a rumpled bed. She too was blond, and her frizzy hair folded away from her face, as rumpled as the sheet over her body.

"I'll see ya later," Al said, and backed out of the room.

Dog was still staring at Leo, shaking his head in disbelief, moving around him in wide circles. Leo had begun to get nervous when Dog said, "Can you talk? Can you talk through that stuff?"

"Yes," Leo said. "Please. I paid."

"Okey-doke," Dog said, throwing his hands up—lines of muscle leaped out of his arms. "What you wanna see, especially? Anything special? We'll do anything you like."

"Just get on the bed with the girl," Leo said.

"Sure, man, I'll get on the bed with the girl. Anything you say, tourist." Dog pushed the underpants down over his buttocks, and Leo saw that the tattoos ended at the man's waistline. "You siddown over there, you get the best view," Dog said, pointing at a chair about four feet from the bed.

Leo finally realized what the apartment's smell reminded him of—chicken soup. He sat on the wooden chair and watched Dog lift the sheet off the passive girl. Dog was already tumescent. The girl's body was childlike except for her large breasts, which spilled sideways off her chest. Dog knelt between the girl's open legs.

Directly before Leo on the bottom sheet was a brown stain the shape of the state of California.

Leo began to groan as Dog pounded toward his climax: this was real, this was what he had been denied in the club, and as Dog shuddered over the girl's limp body, Leo gasped and trembled.

"Okay, man," Dog said, pulling himself out and sitting up on the bed. "That's what you paid for. Right? You got what you paid for, right?"

Leo nodded, standing up.

"Well, they give us tips, man," Dog said, moving off the bed. The girl was still staring at Leo, and her mouth was open. Dog put himself between the door and Leo. "We sort of appreciate tips, see."

"Of course," Leo said through the hole in his bandages.

He pulled a twenty-dollar bill from his pocket and passed it to Dog.

"You're real different," Dog said. "Hey, you want Mona now? Lotsa these guys do. Another fifty, you can do anything you want with her. Mona'll suck your bandages, man, suck 'em right off." He reached out and gave Leo's chest a hard tap.

Leo groaned, and Dog took a step backward, holding his hand up as if it had been burned. Heavy brutal lines had appeared in his face. "What the fuck are you made of, man?" Dog's entire face had changed, become leaden and suspicious. "Jesus, man." He looked over his shoulder at the girl. "Jesus, Mona, look at this guy's coat. Look at your coat, man."

Leo was breathing hard, experiencing a dreadful *loose* sensation in his chest. The front of his coat had a large dark spreading stain. "Leave me alone," Leo said frantically. "Don't touch me. Just let me get out of here."

Dog stepped toward him with his face bunched up and his eyes contracted so tightly they seemed to have no pupils at all—Leo threw his hands up. Dog dented his jaw with a short left jab, and then hit Leo hard in the temple with his right fist.

The bandages around Leo's head flew apart. White froth scattered across the room like blown suds. Leo toppled to the floor and the frothy white substance poured out of the wrecked bandages. In ten minutes Leo Friedgood was an arrangement of wet clothes, shiny bone, and a damp spaghetti of bandages in a pool of slime. He had been carrying only cash, which Dog removed from his coat pocket.

Leo Friedgood had just disappeared completely from the world.

Thirty minutes later, Grover Spelvin and Junior Bangs saw Dog and Mona Minnesota coming down the front steps of the Hotel Spellman. The two men had been leaning on a lamppost across the wide street, and as Dog's thick body sidled around the door, Grover straightened up smartly and punched Junior Bangs in the side. "It's them," he said. "Come on, Mummy." Mona Minnesota slouched out into the hot sun after Dog and trotted after him down the steps. Both Dog and Mona were carrying brown paper bags bearing large irregular stains.

Grover and Junior crossed the street against the light and began following Dog and Mona south on Eighth Avenue.

"Where's the damn Mummy?" Junior asked. "We been waitin' all day, now where the hell is he?"

Dog stuffed his paper bag into a trash container and waited while Mona put her bag in on top of his. Then they continued at a slower pace down the avenue, looking, as both Grover and Junior instantly recognized, like a young couple out to buy a serious quantity of drugs.

"Shit," said Grover.

"God damn," said Junior.

"Ain't no more Mummy," Grover said. "Dog done took him out."

The two men approached the waste bin where the two bags sat like ornaments on a hat. Junior Bangs delicately plucked at the lip of Mona's bag and peered in. Then he giggled; when he saw how Grover was looking at him, he let out a great roaring laugh. "Grover," he said, bending over with his laughter, "Dog drownded the Mummy. He drownded him in shaving soap. Haw haw!"

Grover Spelvin gloomily hooked a finger into the bag. He peered in. Then he shook his head. "That ain't shaving soap," he said. "That is the Mummy. God damn. You know what?" He turned to Junior with something like a sense of wonder on his broad face. "Dog took him out all right, but that dude was the real Mummy. Like in the old movies."

"Fuckin' Dog," Junior said, shaking his head.

"Inside those bandages he was all *juice and bones*," Grover said. "The real Mummy. God damn."

"The Mummy," Junior said.

"I wonder how much money he had," Grover mused.

4

"I'm so glad you're willing to help," Sarah Spry told Ulick Byrne that night. "You know, I've never needed help of this sort before—used to doing things by myself."

"I know, I know," the lawyer said. "I'm the same way. But we're friends, Sarah. And I guess this is something you don't want Brockett and the other people at the *Gazette* to latch on to before you're ready for them."

"Exactly. I'm just working on a hunch, Ulick. Brockett would think I was crazy. So if you can, you know, just look into the records for me and see if there were any industrial accidents, anything like that, in our vicinity in the past six weeks to two months. If there hasn't been anything, maybe you could check on sunspot activity for me. I'll be working on another line, and of course I'll share anything I find with you. Things are going too crazy around here.''

But that was scarcely news to Ulick Byrne. During the past week or two, half of his clients seemed to have bloomed into full-fledged psychosis. In fact, so many things had gone wrong that Ulick Byrne himself thought he was probably going crazy. The O'Haras of course had a reason for their present instability; and perhaps the Johnsons did too—their four purebred Lhasa Apsos had all run out together and been puréed by the wheels of a Druze Cement Company truck. But another of his clients had actually jogged herself to death. Forty pounds overweight, she had never done anything more strenuous than pick up the remote-control device for her television set. Then one morning she was up running down Sawtell Road before breakfast, and she would not stop even when her husband cruised along beside her in his BMW, pleading with her to come inside. Half an hour later, after three solid hours of jogging, her leg muscles had given out and so had her heart.

In fact, Ulick Byrne thought, if you took a look at what his clients had been up to lately, you had a better picture of what was happening to Hampstead than you wanted—because no one would want to get so close to all that madness. Besides Jane Anderson jogging herself into a heart attack on Sawtell Road, there was George Klopnik, an accountant with a firm in Woodville—George, Ulick knew, was about as successful as a Woodville accountant could be without actually being a partner. Yet George had entered Ulick Byrne's office with a glinting, warped look in his eye and a conviction that he should sue the government of the United States: for giving him false expectations. George was convinced that in the case of *Klopnik vs. the U.S.* a jury of his peers would award him twenty million dollars in punitive damages. Ulick had gotten him out of the office only by promising to look up the precedents on cases on false expectations. Even worse than George was Rogers Thornton, the patrician head of a large furniture-importing business. Thornton had the silver hair, the pinstriped suits, and the wonderful manners appropriate to a house on Mount Avenue and the presidency of a successful company; he had also, in the afternoon of Tuesday, the seventeenth of June, come up to a pretty high-school girl standing outside of Anhalt's on Main Street and said, "I am the possessor of a particularly beautiful whanger. Would you care to see it?" Now Thornton was out on bail, but the girl's parents wanted him put away for life if they couldn't get him castrated, and Thornton was serenely unaffected by all the fuss. "You don't understand, Mr. Byrne," he had told Ulick. "I really am the possessor of a particularly beautiful whanger. Surely that will count in my favor?"

And we cannot leave Ulick Byrne's tribulations without mentioning Maggie Nelligan of Revolutionary Circle, who with her friend Kathryn Hoskins of Gravesend Avenue had gone into Bloomingdale's in Manhattan one morning and ordered a hundred and seventy thousand dollars' worth of goods in the fur department. Mrs. Nelligan and Mrs. Hoskins had been requested to have a chat with the fur-department manager in his office, which they happily agreed to do. When the manager asked how the ladies intended to pay for the furs the ladies grew indignant. Surely the manager knew her, Mrs. Nelligan protested. Surely he knew her name? The manager regretted that he did not, but if she would be so kind as to refresh his memory . . .? "Why, I own this store," said Maggie Nelligan. "I would have thought that you'd know that." "And I own it too," said Kathryn Hoskins. "We both own it." Maggie Nelligan nodded vociferously. "Now we'll have our furs, please," she said. In the end there had been shouting, blows—the poor fur-department manager required stitches—and the police had been summoned. A very grumpy Maggie Nelligan and Kathryn Hoskins had been charged with assault and attempted larceny and locked up in a cell. Mr. Paul Nelligan had called Ulick Byrne the next day.

Also, there were the signs of disorder that Byrne had seen around the town . . . the garbagemen hadn't come to his house for a week straight, and then they showed up twice on the same day, grinning like lunatics; the taxi driver who had taken him from the station to his house on Redcoat Grove late Friday night had managed to get lost, though he'd taken Byrne home at least twice before; a girl working the register at Greenblatt's had tried to charge him six times for the same veal roast and had broken down in great whooping sobs when he protested; and he was sure he had seen through his office windows an old woman furtively eating dirt and grass from one of the big planters in the building's parking lot. And didn't there seem to be more fights than ever before, shorter tempers? In that same parking lot two days before, he had watched a pair of high-school boys slug each other half-senseless. . . .

Helping Sarah, he thought, might also help take his mind off these things.

He called her back two days later: his research had turned up only one item. "And I'm not sure it fits into the pattern you're trying to build, Sarah. But here it is anyway, just to show you I believe in the cause—on the seventeenth of May a couple of guys died in an accident at a chemical plant in Woodville. Woodville Solvent, to be precise. The reports all indicated that the men died of carbon-monoxide poisoning."

"Humpf," Sarah said. "Not much help there. I was hoping there'd have been some big spill, maybe on the highway . . . but wait a second. That was on the seventeenth? That's our day. *That is our day.* Mrs. Friedgood was killed on the seventeenth of May. And I'll tell you something else that happened then, there was a terrible smashup on the highway that killed eight people. Doesn't it look like we might just be stretching the bounds of coincidence here, Ulick?"

"Jesus, I have a terrible headache," Byrne said. "But yeah, I agree with you. Because—"

"And just look at the *eighteenth,*" Sarah said, her voice rising. "Do you remember what happened on the *eighteenth?*, Ulick? Five people dropped dead. It's all in the *Gazette.* We were all so wrapped up with that terrible murder that we never stopped to think there might have been any connection. But you know, it's really too early for me to bother anyone else with my nutty ideas about all this, but I think there might be some kind of pattern."

"Well, that's in line with what I was going to say," Byrne told her. "I'm damned if I can tell you what it is. But, Sarah, what I was going to say is, I think there might be some kind of pattern because of Leo Friedgood."

"The husband," Sarah said.

"Right. Leo Friedgood is some kind of officer of the Telpro Corporation. They're heavily into defense work, along with lots of other stuff. Well, Telpro owned Woodville Solvent—I did part of the paperwork on the transfer. They didn't want a Woodville attorney involved."

"Well, we're onto something, but I don't know what," Sarah said.

"Let's find this Friedgood and talk to him."

"And then I'll try out some of my funny ideas on you."

"I could use a good laugh," Byrne said. "All my respectable clients seem to want to end up behind bars."

5

When Richard Allbee arrived home on that Tuesday, Laura opened the front door for him: he dropped his suitcases on the floor and hugged her until she said she couldn't breathe. Then he stepped backward and, still holding her shoulders, looked at her. Her face was glowing, her hair clean and soft, her belly somehow visibly larger: a dozen cornball remarks about Grecian vases formed in his mind, but all he said was, "God, did I miss you. You look so good."

That night he told her all about Morris Stryker and the house on College Street—about the endless meals in second-rate restaurants, the shifty men consulting with Stryker, Stryker's rejection of his plans, how he had almost run down the client in order to escape him. "That means our income is effectively cut in half," Richard told her. "But I don't want you to worry about that. Something will happen. I know it will."

"I'm even surer of that than you," Laura said. "I bet you that in two years, at the most three years, you'll have so much work that you'll be turning down some clients. Trust me. I have a crystal ball."

And it was true that though the Allbees had less cash in their pockets, they survived each month's deluge of bills all during that summer and fall. During this time, with Richard working just up the road in Hillhaven, they became closer than they had ever been. One day a week, even as Laura's pregnancy developed, they went to New York and wandered through galleries and museums—and this exposure to Manhattan, as well as the healthy growth of her baby, melted away Laura's depression at leaving London. They agreed that when Richard's business would allow them to spend more money, they would rent a small apartment somewhere on the West Side to use on the weekends.

On the September night that the baby was delivered, Richard stood beside the bed and said the helpless but encouraging things fathers say: "You're doing a great job, darling. Now it's going to be time to push again. That's it: push, keep pushing, keep pushing, really *push* now. That was wonderful, Laura." He was babbling, too excited and too proud of Laura to really remember the lessons they had taken. What most impressed Richard about the process of birth was the courage, even the heroism of women—he thought that if men had babies, there would be a lot fewer people.

After ten hours of labor, Lump was born in Norrington Hospital on September thirtieth, weighing seven pounds one ounce, twenty-three inches long, normal and healthy in every aspect, and female—as Richard had known she would be. The following day, Richard and Laura decided to name her Philippa, for no reason other than that they both liked it. "Philippa?" asked the nursery nurse, a big good-natured black woman with a thick wiry corolla of hair. "Whatever happened to good old normal names like Mary and Susan? Seems like nobody uses those anymore." Four days later the Allbees took their daughter home to the lovely new house on Beach Trail. Richard had managed to decorate the room they had chosen as the nursery, but in much of the rest of the house the walls were unfinished and exposed pipes rattled against plaster surrounds and junction boxes sat like spiders in the centers of immense metal webs. It was as Richard had explained to Laura years before: the restorer's house was always the last to get restored. "I'm glad you're not an obstetrician," Laura said.

As Philippa grew, she resembled Laura—her hair was that same delicate watercolor shade of red—much more than Richard, and from the start, this sweet, sober, questioning child owned her father's heart. Richard and Laura never tried to have another child; Philippa seemed to take so much love from them, and to create as much as she took, and the Allbees never seriously considered filling a void they could not see or feel. When Philippa was five, they enrolled her in the Greenbank Academy.

By then their house was restored, and Laura's prediction had come true, though a year or two later than scheduled: Richard had offers of so much work that he could only take half of it. By now they were thinking seriously about that apartment in New York, the more so since Laura knew that she wanted to look for a job when Philippa was a few years older.

When Philippa was in the fifth grade, Laura began interviewing for jobs on magazines, with publishers of all descriptions . . . and in six months she had found a job as an assistant editor with a paperback company.

Laura flourished in this job, but the Allbees' marriage became shakier than at any time since their move back to America. As Laura became more experienced with publishing, Richard could not help his resentment over how much time she spent away from the house, away from him: he had to accept that Laura's job had become almost as important in her life as her marriage. The Allbees fought and strained with and against each other for eighteen wretched months.

By the time that Philippa went off to Brown University (Richard drove her up to Providence, and looked up Morris Stryker in the telephone book while he was in Providence, expecting not to find him, and did not—either dead or unlisted), Laura had been named editorial director at Pocket Books; and Richard had become more successful than he considered he had any right to be. He spoke at convocations and symposia around the world, he and Laura had made many trips back to London, and he had an office in New York as well as one in Hampstead. He employed two young architects passionately interested in restoration work (and one of them, he thought, seemed as passionately interested in Philippa). In Philippa's junior year at Brown, one of Laura's young discoveries wrote a book that instantly began to sell more than twenty thousand copies a week, and went on to sell steadily until they had printed more than two million copies; and Richard got the most important commission of his life, to restore a famous Victorian country house designed by Sir Charles Barry.

That Thanksgiving, Laura and Richard and Philippa had a long, consciously celebratory dinner in their Hampstead home. The Allbees drank a bottle of Dom Perignon before dinner, and then went into the dining room to feast on the goose their cook had roasted, and all the other, more traditional foods she had made—the stuffing, the acorn squash, cranberries, potatoes, mince pie.

The doorbell rang just as they sat down. Richard groaned,

saying that it might be a delivery of plans from the New York office. No, Laura said, it could be the messenger service delivering her new star's next manuscript a day early; she stood up and left the table as Richard started to carve the goose.

When Laura opened the door, Richard glanced sideways— a chilling blast of wind, wind so cold it felt black, had whipped into the dining room. "What?" Richard said, putting down the long carving knife. He turned toward the door, and in that second saw Billy Bentley walk forward toward Laura through the door: Billy walked in on that rising, whipping black wind and his eyes were glowing. In the next second he slammed a knife into Laura's stomach and hauled it upward toward her heart with gleeful and inhuman savagery.

All of this could have happened, and some of it did, but not in that way.

Richard rolled over in bed and blinked up at the ceiling: he did not feel sane, but whatever sanity he'd had was the inventor of this elaborate and cruel fantasy. At times he had almost believed it; no, at times, prostrate here in this bedroom, he *had* believed it. He had seen Philippa being born, and he had seen her face when she was able to ride her first two-wheeled bicycle, when she had been first in her class in a test. He had *seen* that page of the Providence telephone directory, the row of names that did not include Morris Stryker's, and heard Philippa's voice asking him, "Who are you looking for, Daddy?" These invented things he had seen had probably kept him at least as sane as he was; and had probably kept him alive too—for the past five days he had been in shock so deep he had almost needed to remind himself to breathe. As Leo Friedgood had dosed himself with alcohol after the death of his wife, Richard Allbee had fed himself on imagination.

About nine o'clock on Tuesday night, the seventeenth of June, Richard had taken Exit 18 off the Connecticut Turnpike, swung down the Sayre Connector to Greenbank Road, crossed over the bridge from which Turtle Turk had threatened to drop Bruce Norman, went past Wren Van Horne's house and the entrance to the beach, and from Mount Avenue turned into Beach Trail. He had rehearsed so many alternatives in his mind—there had been a power failure, there had been a burglary, Laura had been trying to dial *him* and was now on the highway to Providence—that all he wanted to do was see his wife and make sure that everything was still all right. Among the alternatives he had considered was a fire, and so he felt easier as soon as he got far enough along on Beach Trail to see the back of his house.

The light inside the back door was on, Richard noticed as he drove into the garage. He got his suitcase out of the trunk and carried it across the drive to the back steps. Then he opened the back door and called his wife's name. He entered; dropped his case just inside the door.

Richard went down the hall toward the front of the house. "Laura?" he called. One of the lights in the living room was on, and he saw that Laura had hung up several of their paintings on the long wall at the back.

He wandered through the living room and out into the hall again. This time he noticed that the front door was open; and when he noticed that, he caught a heavy, unfamiliar odor on a drift of air: it had come from deep within his house.

Standing there in the empty hall beside the open front door, Richard had wanted to go back out the rear door, take his car out of the garage and drive all the way back to Rhode Island—all the way to Maine, all the way to the Arctic Circle and the end of the world, if need be. His heart had lurched in its rhythm, and for the last time he whispered her name. He touched the open door, swallowing hard, and pushed it shut. Then he turned to face the house.

Richard went into the dining room, saw that their round antique table had been polished and the chairs taken from their protective packing. He turned on the light in the kitchen and stepped in.

The kitchen was empty. On the counters were swirls left by a damp rag. Beside the sink—like a severed hand—lay the red receiver for the telephone. On the little table were boxes of unpacked glasses. One of these boxes had fallen to the floor, and a bright scattering of broken glass lay on the tiles. Such small signs of disorder.

At the far end of the kitchen was a pantry Richard was planning to remove. It was a small enclosed space with aluminum tubs, a washer and dryer, and handmade shelves all the way up to the ceiling. Richard forced himself to open the door to this pantry; then forced himself to pull the cord that turned on the light.

At first he saw nothing but the washer and dryer. He held

his breath and walked into the small square room. He looked at the shelves and saw a thick layer of dust, an old pair of striped work gloves. Dusty fruit jars with red caps had been tented within a furry spiderweb.

When he looked at the side of the washing machine he saw a splash of blood.

She had answered the door, come into the kitchen with her guest . . . then she had known she was in danger, and she had picked up the telephone. The man had cut the phone line. Laura had run into the pantry and squeezed herself down beside the washer. She had already been hurt.

What then?

He did not know if he was strong enough to know what had happened then.

Holding his hands to the sides of his face, he came out of the kitchen by its back door and went down the narrow back hall. At the bottom of the steep narrow back staircase, in the old days the servants' staircase, he found another splash of blood.

So she had burst out of the pantry and climbed the back stairs. He groaned, set his foot on the bottom step. His body seemed paradoxically heavy enough to flatten the step, so light it could float upward at the slightest push. He walked up half a dozen steps, breathing in short agitated gasps.

Halfway up the back staircase he saw a bloody palm print on the wall above the handrail. On the top step lay another splash of blood, already dried and brown.

He went straight ahead to the room they had chosen as Lump's nursery. It was the nearest room; it was where she would have run. Richard stopped before the nursery door, kneading his hands together, and all at once caught that unfamiliar odor again; now he recognized it as the smell of blood. He gently pushed open the door of the nursery.

Just inside the door a silver-and-brown thing lay on the old carpet. It took Richard a moment to recognize it as human flesh, another moment to identify it. Laura was frozen back against the nursery wall, her blood splashed like a bucket of paint over the window above her body. Richard moaned like an underground animal: like a wounded badger. He stabbed on the light, starting to give in to the frightened weeping that had been building within him. Lump too had been riding on the Dragon's back, the shapeless little thing that would have become his Philippa. She was beside Laura, what there was of her.

Laura's mouth was open, her eyes stared at him; Lump's mouth, too, was open. Richard stood before them, so incapable of movement that he could not even tremble. Finally he saw that the opening torn in his wife's belly was filled with flies, and he screeched so loudly that the effort let him move backward out of the nursery and into the hall.

6

The being who had once been Dr. Wren Van Horne sat in his darkened living room and faced the old mirror the doctor had bought. What it saw in the mirror were scenes of devastation and ruin—smoking rubble and heaps of shattered bricks—the timeless scenes of its landscape. Streets heaved upward into impassable mounds of broken concrete, buildings burned down to their foundations, bridges sunken into the water they were supposed to cross, huge piles of ash flaring up, tongues of fire flickering around their circumferences as a bitter wind rustles through, then subsiding again, breathing out a sullen smoke. . . .

Then a shuffled deck of pictures rolled across the surface of the mirror. The faces of screaming children, troops moving across a wide street, the trenches and mud and barbed wire of the First World War, the emaciated bodies of concentration-camp victims—bodies starved down to catgut and gristle . . . these images too were timeless, and represented both past and future. Children with swollen stomachs and the faces of old men, hunched men and women picking their food off a barren hillside.

Now the being saw suspended in a towering wave of blood the faces of all those who had died since the seventeenth of May. Joe Ricci, Thomas Gay and Harvey Washington, Stony Friedgood and Hester Goodall, Harry and Babe Zimmer and fifteen firemen, Bobby Fritz, all the others—their faces and bodies floating in the red wave.

Then the towering wave subsided, and the being in Wren Van Horne's living room saw platoons of children swimming off Gravesend Beach, forcing themselves to go beyond the markers, making themselves swim when they were so exhausted they could scarcely make their arms lift out of the heavy pink water . . . then he saw them swimming back toward shore, their bodies dark with bottom-mud and hung with ropes of weeds.

He turned in his chair to look hungrily out of the wall of windows facing the Sound.

Yes.

Standing on the seawall at the edge of his lawn was a silent crowd. He moved to the windows to let them in.

The first one to step in through the opened windows was a small boy wearing the torn and faded remains of a blue T-shirt. On the shirt there still lingered a barely visible photograph of Yoda.

7

With burning bowels and a pounding head, Turtle Turk worked the traffic light on the corner of Riverfront Avenue and the Post Road the following morning. He was recovering from the worst bout of flu of his life, and by now he knew that he should have stayed home another day. He saw double for a few seconds, and shook his head. His guts squirmed; soon it would be time for another of his half-hourly visits to the crummy little toilet in the back of Abrazzi Liquor—the liquor store stood right behind him on the south-east corner. It was just his luck, Turtle thought, that he got the flu so late in the cycle: by the time he fell sick, everybody else had been over their flu so long they didn't even remember how rotten it had made them feel. All they cared about was covering his place on the duty roster and subtracting sick days off his schedule—Turtle could still work himself up into a fine hot resentment by thinking that none of his fellow officers had even visited him at home. (The warmth of his resentment probably kept him from seeing that his frequent loud diatribes about the assholes who called or came by his camper at night had decided everybody else that Turtle hated to be bothered at home.) But this morning Turtle had enough to make him percolate with resentment without rehearsing the callousness of the younger policemen.

First there was the damned button, and second there was the urge to grow hair on his palms that affected every civilian once he got behind the wheel of his car. Any cop who did this duty had seen mild little people who would cry if shouted at suddenly act like savages in traffic—screaming out the window, blasting the horn, squealing their tires—but today it seemed worse than ever. Turtle *knew* that a couple of kids had deliberately swept so close to him they had almost run over his shoes. There was more than the usual amount of horn-leaning from the cars stuck behind the red light on the Post Road. Some of that was the fault of the button, but mainly it was just impatience—as if the places these civilians had to get to were any better than the insides of their cars. Worst of all, there had been two fender-benders this morning, and that was unusual for this corner; and in the second little accident, a big guy in a glen plaid suit had come boiling out of his Audi and run back to the little fatso in a Ford who had banged him—the big guy had torn open the door of the Ford and was battering on the fatso's face before Turtle could get to him. And then he had only stopped the big guy by clubbing him with his nightstick. All that wasn't easy on a man with a headache and a sick stomach. On top of everything else, he had a complicated report to write up when he got back to headquarters.

And if that wasn't bad enough, some lady with frizzy Chiquita Banana hair and a cigarette plastered to her oversized lower lip had leaned out her window and screamed at him that there had been *four murders, damn it! What are you morons doing about it? Picking your noses?* Of course civilians were dumb as dogs, they didn't know that the state was now running the murder investigations. And if they did, they probably thought that someone like Turtle would resent it—but Turtle thought the situation was just fine. Let the state do all the dogwork. A young jerk like Bobo Farnsworth probably thought that investigation was good for his soul, but Turtle knew that it was mainly just hard on the feet. If the state guys identified the killer, it would be the Hampstead cops who would take him in. That part was all right with Turtle.

"Well, me, lady, what I'm doing about it is, I'm giving the killer your name as soon as I run your license number through state records," Turtle muttered to himself.

Then the button got stuck again. Turtle shook his head, getting purple in the face with rage. When he pushed the button on the little hand-held metal box, the signal was supposed to change on the traffic lights. And when it got stuck, as it did every other time this morning, he had to get across the street through the traffic and open the console on the sidewalk and jiggle a switch in the junction box; then he had to run back across the street and see if it worked. Sometimes the light just bit down on red or green and Turtle had to get out in the middle of the white circle and direct traffic with his arms and his whistle until the machine decided to work again.

He held up his hand and stepped off the curb. Horns blasted, the cars began to stack up on either side of the road. Turtle stepped between two cars and glared at a weedy baldheaded idiot leaning on his horn. On the other side of the yellow line, right-turning cars from the Post Road cruised by unstoppably. Turtle stuck his arm out again and blew a piercing command on his whistle: two more cars went by, and finally the third, a Jaguar driven by a blonde with short upturned hair, stopped. Turtle stepped in front of it, and the car crept forward another five inches and touched Turtle's knee. He blasted the whistle loud enough to shatter the windsheld, and then took the whistle from his mouth and with a beet-red face yelled, "What's the big idea, lady? You tryna—"

Another car making a right turn from the Post Road crumped into the woman's car. Turtle felt a sharp pain in his knee as the Jaguar's bumper struck it, and he bellowed, "Out! Out of the cars! Both of you!"

Savagely he hit the switch inside the junction box, and through the furor of the horns heard the loud *click* as the light changed.

"Now get those cars moving and settle your problems!" Turtle bellowed, not sure why he'd tied up traffic by making the blonde and the man behind her leave their cars . . . through his headache floated an image of his whipping both of them with his stick, flattening the man's nose and breaking the woman's jaw, scattering teeth and blood . . . He glared at them with such peculiar intensity that they each hurriedly got into their cars and drove on until they could pull into a parking lot to swap insurance cards.

Turtle ground his teeth and stepped down off the curb again to limp across to his station. His bowels stirred, and in a very few minutes he would have to be back in Abrazzi's stinking three-foot square toilet. He wondered what would happen to him if he used his nightstick to crack open the windshield of the next expensive piece of foreign tin that went past—he guessed that the pleasure of it would far outweigh whatever punishment the department gave him.

Now he had to contend with the left-turners from the other side of the Post Road. He stuck out his hand and put his foot across the yellow line. A car ignored his signals and rushed right past him, the rear window passing no more than two feet from his face. Turtle never noticed who was driving—except that he had a dim, uneasy sense that *no one* was driving—but when he looked furiously through the rear window he saw the torn and scarred face of Dicky Norman staring back at him.

It seemed to hang in front of his eyes for an impossibly long time. Dicky's face was that fishy white of all dead skin, except for the black lines where a surgeon's knife had cut through his forehead and scalp. His eyes were faintly yellow around the pupils and as lifeless as the face. Dicky's tongue moved thickly as Turtle peered into the rear window—Dicky was struggling to speak. Then the apparition flew past him: the car was gone, already moving through the intersection.

Turtle stumbled blindly into the traffic, holding his hand out without looking to see if he was stopping any cars. The whistle hung slackly from his lips.

He made it safely to the curb and went up the steps into Abrazzi's without even looking back at the traffic. Mike Abrazzi, the old man behind the sloping counter, said, "You sure got the runs, huh, Turtle?"

"Shut the fuck up," Turtle growled, and rushed into the little toilet and got his pants down just in time. He kept trying to blot out the picture of Dicky Norman's face.

When he came out, trailing some of the odors from the little room at the back of the liquor store, he saw that the traffic was for once streaming past normally, and he looked up the Post Road—up past the bridge, going toward the near end of Main Street, he saw a little group of people that took his attention by its incongruity. He first recognized Graham Williams, a man for whom he had only scorn—Williams had run out on his country instead of trying to help it. Then he recognized Richard Allbee, the husband of the last victim; and beside Allbee was Patsy McCloud. Turtle had seen her grow up in Hampstead, and he knew she'd married that football player from J. S. Mill, Les McCloud, who had creamed himself on the highway a week or so ago. Patsy was a pretty girl, with those big eyes and that long hair. With these three went a teenager, some boy Turtle did not recognize. For an instant before turning his attention back to the traffic, Turtle watched these four make their way in the sunlight toward

Main Street—and the second oddest thing of the day happened to Turtle Turk.

He envied those four people. It went through him with a peculiar, poignant sharpness that they were a kind of family, so great was their affection for each other. For a moment in which he was surprised by the clarity with which he saw these four—as if they were outlined in bright sunlight. He wanted to be with them, to be a part of that closeness. And in that second he permitted himself to feel envy.

But then they turned the corner, he could see the hump in old man Williams' back, and they were just ordinary civilians again. Turtle stabbed at the button again, and again it stuck. He started to swear, and then again was assailed by the sight of Dicky Norman's face looking blankly at him through the car window. He closed his eyes, exhaled, and pushed the button gently with his index finger. The lights changed with a loud decisive *click*. Turtle opened his eyes again, tingling with relief. Christ, for a second there he'd almost believed . . . He scowled at the cars gunning through the intersection. For something like that, they could take his pension away.

Richard Allbee would have talked about what he thought he had seen: indeed, as Turtle watched him turn into Main Street with his friends, Richard was ignoring the tears that slid down his cheeks and telling the other three about his days' long fantasy about Laura and his child, and before the end of the day he would be telling them about Billy Bentley and the dream of making the earth spout blood. Even Les McCloud would have found someone at a bar—not Patsy—to amuse with his crazy story of seeing a dead face through a car window. But when Turtle's eight hours were up, he reported back to the station and laboriously typed up his report on the fender-bender, changed out of his uniform, and went home to his Winnebago. There he drank five beers and fell asleep while watching a ballgame on television.

At eight o'clock Turtle awoke, muttering "catch up" to himself. He went into the camper's little toilet—smaller than Abrazzi's but not much cleaner—relieved his bladder, shaved, splashed water under his armpits. He left the camper to drive up the Post Road to Billy O's.

Billy O's was a bar in a section of Bridgeport mostly inhabited by black people, but no black person ever went into

Billy O's. It was a cop bar. The owner, Billy O'Meara, had been on the Old Sarum force for twenty years before a kid in a stolen car had run into him and broken his pelvis into toothpicks. Now he limped from one end of his bar to the other, endlessly explaining that most human beings were good for shit, but especially kids, Jews, Protestants, Dagos, Puerto Ricans, women, and most especially jungle bunnies. If a black man had dared poke his head into Billy O's, Billy O'Meara would probably have dropped dead on the spot of racist's apoplexy.

When Turtle walked in, the six or seven guys at the bar glanced at him and immediately stopped talking. That meant, Turtle knew, that they had been talking about Royce Griffen. The only policeman in this part of the state to have shot himself in the past ten years, Griffen was the subject of a lot of conversation in cop bars and department locker rooms. Turtle was sick of it: it seemed to him that a bunch of loaded cops talking about Royce Griffen was even more boring than Billy O'Meara talking about how many black guys had tried to break into his storeroom.

"Aw, Jesus," he said. "Are you fuckin' guys exhuming Roycie again? Let the little bastard get a little sleep, will ya? He ate his gun, he ate his gun, nattata nattata nattata. Give it a rest."

A Bridgeport police sergeant named Danny Salgo said, "Word is you rode him pretty hard, Turtle."

"Sure I rode him hard," Turtle said. *"Everybody* rode him hard. What the hell you trying to say?"

"Nothing, Turtle," Salgo quickly said.

"It better be nothing. A department gets one foul ball who freaks out, and everybody for a hundred miles around starts doin' a ten-year post-mortem." Billy O'Meara put a glass of beer and a short glass of Jack Daniels over ice down in front of Turtle; Turtle sipped the bourbon, then took a long draught of the beer.

"Gimme some good news, Turtle," Billy O'Meara said. "With these other guys, all I get is the bad. So-and-so flunked the captain's test, some other dumbbell totaled his car, blah blah blah. Johanssen down the end there, he's so full a gripes he's goin' to Los Angeles next month, take the tests to get onto the force there."

"Los *Angeles?*" Salgo said incredulously. Johanssen was a twenty-four-year-old policeman in Hampstead. "They takin' babies out there now? Why the hell you wanna go all the way out there just to meet a lot more spics? You're a little puppy, Johanssen—they'll take you apart out there.''

Johanssen shook his blond head, wisely keeping his temper. "I just got sour on this place," he said. "Even Bobo's thinking of going out there, I hear. You make about three times as much money, for one thing.''

"Bobo Farnsworth, the world's only tee-total cop," Salgo said. "A coke-sucker.''

Turtle suddenly felt weary. "Bobo's a good cop," he said. "So's Johanssen down there. He's a kid, but he's a good cop." Then Turtle laughed. "You want to hear the good news, O'Meara? Hey, Johanssen. You comin' to *The Choirboys* next week?''

Johanssen nodded into his beer glass.

"There's your good news, Billy. Another midnight special for the Hampstead and Old Sarum boys. This one is gonna really be wild. You'll be lucky to have a bar left.''

O'Meara was already laughing—he was remembering, as all the men in the bar knew, what had happened after the First Annual Midnight All-Police Movie at the Nutmeg Theater behind Main Street. The movie had been *Klute,* and about a hundred and fifty Hampstead and Old Sarum police officers had attended. For three dollars apiece, they had had all the beer they could drink and about six pounds of popcorn each. By the time the movie was over, the theater was full of crushed popcorn and flattened beercans, and the more boyish of the boys—who had screamed and shouted for an hour and a half—were ready to have a little serious fun. A bunch of cops had taken a short detour on the way to Billy O's, and at two o'clock, the little bar locked its doors on nineteen drunken cops and three local working girls. By four o'clock the place smelled like a high-school locker-room; by five, the girls stopped charging, having made about two months' worth of money; by six, everyone but Billy was on the floor, all the girls naked and most of the men, too. Heaps of wet five- and ten-dollar bills lay here and there, stuck together with spilled beer. At six-thirty Billy gave everyone a free drink and kicked them out. Two or three of the men, among them Johanssen, had driven straight to the police station to work out on the firing range before their shift began.

"Hey, I'd like to make it to that," Salgo said.

"I don't think they're inviting firemen this year, Danny," Turtle said—an old police joke.

Turtle and the others settled into the familiar rituals of a night's drinking; and no one said anything he had not said many times before; but in the middle of the night in the bar, Turtle felt as though maybe he did have whatever he had envied in the little group of Patsy McCloud and Graham Williams and the other two that morning—had as much of it as he wanted anyhow, as much closeness as he could stand, and the little cop's bar in a Bridgeport ghetto gave it to him.

"I had enough," he said at ten minutes past one. "I'm seeing things. Gotta get home. Pretty soon I'll be like that old Josephine Tayler. Saw her grand-daughter today. Argument for rape. Goodbye."

At one-thirty Turtle got out of his car and began to push himself up the weedy bank that separated his camper's site from the road. The Winnebago sat on a half acre of cleared ground Turtle had bought from the town in 1941. Next to Turtle's land was a run-down grocery store that doubled as a gas station, behind it was another half acre of trees. When Turtle was half way up the bank, he heard somebody moving around in back of his camper—loud footsteps from somewhere in front of him. "Pardner," he whispered to himself, and fumbled getting his gun out of its holster. Someone was trying to break into the Winnebago: that was his first thought.

"Come on out where I can see you," he shouted, thinking that it was probably a couple of kids who would cut and run for the trees. "Get out here, you scum."

Panting, he reached the top of the bank. He crouched over and waddled as quickly as he could to the white fence on the other side of his property from the store. From there he could see the front of the Winnebago. No one was hiding there, flattened up against the camper's stamped metal. "Come on out," he shouted. No one responded. Turtle ran across the back of the camper and circled up around the far side. Now he was sweating and breathing hard enough to strain his belly against his belt. Despite what he had heard, there were no kids larking around his camper.

Then he heard the sound again—a heavy body moving. It came from the trees behind his land.

Turtle wiped his forehead with his sleeve. The sounds still

came toward him from the trees. "What the hell are you doin' in there?" he screamed. "Is this supposed to be a *game*?"

Turtle thought of what he had seen that morning. Dicky Norman's awful face—

but of course he had not seen it.

"I'm a cop and I'm armed!" Turtle yelled.

Then he could see the body coming out through the last of the trees.

Too much Jack Daniels and too much beer. The body, now emerging onto the cleared land, was Dicky Norman's, and it was naked and so white it seemed to reflect back the moonlight.

"I don't know what you are, but you better leave me alone," Turtle said, aiming his pistol at Dicky's chest.

As soon as Dicky took another step, Turtle could smell him. It was the smell, unforgettable, that Turtle had been subjected to as a young cop when they had discovered the body of a hunter locked in his car out behind the Rinker Brothers' icehouse in the late forties. The hunter had got lost in a snowstorm, and the cold froze him to death in mid-January: it was April when they found him. Turtle had opened the door of the hunter's car, and he'd thought that he would puke for an hour.

Dicky said something that was lost in the buzzing of a thousand flies. He took another step toward Turtle.

8

Two hours after the death of Turtle Turk, Mikki Zaber O'Hara dreamed again that she was sleeping with her son Tommy. She cradled his thin cold nine-year-old body, peeled the wet strands of weed from his forehead, kissed his cold wet cheeks. She rubbed her hands over his back, sleepily trying to warm him. Oh, she loved Tommy! Her hands pressed his shoulders into her, and beneath her hip she felt grit: she unthinkingly knew it was sand. Her husband snored on behind her, and Mikki ran her hand lovingly down her son's cold flank. Mud slowed her fingers, slimed against her palm. Gradually, still sleepily, Mikki understood that she was not dreaming. She was awake, and Tommy was miraculously beside her. She cradled his face; Tommy's eyes fluttered.

The boy had given her a chance to join him: all she wanted was to join him.

In the morning both their bodies were gone. Hampstead had crossed another threshold, and now stood—as Mikki Zaber O'Hara had for a phantasmal, lyric moment—on the border beween life and death.

PART THREE

Dominion

Why didst thou leave the trodden paths of men
Too soon, and with weak hands though mighty
  heart
Dare the unpastured dragon in his den?

—Shelley

PART TWELVE

Defining

1

The Belly of the Whale

1

Lyric; phantasmal; such words mean only that there was a disorder in the very stuff of reality, and that this disorder affected people in various ways, some of them surprisingly pleasant. Reality was on a bender, and if what the bender led to was a theater of horrors in the basement of an abandoned house on Poor Fox Road, only three people were present to see them: metaphorically, most other people in Hampstead had their eyes sewn shut, and the peculiar visions that danced across the inside of their eyelids sometimes delighted or lulled them, as absurdities can delight or calm a drunken man. Otto Bruckner had foreseen that about eight weeks after the accident at Woodville Solvent, Hampstead and Patchin would be held squirming in the grip of his invention—that horrors like those that lived in Bates Krell's basement would pour out through the streets—but of course he had no idea that his invention would shake hands with an enigmatic colonist named Gideon or Gidyon Winter. He just knew his thinking cloud, and that was enough; he did not have to know any more to find the next world preferable to this one. But people in Hampstead did not have his foresight, they had no idea that they were crossing a border: what they, including our four friends, mostly knew was that it became more and more difficult to separate what was actually happening in the world from what was going on in the mind. The thinking cloud had settled over them too. So what Patsy and Tabby saw together, what Graham and Richard and Patsy saw as they struggled to save Tabby's life at the bottom of a mirror, in the world's bowel, had to be taken as it came: to be met on its own terms, however bizarre those terms appeared.

Desmond O'Hara, who had flown back from Australia to bury his sons, met those terms when he awakened to find his

wife gone from their bed. He searched all through his house,
chill with the thought that she too had gone down to Gravesend Beach in the middle of the night. He still had jet lag, and
found himself falling asleep in the middle of that day, as
scared as he was, and imagining that Mikki was talking to
him, asking him about the price of opals in Coober Pedy,
laughing at him! When he woke up at midnight, totally disoriented, he imagined that he could still hear his wife's voice.
Crazy, he thought, and when he checked through the house to
see if she had come home, thought he was crazier yet when
he saw or imagined he saw her looking at him out of a long
mirror in their dining room.

Now, was that *lyric*? Was that *phantasmal*? For Des
O'Hara, still groggy from the long flight from Australia and
the experience, eight hours later, of burying his two children,
seeing his wife in the mirror had something of each of those
qualities in it: without knowing how, he understood that he
would never see her again. She was very clearly on the wrong
side of the mirror—on the inside, looking toward him from
around the back of the frame. The flowers she had put on
their table gleamed whitely, the wallpaper behind them made
a dark plane intersected by white stripes, and these familiar
things occupied the same world as himself: Mikki's broad
stricken face loomed toward him like a face trapped beneath
the ice of a frozen river. Her terror made her seem to be
smiling. When he turned on the light she was gone.

It is likely that many people had such experiences. Without
knowing it, they were in the belly of the whale.

Superficially the town looked the same. If you let your eye
glide over the anomalies you saw the old pretty Hampstead,
the big houses and the acres of lawn. But what you'd be
overlooking would be that many of those big houses were
vacant, their windows blank empty staring eyes, and that the
long lawns were rapidly turning back into meadow. People
tended to stay at home after nightfall, so they did not see the
fires that sprang up here and there around town—they might
hear the loud voices of the wandering kids who set fire to the
abandoned houses, but they closed their ears to anything else.
*Screams? Shouts? When, last night? Why, we didn't hear a
thing—of course we've been awfully busy packing these past
few days, it seems like we fall asleep all over the house,
scarcely have the energy to get to bed, and then we have
these funny dreams . . .*

If they were sane, they closed their ears and kept on packing. If they saw men brawling on Main Street—well-dressed men, men who had to put down their briefcases to get really into the bloody work of eye-gouging and nose-biting—they shrugged and hurried home. They were putting their stuff in storage for a little while, that's what they were doing, and wasn't it too bad about the climate of violence you saw everywhere in America these days? Why, just yesterday on the Phil Donahue Show . . . Why, the world's a crazy place, everybody knows that now. . . . If they were sane, they mumbled such things to themselves, kept on packing, and hoped the crazy outcries on the street—cries like those of pigs and dogs and wolves—would keep on moving down toward the end of the block.

Sometimes at night, Patsy and Tabby could hear these voices of the so-called sane mumbling in their heads.

Yeah, we sure managed to get a lot of stuff in the old wagon, we're thinking of taking the kids out to see John's boys, after all they have the same father, it's all one family. . . .

No, I haven't seen old Mrs. Ellis around lately, funny, I haven't even thought about her in a couple of days and we used to say hello every morning. . . .

A man all in bandages, you say? Must have been the world's worst case of poison ivy, don't you reckon? . . .

Burned? The Ellis house? Why, I can't believe I didn't notice that, I go past that house twice a day, I guess my mind's just been on getting our things together so we can get off to Kiowah Island tomorrow morning. . . .

And underneath the false calm of these mumbled sentences is a frantic, driven urgency, not at all sane, which is saying *let's go let's go let's get outta here, don't listen to them, just go GO GO GO GET GOING BEFORE IT HAPPENS. . . .*

Patsy and Tabby could hear that too; by the second week of July they had seen a couple of people with shining, ruined skin, and one day Patsy heard a gang of children shouting, "Leaker! Leaker!" and saw them throwing stones at a bandaged man trying to scurry around in back of Greenblatt's; and they were none too sure of their own sanity, but they could not get out of there, they could not GET GOING, and they had to listen to whatever came their way.

Tabby could see his father's life and his own sliding toward the condition of the earliest, worst days in Florida. Clark was drinking steadily from noon onward, and Tabby often had to try to bully him into eating. He hated doing this—shouting at his father, banging a pan against the stove in an only half-simulated rage—and hated even more that it worked. Sometimes Clark shouted back at him, and sometimes he stalked away from the table, but usually he bowed his head like a child and ate the food Tabby cooked for him. If Berkeley Woodhouse were there, she'd finger a little food into her mouth, laugh at both of them, and roll back to the television. Television and bed seemed to be all his father's mistress cared about. As the day went on, her bright lipstick began to drop off her mouth and go staggering down the side of her face.

Tabby kept Patsy away from his house—he wouldn't have minded if Graham had seen Berkeley and his father at the end of a day, but Patsy's seeing them would have humiliated him.

It was as though he had looked away for the blink of an eye, and in that blink his father had somehow contrived to ruin himself. At least in Florida Clark had had to find work, he had kept moving, he had changed his shirts and his underwear; but now with his own father's money to cushion him, he had become as torpid as a lizard on a rock. Tabby imagined that if he sniffed his father's palm, if he smelled his old T-shirts, he would be smelling booze—so soaked in it were Clark's pores. And one night, looking at his father glumly poke a forkful of instant mashed potato into his mouth, Tabby thought he saw a dim light hovering behind Clark's head, a little spectral light that moved when he moved. Berkeley was noisily fiddling with the ice cubes, so he could not ask her, but it seemed to him as though all the alcohol in his father had taken visible form. A fly circled in from nowhere and landed on Clark's hand. Clark stared at it as if it were an exotic bird, clumsily raised his hand: and then smashed the hand down on the table. The fly zipped off to investigate Clark's hair, and on the surface of the table—or just *beneath* the surface of the table—a pool of blood seemed to rise up out of the wood. Tabby stared at it: the blood flattened out like oil beneath the pressure of his father's fist. Just for a moment—and this was *phantasmal,* it made poor Tabby shake—he saw Berkeley's lovely blurry face beneath that fist, staring in terror upward through the film on the top of the table. He turned around, and she was still knocking the ice tray against the side of the sink, her Tareyton lolling against her lower lip; one hip was elevated to get more power into the *chop chop chop* of the ice tray against the aluminum. That was reality, and the face pressing up in terror against the surface of the table in a flat puddle of blood was only vision. When he looked back at his father, he saw that smudge of whitish gray behind his head dimming out, disappearing like the gray cat Richard had described. Tabby went back to his desultory conversation with his father, and heard again the racket Berkeley was making at the sink; he had not been conscious that a noise in his ears had deafened him. The gold at Berkeley's wrist looked red.

Des O'Hara, who had lost everything and did not comprehend how, and who understood much less than Tabby of why, carried a full bottle of Delamain cognac out to his garage at six-thirty on the morning of Wednesday, the ninth of July. He got into his car, started the engine, turned on the radio, and drank cognac and listened to a tenor saxophone player named Scott Hamilton tenderly make his way through "I Would Do Anything for You" on WYRS as the carbon monoxide stole his life from him. He was in the whale's belly and he knew it, and he wanted it no more.

Richard Allbee, who was walking up Mount Avenue to his job every morning, also thought that either the world or he was slipping a gear—he saw such oddness on these walks! Both John Roehm, the contractor he had hired for the Hillhaven job, and the client knew what had happened to Richard; the client had asked him if he wanted to put the job off for a couple of months, but Richard, who knew that John Roehm had his own bills to pay, had insisted on starting the work on the agreed day. This had been a good idea. After his first period of mourning—that period of deep shock, during which he had almost had to remind himself to breathe, when he had burrowed deep inside his fantasy—and after he had talked and cried with Graham and Patsy and Tabby, working helped to carry him out of himself. In fact, he could leave his misery for minutes at a time just watching John Roehm work. If carpentry were an art, John Roehm would have been a Rembrandt: he'd lay his big hands on a piece of heavy unwieldy oak and make it dance and sing, he was so good he could practically whittle the porch pickets they had to make as part of the Hillhaven job. And an old-timer like Roehm appreciated the techniques Richard wanted to use in the interior of the house—making molds to replace the broken plaster ceilingwork, cutting the beads in at the corner of the window trim and doorjambs where someone twenty years ago had "modernized" them away. Roehm was also interested in testing the library paneling with mineral spirits and lacquer thinner to determine its original shade. All this spoke right to Richard's heart, and sometimes he felt tears jumping to his eyes as he watched white-bearded old Roehm execute some dazzling and offhand bit of craftsman's artistry with a saw and a section of oak. It is possible that John Roehm and the Hillhaven restoration saved Richard from Desmond O'Hara's fate—he had to do a lot of the lifting and carrying, since his and Roehm's assistants kept quitting, and even though he looked five years older than he had in May, he was gaining new muscle. At night he fell down straight into exhausted sleep. He broiled something in his kitchen, not looking at the place on the counter where the severed telephone receiver had lain, ate his pork chop or steak with a cold bottle of beer, and started yawning before eight-thirty. So his days were okay: apart from his feeling, at any unguarded moment, that his stomach and heart and probably his lungs too had been blown away on the seventeenth of June, Richard was okay at work. If he watched the direction in which his thoughts were taking him, and took the hammerblows when they came because he was half-prepared for them, he was fine at work. It was during his walks up to Hillhaven on Mount Avenue that he most doubted his capacity to get through the day.

It was a good and useful walk, and it got him to work with his muscles stretched and ready. Between the big houses on Mount Avenue he could see flashes of the Sound, and when he turned the last corner, pausing to look at the massive ivy-covered house where Graham had met Dorothy Bach at the end of the twenties, he had arrived at low flat Hillhaven beach. By the middle of summer, this beach was filled with people all day long, and from them rose a dense compacted odor of sun and salt, of tanning lotions and sweat. In the mornings the tide was in, and the blue-black water muscled right up to the first row of sunbathers, stretched out on their towels across a rack of drying seaweed; in the evenings as Richard walked home the beach trailed off into a bumpy landscape of glittering salt pools and shells through which brawny seagulls hunted and pecked. These visions of ordinariness, of the world going through its customary cycles, helped Richard wean himself from the considerably less ordinary visions he had passed on his way to Hillhaven beach.

The first odd thing Richard saw, back at the start of the Hillhaven job—the first day, in fact, that he had decided to start walking the two miles between his house and the new job—was that Charlie Antolini had at last got himself out of the hammock and was now painting his house. All that was odd about Charlie's paint job was the exuberant cheer of the painter and the color he was slopping on his house. Charlie Antolini grinned down from his scaffold when he saw Richard going past, he shouted out, "Hey, buddy! Great day, huh? Un-fucking-*believable!*" From the big paintbrush in Charlie Antolini's extended hand dripped strings of bright pink—pink so bright it seemed to sizzle when it fell on the grass and bushes beneath the scaffold. On the house, this paint had a Day-Glo aggressiveness. Charlie, that first morning, had covered half a side wall of his barnlike colonial. It took Richard a moment to see that he had also covered the shutters, the sills, and the windows with this glaring glossy pink.

As the days went on, Richard saw Charlie Antolini not only cover all his windows with the paint and slop it on the front door in the spirit of a man christening a ship, but ("Let's make this ol' momma really *shine,* hey? Whaddaya say?") climb up on the roof and start slapping it on the shingling there. Richard stopped walking, called something back to Charlie, and held his breath as he saw his neighbor approach his enormous television antenna. Would he upend a bucket over the skeletal contraption, or would he try to trace all those angles and lines with his brush? He saw Charlie briefly consider the problem, and solve it pointillistically. He dabbed pink swabs on the main post of the antenna, and waved his brush over the rest to speckle it; then Charlie winked at Richard, happy that someone had witnessed his ingenuity.

Along about this time Richard also witnessed Flo Antolini speeding off down Beach Trail in a car so full of suitcases that the rear window was blocked.

Yes, those things Richard certainly saw, there was no doubt about them. But other things were not so easy.

Did he, for example, really see a tall spindly man dressed in a shabby frock coat and droopy gray leggings jogging past him as he took his walk to work? The man resembled some foolish frog-hunting bird, or a scarecrow so hapless that his fields were picked clean of seeds in minutes, but he resembled something or someone else even more, and Richard turned to watch him clumsily thump past, trying to find the resemblance in his memory. He saw jug ears redly irradiated in the early light, and then he had it: *He was tall, but exceedingly lank, with narrow shoulders, long arms and legs, hands that dangled a mile out of his sleeves, feet that might have served for shovels, and his whole frame most loosely hung together. His head was small, and flat at the top, with huge ears, large green glassy eyes, and a long snipe nose. . . .* It was Ichabod Crane, the Connecticut schoolteacher of "The Legend of Sleepy Hollow." Richard watched him thud along Mount Avenue, his flat head bobbing in time with his steps, Ichabod Crane with flapping hands and feet, and when he turned into a curve, Richard went out into the middle of the road to be able to see him a moment longer.

Ichabod Crane. On Mount Avenue. In a world where his wife had been so brutally killed, that was as possible as anything else.

The oddness increased. The day after seeing Ichabod Crane jog past him, Richard looked into a car driving down Mount Avenue and saw an apparition from the twenties in Berlin— from the Berlin of Christopher Isherwood. Behind the wheel was a blond woman dressed in male formal wear, black evening clothes, jetty studs winking from the starched white shirtfront, neat black tie strapping a wing collar. She wore a monocle and smoked a yellow cigarette in a long ivory holder. Her hair was cut like a boy's, and in the instant Richard had of her, he saw that her skin was cratered with tiny scars. Her eyes slid toward him, and he froze in midstride: she was not from his world, she was malignant as a tumor, and her glance on his skin felt like the cut of a knife. Then the woman sped down Mount Avenue, and Richard was sure that the earth opened to take her car the instant that she rounded the curve in front of Tabby's old house.

The next day Richard saw a man whose entire body seemed to be wrapped in bandages duck behind a gatepost on the inland side of Mount Avenue as he approached, but this he knew was no hallucination. The man was a "leaker"— Richard was not even sure where he had first heard the awful term, but he knew it. There were children in Hampstead who chased these poor dying creatures through the streets, trying to pierce the protective shell of bandages and let the life out of them. It was no wonder the poor leaker fled when he saw someone coming. Richard could hear the man breathing huskily from behind the thick concrete gatepost as he walked by, and he started to say, "It's all right, I'm just walking to work," but he got no further than the first word when the panicked leaker jumped up from his shelter and flung himself down the road away from Richard. Richard's heart moved, watching the poor doomed creature flap off down Mount Avenue—this was worse than seeing the woman from hell, for the suffering leaker, a fellow being in distress, spoke more directly to him, gave him back an image of himself. Desperation, extremity, panic.

And several days later, as if the torment of these moments were ordained to grow in a geometrical progression, what he saw was much worse. After that, he drove up Mount Avenue to Hillhaven and kept his eyes straight ahead.

It began simply. A nondescript black car came up from behind Richard only a few minutes after he had started to stride up the Golden Mile, flashed its brake lights and pulled over. The driver would have the Hagstrom Atlas for Patchin County open on his lap, and as soon as Richard came near enough to be seen through the side window, he would ask, "Is this Mount Avenue?" Or "Am I going the right way to get to Hillhaven?" Any pedestrian on Mount Avenue was likely to be buttonholed by a driver made insecure by the absence of road signs. The black car—some kind of Chevrolet, Richard saw—sat quietly by the side of the road, waiting for Richard to draw up beside it. It trembled once, like a sleepy dog.

The car had stopped directly in front of the old Smithfield house.

Richard stepped forward, eager to be helpful, and the driver's door opened. Then the passenger door swung open too. Richard hesitated for a moment, and the hesitation may have saved his life. One of the rear doors, the one on his side, also opened. Richard took a step backward—suddenly the innocuous little car seemed surrounded by a sinister light. Three of its doors open as it sat beside the road on the sunny July morning, the black Chevrolet resembled a squatting insect, a beetle. A fly. For a second nothing happened except that Richard's mouth dried: he did not know why, but he was afraid of whatever was in that car.

Then Laura stepped out of the passenger side of the black Chevrolet.

Richard groaned: all the other things he had seen had led him to this one unbearable sight, his wife getting out of a nondescript black car on her long legs and turning to look at him with a face in which expression seemed too tightly packed to be readable. Her hair moved in the slight breeze from the Sound.

A man got out on the driver's side and like Laura turned to stare at Richard. He wore a torn madras jacket; a bright yellow Lacoste polo shirt smeared with mud covered his oaken belly. Another man, older than the driver and with a dull, clay-colored bald head, stepped out from the backseat. The three of them stood mutely beside the black Chevrolet and gazed at Richard. Their faces were alike, he saw: not crowded with conflicting expressions but empty of all expression. Their faces were dead.

Laura opened her mouth, and Richard instantly reacted out of horrified instinct—he clapped his hands over his ears. Whatever this dead Laura had to say was what he did not want to hear. He took several slow steps backward, and saw the two men begin to move slowly down the sides of the car toward him.

Richard stepped backward once, twice more, said, "No, go away, get out of here," and when they kept up their slow progress toward him, turned and ran—flung himself down the road, like the previous day's leaker. Desperation, extremity, panic.

Fifteen feet before him was a drive of crushed red rock between brick pillars. Richard wheeled into it and pelted up the drive between a line of maple trees and a tennis court behind a tall chain-link fence. Finally he saw the gray stone mansion at the end of the drive. Behind it, the sea flashed light at him. The downstairs curtains were drawn, and the house had a heavy, brooding, unoccupied look. Richard had no idea what he would say if someone opened the door to his knocking.

He jumped up the steps and leaned on the bell. In his mind he saw Laura moving inexorably down the road, turning into the dusty red drive . . . Richard kept his finger on the bell.

Footsteps came toward the other side of the door, paused; a bolt slid into a latch. The door opened an inch or two and a white suspicious face looked at him over a taut length of chain.

"I live across the street," Richard said, playing the card that would mean the most on Mount Avenue. "Some people out on the street are . . . uh, I think they'll kill me."

"So you say," replied the old man behind the door.

"I'm scared to death," Richard said.

"Right now, that's not too dumb," the old man said, and unhooked the chain. He raised his right hand and Richard saw that in it was a flat sleek black automatic pistol. "That's not too dumb at all. So you came up here for help?"

Richard nodded. "They stopped their car in front of me—in front of the old Smithfield house."

"The old Smithfield house." The man nodded; lowered the pistol. "Yeah, Monty used to live next door there—had the whole family in with him. You suppose they're still there?"

Richard nodded.

"Well, I don't mind giving you a hand. I'll just run 'em off with this thing. She has a full clip in her too, in case we need a little firepower."

Richard was so rattled that he never stopped to think: why would a pistol frighten people who were already dead?

He and the small white-haired man set off down the drive. Richard had to walk fast to keep up with his savior, and as they skirted the tennis court, he learned that the man's name was Charles Daisy, that he was a widower with six grandchildren, a retired lawyer. "Got a little target range down in the basement, that's why I'm pretty handy with this old girl here, 'course we all shoot skeet out at the Wampetaug Country Club from November to February, that sharpens up the eyes like you wouldn't believe . . ." They had reached the end of Daisy's drive. "Where were they?" the old man asked, looking perkily up and down the avenue. "Where do you suppose they went?"

Richard was looking right at them—they had not moved since he had turned and run. Laura's impassive face stared toward him; a thousand familiar but drowned feelings were latent in her flesh. He saw a few delicate bloodstains—feathers of rust—rising up her neck from the top of her blouse.

"They cut and run, didn't they?" crowed Charles Daisy. "They were just scum, son, that's all, scum looking for a soft place to settle. They won't bother you now." Daisy looked at him and amazed Richard by winking one of his webbed blue eyes. "I recognize you, you know. Took me a second, but then I had you. You were the boy in that series. Spunky. You were Spunky."

Richard knew that he was making a serious mistake, but he could not help himself. He asked, "Can't you see them?"

Daisy cocked his head.

"They're right there. Right where they were before. Two men and a woman. I could even tell you the license number of the Chevy. It's TBC 67—"

"You get the hell out of here," Daisy said to him. His white little face had turned pink. "You just take off down the road, actor boy, or I'll put a bullet in your throat. I mean it. Get moving."

"I'm not crazy," Richard said.

"Thought you'd get old Charley Daisy out here on the road and jump him? Thought you'd get yourself a nice place on Mount Avenue? Is that what you thought? You didn't know old Charley Daisy very well, did you?" He flourished the gun in Richard's general direction. Richard saw that if he wanted to, he could just snatch the gun from Daisy's hand.

"I just wanted your help, Mr. Daisy," he said.

This made the old man even more furious. *"Move! Get away from me!"* Daisy backed away from Richard and leveled the gun at his chest.

Richard moved. He dared say no more. He turned his back on the man and walked toward the little group around the car. In agony, he glanced once at Laura's face. Eyes open, she looked asleep. She was not there, except for him. And she and the others could not take him while furious Charles Daisy watched him go. Either that, or the Dragon had worked out some new trick for him. He got so far off to the right side of the road that his shoulder scraped and rustled in the thick bushes. Old Charley Daisy was still behind him with his fat pistol pointed at his back, but that was not why Richard's stomach felt knotted tightly as a boot lace. He glanced sideways and down as he went past the car, and saw that the driver, the one with the madras jacket and the polo shirt, wore nothing on his feet, which were plump, white, and crusted with filth. But for the dirt, they were very preppy feet. The skin had peeled itself back over a couple of serious abrasions, but those feet had not bled. The skin had parted, but there had been no pain and no blood.

He was terrified that Laura would speak to him until he had gone at least thirty yards down the road.

When he got to the job, John Roehm was sitting on the tailgate of his pickup in the client's driveway. To his right, extending over the edge of the tailgate, was a stack of white, freshly sawn oak boards. Roehm looked like Santa Claus in a flannel shirt and red suspenders, sitting beside his treasure. "Thought we could begin on those shelves today, after we test the paneling. Happened to find some pretty decent oak yesterday evening. Best I ever seen, to tell you the truth."

"If you like, John," Richard said.

Roehm tilted his massive head. "Another beautiful day, boss."

"I guess it is, John."

Looking at him, Roehm saw everything; saw enough, anyhow. "We'll just take it little by slow, boss. Little by slow." And meant everything that he said. Richard helped him carry the oak boards into the house.

2

As Richard Allbee discovered later, he was right to have run from the three apparitions that climbed out from the nondescript black Chevy; they represented danger, they had meant to kill him; there was no mercy in what was left of his wife. The last two direct victims of Hampstead's dragon, the fifth and sixth persons to die at the hands of Wren Van Horne, did not have Richard's luck. They too met apparitions, but they met them unaided; and with the apparitions they met Dr. Van Horne not long before Graham Williams' old friend endured the second great alteration of his life. Dr. Van Horne treated them as he had treated his four earlier victims: and so they too, or at least one of them, experienced what we have called the "phantasmal." But by this time, as General Haugejas would soon see, you could get the whiff of the "phantasmal" simply by moving through the streets of Hampstead.

The last two people to die directly at the hands of Hampstead's most respected gynecologist were Franz Holland and his wife, Queenie.

Queenie Holland owed her first name to her father, a cockney named Albert Martin who had come to America as a young man of not quite twenty and discovered that his accent in an American ear resounded as grandly as a duke's. Albert found himself a well-paying job at Macy's in New York, married a woman in the dress department, found time to chase nearly every attractive woman he saw, charmed all with his amoral but practical Londoner's wit, and eventually saved enough money to buy a woman's clothing store in Hampstead, Connecticut.

Queenie was intense and practical, but grew up loving the ideal of the gentleman, of which class she mistakenly took her father to be a representative. With Franz Holland, the son of the funeral director, she was closer to the mark. Even as a teenager, Franz was stuffy, but inside the affected social manner he was gentle and kind; and Queenie, who had part of her father's calculation, knew that he was growing up in a business where the customers would never stop coming. It was like making toilet tissue, Franz once told her in all seriousness, people would always need his product. If Queenie said *shit and death, you bet,* to herself, she gave no sign of it to Franz. They were married two years out of high school. Very quickly Queenie made herself indispensable to the firm of Bornley and Holland, doing the correspondence and working on the books. Her practicality, her best inheritance from Albert Martin, had found a worthwhile outlet.

So by 1980, when they had been married better than thirty years, Franz Holland could not separate the running of the funeral home from what his wife did in her office all day. And that was what made Queenie's recent behavior even more troubling than it would have been otherwise. He could have done the books by himself, though it would have taken him twice the time it did his wife; but he had no idea anymore how she did the ordering—he barely remembered where they kept the catalogs.

For thirteen days Queenie had done nothing but watch television. She did not even bother to dress. She got out of bed, brushed her teeth, and switched on the old Sylvania in the bedroom. Then she sat on the edge of the bed and went crazy—that was how it looked to Franz, anyhow. She had started, thirteen days ago, by talking to Tom Brokaw, she sulked when Jane Pauley took over the screen, and then brightened up again when Gene Shalit came on. She had conversations with the people she saw on television—Queenie did not just talk *at* Tom Brokaw and Walter Cronkite and Ted Koppel and all the other men whose faces filled the Sylvania's screen all day, she talked *with* them. When the host of the *Today* show said, "Many people today are caught in a financial bind in part because of tuition rates at our nation's colleges and universities," Queenie chimed in with, "Oh, don't I know it, Tom! Why, I'm beginning to wonder if college is only for the wealthy these days!" She went on like that all day. At first Franz had assumed that Queenie was making fun of him for some reason—Franz was in the habit of telling commercials that they were rubbish—but as she had kept on he had realized that his wife had lost her mind. What else could you call it when someone thought those moving faces in there were real people?

Queenie would not even eat. He had to bring her sandwiches, carry them into the bedroom from the little kitchen on the second floor of the funeral home, watch her distractedly swing her eyes toward him and say, "Thank you, dear," and then turn back to her conversation with Robert Reed on *The Brady Bunch* or Carter Oldfield in *Daddy's Here*. The sandwich gradually dried and curled during the day, and when he brought in her soup at six o'clock he took it out with him and threw it away. She did drink—Tab or Mello Yello or whatever was being advertised. These sickly soft drinks were what was keeping her alive, he supposed.

So Queenie sat upstairs hypnotized and perky before the television, and Franz worriedly dealt with the bereaved—more of those than ever, now—and the salesman from the supply houses and the mail and the bookkeeping. Often as he moved through the public rooms downstairs, which were much grander than their shabby rooms on the second floor, he could hear the theme songs of the programs Queenie would soon be joining. A forties-style swing band pumping out a rhythmic version of "When the Red, Red Robin Goes Bob, Bob, Bobbin' Along" meant that in sixty seconds Queenie would be deep in serious discussion with Carter Oldfield; an equally familiar *da da da, da da DUM de dum* indicated that it was time for *I Love Lucy* and Queenie's reflections on the present state of Cuba with Desi Arnaz. He had never before realized that the sounds from their living quarters were audible downstairs. This had come to his attention shortly after the morgue drivers had delivered the body of Desmond O'Hara to his back entrance—they had loaded the cyanotic body on the table in the preparation room, Franz had signed the forms and was walking the men back toward the rear door, and the unmistakable sounds of "When the Red, Red Robin" had drifted down the stairs. One of the drivers had burst out laughing; the other one looked startled but pleased, and said, "Hey, that's *Daddy's Here*. You watch that too?"

Queenie directed only two personal remarks to him during this period. The first came at the end of her first day of madness. She left the bed, set her untouched bowl of soup on the floor, said to Johnny Carson, "Oh, I know that's right, Johnny, those Hollywood people are just a big bunch of dingbats," and switched off the set. Then she went back to the bed and climbed in beside her trembling husband. "Oh, Franz," she said, "I've had so much *fun* today." The second remark came in the fourth day of her madness, and after Franz had pondered it for a day or so he thought it might be the explanation for Queenie's breakdown. He had come in with her sandwich—tuna salad on white bread—and a can of Tab. She was raptly talking about feminism with some glossy-mustached soap-opera actor Franz did not recognize. Queenie sipped from the Tab. She said, "I know you don't care what a mere woman has to say, Amory," to the television, and then disturbed Franz by locking his eyes with her own. Her face trembled for a moment—it looked like a face seen through a veil of water. "I'm glad now that we never had children," she said in her real voice. "All those poor dear children drowning . . . all those little corpses. I'm glad we're childless."

Franz Holland thought that he might be following his wife into madness. It seemed to him that ever since Patsy McCloud had suffered her peculiar fit in his casket showroom everything had been getting dark, dark, dark . . . all those firemen had died and then everything went somehow *wrong,* every day there were more new funerals to plan and schedule—it was like Jonestown! Exactly. Every funeral director he knew, including himself, was fascinated with Jonestown and the technical problem it presented, and here he was, Franz Holland, trying to solve these problems all by himself in Hampstead.

He could still remember that pretty Tayler girl, Patsy Mc-

Cloud as she was now, dropping her mouth open and getting that scared crazy look in her eyes and yelling *"Don't touch me!"* at him as if he had just turned into something loathsome. His feelings had curdled. Franz Holland was a man extremely self-conscious of the way he looked, and Patsy's shouting like that at him—the very expression of her eyes—had been like a knife in his gut. And ever since that day, ever since he'd been made to hide out of sight around the corner in the casket showroom while she called her friends, he had begun to fret even more than usually about vandalism and break-ins downstairs.

Queenie might have been the bookkeeper, but Franz knew that most of his investment, which is to say most of his money, was in the public rooms. In the vestibule were antique tables his father had bought just before the First World War, massive Chinese vases now worth so much Franz's heart stopped whenever he dusted them, and a little Oriental rug, also bought by Franz's father, which was above insurability the way some characters in a detective novel are above suspicion. In the room beyond the vestibule was an enormous Kirman rug. All of these costly worldly things haunted Franz as he lay in bed at night. He heard scratches at the door, soft thumps against the big downstairs windows. Since Patsy Tayler McCloud had twisted the knife of his ugliness in his gut, Franz had known that some wild kid was going to break in and piss all over the Kirman; snub out a cigarette on the antique table. Lying in bed, he could actually *hear* this going on. The door thumped, glass discreetly broke, footsteps entered. Splash, splash on the big rug, those lustrous fibers eagerly drinking up the fluid. Some nights he could almost hear the zipper raspily sliding down just before the kid ruined the rug.

And voices—there were voices too, from down there. He did not want to hear them, but they drifted up the stairs, whispery and hot. The first few nights, he had gone down to investigate, but of course had seen nothing. There had been no scratching at the door, no subtle chiming of broken glass, no unsteady footsteps across the irreplaceable rug. The grand empty rooms had greeted him like a reproach. All those invasive noises had happened only in his head. Two or three nights running, Franz had wearily trailed through the waiting rooms, the chapel, and the showrooms and seen only his inventory. And when he got back upstairs and stretched out

beside gently whiffling Queenie, he heard the voices all over
again—the hot, teasing voices. *Franz? Franz? Didn't see us,
did you? Try again—try again, ugly Franz . . .*

Ugly little Franz . . .

Shortly before midnight on the day that Richard Allbee was
allowed to walk past his wife's specter unharmed, Franz
heard the entire sequence of noises yet again: the soft sounds
against the door, the quiet breaking of glass, the footsteps
across the vestibule. *Can you find us, ugly boy . . . ?*

Someone chuckled. Splash, splash—the urine pounded into
the carpet.

Franz groaned. He would have to try again. *Find us, ugly
little Franz? Find us?* Still he could hear the awful sound of
the huge Kirman being defiled. He threw back the sheet and
left his bed.

"Oh, you're nothing but a real old rogue, that's what you
are," Queenie said to a white-haired man in a Peugeot
commercial.

Franz wandered out of his room and felt for the switch that
would illuminate the great front staircase. If someone really
was down there, maybe the light would scare them off: Franz
had no interest in heroics. He paused at the top of the curved
staircase and listened intently.

Ignoring the hot whispers from the depths of his public
rooms, he decided to do no more than to peek into the rooms.
He would not even bother to turn on the lights.

Just a quick turn around the downstairs, then back up.
Franz set off into the Tranquillity Chamber, which he had to
pass through to get to the other rooms. As he had decided, he
did not switch on the lights, but he saw perfectly well that the
big Kirman, all its complexities resolved into a single field of
black, was safe and the velvet curtains unmarked. He passed
through a door and was in a wide circular hallway interrupted
by arched doorways to other chambers. It was in this hallway
that Patsy McCloud had seared his self-esteem. All the heart
left him suddenly: if he had not heard the *Tonight Show*
audience roar like a zooful of beasts, he would have gone
back upstairs on the momentum of his next breath. But the
audience screamed and roared, and Franz saw Queenie tilting
her head and making some chirpy comment—and he walked
across the dim hallway to look into the first arch.

Here was his casket showroom: perhaps two hundred
square feet with ranks of caskets displayed on pedestals. He

knew this room would be empty. Since the Tranquillity Chamber was empty, all the other rooms would have to be empty too. Now his check of the rooms was merely a formal gesture. He just glanced in, and then turned away.

And then he turned back again, uncomfortable. That smell—he had smelled something. He was suddenly jarred by the recognition that his showroom stank of urine. It smelled like an Army latrine, in fact, the stench blossoming out around him as he stood transfixed in the door of the shadowy room. "Now, then," he said. "What in heaven's name . . . ?"

Franzie, you found us!

Franz felt all the air leave his body. In the midst of the incredible urine stench, now so strong that he could almost *see* the fumes coiling in the air, two bulky figures were visible back behind the second rank of caskets.

Found us! Found us! You win the prize, Franzie!

"Prize, what prize? What in the name of heaven . . . ?" He was so shocked by this realization of his worst fantasies that he could not really take it in properly. Two men, *these* men, had broken into his building and . . . *peed* on his inventory of caskets! "Get out of here," he said, outrage beginning to take root in his fear and shock.

His hand tremblingly found the light switch. He punched it in and the showroom jumped into being, awash with light and rich with the burnished surfaces of the forty caskets on their mahogany pedestals. And then he knew that he was crazier than six Queenies. The men were Chief Tony Archer and his deputy, both of whom were dead.

Filling the air in the right half of his showroom he saw what must have been a million flies; as the concentrated noise of their buzzing blew him back in revulsion—into the left side of the room, so he knocked aside two of the red leather chairs against the wall—the smell of dead urine towered up around him.

Then the solid, writhing mass of flies whirled apart and scattered through the showroom. Just now rising from one of the red chairs to the right of the entrance was a gray-haired man in a soiled white suit. His face was slick and shiny. As Franz focused on the man he took in two things simultaneously: this man in the dusty white suit ridged with dirt was Dr. Van Horne, and the doctor had become a leaker. Like Richard Allbee, he was not sure where he had first heard the term, but he recognized the symptoms. Wren Van Horne was only a week or two from having to bandage himself together—his skin seemed to be in constant motion, sliding minutely, checking, moving again.

"Oh, I'm sure, yes," Dr. Van Horne said. "You want the prize, don't you?"

"Prize?" Franz numbly repeated.

"Why, you finally found us," Dr. Van Horne said, and held out his right hand. In it was a delicately curved scalpel. The doctor stepped toward Franz, his face jigging, and laid open the undertaker's neck with one rapid sweep of the blade.

When he was done with Franz Holland, the doctor went slowly upstairs, where Queenie was telling Jack Nicholson that if he washed more, just like she did, he wouldn't feel so downright rotten all the time.

3

"You wouldn't believe what happens in my office. *I* can't believe what happens in my office."

Ulick Byrne and Sarah Spry were taking their time over lunch at a pretty little restaurant on the Post Road called Sweethaven—this had been Sarah's choice. Sarah liked the ferns, the pale polished wooden floor, and the crêpes and salads and quiches on the menu were what she considered a substantial lunch. That they had only a wine license was a matter of indifference to her. Ulick Byrne had resigned himself to the absence of gin and in fact felt too ill to lament the absence of anything he considered actual food. At all the other tables in the room women sat and talked, sat and smoked, deliberated over whether to order the crêpe with shrimp, scallions, and white wine sauce or the crêpe with asparagus and what the menu called "a delicate, creamy cheese of cheeses from the French." He was the only man in the restaurant, and felt, on top of his illness, like an odorous old bear invited into a dollhouse.

Sarah said, "I'd believe it. Have you taken a look at the newspaper lately?"

Ulick unhappily prodded what was left of his Crêpe Surprise. He had eaten everything in it that resembled meat, and he wondered if he'd cause a scandal if he asked for catsup to cover up the taste of the yogurt or whatever it was that had been in there. "To tell you the truth, I hardly ever did read the *Gazette*. Sometimes I used to look at your column, like everybody else. But I have too much to read at work. I barely have fifteen minutes for the *Times* in the mornings."

"Well, the old *Gazette* isn't half-bad, for a little tabloid that comes out twice a week. We do a good job of covering this town. If I do say so myself. But—and this really gripes me—even if we came up with a great story about the cause of everything that's going on here, and I mean a *great* story, Pulitzer-prize-great, nobody'd be able to read it. Because it'd be so full of misprints it'd look like an eye chart."

Ulick was staring at a woman across the room and deciding that he could do without catsup after all. The woman, slim and unsettlingly like Stony Friedgood in appearance, with sharp neat features softened by a wealth of dark hair, had smeared her lipstick from the base of her nose nearly to the point of her chin. When she opened her mouth, Ulick noticed that she had not neglected her teeth. Neither of the woman's two companions seemed to mind that their friend's face looked like a road accident.

"I thought the paper looked a little funny the last time I saw it." The headline, he thought, had read REASSESSMENT MEANS EXTRU EASTWOOD AND TIME FAIL.

The plump blond woman seated next to the lipstick lady nonchalantly unbuttoned her blouse and folded it back over a large sun-tanned breast. She hefted the breast in her hand for a moment, making some conversational point, and then popped it back inside the cheesecloth blouse.

"It always looks funny," Sarah said. "My editor reads the proof every morning, he slaves over it to check all the errors, and about half the paragraphs come out one hundred percent dogfood. You're not eating. Don't you feel well?"

"I *feel* like dogfood," he said, not adding that he also felt as though he had just eaten it. "My stomach's no good. Maybe I have a temperature, I don't know. To tell you the truth, I don't even care much. I've been losing my temper a lot too. My secretary's about to quit because of the way I've been shouting at her."

Sarah reached under the table and patted his knee.

"What's that for?"

"Just to tell you to take it easy, assistant. Too many men are losing their tempers around Hampstead these days. I don't want you to get in any fights. Especially not with your secretary."

"The way I feel, she'd walk all over me. Have you any idea of what's going on in my office? I don't know what I am anymore—some kind of shrink, maybe. People come in, clients I've had for years, they say hello, they sit down, their faces go all funny, and they burst into tears. I just can't sit there and watch people cry. It drives me up the wall. I'll tell you something else. Two of my clients killed themselves in the past three days. These are *guys*. One guy shot himself in the head, the other one drank a bottle of weedkiller. They had good jobs . . . hell, they had great jobs. I can't figure this shit out anymore."

"Yeah. If I didn't have something interesting to show you, I'd get depressed, and then I'd start to cry, and you'd have to find something to break."

"Something to show me?" He unthinkingly glanced over at the plump blond woman in the cheesecloth blouse.

"Don't worry, Ulick. I'm not going to disrobe. I wanted you to see this picture from the *Woodville Herald*. They're owned by the same chain that owns us, and some of the features are shared, but of course most of it is entirely different. I sent over a request to see their issues for the third and fourth weeks of May. On the front page of the May nineteenth issue I saw a photograph that interested me. I got their photo editor to send me an enlarged glossy. I think you'll be interested too." She bent down, picked up her bag, and took out a manila envelope. From the envelope Sarah extracted an eight-by-ten shiny photograph.

Ulick took it from her. He could not imagine why she thought he would be interested in the photograph. It depicted, in harsh clear black and white, a group of men standing in what looked like a parking lot. The two men in the center were apparently being questioned by the others, who stood about them in a rough circle. Byrne could identify none of their faces "So?" he asked her.

"The two men in the center are the scientists who were in charge of the Telpro installation in Woodville, Theodore Wise and William Pierce. This photograph was taken at a sort of impromptu press conference on t. e day those people died in the plant."

"Okay," Byrne said. "What's the point?"

"Him." Sarah tapped a fingernail on the bulky figure of a fuzzy-haired man in a sweatshirt. The words KEEP ON

TRUCKIN' were dimly legible across the front of the shirt. "Do you know who that is?"

"Some greaseball."

Sarah permitted herself the indulgence of a taut little smile. "That greaseball is Leo Friedgood. A friend of mine in the police department identified him for me."

Ulick's eyebrows contracted; he raised the photograph closer to his face. "Friedgood was there? On May seventeenth? He was at Woodville Solvent?"

"Obviously."

He put the photograph down on the edge of the table. "I'm damned if I can figure this out. But if Friedgood was there, then Telpro sent him there. And if they sent him there, they wanted him to do something. They must have felt that . . ." He paused, thinking. "They must have felt that more had gone wrong than the staff on hand could manage. The question is, what's happened to Friedgood? He hasn't been in his house for weeks."

"Telpro," Sarah said.

"You have it all figured out, don't you? Telpro. Iron Hank Haugejas. They put Leo away somewhere—they're keeping him out of sight, because he's the only person not directly related to Woodville Solvent who knows what really happened there."

"Who knows Telpro's level of responsibility for what's going on in Hampstead." Sarah neatly inserted the photograph back in the envelope, the envelope back in her bag. "Do you know what I want to do? I'd like to rattle General Haugejas' cage a little bit. I think it's time to do something drastic. I want to go to his office and see what he says about Leo Friedgood and Woodville Solvent."

"In that case, you'd better take your lawyer with you."

"Did you have any plans for the afternoon?"

Ulick Byrne did not want to admit it to himself, but he was professionally as well as personally excited about what might arise from a meeting with General Henry Haugejas. He was convinced—even on the tiny evidence he and Sarah had—that Haugejas and Telpro had conspired to hide whatever had really happened in Woodville on the seventeenth of May. Haugejas was a rough customer, and Telpro had a million lawyers, but suppose that he and Sarah could catch them with their pants down? Ulick could sniff out the beginnings of a series of lawsuits that would add up to billions of dollars. It would be a scandal many times larger than Watergate, and every bit as clear-cut, as black and white: the principal lawyer for the citizens of Hampstead would become famous overnight, especially if he had personally helped to uncover the scandal.

Sarah noticed that as Ulick Byrne drove toward Manhattan on I-95, as he crossed over the Triboro Bridge, as he putted along in the traffic down FDR Drive, he now and then looked as though he were trying not to grin.

When they reached the Telpro building on East Fifty-ninth Street, Sarah bustled him past the guard's desk in the lobby and led him into a waiting elevator. "How do you know where you're going?" Ulick asked her.

The elevator doors silently closed, leaving them alone in a humming wood-paneled box. "I'm a reporter," she said. "I'm also a reporter who is a lot older than you. When Iron Hank retired, so to speak, from the military, he made a pompous speech about how all his future battles would be fought from behind a desk on the twentieth floor of a building on East Fifty-ninth Street." She pushed a glowing disk on the elevator panel. "So we're going to give him one of those battles."

Byrne shrugged. "Of course he might have moved offices a dozen times since then."

"Then we get directed to the right floor. But the main thing is, we got past the desk."

"Now we have to get past his secretary."

On the twentieth floor they stepped into a wide corridor leading to a glass door with SPECIAL PROJECTS painted on it in stark black letters. Behind the desk a red-haired secretary or receptionist sat at an elaborate desk. She lifted her head and smiled as the two of them came through the door and across the thick tan carpet. Ulick was forced to admit that Sarah Spry managed rather better than he did the business of getting over the width of carpet with the air of having a perfect right to be there. "May I help you?" the girl asked.

"We'd like to see General Haugejas, please," Sarah said firmly. "But we'd like to have a word with his secretary first."

The girl behind the desk looked puzzled. "Do you have an appointment with the General?"

"Please let us speak to his secretary," Sarah said. She silenced Ulick with her eyes. "You can tell her that a journalist from the *Hampstead Gazette* and an attorney have come in connection with the events that took place at Woodville Solvent."

"Woodville Solvent? The *Hampstead Gazette?*" The girl lifted a telephone receiver the same color as the carpet, punched a single digit, and spoke softly into it for a moment. She looked up wide-eyed at them. "May I have your names?"

"Mr. Byrne and Mrs. Spry," Ulick said.

The receptionist spoke quietly into the receiver again. Then she smiled brightly at them. Mrs. Winthrop would be coming out any minute to meet them.

Any minute turned out to be thirty-one minutes later. Mrs. Winthrop turned out to be a Chinese woman in her late twenties. In a crisp dress the same flat black as her hair and large round glasses tinted amber past the level of her eyes, Mrs. Winthrop possessed a beautiful smile and a force of personality that immediately vaporized the red-haired receptionist. She took Ulick Byrne's hand while she pronounced his name and fried him with her smile, and shook it like a man. He felt as though he had just been weighed, measured, and sent out to be washed. She had moved on to Sarah. Byrne found himself wondering what Mr. Winthrop was like.

"Won't you please come back to my office?" she said, and turned smartly around to lead them down another softly lighted corridor. After several twists and turns, she opened a large blond oaken door and showed them into an office with a wide black desk and a long black leather couch. Bright abstract paintings decorated the walls. Mrs. Winthrop moved luxuriantly around the back of the desk and sat down. "I must explain that General Haugejas never sees anyone who does not have an appointment, so even if he were here this afternoon it would be impossible for you to meet him."

"He isn't here?" Sarah said.

"He isn't even expected back until tomorrow, Mrs. Spry. But I'm sure that he would want me to find out what concerns you so that he can get back to you about it. I wonder if you could explain to me why a gossip columnist on the Hampstead newspaper and a lawyer who chiefly specializes in real-estate transactions are interested in General Haugejas?''

And from that point on—we must assume, judging by the quickness of the General's response—Mrs. Winthrop recorded every word pronounced in her office. The tape recorder would have caught Ulick's growing annoyance, Sarah's increasing distemper, their obvious belief that Henry Haugejas was on the other side of the door behind Mrs. Winthrop's desk. (In this they were wrong—the General was attending the board meeting of a bank down on Wall Street that afternoon.) The recorder would certainly have stored Ulick's remark that Telpro had killed children in Hampstead, Connecticut, and his frequent questions about the presence of Leo Friedgood at the plant in Woodville. Feng-chi Winthrop, who had sent him there, merely looked vaguely puzzled at the barrage of accusations which came from the two doomed and frustrated people on her leather couch.

4

On the next day, Friday, the twenty-fifth of July, General Henry Haugejas, accompanied by two aides, ceremoniously arrived in the streets of Hampstead—not in the front seat of a flag-bedecked jeep, as he had arrived in certain carefully chosen Korean villages, but in the backseat of a limousine.

The Friedgood house was empty and clearly had been that way for some time. The neighbors were unhelpful. They did not know what had become of him and they did not know why they should open their houses to be searched by three strangers. When the General identified himself and explained—with a total lack of graciousness—that the location of Mr. Friedgood was important to national security, the residents of Cannon Road, Charleston Road, and Beach Trail usually opened their doors to the General and his two large mascots. But all of these delays, all of these explanations and hesitations and half-hidden hostilities, had chipped away at the three ex-soldiers.

It was their failure as much as the repeated explanations and the sour breath of class privilege that bit at them. By the time they had looked through twenty houses, the General and his aides were keyed taut as piano wire. They had begun seeing themselves as essentially military once again, and they were sick of the problems given them by civilians. The aides, whose war had come after the General's, thought with longing back to the days when they could charge, dripping with weapons, into any hootch they wanted to turn over; and how all the people in the hootch would bow and smile so vigorously they looked like they were simultaneously going to break their backs and their jaws. It is likely that they expected the Hampstead police to act that way—like Vietnamese peasants.

And that was what caused their trouble—in a way calculated to raise the hackles of any police officer anywhere, General Haugejas and his aides assumed that the officers existed to follow their orders: that they were all in the same army, but the policemen far down the chain of command.

Sarah Spry's friend, the desk sergeant Dave Marks, was the first to meet the three of them, and their manner immediately annoyed him. The big old guy with the iron-colored hair tried to stare him down, and the two bozos with him flanked Dave across the desk the way the terrorists did in the police training films. One at each side, about eight or nine feet apart, so that if he looked at one, he wouldn't be able to see the other. These three looked like trouble and delay, and Dave Marks wanted neither; what he wanted was to end the shift, take a shower, grab some food, and get to the midnight showing of *The Choirboys* at the Nutmeg Theater, on the other end of the municipal parking area from the station. That was what all the cops on duty that night wanted; all of them felt an extra tension and anticipation, and so they all felt an increased impatience with pushy outsiders.

The General smoldered at Dave Marks from a point equidistant from the door and the desk, and ordered Dave to get the chief.

"Chief's out," Marks said. The chief was home in bed, but he saw no reason to tell that to his visitor.

The General approached the desk.

He placed a card in front of Dave Marks. "I don't think the chief here would mind if you let us see whatever you might have on the whereabouts of Leo Friedgood."

Marks pursed his lips and read the card. "Telpro Corporation," he said. "Didn't you used to be his boss?"

"Mr. Friedgood is an employee of the Telpro Corporation, that is correct. As your chief is out, I am requesting you to get your file on Mr. Friedgood."

Marks raised his eyebrows. "The file."

"It is not an ordinary matter, Officer. This is a question of security."

"Now, wait a second." Marks bent over the card again. "This doesn't say anywhere on it that you're still with the government, General. Even if you were, I'd need a special request form before I could let you look at our files. But you're not. So you're not even going to get a special request form. So that's that."

"I want to speak to your chief."

"Come back tomorrow, General."

"And while I am speaking to your chief, I want you or one of your fellow officers to locate Mr. Friedgood's current address."

"You'll have to talk to the chief about that. But, sir, he isn't going to give you anything."

"I am going to give your chief an unfavorable report on your behavior this afternoon, Officer Marks."

Three or four other officers had drifted up toward the desk: the General should have noticed that they moved very quietly, with an almost protective solidarity.

"I don't care what you do, General. All I know is that you are a private citizen who thinks he has the right to give commands to police officers and roam through police documents. I think you got a problem there, General."

The General's face had grown even redder than it was normally. Now at last his battle had begun. "I am going to give you a telephone number in the Defense Department. I am going to ask you to call that number and listen to what they tell you. I am going to order you to do those two things. And then I want to see your file on Leo Friedgood."

"I am going to ask you to remember where you are, General," Dave Marks said. "You can't order me to do anything. I want you and your goons to get out of the station right now."

"Hey," one said. "Hey, all we want is—"

"Out," Marks said. "I mean it."

"You are being foolish and self-destructive," General Haugejas said. "I have a right to be here, and I have a right to the information I requested. If you will simply call the Defense Department—"

"Who the fuck are you, anyhow?" a blond young policeman asked—his face too was red. "You think we're in your army? You've been ordered out of this station, buddy. Don't you think you ought to get going?''

Greeley, the aide who resembled a blond ape, stepped toward Johanssen and grabbed his arm.

"Stop that," Johanssen said.

"Hey, nobody wants any trouble," Greeley said. "We been looking for this AWOL all day, man. We're gonna find him eventually, and you guys are gonna help us find him."

Johanssen turned to the little group of policemen with a *do you believe this guy?* expression on his face. As he turned, his hand brushed against Greeley's pistol in its harness. Without thinking, acting out of pure fury and pure reflex, Johanssen kicked Greeley's legs out from under him, dropped to one knee on astonished Greeley's chest, and reached inside his jacket for the pistol.

"Leave my men alone!" General Haugejas shouted.

A burly young cop named Wiak gripped the General's arms from behind, and his partner stepped forward to remove the General's guns, now visible, from his waist. Another pair of policemen had taken the other aide's pistol in the same fashion.

"I am ordering you to release me," the General said. "My name is Henry Haugejas, *General* Henry Haugejas, and I demand my release and a telephone."

"What kind of arsenal do you guys walk around with, General?" asked Dave Marks. "You're loaded for bear. If I was Leo Friedgood, I'd want to stay upwind of you."

"I want a telephone!" Haugejas shouted. "You *will* permit me to the use of a telephone."

Greeley unwisely tried to wriggle out from under Johanssen's knee, and the young policeman rolled him over with one deft twist of his arm. Mark Johanssen planted a foot in the small of Greeley's back, then reached down and cuffed Greeley's hands together behind his back.

"You *idiot!*" the General shouted. "Release that man!"

"I told you, I'm not in your army," Johanssen said, and stepped over Greeley toward the General.

"Get them in the cells," Marks said quickly. "Just get them in the cells, we'll sort it out tomorrow."

"Well, this son of a bitch assaulted me," Johanssen said, pulling Greeley painfully to his feet. Greeley turned his head and spat on the lapel of Johanssen's uniform. "Holy *shit!*" Johanssen said. He slammed his fist into Greeley's belly, and when the aide doubled over he hit him in the side of the head, knocking him into the first of the row of little cells off the reception area of the station. *"Shit!"* he repeated at the yellow blob reposing on his lapel. He tore off the uniform jacket, jumped into the cell where Greeley lay panting against the concrete wall beneath the sink, and wiped the stuff on Greeley's chin. "I oughta make you eat it, cocksucker," he said, and left the cell, locking the door behind him.

Larry Wiak was propelling the General toward the second cell. The General's face now was utterly distorted by rage and disbelief—it had never occurred to him that when he began the battle he might end it in defeat. *"Get your hands off me!"* he was screaming. *"I'll cut your nuts off!"*

"I never did like generals much," Johanssen said, gloating as Wiak pushed the General into the cell.

"You guys really ought to do yourselves a favor and call one of those numbers," said the second aide as he was being led toward the third cell. "Tomorrow the shit really hits the fan."

"Generals are always willing to take off someone else's nuts," Johanssen said.

Iron Hank continued to rant loudly and furiously—but he had finally recognized that in a town where everyone had been exposed to DRG-16, nothing kept the police from going batty along with everyone else.

"At least these three turkeys aren't going to keep us busy tonight," Larry Wiak said to Johanssen.

Johanssen listened to the General bellow and threaten. "Not unless the old fart gets to a phone and has the station nuked," he said.

"Nuked!" the General yelled. *"You'll think that's a pat on the behind!"*

5

"You want to go. I know you do."

"I did want to go, sure. That was before you got sick. Jesus, Ronnie."

"All your friends are going to be there."

"I see all my friends at the station anyhow. Seeing them get tanked up in a movie isn't any big treat."

"And you had such a good time last year."

"*Last* year you were healthy. For God's sake, Ronnie. You didn't even touch the food."

"Well, part of the reason I'm not hungry is that I'm worried about you. I don't want you to be any big martyr, you know. I'm still going to feel crappy if you go to the movie or not. So I think you ought to go."

"Jesus, Ronnie. I'd feel terrible if I went tonight. It's just a movie. I want to stay home and take care of you."

"Take care of a sick old lady," Ronnie said, and turned her face sideways into the pillow. A sick old lady was just what she looked like, Bobo thought—he could see how her skin had dried out in the weeks of her illness, how her cheeks were sinking in past the line of her jaw like those of a toothless mountain woman. At nine o'clock that night, Bobo sat beside Ronnie's bed in a darkened room, randomly moving her untouched plate back and forth, an inch at a time, on the aluminum tray. Ronnie had closed her eyes, and her lids lay against her face like veined gray stones. She sighed; shifted her face deeper into the pillow. Lines cut deeply into her forehead, sank into the flesh at the corners of her mouth. For a fugitive and disloyal second Bobo regarded Ronnie Riggley with utter dismay—for himself, not his lover. Could he really tie himself for the rest of his life to a woman so much older? Live with this woman and watch this ghastly worn face slowly overtake the face he knew? A web of lines and faint wrinkles seemed to lurk just beneath her skin, sucking her face into it. For a moment Bobo wanted to flee: he felt like an orderly at a nursing home. In the next instant these thoughts rebounded. He pressed her hand, feeling a shameful guilt; yet the thoughts which had given rise to the guilt lingered.

"Go," Ronnie said. "Don't let me hold you back."

"We'll see," Bobo said, and the words reverberated with a double meaning for him. He picked up the tray and carried it out into the kitchen. Behind him Ronnie sighed again, in pain he thought.

The problem was—and now Bobo had to restrain himself from slamming his fist into one of Ronnie's cupboard doors——the problem was that his murder case, all these murder cases, had somehow mushroomed out, spilled out of themselves in some way he could not define, and poisoned the town. That was how it seemed to Bobo: as though the sickness in the killings had in some way gotten out of the killings themselves and begun to blossom on the walls and sidewalks.

Now Bobo never enjoyed his nightly rides through Hampstead. He saw too many crazy things, and the fun had forever gone out of madness for him. A couple of times a night he had to break up mysterious brawls; when he talked to the bleeding fighters after pulling them apart, they could not, exactly, remember why they had been fighting. Another commonplace now was a perfectly ordinary person—who might have shown some signs of depression in the past few days, but this was not always so—suddenly frozen in an inexplicable mania. So many people had decided that window breaking was socially acceptable that Main Street looked permanently boarded up. Bobo himself had answered the call when Teddy Olson, a druggist on Main Street, had driven his Camaro right into a group of high-school boys and killed four of them— Bobo wasn't sure how he knew this, but he was positive that if the killer hadn't come to Hampstead Teddy would still be measuring out Valium behind his counter instead of waiting out his trial date in the Bridgeport jail.

In fact, right now in Hampstead, Bobo reckoned, there were about a hundred people of all ages and both sexes who looked crazy enough to be the killer. Some of them were cops: and that was another part of the problem that made Bobo want to start punching Ronnie's kitchen cabinets. The whole department was going bughouse because they had not been able to nail the man; the state police were also looking angry and desperate as they chased around the same diminishing circle of unhelpful leads. Worse for Bobo was the look he saw in the eyes of cops like young Mark Johanssen and his friend Larry Wiak—a look that said they wouldn't mind really pounding the crap out of the next guy who crossed them. This was more than just a look in the eyes. Wiak had savagely flattened two people he had separated in a brawl in the parking lot behind Main Street that morning. One man was lucky to have escaped concussion, and the other had lost three teeth. But even worse than Wiak's delight in having pounded these citizens and the approval the other officers gave Wiak for it was the sense Bobo had that Larry Wiak really wished he had been able to shoot those two men instead of merely hitting them.

He tipped the uneaten food into Ronnie's garbage disposal, rinsed the dish, and placed it in the machine. He leaned on the sink with both arms outstretched and looked at the blurry reflection of his face in the window. And for the first time, perhaps since the murders began, the midnight showing at the Nutmeg Theater caused him a little thrill of apprehension: while everybody else was shouting and chugging beer, it might be better if Johanssen and Wiak and a few others just went out to a quiet bar by themselves.

6

The policemen who survived the Second Annual All-Police Midnight Screening were never able properly to explain how things went wrong so quickly. They, like Bobo, had an excellent grasp of the reasons why the screening had turned into a disaster; they were as aware of their frustrations as he; but what they could never quite get straight was the actual sequence of events which turned a hundred exuberant cops in something under half an hour to a hundred hysterics waving pistols. There were a few things all the survivors agreed upon—shortly before the carnage began, Larry Wiak had taken off all his clothes and jumped on the stage in front of the screen; and an old patrolman named Rod Fratney had begun yelling in a high-pitched squealing voice that he had seen Dicky Norman. And the thirty-two survivors of the Nutmeg Theater also agreed that a man seated on the far right of the theater had screeched as soon as Fratney uttered Dicky's name. They agreed that Larry Wiak was the first to die: but eleven of them swore that Fratney had killed Wiak, sixteen said the unidentified cop who had screeched shot naked Larry Wiak, four said that both of the men simultaneously put bullets into Wiak's chest; and one man swore to Graham Williams that while both Rod Fratney and the unidentified man had their guns out and were firing, their bullets hit the screen—what killed Wiak, the man swore, was a lightning bolt that began just beneath the ceiling of the theater and angled lazily and surely toward the big naked man standing in front of the screen. "When it hit him," the policeman told Graham, "it was like nothing else you ever saw in your life. A BAR wouldn't do so much to a guy. It just tore that big fucker apart. He went off like Old Faithful, and that's when all the guys went stone crazy."

That sounded right to Graham, it sounded in the Dragon's key; and so he went back and asked some of the others if they were sure about either of the two policemen shooting Wiak.

In a Bridgeport police bar named Billy O's, a forty-three-year-old sergeant named Jerry Jerome gave him a weary look and said, "You mean the lights? Somebody told you about the lights?"

"You tell me about the lights," Graham said.

"Right as soon as we all got in there. As soon as we all had a couple of beers apiece—those guys, it was like they were chugging right out of the can, I never saw 'em drink so fast before—and right when we were ready for the movie. Everybody stopped yelling the way they were doing, and the lights went down. Johanssen and a couple of other guys, Maloney and Will and I don't know who else, were still farting around in the aisles, but everybody else was sitting down. You could sort of hear everybody sigh—because this was it now, this was what everybody'd been waiting for all week. When that curtain started moving away, folding up, a few guys clapped, but most of us—hell, I could feel it!—sort of mentally came to attention, you know what I mean?"

Jerry Jerome took a big swallow of his Jack Daniel's, blinked at Graham Williams, and asked, "Do you know about 'Spigger'? Did anyone tell you about 'Spigger'?" When Graham shook his head, Jerry Jerome smiled a pale little ghost-smile and said, "That came a little later, and that was how come I thought maybe the lights were just my eyes. Because if the guy who shouted it saw what I saw, I didn't think he'd be able to make a joke right away. I was still trying to figure out if my head was screwed on right."

He tilted his head and looked at Graham. "Buster, if you laugh at me, at what I'm going to say to you right now, I'll smash this drink right in your face. Okay? Okay. I thought I saw the northern lights. You know? *Streams* of light, pouring down from the ceiling toward the screen—almost like fireballs, some of 'em were. Blue and yellow and red . . . all sparkly and electric-looking. I saw it, man. I was so scared all of a sudden I thought I'd shit. I was sure the whole damn theater was on fire. Reminded me of night artillery practice when I was at Fort Sill. Zoom, zoom, zoom, you know? Fuckin' air was full of that stuff—and then it all ran right into the screen. So . . ." He sipped at his drink and looked hard at Graham, a real cop's stare, to check out how he was reacting to all this. "So when I saw Wiak—when I saw something crazy come at Wiak and blow him into cottage cheese, I thought it was the same thing."

"Spigger" turned out to be easy. Nearly all the survivors remembered it, and most of them remembered that the man who had made the joke was one of those larking about in the middle aisle when the lights went down. They agreed that it was not Johanssen—his humor was not so crude. Maloney seemed the best bet, Artie Maloney, who came back from 'Nam with a boxful of medals he would take out of his desk at home sometimes and show if you were both drunk enough. It seemed likely that it was Maloney who had shouted out "Spigger!" when the first black man who was not a policeman appeared on the screen. "Spigger! Half-spick and half-nigger!" The boys went crazy. If there was beer in their mouths, it went all over the head of the guys in front of them. *"Half-spick and . . ."* You could hear Maloney's phrase echoing through the Nutmeg Theater—but the truth is that Maloney's joke was not really so good. It is quintessentially the sort of thing a half-drunk twenty-eight-year-old Irish cop would say when he had his feet up on the seat in front of him and felt he could get away with saying anything that popped into his mind. Older police officers like Jerry Jerome and Rod Fratney ordinarily would not even dignify such a crack with as much as a smile.

Why, then, was Maloney's dull remark so successful? It occurred to Graham that it might have represented at least a release from extraordinary tension. What if more than Jerry Jerome had seen the streams of light like tracer fire blazingly enter the screen? What if every man there—every man but Artie Maloney—had seen the lights, and wondered if he was losing his mind? "Spigger" might have brought them back to themselves, jerked them out of their bewilderment.

But perhaps not all the way out, and maybe "bewilderment" is the wrong word for their condition. For there is one more thing that most of the survivors of the Nutmeg Theater gradually confessed to Graham Williams; in all the confusion, one more area of agreement.

It was a twenty-year-old kid who first hinted it to Graham, and he looked as embarrassed as Jerry Jerome had in the Bridgeport bar. The boy, Mike Minor, once might have looked authoritative in his uniform, but in a KISS T-shirt and jeans, sitting on a wooden rocker in the kitchen of his parents' house, he still seemed undone by the events in the Nutmeg Theater. His eyes were too large for his head, and a vein in one lid kept insistently bumping and bumping, as if it wanted to go somewhere else. He had quit the force in September, and was thinking about trying to get into computer training somewhere: to Graham it looked as though he would be better off waiting another six months. His attention span was roughly equal to that of a four-year-old. "I thought I saw maybe something like spiderwebs way up there when the lights went down, yeah," he told Graham. "Not lights exactly, but something that was sort of floating, sort of floating lines . . . spiderwebs. You want a Coke or something?" He twitched over to the refrigerator and took out a can of Diet Pepsi, brought it back to the butcher-block table, snapped off the tab and poured about half of it down his throat.

"Man, I just couldn't figure it out when Larry took off his clothes like that. And I couldn't tell you why he did it. He was nothin' but a goddamned animal, if you want to know the real truth about Larry Wiak."

Mike Minor nervously drank the rest of his Diet Pepsi in two huge swallows. "When he came walking out of those shadows all big and white like that, he terrified me, man." The boy nodded, ducked his head like a puppy who fears a blow. "And when Rod Fratney yelled what he did, and that other guy over on my side screamed just like a girl in a horror movie, I could have pissed my pants. Because I knew he was there, man, he was right where I was." He glanced at Graham, who was already nodding with the boy. "Man, he'd seen it too. Just like old Rod. And me."

"He had seen Dicky Norman, you mean." Graham had expected this.

"Well, two nights before we went to that *Choirboys* show, supposed to be the biggest party of the year and all that, two nights before that I was out on patrol. And I got lost. I was somewhere near the Academy, but I couldn't get my bearings. Some road—some narrow road with no street signs. I couldn't even remember how I got there. It was like being in a bad dream, man. For a second I was real panicked, like 'Where am I, man? I'm a cop and I don't even know where I *am*!' There was nothin' but these big trees all over. I couldn't even remember what part of town I was in for a couple of seconds. I decided to turn around and go back the way I came until I saw something familiar. So I get the car pointed into the trees, and I put the car in reverse, and I look in the rear-view mirror . . . and I saw Dicky Norman. Man, it's crazy, but that's who it was. His skin looked red because of my taillights. He was just coming out of the trees on that side of the road, like that's where he slept or something, and one of his arms was all torn off and that big round face looked gray and tired and . . . waxy. He was moving right toward me. Boy, I pushed that car into Drive and spun right out of there—gave the right-front fender a huge big dent.''

"So when Larry Wiak started coming out of the shadows toward the screen . . .'' Graham did not have to say any more.

"Yeah. I mean, nobody can ever ask Rod Fratney anything ever again, but I know—I *know*. He saw him too.'' He looked defiantly at the old man across the butcher-block table and concentrated on flattening out the aluminum can with the palm of his hand.

"I'm sure he did,'' Graham said, and the boy glanced suspiciously toward him. "I saw a lot of funny stuff myself, last July and August.''

"Yeah.'' The boy ducked his head again and tamped down a wrinkle in the seam of the can. "Yeah. A lot of funny stuff.'' When he next looked at Graham, his eyes seemed inflamed. And then he dropped his bomb: not all at once, for he was still not sure of Graham's trustworthiness, and not at first directly, for among those he distrusted was himself: but Michael Minor took Graham a long way toward understanding what actually happened in the Nutmeg Theater. "Did anyone tell you about the movie?'' he asked.

And that was one thing that none of the survivors had mentioned. Graham looked at the boy's painfully strained eyes and said, "Tell me about the movie, Mike.'' His stomach tightened, and he knotted his fingers together so they would not tremble.

"I don't know what I *can* tell you,'' the boy said. He was silent for a long time, scratching the back of his left hand. "Like it was about us?'' He cocked his head, looked sharply at Graham, and went back to scraping his nails across the back of his hand. "But then it sort of changed. It got *different.*'' Graham waited impatiently while Mike Minor struggled with his inadequate vocabulary.

"It got different, you said.''

"Oh. Yeah, it got different.'' The boy straightened up in the rocking chair, and his face drew into itself. A cold light like hoarfrost from the window beside him lay across the plane of his cheek, made it as blunt as the side of an ax.

Suddenly the boy looked ten years older to Graham. "It got like it was a 3-D show. I could see *into* it just like into a room."

The boy stirred in his chair. "Then I saw what that room was. It wasn't the police station in the movie anymore—I mean, it was a police station, but it wasn't the same one. You know, it sounds dumb, but it took me a long time to recognize it. It was the Hampstead police station. The one we'd all just left. Mo Chester, the night deskman, was up there, and McCone, his partner . . . ah, this is where some of the guys started making noise. I can't tell you why, but it didn't seem funny that our own station and two of our guys should show up in the middle of *The Choirboys*. It seemed *great*. Then they showed the muster room, and every cop we had was in that room, even the ones who didn't come to the show. Royce Griffen. That was what I noticed first: Royce Griffen's hair, that real bright red hair he had. And then I noticed the back of his head."

Minor crossed his legs and put one hand up to the frozen-looking cheek. "It was like hamburger. Just gross. And I saw that every guy in there was dead. They had these big *wounds*, these big mushy *wounds*. And their skin was all sort of green-ish . . ." He was trembling now, and Graham understood that his peculiar posture was supposed to keep him so rigid he could not shake. "That's what I saw, anyhow."

"That was all that you saw?"

"One other thing—but it was just short. We had these little cells, holding cells, where we kept drunks overnight. Or where we put kids until their parents could come and pick them up. Six of them, all in one row. I didn't know we had anyone in there that night, because I was on day shift. The camera went right through the door to the cells, and it showed the first three cells. It looked like a butcher shop in there, man. Cut-up bodies, bodies all ripped open with all this stuff hanging out of 'em, blood all over everything . . . their clothes all mixed up with their insides." Mike Minor locked his hands around his upraised knee. "Right after that I thought I saw Dicky Norman stumble toward the screen. And that's when it happened."

The boy was shaking so uncontrollably now that even his voice trembled. "Guys were crying and yelling . . . I saw the guy right next to me, Harry Chester, Mo's brother, catch a round right in his throat and jump up and have his head opened up by what must have been a .357, and I hit the floor and got my own gun out. I was sure Dicky Norman was coming for me again, and I just started shooting up toward the front of the theater . . . I probably hit a couple of guys, I don't know. . . ."

Graham stood up and went toward the shaking boy. After a second of hesitation he patted him on the back and went hunting for brandy. He found a bottle, poured an inch into a wineglass, and gave it to Mike Minor, saying, "It's okay, son. It's okay. It's all over now. Anyone you hit was probably hit by a dozen other men, too." Because first he had been hit by the movie.

When he knew enough to ask some of the other survivors about the film, he heard a dozen variations on Michael Minor's story. No two had seen the same thing, but after the first few minutes, none had seen *The Choirboys*. Some had seen their wives and daughters making love with other cops, a few had seen their children's bodies pulled from the gentle surf on Gravesend Beach. A cop named Ron Rice had seen something like a sea monster—a huge underwater reptile with a wide savage mouth—swimming along and biting children in half, tearing their bodies apart and turning the water red. Most saw dead people moving as though they were alive. Two or three more of the men Graham talked to saw red-headed Royce Griffen. Many of them saw the drowned children and were chilled by their white cold faces. A cop named Lew Holz told Graham, "The way they looked! You know, I maybe saw them for only about a minute or two, if that long, but . . . they looked damned funny. They weren't kids anymore, they were something else, something you never want to see in this life, mister, and I don't either. They looked as though they had been fathered by rattlesnakes, that's how they looked." Holz had not seen Jerry Jerome's lightning bolt; like most of the others, he thought that Larry Wiak had been killed by Rod Fratney—even though Fratney was generally regarded as one of the worst shots on the Hampstead force. But by the time Graham spoke to Lew Holz, he no longer thought the question of who or what had killed Larry Wiak was the most important one he had to ask.

Therefore, the second time he talked to Bobo Farnsworth

about what he had discovered that night, he asked him, "When you got into the Nutmeg after running down from the station, did you happen to see what was on the screen?"

For the movie was still running when Bobo ran into the theater; the projectionist, hit by a stray bullet, was alive but incapacitated on the floor of his booth; the screen was in tatters but *The Choirboys* or whatever the Dragon had put in its place was being screened on the shreds of fabric and the blank wall behind them.

And Bobo, standing in the topmost part of a darkened room filled with dead men and dying men, had seen it.

7

Ronnie had fallen into an uneasy, twitchy sleep shortly after ten o'clock. Bobo hovered by the side of the bed, unwilling to leave her—drained by her lengthy illness, Ronnie looked translucent in her sleep, and Bobo feared that she might trip over from flutters and twitches into outright convulsions. He stroked her hand, then picked it up: it felt hot and dry and no heavier than a hummingbird. Holding her hand while she slept made him feel somehow false to himself, and he gently set her hand back down on the sheet. Then he went into the bathroom, soaked a washcloth in cold water, wrung it out, and returned to Ronnie's side. He delicately patted the cold cloth over her forehead. Ronnie muttered something that sounded like *Voon*, but did not awaken. Bobo rested his fingers on her forehead and thought it felt a little less feverish.

Nursing, Bobo had discovered, was more exhausting than police work. He had reported for the day shift, come home to take care of Ronnie, and now he felt as though he had gone thirty-six hours without sleep. Most of the exhaustion, Bobo thought, was a product of the anxiety he felt about Ronnie's condition, but being in attendance on her for six or seven hours without letup had given him sore feet and a backache. He would have climbed on the bed beside her, but he did not want to risk waking her. He sat down by her side, took her hand again, and closed his eyes; then he went across the bedroom to an old overstuffed chair, removed the clothes from it, and dropped them on the floor, and then dropped himself onto the spongy seat cushion.

Several hours later he awakened, disoriented—sleep had come so swiftly upon him that it took him a moment to recognize that he *had* slept. Bobo leaned forward, and his back complained; trapped in his tightly laced shoes, his feet felt swollen and tender. Across the room, Ronnie was moving her hand exploringly across her face. Then she opened her eyes and saw him.

"Oh, you sweetheart, you stayed with me," she said. "Um. I'm so *dry*."

"Just a sec." Bobo bounced out of the chair and brought her a glass of water from the bathroom. "How do you feel? I think you must have slept a couple of hours."

Ronnie tilted her head, considering; she sipped at the water. "I do feel better. You know, I think I could even eat something now. A little soup, maybe? Would you be a real sweetie and make some for me?"

"That's what I'm here for," he said.

When he returned with a bowl of mushroom soup he sat on the edge of the bed and watched her eat nearly all of it. As she handed him back the bowl, she yawned hugely. "Oh! I'm sorry," she said. "Bobo, I feel limp as a rag. I think I'm going to sleep for the next three weeks."

Bobo smiled at her.

"What time is it? About twelve-thirty? Bobo, why don't you go down to the movie? It probably started late, so it won't be like walking in in the middle—you'll only miss a couple of minutes, I swear. All I'm going to do is turn off the light and go back to sleep. I'll be all right. I promise."

"Well, maybe I will," Bobo said.

He did not go straight to the Nutmeg, but walked up to the old brick station house after he had parked his car. The theater was only a few minutes' walk across the sloping municipal parking lot, and Bobo was interested in what had happened during the second shift. A few more cases of arson, an anonymous body rotting in a shed, a high-school boy who had tried to fly off the roof of his house? The night deskman, Mo Chester, would have something funny to say about the afternoon's supply of weirdness. Mo Chester could always make Bobo laugh. Also, Mo would be chafing about having to miss the movie and the inevitable party afterward, especially since his brother could go to them.

Bobo went up the steps and pushed open the massive wooden door, already smiling about Mo's probable response to the surprise of his appearance.

"Well, guess who's here?" he said, clapping his hands together. "Can I get you any beer from the . . ." *Theater,* he was going to say, but the absence of an audience stole the joke from his throat. Mo Chester was not seated behind the desk, a telephone glued to his ear and a wry smile on his face. The desk was vacant. Gance McCone, Mo's partner, was gone too, and that was doubly odd. Bobo could not remember ever seeing the desk completely abandoned.

"Hey," Bobo called out. "What's the big idea, Chester? You and Gance on strike today?"

His words went out into the depths of the station—it was as if he could see them go. Bobo was suddenly convinced that he was the only person in the station. At this point he had not become aware of the smell. He stood absolutely still in the wide entry of his station; then by reflex he reached for the place on his hip where his gun should have been. Danger bells were ringing very loudly in Bobo's mind, and it was only when he touched his belt that he realized he was out of uniform.

"Anybody?" he shouted.

The phone rang just before Bobo went across the floor to look over the top of the desk, and the sound of the ringing is half of what triggered Bobo's *déjà vu.* He suddenly felt as though he had been in this moment before: the shock of the empty station, the shrill insistence of a telephone: himself standing in precisely this way, flat-footed and off balance.

Then Bobo became aware of the smell that pervaded the police station, and for the first and only time in his life he could identify the causes of the *déjà vu* experience and locate the real moment which lay behind the illusion of having been in precisely this same moment at an earlier time. Because he smelled blood—had just become aware that the odor of blood was so strong that the walls might have been smeared with it—and because the telephone was jangling and jangling, he had been put back into one of the unhappiest hours of his life: the time when he had responded to the call from Hester Goodall's brother and after seeing the mess in the kitchen had telephoned the station and waited for the other men to come. Mrs. Goodall's telephone had shrieked at them, but the priest apparently did not hear it and Bobo did not want to get involved with answering calls. The captains and the state cops could deal with Mrs. Goodall's friends and family.

The station stank of spilled blood like the Goodall house on that May afternoon, and Bobo went apprehensively toward the desk. When he reached it, he rose up onto his tiptoes and peered over the top. He saw the padded chairs the desk officers used, their telephones and notebooks and cigarettes; and he did not see what he had feared. No bodies lay twisted together on the raised floor behind the desk.

"Chester! McCone!" he shouted. "Anybody!"

He ducked into the hallway that led to the offices and the muster room and the interrogation rooms, but he saw no one. Behind him, the shrilling of the telephone continued. Before he went prowling through the rest of the station, Bobo turned around for another look at the entrance. And then Bobo saw, as he had not earlier, that the door between the main part of the station and the six little holding cells was open an inch or two.

This door was always kept locked, even when no prisoners were being held; it was a rule as conventional and as rigidly kept as the unwritten command that always kept at least one officer at the desk.

Bobo went slowly back across the white floor. He touched the barred metal door; swung it open. The stench of blood, now combined with the dark unmistakable odor of feces, rushed out toward him. Bobo looked down and saw a red stippling on the floor.

He was sure that the bodies back in there would be those of Mo Chester, Gance McCone, and any other officer who had been caught in the station.

Bobo stepped into the corridor and quickly ran down the length of the cells, seeing that there were three bodies. None of them were the bodies of policemen. The cells' doors were still locked. Behind the bars, the bodies lay disarranged and savaged in their separate cells. Bobo was not breathing now; he was barely thinking. On the floors of the three cells, blood lay in a thick glaze. Behind him the telephone finally stopped ringing. One of the three men—this was Greeley—had been so clawed that his face was only an assemblage of wet ragged strings; Bobo looked hard at the second bloody face and thought it looked almost familiar—as though this man had once been in the newspapers or on the covers of magazines.

It took him less than thirty seconds to pound downhill

across the length of the municipal lot. For one night, the manager of the theater had arranged that the marquee read: WEL-
COME POLICE OFFICERS OF HAMPSTEAD PRIVATE SHOWING. He
raced toward these tall black letters.

The lobby of the Nutmeg was brilliantly lighted and as
empty as the station house. Loud noises echoed through it—
from the soundtrack of *The Choirboys,* Bobo assumed, piped
in from the main section of the theater. He identified a biting
odor as familiar to him as the fragrance of beer.

It was cordite—the odor of the firing range in the basement
of the police station.

He trotted past the ticket post and burst through the twin
swinging doors into the theater. Cacophony erupted from the
speakers: shouts, grunts, bursts of loud and irrelevant music.
The beam from the projection booth illuminated the last swirling traces of smoke.

All the seats seemed empty. Bobo took a few uncertain
steps down the sloping aisle, uncertain because his eyes had
not yet adjusted. "Hey," he said, "guys?"

Then he saw a leg extended into the aisle, draped over an
armrest. "Hey, you all drunk?" He heard a groan rising
softly from beneath the mad roars and giggles on the soundtrack. Bobo touched the upraised knee; shook it.

"Where are the lights in this place?" he yelled.

And then either the screen turned brighter or his eyes adjusted, for he saw wounded and dead men sprawled across
their seats in every part of the theater. It looked like some sort
of ghastly joke: wherever Bobo looked, ahead or behind, to
either side, he saw lolling heads, outstretched arms, bodies
pitched over the tops of seats and bodies jammed into the
filthy popcorn-strewn aisles between the seats.

For a couple of seconds Bobo Farnsworth probably lost his
mind. He uttered a long wavering scream. He ran down to the
first row and saw Mark Johanssen's body lying faceup in the
wide aisle at the front of the theater. Johanssen's blond hair
was laced with a dark substance that resembled chocolate,
and his mouth was open. On the stage four feet from Johanssen's corpse was a thick slime of blood and wet organs, in the
midst of which sat a fat human hand like a fleshy spider.

Bobo thought he was the last policeman left alive in
Hampstead.

Just before his professionalism released him from his
shock, Bobo heard a mingled subtonal whisper coming up, it

seemed, from the ground, from beneath the floor. The noises on the soundtrack ceased as if cut off by a knife. The whispering sounds resolved into groans.

Not all of the men were dead.

Bobo ran, slipping on blood, back up the aisle. When he reached the rear of the auditorium again, just before he went to the telephone and called the state police, and then the ambulance services in Hampstead, Old Sarum, and King George, he took one look back into the theater.

And the screen claimed him, took him in.

"I saw something crazy," Bobo told Graham Williams months later. "It was hard to see, because the screen was all torn up and most of the picture was being projected on this wall behind it and that kind of threw the focus off a little bit."

They were in Graham's house, and Bobo nervously stood up and jammed his hands in his trouser pockets. "You had that girl living here with you for a while, didn't you? That Patsy McCloud?"

"Yes, she was here," Graham said.

"Not anymore?"

Graham shook his head.

"Well, the reason I bring it up is—this won't make sense to you, Graham, but I'll tell you anyhow. The reason I bring that up is that when I was standing there looking at the screen I suddenly thought of her. I saw her face, thought of her face I mean. And I wanted to see her. Like she could help me. I really did want to see her."

"That makes sense to me," Graham said. "You don't know how much sense that makes."

Bobo gave him a gloomy, almost sour look. "Maybe it does. Yeah, I remember that day—that day down on Kendall Point. I'll never forget that, I promise you. The way I thought Ronnie was dead, and what I thought was down there in that gulley . . . and that girl Patsy there with you and the other guys. You know what? You all looked beautiful. *Beautiful.* Even now, you humpbacked old monkey."

"Since Patsy is about ten or fifteen years older than you, maybe you should stop calling her a girl," Graham said. "And I don't have a hump on my back."

"Neither did that bell-ringer at Notre Dame," Bobo said, pronouncing it like the university in Indiana.

"Do you know we have a complete force again? It didn't even take a month and a half—we had kids applying from all over to get on our force. I thought it would take a year. More." Bobo wrapped his arms over his chest and took a couple of steps toward the typewriter table. "Anyhow, I sort of fell in love with Patsy then, just looking at her. And you know how worried about Ronnie I was. But that girl—pardon me, that woman—she just knocked me flat. I would have died for her."

"Let's get back to the Nutmeg Theater," Graham said.

Bobo stopped perambulating aimlessly between the couch and the typing table and went back to sit across from Graham. "Yeah. That's what you want to know about, isn't it? And the funny thing is, I promised myself I'd never tell anyone about the stuff I thought I saw on that ripped-up screen. I didn't want to sound like a candidate for the booby hatch."

"Most of the men there made the same promise to themselves."

"And broke it to you."

"Some of them."

Bobo laughed. "Well, to hell with you. I never would, except for that day I found you on Kendall Point. That's the only reason—and I still don't know what really happened there."

Graham merely kept his gaze fixed on Bobo.

"Okay. Fine. I'll tell you. Remember, I've only been standing by the door for a few seconds now—and the whole thing only took a couple of seconds. It just went bang, bang, bang, like I said." He inhaled loudly and opened his eyes again. "Anyhow, what I saw was Ronnie." He stuffed his hands in his pockets again, and Graham saw sudden deep strain on his face. The hands in those pockets would have been clenched, and part of the strain would have been the effort of not giving in to whatever powerful impulse ran through him at that moment—to weep, to scream, to begin shaking uncontrollably. "Just for a couple of seconds, if that long, but it was enough."

"You don't have to—" Graham began, but Bobo cut him off brusquely.

"Oh, I want to. Yes, Graham, I do. Isn't that what I'm

here for? I saw her buried, I saw Ronnie in her coffin, and I saw things eating on her. Rats. Big white worms as long as snakes. Taking chunks out of her. But she wasn't dead yet, and she was screaming, Graham, she was screaming her lungs out. And she was going to go on until she died.'' Bobo bent over, grimacing, as if his stomach hurt him. "And I'll tell you what I realized as I went away from that horrible sight toward the phone in the lobby. That I was just looking into my own mind. Okay? You follow that? Part of me wanted Ronnie to die that night, Graham. Part of me was sick and tired of taking care of her. So I put her in her coffin, Graham, and I buried her deep. And because she was still alive, she was down there screaming to get out.''

Graham opened his mouth to say something fatuous, but Bobo cut him off with a wave of his hand. "Don't. Just don't. You don't know the rest. Ronnie fell asleep that night all right, but do you know what she dreamed about? Can't you guess what she dreamed about that night? It went from my mind right onto the screen, or what was left of the screen, and straight into her mind. And that was nearly it for her— because she knew, all right, she knew where that horrible torture came from. She never admitted it, but she knew. And that almost killed her, Graham. When I got back to her house, she had fallen on the floor and puked all over herself and her skin was so dry she felt like a goddamned desert. I bet she had a fever of a hundred and two or three. I know she did. She almost died that night. And if she had died, it would have been because I killed her.''

"No,'' Graham said, but he knew that what Bobo said was at least half of the truth. And that Ronnie had at least half-known of this truth, for Bobo was no longer living with her. Between them had come Gideon Winter, with his dragonish insights into the ambiguities of human affection.

8

"You know,'' Sarah said to her new partner, "I'm getting a funny feeling.''

"I've had a funny feeling for a week and a half now,'' Ulick Byrne said. "I can hardly eat.''

"Oh, poor baby.'' She dryly patted his hand. "An Irishman who can't eat. It must be agony for you.''

"My gut's gone all sour. So what's this *idea* of yours, to use the proper word?"

Ulick had walked over to the newspaper office after sending his secretary home an hour early; now he and Sarah were back in the records room, and everyone else had gone home. "Bixbee" lay open on the long table between them, open to the entries on Murder.

"Well, you noticed the dates for these stories. About every thirty years, something awful happens in Hampstead—and we're assuming that Telpro is behind the latest events in the cycle."

"We know Telpro is behind them," Ulick said irritably. "I must have called Haugejas' office five times today, and all I've heard is the silky sound of that Chinese powerhouse telling me that the General is still in conference. They're planning something. Besides, we've got that picture of Leo Friedgood."

"Was Telpro behind the murder of Stony Friedgood? Is that what we're saying, Ulick?"

He pursed his lips. "No. I don't think we are saying that."

"But it is behind the other deaths."

"All the deaths on the eighteenth of May, yes. All the deaths of children, yes. I'm not sure we can blame those homicides at the start of the summer on good old Telpro."

"Well, I think we can. Anyhow, I'm sure that all the troubles are connected—in fact, I think that everything is connected. Everything that's happening is part of the same cycle. I think Leo Friedgood is connected to this stuff about Bates Krell and Prince Green. John Sayre thought he was connected to those two. I'm sure I told old Bixbee about seeing those names on Sayre's telephone pad, and that's how his name wound up in this column."

"I don't see quite where this line of thought takes you."

"Well, maybe I don't either, Ulick. Maybe we have to work on it a little more."

"Oh, don't take my head off, Sarah. I grant you, in the twenties there was a series of murders much like the ones we've just had. Bates Krell disappears. The murders stop. In 1980, Leo Friedgood disappears. But the killings don't stop, do they? We don't really know when Leo vanished. Do you think Leo killed his own wife?"

"We know he didn't. He was at Woodville Solvent all day."

"Oh, crap. My mind's going, along with my stomach."

"Well, all I'm really saying is that we might start looking for ideas about what's happening now in what happened way back then. If there really is a thirty-year cycle, maybe we ought to be paying more attention to what happened on the earlier turns of the wheel. We can't really do much with the 1952 occurrence—I was there, and not much really happened. A man blew his brains out. But he pointed backward for us, and I think it's about time I took the hint."

"I still don't see how that helps us nail Telpro."

"I think it probably won't. But it might help us see how Telpro fits into the picture in the first place. The cycle—the *pattern*—was there before Telpro was ever thought of."

Ulick shrugged. "We can't exactly call up this Bates Krell and ask him what went on. Or drop in unexpectedly on Robertson Green and hope to surprise him into telling us something."

"No," Sarah said. She was smiling, and Ulick knew that he had fallen right into whatever scheme she had concocted. "It's true, we can't call them up or drop in on them. But we could see where they lived. We could take a look at their houses. Who knows, Ulick? We might learn something."

"You have their addresses, don't you?"

"Of course I do. The *Gazette* printed them."

"So you want to drive around and have a look? That's fine with me."

"Well . . ." She tilted her head. "So that we don't waste our time, I was wondering if a certain young attorney would mind taking the addresses over to Town Hall and seeing if there's anybody in these houses now, or if the houses even still exist."

"Oh hell, give them to me," Ulick said. "But how did I ever get to be your flunky?"

"You had such pretty eyes," Sarah said.

She stayed with the outsized, now almost mysterious pages of "Bixbee" while Byrne walked the few blocks to Town Hall. Had she told the old man about seeing those names in John Sayre's office? There would have been no reason for her to have done so. Sarah could remember asking the editor of those days, a fat happy loafer named Phil Hackley, about the names; the editor had assured her that they could not be important. Had Bixbee overheard? The compositor had been a

wraithlike, unsatisfied-looking man, thin and gray—he'd had
the personality of a tired old hound. Few had taken notice of
him, even when he came in to work in the records room after
his retirement. Sarah had perhaps had four or five conversations with Bixbee during the fifteen or so years they worked
in the same offices. Only one of these had been even faintly
memorable—and that was because of an odd thing the old
compositor had said. He had wandered in out of the print
room on a cigarette break, and Sarah had been talking with
Hackley about the town council's seeming indifference to development on the Post Road and Riverfront Avenue: at the
time, twenty-five years ago or more, these major streets were
just beginning their slide into ugliness—fast-food franchises
next to dry cleaner's next to supermarkets, bars and body
shops jumbled up in a litter of neon signs. "Well, what do
you think about it, Bixbee?" Hackley had asked, leaning
back in his chair with his arms folded behind his head and a
superior smile on his face. Bixbee's thin gray face had contorted; for a second Sarah had feared that he was going to spit
on the editor's carpet. "I don't think it makes a blind bit of
difference," Bixbee had said, and Hackley's eyes had nar-
rowed in enjoyment—*get this old Yankee swamp rat,* he
seemed to be beaming toward Sarah. "No difference at all.
Nothing can save this town."

"Save?" Hackley had asked.

"Nothing," Bixbee insisted. "Hampstead's always been
rotten as a bucket of month-old oysters. Those roads'll get so
they look like a dog's breakfast. And nobody is really going
to notice. You look into your history, Mr. Hackley. You'll
see."

"Why, I didn't know you cared so much, Bixbee," the
editor had said, barely able to keep from laughing.

"I suppose there's a lot you don't know," Bixbee shot
back at him. "You don't know your history, Mr. Hackley."

The editor raised his eyebrows, no longer quite so amused.

Then Bixbee had saved his job—saved it by showing in
effect that he was crazy. And he had mentioned Bates Krell!
Sarah sat up straight at the table in the records room, remembering this conversation more than twenty-five years after the
fact. "I bet you never heard of a man named Krell, Mr. Hackley, a man named Bates Krell. He took bites out of this town—
big ones. He had black wings, Mr. Hackley." Bixbee's
mouth had twisted into something like a smile. "You tell

me, Mr. Hackley, if we're ever going to have another black summer in Hampstead.''

"Black summer?" Hackley exploded. "Black wings? Jesus, Bixbee, I'm sorry I asked.''

Bixbee had shrugged, retreating into his usual personality; cupped his cigarette in his hand; faded back into the print room.

Black summer. Black wings.

And there had been more—Bixbee had said something else that the intervening twenty-five or more years had stolen from Sarah. Something about Bates Krell, she was sure. . . .

. . . something about his house?

That felt right; in fact, Sarah thought, it was why she had suddenly remembered this conversation; it was the link between that day in the office and what Ulick Byrne was doing right now over at Town Hall.

When Ulick reappeared half an hour later, Sarah already knew what she wanted to do. She had the address written down on a sheet of *Hampstead Gazette* letterhead.

"Well, I got the information, but it took twice as long as it should have,'' he said, sliding into his seat across the table. "The Green house was easy. It's been in continuous occupancy for a hundred years or more. A man named John Scully lives in it now, and has for twenty-two years. He's a publisher in New York. I don't know, Sarah, but I don't get the feeling that we'll learn much about Prince Green if we go to this Scully guy's house.''

"I agree,'' Sarah said. "But what about the other one?''

"Well, that's what took all the time. That place is on Poor Fox Road—you know, that little street that borders the Academy's land—and all the property there was once owned by the school. They used to keep those houses as residences for the teachers and for the boarders they used to have, back twenty, thirty years ago. Now the fact is, as I eventually worked out, that absolutely no one has lived in the Krell house since the owner died or left town. The town eventually seized it to pay off the back taxes, but it looks like they could never get anyone to take it off their hands. It's just been sitting there as town property for the past fifty years. For some reason, it was the only building on that street that the school never owned.''

"I want to go there,'' Sarah said.

"A building empty for fifty years? Probably none too

steady to begin with? Have you ever seen those places on Poor Fox Road?''

"Bates Krell's house, the way he left it. Could you really pass that up?" Sarah asked, flaming out at him.

"Not if you really want to go there, Sarah," Byrne said. "If I'll take you to New York, I'll certainly take you to Poor Fox Road."

"On the way," she said, mollified, "I'll tell you about a conversation I was just remembering."

9

"This is about where the mailman found the body of that gardener, Bobby Fritz," Ulick said as they went slowly up Poor Fox Road. "He was lying down in those weeds."

"Ugh," Sarah said. "With that crazy poem inside his chest. You know, I've lived in Hampstead most of my life, but I don't think I've ever set foot on this street before." She peered through the window of Byrne's car at the tangled greenery bunched so thickly beside the road. Behind the wall of vine-choked bushes and trees she could see a tall sagging fence of wire mesh. The grounds of Greenbank Academy lay on the other side of this fence.

"Hardly anyone ever has. It's just stuck back here by itself. Sure doesn't look much like the rest of Greenbank."

Sarah was about to agree, for scarcely anything could have been less representative of Greenbank than Poor Fox Road, but then they went around a bend in the road and saw the houses; and Sarah no longer felt like talking. She knew which house was Bates Krell's, all right.

"I don't think anyone is living down here anymore," Byrne said, but Sarah thought she would have known that anyhow. "The Fritz boy's parents left their house after his death—I guess the boy more or less kept the family together. There was another neighbor or two, but they're gone now. I guess this place got a little spooky for them."

"Spooky?"

"A lady at Town Hall saw what I was looking up, and we had a little talk about it. She knew a painter who lived in that one"—Byrne pointed at a two-story frame house beside a lot filled with wrecked cars—"and he apparently moved in closer to town because he kept hearing funny noises at night. Apparently he never quite got over the Fritz boy's being killed so close by.''

"Funny noises. Everybody in Hampstead hears funny noises at night.''

He was pulling off to the side of the road in front of a house which had no number. It needed none.

"I know,'' Byrne said. "This damn town is turning into a funhouse. Well, this, obviously, is it. The house that Krell built.''

Small, one story high, with its once-brown clapboards split and jagged like broken teeth, the house could have seemed either bereft or sinister. The two little windows on either side of the door had long ago been broken in, and the roofline sagged. Whatever grass had once grown outside that door had years ago given up, yellowed, and died under the thick pelt of weeds crowding what should have been the short front lawn. Just an abandoned cottage by now almost too far gone to be repaired, the house should have seemed pathetic—a place too shabby even for memories. But to Sarah it did not seem so. The little house was decidedly sinister, and precisely because its memories had never left it.

Ulick Byrne must have felt something similar, for he said, "Are you sure the old guy isn't still hiding out in there? About ninety years old, and still, shall we say, aggressive?''

Sarah did not want to leave the safe asphalt of the roadbed to step onto the overgrown path; she did not want to get any nearer that house than she already was.

"There isn't going to be much in there, you know,'' Ulick said off to her side. "Not much besides that wonderful atmosphere.''

"Let's have a look,'' Sarah said, wondering why she always had to be braver than whatever man she was with. "It's just an old house. We'll scare all the mice.''

"I think I understand those mice,'' Ulick said, but he followed her small vehement body up the path.

She waited for him beside the flimsy-looking door. "What if it's locked?'' he said. He sounded almost hopeful.

"I think you could break it down, Ulick.''

She wanted him to open the door, and she could feel his resistance; then she felt him give in. He reached for the doorknob, which was pocked and darkened, but of solid bronze. *Mr. Krell wanted to be able to lock his door,* she thought; *closing this door and keeping it closed was important to him.*

This impression lifted off the serious and anomalous brass
knob and spoke directly to her—an impression like music
trapped in the grooves of a record. And when it came to her,
another thing came to her with it.

It was not about the house, though. She had remembered
that Bixbee had won so many of the office pools—at least
three-fourths of them—that people had stopped betting on
them.

Byrne's hand touched the knob. He glanced questioningly
at Sarah, twisted it, and pushed: the door creaked open.

"Come on, Galahad," Sarah said, and stepped over the
threshold.

She was standing in a small dusty room only dimly illuminated by the two broken windows. A window at the rear of the
room had been covered over with yellowed newspaper taped to
the wall. The cheap pine flooring, buckled up here and there
like overlapping teeth, had never been truly straight, and now
ran noticeably downhill to the far wall, thus adding to the
slightly false perspective given by any empty room: it was like
one of those curved backdrops into which people can seem to
run for miles, an optical illusion. The walls and ceiling had
been darkened by the relief maps drawn by generations of
water stains.

"Oh, yes," Sarah said. The house was, very simply, bad,
and she could feel its badness: it rejected her as it had rejected
all for the past fifty years, it was like a wound that wanted
only to close around itself: but Sarah felt a paradoxical relief.
She was here, inside this place, and she could handle it.

"Completely empty," Byrne needlessly pointed out.

"In a way," she said.

Byrne shot her a dour look and began to knead his stomach
with his right hand. "Place makes me feel worse," he said.
"How seriously do you want to inspect it? There isn't anything to see, really." He advanced a few steps farther than
she into the room, as if to demonstrate his courage.

"I want to see the whole thing."

Sarah wordlessly set out toward the gaping doorway to the
left, taking care to skirt the most jagged places in the floor.
What she entered was another, smaller room, also completely
bare. A light cord dangled from the ceiling. The window here
had been papered over like the window in the living room,
and in the darkness the roils of dust on the floor seemed solid,
almost bulky.

"Where Bates lay his sleepy head to rest, I suppose," Byrne said from immediately behind her.

"The kitchen must be on the other side." Sarah turned around, ducked under Byrne's outstretched arm, and marched back across the living room.

She had almost made it to the arch on the other side of the room when a peculiar sensation overtook her. The pitched floor seemed very slightly to *sway*, to roll against its slope as if to straighten itself, and Sarah stopped moving. The floor gently swung back to its original position. "Ulick," she began, "did you just . . ." She lost the sentence. The little room appeared to be extending itself around her, multiplying its length: for a second it was as if she stood in a vast vaulted cavern.

"Did I just what?" Ulick said from behind her.

Bates Krell's house had its tricks, she saw, its own once-powerful concentrations and plans; these were the distillations of the memories she had sensed when she had first seen the house. It was good that Byrne was here with her: the tricks may have lost much of their potency, but Sarah knew that if she were in the Krell house by herself, these three rooms and a basement could grow into a maze.

"Did I just what, Sarah?"

The room was folding back into itself—she lost the feeling of being a speck in a vast and terrible space.

Sarah knew that, whatever Telpro's role had been, this house was crucial to everything that was happening in Hampstead: she did not yet understand how the parts fit together, but Bates Krell's sinister little house was one of the largest; eventually she would understand. Old Bixbee, who had a gift for picking winning numbers, had understood before her, and she would go through his index the way Billy Graham went through the Bible.

"Sarah?"

"Excuse me, Ulick. I had an odd sensation just now. I wondered if you felt anything."

"An intense desire to get out of this place."

"One more room and then the basement. I think we really have to see it all." She continued on her way toward Bates Krell's kitchen.

Here the window had not been covered, and harsh light revealed the jagged tears in the crusty linoleum, the webby constructions of dust and hair which floated up a bit in the air they disturbed as they entered. A gray metal sink the size of a washtub bolted to the exterior wall; rusty pipes ran along the floor beneath it.

"Where Krell made his renowned Krellburgers," Byrne said. "We dare not ask of what."

He went forward, bent at the waist, and peered out the window. Two rusting cars with shattered windshields grazed in tall yellow weeds. "I bet we could get this place cheap," he said. "Do you suppose the pipes still work?"

Sarah shook her head, but Byrne was already twisting one of the spigots over the metal sink. A pipe banged against the wall, and a wad of dust shot out of the spigot and puffed into nothingness against the sink. The pipe thumped the wall again. "I think there's still water coming here," Byrne marveled.

The spigot shook atop the sink, vibrating with a drumming, gathering intensity.

"Turn it off," Sarah said, but Byrne merely glanced at her.

In the next instant the handle exploded off the spigot and a thick yellowish substance sprayed into the room, spattering both of them. "Hey!" Byrne shouted, jumping back. A fat stream of the yellow fluid was still jetting across the room, but in seconds it subsided to a sluggish steady flow from the spigot into the sink. The fluid stank—it smelled like illness to Sarah, like something drained from a dying man. Already it was halfway up the side of the gray sink. Where the fluid had hit the floor it lay in congealing puddles, like cloudy Jell-O. The smell of it filled the kitchen.

"There's no way to turn that thing off," Ulick said, half in a panic. "My God, what *is* that stuff? It's going to run out on the floor any minute."

"I think it's the secret ingredient in Krellburgers," she said, paying him back a little. She inspected a fat wad of the stuff which had landed on her skirt and now clung there. Sarah took a tissue from her bag and dislodged it.

The pipes still roared: Sarah could see them moving beneath the sink, jittering into each other, knocking between the floor and the wall. The whole house seemed affected by this agitation, to tremble in rhythm with the loud pipes.

"Let's get out of here, Sarah," Byrne said. "I'm covered with this stinking goo, and I really think we can do without the basement."

There was only one more door in the little kitchen, and Sarah pulled it open. The hinges squealed; behind the door was musty blackness. "Bingo," Sarah said.

"I think we should go."

"You go, then. I'm taking a look at the basement."

She turned toward the rotting steps which led down into the blackness, and as she knew he would, Ulick said, "Then you'd better let me go first." He was brushing at his jacket with a noticeably unsanitary handkerchief. He balled this object into his pocket and went around her to feel his way down the stairs.

"There's some light at the bottom," he called up to her, and as she stepped onto the packed earth of the basement floor she saw why. The stairs ended just before a stone foundation wall, and when Sarah walked around to the side of the staircase she noticed the glass bricks set at the topmost level around the perimeter of the basement, two on each side. Less transparent than the usual basement windows, they at least admitted a cloudy light.

Sarah's skin shriveled on her back, her scalp, her hands. As soon as she had stepped into the main area of the basement, she felt intensely uncomfortable—it looked much more like an ordinary basement than the house like an ordinary house, but it was not ordinary. Here was where the memories were strongest, most concentrated. When evil had taken root in this house, it had grown here first.

Ulick Byrne must have felt it too, for he said, "My God Sarah, this is a terrible place."

She looked at him curiously. Then she looked straight and strong at the basement: it was merely a wide-open area bounded by irregular stone walls, floored with dirt. Unclean light showed them a long flat wooden table at the far end—once it might have been a workbench. Even where they stood, they could see the dents and scars on its edges. Every cell of this place, every atom, shrieked against her nerves.

Byrne said, "You know, before I started concentrating on real estate, I spent a lot of time in courtrooms and I saw my share of jails too. I know when I'm somewhere where people have been scared and miserable. You can feel how trapped the people were. But Jesus, Sarah, this is the worst one I've ever known. I don't even want to know what used to happen down here."

"Me too," she said. "I've seen enough. Let's go."

Byrne sighed with relief, and the two of them turned back toward the staircase.

Upstairs, a door slammed shut.

Sarah and Byrne froze. Footsteps traversed the living room, entered the kitchen. They looked at each other with wild fear: the footsteps were going directly toward the stairs. Perhaps both of them imagined that Bates Krell had returned and was bent on slaughtering them—it would have been almost an inevitable thought, in their circumstance: but Sarah recovered a fraction of a second before Ulick and whispered, "It's some kid. It must be."

Ulick nodded, but with little conviction. When the door at the top of the stairs creaked open, he took Sarah's arm and pulled her toward a corner from where they could see whoever was coming down the stairs before they themselves were seen.

He pulled her in next to him, backed against the wall, and then recoiled. The wall had been furry and it had been in motion. Ulick gasped and turned his head to look at the treacherous wall. He nearly screeched. Blanketing the wall were thousands of small red spiders. He felt a sharp stabbing pain in his hand and saw that one of the spiders had just bitten him. He bit down on the pain and flicked the spider away.

The person coming down the stairs was no child. The steps were slow and cautious, the weight behind them that of an adult.

The head came into view. Silvery hair. Both Sarah and Byrne relaxed by an unconscious fraction. Then the face turned unknowingly in their direction, and their relaxation froze again. The man's face was a grotesque parody of humanity. Nearly dead white, it was puffy and ridged with excess flesh. The forehead seemed swollen and bulbous, the chin dewlapped.

Again Sarah was there first: she suddenly realized that the man was what the children called a "leaker" and that he must be using this abandoned house as a hideout. He was only a week or two away from the stage of the disease which would require him to bandage himself—at that point he would need a safe place to hide, where he could tend himself away from the threat of destruction.

A wad of flesh on the man's cheek slid toward his dewlapped chin, and Sarah's heart moved for the man.

"Leaker," Ulick whispered in her ear; she glanced at him in annoyance, and just as she saw that a small colony of spiders was burrowing into his thick woolly hair, she realized that she had recognized the leaker.

The man who had just crept down into Bates Krell's terrible basement was her gynecologist.

"Your *hair*," she hissed to Byrne. "Your hair—*spiders*," and then she stepped away from the corner and said in an almost normal tone of voice, "Dr. Van Horne? Please don't be alarmed. It's me, Sarah Spry."

The doctor turned toward her voice with awful slowness.

Now she could see the extent to which he had been mutilated—that is what she would have called it—by the disease. His face was only barely recognizable, and shone with a slick white moisture. Flaps of skin folded over his eyes, retracted, fell again. She thought he seemed alarmed. Behind her she could hear Ulick hissing, frantically scratching at his scalp as the spiders began to chew on him.

"We intend no harm, Doctor," she said. "Remember me? I'm a patient of yours. Sarah Spry?"

It was terrible, she thought, that a wonderful old man like Wren Van Horne should have contracted that loathsome disease.

Van Horne seemed to be smiling at her, and she stepped toward him, meaning to give him any comfort she could. Her shoe sank into a cool wet pool, and when she looked down in surprise, Sarah saw that she had stepped into a small lake of blood.

"Sarah Spy is a better name for you," said the grinning man at the bottom of the stairs.

She almost thought that the palm of a childish hand was pushing up on the bloody sole of her shoe: for a second she felt that pressure, and the disturbed, unhappy image leaped into her mind. She moved back, afraid to look down, and said "What?" to the doctor. His face seemed to be altering, lengthening, the eyes swimming out from under the flaps of moving skin—

(*Spy*, whispered the doctor)

—and when she heard another sound from the stairs and knew that she and Byrne were saved she ran toward the sound and then stopped and backed toward the corner where the lawyer had taken her—it was the last place she had felt safe, and she returned there by instinct. For on the top step of the staircase to Bates Krell's kitchen she had seen dead little Martin O'Hara staring down at her. His brother, Thomas, stood behind him and looked over Martin's shoulder with the same indifferent gaze.

2

The Fire-Bat

1

All the next day, Clark and his mistress drank with a dedicated abandon—as if they were in a contest and expected a prize. They began with beer, cold bottles of Molson's ale from the refrigerator as Berkeley woozily cut open a package of bacon and slapped the entire slab into a blackened pan, switched to hard liquor around eleven (Jameson's for Clark, for Berkeley Stolichnaya vodka kept so cold it was treacly); opened a bottle of wine to have with lunch. This was liver sausage on rye bread—even sober, Berkeley Woodhouse thought of cooking as a menial task best done by other people—but the wine was a Napa Valley Chardonnay. Up until a couple of hours after lunch, Tabby thought that his father and Berkeley were handling their drinks a little better than usual, and would probably just pass out watching television. They did that every few days, and Tabby turned off the lights and stepped over their legs to go to bed. He thought, in fact, that they seemed less driven than usual: Berkeley ruffled his hair once or twice, and his father made a joke for the first time since the departure of Sherri Stillwell.

"Jesus, Clark," Berkeley said, "I just realized that you were married twice, and I bet you weren't happy with either one longer than six months."

"Happiness can't buy you money," Clark said.

Berkeley barked out a laugh, and Tabby looked up in amazement: the joke disguised a lie, but it was a joke nonetheless, despite its bitterness.

After lunch even this fragile lightness disappeared.

Clark and Berkeley went into the bedroom, "for a little nappy-poo," Berkeley said. The arch euphemism made Clark knot his brows together. "That means for a bump, kid, you get me? 'Nappy-poo,' for shit's sake.'' He pushed her toward the door.

Tabby was familiar with most of the noises that accompanied his father's lovemaking, and rather than hear this array of snorts and grunts one more time, he went into his own room. Twenty minutes later he was surprised to hear sounds coming from Clark's bedroom—usually they did not penetrate so far. And the sounds themselves were not the usual barnyard impressions. Tabby thought he could hear his father crying.

Around two o'clock Clark and Berkeley found their way back into the kitchen, where Tabby sat at the table reading an H. P. Lovecraft novel he had found in the library. Berkeley had large black smudges beneath her eyes, and his father's hair was mussed. Clark's mouth was set in an unhappy curl.

Berkeley went straight to the freezer compartment of the refrigerator, took out the Stolichnaya bottle, slopped several inches into the glass she had used that morning, and then dropped in a handful of ice cubes. "Clark?" she asked in a tentative voice. "You want some Irish?"

"What else would I want?" he growled.

Silently she poured his drink.

Clark gloomily swallowed; grimaced.

"Don't have to take my head off," Berkeley said.

"Give me two good reasons not to," Clark muttered.

Tabby cleared out—he thought that these two miserable people barely noticed his going. When he got back upstairs to his room, he first thought that he could hear his father sobbing again; then that he could hear him shouting. He closed his door; eventually he put his hands over his ears. When the loud shouts ceased, Tabby put a record on his turntable—*The Doctor Is In*, Ben Sidran—and blotted everything out by cranking the volume up as high as he dared.

At four he went back down to the kitchen for a Coke. Clark and Berkeley had left the refrigerator and freezer doors open, and Tabby closed them when he had taken his bottle out. Greasy dishes several days old were piled in the sink, and after sipping from his Coke, Tabby squirted soap over them and turned on the hot water. Berkeley thought no more highly of cleaning than she did of cooking. When his father washed dishes, he broke them on purpose. Tabby quickly washed all the dishes in the sink, dried his hands, and wandered into the library. This was one of the four rooms with a fireplace, and a small smoky blaze stuttered in the grate. Tabby saw that whoever had built the fire had merely used newspaper for kindling and had then tossed more folded newspaper onto the feeble flames. The television set blared out a denture-cream commercial to an empty room. Tabby smelled burning paper, whiskey, some fuming and bitter emotion—while he still thought the room was empty, the bitterness of feeling that had been spilled there was as strong as the odor of his father's Irish whiskey.

And then for a moment he saw the walls sway and ripple. He had the faintest impression that they were sliding toward him, and he flinched to one side, remembering what had happened to him in the library . . . a man with tea-colored eyes raising a gun as a storm boiled overhead . . .

You should have gone to Fairlie Hill, boy, with the others.

His mouth dried; his heart banged.

If he had not heard his father wetly belch at that second, he might have fainted.

Tabby spun toward the sound, and saw Clark leaning against the brown curtains covering the window—glaring at him. He precariously held a tumbler filled with brown liquid. His father's hair had fallen over his forehead. Clark seemed almost to blend backward into the curtains, to be on the verge of invisibility. A pair of flies swooped past his face. Then Tabby saw that Berkeley Woodhouse lay on the couch against the far wall, her skirt rucked up carelessly and her hair fanned half across her face. She too looked almost ghostly—as if the Russian vodka had stolen half her substance.

"Go," his father said. His voice was husky, ragged; fractured by emotion.

Tabby backed out of the room.

He sat on the stairs for a time, too confused about what was happening to him and his father to know what he ought to do. Twice while he sat there, his arms around his knees, Clark stumbled past the bottom of the staircase, going to the kitchen for fresh drinks and unsteadily bringing them back. The messy little fire backpuffed smoke: Tabby could smell its acrid breath. From the library, the voices on the television set contended with Clark's drunken ranting.

"Gutter," he heard his father say. *"Gutter."*

And "Not my fault," he heard him say.

He smelled the sour breath of the hearth and for the first time thought to wonder why his father had troubled to light a fire on a warm day in August.

Clark tossed another heap of newspapers on the smoky blaze, and Tabby heard Berkeley moan. "Four Hearths" seemed filled with night; with shadowy intentions that required the blankness of night and drunkenness. Tabby was chiefly sure of one thing: his father was in torment, and would damage anyone who tried to aid or deflect him. Tormented too, Tabby returned to his room. He clamped headphones over his ears, closed his eyes, and swam as far into his music as he could.

An hour later he emerged into a hallway that was too hot—the air was dry, so gritty it felt sandblasted. The smell of fire and ash rose toward him from the ground floor. Tabby went toward the top of the stairs.

"Dad?"

That drunken, agonized voice went on down there—slowed by the liquor, but inexhaustible. Tabby heard the firescreen in the living room scrape shut.

"Dad? What's going on?"

"Huh," he heard Clark say. Loud footsteps came toward the bottom of the stairs; then his father appeared, clutching the green neck of his whiskey bottle with one blackened hand, streaks of ash dividing his face. "Making fires, that's what. Fires in the fireplaces of 'Four Hearths,' that's what. To get this place warm again. You going to help?"

"How can I help?" Tabby asked.

"Get more wood from the pile outside—lots of it. Berkeley just threw papers on the goddamn fires, that's not how you do it. Go on out and bring some more wood back in."

"Are you cold?"

"Not anymore," Clark said. "I think I just about got it right."

His eyes were glassy—they looked like painted shells. The streaks of ash seemed to be hardening on his face; whatever emotion surged through Clark hardened there too. "Do you feel all right, Dad?" Tabby asked.

"Are you going to get that wood inside or do I have to make you do it?" The armored face with its stony, painted eyes stared up at him.

Tabby moved swiftly down the stairs and past his father; he dared not look at him.

Prudent Monty Smithfield had bought three cords of wood every winter, and every winter burned just less than two in the fireplaces of "Four Hearths." Now split and sawn lengths of wood were stacked against the long back fence—enough for at least three extravagant winters. Some of it was so dry that the bark had lifted away from the gray wood, peeled back like a rolled-up shirt. Tabby remembered to take the carrying sling from the hook beside the back door, and went out onto the shaggy grass. He smelled woodsmoke from the chimneys, and looked up to see it coiling over the house. Black rags that must have been newspaper ash sifted down.

Tabby laid the sling on the ground and stacked as many pieces of the oldest and driest wood as he could lift within its webbing. Breathing hard, he lugged the heavy sling back through the door, banging it against the frame.

"Okay," his father said, glowering at him out of his ash-striped face. "Get that stuff into the fire in the library."

"All of it?"

"Then go out and get more. About as much as you have there. And put it in the living-room fireplace."

"Dad—"

"We need it, Tabby," Clark said. He took a pull from his bottle.

Tabby effortfully lifted the sling and, using both arms, carried it before him into the library.

The room was hot as a sauna. He set down the sling, pushed back the firescreen, and began lifting pieces of the wood off the little heap and setting them atop the sputtering fire.

A cat's tongue of flame curled through a chink in the piled-up wood; an arm of flame, red and muscular, followed it. The dry wood ignited like a bonfire of dead leaves. Tabby recoiled from the sudden intensification of the heat and painfully struck his back against the brass edging on a coffee table. He stood up, rubbing his back.

Behind him, Berkeley Woodhouse groaned on the couch. Tabby whirled to look at her, having almost forgotten she was in the room. She was holding out a lipstick-blotched glass, and Tabby moved quickly to her side and took it from her.

"Fix me one more, will you, sweetie?" she asked: Tabby was certain for a moment that she took him for his father.

But then Clark was looming up behind him, and Berkeley blinked, and her face shuttered: she had known who he was.

"The boy has work to do, and he's going to do it," Clark said, and roughly took the glass from Tabby's hand. "I'll get you another drink, if that's what you think you need."

"Why are you . . . ? Why are . . . ?" Berkeley struggled with the sentence for a moment, but flopped back against the couch, letting it go unfinished.

"Move," Clark ordered Tabby. "Wood, remember? You're not the bartender around here." Misery still seemed to flow from Clark, but now it was an aggressive misery.

"You want more wood," Tabby said flatly. "For the living-room fireplace. Then for the kitchen fireplace. Then the one in your bedroom."

Clark simply continued to stare at him.

"Well, sure," Tabby said. "If that's what you want."

"What *I* want," Clark said. "That's it. You and this dumb bitch remember that." He grinned fiercely at Tabby, and then swung the hand gripping the green Jameson's bottle at a pair of flies that had circled in toward his mouth.

As the sunlight faded, the rooms in "Four Hearths" reddened with the fires; Tabby kept moving from the rear door to the woodpile and back again, and as it grew darker he saw the downstairs rooms and his father's bedroom become almost unrecognizable—the jumping flames altered the dimensions of the rooms they colored, pulling in one red wall and pushing out another, more shadowy wall. Throughout the house Tabby could hear the insistent sucking sound of air rushing up the chimney stacks; he was slick with sweat, and his face, like Clark's, was smudged with ash and soot. As the hours went past, Tabby ceased to wonder why his father insisted on turning the house into an oven—it was another drunken notion, necessarily bad, and by the next day it would be forgotten—and concentrated instead on making Clark happy in his obsession. His arms ached, his head throbbed; after stoking his father's fires for several hours, Tabby could scarcely remember his name. He was half-conscious of Berkeley Woodhouse weaving through the house, ignored by his father. And he thought on one of his returns into the house with the sling filled with eighty pounds of firewood that he had heard his father weeping again, saying, "Jean? Jean?"—as if he were seeing his late wife's ghost. But that was impossible, and anyhow Tabby was by then so exhausted that he scarcely recognized his mother's name.

Berkeley eventually banged open the refrigerator door and took out an ancient summer sausage from Greenblatt's, on which she began to gnaw; the heat and the ache in his muscles killed Tabby's hunger. He went upstairs finally to wash his face and hands—too tired for more elaborate cleaning—and left his father downstairs grinning into the blasting red flames.

On the wall of a room that he assumed was his he saw an unfamiliar pennant—a college or high-school pennant. He stared at it as he staggered toward his bed. ARHOOLIE. *Arhoolie?* This too he could not identify. As he fell into bed the room seemed to distend, to warp about him. His skin felt as though he'd been broiled under a grill.

"A whole plate of fire!" he heard Clark screech just before he fell into numbed sleep.

He dreamed, vividly, of traveling toward a great forest. Huge trees fanned across a plain, their shadows darkening the land before them. Their leafy heads fanned too; bent toward walking Tabby, shook at him. He should run, he knew, he should turn tail and run like hell—even the trees were telling him so. From the great forest came a wave of bitterness, of evil—of what felt like evil to the boy because of the strength of the bitterness. He should have run away, but he had to get nearer, had to *see* what lay hidden between, beneath those reaching trees. As he drew nearer, he gradually began to hear the noises of animals—of animals in pain, screaming or whimpering in terror and agony. Accompanying these terrible sounds of pain and death were the violent noises of the battles still going on: bodies cracking against trees, the earth shredded by claws and hooves. Some animal screamed out in a woman's voice, high-pitched and fearful. In the forest the animals had turned against themselves; and if Tabby took one step between the thick leaning trees, they would leap upon him and rip his heart from his body. That scream like a woman's unfurled over his head.

When he opened his eyes, his hands gripping the warm top edge of a sheet, he saw a glimmering, twisting pool of white light in the middle of his dark room. He had seen this earlier, he could not remember where. And then he remembered his father seated drunkenly at the kitchen table a few days before, this same light playing behind his head.

Tabby's bedroom had become stiflingly hot. The smell of

woodsmoke, prickly but comfortable, filled the room.

The twisting pane of light just past the end of his bed was drawing into itself, concentrating. All those mad animals in the forest . . . Tabby shrank down into his bed, aware for the first time of how his perspiration had dampened the sheets.

The shifting pane of white drew into itself, twisted down into a characterless face. Tabby's body tightened on the damp bed, and he inhaled a great gulp of smoke-perfumed air. The white face before him, still changing, was blank and babyish: but the forehead tilted back and erupted into bulges over the eyes, the chin grew out like a spade, the ears lapped over. The face before Tabby hardened into itself and grinned.

It was the face of Gideon Winter, the true face beneath the one he had shown the world.

Gideon Winter's white face leaned toward him as had the brutal trees in his dream. Tabby was faintly conscious of black clothing imbued with the pervasive smell of woodsmoke. The huge mouth opened: pointed teeth. A tongue like a long snake coiled obscenely out toward Tabby.

From beyond his window the wounded animal screamed again. But it was not an animal, he recognized; that was the cry of a woman.

The face before him evaporated down into itself and wavered in the air like a wisp of smoke. Then it twisted into nothingness, leaving only a bitter smell in the air.

Shaking, Tabby left his bed—now he registered that his room was filled not only with darkness but also with smoke. He reached the window just as another pitiful scream carried toward him through the night. When he looked down toward the front lawn of "Four Hearths," he saw two people struggling in smoke and night. He had seen many such scenes over the past weeks; everyone in Hampstead had seen these obscure but passionate battles; and that may be why it took Tabby a moment or two to identify the two people fighting on his front lawn.

But even when he had seen an unmistakable arrangement of features, even when he saw a familiar blur of lipstick, he did not want to identify these brawling people: his mind fought to reject their identities. His father; Berkeley Woodhouse.

Clark seemed infused with glee, strong enough to fell an oak with the flat of his hand; so even after Tabby had admitted that the man down there was his father, he found himself doubting it. Clark had not demonstrated such energy, such physical confidence, since the barely remembered days of his tennis victories. One of the first things Tabby saw was that his father had not had such a good time in years.

And then he saw that Berkeley's symmetrical face was blurred with blood, not lipstick.

Clark's back muscles laughed again, and his fist smashed her nose to a squashy pulp. As Berkeley's hands came up to her face, Clark kicked her legs out from under her. As soon as his mistress struck the ground, Clark kicked her with joyous accuracy in the ribs. Another of her terrible wails rose toward Tabby. Clark did an impatient, jittering jig—adjusting his stance—and then kicked her squarely in the head. Berkeley moaned, and Clark jigged down the grass toward her midriff. Her long legs were trembling, flailing against the grass. Clark aimed a particularly forceful kick at her belly; her body was thrown back a foot.

Berkeley convulsed again—a coil of white smoke momentarily erasing her face—and Clark was able to smash at her face without the inconvenience of moving. Tabby saw Clark's leg move twice, pistonlike, and immediately after saw the grass at his father's feet take on an added sheen, an extra darkness. Red dots spattered Clark's trousers. The white drift of smoke lazed off, and Tabby saw what had become of Berkeley Woodhouse's face. Then he could move.

Tabby threw up the window, leaned out into gritty warmth. "Dad! Dad! Stop!"

Clark turned around and looked up at his son. His face was as joyous as Tabby had feared it would be, unconsciously radiant.

"Turn around, Tabby," Clark said. "It's your turn now."

"Dad," Tabby breathed out. "I'm going to call for the ambulance."

"Look around you, Tabby," Clark said in a lightly teasing voice. His father smiled at him—a smile that seemed somehow not Clark's at all, but sweeter and more formal—and walked back toward the house, leaving Berkeley's body carelessly behind him on the shiny black grass.

Clark disappeared beneath the roof of the porch. Tabby heard the door slam shut. He glanced in agony at the still form of Berkeley Woodhouse, hoping that she would groan or move . . . he knew that she was dead.

An inner door slammed—the library door.

Tabby turned around, and it was as if all of "Four Hearths" laughed.

The room was not his. It was smaller, more crowded with *things:* he saw skis leaning against a closet door, a trombone case beside the bed, a music stand before the window opposite. Tabby did not ski or play the trombone; he could not read music; and there was no window in that wall. The ARHOOLIE pennant he had seen before, the harbinger of all this change, glowed down at him from its place over the bed.

Still he could smell the pervasive woodsmoke, though he could no longer see it.

Tabby went cautiously across the unfamiliar room to the window. What he saw when he looked out was not Greenbank. He was looking down on a longer lawn, ending not in a slope to the road but at a white fence. Across the street were modest frame and ranch houses, much closer together than the houses in Hampstead. The trees were different—they reminded Tabby of the trees he had known in northern Florida. Black lines of tar wetly streaked the road. Down at a corner—a corner that did not exist—a street sign was visible on its tall pole. Tabby squinted to read it. MAPLE LANE.

Like the contents of the room, this too was unfamiliar, yet somehow known; as if met in a dream.

Downstairs his father roared like a beast—Tabby's chest tightened when he recognized the sound as laughter.

Maple Lane. A room with ivied wallpaper and skis leaning against a closet door. Arhoolie. He thought he *almost* knew what he would find beyond the door. He wondered: if he went to the telephone, would he get the Hampstead police station? Or the police of whatever invented world this was?

Outside the room was a hallway thick with invisible smoke. It rubbed sandpaper against Tabby's eyes, threw salt in his lungs. "Help!" he called. "Dad!"

"You want something?" his father's voice asked calmly from behind him. Tabby whirled around, so frightened he wanted to pee.

His father's voice, but not his father. A slim, much younger man separated himself from the wall. His face was pitted with small acne scars; he looked to Tabby like someone who would have sought out the Norman twins—he looked criminal. He wore a cap on his head and what Tabby only now recognized as a gray tweed suit that belonged to his father. Tabby stepped backward.

"Get back in your room, Spunks," this creature said. "I got a whole plate of cookies for you." He smiled at Tabby, and the smile froze the boy. "Whole plate, my little buddy."

"Dad," Tabby said.

"Daddy's here," the creature said in his father's voice, and began to glide toward Tabby.

Tabby turned around and ran for the staircase he mysteriously knew was at the end of this corridor. Behind him, the creature with his father's voice started to laugh.

The heat intensified as he rushed down the stairs. He could hear, but not see, the fires in the living room and library . . . noise of kindling, snapping flames taking all the food they could. He hit the bottom stair and ran into a living room decorated with a chintz couch and frilly curtains on the windows. A grandfather clock stood on a hooked rug beside a stone fireplace. The room seemed hot enough to burst by itself into flame. Wooden Dutch doors separated this room from the big kitchen, and Tabby ran through them, wanting only to get outside—to the real outside, to Greenbank.

A woman who had been standing at the sink turned to smile at him. And that was when he realized for the first time where he was. In a modest brown dress with a white Peter Pan collar, Grace Jameson—Grace Jameson with his real mother's face—was greeting him in the kitchen of *Daddy's Here,* where so many confrontations and accommodations had been met. Along with the simple, primitive smell of fire he caught the odor of pot roast. He stopped moving; stopped breathing.

"Oh, darling," his mother said. *"Here* you are. We've been waiting such a long time. Dinner's almost ready. Shouldn't you go back up to your room and wash up? Your daddy's waiting for you, you know."

"Billy Bentley," he breathed out, his eyes avidly on the face of Jean Smithfield—she looked just as she had on the day of her death ten years before. She was different from the way he remembered her: his memories had been indelibly shaped by photographs Clark had saved, and now he saw that for photographs she had pursed her mouth, had generally tightened up. Aged twenty-nine, his mother was shorter than he had realized, sweeter, more fragile.

"Now you're just being silly," she said. "Back upstairs with you, young man."

"Mom," he said.

Jean Smithfield stepped toward Tabby, an expression of profound love mixed with reproach for a difficult child printed on her face. Then she smiled, and playfully reached out for his shoulder.

Tabby looked at her and wanted to run into her arms. But a wave of hot air as from a blast furnace—air that seemed hot enough to melt iron—flowed toward him, and he stepped back, startled.

His mother was still smiling at him, but her hands were the centers of twin balls of flame; in an instant, the flames had coursed up her arms and leaped into her hair. Beneath the smiling face, Tabby saw white glowing bone. He jerked backward again, and his mother tottered toward him, the flames spreading across her face and down her chest.

Not looking, Tabby held out a hand to one side and felt it encounter the intense heat of an invisible fire: he screamed at the pain, and his mind nearly balked like an overloaded machine. The house was burning around him, and he could not see the flames.

His mother sank to her knees, still reaching out for him. Tabby dodged away from the side where he had met the flames, but could not take his eyes off his mother. She was a shapeless mound of fire from which protruded two upraised arms.

His burned hand pulsed and fluttered with pain. Even before he looked at it he knew that it was blistering, turning red.

His father started to laugh behind him, and Tabby whirled around, bracing himself to see Billy Bentley. But it was his father, dressed in the gray suit, holding a tumbler full of Irish whiskey. When Clark splashed some of the glass's contents on the floor, little fingers of fire snatched the whiskey away as soon as it struck.

"Ain't this lovely?" Clark said. "All of us together again for the very last time—and on television, too!" Clark staggered to one side, wiped the sweat from his face. He was grinning like a dog, mindlessly. "Upstairs, your mother said—you heard her, kiddo. You get on up there and get ready for dinner."

Fibers on the left sleeve of his jacket had begun to smoke and darken.

Within the twitching mound of fire that had consumed Jean Smithfield, a form Tabby had seen twice before was struggling to be born—stretching itself, finding its wings. Heat roared around Tabby's head.

"A whole plate of fire," Clark said reflectively. "That was it, wasn't it? 'A whole plate of fire.' I can remember you saying that so many times. Right here in this kitchen."

Richard: this was about Richard Allbee, not him. The Dragon was telling him that Richard too was going to die tonight; the Dragon wanted him to know that.

"I'll help you get upstairs, Spunky," his father said, faltering toward him. Tabby moved another step away from the hottest part of the room and glanced again at the yawning blaze in the middle of the kitchen floor. Almost, he could see the head with its wide empty eyes—eyes filled with night—rising up. Then another movement took his attention, and he looked across the stretching flames and saw Billy Bentley leaning against a blazing wall, gently smiling at him from the depths of his pitted face. Billy uncrossed his arms, brought down a hand, and produced an extended middle finger like a rabbit from a hat.

"We gotta get going," Clark said uneasily. "Time . . . there isn't much time . . ."

Tabby was retreating, not knowing where he was going but wanting only to get away from the almost solid-looking moving pyre in the middle of the kitchen. He felt his eyebrows crisping, the small hairs in his nose threatening to burn. Billy Bentley was still giving him the finger while leaning on a burning wall.

"Is this the end of the series?" Clark asked, blinking. Billy's mouth opened in a noiseless shout of laughter.

He was going to die. The house was burning, and he and his father were so trapped in this hallucination about *Daddy's Here* that they could not even find the way out. Tabby backed farther away, now seeing the head of the fire-bat lift out of the pyre, scanning toward him with its empty eye-holes. Once the fire-bat saw him, he would die—the whole kitchen, the whole house, would explode like the Death Star in *Star Wars*.

"Hey, kid," Clark asked. "What the shit happened to Berkeley? Jesus, why's this damn drink so hot?"

"Dad," Tabby said. "Get out! Out of the house!"

The head of the fire-bat turned hungrily toward Clark; one great wing crackled out of the flames and unfurled across the width of the kitchen, slamming his father into the sink and instantly covering him in flame. Tabby saw Clark's drink ignite; then saw his clothes fly off his body. His father screeched in agony as his skin began to fry.

"Noooo!" Tabby shouted, helplessly seeing his father die.

Another huge wing crackled out of the flames.

With a hopeless desperation, Tabby whirled around, sobbing, and ran away from the heat—he did not know where he was going in the real house that lay concealed beneath this vision of the house from *Daddy's Here,* but the temperature of the air told him where the fires were weakest.

His fingers touched a hot wall. He heard the crackling of enormous wings behind him. He slid his fingers along the wall, hoping that he was wrong and knowing that he was not.

A wooden molding slipped beneath his moving fingers. He found the edge of a door and tore at it, scarcely believing that it was there—cool air rushed up at him, and he threw himself through the opening.

A searing line stroked across his back, as if he had been grazed by a flaming sword, and he was falling into darkness, out of control, his head and arms and back thumping, cracking against hard wood . . . he rolled over and struck the bottom. His face was wet, cold. He thought he was bleeding: his head throbbed in a dozen places where he had struck it, and his lip was swelling. The air seemed frigid. He opened his eyes cautiously and saw only darkness.

Gradually he realized that he was in the cellar. The wetness on his face was perspiration, not blood—the cellar felt like an icebox after the intense heat of the house. He pushed himself back from the foot of the stairs, afraid that the thing upstairs would send flames shooting down after him. His legs and arms complained, but moved: he had not broken anything in his tumble down the stairs. Tabby made himself stand; for a moment he simply stood, waving his burned hand gently in the air, breathing slowly. He walked backward into a wall and propped himself against it. He *felt* more than knew that he was crying.

Tabby walked himself along the wall, keeping his shoulders against the concrete block, moving into the area of greatest darkness. From the floor above him came noises of war and tumult—he could hear the fire gaining strength, claiming more and more of the house. And in the midst of that noise, he heard an undercurrent of voices calling out an indistinguishable sound that must have been his name.

He inhaled and held the breath, trying to stop his pointless crying. He wiped his face with his undamaged hand.

Tabby moved as far from the staircase as he could get.

A single voice called out, "Come up here, son." It was his father's voice. Tabby saw Clark jigging down on the lawn, kicking the life out of Berkeley.

"Get up here. *Now.*"

Tabby turned around and pressed his bruised face into the hard cool concrete block. It was gritty, and sent needles into his skin. Tabby hugged this uncomfortable wall, shaking.

A roaring entered the cellar, and a cloud of heat—Tabby turned his head away, but not before he had seen a wall of fire come blasting down the stairs. He flattened himself against the wall.

He heard the fire take the staircase and begin sucking at the ground.

Tabby looked up and saw the burning earth reflected in one of the little cellar windows.

2

Nine hours earlier, Graham Williams had been glaring in exasperation at a young man in a red-striped shirt, bow tie, and blue blazer who was seated at an antique desk in an elegant bow-fronted Georgian building on the Old Post Road in Hillhaven. The building housed the Hampstead-Patchin Historical Society, and the young man—the only person in the building apart from Graham—was one of the graduate students on its staff. Though momentarily flustered, the young man seemed utterly at home in the Historical Society, and this was a part of Graham's annoyance—this squirt acted like he'd been born back in the reference stacks.

"You have more problems than you know, kid," Graham said, shoving his hands deep into the pockets of his baggy trousers and hunching over even farther than usually to nail the boy to his leather chair with a scowl. "Forget about this new so-called rule you just invented. Forget—"

"I *told* you. The director insisted on it. We can't allow the public back into the stacks anymore. We had too many problems this summer—you wouldn't begin to believe some of the—"

"And don't interrupt me, buster. You have a *real* problem,

if you call yourself a historian. You're ignorant. You never even heard of the Black Summer. One of the most crucial periods in the history of this region, and to you it's only a blank page.''

The boy sighed, leaned sideways in his opulent chair, as if he wanted to get out from under Graham's gaze. "I'm in European History. You're talking about regional interest here—I don't feel you're qualified to attack me as a historian anyhow—''

"I've *seen* more history than you've read about!''

"Mr. Williams. We're not getting anywhere. I have in fact heard of the so-called Black Summer, though it is true that I'm not really up on what happened then, and if you would be seated at one of the tables, I'll go back into the stacks and dig up everything that seems even faintly relevant to it. Is that good enough for you?''

"I'll settle for it, but the answer is no.'' Williams took a step backward and ceased trying to murder the boy with black looks.

"Now we're getting somewhere.'' The boy stood up, buttoning his blazer. He looked smug, a little prissy to Graham; he made his way around the desk with an almost invisible smile of self-congratulation on his lips. "If you'll seat yourself in the reading room, Mr. Williams . . . ?''

Graham scowled at him again. "You've heard of it, you say. What have you heard?''

The boy tossed his head. "I'll try to remember when I'm getting your books from the stacks.''

Graham turned his back on him, disgusted, and stalked out of the mahogany-paneled anteroom into the much larger area the Historical Society had filled with long library tables. Framed maps and portraits of both men and houses lined the walls; cases against the walls held bound manuscripts and books of drawings and sketches. Graham dropped his pens and pads of paper on one of the front tables as noisily as possible. Then he shoved his hands back in his pockets and made a rapid tour of the paintings, all of which he had seen many times before. He ended before a hand-painted map of the Hampstead-Patchin seacoast; marshes and wetlands had been sketched in, an Indian raised a bow at the site of a massacre in 1645, a redcoat soldier stood at attention on Kendall Point. The mapmaker, who had made wildly inaccurate guesses about the shape of the coastline and the distances between his various landmarks, had inked in the date on the bottom-right-hand corner: 1803. Graham had often wished that he could meet the anonymous mapmaker: could suggest that he wait another eight years before finishing his work. If he'd drawn the map in 1811, Graham was sure that he'd have had a more interesting image to place on Kendall Point.

"Mr. Williams? Mr. Williams?"

Graham turned sharply, almost jerkily away from both the hand-painted map and his preoccupations. The young man was standing before a mound of books and papers; he looked even more pleased with himself than he had before.

"I found quite a lot of material," he said. "You've got copies of the New Haven papers and broadsides for the summer months of 1873, copies of the Patchin newspaper, all the books I thought might even be a tiny bit helpful—and I remembered that other thing I mentioned." With his index finger he pushed forward on the table a slim book in a gray library binding. "Ever heard of Stephen Pollock?"

Graham impatiently shook his head.

"Pollock is supposed to have influenced Washington Irving. Anyhow, Pollock wrote a book called *Curious Voyages* —a travel book. And that's what I thought of earlier. He was in Connecticut in 1873, and he took a coach from New York to New Haven." He smiled brilliantly; pointed to the front door with a gold ball-point. "Which means that he passed this house. He was on the Old Post Road."

Graham put the Pollock book aside, intending to look at it later, and spent several hours looking through the mimeographed newspapers from the summer of 1873. What was most startling, he thought, was the deadly indifference—the calm—into which the Black Summer had fallen. Now and then there was a reference to the change in the coach schedules, or the shipping patterns; and in the Patchin newspaper he caught a jocular reference to the sudden prosperity of the area's undertakers, the profusion of coins in the gravediggers' pockets. What was most startling was that no one had seemed startled—half a town had died, and in the neighboring towns people shut their eyes and made jokes about rich gravediggers. They had spent years pretending that Hampstead no longer existed.

Still not picking up the Pollock book, Graham sent the graduate student back into the stacks for information about the burning of Patchin in 1779—he wanted to let his mind play over various events of the thirty-year cycle. Tryon landing at Kendall Point: the English and the Jaeger mercenaries swarming up over that wooded, stony land: in a violent storm, putting houses and farms to the torch.

The soldiers had trampled across Gideon Winter's grave to sack the town.

Kendall Point. Sometimes Kendall Point seemed to reach out toward Hampstead, to grasp at it . . . as though it fed on the town.

A chill went over Graham's body, and he saw himself as he was, a bent old man, no longer very strong—the strongest part of him now was his voice. And this was what he proposed to set against Kendall Point and Gideon Winter; because of ideas he had been chasing for fifty years; because once he had fought a madman on a boat and imagined that he had been fighting even more.

How long had it been since he had seen Kendall Point? Graham realized that he had not been out there since he had begun looking into Hampstead's history—in those days, still really a boy, he had gone out for a look at the place. He had seen . . . nothing. He had looked at trees, rocks, the water. He had walked down into the ravine left behind by the events of 1811; and there too he had looked at boulders, exposed earth, caverns washed out by erosion, tough ropy weeds crawling over all; nothing. He had looked but not seen. He had been thinking about Tryon's soldiers and how they had landed; he had not paid enough attention to the Point itself, to the heart of what was all about him.

Almost without realizing he was doing it, Graham pushed himself back from the long table and stood up. Still he could feel traces of his goosebumps scattered across his back and down his arms.

He turned to the painted map. In its light wooden frame, it had a decorative, pastel look, like something found in the room of a small child. Graham walked toward this innocent, inaccurate map.

Where Greenbank was, the mapmaker had drawn two little farms and sketched in extensive marshland. Graham stared moodily at these for a moment, then looked once again at Kendall Point.

It was larger, more bloated than in reality. The redcoat stood at attention in the middle of this distorted Point, his musket propped on his shoulder. Graham squinted and leaned closer to the framed map: he had never really looked carefully at the face of the little redcoat.

Then he was frozen there, bending over with his own face only inches from the glass covering the map, because he had seen the little figure move. The redcoat was lowering his musket, spreading his legs.

The little figure's mouth split open in a wide grin: He was not a drawing anymore, he was antic and alive, and he was unshouldering his gun. Graham was dimly aware, in the midst of his astonishment, that the lines on the map were flying about, making jagged patterns around the little figure. The redcoat winked at Graham, raised the gun and sighted down the barrel. When he pulled the trigger Graham heard a *pop!* like the explosion of a small balloon.

In the next second a tiny starburst appeared in the glass covering the map.

Graham jumped back, fearing for a second that he'd been struck by the ball. Then he saw it, embedded in the broken glass—a black metal dot, gnat-sized. A tiny flame sprang up in the middle of the redcoat's chest.

Just before the young man in the bow tie rushed into the reading room, Graham finally noticed what had happened to the lines on the map. The seacoast from New Haven to the Norrington border was the snouted, horned profile of a dragon. He groaned—feeling as if he had caught a real bullet in his intestines, a sharp twist of sudden agony.

"Mr. Williams? Anything happen?" the young man said. He'd come in such a hurry that he had left his jacket unbuttoned. Then he saw the map.

"What did you *do?*" He gaped at Graham, then back at the wall. Flames were sprouting beneath the glass, curling over the distorted depiction of Kendall Point. The figure of the redcoat had blackened and shriveled. "My God," the boy said. He ran to the map, and touched the frame to take it off the wall. Immediately he snatched his hands back, wincing. "It's burning!" he said, still stunned. He threw off his blazer and used it to grasp one side of the frame. The boy awkwardly wrestled the map off the wall, and the glass struck the boards. "What . . . ?" the boy said, looking wildly at Graham.

"Fire extinguisher," Graham said. "You need a fire extinguisher."

"You wait here, Mr. Williams," the boy said. "I mean it. You just wait right here."

"I think you'd better hurry," Graham said.

The boy looked in anguish at the little flames lifting up from the map, turned around, and ran out of the reading room.

Graham went nearer the map. He stepped on the flames and ground them out. In the depths of the building, the boy slammed a door. Graham went slowly to the long table and picked up his pens and notepads. He slipped Stephen Pollock's *Curious Voyages* into the stack of his papers. He was out the front door and halfway down the cobbled walk to his old car before the door deep in the building slammed again.

Breathing hard, he turned on the ignition. Just before he drove away he looked sideways at the bow windows of the Historical Society and saw the face of the young man inside shouting something at him. Graham threw the car in gear, stepped on the accelerator, and made one of the most impetuous departures of his life.

He was pointed in the direction of Patchin, away from Hampstead, and flicked on his turn signal before going around the block; but after he had turned seaward, he continued straight on Harbor Road and did not circle back toward Mount Avenue and Greenbank. He was going to Kendall Point.

Where the road ended in a sweep of gravel before a crumbled wall, Graham parked his car and went slowly across the broken surface of the asphalt to the gravel. He put a shoe on the low wall, feeling a barely suppressed excitement. It was the *tone* he had not understood before, that hectic, gleeful *tone* of the Dragon's.

Looking out at Kendall Point, Graham felt twenty years drop away from him—thirty years. He had his little pain in his chest, his right knee throbbed, and his back was giving him regular twinges, but he was on the verge of discovery: of breakthrough. He knew it. And the Dragon knew it too. Like Tabby Smithfield alone on Gravesend Beach, Graham could have shouted, "Show me!" and meant all of Tabby's defiance.

Before Graham was a leafy gorge perhaps twenty feet deep, with gentle sides and huge boulders on the bottom to make it an easy matter to cross over to the other side. Beyond the gorge was a flat grassy plain with a stand of ancient oaks and white spruce in its center; at its edges, this plain degenerated into marsh, which itself degenerated into stony beach just before the waterline. From where Graham stood, at the end of the roadway, to the farthest tip of the Point was a distance of perhaps two hundred yards.

The inhabited land reached by the end of Harbor Road—the territory behind Graham now—still looked surprisingly as it had the last time Graham Williams had come out to Kendall Point. The Depression had somehow hit this obscure corner of Hillhaven ten years early and had never left.

As Graham saw it now, the Dragon had spoiled this place. Directly beside the curved end of the road stood a white building with a concrete terrace partially visible behind a tall fence. The building had a long ground-floor window facing the Sound, and ranks of smaller windows in the upper floors—in one of these a pair of tights dried on a line, in another a Budweiser lamp flickered. Graham had always felt certain that this building was a bar, but it had no name, no sign; for that reason and because of the line of little windows, he assumed also that it was a whorehouse. It *looked* like a whorehouse; like a bad one, a place where you just might get robbed. Down the rough street going past the white building stood a half-dozen little houses—they were what Hillhaven had instead of Poor Fox Road. Just as they had a generation and a half ago, these houses seemed abandoned, leeringly empty, invitations to tragedy. Graham felt now, looking at the row of dilapidated and leering houses, that they were waiting there for their victims.

Graham stepped up onto the low wall, looked back at his car and the cluster of buildings, and then jumped the eighteen inches down into Dragon's land.

First he had to get down into the gorge, make his way across the tops of the boulders, and then go up the opposite slope onto the Point itself. The slope down to the boulders looked easy enough—if he had been a child, he would have tried to slide down on the soles of his shoes. The wild rhododendron bushes growing down the sides of the gorge now seemed almost to invite Graham to use them for handholds, or for brakes if he found himself moving too quickly.

Moving very carefully and heeling over to his right,

Graham began to inch his way sideways down the slope. The earth held solidly beneath his basketball shoes. He stuck his left arm stiffly out for balance, and went down a few more steps. Soon he would reach the rhododendrons and be able to cling to them nearly all the way to the boulders. Down a few more steps, his ankles already beginning to grumble at the way they were bent. Graham bent to the side a little more and put the fingers of his right hand against the ground, steadying himself.

His left foot found a grip six inches down the slope; his right awkwardly crossed over it and found its own place. Graham exhaled, nearly grunting: this was more work than he had expected. He dropped the left foot again, and felt moss slither under the sole of his shoe. For a moment he wobbled, almost going over, and dug his fingers into the grass: his leg slipped out from under him until the basketball shoe found a patch of bare earth and clung.

Jesus, why am I doing this? he thought, straddling three feet of sloping ground as he drove the fingers of his right hand deep into the earth, gripping roots and a pelt of grass. *Why did I come down here?* He looked back up toward the top of the gorge and saw the sky wheeling blackly over the rim, the land rearing up as dizzily as a roller-coaster track.

Graham groaned out loud. The slope he clung to was canting up like a ladder jerked suddenly perpendicular. The light had winked out. Graham was crazily conscious of the glowing dial of his radium watch—and of a wheezing, asthmatic sound he thought was the laughter of the rotting houses until he realized that it came from his chest.

His head was swinging backward, his feet forward, in sudden night. Where he had dug his fingers into the ground, the earth scalded his hand. A tubular root against his palm suddenly burned like a hot water pipe.

Graham flailed out with both hands, reaching for any support he could find, and immediately slipped five or six feet down the slope, scraping his belly and his face against rough stones. Then it was as if a rhododendron had twined its stalks around his hands, voluntarily stopping him from sliding onto the boulders. Graham gripped at the bush, felt it accept his hands and then find his legs. For a moment he was secure.

"Help me!" he called out, thinking that one of the girls from the bar might hear him. *"Help me!"*

He knew, and wished he did not, that the girls in that place would have heard and ignored many strange cries from Kendall Point. *"Helllp! Helll . . ."*

The bush or the steep hill, or both, flexed and threw him off. He felt the muscles of the earth contract, the twigs and leaves of the bush he clung to coil into themselves and *bulge* monstrously, and after that he felt only air rushing away from him and his stomach falling faster than he was.

After he struck the boulders he felt nothing.

A long time after, Graham opened his eyes onto a red immensity of pain. He moaned, licked his lips, moved his legs. All of him hurt so thoroughly, so comprehensively, that he was not aware of any special injuries: he himself was the injury. Yet after a few minutes, individual reports began to come in: his head was muffled in an enormous ache, and his right cheek had grown out to twice its size; his right arm sang out with pain when he tried to raise it. His hips sent up messages of drowsiness and confusion.

He blinked twice rapidly, then twice more. He raised his left hand carefully and explored his face; wiped at his eyes. Above him the world was again taking shape, reforming itself out of the redness.

The rim of the gorge lay like a black line beneath the sky's starry and dark blue. Graham did not at first remember why he was outdoors, and he puzzled over the odd vertical landscape before him. He could remember staring at the map in the Historical Society . . . after that, all descended into a rushing blackness.

He remembered a starburst exploding across the surface of a pane of glass. What had caused that?

Graham used his left arm to prop himself upright. The world went red again and swung around him in big dizzying orbits. He moved his right arm, and the elbow reacted as though he had been kicked there. Hissing with pain, Graham opened his eyes again and saw how close he was to the top of the gorge.

The agony in his elbow ceased as he cupped it in his left hand. Graham thought he was ready to move. He carefully lowered his right arm and put his left hand flat against the smooth surface of the boulder so that he could help himself stand. His hips agonized, but he thought he had just bruised a bone or jarred the ligaments—in fact, at this moment Graham was congratulating himself on having survived his fall with so little real injury. Looking at the slope now, he could see dark scars which were the marks torn by his shoes as he stepped down—they ended about twelve feet from the boulders, and halfway between the last mark and the rock was a patch from which the moss and grass had been erased, rubbed away. Graham's hip, its track. He was very lucky to be alive, luckier still to be whole. He tried to persuade his legs to get under him.

His hand came down into a puddle of something sticky and wet, and Graham glanced at it more in curiosity than surprise. It was black—in the starlight it looked black. Graham did not identify this fluid as blood until he smelled it, and then he gently shook his head, wondering if the wound on the side of his face were worse than he had thought.

He swept his hand to one side, confused, and touched another body that had been lying beside his. It was smaller than an adult body. Graham groaned again and this time forced himself to his feet. Then he tottered around the perimeter of the boulder so that he could see the face. He bent forward on his painful hips. His heart and gut contorted; the face was Tabby's.

Tabby's neck had been sliced open, so savagely the boy had nearly been decapitated. He had been killed up on the rim of the gorge and then his body thrown down beside Graham: the body had the boneless ease of a discarded toy.

"Oh, God," Graham said. "Oh, dear God." He had begun to cry, and unthinkingly he lifted his right hand toward his nose—the elbow screamed. Graham inhaled sharply, gripped his right wrist with his left hand, and supported the right arm atop the left while he scrubbed his nose with his sleeve. "Oh, dear God," he repeated, and fresh tears jumped to his eyes. "Tabby."

Tabby opened his eyes and froze Graham to his foot of rock. "I'm dead. I'm dead, and it's your fault."

Graham almost fell off the boulder. Tabby's face was merciless.

"You should be dead, not me," Tabby said. "He wants you to know that."

In Tabby's eyes the old man could see the pinhead dots of light which were the stars.

"He killed me—he killed me because of your meddling— he killed me because you took us to that marker and read us his name—*God damn* you! *Damn* you!" The boy's head lolled back against the rock, blood drooled from the ragged second mouth. *"You asked for this, and I damn your soul to hell!"*

"Tabby," Graham began, "if you are Tabby, you know I would never—"

The boy's head rolled back again. "You know what happened in the Black Summer, don't you? Don't you? *Don't you?"*

Graham shook his head. "Not everything. Tabby—"

"You don't—you don't know anything. Because *this* is what happened. *This."* The head rolled to the side, fixing Graham with a look of idiot glee. "Me. I'm what happened. Me. This isn't even what I look like now—you don't know that either. You wanna see? You wanna see what I'm like now? You might as well know what you're looking for."

"Looking for?"

"'Four Hearths' is just one hearth now, Graham." The drooling mouth split with laughter and then the whole body instantly shrank, blackening, to a dwarfish mummy. The dry little husk whispered on the flat surface of the rock. Ashy sections crumbled off.

Graham looked in horror at the blackened remains of Tabby's body. Shaking, he bent forward, no longer noticing the agonies in his elbow and hips, and laid his fingertips on the black crust. As soon as he touched it, the little husk cracked into uncountable pieces—gray dust rose up, lighter than air, from the fractures. The thousands of shreds of ash on the surface of the boulder stirred, broke into particles the size of houseflies, spun crazily apart.

Still trembling, Graham painfully straightened himself. For a second the world turned red again and canted up like the deck of a boat at sea—he was gripping his right elbow, his face locked in an old man's Mayan grimace. Tabby was dead. "Four Hearths" had burned down and Tabby had been killed there. The Dragon had turned lovely Tabby into a thing like a blackened cocoon. Holding his flaring elbow close in to his ribs, Graham wept for Tabby—for his own weakness too.

Finally he wandered off the boulder's flat top back onto the slope of the gorge. Damn you, Tabby had said to him through his blood-spattered mouth. I damn your soul to hell. Graham's tired feet found themselves moving sideways up the mossy slope: through wet eyes, he saw where he had torn the side out of a bush. I damn your soul to hell. Damn you. When he pulled himself over the top of the little gorge, the lights of the bar's windows struck his eyes like needles. Behind the glass, men and women, damned too, filtered back and forth through an underwater light. Fish in a bowl, Graham thought, fish in a barrel. He fell once on the way to his car.

3

Three days earlier, Richard Allbee had begun walking to the job up in Hillhaven again. John Roehm, who knew nothing of what had happened on Richard's last walk, had been unsubtly encouraging him to leave his car at home—Roehm evidently believed that when you were thrown off a horse, you got right back on again. "Best exercise in the world," Roehm said as sawdust flew from the ripsaw into his beard and fell like golden dandruff to his red shirt. "You'll stay healthy all your life, long as you walk a couple miles a day." Richard had given in—and maybe surrender was best, for despite his fears the walks had gone uneventfully.

John Roehm's benign bearded smile of total approval greeted him on the first two mornings like a reward. On the third day—the day of the fire at "Four Hearths"—the smile was there, but Richard was less sure of the wisdom of applying horse-training metaphors to Patchin County.

He had been approaching the point on his walk where trouble always seemed most imminent, where that emotional disaster he feared blew trumpets and bugles at him as soon as he drew near—it was the section of Mount Avenue that traveled from one stone gate to the other, thirty yards down, of Tabby's childhood house. Walking past that gray mansion, Richard pulled back his shoulders and increased his pace, he sweated out the distance, wanting only to make it well past the other end of the drive.

On the day that "Four Hearths" would burn to the ground and kill everybody inside, Richard Allbee had gone no more than half the distance between the two stone gates when he saw that he would again have welcomed the sight of feverish little Charles Daisy. A woman in a long dress he remembered stepped out from behind a tree and waited for him. Her feet were bare and pale in the dark myrtle which grew between the iron fenceposts and the road. The woman was Laura. As soon as he had seen her, she began coming toward him.

Sweat burst from him and instantly soaked his shirt. He clutched the handle of his briefcase, clamped the rolled plans more firmly under his arm, and as firmly kept his eyes on the surface of the road before him. Pebbles, cracks in the asphalt, a pigeon feather ragged as an old toothbrush, loomed up as if magnified, and disappeared when he stepped over them.

She wanted him to look at her, but he would not, could not. His body would not let him see how badly hers had been treated.

He *felt* her pleading, and shook his head. If he saw her mangled and destroyed—saw her once again—that was the end of him. She would have him, then. He heard her feet whispering through the rubbery myrtle. Her silence was worse than speech would have been—he heard also how the dress slid across her hips, brushed against the little plants. He squinted, ground his teeth, plunged ahead.

He passed the second gate—the other end of the long drive up to Monty Smithfield's former house—and groaned out loud when Laura's specter did not disappear. Still he would not look at her. The myrtle had ended, and Laura's feet were moving over gravel, causing a sound like rolled dice.

She did not leave him until he reached the bend in the road just before the long white stretch of Hillhaven's beach. No children there now—parents were terrified of letting their children get near the water—but a few intrepid women in bikinis lay on the sand, reading the summer's novels and deepening their tans. Richard's eyes were nearly closed: he was squinting so that he could see as little as possible without walking in front of an oncoming car. He sensed, then saw the approach of the beach through his filmy eyes; then he knew that she was gone. All he heard was the water slapping itself into the mild froth that hissed into the shingle; he registered her subtraction from his side as a sudden push of warm air against his ribs.

At the job, John Roehm took one look at him and left him alone all morning—a sacrifice of self, for the old man loved to talk. Richard knew that he was getting ready to put boiled linseed oil on some of the new flooring they had cut into the dining room, and that he wanted to hem and haw about the amount of coloring to use in the oil. John Roehm could cook up a good thirty minutes of ideas about such a topic. But Richard conferred with the client, who appeared to notice nothing wrong or unusual about him, marked up his plans some more, and did two hours' lonely work on the roof trying to shape up a cornice. Still he bit down hard on nothing; in his inner ear he kept hearing bare feet whisper through tough green myrtle.

Laura returned for Richard while unconscious Graham Williams stirred on a flat boulder; while Tabby Smithfield flattened himself against the cellar wall and tried to shut out the voice, his father's, which came from a being not his father. She came at night, and Richard was almost prepared for her.

He had gone to bed early, promising himself that he would walk up Mount Avenue the next day, and the day after that, and every day until Laura stopped appearing. He would not even cross the street: he would do just as he had done, walk blindly on, refusing to look at or speak to her. Richard opened the book he had been reading, *The Woman in White*, and tried to lose himself in the plight of Marian Halcombe. The print kept receding away from him, and more than once he read the same paragraph without noticing: Richard had assumed that he would have difficulty falling asleep, as he usually did these days, and the assumption kept him from realizing that he was in fact already drowsing. For a time he struggled with Wilkie Collins' prose so stubbornly that he twice picked up the book after it had fallen from his hands. The third time the book dropped onto his chest he put the marker between the pages and placed the novel on the bedside table. Just as he did so, he realized that he had not only assumed that he would be awake most of the night, he had wanted to be awake; wakefulness felt like protection. Once the thought became conscious, it was foolish. Richard turned off his light and slid down between his sheets. The house was dark.

A moment later the lights in the hallway went on and spilled brightness into the room. Richard's heart gave a great startled thud. He sat up and saw the open doorway, the hall filled with light, and the door to the nursery, also wide open. That door had been closed since the last policeman walked out of the house. Richard had not wanted to enter the nursery ever again. If he'd found the key, he would have locked the nursery and kept it locked. "Who's there?" he called out, hoping that the old wiring had blundered into itself and caused the light to switch on. "Who's out there?"

Laura stepped through the nursery doorway and into the

bright hall. For a moment she stood outside Richard's room, perfectly still. Her face and chest were streaked with blood, blood had clotted her hair; below the thorax she was an open wound. This time he had to look. He did not dare to take his eyes off her. She wanted him to know, or the Dragon wanted him to know, what had happened to her.

He looked at the mutilated body of his wife and eased himself out of the bed. The Dragon had sent her; or she herself was the Dragon. He remembered that night after the Mc-Clouds' awful dinner party, when he and Laura had undressed together and made love in their rented house. Waterbed love, potbellied-stove love. She had looked totemic, wholly beautiful to him. *I don't want to lose you, Richard.* He was shaking, whether with fear, disgust, or rage, he could not tell. Instead, he had lost her.

Laura stepped nearer, and Richard backed away toward the bathroom, keeping the bed between himself and Laura. She slowly stepped out of the light into the darkness of the bedroom—for a long moment she was only a shadow, a Laura-shaped outline against the light, and Richard almost melted onto the floor: his wife had come back. Then he was assailed by those odors another specter, Billy Bentley, had pushed toward him from an elevator in a Providence hotel: rot, sewage, evil swamp gases, feces, death.

"Get out of here," he said.

She moved toward him, circling down toward the foot of the bed. Her eyes gleamed whitely. The wound in her belly flapped like a shirttail.

"You're not Laura," he said.

The end of her mouth lifted in a taunting half-smile.

"Are you going to try to kill me?" he said. "Fine, kill me. I can't take this anymore. I went crazy when you died. Do you think I want to live here all by myself?"

She passed through a stark vertical shadow, and when she emerged again into the light from the hallway her skin was whole. The blood and wounds had gone—as if Richard's memories had created her fresh. Now she was his wife again, stepping nearer and nearer through the dim light.

His breath caught in his throat; his skin tingled, suddenly cold.

Laura stepped right up before him, still with the half-smile playing on her mouth. She reached out to him, and he stepped backward—her fingers just grazed his bare chest.

His skin raised and blistered where she had touched him. The pain sank into him like knives—Laura or not, she was real enough to kill him. Smiling, she came forward again, reaching out.

"No," he said, moving backward toward the bathroom door. "Go away. I can't fight you."

She forced him into the bathroom, and he continued backing away. The whites of her eyes shone in the darkness of the bathroom, and Richard's skin moved in revulsion.

He could back out of the hall entrance to the bathroom, he was not cornered; all of the house was available to him. Laura crept nearer, and he jumped back, feeling behind him for the knob of the hallway door.

"Go," he said. "Get out of here."

She crept nearer, and his hand found the knob. He jerked the door open behind him and walked backward out into the hall.

Here the light above the staircase, the light which had announced Laura's presence, cast everything into banality— they were not in the chiaroscuro of the bedroom, but at the top of the main staircase. In real light. And his naked wife was coming playfully for him out of the bathroom door, real light falling on her real flesh and catching in her hair. She was smiling a typical Laura-smile. Richard backed slowly away from her, touching the top of the banister. Here in the light, Laura's presence seemed almost ordinary. She tilted her head, then made a playful little darting movement toward him, and he jerked back.

They stood unmoving at the top of the staircase for a moment. Richard knew that she meant to kill him, and here in this banal everyday light it seemed impossible that he should ever have been willing to die. She was a creature of the Dragon, not Laura. Laura had belonged to the world of affections and friendships and work. This thing before him, so perfect, was a betrayal of her.

Richard, who knew every inch of his new house, knew that one of the pickets supporting the banister was like a loose tooth—twenty times he had jiggled the picket, promising himself he would get around to fixing it. Watching Laura very carefully, Richard took another step backward and reached sideways and down: his hand fell on sculptured wood that rattled in its socket at his touch. He pulled as hard as he could, and the picket splintered away from the single nail holding it. Even before the two-foot-long piece of wood was securely in his hand, Laura was rushing at him.

He had time only to try to jump out of the way and club at her. She groped for him, but he moved sideways, bringing down the picket. It struck her smooth shoulder and knocked her into the banister: where it had touched her skin, it darkened and released a wisp of smoke.

Laura straightened herself, then deliberately touched the top of the banister with her forefinger. An orange flame the size of a match sprouted on the molded banister, blistering the layers of paint. Richard remembered how that touch had felt, carving into him. The little flame guttered out. Laura dashed at him, and again he swung hard at her, connecting with one of her arms. A tiny flame shot up on the picket, disappeared when Richard swung his weapon around in the air.

That terrible odor of rot and death boomed toward him again. He saw that where Laura's feet had trod, the carpet had blackened and scorched. She charged at him again, driving him backward through the open nursery door.

As she entered, he swung at her head and she raised her arms too late to deflect the blow. The impact knocked her sideways; she sprawled onto the hardwood of the nursery floor, blackening the varnish. Richard jumped forward and brought his club down again, smashing her forehead. What he was doing seemed almost geometric to him, a series of steps he had to go through cleanly, in perfect order and without emotion. Long bruises were already appearing on Laura's skin; her right arm dangled. He chopped down at the head again, and she reached out and grasped his ankle with her left hand.

Searing pain knocked him down. She was grinning at him, and an alligator had closed its teeth on his ankle. In a rage now, Richard drove the ragged end of the picket into her face. The picket jumped into flame, and she released his ankle.

Richard got on his knees and battered at her as she tried to crawl toward him.

Then something happened that he did not understand, was not even sure had actually happened, until Graham Williams talked to them all late that night. The picket, now burning like a torch, seemed to tremble in his hands—it seemed living. He smashed it down on the Laura-thing's head, and for a moment it seemed lit from within, golden. He raised it and battered down again, and it quivered in his hands like a bird. *"You're not Laura,"* he breathed, and smashed once again at her head. She had ceased to move. He pushed himself across the floor away from her.

A film of blue flame ran lightly across the naked body on the hardwood floor, flickering lightly across the splayed legs. Richard sat up and watched the flames feed upon each other, redden and grow. He had not been geometric, he had beaten this thing into defeat in the same room where his wife had been murdered, and now he was drained by his feelings of rage and triumph.

A shape stirred and expanded within the fire over Laura's body: before it became definite, Laura rolled up *into* the flames and was consumed. Then the flames concentrated, and Richard saw big wings flicker out of the center of the fire—he drew back from the suddenly intensified heat, and a bat made of flame lifted from the charred floor.

Heat rolled over Richard, rolled into him, and the force of it pushed him back into the wall—as if a giant hand had given him a shove. For a moment the entire room shimmered—blue lines of fire chasing wildly over the floor and walls—and then the window exploded outward, and the flexing fire-bat exploded out with it.

Richard peeled himself away from the wall. His face felt sore and dry—sunburned. The nursery was full of drifting ash and the smell of frying wood. On the floor was a large charred circle on the perimeter of which lay his picket, or what was left of it. The stub of the picket was black too, and glints of red rose and died along its length. Richard managed to stand. He went slowly across the blackened floor to the hole where the window had been. A furious, raging fire rode on its own wings into the black sky. When he looked down, he saw Tabby Smithfield standing down there on his front lawn, staring up at him with a face like a white smudge.

"And I looked down," Tabby told him in a shaking voice, "and I saw a lead pipe—just lying on the floor of the cellar. So . . . so I picked it up and smashed the window, just smashed it . . . and then there was some old stuff in there, trunks and stuff from my grandfather, and I piled it together and climbed up on it. And then I climbed out of the window. I cut myself, but not too bad. Anyhow, I got outside . . . I saw my house burn right up—it was like one big sheet of flames, the whole house . . . and I knew my father was dead. So I ran over here."

"And you saw the fire-bat. That's what you call it?"

Tabby nodded.

"Where have you seen it before?"

"One night when I was on the beach—that night all those houses on Mill Lane burned down. And all those firemen were killed."

"Jesus," Richard said.

"And in my house—tonight. But it was like I was in the *Daddy's Here* house."

"Oh, my God," Richard said, remembering the nightmare from his earliest days in Hampstead. "Billy Bentley."

"He was there. Shouldn't we call Mr. Williams and Patsy? Don't you think we ought to see if they're all right?"

Richard did not want to tell the boy that he had already tried to call Graham and Patsy; while Tabby had been washing his face in the downstairs bathroom, Richard had dialed both their numbers. Neither Graham nor Patsy had been in. He said, "Look, it's almost eleven at night. Graham'll be in bed, sound asleep. Patsy too, probably. We'll try to call them in the morning. In the meantime, I guess this is your home now, if that's all right with you. I wouldn't mind the company."

Tabby had pushed himself deeply into Richard's guest bed, and now he rolled over and locked his face into the pillow. His shoulders were trembling; Richard, too tired to be perceptive, finally understood that the boy was crying. He patted Tabby's back and sat with him for some minutes. Finally he said, "Your father and my wife. I suppose we could be sorry for each other, instead of being sorry for ourselves. You want to try that?" Tabby nodded into the pillow. Richard stroked his back and said, "Besides that, you need someone like me and I need someone like you. Tomorrow we'll go get you some clothes and anything else you need. Okay?" Still crying, Tabby nodded into the pillow again—he did not want Richard to see his face. "I'm going to bed," Richard said. "My room is right down the hall, in case you need anything."

Richard did not think he could sleep—he was exhausted, but his inner pulse raced. He lay in his own bed with all the lights off, trying to calm that inner engine that chugged and chugged, wanting him to get dressed and go out to search for Graham and Patsy—he would have, if he'd had a single clue as to where they were. He and Tabby had escaped the Dragon; could Patsy and Graham do the same? Interspersed with his anxious thoughts about the other two were worries about the boy now sleeping down the hall—part of Richard knew already that he wanted Tabby Smithfield permanently in his life, but would the boy accept him as substitute father? And could he really *be* a substitute father? Wouldn't Tabby resent any attempts to replace his true father? And wouldn't he have relatives—family—whose proper role it would be to raise him? But when Richard Allbee thought of Tabby Smithfield's family, he saw himself and Patsy McCloud and Graham Williams. And where were they now? Did the fire-bat visit them too? Were they alive? In the midst of these spinning circles, Richard fell asleep. And was instantly dreaming. . . .

He was carrying a huge heavy sword in his hands—so large that he had to support it across his forearms, so heavy that all the muscles in his arms were shrieking. But he could not stop, he could not rest. Around him was the pure, the primal Bad Place: a dank countryside of craters and leafless trees, of burned farmhouses and stinking pools. Richard trudged forward, his arms shaking with pain, toward a flat yellow horizon. When it was time, and when he had reached the right place, he stopped. Now the burned farmhouses were far behind him; on the surface of the gray tarn some twenty feet before him smoke or fog corkscrewed up. He planted his feet on the damp ground. In his arms the sword was becoming lighter; had begun to glow. He grasped the handle with both hands and lifted the sword as high as he could in the air. Then—already bringing it down—he saw that Laura lay on the ground directly before him. Richard screamed, but he could not stop the descent of the sword: it cleaved through Laura's body and bit into the earth. From both wounds, a fountain of blood erupted, drenching all the landscape and instantly soaking him. Richard moaned, opened his eyes and expected to see a red world—instead he saw Tabby's face, so worried it was pinched far down into itself.

"It's Patsy," Tabby said. "She's going to die."

4

Patsy, lonely, had tried to call Graham Williams; when Graham had not answered, she dialed the first four digits of Richard's telephone number, and then hesitated—she was not sure she could trust herself around Richard Allbee. Especially this late in the evening, and especially in this mood. Patsy had been feeling restless, indeed almost reckless, most of the day; and she'd had very little to do except read and watch television. She had found a copy of one of Graham's books, *Twisted Hearts,* at Books 'n Bobs, and was halfway through it, but she did not want to gulp it down—it was too good for that, Patsy thought. She was a little surprised at how much she liked Graham's novel. But she did not feel like reading now; and television offered only the usual popcorn. She would have liked to spend several hours with Richard, just seeing what would happen if they were alone in the same room. But Richard, she knew, would never begin anything with her—he was out of practice, he had been married too long. He was unsure of himself. And Patsy was unsure that she could initiate anything with Richard, or indeed that it would be right to do so. Richard was still deeply in mourning, his emotions were scrambled. If she began anything with him, he would make too much of it—it would touch him too deeply. And wouldn't it seem too pat, almost cornball in fact—the widow and the widower? That was unaesthetic. Patsy gently put down the receiver. She could always take a bath. If she still felt this way tomorrow, she would go out and spend too much money on clothes. When she pulled out her credit card, only she would know how virtuous she was being.

She got about six paces away from the phone when she decided that she would call Richard anyhow—she didn't need a bath, and she didn't like shopping. Patsy turned around, and that was when her telephone rang. She would have bet a hundred dollars that the person on the other end of the line was Richard Allbee.

But she would have lost her bet: the caller said, "Patsy, I'm really glad you're home. This is Graham."

"I just called you!" she cried. "You're not there!"

"I just got back. Patsy, I've discovered something, and it

could be the clue to everything—I think I know where he is, Patsy. And who he is.''

"Tell me," she said. "Can you tell me over the phone?"

"Not now," Graham's voice said. "Trust me, Patsy, there's a reason. I want you to meet me someplace."

"Well sure, okay," she said, pleased and a little flattered. "You name it."

"Do you know Poor Fox Road? In Greenbank?"

"I never heard of it," Patsy said.

"It's a little obscure, but it's . . ."

"Oh. I know. It's where that Fritz man was killed. I remember. The gardener."

"Can you find it? It's just across Mount Avenue from the entrance to Gravesend Beach. You have to look hard to see it—it's not marked. It looks more like a driveway than a town road."

"I think I've seen it," Patsy said.

"Well, there are three or four houses down the end of that road. They're all vacant now. I want you to meet me at the little brown clapboard place next to the house with all the junked cars on the lot."

"Doesn't it have a number?"

"No number, but you can't miss it. Brown clapboard. Sagging roof. Just look for the place you'd choose if you wanted to store your shrunken-head collection. Just go inside. If I'm not there, I'll be along in a second. I have to get some things together—some things I want you to see."

"Brown clapboard, sagging roof, shrunken-head collection. You seem very excited, Graham."

"You'll see why. I'll see you on Poor Fox Road as soon as I can get over there." He hung up.

Patsy went straight to her bag, which was sitting open-mouthed on the kitchen counter, and began to search inside it for her car keys.

Only five or six minutes later she was pushing down her brake pedal, looking out the windshield of her car at what almost had to be Poor Fox Road.

Her headlights illuminated a narrow track over which the overgrown trees and tall bamboolike marsh grass seemed to lean. Patsy caught a disturbing glimpse of the moon sailing up into the sky—just an image of it between two black looming maples—and did not recognize until a moment had passed that she had been disturbed because the moon had seemed too large, almost twice its normal size.

She was traveling very slowly, still not absolutely certain that she was on the right road, and when she went around the bend where Bobby Fritz had so happily met Dr. Wren Van Horne, she began to hear what sounded like the noise of working machinery—a pounding, a drumming. Patsy assumed without even really registering the thought that the Academy was the source of this sound. Then her headlights found the first of the houses; then the second, which sat in a sea of junked cars; then the third. And her heart sank.

It was brown, or something like brown, and clapboard; and the roofline noticeably sagged. Black windows gleamed at her as she drew her car up before it: but she immediately saw that she had been mistaken, the glass was broken in, long gone. The mistake seemed of a piece with the house. What had caused her despair had not been the shabbiness of the house, she had expected that; it was the atmosphere which surrounded it, of being permanently apart—selfish. She did not want to go in there. The headlights of her car brought the little building forward, emphasized its isolation and starkness. Patsy cut off her ignition and turned off her lights.

She contemplated the house. She examined the sharply defined masses which were trees, and the hulks of abandoned cars—somehow made almost beautiful by the streaming moonlight. She gazed without interest at the other houses she could see, and saw that none of these were inhabited. Poor Fox Road was a little ghost town. She looked back at the house and found that it had lost whatever particularity it had previously had. It was just another empty building. Really, there was no reason not to take a look at it—and Graham had been so excited.

Patsy opened the door of her car and stepped out. The machinery sound, that pounding as if jackhammers were at work in the center of the earth, abruptly ceased. She looked over her shoulder at the school property, startled, but saw only the mesh of the fence crowded with moonlit leaves.

In front of the house she hesitated for a moment, hoping to hear Graham's old car grinding toward her. There was no real path up to the front door anymore, only a mat of weeds. Patsy looked down the narrow track of the road again, really expecting to see Graham's headlights sweeping through the moonlight. Patsy thought for a second: *he's never going to come:* and then shook her head at her foolishness.

She went up through the thick weeds and felt the remains of the path through the soles of her shoes. "Come on, Graham," she said aloud. The house, she thought, must have been connected to whatever happened to Graham in the twenties; as she put her hand on the brass doorknob, Patsy realized that this mean crumbling house must be an important part of the story that involved all of them. Patsy decided to follow orders.

She turned the knob and pushed open the door, and a squeaking bat swooped out of the house and clamped itself over the side of her face. Too startled to scream, Patsy tried to tear the creature off her face and felt its tiny claws digging into her hair, into her cheek. Her fingers found the small furry body. The bat's high-pitched squeaks drilled into her ear. She felt its head moving, burrowing in her hair. Her eyes closed, dancing frantically back and forth, Patsy half-stumbled over a sill as she entered the house.

The door slammed shut, but in her terror Patsy hardly heard it. The bat's furry body revolted her, but not only did she have to touch it, she had to wrap her fingers about it. Slapping it with her hand had only increased the frequency of the shrill hate-filled noises echoing through her head. She could feel its tiny teeth working on her scalp. Patsy's breath came in short, rapid surges, and she heard herself begin to release an eerie un-Patsy-like wail as she worked her fingers under the body of the clutching animal. At last she thought her grip was secure enough to dislodge it—the bat's heartbeat throbbed like a bird's in her hand—and she tore it off her head.

The bat had gone sailing away as soon as it was free, and as Patsy opened her eyes, she threw out her arms and moved in an agitated circle. Her eyes told her nothing—she was in a black, flat environment. Holding her arms and hands over her head, still panting, Patsy started to move quickly across the room. That jackhammer-drumming sound seemed to envelop her, to rise up all about her. Patsy could not really see the floor at all: she was vaguely conscious that it was a pattern of darker and lighter patches, but had no time to imagine what that meant. She was now as terrorized by that overwhelming sound as by the possibility of the bat making another pass at her, and she moved straight toward the door. That sound seemed to boil out of the walls. Patsy had taken only a couple of awkward and hasty steps when it seemed that the floor rose up and slapped her down.

She landed on her side, grunting. Now she could see what had felled her—before the moonlit square of window a broken floorboard slanted up like a broken spar. Her head was only inches from the ground. Above her she was suddenly conscious of black wings, of more than one body zigzagging through space. Patsy crawled forward around the hole in the floor. The boards pitched beneath her. That pounding noise rose straight up through the floor. She scrabbled across the treacherous floor, scraping her palms on broken boards, for what should have been twice the distance to the front door. The bats whickered overhead, how many she could not tell. When her hand touched a sticky metal pipe, she cried out— she had gone deeper into the house. All her crawling had taken her farther away from the door.

Patsy used the pipe, then the metal tub above it, to lever herself to her feet. Something slimy and foul covered her hands; she felt it on her legs too. Then she saw two bats whirl past the square of window—hadn't there been *two*? *two* windows?—and shrank away just as she took in that their faces were white. The two bats swooped past her, squeaking in fury, and Patsy saw that one of the bats had flowing red hair and a woman's face.

The door just opposite her flew open, revealing a solid wall of flies that instantly dissolved into a million buzzing particles. They instantly covered her, fell on the sink, blackened the air. Patsy lifted her hands to wave them away, and was given a sudden vision, as if it had been beamed into her head, of Les McCloud yelling and stamping down on the accelerator in the last seconds of his life.

Through the screen of flies a reddish light had begun to filter, pulsing with their comprehensive buzzing. The cellar door, the source of this reddish light, threw itself fully back against its hinges.

Patsy stood transfixed as the red light washed over her: the flies exploded up into the air again. At the bottom of the cellar steps, a red liquid washed and lapped over the wooden treads. This liquid blanketed the floor—it appeared to be at least several feet deep. In pulsating red light, it surged up to take another of the treads. Then Patsy saw a red hand break the surface of the turbulent lake. Another hand broke free. A head followed—small, well-shaped, the head of a young person.

The streaming body tried to find its footing on the bottom step. Another hand broke free of the surface behind it; then another. The first body was that of a boy or young man, Patsy saw: it grasped the rail with one hand and yanked itself forward and up. She could see the filmed eyes moving sightlessly, painfully. Another swimmer's head broke through back in the vault of redness, the mouth wide open in a soundless shout of triumph.

Tabby? Patsy sent out unthinkingly. *Tabby? Where are you, Tabby?*

Tabby? Tabby?

Patsy, Tabby thought, coming abruptly out of a miserable half-sleep tormented by images of Gravesend Beach lathered with a bloody surf. *Patsy?* He felt as though he'd been tickled by a cattle prod—as though a powerful wave of electric current had just gone straight through him.

Patsy was in trouble: mortal trouble. Tabby threw back the sheet and sat straight up in bed, more alarmed even than he had been in his own house.

Patsy are you all right are you are you

He felt nothing before him but the conviction of mortal danger.

Tabby jumped out of bed. He felt small and frantic. Where was Richard's room? *Patsy,* he thought despairingly, and suddenly saw a barren room with an oozing sink and a ruptured floor. Tabby turned blindly into the hallway, going toward the main staircase through the darkness. He heard deep, even rhythmic breathing, interrupted sporadically by snorts, and turned toward the sound. Tabby held out his hands, whimpering because of his urgency, and groped until he felt the edge of a doorframe. He eased through the empty frame, and then wiped his hands up and down the wall until he found the light switch. Tabby flicked on the lights.

Richard Allbee lay back on his bed, openmouthed and snuffling. The sudden light did not awaken him.

Tabby ran to the side of the bed. Richard snorted loudly but did not awaken. Tabby shook Richard's shoulders, hard. "Wake up!" he said. "You have to wake up! Richard!"

Richard's eyelids fluttered, his mouth smacked. He uttered a half-audible moan. "Hey," he said.

"It's Patsy," Tabby said. "She's going to die."

"What?"

"She's going to *die*," Tabby said, and his voice broke. "She's in some terrible old house, and something's going to kill her, Richard. We have to help her."

"Help her how? How do you know this, anyhow? What can we do?" Richard was now wholly awake, but not yet fully in command of himself.

"Call Graham," the boy said. "He'll know where the house is—he *has* to know."

"You're sure?" Richard said, then wiped his face and looked at the boy. "Of course you're sure. I'll call him right now. I just hope he got back home."

Richard lifted the bedside phone and put it in his lap and began to dial.

For Tabby, everything was moving with agonizing slowness. He turned his back on Richard, hearing the maddeningly slow clicks of the dial, and closed his eyes.

oh Patsy Patsy hang on please

we'll find you Patsy—God we will

don't don't don't die I love you

Behind him a surprised-sounding Richard was talking with Graham: when Tabby heard him say, "You think you know the house?" he could concentrate no longer. "You think your *arm's* broken?" he heard Richard say, and that snapped his concentration for good.

"Get your shoes on," Richard told him. "Graham's coming over right now—I'll just throw on a bathrobe and we'll get going in my car. He thinks he knows where she is."

As much as she heard Tabby speaking in her mind—and that was only dimly—the air about Patsy seemed charged with a particular Tabby-ness, a fresh sprinkling of his personality that was curiously detached from Tabby as a person; the essence without the form that gave the essence its meaning. Instantly the crowd of flies filling the air seemed to lessen.

Down there, the redness and the pulsing light were diminishing second by second. The blood-soaked creature on the cellar stairs retreated, still holding out one arm toward Patsy as if he expected her to help him escape. Even after his head had disappeared beneath the red tide, the arm still reached out, imploring. Watching that arm sinking slowly into the red tide, going to the elbow, then to the wrist as the fingers stretched hopelessly out, Patsy began to weep. The tide of blood in the basement fell back slowly from the stairs, going down some invisible cosmic drain.

She looked toward the spotted ceiling. Hundreds of flies buzzed in circles up there, throwing themselves against the crumbling fabric, trying to get out.

Patsy stumbled, then went blindly out of the kitchen. She stepped over the holes in the floor, skirted the board that had brought her down earlier. Now she could see the door clearly in the moon-washed interior—it was even open a crack, and an oblong of light had fallen into the room. Across Poor Fox Road black and white leaves stirred and whispered.

She waited in the middle of the road. She busied herself in plucking drying flakes of yellowish gunk off her clothes. When she chafed her palms up and down her calves, most of the pasty yellow stuff shredded away. Patsy crossed the street to her car. A few seconds later, headlights poked around the bend of the little overgrown road.

She could see their faces through the open side window of Richard's car—three white ovals pressing toward her. Patsy saw that Graham's right arm was in an impromptu sling made from a red paisley bandanna. An enormous bruise purpled his right cheek.

From Tabby, she felt a warming uncomplicated blast of concern and love.

"Can you drive your car, Patsy?" Graham boomed at her. "We shouldn't leave it here all night."

Patsy nodded.

"Sure?" Richard asked, leaning over Tabby to get a closer look at her. "Why don't you let me come with you?"

"Yes. Okay. I'd like that."

"Then drive back to my house," Graham said. "None of us is going to get any sleep tonight."

5

Patsy and Richard sat on Graham's old couch, Graham straddled his typing chair and sat facing them across his coffee table, scowling. Tabby sat cross-legged on the floor before Richard and knew that the scowl was chiefly meant for him: he could tell, too, that Graham was as angry at himself as at him. Now they all knew what had happened to one another that day, and each of them, Tabby thought, was thinking that his luck must be running out.

"I asked you a question, Tabby," Graham said. "How did you know that Patsy was in trouble? And how could you describe the setting so well that I could identify it? What's going on here, Tabby?"

"I just knew," Tabby said.

"Just knew. Pah! Don't you realize, son, that *everything* that happens to us is important—part of the pattern? And that if we can't read the pattern we can't do our job? You can't hide anything from me, Tabby, not if you're serious about helping us."

"I'm serious, all right," Tabby said. He didn't mind telling Graham and Richard about the connection between Patsy and himself, not if Patsy didn't mind, but he could *not* tell Graham Williams and Richard Allbee what he had been doing the night he and Patsy had discovered the connection, even though he felt closer to them than to anyone except Patsy. They would not understand—Tabby himself barely understood anymore how he had let himself get talked into going with the Norman twins. Tabby *was* serious; how serious, Graham and Richard would learn when they found out that he had destroyed the Dragon.

"Prove it to me," Graham said.

You bet I will, Tabby thought, and said, "Okay. You want to, Patsy?" He looked up at her, and she was nodding at him. "Okay. I don't know what you call it, exactly, but Patsy and I, we, uh, we can . . ."

"Telepathy," Patsy said. "We can send messages to each other."

Behind Tabby, Richard Allbee inhaled sharply.

"Ah," Graham said. He was smiling. "Of course, it had to be that. I knew the first time I saw the two of you together that you were two of a kind. Good. Thank you for telling me. When did you first notice that you had this ability?"

This question led to paths Tabby did not wish to take. He said, "It just happened."

"Nothing 'just happens.' Patsy?"

"It was the first night all four of us were together," Patsy said. "The night I had the fit and saw the dragon-head coming out of that book."

Graham straightened up, and adjusted the sling on his arm. "As long ago as that," he said. "But it does *fit*, do you see, it fits beautifully. Because *we* came together and *we* fit. And we fit because we had to: and the reason we had to is that our enemy was just finding his real strength then. He and the four of us turned a corner together. Tabby! Do you have anything to tell us? Anything to add?''

Tabby shook his head.

''Well, let me tell you what is in store for us—let me tell you about the Black Summer, and then you might want to change your mind. Of course, by now you can probably guess what went on then. At least some of it. Because it's going on around us now—I think Gideon Winter is trying to reenact the summer of 1873, and I think he's doing a pretty fair job. We have people moving out of town, we have the fires and all the deaths . . .'' His face pinched with pain, and he carefully adjusted his improvised sling again. ''Pretty soon the trains'll just go past the stations here—Greenbank and Hampstead. The drivers will just 'forget' to stop one day, and then pretty soon they'll 'forget' again, and before long they'll hardly even see those stations when they run past them. Once in a blue moon they'll look and see the big red HAMPSTEAD sign and they'll scratch their heads and wonder why it gives them a twinge. And you know, it won't make any difference at all—no one's going to be waiting for the train anyhow, those platforms'll be deserted. We're going to be sealed off, friends, and the town is going to accept it—it's already half-way there. And Hampstead could be nothing but a big grave-yard for the next two years, the next five years, the next ten . . .''

Graham fixed them all with his glare, then rubbed his throat with his left hand. ''Dry. I'm gonna need some lubrication. Tabby, you step over to the refrigerator there and get me a bottle of beer, will you? Patsy, you want anything? Some of that gin? Richard? Might as well settle down, it'll be a long speech. I'm going to tell you about that summer of 1873, but I'm also going to let you in on what happened between me and Mr. Bates Krell, whose house we saw tonight. It's about time you kids let me get all that off my chest.''

Tabby got a beer for himself, too.

3

The Burning River

1

"I was twenty," Graham began. "Closer to Tabby's age than either of yours, which is something you ought to remember as we go along. I was working on my first novel—one I published eight years later. I thought I had a pretty good subject for a novel, and in fact the subject was going on right around me, because I wanted to deal with the disappearances of women from Hampstead. My parents had known one of these women, Daisy West. And I knew that Daisy's husband, Horace, who was actually a very mild man, had fallen apart when Daisy vanished—he went down to the police station and threw a punch at Nails Kletzka, the chief. And Nails put him in a cell for the night. That was the sort of thing I wanted to work on. The effect on other people when somebody disappears, how lives are changed by that.

"Anyhow, I had me a little notebook in which I'd scribble my ideas, and I'd take long walks, getting away from people—my family, I guess I mean—and write down the little things I thought of. And most days, where I walked was alongside Rex Road—that road that runs along the river from Greenbank Road all the way into town. In those days almost all the left side of Rex Road was open field, right down to the river. You could walk for two, three miles and never lose sight of the water. I'd watch the traffic on the Nowhatan, write down some notion, and amble along. When I got hungry I'd sit down and take a sandwich out of my canvas backpack—I always had a couple of books in there too, maybe a little volume of John Donne or Rupert Brooke. I was a high-toned young fellow, if I wasn't always as discriminating as I imagined. High-toned. Naive—and about as capable of writing the book I wanted to as a hamster. Me and my Donne and

Rupert Brooke—they weren't the weapons that let me survive that summer.

"Well, one day I was sitting there in the field beside Rex Road, watching the boats on the Nowhatan and eating my sandwich. I looked up, and my eye was caught by a man puttering around on the deck of a chunky little lobsterboat making its way toward the Sound. He was bearded, a big guy, with a heavy blue coat on his back and a cap jammed slantwise on his head. For some reason I felt a sudden disturbance—I mean, I felt disturbed, but I mean more than that. I felt a *disturbance*, a hitch, an error in the pattern of things somehow: as if I'd glimpsed two moons in the sky. I felt a sudden wrongness; maybe that's the best way to put it. I put down my book, and the sandwich went dry in my mouth. The boat swung out, shifting itself in the current, and the man in the cap held on to the railing beside his cabin and raised his head. He was looking straight at me, as if all along he'd known I was there on the bank."

Graham stopped—Patsy's face had gone white and alarmed. Her eyes looked widely dilated, and he knew that whatever she was seeing, it was not the four of them in his shabby living room.

Then Tabby said, "You knew," and he looked at the boy, who had the look of kinship to Patsy that Graham had seen the first time he met them—Tabby's face too was frozen and white.

"You knew," Patsy echoed.

They were seeing it with him—seeing it better than he, because he was looking back through his memory and they were seeing it freshly, directly.

"Yes, I knew," he said. "I knew that I had seen a devil. The way you're seeing him now."

"My God," said Richard. "Are you, Patsy? Tabby?"

They nodded, almost in unison.

"My God," Richard repeated. "I suppose we ought to be getting used to things like this by now, but . . ."

"You saw the world go crazy," Tabby said.

"Once in my life I was like you two. I had some kind of a vision, and it *rocked* me. I saw the world turn black, or maybe my sight went black for a second, and then I saw smoke lifting up off the ground, and I saw flames covering the surface of the Nowhatan. The river was nothing but flame. It stank like a dump. Then the vision went away. I was just looking at the good old gray Nowhatan again, and a tubby little lobsterboat was putting out to the Sound. That man on deck had paid no more attention to me than he would to a dog.''

"So you felt you had to follow him," Patsy said, and Tabby chimed in with, "To find out about him."

"I was back there the next day, and I had my notebook and my lunch but I wasn't hungry and I hadn't written anything. I was tense as a whippet. You know, I think I was waiting for that terrible vision to repeat itself—and I was sure it would. It was the confirmation that I wanted—confirmation that there were realms of existence, realms of being, beyond anything I had known before. I couldn't take my eyes off that little boat docked only a little way downstream. Well, the man appeared; he started up his engines; he went right past me, just as he had the day before. And just as he had the previous day, he lifted his head and saw me standing on the bank—his glance just glided over me. He was a stocky, powerful-looking man and I could still feel the touch of his eyes. The boat chugged past me. Nothing at all happened. I stood there, like a rejected suitor, and watched it go. I felt empty and flat. The boat went on, an ordinary lobsterboat, around a bend in the river . . . and me standing there with my mouth open.

"So you're right," Graham went on. "I had to find out about him. Late that afternoon I was across the river. I pretended that I had a message for one of the lobstermen but that I had forgotten his name. 'A big man,' I said, 'with a beard. He wears a cap. This is where he docks his boat.' A scrawny little mate grinned at the others and said, 'It's Krell. He means Bates Krell.' He turned back to me, and I saw sheer malice glinting in his eyes. 'Have a message for Bates Krell, do you? He'll have one for you and all, boy.' They all laughed, and another fisherman said, 'He'll have more than a message, sonny.' Of course I didn't understand then what they meant, but I understood something—they were afraid of the man.

"Well, I waited for him to come in with his catch. I didn't have a clue about the meaning of what had happened, but I *thought* I understood that this man Krell was in some way responsible for the very thing that had led me to my first sight of him—the disappearance of Daisy West and those other women. Krell brought his boat in just before sundown. He had a small catch and I hung back on the edge of the docks and watched him as he negotiated a price for his lobsters with the fish merchants who came there for that purpose. He seemed surly, aggressive, not at all stupid—he seemed ordinary, but I knew he was not. I wanted to know where he lived: I wanted to know all about his life. The aura of that extraordinary vision I'd had clung to him, and I felt a kind of obsession with the man.

"When he went home I followed him. I didn't think he saw me. He walked those two or three miles up Greenbank Road just looking straight ahead, just marching along in his rubber boots and little cap, as if the whole world belonged to him. It had grown dark, and there was nothing on either side of Greenbank Road in those days but fields and marshes. No lights. I went through the fields, covering myself in burrs and thistle, ruining my shoes and pants.

"So that was how I learned where his house was—and as soon as I saw it, I knew that it was no more ordinary than its owner. It was absolutely his. Or he was its. I hid in the trees on Poor Fox Road and watched him slouch up his path, open his door, and go inside. That terrible little house closed around him like a fist. I backed away, almost with the sense that the house itself was seeing me with Krell's eyes—I was suddenly spooked, everything around me seemed threatening, and I took off for home. And when I got there and survived the treatment I got from my parents for showing up so late and in such a shabby condition, I had to think of what I could do next—for, knowing what I was pretty sure I knew, I had to do something. I couldn't just write a book about a fisherman who killed people: I had to step over the line and act. I think I had the worst nightmares of my life that night.

"But in the morning, I knew what I was going to do. I was going to get the evidence that would send Bates Krell to jail. And I was going to get it by secretly boarding his boat in the middle of the night and finding something that one of the women had dropped there—as a fisherman, I'd realized, Krell had the biggest pocket in the world to hide things in. The Nowhatan; Long Island Sound; the Atlantic Ocean. He could have thrown half the women in Hampstead overboard, and as long as he'd taken the precaution of weighting them down, no one would ever find them."

Graham, intent now on his story, did not see the odd expression, half of apprehension and half of stubborn determination, that went across Tabby Smithfield's face.

2

"Two nights later," Graham continued, "I did it. I got on board Krell's boat. I found something, but it wasn't what I thought I was going to find.

"I had to wait until my parents were asleep, and then make damn sure I didn't wake them up. You know what parents are—*everything* wakes them up. So I didn't get moving until after midnight, and I just crept into my clothes and went down the stairs like a ghost, terrified that my old man would start shouting. When I got outside, I closed that door so quietly even *I* didn't hear it click. Then I tiptoed into the road and got about fifty paces away—and then I ran like hell.

"And I didn't stop running until I got to the bridge. I hadn't seen a living soul the whole way—not even a car. Hampstead was really just a small town in those days, and small towns go to bed early. I flew: I couldn't have walked even if I had wanted to, my body wouldn't have let me. I suppose my footsteps might have disturbed the sleep of a citizen or two, but I thought what I was going to find would be much more disturbing—proof that Daisy West and the others had been murdered, just like the women before them, back at the start of 1924. By the time I got to the bridge I had run about two and a half miles, and my legs were pretty sore, but I don't think I was even breathing hard. That's how keyed up I was! I leaned on the iron railing of the bridge and looked up the river. I could see it. Krell's boat, the *Fancy,* was docked just where it had been the day before. There wasn't a single human being in sight.

"I walked the rest of the way. There were a couple of taverns down that way even then, speakeasies they were, and a few late-night drinkers went past me on Riverfront Avenue. I turned my head away, and I suppose they did the same. As soon as I could, I ducked between the buildings and got closer to the river.

"It was slapping against the pilings. The smell of the water seemed to be much stronger than during the day, but maybe that was because my senses were so . . . so *refined.* Every little detail went through me like a knife—I remember that in the moonlight the pattern of the grain on the boards of the dock seemed to ripple, to *flow* down the dock. . . .

"Bates Krell's boat was lifting and subsiding with the

movements of the water, rubbing itself up against the dock like a big old dog. All I had to do was jump on board. There wasn't another person in sight. The boat almost seemed to be welcoming me, inviting me on board, with those little sighing lifts and bumps. But I hesitated—was I really going to bite the apple? Commit a crime? I rested my hand on the rough wood of the boat—up and down, up and down . . . and then I mentally said *to hell with it,* and vaulted onto the deck of the *Fancy.*

"My shoes raised a cloud of dust. I could smell fish and mold. When I took my hand off the railing, it came away black—Krell's boat was one of the filthiest things I've ever seen. I crouched down below the level of the railing, just in case anybody might happen to be looking my way, and sort of duck-walked across the deck. I didn't know what I was looking for, exactly, but I guess I had the idea that maybe Krell had kept souvenirs of his deeds. My fantasy was that I'd open a little locker somewhere on the *Fancy* and find a cache of women's handbags or shoes.

"The trouble was, I couldn't seem to find this locker anywhere on the deck. I made a complete circuit, crouched over like that, and all I got was a backache and smudgy marks on my clothes wherever I'd brushed up against anything. I'd found nothing at all in the wheelhouse. The only place left to look was the hold, and there were two reasons why I was reluctant to go down there—I'd smell of fish and lobsters for days, and once I was down there, I wouldn't be able to tell if someone was coming. The last thing I wanted was to be caught on board the *Fancy!* Then, almost by accident, I saw something I'd missed before.

"The moonlight was touching a small brass handle just a little bit farther down the deck from me—it was about six inches beneath the railing. I thought I could see a kind of a shadow-line beside the handle. It looked just like a secret cabinet Krell had built into the side of his boat. This was it! I knew what was going to happen: I'd slide that door open, and all sorts of necklaces and rings would spill out onto the deck. I was going to find treasure, *real* treasure, and to get rid of Bates Krell all I'd have to do was take a few baubles to Kletzka—the murderer would be salted away before the sun came up.

"I scuttled over to that gleaming handle and shoved it to one side—that sliding door moved like it was greased. My

eyes must have been like dinner plates. By now I was convinced that I was going to see not just a heap of women's
shoes, but a fortune in jewelry.

"But that little cabinet Krell had built into the side of the
Fancy was almost empty. There was a stained old coffee cup
in there. And beside it was a wineglass. That was all. A cup
and a wineglass. I didn't understand—not at all. I took out
the wineglass and looked at it. The crystal was etched with
leaves and blossoms and was about as heavy as a square inch
of air. It caught the moonlight; it sparkled. This fancy damn
glass spooked me a little bit, surrounded by the filth of that
boat. It was like holding a flashlight. I put it back in the
secret cabinet and slid the door back. Now there was only one
more place to check. The hold. I decided I'd just *look* down
there; not actually climb in.

"You opened the hold on the *Fancy* by using a polished
length of wood maybe eight inches long: you slid it into a
catch, and then used the piece of wood to lever up one of the
big doors. I worked this out when I saw the wood hanging by
a thong on an upright next to the hold doors. I lifted the
wooden lever off its peg, pushed it into the catch, and swung
hard on the door. It opened; and I almost fainted and fell in.

"What I saw down there was a lake of blood—that's right,
just what the rest of you have been seeing. It looked like it
was rising, coming right up to the top of the hold and the
doors. It was *seething,* and for a crazy second it looked somehow conscious. I wobbled on my feet, and only just managed
to drop the door before I blacked out and fell in.

"Then of course I had to be sure that I'd seen it. As soon
as I was steady enough, I pulled the door open a bit—but this
time I smelled only the old odors of fish. There was no smell
of blood at all. I opened it farther, and saw that I was looking
down into an empty hold. That was it for me. I got off that
boat as fast as I could, and I wasn't breathing normally again
until I was back on the bridge, going home.

"The next day I worked out another strategy. Two damn peculiar things had happened to me, and I wasn't about to
quit—if anything, I was even more positive now that Mr.
Krell had killed all those women. And that for some reason, I
was meant to bring him down. It was my job, mine. So I
worked out another plan.

"I was sure that he'd had assistants—all those lobstermen

did. No man, no matter how strong, could do the job by himself. Usually their sons helped them, or they hired the boys who hung around the docks. In later years, you always saw teenage boys fooling around in gas stations: hoping for jobs, most of them. In those days, in this part of the world, the same kind of boy haunted the docks. I was sure that I could learn something if I could find one or two of Bates Krell's old deckhands. Well, it turned out to be a lot more difficult than I thought it would be.

"I asked questions around the docks, and I asked questions in the little speaks down along the river. The Blue Tern—that was one of them, and it's still there. I made up some elaborate story; maybe it didn't fool anyone. Maybe they just didn't want to talk about Bates Krell. One old river rat I cornered in the Blue Tern finally told me, after I poured about a gallon of rye down his scrawny throat, that Krell abused his deckhands. 'They runs away on 'im,' he said. 'They clears out in the middle of the night, and so would I. You can be hard and a boy will respect you, but no boy today will stick out bein' half-kilt. When I was that age you took what you got and was grateful for it.'

"I asked him if he knew where any of those boys were now, and he said he imagined that they'd gone upstate, getting as far away from Krell as they could.

"'All of them?' I asked. 'Isn't *one* of his old hands still in town?'

"He chewed on it for a bit, and I poured more rye into his glass. Rye is what they called it anyhow—I think it had been in a barrel just long enough to lose the chemical smell. 'Might be one,' he finally said. 'Boy named Burgess. Pitt Burgess, he called himself. A funny one. He quit on Krell— brave like a crazy dog can be. Never came around the docks after that, and nobody missed him. Never took to him, d'ya see. None of us here ever took to him.'

"'Where does this Burgess boy live?' I asked.

"'In the marshes,' he told me. There was an evil old glint in his eye, too.

"Now there are no more shacks down on the marshes, but in the twenties—right through the Depression, in fact—there were people who lived in tarpaper houses on that swampy ground just inland from Gravesend Beach. Lone men, mainly, who lived on the shellfish they caught at low tide. So I knew where to look, though I wasn't very happy about it. I was going to ruin another pair of boots. And those shacks on the marshes . . . well, nobody in his right mind would relish the thought of going down there. Those few crazy loners were a law unto themselves. But I thought this Burgess boy was probably my last chance to find out about Krell. So the next afternoon I hiked down Greenbank Road to the entrance to the beach and jumped over the little tidal estuary there. Then I squished off through the marsh and went toward the shacks—there were six or seven of them, strung out from the waterline back toward the direction of the Millpond.

"I wouldn't have known which one to approach first except that I saw a tall skinny kid with dirty-blond hair messing around outside one of the most distant shacks. The kid saw me, and didn't think twice—he just ducked inside his door. *My boy,* I thought. I plodded over the wet ground to that hovel and knocked on the door . . ."

3

. . . and a frightened-looking boy pulled the door open and blinked at Graham. He was no more than seventeen. His eyes seemed froggy: Graham finally noticed that he had absolutely no eyelashes. "Get away," he said. "You got no business with me."

"I need your help," Graham said quickly. "I'll pay for it. Look—I brought you some food." He thrust forward the wrapped package in his hands: in it were cans of beans, some sliced meat, and three bottles of beer. The boy reluctantly accepted the package, and began prodding and fondling it with his hands. They, like his pinched face, were gray with dirt. "You're Pitt Burgess, aren't you?"

The boy glanced up at his face as a convict does at a guard's, then nodded. "This is food?"

"I tried to figure out what you might need."

The boy nodded again, and looked almost stupefied. Graham realized sinkingly that he was semiretarded, on the bottom edge of a normal intelligence or beneath it.

"Some beer, too," Graham said.

Burgess licked his lips and smiled at Graham. "What kind of help you say you need?"

"Just some questions."

"You ain't gettin' any of the beer."

"It's for you."

Burgess nervously backed away from the door, and Graham went into the dingy single room. It was stiflingly hot, and as dirty as the boy himself. While Burgess clawed at the package and opened one of the bottles of beer, Graham noticed how beads of water adhered to the inside walls and the rungs of the two cane chairs. Moisture had instantly appeared on the side of the boy's beer bottle. The plywood floor was furry with mold. A picture of a Marmon coupé torn from a magazine was tacked to one of the walls. "Beer's good," Burgess told him. "Guess you can sit, if you like."

"Thanks," Graham said. He did not want to alarm Pitt Burgess. The boy still seemed as nervous and liable to bolt as a doe in the woods. "Do you mind answering some questions?"

"You ask and I'll see."

He watched the boy take another swallow of beer.

"When was the last time you worked?"

Burgess squinted at him and washed beer around the inside of his mouth. "Who sent you, anyhow?"

"Nobody sent me, Pitt. I told you: I need some help you can give me."

Suspiciously the boy cocked his head. "Okay. I was working about four, five months ago. That was the last time."

"What was the job?"

"Deckhand on a fishing boat."

"Why were you fired?"

"Hey, mister—I quit. Nobody ever fired me. I quit. You hear I got fired? Is that what you heard?"

"Why did you quit, then?"

Now the boy seemed even more nervous than usual. His unprotected eyes could not remain still. "Wasn't treated right," he muttered.

"Did he beat you? Did Krell beat you?"

Then nothing changed in the room, but everything was different. Beneath his layer of grayish dirt, the boy had gone the color of curdled milk: even the slow drops of water sliding down the wall seemed to stop and tremble where they were.

"I have nothing to do with him," Graham said. "I've really only seen him once or twice."

"He hit me," Pitt Burgess said softly. He was relaxing from the outside in, in concentric circles. "Yeah. That's why I quit."

He still would not look at Graham, so Graham stayed quiet—cannily—winning the boy's confidence the way he would a dog's. He looked at the picture of the Marmon and did not move.

"He hit me a lot," the boy finally said.

Another long pause. Graham was afraid he would fly apart from sheer muscular tension.

Then Pitt Burgess said softly, "And he began to look younger, didn't he? Younger. Sure he did. Handsome."

"Did you think he was handsome, Pitt?" Graham whispered.

The boy nodded, and his Adam's apple jerked in his throat. Then the boy's naked eyes for the first time in thirty minutes found Graham's face. "He was. He was *awful* handsome. Sometimes you don't mind things s'much, y'know, if . . ."

A vein in Graham's head began to pound. He was getting a headache. "I see," he said.

"You're nice, bringing me food," the boy said. He paused, as if giving Graham room to express something he did not trust himself or the situation enough to say.

"That's all right," Graham said, horribly embarrassed now.

"I was ascairt of him when he got s'handsome," Burgess said after another of his pauses. "I was thinking about what he done."

"To look younger?" Graham asked.

"What he done *before* he started to look younger. He had boys before me, mister." Pitt Burgess stared at Graham with a new expression in his eyes—there was calculation in it, and shame, and bravado, and some mysterious thing that made Graham want to run from the shack.

"And he beat those boys, too. How many were there? Three or four?"

The boy cleared his throat. "About so many. Three. Four. He took them home with him. I wouldn't let him take me home. He made me ascairt."

"Pitt," Graham asked, "I'm not even sure what I'm asking, but did you ever see anything funny on board the *Fancy*?"

The boy had coiled up inside himself again, and his eyes looked reptilian.

"Look," Graham said, "it sounds strange as hell, but did you ever see anything like a lot of blood?"

Pitt shook his head.

"Did you ever see *anything* that wasn't normal?"

From the oddly intelligent (because ironic) look on the boy's face, Graham knew that nothing aboard the *Fancy* had been entirely normal. "Maybe I'm not asking the question the right way," he added miserably.

"I know," the boy said. "I know what you want. Something he wouldn't like me to say. But I'll say it—to you. One time I heard this terrible noise. I looked at the wheelhouse. I couldn't believe it. The whole wheelhouse was filled up with flies. Maybe a million of 'em in there. But I knew something—I knew they weren't really there. He hit me because he knew I saw 'em, though. He liked to hit me." This last sentence was almost flirtatious.

"Oh," Graham said.

"He took the other boys home with him," Burgess said. "I don't know what else he done, but he took them boys home with him. And nobody ever noticed."

"Noticed?"

"Those boys went off upstate, I guess. Looked for jobs on the New Haven docks, I guess. I guess nobody ever saw them again."

"Oh, my God," Graham said, finally understanding.

"Nobody," Pitt Burgess said, half-smiling at Graham. "And nobody cared. They was just nobodies from nowhere. So I quits him and slides off up here to the marshes, and I never have seen my handsome Mr. Krell since that day."

Flirtation—this was a flirtation.

Graham stood up, having learned both less and more than he had come for; uttered a conventional and inappropriate and panicked leave-taking; got out as quickly as he could. As he squelched back across the marshes, he could feel Pitt Burgess standing in the door of his squalid shack, watching him go. With what emotion, he could not have said.

4

At home Graham took a long bath—he felt as though the greasy, damp atmosphere of Pitt Burgess' shack had sunk into his skin, and he scrubbed himself with the loofah until he thought he'd blister. He had never before felt real moral revulsion, and never before had he met anyone he had considered degraded: but Pitt Burgess was degraded, and Bates

Krell was responsible. Graham felt as though he had seen down deep into a pit, and had escaped with his life—one more step, one more second, would have seen him fall into it.

Very likely that was the reason for his nightmares. Three nights running, Graham's nights were troubled, feverish. He dreamed he was sleeping in a coffin in a room curtained with black velvet. His hands, his mouth, were stained red. He wanted to fly, to rise out of the coffin and sail through the night sky. The following two nights, the dream altered: he slept beside a pit in a deep wood. He thrashed, moaned in his sleep. At the bottom of the pit was something awesome and powerful, an object or group of objects that called and called to him. He could not look; he would not be able to endure it if he were to crawl to the edge of the pit and stare downward.

These second two mornings Graham awoke with the distinct, particular feeling of having looked backward in time. He found himself unable to speak to his parents. When he looked into their kind, successful and blinkered faces he felt himself an outcast: he wanted to cry, or to run away. He ran. He locked himself in his room. He was polite when they came to his door, but he would not leave his room. If they left food outside his door, he would eat. If not, not. After a very short time, he could feel his parents' misery lapping at him—could feel their questions scratching at his locked door. This period of madness-in-effect, Graham's mini-breakdown, lasted four days. On the fifth day he awoke feeling shaky but himself again: there had been no nightmares for two nights. He had lost the sense of some monstrous self heaving beneath his own skin.

He came down for breakfast and apologized to his parents for his behavior. He implied that he had been working too hard on his book. And as soon as he was done with his breakfast he gave in to obsession and walked all the way down Greenbank Road, crossed over the bridge, turned up Riverfront Avenue and went back to the docks.

The *Fancy* was in its slip—Graham hadn't quite expected this. In coveralls and a blue knit cap tugged down over his head, Bates Krell staggered back and forth from a disorderly pile of lobster traps, throwing them on the deck of his ship. When Graham saw him this time, instinctive and unreasoning fear leaped out at him from his own heart: he thought of those three or four boys Krell had taken home with him, and who

had never been seen again. Graham was unable to take his
eyes off Krell, but he did not want the man to see him. He
went slowly backward until he was in the narrow alleyway
between the fish market and the Blue Tern. And there he
hovered, mutely watching Krell load the traps onto his boat.

The world did not tremble; the river did not burst into
flame. There were none of these gaudy supernatural signs. A
bull-like man in a blue knit cap threw boxy traps onto the
deck of a boat. Graham watched him as if he had been put
under hypnosis. Krell's face was unreflective and flat, his
eyebrows thick and black, like his beard. A man given to
sudden storms, you would have said, to meteorological outbursts; but nothing more.

Graham found that he was panting, taking in air in short
quick gasps.

A small man darted out the door of the Blue Tern, gave
Graham a look of startled recognition, then sloped away toward the docks. It was the scrawny ex-fisherman who had
given him Pitt Burgess' name. Graham's stomach tightened
as he saw the man weave toward the diminished pile of traps.
Then the little man's head jerked sideways and Krell stopped
moving; the little man had told him something.

Now the thin old man was wandering away down the
docks. Krell had stopped his work and was standing, head
bent so his chin was on his chest, hands in the hip pockets of
the coveralls.

Get out, get out, Graham thought: *he knows!*

Krell turned sideways, tilted his head, and fixed Graham to
the side of the Blue Tern with his eyes.

Graham straightened up: above his panic floated the realization that ordinarily these theatrical bully's mannerisms
would have amused him.

Krell half-smiled, then took a step toward Graham, who
moved out of the narrow alley to meet him on the dock, in
plain view.

The man stood directly in front of him, only inches away.
The odor of fish and dried sweat, chiefly the former, clung to
him. He was about Graham's height, and his muddy eyes
went straight to Graham's. A surprising quantity of suppressed gaiety lived in those eyes. A second after looking into
them, Graham wondered how he had ever thought them
muddy.

Graham first felt the threat of the man; a second later he felt what he could only have called charm.

"You know," Krell said in a husky, high-pitched voice, "I can't help myself. I'm interested."

"Yes?" Graham said.

"Interested." Krell nodded. "I just can't figure out why you should come down here asking questions about me. I've seen you before, though, haven't I? You were on the side of the river."

"Yes," Graham said. "Yes, I was."

"Well, let me in on the secret. I don't suppose you want to invest in a lobsterboat."

Millions of contradictory impressions were streaming toward Graham—he sensed violence flickering about Krell, but along with the violence came the sense of a powerful, and powerfully unified, personality. Krell was an unregenerate being with the native appeal of those who are wholly themselves: everybody Graham knew would have thought Bates Krell awful, but the man had accepted his awfulness so thoroughly that he had nearly succeeded in making it a positive quality.

Then Graham understood something else: that this man would have been very attractive to women.

He told as much of the truth as he dared. "No, no, of course not. I'm a writer—I'm just beginning, actually. My name is Graham Williams, Mr. Krell."

"A book writer?"

"I'm trying to write a book. When I saw you that day I thought, ah, I thought you'd make an interesting character."

"Was that the first day you saw me, or the second?" Now the eyes were positively sparkling.

"Both."

Krell took a step backward, still half-smiling; he glanced toward the *Fancy*, then back at Graham. "A character in a book, eh? That's something new. A book by Graham Williams. Now I have an idea for you. I'm going out for a couple of hours right now, as soon as I get the last of these new traps on board. Why don't you come along? You can see if you really want to put a lobsterman in your book, Graham Williams." He suddenly left Graham and returned to the little heap of traps. He tossed another on the deck while Graham stared at him, and then turned around with an appraising look. He wiped his hand down his handsome beard. "I'll even give you a glass of wine while you see the work. I understand you writer fellows have nothing against a sip now and then."

Graham remembered the sparkling wineglass in that dusty cupboard. The memory was darkened with threat: and he said to himself, *this man kills people*. But if the story he had told Krell were the truth, wouldn't he accept the invitation? And if Krell were suspicious of his motives, wouldn't that somehow be more apparent? The man was anything but an actor. If he went out on the boat, Graham thought, and kept his eyes open, he might learn something that would help to convict Krell.

Graham went forward and picked up the last two traps. "Let's get going," he said.

Krell lifted his thick eyebrows, nodded; smiled. He waved Graham onto his boat with a mockingly courtly gesture.

A moment later they were chugging up the Nowhatan against the tide. "How do you remember where you put your pots?" Graham asked. He was looking at the spot on the bank where he had been standing the first time he had seen Bates Krell.

"Markers," the lobsterman said. "You'll see them when we get out there."

"The town looks so different from the river," Graham said. "I've never seen it this way before. It looks . . ."

"Wild and woolly," Krell shouted from the wheelhouse. That was not the term Graham would have chosen, but it fit. From the middle of the Nowhatan, Hampstead looked raw, unfinished; a frontier town. The backs of the buildings seemed to droop toward the river. When they had passed the last of the buildings and the final series of docks had washed behind them, the riverbanks looked as though they led off to an infinity of marshland and tall waving broom grass.

The illusion broke when the *Fancy* rounded the headland at the mouth of the river and swung out into Long Island Sound. On the bluffs above their private beaches the houses of Mount Avenue, far up the coastline, hung like colored lanterns between their wealth of trees; nearer, the town's beaches luxuriated against the edge of the water.

"How far out do you go?" Graham called to Krell, who merely waved toward the upper end of the Sound.

A light, bluish haze in the air subtracted Long Island.

The *Fancy* pushed itself through the water, going always farther from the land—soon the Mount Avenue houses were the size of matchbooks. Dwarf trees curled over them. The Hillhaven beach, just to the right of the tiny houses, hovered above the water like a puff of smoke.

Graham saw a flash of yellow bobbing on the water, then two more a long way ahead, appearing and disappearing with the folding, unfolding of the waves. Krell's markers. He was about to turn toward the wheelhouse and ask about them; and then decided not to, for the first of them, now identifiable as two painted sticks nailed together to form a cross, was already slipping past the bow. Krell had not cut his engines. Someone else's markers, then. Graham leaned against the rail.

And then his intuition—or the gift he had momentarily shared with Patsy and Tabby long before either of them was born—saved his life. He suddenly caught the smell of blood, as if an ox had been freshly slaughtered on the deck behind him.

And some animal was behind him—a grotesque thing, a monster. He knew this. It was a thing so terrible that the sight of it would turn his muscles to rubber. Yet it would kill him where he stood if he did not turn around. In his mind was a picture of a spider the size of the wheelhouse, and he turned to face it.

Bates Krell was halfway across the deck toward him. The door to the wheelhouse sagged open. Krell was holding a long wooden rod fitted with a sharp metal point like a bayonet. Coming toward Graham in order to gaff him, the lobsterman smiled. His eyes blazed beneath the thick demarcations of the eyebrows. Krell's entire face was a mask of joy, power, purpose. . . . *I was ascairt of him when he got s'handsome,* Graham remembered.

Krell laughed out loud and stepped closer.

5

"So there I was," Graham said, "without a weapon—and that madman circling in toward me with a gaff. He was going to open me up, I could see that all right. He was going to slice me from gullet to bellybutton and then feed me to the fish. Bates Krell. He couldn't have looked happier if someone had given him a steak dinner.'' Graham closed his eyes. For a moment, sitting backward on his typing chair, he lowered his head. A few lone white hairs protruded through his scalp. When he raised his head again, his eyes seemed very large. ''And it should have ended that way. I could never have defeated Bates Krell in a fight.'' He blinked, and—just for a moment—he looked very young to Tabby, as young and as frightened as he had been when he had faced a murderous Bates Krell on the deck of the *Fancy*. ''But I did defeat him. Tabby knows. Tabby saw it happen, the first time we met. But I don't suppose you understood it, Tabby.''

''I don't know,'' Tabby said, looking up at him. ''What did I see? I saw you pick something up—didn't you do that? Wasn't there something . . . ?''

''Well, what is it?'' Patsy asked. ''A club? I have an idea . . . it's like a club, isn't it?''

''No, not a club,'' Graham said. ''But it was the only weapon I could think of then—that eight-inch polished piece of wood that I'd used to open up the hold. I looked sideways, and there it was, still hanging from its thong. I sort of darted to the side, and Krell jabbed at me and missed. He didn't care. He knew he was going to get me eventually. A little thing like that wooden pin wouldn't stop him. He jabbed at me again, and I ran for it—I lifted that little wooden pin off the upright and held it in my hand and faced him just like I knew what I was doing. Just like I had a chance.''

Graham looked at them all, having come to the hardest part of his story. ''And Krell came in for me, sort of twitching that deadly gaff at my gut. He said, 'You know nothing, Williams. *You know nothing.*' I damn near fell apart—I was panicking. Right then, I thought I heard the buzzing of a million flies—my back was to the wheelhouse, and I remembered what Pitt Burgess had told me and thought they were in there, a million flies blacking out the windows. And then . . .'' He scanned their faces, and saw that he had carried them with him so far.

''This is just the hardest thing to say,'' he said. ''Somehow . . .'' The expression on Patsy's face stopped him.

Patsy was glowing like a candle; she had seen. She was looking straight down into the triumph he had made of that day, and feeling that triumph as if it had been her own— seeing all that in her face, he could have melted with love for her. He reached out and took her willing hand.

"Oh, you had a sword," she said, her eyes glowing and looking back more than fifty years. "Oh, Graham, you had a sword. You had a sword and you were *beautiful*."

She had carried him right through the difficulty; it was she who was beautiful.

"It's what happened," he said. "I felt about eight feet tall. I felt as strong as God. And that damned little eight-inch piece of shiny wood in my hand . . . it was a sword, just as Patsy said." Graham put his free hand over his eyes and was silent for a moment. "A *sword*." His voice trembled, and he shook his head. "I'm not going to cry, I'm not. But you know, I'm living through all this again . . ." He shook his head decisively, and took his hand away from his wet eyes. He put that hand too over Patsy's.

"The whole day changed—I felt a sort of crazy radiance all around me. Krell was screeching at me. His eyes were different. They were *big:* big as golf balls. And they had no whites and no pupils in them anymore. His eyes were black, jet-black, with a kind of a golden pattern across them—they looked like stones. Precious stones. He rushed at me, screeching like that, and I knew what he was feeling—the same wild triumph that was charging through me. But I knew I was going to win. Everything had turned inside out, and I was going to destroy Bates Krell. I swung that sword through the air, and it bit Krell's gaff in two. Krell screeched again, and then he threw himself at me."

Graham straightened up on his chair: he still gripped Patsy's hand with both of his own. "And I swung that sword again, knowing just what was going to happen. Or it swung itself. Krell's face was only a foot from mine when the sword went into him, and I thought I saw two faces there—both of them crazy with evil and that wild joy. I felt the sword slide into his middle, and I put my muscles into it. Krell's face looked like it was magnifying, bloating up like a balloon: and then I felt the sword sever his backbone, and I really hauled at it, and it came out on the other side of him. Blood shot out like out of a hose. The momentum of the sword, and the weight of it, nearly took me overboard. Krell's face changed again—went blank—and his top half fell over and splashed onto the deck. His legs stayed upright for a moment longer, and then they went down too. I felt like singing—I had a moment of pure elemental fulfillment. The strongest moment in my life. Jesus!

"And then it faded—everything faded. The day went back

to being just a day: that gold sparkle went out of the air, the boat was chugging around in circles; and my sword was just a wooden pin again. Blood was still spilling out of Krell's corpse, and I watched it foaming into the cracks between the deck boards.''

Graham gently released Patsy McCloud's hand. "Kids, when I got into trouble in the fifties, the power of this memory is what saw me through. I'd fought a devil, I thought, and some power had saved me. Then all my strength flooded out of me, and I almost had to sit down, I was so weak. Already that strange, wonderful moment was getting mythical; vague. Two halves of a man were oozing blood onto the filthy deck in front of me. It almost made me sick, but I had to get rid of them. That was what was uppermost in my mind: I never considered the consequences. It never occurred to me that no one would believe me!

"I closed my eyes tightly and grabbed his trunk by gripping it beneath the arms. I hauled that part of him up and dropped it over the railing. Then I heard it splash into the Sound. Like a good old dog, the *Fancy* toiled around the place where his head and chest went down; like it was waiting for him to come back. I grabbed one of his ankles with each hand and flipped the rest of him over the side. I leaned over the railing and watched his boots disappear under the water— they sank like stones, they went straight down. Then I turned away. The wooden pin I had been holding was rolling across the deck, and I snatched it up a second before it rolled into all that blood. Then I threw that overboard too.

"I went into the wheelhouse and straightened the boat out—for a second I thought about just sailing straight up the Sound, pushing straight out into the Atlantic and never coming back. But I turned the boat around and went back toward the mouth of the Nowhatan.

"Of course I didn't have a clue about how to dock a boat like the *Fancy*. Sailboats were more my league, and luffing in toward a slip was tricky enough for me. Once I spotted the rear windows of the Blue Tern, I turned the wheel in toward the pier and cut off the engines and hoped for the best. Well, the *Fancy* hit that dock like a truck running downhill out of control, and chewed a big hunk out of civic property. I probably knocked a few glasses off shelves inside the Blue Tern, too; and I put a sizable dent in the side of the boat. I jumped off, tied the lines to the nearest posts, and took off at a dead run for the police station.

"That magical rightness had left me, all right. I sat in Nails Kletzka's office and told him everything—from my first sight of Krell all the way to bruising the hell out of the dock in back of the Blue Tern. And he just thought he was listening to a boy who'd gone out of his head from reading too many books. Nails Kletzka was a good chief, and he was a tough boyo. He was even good enough at politics to hang on to his job for more than thirty years. But what I was saying was too much for him—and of course I should have known it would be. I should have known enough to soften that story up, to make it more acceptable to a Polish roughneck in his first year as chief. I should have bowed to the realistic tradition. I sat there pouring out my crazy story, and I saw Nails getting at first more and more uncomfortable and then downright fidgety and finally just plain angry. When it came to Krell's death, I said that I grabbed the gaff away from him and stuck him with it—pushed hard enough on that gaff to force Krell over the railing. I had that much sense anyhow.

" 'So you decided that this Krell fellow murdered those women. All those women. And that fruitcake boy out on the marshes persuaded you that he'd killed his deckhands, too. Three or four of them.' Nails looked at me, and I saw that he'd just as soon lock me up for wasting his time with a story like that.

"I told him that was right.

" 'So how many citizens did you decide this Krell did away with altogether? Seven, eight? Ten?'

" 'Something like ten,' I said.

" 'So where are the *bodies?*' Kletzka shouted at me. 'I mean, where are all these dead boys? Where are their mothers—why hasn't anybody listed them as missing? And what sort of proof do you have that Krell had anything at all to do with the women who've disappeared? Or even the poor women we found dead? Is there any goddamned proof at all?'

"I had to shake my head.

" 'We don't even know for sure that you killed this man in self-defense and threw his body overboard.'

" 'I did, though,' I said. 'You can see the blood on the deck of his boat. That's some kind of proof.'

" 'Proof of nothing,' he said.

"I want to tell you that I spent the whole day in that office. Kletzka sent a man down to the docks, and the officer came back with the message that, yes, the *Fancy* did seem to have been amateurishly berthed, but that no one had seen it come in. No one had seen me leave the dock with Krell. There was some blood on the deck of the *Fancy*, but that proved nothing. Anyhow, in 1924, we didn't have the sophisticated blood tests we do now.

"Finally, though Kletzka never said it directly, I began to get an idea—and it helped explain some of his anger. I began to see that some men in town had been complaining about this Bates Krell: they thought he had been bothering some of the local women. Their daughters—or their wives. Somebody had thought they'd seen Krell entertaining a woman on board his boat one night. And I started to see that I had botched up Nails's investigation, to describe it charitably. He hadn't been able to begin any real investigation because all they had against Krell was the suspicion of a guy who thought he might be a wronged husband.

"At the end of the night I understood one thing more. Kletzka was half-inclined to believe that I had killed Bates Krell: but he was never going to arrest me for it. In fact he was going to pretend I never came in. He'd tell his department that I was 'that young would-be writer'; that I had too much imagination. And he was going to wait and see if the disappearances and murders would stop. It was rough justice, but he knew that was better than none. I went home that night with no charge against me, and I burned every note I'd taken. The deaths did stop; and what had happened to me out in the middle of Long Island Sound began to seem more and more a fever-dream, something I'd imagined.

"I didn't see Chief Kletzka again until 1952, twenty-eight years later, when I was pretty much a disgraced character. I was riding the bottle pretty hard in those days, and I wasn't sure of my legal status. Most people here had decided I was a threat to the American Way of Life, if only because Senator Joe McCarthy seemed to think so. Not to mention Martin Dies. I was about to go back to England; I wanted to go while I still had a passport. One man in town stuck up for me. Johnny Sayre. He knew I wasn't a Communist—Johnny Sayre knew that for me people on the left were better company, better talkers, and hell! just more interesting than your usual fifties Patchin County Republican with his three-piece suits and his recipe for the perfect brandy alexander. So he made sure that he invited me out to dinner with him. At the country club, where everybody would see him with me, and me with him. We were going to get together in London on his actual birthday—he and his wife were going over in a day or two, and I was to follow shortly after—but Johnny wanted Hampstead to see what he thought of me. And at the end of that evening I was having my first conversation with Nails Kletzka in twenty-eight years.

"So much time had passed that nobody but an old-timer like me called him Nails anymore. He hadn't done his carpentering since before World War Two. He was just the Chief. By now he had a great big belly and a lot of lines on his face. But he remembered me—I saw in his eyes that he remembered that day in his office, and all those women that had died. And there we were, standing over the body of one of the best men ever to live in this town. *What is it with you, anyhow?* I could almost hear him ask me. By then I thought I knew, though I couldn't have told him any more than I could have in 1924.

"The next day we went in a little party to Johnny's office—me, John's widow, Chief Kletzka, and that little red-haired reporter from the *Gazette,* Sarah Spry. The one who writes that social column. I was just along to hold up Bonnie Sayre, and Nails didn't much want me there, but he couldn't refuse the widow's request, could he? It was Sarah Spry, the woman from the paper, who first saw John's telephone pad. 'Anybody know who these men are?' she asked. Nails and I leaned over to look at the pad and we both saw that name at the same time. Bates Krell. I thought someone had just clubbed me. Nails didn't say a word. He just walked out. I didn't even have time to ask him if he knew the other name on the pad. Sarah Spry kept asking 'Does this mean anything? Does this mean anything?' and her voice grated like a fingernail on a blackboard. But I didn't blame her: it was a reporter's question, and she had been one of the first people to see John's body. *I* couldn't tell her. I went downstairs to talk to Nails, but he was already gone.''

6

"After that episode between myself and Mr. Krell I started to look back into this town's history," Graham told them. "I didn't have any idea of what had happened to me—after a couple of weeks I could hardly be sure anymore that *anything* had really happened. It seemed more and more like a dream. I'd go down to the docks and stare at the *Fancy* and try to convince myself that I wasn't as crazy as Nails Kletzka thought I was—if I had any proof of my sanity, it was that Bates Krell had disappeared for good. His boat sat there getting dustier and increasingly battered, and six months later the town of Hampstead sold it to pay off the taxes.

"There was another factor that gave me the impetus to start investigating local history. When Daisy West had disappeared, I'd overheard my father say something to my mother about a black summer—he clammed up pretty soon when he saw that I was paying attention, but the phrase stuck in my head. Black summer. I'd sort of had my own black summer by then, you know. And then I had a feeling—one of those feelings you can't ever prove to be true, but which you think is true anyhow. That feeling was that things had always been funny in Hampstead: that Hampstead was a natural place for black summers. So I began to dig around in the old newspapers and in *History of Patchin*, and from there eventually to Dorothy Bach herself—and to all my researches into what happened during the Black Summer. And I'm still learning about it. An offensive young snob at the Historical Society gave me another clue just this noon."

Richard could not hold the question in: "Well, what did happen, Graham? From what you said before, I guess the town was somehow cut off . . ."

"Gradually but surely," Graham said. "And because of that, Hampstead almost died altogether—no mail, no coaches stopping, no ships arriving. None of the trade and contact that keeps a town alive. Of course it didn't start that way. Like this summer, it started with a series of brutal murders. Then the Dragon became more powerful—as he clearly has this summer. There was a terrible fire on Mill Lane. Where that fire this summer killed most of the firemen in three towns. Well, think of that! Just about a hundred years before the Black Summer, General Tryon's men, aided by one of our local gents, burned down most of Greenbank and Hillhaven. That's three major fires, roughly a hundred years apart . . . a Williams and a Smyth died in 1779, at least one person from each of our families died in the Black Summer, and serious attempts have been made on our lives this summer. I'm just suggesting to you that the Dragon seems to be strongest and hungriest just about once every hundred years.''

They were looking at him, but for a moment their eyes were vague: they were remembering what the Dragon had done to them that day. Curiously, Tabby Smithfield, who had been left an orphan by the events of that day, was the most intent. He had finished only half of his bottle of beer and was leaning forward cross-legged, his jaw muscles working.

"What was on Mill Lane in 1873?'' Richard asked. "Houses?''

"A cotton mill,'' Graham said softly. "The Royal Cotton Mill took up that whole peninsula. Royal Cotton wasn't one of the biggest in the country, and the cotton business was always a little slow in Hampstead, but Royal Cotton was an important part of this town. It employed hundreds of people. And if it had prospered, the entire nature of Hampstead would have changed—its character would be entirely different by now. What are we, really, but an affluent bedroom for New York? We could have been a town that supported *itself,* that depended upon *itself* for its destiny . . . do you see what I'm saying? When Royal Cotton burned to the ground in June of 1873, Hampstead lost its significance.''

He stood up; put his left hand in the small of his back and stretched backward. Graham took a few aimless steps toward his desk, then turned and faced them again. "Nobody ever found out how the fire started. Or how, once it had started, it spread so quickly. This was a genuine mystery, my friends, and it still is. Royal Cotton had no furnaces. It had fireplaces in the managers' offices, but in June they would have been stone cold. Was it arson? No one knows.''

He touched the bruised side of his face. Graham looked unnaturally white now, as if the effort of talking had drained him of most of his strength and energy. Even his resonant voice was frayed and tired. "Royal Cotton had been supposed to bring prosperity to Hampstead, but instead it brought ruin. The fire spread across the marshes from the mill, jumped right across that little estuary beside Poor Fox Road, and gobbled up houses all through Greenbank and Hillhaven. The area must have looked much as it did when Tryon's men fled back toward their ship. And it spread the other way, too, burning the crops and the houses nearly all the way to where the country club is now. The town was ruined. Its throat had been cut. Hundreds were dead." Graham turned toward the window as if he wanted to face down the mocking ghost there. "But that wasn't the worst thing that was going to happen to Hampstead."

He went to the coffee table in front of the other three and picked up a small gray book. "Half of the people in town picked up and left. A lot of them just walked out on everything they owned. I think they *felt* something—they had the shivers, and they wanted to get out." Then Graham gave a long, despairing sigh. "They knew worse things were coming.

"And we know what those worse things are, we've seen them now. Richard has seen it—I saw it on the bottom of a ravine. Tabby heard it calling for him. Patsy . . ." His face showed his torment. "Patsy saw it coming for her, and only Tabby could save her." He shook his head. "Those who left the town—they did the right thing. It was the ones who stayed behind who made the mistake. Let me tell you about this book."

He held it up. "*Curious Voyages,* by Stephen Pollock. If he's remembered today, as I have just learned, it's for only one story. 'Dread.' It pops up in anthologies every now and then. But Washington Irving met Pollock and wrote 'The Legend of Sleepy Hollow' after Pollock had talked to him. The real setting for 'The Legend of Sleepy Hollow' isn't Tarrytown, New York, or the other villages that are sometimes mentioned—the real setting is Connecticut. Where Ichabod Crane, according to Irving, was born and raised."

Richard Allbee raised his eyebrows. For a moment he almost seemed to smile.

"Yes, Richard. Ichabod Crane. One of the visions from Mount Avenue. Shown to you because you were the only one of us who would recognize him. The Dragon was having fun."

Graham turned his chair around and sat. "In one of the chapters in this book, Pollock describes a journey he took by coach from New York to New Haven during the summer of 1873. I want to read you a couple of paragraphs. It won't take long."

He opened the book and began to read. "*My companions*

*in the coach began to manifest all the signs of nervous dis-
comfort as we drew nearer to Hampstead. This was latterly a
village of some charm situated most pleasingly on the coastline of Connecticut, but some months previous laid waste by
fires.*

*"These poor beleaguered citizens of America, each the
girth of a hogshead of ale and blessed with excellent health,
functional teeth, and the Republican absence of excessive hu-
mility, found that they could not bear the mention of Hampstead—far less the spectacle! Nothing would do but that the
coach's curtains be drawn, and as tightly as possible.*

*"Soon we had reached the place itself, unfortunate Hamp-
stead. The others in the coach ceased their conversations; the
two women closed their eyes with what looked to be painful
severity, and their husbands fixed their eyes firmly upon nonexistent horizons. They had paled, all four. Gradually it came
home to me that my companions were one and all fairly paralyzed with fear.*

*"As their terror grew, my curiosity imitated it. What on
earth could have inspired this superstitious dread of an
obscure coastal village? I was determined to peek through the
curtains and see the place for myself. The coach was rattling
along at twice its normal speed, and the five of us were con-
sequently thrown about within the interior. As soon as I was
pressed against the window beside me, I snatched at the curtain and looked without. One of the women screamed, and
her husband made to sever the offending hand from its wrist.
I dropped the curtain and pacified him. I hoped the speed of
our carriage would double, then double again. None of us
breathed properly again until we had crossed over the border
into Patchin.*

*"Two nights later, at my temporary lodgings in the univer-
sity town of New Haven, I wrote to postpone the appointments
I had made and devoted myself to the telling of a tale. Within
the passage of a few fevered hours I set down my story
'Dread.'"*

Graham closed the book. "He took a look at Hampstead,
and two nights later he wrote 'Dread.' Do you know the
story?"

"I do," Richard said. "I read it in high school. It's about a
man who fears that he is living in a city populated only by the
dead. In college one of my teachers said that it was supposed
to have had some influence on James Joyce."

"What did Pollock see in those few seconds? I think I know—and I think you do too." Graham looked at them each directly, unsparingly. "I think he saw, or thought he saw, corpses moving through the street. Because I think that's what happened to Hampstead. And I think that's what is happening now. Do you doubt me, Richard?"

Richard shook his head. "I can't, after tonight."

"And you, Patsy? You, Tabby?"

Patsy said, "I don't . . . I don't think I doubt you." And Tabby merely nodded his agreement with Patsy and Richard.

"That's the Dragon at his most powerful," Graham said, standing again. "What the devil time is it, anyhow? Four-thirty. Too late for an old man like me to still be making sense. You people are going to have to let me go to bed pretty soon. Though as soon as we can, I think we ought to talk about changing our living arrangements. We can't afford to be so scattered anymore. We'll have to work something out."

"I want to ask you a question," Tabby said.

Graham nodded at him.

"What makes the Dragon be more powerful in some years? Like he is now."

"I think I know the answer to that," Graham said. He went to his desk and switched off the lamp that had been burning there. Instantly his living room filled with shadows and looming spaces. "Our families each had at least one person employed at Royal Cotton. And I think people from our families, at least one person from each of the four families, stayed in Hampstead during the Black Summer. Stayed to fight the Dragon. And I think they eventually located him and killed him." He crossed his arms over his chest. "But he has never been as strong as he is now. I hate to say it but I think *we* make him stronger."

Patsy asked, "Is the Dragon always a man?"

"In Dorothy Bach's book, there is a reference to a woman named Hester Poole, who was interred on Kendall Point in 1812. 'For having grievously transgressed,' was the explanation. No, I don't think the Dragon is always a man. I just think it feeds on us for as long as we let it." He threw up his hands in a gesture almost despairing.

The others stood up and began to move awkwardly apart. Tabby went to Richard's side; Patsy hovered alone by Graham's typing table.

Graham opened the door and let Richard and Tabby out;

for a moment he stood in his door and watched them go across the street in the dark. Then he turned to Patsy.

"I don't want you to think I'm forward," she said. "But I'd like to stay here tonight." She smiled at him, and exhaustion showed starkly on her face. "Do you have a spare bed somewhere in this library?"

Graham smiled back. "There's one buried under a mound of books—across the hall from me. You even have your own bathroom. I'll get you some sheets and a pillowcase. You beat me to it, you know. I was going to ask you."

"I don't think I could stand being alone in my house," Patsy said. "Not after today."

"You shouldn't be alone anywhere," Graham said. "None of us should, really. It's too dangerous. I should have known all this was coming, that first night—when we went to the marker stone. In fact, I did know. I just didn't believe it."

Patsy suddenly yawned.

"Oh my, let's get you upstairs," Graham said. "I just want to give you one more bit of advice. Okay?"

She tilted her head. "Shoot."

"If you hear somebody rapping on your door tonight, don't let him in."

Patsy laughed out loud and put her arms around Graham's neck.

4

The Bottom of the Mirror

1

In the second week of August, while Tabby Smithfield readied himself to imitate Graham Williams and attack the Dragon single-handedly, two seemingly unrelated events occurred which might have been supposed to affect the life of every human being in Hampstead, Hillhaven, and Patchin. But of course nothing was what it seemed and the two events—Dr. Chaney's first announcement of "Dobbin's Syndrome" and the press conference conducted by Dr. Theodore Wise and Dr. William Pierce in a Butte City motel—were intimately connected; and Hampstead and the other towns rolled on as though nothing had happened. That was confirmation of their madness, if any was needed; after the press conference, none was.

The dozen or so surviving "leakers," in fear of their lives and tired of hiding in abandoned houses, had found their way to the safety of the Yale Medical Center. There Dr. Chaney supervised their cases and worked out an increasingly brilliant series of life-support systems for them. Chaney finally designed a foam-and-fiberglass structure that could be molded to the patient's changing requirements—when the patients were in the final stages of the disease, they were surrounded by a kind of exoskeleton, a dish of a firm but pliable rubbery substance with a strong resemblance to an egg coddler. Dr. Chaney thought he was ready to announce the appearance in Patchin County of "Dobbin's Syndrome" in a splashier forum than *The Lancet*, which had been sitting on his article for more than a month—"Dobbin's Syndrome," if not Dobbin himself, had become his cause. He invited a medical reporter from the *New York Times* to New Haven and drove to the train station himself to pick the man up. In the black leather folder clamped under his arm as he waited at the top of the ramp were twelve eight-by-ten color photographs that would help prepare the young reporter for what he would see at the medical center. The reporter, it is safe to say, had never seen anything like Chaney's photographs; nor had he ever seen anything in the line of his work that affected him like the sight of what remained of Pat Dobbin—at that point the illustrator was suspended in a container like a small pink bathtub.

Ted Wise and Bill Pierce read the reporter's article on their computer screens in Montana—since the disappearance and presumed death of General Haugejas, their division had been stripped down to just the two of them and a secretary. Their laboratory had been dismantled sixteen days before, all the other scientists scattered to Telpro plants and installations, some of them in universities, across the country. Wise and Pierce had supervised the virtual destruction of the project they had headed for nearly two years, sent off the rest of their staff and carefully isolated and bottled their entire stock of DRG-16. They knew they would never create a DRG-17. In the afternoon of the eighth day of their existence in an essentially jobless limbo, a Telpro truck driven by an Army Spec 4 in civilian clothes carried away the padded crate which held the big metal bottles. Wise and Pierce had loaded the crate onto the back of the truck themselves. The Spec 4 jumped up into the truck's bay and slapped a gummed label to the crate. MACHINE TOOL PARTS.

"What do you suppose they'll do with the stuff now?" Bill Pierce asked his boss as they stood by the gate and watched the truck turn east on the dusty road toward the highway. The truck already looked very small, dwarfed by the immense desolation of the landscape.

Wise knew. "It'll go in the drink," he said. "They'll put it in another container and drop it off a boat and hope the stuff'll sit on the bottom forever. There won't be any records on it."

"Do you think we'll get another project?" Pierce asked. The truck was still in sight, the size of a Matchbox toy.

"What do you think?" Wise said. His lips were dry and chapped, and the prominent front teeth looked dirty.

"I say we got a chance."

"Sure. If Haugejas turns out to be immortal." He ran his tongue over his front teeth. "Remember Leo Friedgood?" he suddenly asked. "I hope that son of a bitch got what was coming to him."

After another eight days of their limbo, Pierce gave a peculiar shout while reading excerpts from the *New York Times* on the computer service. Wise looked up blearily from his cot in the office. "They find Haugejas?" he asked.

"Oh, God," Pierce said. "Come here and take a look at this."

Wise staggered over to the terminal. After he had read the first two paragraphs of the article the young reporter had written about Pat Dobbin and the others, he no longer felt tired. "That's it," he said. The memory of Tom Gay screaming behind a glass wall, never far from his mind, momentarily blotted out the green-on-charcoal words on the terminal. "That's really it. A wild card—that's what I told Friedgood, isn't it?" He rubbed his eyes, then leaned closer to the terminal, as if that might change the words.

"What do we do now?" Pierce asked him. "I think I know what I want to do. I think I'll do it even if you don't agree."

Wise gave him a look that for a moment was purely fearful. "You know what the consequences will be, don't you?"

"No. Neither do you. But I think we've been sitting on this too long already. I say we call up this reporter, and his editor, and anyone else we can think of, and start telling the truth."

Wise passed his tongue over his front teeth. He looked at the glowing terminal again. "That's what I say too."

Two of the consequences Dr. Theodore Wise had foreseen took place immediately after the impromptu press conference at the Best Western just outside of Butte: he and Dr. William Pierce were fired, and half an hour later were held for questioning by the Montana state police on the telexed request of the state police of Connecticut. The press conference had been a wilder affair than he had imagined: television cameras had materialized around him, reporters had shouted questions at the tops of their voices, someone always seemed to be running into the suite with a headset over his ears and another loud question.

"How does it feel to know that you killed all those children?" a woman in sunglasses and a fringed buckskin jacket asked him.

Wise swallowed: he tasted cigarettes, though he did not smoke. "Well, that result . . ." he began, trying to answer the question honestly. "That result was one of the reasons Dr. Pierce and I assumed that our work was unrelated to the tragedies in Connecticut. Our results fell within certain parameters, and that was really pretty far off the map. Children drowning themselves, I mean." His face reddened. "I still cannot think that our product was responsible for such a thing. Agreed, it is morally shocking. But in our subjects we never saw any inclinations toward suicide, whether individual or mass."

"Your subjects were *apes!*" a man in a plaid shirt yelled from the back of the room.

"No, they were monkeys," Wise said. "We did see frequent cases of instantaneous death, to a total percentage of five to eight ranging through all categories of DRG."

More pandemonium, and such a flurry of questions that Wise answered the only one he was certain he had heard correctly. "Yes, I would assume that the DRG was responsible for a portion of deaths in the area on the day of the accident."

Bill Pierce stood up; he had seen two policemen enter the suite.

"What should they do in Hampstead?" a man's voice called through the shouting evoked by Wise's answer.

"Put a fence around it," Pierce said.

That was only the first of dozens of news conferences dealing with Hampstead and DRG. The Telpro press officer held one, then another, and then another: at each of these appearances he denied what he called "the allegations"; he defended the record of General Henry Haugejas; he promised a full review of the situation. He said nothing. The Pentagon press attaché said no more, but said it only twice. The parents of Harvey Washington, one of the three young men who had died, held a press conference in their living room to accuse the Telpro scientists of racism. The Secretary of Defense, questioned about the Hampstead furor—for it was that by now—said, "Happily, we're in a condition of complete deniability on that." So many demonstrators were appearing in front of the Telpro building every day that the New York police cordoned off the sidewalk on East Fifty-ninth Street to keep the pedestrian traffic moving. A Senate subcommittee was formed; the subcommittee subpoenaed a truckload of files and documents from Telpro, and then it promptly got lost in them. Two film deals had been nailed down before Dr. Wise and Dr. Pierce had spent as many weeks repeating their story. *Time* magazine ran a feature titled "The Strange Story of Patchin

County.'' *Newsweek* asked: ''What's Happening in Hampstead?'' *Newsday* wondered: ''Did DRG Create a Killer?''

As Graham Williams had predicted, the commuter trains no longer stopped at the Hampstead, Greenbank, and Hillhaven stations—once Pat Dobbin had pitied the men so driven that they lined up on those platforms even on a Saturday, but even if Dobbin had pity enough now to give some of it away, there was no one left to take it from him. The trains swept by empty platforms. Now and then a man, not always the same man, showed up where he had been used to catching his train to Grand Central. His suit was very likely misbuttoned and his hair uncombed; his briefcase was empty; he could not have explained what, precisely, he was doing. In any case, he had arrived at the wrong time. This composite man rubbed a bruise on the side of his face or nudged a loose tooth with his tongue—he had a murky but satisfying memory of a fight in the parking lot at Kiddietown (or at the bar in the Chez Normand, or in front of the checkout counter at Grand Union) but could not quite remember why he had been fighting nor why it had felt so good. Eventually the man wandered off or jumped down to poke around on the tracks or took off his clothes or smiled and tossed his briefcase through a station window or . . . whatever it was he did, if he was still there when the next train rushed past, the noise and furor and color of Conrail's hasty visit probably frightened him.

Graham Williams had not foreseen that the state police would install roadblocks on the thruway exits and entrances for Hampstead and Patchin, but he would have known that the effect of the state closing off these towns was almost negligible, at least in the towns themselves. Hampstead people could not drive to New York anymore, not unless they took Route 1 up to the far end of Patchin and could talk their way through a police inspection post—but Hampstead people did not often feel like coming out anymore. By the time of Wise's press conference, all those who wanted to go had left. Those who remained had enough to think about without bothering themselves with trips to Bloomingdale's.

For even the most deranged and the most violent, for even the fifteen-year-old who had discovered a mad blooming joy in splashing gasoline on a wooden house and throwing a blazing book of matches at it, Hampstead had come to be filled with odd dreads and terrors: as if they too secretly were ''leakers'' and could be tracked down and destroyed. Hampstead people heard voices at night, drifting down the attic stairs or whining outside the bedroom window. The voices were almost but not quite recognizable . . . it may be the mind *fought* those recognitions. Even the craziest, even the most violent, made sure now to lock their doors at night, and to lock the bedroom doors too. Walking the tree-lined streets, people kept their eyes straight ahead; golfing, they silently agreed to skirt certain fairways—there were places that made you feel funny, that was all, and you stayed away from them.

More and more, sudden holes appeared in the fabric of daily life, holes that once had been filled with people. Both Archie Monaghan and his partner, beefy Tom Flynn, just stopped coming to their office in the last week of July. Their secretaries continued to come to work until they had typed up the last land contract, duplicated the last will, filed the last deposition. Then they found their way down the hall to the offices of another law firm, Shobin Schuyler Mink Fine & McFeeley, where the secretaries had brought in a television set and spent the days engrossed in soap operas and game shows—they sent out to the deli for lunches. Shobin and Fine had left town in early June, Schuyler a week later. Mink had been killed in a hit-and-run accident outside the Framboise restaurant, and McFeeley's body was later found in the same spot of rough on the golf course that yielded up the bodies of Archie Monaghan and Tom Flynn. The women felt better being together; they wanted one another's company.

Around the Krell house on Poor Fox Road, the weeds had started to die: no one saw, so no one asked why, but the crabgrass and dandelions, the wild timothy and ragweed, were beginning to shrivel and turn black around the edges. On Kendall Point the plants were dying too, and sometimes the ground seemed to breathe out a gray dingy smoke—but that must have been mist.

2

A troubled Tabby Smithfield was walking down Beach Trail in late-afternoon sunlight three days after the long night in Graham's living room. For these three days Tabby had spun back and forth across a difficult internal point—knowing that he had to make a decision, he had succeeded only in confusing himself. Tabby had withdrawn a little bit from the other three, afraid that his uncertainty might force him into saying too much. He did not want to discuss what was on his mind with anyone until he was sure of his feelings; and even then, he wanted to talk about his decision with Patsy alone before the two men got involved. With any luck, they would not get involved until everything was over: Tabby knew that Richard and Graham would never approve of his going alone against the Dragon.

When Tabby reached the end of Beach Trail he turned left. He looked over his shoulder and ran across Mount Avenue, the simple physical release of pushing himself off the crumbling blacktop momentarily blotting out his problems. After a few seconds of comparative bliss, he slowed to a walk again. A moment later he again looked back over his shoulder. All he saw was the gently curving length of Mount Avenue unreeling itself beneath the oaks to Gravesend Beach. Tabby paused, put his hands in the pockets of his tan corduroy jeans, and made sure no one was hiding behind one of the big old trees. Finally he shrugged and turned around; began walking again toward the house where he had been born.

He still had the nagging, persistent feeling that someone was following him.

When he looked around again he saw only the crumbling and pitted road, the massive old trees, the glossy banks of myrtle before brick walls. Sunlight trembled on the road, cut into patterns by the leaves. Tabby lifted himself onto the balls of his feet and started walking forward again.

Still that prickly feeling persisted.

The four of them had eaten their meals together since that long night of talk; Graham and Richard spent most of their time trying to figure out if there had been any pattern in the kind of person chosen by the Dragon, or if the killings had revealed anything they might have overlooked. Patsy sat in on these discussions, she pretended to be thinking as concentratedly as the two men, but Tabby had always felt her sliding away—sending him little questioning darts. He had resisted these, but the notion of rejecting anything Patsy McCloud offered him contradicted everything he felt about her and helped send him back into himself. At meals he ate little, said almost nothing.

He could *do* it: he held to that. Graham's long story about Bates Krell had been narrated in a kind of code he alone had understood; deciphered, the code meant that only Tabby Smithfield, of the four of them, could destroy the Dragon. But did it mean that he had to act single-handedly, as Graham had? Much of Tabby wanted to do it alone, to prove himself to the others at the same time as he kept the secret of the attempted burglary—all of that now swarmed with shame and blackness for Tabby, he could not imagine or remember how he had wound up crouched in the back of Gary Starbuck's van, everything leading to that moment had been like a whirlpool hauling him down into itself against his will.

Graham had made a point of stressing that when he met Bates Krell he had been closer to Tabby's age than to Richard and Patsy's. And at least to Tabby, most of the emphasis of Graham's story had been on his isolation. Graham had trusted himself to act alone, and when he had needed help he had found it. You could not go bob, bob, bobbing through as many schoolyards as Tabby had without learning that the great gifts in life went to those who acted all along as though they expected them.

When he thought about that long wing of fire lashing out to murder his father, Tabby knew that he had to kill the Dragon: it was only when he actually thought about doing it that he had to confront his fear.

When he thought about going back into Dr. Van Horne's house, his stomach froze.

Now Tabby stood before the iron pickets of the fence, looking across the yellowing lawn to the house his grandfather had owned—the house Monty Smithfield had probably assumed would pass in time to Tabby. On this land three hundred years ago Gideon Winter had set in motion the series of events that would irrevocably alter Tabby's life. For Tabby that was the strongest proof that he was meant to destroy the old man in the house above Gravesend Beach. The very fact of his birth in this house was part of his having been chosen.

Yes, Tabby said to himself. The killing of Wren Van Horne was his job.

A shadow fell across the baking grass just before him, and Tabby jumped—he had been deep in his private world. He whirled to face the shadow's owner, frantic, convinced that Wren Van Horne had followed him up Mount Avenue and was now going to try to kill him: and instead of the doctor he saw before him the one person he would truly have been willing to see.

"I'm sorry," Patsy said. "I guess I sort of sneaked up on you—I didn't mean to startle you, Tabby."

"Oh, Jesus," Tabby said. "I mean, okay. I guess you really did startle me. Wow. I must have jumped about a foot."

They smiled at each other, and Tabby felt her mind brush his. He deliberately shuttered his thoughts, and felt the brusqueness of it: if Patsy had excluded him in that way, it would have felt as though his fingers had been caught in a door.

"Sorry," Patsy said. "I shouldn't have done that."

Tabby shook his head. "No, it's me. I guess I'm nervous or something. What are Richard and Graham up to?"

"The same thing they were up to when you left. Talk, talk, talk. I think they're actually having a wonderful time, in spite of their frustrations."

"And so you decided to follow me. Or did Graham tell you to follow me? I guess everybody thinks I'm holding out on them."

Patsy shook her head vehemently. "Of course Graham didn't send me after you, Tabby, and if he had, I would have told him to go to hell. I came here because *I* wanted to talk to you and I thought that I'd find you here—nobody sent me. I'm not spying on you."

"Yeah, I guess I believe you." He smiled back at her.
you do believe me, don't you? it's important.
I do you know I do
but you're still holding out on us
Patsyyyy . . .
I think you want to tell me—I think you want help
yes yes yes okay
"Okay," Tabby repeated. "You're right, I do. I do want help. But only yours."
mine is the only help I can offer
"You know what I mean."

She nodded. "The only thing I don't know is why."

"Didn't you ever do anything that embarrassed you? Can't you understand that?"

A faint trace of color appeared in Patsy's face.
you'd risk all our lives because of embarrassment? *Is that all that kept—*

"No, that's not all," Tabby said quickly. "Maybe 'embarrassment' is the wrong word."

"I bet it's not so bad," she said, coming nearer and daring now to put her hand on his shoulder. "Whatever you were doing, Tabby, it wouldn't seem so terrible to us."

He shook his head.

"But you know also that you can't keep silent any longer. If you know something . . ."

Their eyes met. "Oh, I know," Tabby said. "I was just thinking about that."

"I watched you when Graham was telling us about Bates Krell. I could tell what you wanted to do—you want to kill the Dragon by yourself, don't you? Just like he did. It was written all over your face."

He nodded: if she had seen that much, then she knew the most important thing.

"I could kill him," he said. "If Graham could do it when he was only twenty, I could do it now."

"You know who he is," Patsy said, finally stating the real subject of all their conversation. "I thought you did."

"I'd like to bring you his head on a plate," Tabby said, smiling grimly. "That's what I'd really like."

There was an electric silence between them for a moment, and then before Tabby could speak again, Patsy said, "I'd rather come with you. Let's both put his head on a plate."

It was just what he had been thinking, advanced another step in reasoning. He inhaled: now she would never leave him alone long enough to do anything anyhow. Patsy had forced his hand beautifully, and made it impossible for him to make any choice but the one he most desired but had not yet come to. He and Patsy would kill the Dragon together.

"He killed my father," Tabby said. "He made everything *be* this way. I saw his face when I was five years old—I was a little boy, and I saw him *murder* someone." Tabby's sense of outrage seethed, then calmed. "I want to do it tonight," he said. "Let's do it tonight."

"Two of us should have a better chance than you alone," Patsy said. "And we've been each other's good luck, haven't we?"

He could see the fear in her face, and knew it matched his own; but she was strong enough to carry both of them through. Tabby's hesitation died.

"Tell me his name," she said.

"It's that doctor who lives in the big house just above the beach. Dr. Van Horne."

"And you're sure about that—I won't ask you how you know, I just want to be sure that you really *do* know."

Tabby nodded, seeing amazement and surprise and, even more than these, confidence in him replace the fear in Patsy's face. "I really do know," he said. "It has to be him. But you have to promise me—you won't tell Richard and Graham."

"I should." She looked into his implacable face. "But I won't. I promise."

"Tonight," Tabby finally said.

"About six or six-thirty? I usually go out for a walk around then. I don't want to make Graham suspicious. And there's something I want to pick up from home."

"I'll meet you out on the street. Richard and Graham are so tied up in each other, they'll never notice we're gone."

Patsy gave him a nervous smile, acknowledging the rightness of this.

"And you really won't tell the others?"

"I promised you."

"You're pretty special," Tabby told her. He was seeing her suddenly and for the first time not as someone separated from him by the disparity of age and sex, but as an equal. A robin began its song. Standing a foot away from Patsy McCloud in the hazy sunlight before his grandfather's old house, Tabby took in this small woman with prominent cheekbones and delicate lines around her large brown eyes—

you too, buster

—and was the adult man he would be someday, looking at a woman he had known so long and with so much affection—

??? what??? Tabby?

—that his imagination could follow hers by instinct. Around Tabby the world wildly swayed, and he was twenty years older, the true partner of Patsy McCloud, and so much information about himself and Patsy streamed out from her that he could not sway with the world: fields of flowers, glistening with rain, lay about them: he took an awkward, lurching step backward, and that broke it. The world was still and Patsy's history, which had somehow miraculously been the history of himself and Patsy, was no longer flowing into him. That odd singing vision had left him; the robin's song had ceased.

what the hell???

Patsy I, Patsy I . . . how?

"What was *that*?" she said to him—her face was wild. She stepped right into him and put her arms around his chest. "My God," she said.

"I can't, uh . . ." he began. "I can't, uh . . ." He blinked rapidly, then stepped back from her, still holding her arms. "Holy mackerel."

They dropped their arms and moved apart from each other. "Okay," Tabby said. "Okay. Six o'clock."

He watched her go away from him—she turned and waved just before she went back up Beach Trail.

Tabby decided to walk up to the hole in the ground filled with blackened rubble that until three days ago had been "Four Hearths." This was his father's only grave.

As he walked up the hill Tabby again had the crawly sensation that he was being followed, but he did not even bother to look over his shoulder. The feeling was a part of that weakness for which Patsy McCloud and "Four Hearths" were the cure.

3

"What time is it, Richard? Should we be getting back inside?"

Richard Allbee, sprawled on a lawn chair, raised his arm and squinted at his wrist. "About five to six. Why go back inside? It's so nice out here. But I suppose I ought to start dinner soon."

Graham took a long draw on his cigar and then released a thick plume of smoke. "I guess I don't associate thought with my backyard. Thinking is indoor work. But if you want to stay out a little longer, that's fine with me. Where did Patsy wander off to?"

"You got me," Richard said. "Maybe she wanted to talk to Tabby."

"Yes," Graham said. The sling was gone; he had not after all broken his elbow but only bruised it. He too lay back on an untrustworthy lawn chair, the straps of which were frayed and rusty. The tallest of the weeds pushed up against these plastic straps, and indeed felt much tougher than them to Richard—if the straps finally let go, the weeds would probably hold him up by themselves. Graham said, "They're very close. Well, they would be, given what they have in common. I'm sorry you weren't there the first time they met."

Richard rolled over on his side to look directly at Graham. Beyond the old man, who was particularly garish this evening in a red sweatshirt and the yellowish-tan tweed trousers of what must have been a forty-year-old suit, the unkempt backyard straggled in a wilderness of weeds and knee-high grass forty yards to an impenetrable wall of foliage.

"After Tabby and Patsy had seen each other, I think Patsy got ten years younger on the spot," Graham said. "They share something we'll never really understand—no more than a person blind from birth must understand the concept of color. But even so, I think it'll work for us. It's part of our arsenal."

"Graham," Richard asked, "what do you think is really going to happen to us? Believe me, I wouldn't ask this if Tabby and Patsy were here, but have we got any kind of a chance at all?"

"Yep," Graham said. "'Course we do. Even after the Black Summer, our people destroyed him. It's harder for us now, of course—everything else has changed, too. A hundred years ago, it didn't matter quite so much if Hampstead was cut off. We grew most of our own food, d'ya see? Most of this was farmland—we lived off the land. But pretty soon, the grocery stores are going to be damn near empty, and things are going to get serious. We're going to have riots over food. People are going to get killed for meat and flour and sugar." He drew on his cigar again, and held it up as he exhaled. "There won't be any more of these, either. Oh, I don't know if the government will really let it get so far, as far as food riots anyhow. I suppose they'll allow in just enough food to keep us from starving."

"You're thinking of that Telpro story on the news," Richard said. "The world thinks *that* is the reason for all our troubles here—they think that stuff is driving us all crazy. And I think it is too. DRG."

"One of history's jokes," Graham said. "The name, I mean. Or it could be a sign that our enemy has a million weapons lined up against us . . . or—get this, Richard. Maybe it's *all* this DRG. Maybe we're completely out of our heads."

"Do you really think that?"

"Nope," Graham said, and was going to say more when a great commotion on the other side of the tangled screen of trees made both men sit up on their stretched-out chairs.

"What the *hell* . . ." Graham began, and looked over at Richard, who was already on his feet. The sound coming from behind the dense gathering of trees had already doubled in volume—it was as loud as a rock band and twice as cacophonous, filling every particle of the air.

"Get up!" Richard shouted, but knew that his words too were lost—Graham seemed helpless, his face working foolishly and his big hands flying up and down. Finally Richard saw that Graham could not get out of his chair, and he grabbed his forearms and pulled him out. A hot breeze, springing up from nowhere, flattened the old man's sweatshirt against his back and pulled at Richard's hair.

The sounds of white-hot metal being plunged into cold water—that was the image in Richard's mind—now were joined by the more obvious noises of fire. Graham got to his feet just as the nearest trees burst into flame.

And then Richard was standing still with his hands clamped around Graham's wrists because what he was seeing had stolen his power to move. The hot wind fried his skin; the furry tips of the weeds nearest the property line were popping into flame like little candles. A fiery ball of light had burst sizzling out of the trees, leaving a smoking black hole behind it. Richard stood openmouthed until the huge ball of light slammed into the ground.

In the middle of a burning circle stood a giant black dog. It swung its head and snapped its jaws at nothing.

Richard and Graham were already moving backward toward the house, and in the sudden clarity of the silence they heard the dog's teeth click together. Its growl seemed to grow right out of the earth—the low powerful sound vibrated in Richard's belly. He was dimly aware of Graham picking up his lawn chair and dragging it along as they moved backward. The dog radared its massive head toward them. Richard estimated that he and Graham were perhaps twelve feet away from the back door—three or four seconds. Graham was moving as quickly as he could, and still fumbling with that chair. Neither of them wanted to turn his back on the dog, which had begun to bristle and crouch. A stiff ruff of hair stood up between its taut shoulders.

The dog's mouth quivered uncontrollably over the long white teeth. Strings of saliva looped out and collapsed into the weeds.

If it jumped at them, it could tear them to pieces before they got a foot nearer the back door.

The huge black head tracked from Richard to Graham; back to Richard; to Graham.

The dog moved slowly toward them, still crouching, tracking the men. Richard felt a blanket of perspiration rise up out of his skin and instantly soak him. A drop trembled from one of his eyebrows and splashed down into his eye, and his vision blurred. He was afraid even to blink. The giant dog crept nearer, slavering and trembling.

At last Richard could no longer bear not knowing the distance to the back door, and he twisted his head and glanced over his shoulder. He was immediately aware of a massive displacement of space—as though a building had taken flight. That rumbling low growl now hung in the air behind him, and Graham's door, propped open for the ventilation, was only a few feet away. He reached for Graham just an instant after he saw the blur of preposterous colors that was the old man convulse.

Richard caught a flailing arm and pinned it to Graham's chest, pulling both of them backward, and realized that Graham had thrown his chair at the giant dog. They fell back into the house and landed heavily, Graham on top of Richard, on the kitchen floor. The dog's muzzle jumped toward them through the door and then stopped suddenly as the animal's shoulders caught in the frame. "Screen door!" Graham yelled, and rolled away. Richard squirmed out of the way of the gnashing teeth and flattened himself against the wall. As the dog snarled and stared at him with black eyes the size of footballs, Richard worked his way around the back of the screen door. He slammed it on the dog's head, feeling the frame bend when it met bone. The dog retreated for a moment, then slammed itself into the doorway a second time, shaking all of Graham's house. Richard heard a *thud thud slap* from the other end of the house—books were tumbling off the shelves. He used all his strength to smash the frame into the dog's head. Now the animal was uttering a crazed set of squeals and roars. Richard's heart was trying to jump out of his chest: he gave the head another battering, running the frame into the muzzle, and the dog violently waggled his head and shook Richard off-balance and onto the floor. *One more charge and he'll knock the wall in,* Richard thought, and got back on his feet.

The black football of the eye swiveled furiously toward Richard. He put his shoulder to the screen door and drove it again into the muzzle.

The dog yelped and drew itself backward, leaving a four-inch-thick trail of drool on the floor. Richard saw a ribbon of blood spurt from the dog's nose and soak into the hairs and whiskers beneath. A red stripe formed down the side of the muzzle, and the dog backed all the way out of the door, making a high-pitched keening sound.

"Got him!" Graham yelled. "Got the bastard!"

The giant dog lowered its head to the ground and clamped its paw over its muzzle. Richard opened the screen door and quickly grabbed the doorknob of the yawning door and slammed it shut. Then he locked it. He could still hear the dog crying outside, as loudly as if the animal had a microphone in its throat. Then he turned around and looked at Graham.

The old man was dancing on the balls of his feet, his long white hair floating around the sides of his head. "Did you see it? Did you see it? I *nailed* the son of a bitch." He danced back a few steps, then forward again, jabbing with a long stainless-steel carving knife. "I shoved this damn thing right into his goddamned nose. Hah!"

"Good work," Richard said. "I think he was just about to break down your kitchen wall."

"What's he doing now? Is he still nursing himself out there?" Graham dashed to the window and Richard followed. The dog was supine on the carpet of weeds. When it saw the men looking at it, the dog picked itself up and barked twice. Then it swung its head around, sending splashes of blood flying onto the lawn, and looked for something to attack. Finally the dog saw the upended lawn chair Graham had thrown at it, picked it up with its long teeth and flipped it up and down until the chair was only a collection of long sticks held together with plastic rags.

"Should we try to get out the front door?" Richard asked.

"And go where?" Graham asked. The question seemed to sober him. He put the knife in the sink and passed his trembling hands over his face. "How far do you think we'd get? We wouldn't make it across the street."

Though it still bled, the giant dog now paced back and forth over Graham's weedy lawn, watching both the door and the window. "Let's try something," Graham said. "You go to the front door. Just look out. Let's see what happens."

As soon as Richard left the kitchen, the dog ceased its pacing and loped around the side of the house. Graham followed Richard through the house and found him peering through the window set in the front door. He did not even have to look outside. The dog was uttering its repertoire of squeals and yelps and interrogatory whines so loudly that Graham would have had to shout to speak to Richard. He tapped him on the shoulder instead, nodded, and jerked his thumb back toward the kitchen.

The dog beat them to the other side of the house and was already pacing the backyard when they looked out the kitchen window.

"We're trapped," Richard said.

"I think that's the point," Graham said. For a moment all his force of character deserted him, and he resembled a weary and badly made-up old clown. "Do you have any idea where Patsy and Tabby are?"

Richard shook his head. He still did not understand.

"That thing out there is keeping us from them. If it had been able to kill us, that would have been fine and dandy, but the main thing is that we can't help Patsy and the boy. Gideon Winter is after them." Graham's eyes looked stricken. "He knows where they are, Richard. And he's going to try to get them. I bet you Tabby got all worked up over my story about Bates Krell and thinks he can do in the Dragon all by himself."

"And Patsy insisted on going with him. Because she would know."

"Damn that boy," Graham said. "I knew it, knew it, knew it. Tabby was holding out on us."

"I'm not sure about that," Richard said. He glanced outside to where the giant dog was trotting relentlessly back and forth through the weeds.

"Well, there's one thing I am sure of," Graham said. "We have to get out of this house."

"I don't suppose you have a gun."

Graham tilted his head, rubbed his hands on the red sweatshirt, drying his palms. "A gun? Christ, I have something around here somewhere. A shotgun. Shells, too. I haven't looked at it in twenty years. Got it in London. Hang on, I'll see if I can find it.'' Graham walked past Richard and went out of the kitchen, almost literally scratching his head.

Richard watched the dog loping back and forth across the backyard and listened to Graham's progress through the house. After a minute or two Graham called, ''Found it!'' from the top of the house. He came into the kitchen with gray ovals of dust on his knees and a long double-barreled shotgun in one hand. ''Up in the attic, still in its case. Never even got dusty.''

He handed Richard the shotgun and thumped a box of shells on the table. ''Here, you try her. I never was much of a shot.''

Richard turned the shotgun over in his hands. The stock gleamed; an ornate pattern decorated the barrels. ''A Purdy,'' he said. ''When you said you had a shotgun, you weren't kidding.'' He looked curiously at Graham, then cracked the gun open and peered down the barrels. Satisfied, he slotted in two shells and then scooped out a handful more and jammed them in his pocket.

''Still couldn't hit anything. That's how I know I'm not much of a shot.'' Graham said. ''But in those days I was young enough to think that if I bought something, it ought to be the best.''

Richard was already pushing the kitchen window up just far enough to slide the Purdy's barrels through. Then he cocked one of them, knelt down, and waited for the dog to trot into his sights.

4

At six-thirty that evening, just about the time Richard Allbee was taking his second futile shot at a giant dog, Tabby Smithfield and Patsy McCloud were standing immediately inside the gates of Wren Van Horne's property. Here were no fields of flowers. The trees beneath which Gary Starbuck had parked his van shielded them from the house—for a moment Tabby saw all the windows in the long white facade as eyes, and was afraid that he would disgrace himself by being too terrified to move. Tabby made himself remember his father standing confused in the kitchen while a long wing of flame whickered toward him; then he made himself remember his father's screams. Tabby bent down and picked up a gnarled stick about a foot and a half long from the packed, needle-littered earth beneath a spruce. Then he turned to Patsy and smiled whatever reassurance he could at her.

"How are we going to do this, exactly?" Patsy asked.

"Just remember Graham's story," he said. "Somehow, when we need it . . ."

"Yes," Patsy said. "So it's simple as that. We knock on his door, and when Dr. Van Horne opens it, you'll cut him in half with this sword you'll suddenly be holding."

"Something like that," Tabby said. "I don't think we knock on his door, though. There must be a way to sneak into his house." He saw the faint lines about her mouth slightly deepen. "Are you making fun of me? You're really a strange woman, you know."

"You don't know the half of it, dear one."

"I can't believe we're standing here joking around when we could be dead in twenty minutes."

Now Patsy gave a real smile. "I can believe it. I'm scared to death. Do you think we'll have as long as twenty minutes?"

"Maybe nineteen," Tabby said.

"You and that silly stick," she said. "I know. I'll ring the bell. Then you jump out of the bushes and saw him in half with your stick."

"Weird," Tabby said.

"Or maybe I just shoot him in the heart."

"Shoot him?"

Patsy nodded, putting her right hand into the waistband of her trousers. When she brought the hand back out from under her loose shirt—one of her husband's, Tabby irrelevantly thought—it held a small pistol.

"Maybe you're not so weird after all," he said. "Should we go?"

"We couldn't maybe give ourselves another thirty seconds?"

"We're going to put his head on a plate, remember?"

For a second they just looked at each other, tasting their own fear and seeing it in the other's face.

okay, champ. take it away
no more sobbin'

They left the shelter of the spruces together. As if by agreement they went slowly up the far left side of the property, out of the direct line of sight of the front windows. Tabby made no effort to conceal himself behind the various trees he walked past, nor did he crouch; Patsy, not sobbin', followed a step behind. He was aware of her as a fluttering presence in his own mind, a warm companionate buzz of emotions.

When Tabby went up the last little rise, he did crouch, and then ran toward the side of the house. Squatting down with his back against the long white boards, he saw Patsy just slipping up beside him. She took several short sharp breaths. The pistol was still in her hands.

now where?

around back

Patsy half-stood, bending over so that she could go beneath the two ground-floor windows on this side, and crept to the corner of the building. Then she looked back at Tabby and nodded. He crept toward her, seeing the Sound behind her grow longer and more massive as he approached the edge of the bluff. Patsy was looking at him questioningly, and when he was beside her at last she pointed to a green bulkhead door set in the ground. He nodded. Anyone in the house would have to be looking right at the door to see them breaking in.

beautiful

locked?

let's see

Tabby slipped around Patsy and ducked into the little screen of bushes around the bulkhead. These continued down the rear of the house to the long wall of windows. He went down on his knees before the door. From the dense, spiky bushes came an odor of sap and green nuts. Tabby put his hands on the bulkhead and leaned forward to try the handle. It turned in his grasp, and he experimentally pulled upward on it. The green door creaked and lifted. He put his feet under him and leaned forward again and swung the door fully open. Just as Tabby was about to turn triumphantly to Patsy, something huge raised itself from behind the bushes and clamped down on his wrist. Tabby went pale with shock. His wrist was in the grip of an enormous and filthy hand. He looked up over his shoulder and saw the dead face of Dicky Norman scowling down at him.

5

Richard braced himself between the floor and the windowsill when he saw the giant dog come to the far end of its circuit and turn back toward him. "Try to get a head shot," Graham said. "Hit him where it'll do the most damage."

"Have you thought about the possibility that that thing isn't even there?" Richard gently put his finger against the trigger. In his sights was the narrow stippled trunk of a sapling.

"It's real enough for me," Graham said. "It did a fair bit of damage to that door."

"It's real enough to do that, all right," Richard said, "but I wonder if anyone but ourselves could see it."

"Here he comes now," Graham said, pulling on his sweat-shirt out of excitement. "Cock both those barrels, sonny. We mean business."

Richard cocked the other barrel and put his finger over both triggers. The black head pushed into his sights, and Richard saw the dog instantly register the fact of the gun. It ceased pacing and lowered its head and trotted toward him.

"He's after the gun! Richard, he's after the gun! Shoot!"

Richard was already pulling back the triggers.

The explosion, loud as a bomb in the kitchen, pushed him back into a chair. Richard felt as if he had been kicked in the shoulder. He looked up as he pulled the shotgun safely inside, hoping to see the animal fall.

The enraged dog threw itself against the window. Richard heard wood splintering—the animal had cracked the frame. The dog retreated, and Richard saw where his shots had gone. At the base of the dog's neck, a spiral of gray smoke curled from a sizzling wound.

"It isn't even bleeding," Richard said, looking up at Graham. "I don't think the Purdy is going to get us out of this one."

"Try for his eyes," Graham said.

The dog threw itself against the window again, cracking the bottom pane. Both Richard and Graham saw the wall bulge in as the heavy body smashed into it.

"For God's sake, reload," Graham said. "Try to get both barrels in his eyes."

6

The vast face swam toward Tabby, dead rubbery skin and eyes that looked as if their color came from swamp water. Another hand locked onto his shoulder. For a terrible second Tabby thought that Dicky Norman was going to take a bite out of his face. He sensed Patsy's almost equal shock and terror booming at him from the side of the house, but could not even tell her to run—his mind was frozen.

"You're a good little fucker, Tabs," Dicky said. "I knew you'd come here. I knew you'd help."

"Help," Tabby managed to get out, and then realized that this monster was holding him with two hands. Dicky had lost an arm on the night of his death. The bloated dirty face before him was inhaling, then blowing out foul air. The dead would have no need to breathe. "Bruce?" he said.

"Yeah, sure," the vast face said, and

Patsy don't shoot don't shoot Tabby sent out as loud as he could.

"Who's *that*?" Patsy asked, lowering the pistol as she came into his vision behind Bruce's enormous arm. He had stopped her a second before she would have put a bullet into the back of Bruce's head, and she still looked as though she thought that was a good idea.

"It's Bruce Norman," Tabby said. "The Dragon killed his brother."

Bruce's eyes moved incuriously to Patsy and took in the pistol she was still pointing at him. He released Tabby's wrist and gently closed his hand around the gun. Patsy backed away from his touch. Bruce had hardly seemed to see her at all. He returned his gaze to Tabby. "Good little fucker," he said.

Tabby gestured with his head. "Let's get around the side, Bruce. Where he won't see us."

Still clamping down on Tabby's shoulder, Bruce Norman allowed himself to be led to the side of the house. The three of them knelt down on the dry grass. "You came to kill Van Horne?" Tabby asked.

"I been following you," Bruce said. "You never saw me, did you? Not once. I knew you'd come back here, Tabs. We gotta kill him."

"Dr. Van Horne killed your brother?" Patsy asked. Bruce made no response: the question just sank into his skin.

The huge moon face lolled before Tabby, gray with fatigue and layered with streaks and splashes of dirt. In Bruce's open mouth yellowing teeth stuck up like fenceposts. Particles of earth, fragments of dead leaves, matted his long Indian hair. "I keep hearing him, Tabs," Bruce said. "You know? It's like Dicky sometimes was right in the trailer with me. I could hear him moving around in the living room. Finally it spooked me so bad I had to sleep outside—I been doin' that for weeks now. And I seen some funny stuff, Tabs, I sure have seen some funny . . ." Bruce's eyes slipped out of focus. "I saw a snake the size of a house come along and swallow a little boy, Tabs, he just opened up this huge fuckin' mouth and picked the kid right up and swallowed him down . . . When I slept on the beach I saw dead kids come out of the water . . . and, Tabs, all this shit is comin' from *him. He's* makin' it all happen." Bruce's eyes darkened. "Finally I wound up sleeping on Dicky's grave, right in the cemetery. That's where I go at night now. Just go to sleep right on Dicky's grave there."

"Does Dicky . . . ?" Tabby began, and then stopped. He did not want to know if Bruce conversed with his brother during the nights in Gravesend Cemetery. Bruce Norman, Tabby now almost unwillingly saw, was what Graham Williams must have been like when he had killed Bates Krell. Everything he had undergone had given him an authority that was undeniable but not sane. This degree of reality had left sanity far behind it.

"So let's go do it," he said to Bruce. The massive dreamy face before him acknowledged Tabby's readiness with a smile.

Bruce led them down the bulkhead stairs into the cellar, and Tabby quietly closed the metal door behind them. In semi-darkness he went the rest of the way down to find the others. The Van Horne cellar was a warren of small rooms and chambers, some of them seemingly filled with stacked wood and others still containing the hooked rugs and headboards of the servants who had once slept in them. Tabby found Bruce Norman confusedly moving through the narrow corridors, and gave him a push around a corner. "Tabs, we got to find the *stairs,*" Bruce uttered in a stage whisper.

"They're right here," Patsy called softly, and Bruce and Tabby turned toward her voice.

In the middle of the vast cellar space stood an incongruously small oil furnace on a circle of bricks that had once supported a multiarmed giant. Overhead, copper pipes and shiny boxy vents cut through a spaghetti of electrical wiring stapled to the joists. Patsy was standing just to the side of a wide straight staircase which came to an end five feet before the little furnace.

Bruce grunted, and they went past the furnace toward the stairs.

Then suddenly Bruce stopped moving. Tabby bumped right into him and felt as though he had collided with a structure made of concrete and angle irons instead of flesh. "What?" he said.

"Tabby," Patsy said from the other side of Bruce. "Look at the gun. It's like what happened to Graham—I think it really is like what Graham said."

Tabby moved around Bruce's side and immediately saw the twisting knot of light coiling and darting on his open palm. A silvery radiance played over Patsy's little pistol, flickering out, then surging into a wide dazzling beam that swept across the busy ceiling of the cellar like a searchlight. "My God," Patsy said.

Tabby could not speak—he was caught between awe and joy, between jealousy and impatience too. He took in the expression of single-minded pleasure on the face of Bruce Norman. "It's going to work," he said, almost as if he had not believed in Graham's account until that moment. The dazzling bar of light flashed out again and for a moment, for something less than a second, seemed to be irradiated with a rainbow of colors: and in that same fraction of a second, something glittering and golden flickered around Bruce Norman.

Then it was gone. The little pistol seemed to suck all the light into itself and shrink it down to a last failing gleam against the barrel.

"I'm gonna *kill* him," Bruce said, and Patsy got out of his way as he tottered toward the staircase.

They came up into an empty hall. The three of them stood indecisively before the open door, each looking a different direction. Tabby realized that he was still holding the gnarled stick from beneath the spruce tree, and gripped it in a more businesslike manner. Bruce Norman was staring heavily down the length of hall toward the big room at the back; Patsy seemed suddenly unsure of herself—Tabby watched her nervously scanning their surroundings.

He took his eyes off Patsy's face and noticed the odd, slimy-looking streaks and stripes along the walls—they looked almost like the tracks of giant snails, but also as though some decaying matter had been repeatedly brushed against the walls. Tabby had time enough to register the strong sharp yeasty odor that filled the house, and then Bruce's hand swallowed his. "He's here," Bruce said, and smiled loonily and turned and dragged Tabby behind him to the living room. In his other hand he held the little pistol.

They entered the long windowed room in a clattering rush, Patsy flying along behind the other two. Tabby pulled away from Bruce's grip, confusedly thinking *there's something wrong, they had a break-in here*—a chair was overturned, a lamp lay shattered on the floor. Then he saw an amoeba-shaped bloodstain six feet wide, gone rusty with age, covering the wooden floor and part of a rug. "*Dicky!*" Bruce bellowed, and Tabby whirled around.

The mirror in the ornate oval frame was doing something impossible. It was at this that Bruce Norman had yelled, but Tabby could certainly not see Dicky in the mirror; nor did he see a reflection of the room and the now rather streaky wall of windows. The mirror's surface had filled with billowing smoke and lightninglike flashes of sudden brightness: and Tabby had the illusion of depth, as if he could put his hand tnrough into this curious storm.

"*Diiicky!*" Bruce screeched, and everything changed.

Suddenly Tabby heard that monstrous rhythmic buzzing of a million flies he had first heard on Gravesend Beach; overlying it now were the sounds of many voices, as if a humming crowd were just outside the door. The air darkened, or Tabby's vision went dark, and he understood that things had just slipped totally out of control, that he and Bruce Norman and Patsy McCloud had no chance against Dr. Van Horne . . . he reached out his mind for Patsy, but felt his panicky fluttery effort crash against something hard and cold.

The air was filled with flies and grasping hands and open mouths, and he had lost Patsy. Crazed, inhuman noises roared in his ears. Tabby shouted her name and could not hear his own voice.

Someone stepped into the room through the door they had just used, and Tabby jumped backward, knocking over a small glass table and dumping a statuette of a dancer to the floor. He had a glimpse, in the confusion tearing through the air, of Patsy backed up against the windows, and staggered toward her.

So you're here at last, Mr. Smithfield, someone said or thought straight into his mind. *Do you like it?*

A few feet away from Patsy he turned around to face the man who had addressed him. Once again he heard Bruce Norman bawl out his brother's name: the air was clear again, and the sounds and the grasping hands were gone.

"You killed Dicky!" Bruce screamed, and lifted the gun.

Then Tabby saw for the first time that Wren Van Horne had become a "leaker." The doctor was far advanced in the disease: his ruined skin shimmered and moved, and he was already wearing gloves on his hands.

"In a way I did," the doctor said. "This is your little raiding party, is it?" He made a ghastly parody of a smile. "You arrive on my last night here. Excellent timing, Mr. Smithfield."

"You're dying," Tabby said, still not quite believing it—that he was doomed no matter how many tricks he could play on their minds.

"Fuck that, you're dead," Bruce said, and aimed the pistol at the doctor's chest. He pulled the trigger.

The explosion was quieter than Tabby had expected, the sound of a branch cracking in half; there was a little gray meander of smoke from the gun. Dr. Van Horne put his hands to his chest and took a neat, almost dancing step backward. When Bruce shot him again the doctor collapsed gracelessly to the floor.

Bruce let the gun fall and stood motionless, as if his will had taken him to the end of its designs. He was panting slightly; he opened his hand and stared without recognition or curiosity at the pistol, then let it drop to the bloodstained rug.

Tabby watched Patsy move forward to pick it up. Then, still stunned by the ease and rapidity of Van Horne's destruction, he looked back at the doctor's body. The right hand was scrabbling in the carpet, the fingers digging into the fibers. He realized that he felt almost cheated: monsters should not die so easily. Tabby took a step nearer the doctor, and saw the grimace on his molten face. The doctor was not dead yet, but he was surely dying.

Well, at last it's over, he thought, moving cautiously nearer to the doctor's body. Maybe this time the Dragon was dead for good . . . maybe the cycle had been ended. He came nearer, barely attending to Patsy's whisper of warning, and looked down at the dying man digging his fingers into the pile of his carpet. Dr. Van Horne turned his face so that he could look into Tabby's face, and the boy was startled by the expression of malicious amusement on the ruined face—it just leaped across the distance between them.

And then, as if all of this were carried on the doctor's glance, cacophony burst into the room and Tabby again heard the millions of flies hovering about him and the keening, exultant voices and saw the arms reaching out for him. *"No!"* Tabby shouted, and went through the crowded air until he stood directly above Dr. Van Horne. He saw white hair fanned across the carpet; the shifting and oddly Neanderthal face of a "leaker"; gleaming, powerful eyes.

In fury and disgust Tabby shouted something—lost in the turmoil of voices around him—and in a deliberate act of revenge for his father's death kicked Van Horne's chest as hard as he could. His foot sank deep into the doctor's body: it had been like kicking a sandpile. Tabby felt loose soft substances, like pillows, crumbling beneath the pressure of his foot. Before he could pull his foot out of the doctor's body, white liquid poured across his ankle.

For perhaps a second the long disordered room fell perfectly silent. Those hallucinatory noises in Tabby's ears abruptly ceased: he was standing over the now undoubtedly dead body of Dr. Van Horne, and warm white fluid was soaking into his shoe: Patsy's questioning eyes found his.

Sunlight glittered on the tall streaky windows.

Then an explosion much louder and more resonant than the firing of Patsy's gun shook the room. Tabby put his hands to his ears as he staggered back from the doctor's corpse—his whole head was still reverberating from the force of the explosion. Someone was screaming, and the room had filled with smoke. Across from him, Patsy was pointing toward the mirror.

Tabby turned his head, his eyes burning from the smoke,

and uncomprehendingly saw that its source was the mirror—greasy blackness boiled through the jagged slivers of glass still adhering to the frame: and within the tumbling clouds, a figure took shape. The screaming behind Tabby raised into a new key and then choked itself off, and still half in a daze from the suddenness with which his triumph had curdled, Tabby turned again and saw what had happened to Bruce Norman.

As the mirror had exploded, its flying glass had shredded Bruce's face. Long splinters protruded like quills from his chest and stomach, but the mooning face was no longer recognizable at all—blood spurted and flowed from every bit of sliced, mangled tissue. Bruce's features had been cut off his face: just as Tabby finally recognized this, Bruce toppled over and hit the floor with a spongy thud.

A tall thin man with an elongated and pale face stepped forward in the room; drifts and curls of smoke hung about his black clothing.

"He . . . he stepped out of the mirror," Tabby heard Patsy say in tones of the utmost disbelief.

Gideon Winter glided toward Tabby between the bodies of Wren Van Horne and Bruce Norman. Tabby, unable to move, saw the black arms raise above him: then his heart burst and his head burst and his life went elsewhere. Gideon Winter wrapped him in his arms.

7

Richard fired both barrels straight toward the dog's head, and this time he could almost *see* the wads of pellets fly—a squad of hornets—across the narrowing space between and sizzle into the wide black forehead. A dozen more smoking holes appeared, all of them concentrated around the eyes, and then the animal crashed again into the back of Graham's house. The window frame slid an inch or two away from the wall, and plaster dust showered onto the floor. Long ragged cracks jumped across the wall. The dog had circled away and was moving toward the back of the yard before it made another run at the house. As Richard ejected the spent shells and dug new ones from his pocket, he could see sparks and flames jumping all across the dog's crown and muzzle.

"One more time and he'll be in here with us," Graham

said, sounding admirably calm. "See if you can shoot his goddamn nose off. I don't know what else would stop him."

"I don't think anything is going to stop him," Richard said. "Do you want to try to run for it?"

He looked up over his shoulder, but Graham was already shaking his head. "Get his nose. Remember how he yelped when I got him with the knife?"

"Whatever you say, boss." Richard braced himself again. He watched the dog turn around and lower his head, preparing to charge the window once more.

Then the dog was flying toward him, and Richard tried to find the dot of blackness which was the nose in the midst of all that other speeding black. He moved the sights in a tight circle, almost getting it, and then he was sure he had it. He began to pull his finger slowly back on the triggers and then blinked. The wall of blackness almost at the wall now was losing shades of intensity: almost instantly it was not black at all but gray, then again almost instantly light gray . . . before he had finished pulling back the triggers he could see that hole in the greenery, still smoldering, through the head of the dog.

Richard lifted his head and relaxed his finger. "Hey," Graham was saying above and behind him. Like Billy Bentley's cat, the giant dog was fading into invisibility, washing away into nothingness, even as it launched itself into the air for its final assault on the window. For a second it was only an outline, a huge shape suspended above the weedy lawn; then it was gone. An almost impalpable gust of warm air gently spent itself against the window.

Richard sat back on his haunches, breathing not at all.

"That means it's over with Tabby and Patsy," Graham said hoarsely above his head. "Whatever the hell was going on is over. I suppose we'd better get out there and see."

"See what? Get out where?" Richard still did not quite trust himself to move.

"Ah, ask me an easy one," Graham said, and patted his shoulder with a trembling hand.

Richard pushed himself up on his feet and looked at Graham. The old man looked slap-happy with relief. "Do you really suppose I could have shot off his nose?" he asked, and was surprised to find himself smiling too.

"That's an easy one, but I don't want to answer it," Graham said. "Let's go outside and check the damage."

As soon as they went out into the back garden they smelled smoke. Richard assumed it was from the sizzling patches of hair on the dog's hide, and took a look at Graham's exterior kitchen wall. The frame was badly cracked, the whole wall bowed in—to Richard's eye, it looked like about fifteen thousand dollars' worth of damage.

"Don't bother with that," Graham ordered him. "Come around the side and look in the direction of the beach."

Richard followed Graham around the side of the house, and did not have to be given any more directions about where to look. A giant column of flame and smoke was erupting out over the Sound, twisting perhaps fifty feet in the air before shredding into falling bits of fire and windblown smoke.

"What in the name of heaven is *that*?" Richard asked.

Graham gave him a look of unhappy compassion. "I think it's the place of my old friend Wren Van Horne. There isn't another house right down there. Unless it's a fire right on the beach."

"That doctor's house? The one right . . ." Richard was remembering the first time he had seen that house, with Laura in Ronnie Riggley's car—he had asked about its cost. On the heels of this memory came another. Wren Van Horne had been Laura's doctor.

"I think our friends went on a dragon hunt," Graham said. He was already moving toward his car, and Richard hurried after him.

Richard slid into the passenger seat just as Graham released his clutch and shot backward into Beach Trail. He twisted the wheel, changed gears, and jerked forward. Graham did not stop at the Mount Avenue corner, did not even look; he stepped on his accelerator and spun around the corner to the right. "I suppose Wren was your Laura's doc," he said.

"Yeah," Richard said.

"I'm just thinking out loud," the old man said, not knowing that he was about to express something that had occurred to, then eluded, Bobo Farnsworth one night outside the Pennywhistle Café, "but you know, the only people who recognized our killer were the women who opened their doors to him. How many men know what their wives' gynecologists look like? If they saw him in Franco's, would they know who he was?"

"Jesus," Richard said, but even he would not have known if he was responding to Graham's suggestion or to the spectacular pyre that they saw commanding the top of the bluff as soon as they had swerved in through Dr. Van Horne's gates. Nearly all of the long white house was invisible behind leaping yellow flames and billowing smoke. From the bottom of the long hill leading up to the bluff the column of mingling smoke and fire was even more impressive than it had been from Graham's back garden.

"Poor Wren," Graham said. "He wasn't as strong as Johnny Sayre."

"Jesus," Richard said again.

As they came nearer to the huge body of fire up the drive, Richard finally saw Patsy McCloud on the front lawn—Patsy was trembling from her shoulders to her feet, shaking uncontrollably like a fever victim, and when he jumped out of the car and ran toward her he saw that she was weeping.

5

Graham Through the
Looking Glass

1

Now I want to talk to you in my own voice again, because what happened right after Richard Allbee and I piled out of my old heap and ran toward Patsy has to be told that way: my faith in the exact old relationship between myself and the rest of the world was tipped over on its head. We went—the three of us, Patsy and Richard and I—into mirror-land, and nothing was real but everything could have killed us anyhow. So these events are like the giant dog, it seems to me, and when Richard Allbee asked me if I really thought that all of us were just out of our minds on DRG I said "Nope," but it was never as simple as that.

All I can do is tell you what I saw with my own eyes—what I thought I saw, was sure I saw. That way I stay honest, and if you want to brood about "reality" you do it on your own time.

While Richard was comforting Patsy and trying to get her to tell him if Tabby managed to get out of the house in time, I was looking at that house, trying to accept that my old friend and fellow widower had been our enemy. Wren Van Horne— that was a blow, one I could hardly begin to come to terms with. He'd been even more a part of Hampstead than myself, one of those men who carry out their duties with the light-hearted grace that illuminates what it touches. He had always been *jaunty,* and old age has taught me that that's a spiritual quality—hanging onto it beyond the age of twenty certainly takes spirit. His patients had respected and loved him, he had been one of those people who instinctively know how to live well, but most important, Wren Van Horne had been one of my people, *my people*. And the Dragon had turned him into garbage. I thought of my admired old friend knocking on women's doors in town, of him picking up Stony Friedgood at Franco's, of all the things the Dragon had made him do, and felt a terrible mixture of emotions.

Richard was still trying to get Patsy to unlock herself from the paralysis of whatever had happened to her, and I walked up to them and put a hand on one of her shoulders. The house before me was rushing into nothingness, consuming itself with an awesome single-mindedness. The rented houses on Mill Lane must have burned down that way—and the Royal Cotton Mill, I realized with a start. The flames had marched straight down the facade of Wren's house and completely hidden it. From somewhere now not far above the top of the first-floor windows the building was solid flame, shooting and twisting far up into the air, and through the windows I saw that the downstairs rooms were a swirl of fire. I heard or imagined that I heard the screams of a score of lost voices from inside the house. Then I looked up to where the smoke and flames were boiling and twisting together so far overhead, and just as Patsy finally found words I saw what I never had seen before this moment, though I have described it to you a couple of times. It was a great bat made of fire, and it spread its enormous wings up in the smoky confusion. Patsy McCloud's dear shoulder jumped beneath my touch, blood surged and pounded in her skin or mine, and I realized that my hand was trembling too. "I think Tabby's dead," Patsy sobbed. "Gideon Winter took him away. And now I can't reach him at all. . . ." Her face strained toward mine, twisting to see me over Richard's shoulder. "I always could," she said. "Always. But now . . . now there's just this terrible *coldness* where Tabby ought to be."

When I looked up again the fire-bat was gone.

"It's all *cold*," Patsy said, and both Richard and I heard the despair in her voice. Her shoulder was calming down, but my hand wasn't—I lifted it off so I wouldn't actually start shaking her. "There's nothing else . . . there's no Tabby there. . . ."

Richard and I looked at each other, and then walked Patsy a few yards down the long lawn away from the fire. I saw in his face that he was no more in control of himself, faced with the likelihood of Tabby Smithfield's death, than I.

"You said that Gideon Winter took Tabby away," I said to

Patsy. She wore a dizzied, glazed expression that made me want to scream out loud or smash something. "Does that mean that Tabby got out of the house?"

She nodded, blinking, and I felt at least a fraction more optimism—I'd been thinking of the husk I had seen on a flat rock at the start of Kendall Point. "Tell us exactly what happened, Patsy," I said. "We'll never see Tabby again unless you help us now."

"Tabby is dead," she said flatly.

"Then I want to give him a burial. But I want to know for sure. And I want to kill the Dragon, Patsy. I want to break him into a million pieces."

That startled her into taking another internal stride forward. Her eyes widened and she lifted her head and began to tell us about meeting Tabby in front of his grandfather's old house; about everything that followed. She finished by saying, "Tabby just crumpled when that . . . that *thing* touched him. He turned white. Then they were gone . . . and I tried to find Tabby but I couldn't . . . I couldn't find anything but cold cold cold . . ."

"They were gone?" Richard asked her.

"They just weren't there anymore. Then the fire started up all around me. I ran. I got outside, and you were coming."

"They just weren't there anymore?" Richard asked, looking first at Patsy and then at me. "What's that mean? Graham, did they kill him or not? And I thought that if someone destroyed *our* Dragon the way you destroyed Krell, that it was over. What the hell is going on here?"

"I think it always was like that," I said and tried to work out what we were going to have to do next. "It looks like Gideon Winter isn't ready to give up yet."

"You think it was Gideon Winter?"

"I hate to say it, but I'm sure of it," I said. "He really is stronger now than he ever has been, strong enough to survive the death of the body he selected." I inhaled a long trembling breath. "The ante's been raised. That's what it is. He took Tabby with him because he wants us to come after him. This time he wants us together and he wants to get us all at once." Those two people who were half of the only real family I had left moved even closer together. "He would have killed Patsy, otherwise," I said. "He wanted us to hear her story, and he wanted, he wants, us to come after him."

"If we knew where to go," Richard said.

"Well, I think I do know where to go," I told them. "Patsy isn't going to like it much."

She stiffened, her eyes darting over my face—she understood, and I was right, she was instinctively resisting.

"Oh," Richard said, and tightened his arm around her. "I see." He was nodding.

"Where several boys were murdered. And both he and I know it. Bates Krell's house."

I turned away from Patsy's desperate face and looked out at the Sound. The water, which should have been calm, churned and boiled, throwing itself forward in a way that had nothing to do with tides.

I jerked my gaze back to Richard and Patsy. She was still trembling, but I saw her strength returning to her and said, "It won't be like going there alone," though I was suddenly as uncertain of that as of everything else. "Well, I'm going anyhow," I said, "I have to. I think Tabby's still alive. He's the bait."

I started walking down the long sloping lawn, at first forgetting completely about my car and then thinking to hell with it. I didn't want to drive to that house; I wanted to go on foot, the way I had in 1924. They could come with me or not. I took a couple of misleadingly determined-looking steps, knowing that nothing on earth could save me if I went into that house alone. This was not 1924, and the game had changed. I took another lonely step, mentally seeing Long Island Sound writhe against the shingle. Then I heard soft footsteps behind me, and an arm took each of mine.

"Cranky old bastard," Richard said. "After all this, did you think you were going anywhere by yourself?"

I looked from Richard on one side of me to Patsy on the other, and thought we were like the three incomplete companions in *The Wizard of Oz*. "I think it's going to be quite a ride," I said.

2

It wasn't until we were going through the gates and back out onto Mount Avenue that I saw Richard checking the shells in his jacket pockets and realized that he was still carrying my shotgun. As usual, at least when he was not tearing bricks out of a cornice or stripping paint off masonry, he was dressed up, which is to say in the way everybody used to dress way back when, even me, in a jacket and real pants—not jeans. Also real shoes instead of those pedigree running shoes guys in Hampstead wear even when they never run as far as the length of their driveway. Anyhow, the point of this is that when I noticed him still carrying my shotgun it somehow seemed a part of him—Richard and the old Purdy and those businessman clothes were strangely cohesive, like Magritte and his bowler hat. The sight of him there at my side as we walked into Mount Avenue gave me a quick boost of confidence. Or at least of willingness to really play out the thread now, to accept everything that was going to happen, as if Richard and his good clothes and the Purdy could give all three of us an irrational amount of protection. Richard Allbee with the gun in his hand had that much authority, and in that second I felt younger than he.

Maybe what I'm saying is that I felt leadership pass from me to Richard, or understood that it had been his all along.

People attracted by the tower of smoke and flame from the Van Horne house had begun to appear on Mount Avenue, walking slowly toward us, their faces tilted up so that they seemed to be watching a high-wire act.

I wondered if my heart was up to what was to come. I wondered if Tabby could really be alive. The three of us stepped onto Poor Fox Road more or less in unison.

The sky changed—without any transition it went from the hazy blue it had been to a gaseous, bubbling red. Patsy stopped moving, and I stopped too. What was above us looked like the expression of an ultimate rage, anger taken to a total limit. A thousand soundless but vivid explosions tore the sky's fabric, sending waves out to thrash and pound against each other. A moment later the sky was bright yellow; then a hard monochrome blue no sky ever was before; then a deep violet-purple; and then it was black. Two moons hung over us, one that ferocious bubbling red and the other white and dead.

All of Poor Fox Road was illuminated by cold moonlight. Patsy gripped my arm so tight it hurt. "Okay," Richard said, and we began to go forward again toward Bates Krell's house.

When we came to the place where the road bends, I saw a

dark shape hanging from one of the big trees alongside the Academy fence. It slowly spun and twisted as we came nearer, a shadowy elongated cocoon. Both Richard and Patsy had seen it, too, and I felt Patsy tighten her grip on my arm again. A second later I saw that it was a body hanging upside down from the tangle of branches.

The body twisted around to face us, and the silver light fell directly across it. The chest had been sliced open and the ribs broken, and the whole middle section of the body was a black hole. Beneath the slashes and wounds, I recognized the face of Bobby Fritz. The terrible face was laughing at us, the mouth split into a Halloween grin. Bobby Fritz's corpse screamed *"You're dead! You're dead!"*

Patsy gasped and pulled at me. Bobby's dangling arms burst into flame. His hair shrivelled and twisted in the heat, and a moment later it too began to burn, making a little *puff* as it went alight.

Richard reached back and gave me a yank, and I pulled Patsy along in my wake.

We moved awkwardly forward for a few paces, and then Patsy seemed to find her rhythm again. "I'll be okay, Graham," she said. "You don't have to frogmarch me." She pulled her arm away from mine, and then looked back over her shoulder. By reflex I too looked back.

The blazing corpse of Bobby Fritz spun around like a mechanical toy, and beneath the flames we could see his mutilated features.

Patsy McCloud snapped her head forward, and her eyes found mine. She said, "I told you, I'm okay," and marched right past me.

Just a few minutes later we saw the Krell house come into view past a wasteland of wrecked cars, and all three of us slowed our pace, as if we thought we could sneak up on it. The windows, or the black holes where the windows should have been, shone redly; but we knew Krell's house was not burning. And we knew we could not sneak up on it; we were walking more slowly because suddenly we were in no hurry to do what we knew we had to do.

Even when I was twenty and straight and pretty well muscled, that house had spooked me. I knew a lot more about it now.

Richard quickly moved on ahead of us, and went right over the moon-washed scurf of weeds to the door. He held the shotgun straight out at his hips and looked back at us. I saw his jaw muscles jumping. Patsy went straight toward him. I came up beside the other two, and Richard said, "Here goes nothing," and turned the knob and pushed open the door with the barrel of the shotgun. Patsy flattened her hands over the top of her head. Red light spilled out over our legs.

You will have worked out already that Patsy covered her hair because of the bats, but I didn't get it until I had looked in. Richard was pointing the shotgun into the room as if there was going to be something he could shoot. Maybe half a dozen bats came wheeling and skittering out of the corners of the room; Richard tried to wave them away with the barrels of the gun, but two of the bats merely circled off and flew back toward us.

Then I saw long red hair streaming from the head of one of the two bats taking another dive past Richard; and I took in that both had white faces. I did not want to see their faces—I knew I would recognize them, and that would have been worse than the sight of Bobby Fritz hanging upside down from the tree.

Richard gasped, and let the barrels sag down: he had recognized one of those tiny faces.

My temper jumped up inside me like a wild beast. Tabby's own face shone in my mind, and I gripped Richard's free arm as he had done mine four minutes earlier, and I pulled him into the house with me. "It's daytime!" I shouted, *"daytime!"*

For a second or two, maybe more, it was—we saw the real sunlight splashing against a wall, the real barrenness of the place. Ruptured floorboards, cracked walls, thick dust: we saw it. There were no bats. Patsy rushed inside and got right up next to me, and I felt strong enough to take on three Bates Krells. My temper still sizzled. Giant dogs and bats with human faces! Two moons! This stuff turned my stomach.

A movement at my side registered in the corner of my eye, and I turned my head and moved forward at the same time. What I saw was Les McCloud standing in the doorway to another room, wearing striped pajamas and a gaping robe and already pulling the trigger of a small pistol. A long line of flame erupted from the pistol's little barrel, squirted just past Patsy and me, and shot harmlessly into the room to our right.

Black night immediately returned, and the blast from the shotgun flared out just as I saw Les begin to fade into noth-

ingness. The wad of shot smacked into a wall. "He's gone,"
I said, but no longer felt like challenging the darkness.

I could hear Richard breathing hard as he ejected the spent
cartridge and sent it rattling to the floor.

We all could see that the source of the red light filtering
through the dark was the room that lay beyond the door where
Les's spectre had appeared. It spread outward from that
room, filling the doorway with a red haze.

"I know where we have to go," Patsy said, flicking a sideways look at me. Her face seemed bony and drawn in the dim
light, neither male nor female.

"Patsy," I said, "no one is going to make you go down
there."

"He's right," Richard said. "Not after the last time. You
could wait outside—you came this far, and that's enough. If
Tabby's down there, we'll find him."

"Tabby's dead," she said with that same flat certainty.
"But I'm still going with you. We have to be together, don't
we? That's what you think, isn't it, Graham?" Her eyes slid
toward me, more bravely than before.

"I don't know what I think anymore," I said truthfully.

"Well, I think I want to end it," she said. Then she surprised us both by pulling her pistol from her waistband—I
guess both Richard and I had assumed that she had left it in
Wren Van Horne's house. "I'll use this, too, if I have to.
There's one bullet left in it, I think. You two guys can wait
out on the sidewalk if you like." She tucked the gun away
back under her shirt and looked at us, just waiting to see what
we would do. She was small and brave and willful, grown far
past the woman who had come running around the corner
toward three men and a boy on that night when the first birds
had fallen from the sky. Patsy had come a farther distance
than any of us.

"Well, let's go then," Richard said, tucking the shotgun
up under his arm. "We all want to end it." He looked at me
and I saw that despite the calm in his voice he too had been
moved by Patsy.

She abruptly turned around and walked through the hazy
doorway into Bates Krell's kitchen. Richard and I followed
closely behind. The door to the basement still hung wide open
on its hinges, and we saw that Patsy had been correct—the
light came streaming up the basement stairs. When the three

of us looked down we saw how strong, how dark it was, how it pulsed. Going down there would be like walking into an enormous heart.

I stepped forward first. If anything were going to happen—if there were booby traps on these stairs—I wanted it to happen to me, not those two. Being seventy-six has a few advantages, one of them being that a premature demise is no longer possible. Still, I took those stairs slow and easy, and kept my eyes open. Like a heart—the image grew more accurate the farther down I went. I was bathed in that redness; the pulsations of the light vibrated through the treads of the stairs and the flimsy handrail.

Richard came up beside me—he too wanted to be between Patsy McCloud and whatever might be in the basement. We moved around the side of the staircase.

I don't know what we expected to find. Nightmares from Hieronymus Bosch, fiends devouring Tabby's body, Gideon Winter flying at us: anything but the wide empty space we were looking at. Glass bricks spaced here and there along the top of the walls glowed with the same redness that filled the cellar. At the far end of the room a battered workbench stood against the wall. That was it.

"Tabby isn't here," Richard said, momentarily perplexed. The anticlimax of coming into a room bare of anything but a beat-up workbench and a lot of inexplicable red light stopped him in the dead center of the cellar. Patsy drifted off to one side, and I went up to the workbench. We had come to the right place, I was sure of it, and thought that maybe I could find something to lead us to Tabby.

In the air around me I became aware of a kind of thickening—as though that pulsing redness had curdled the air. What was happening was the gradual heightening of a condition present since we had come down the stairs. We were getting over the shock of not being shocked, to put it like that, and the real character of the place was finally reaching us.

Krell's basement, not empty, was crowded with the emotions which had been set free there. Terror, despair, a soup of human misery roiled in the air around us. Until the summer of 1980 I would have rejected the notion that such an experience was anything but the projection of a suggestible observer. But in Krell's basement I knew I was not projecting all that misery. My stomach cramped into a bitter knot. The *wrongness* of the place, the monstrosity of the pleasure given by torture, had assailed me. I wanted to get back outside as fast as I could. The big heart of the basement beat almost audibly around Patsy and Richard and me, and for a second I saw the walls thronging with spiders, hideous black shapes circling toward me, a body stretched in agony on the workbench. Those pictures were all from books I had read in childhood. The three of us had to get back outside.

I started to move toward Patsy, seeing on her face that she too had been poisoned by this place, and the packed earth beneath my feet trembled and nearly threw me to the floor. A hand thrust up through the surface of the floor. Then another shot up out of the earth. Another pair of hands almost immediately pushed up only a couple of feet away.

"Let's get out of here, for God's sake," Richard was saying, clubbing away the first pair of hands with the stock of the shotgun.

Patsy said, "I don't know if we can make it to the staircase," and I saw what she meant. The earth between us and the stairs seemed to be shredding into brown sugar, granulating.

"You won't believe this, but there's a door over there," Richard said, and as we turned he pointed to the nearest wall. Set into the concrete blocks was a wooden door with big iron hinges and wide black iron crossbraces. It certainly had not been there earlier, and for a moment it looked as sinister and forbidding as everything else in Bates Krell's little playpen.

Both Richard and I went forward, trying to figure out if running for the stairs was worth the gamble. Richard pulled Patsy into a clear area, and as he did so the head and torso of a boy in his early teens broke through the crumbled earth.

A vision or hallucination Richard had described during our long talks came back to me—the cemetery ripping itself apart, vomiting out its dead. Richard's vision was our truth, I saw, and then thought: *of course, that's how the Dragon works.*

"Graham?" Richard said. "The door?"

He was thinking that maybe we still had a second or two to reach the stairs, if we ran like hell—and thinking that, then he would be the only one to make it. I couldn't move that fast, and Patsy looked ready to keel over.

I backed toward him, and he put an arm around Patsy's waist and got her moving. I checked on them over my shoulder, and saw Patsy recover herself and almost visibly accept the idea of using that door, even if it did look like it could lead only to another torture chamber.

Richard pulled the door open and we hurried through. I had to bend my neck to avoid clubbing my forehead on the lintel.

3

You see why I wanted to describe this series of events in the first person: why the pose of an objective narrator would be no good, a lie to you and me both. That heavy crossbraced door *wasn't there*. I went through it, and if I hadn't ducked I would have banged my head on it, but even then I knew that no such door had ever stood in Krell's basement. And Richard Allbee and Patsy McCloud knew that as well as I did. The door was the dream of a door; our dream; but also the Dragon's way of taking us where he wanted us to go.

The other thing we all knew was that there was no less danger on the other side of the door than in Bates Krell's funhouse. Our door was not an escape—but we could not go back, once we had chosen it.

We found ourselves in a foul-smelling tunnel so narrow that we had to go in single file. Richard first, then Patsy, then me. I brushed my hand against the curving wall of the tunnel and then quickly jerked it back—damp, spongy, resilient as rubber, it had felt like living tissue. Far ahead of Richard dim hazy light came leaking around a bend in the tunnel, seeming to promise that we would come out aboveground somewhere on Poor Fox Road or the marshy land just beside it. As we moved toward the light the walls gradually widened out, and eventually we could almost walk three abreast.

"I hope we're going to get out of here soon," Patsy said. "Are we going to wind up outside?"

I shrugged.

"It stinks in here," Patsy said. "Like a sewer."

"As long as we get away from that house, I don't care what it smells like," Richard said. "You saw the women, didn't you? Krell didn't drop them all overboard. And he killed a lot more people than anyone suspected."

That had occurred to me too. By the time we had fled through the door, at least thirteen or fourteen boys and women had broken out of their shallow graves. Krell's basement had earned its powerful echoes and resonances.

We came to the bend in the tunnel and were suddenly walking into a light so strong that it obliterated detail. For a second I was blinded, and my eyes stung, and I covered them with a hand. We had stopped moving. When I put down my hand I squinted into the dazzling light and saw that a person was standing against the tunnel wall up ahead. It was just a black shape, unsexed. "Okay?" Patsy asked, and I nodded. We started to go forward again.

"Who are you?" Richard called out. He raised the gun at his waist.

Just then I had an idea about where we were—about what this tunnel was supposed to be.

We came forward far enough to see that the person up ahead was a woman; and even before we were able to see anything of her face and clothing it was clear that she was crying.

"Patsy?" the woman said.

Patsy did not say anything. She took my arm with her left hand and Richard's with her right.

Her plain, dogmatic face swam out of the light. Severe black glasses, limp hair. The woman wore a rusty tweed suit that turned her body into a fuzzy tube. She did not look like someone who cried much.

"Oh, my God," Patsy said. "Marilyn Foreman."

"Get out of here. Get *out* of here. You're dead already, just like the boy. The farther it goes, the worse it gets."

Patsy moaned, and lowered her head and practically pulled Richard and me after her. "Leave me alone."

We were going past the woman now, and she curled her hands into her waist and hissed against the tunnel walls to let us by. I brushed my arm against her clenched hands and felt their pure and burning cold.

But we were already past her, and Patsy McCloud was still hauling at us like a mother marching two boys toward the woodshed. Her face was entirely grim. The woman behind us hissed again.

Patsy paused, and her grip on my arm relaxed.

I looked around. Richard Allbee did the same. The tunnel was empty.

"Did we just see a homely little woman who looked like a

grade-school teacher?'' Patsy asked. ''Did she tell us to go back?''

''We saw a homely little woman and she told us to go back,'' Richard said.

We began to move forward again.

''Thank God,'' Patsy said. ''If we're going crazy, at least we're doing it together.''

We took another step, and the light intensified with brutal suddenness. Patsy twisted away. My eyes painfully curdled, as if they had been poached. I stumbled forward, suddenly alone, and when I could open my stinging eyes again I too was grateful to have company in my delusions.

We seemed to have left the tunnel and come into a long book-lined room; yet the room had the same stink of sewer gas as the tunnel. Patsy and Richard, some yards away from me, moved closer. I think they must have recognized the room before I did. I looked sideways at a brown row of un-jacketed books and saw that it was familiar stuff. Like Krell's basement, this place echoed with unheard miseries, with a sordid emotional life. It too was one of the Bad Places. A wad of tarry goop dripped down the spines of a couple of adjoining books. More of the goop oozed down over other shelves and onto the floor.

The room was very hot: everything in it exuded a faint burning smell, as if it were smoldering somewhere deep within. *Where are we*, I wondered, *what is this terrible place?*

Then I saw a familiar typing table down at the far end of the room, set before a familiar window. They seemed an acre away. The window was black. I jerked my head sideways toward Richard, almost expecting him to deny what I already knew, and behind his worried face I saw the *Glenda* poster leaning against the bookshelves. We were in my living room. It had been stretched out about three times its length, but the Bad Place was my living room.

''Hey, Graham,'' Richard said, ''don't—''

''Don't *what*?'' another voice screeched from far down at the other end of the room. Oh, I thought I knew that voice too. I turned to see that a squat man in a double-breasted suit, his meaty face bristling with five-o'clock shadow so dark it was like a tattoo of a beard, was standing up behind my desk. Him. ''Don't you want your pinko friend to understand what's happening to him? Williams!'' The Senator poked a thick forefinger at me. "You're a lousy Commie, do your friends know that?''

"I was never even a halfway decent Communist, much less a lousy one," I said.

"You were *weak!*'' he bellowed at me. "You're a *drunk!* A lousy *alkie! Lush! Boozehound!* You abandoned two wives— are your friends aware of your despicable record, of your cheating and lying, are they aware of how you weaseled yourself into marriage twice and then betrayed your wives? I have here, Mr. Williams, I have a list in my hand which contains not only all of your extensive Communist affiliations from 1938 to 1952, but also your sex partners during that period." He was brandishing something that looked like a grocery receipt. "This is a disgusting record, Williams, this is evidence of moral degradation. You're disgusting because you're weak. *Weak!* You're a weak, treacherous Commie drunk."

"A drunk I was," I said. "I cheated on my wives too, just about as much as they cheated on me. But I never abandoned anyone." I was starting to get the shakes.

That shifty tattooed-looking face suddenly was only a foot or two from my own. "Weak and treacherous." I could smell the booze on his breath, also onions. "Tell me this, Williams. Don't you know that Tabby Smithfield would still be alive if you hadn't infected him with your sick fantasies?"

I started to throw a punch at his gloating face, but the face had changed before my fist had even picked up any momentum. He had turned into a capering red devil. Now he was at least two feet taller than I and he bent over me, grinning, and a forked tongue slid out of his mouth. Searing heat came off him. I felt Richard pulling me backward, and I forgot about hitting anybody and concentrated on backpedaling. If I hadn't started moving my feet, Richard would have yanked me right back on my keester.

That burning devil reached out for me: his hand came so close to my face that I saw how it was composed of a million interlacing flames, little jets of fire so tightly bound together that they formed a solid body, solid flesh. He would have taken off my face if he had closed that hand on me. Richard was moving me backward with the reckless power of a flood or a tornado, and I stayed on my feet, and the red hand just flicked past me.

Past most of me, anyhow. His hand grazed mine—the one

with which I had intended to hit him. A hundred daggers pierced my skin, acid splashed over the wounds, I yelled incoherently; and everything went absolutely black, but not before I had heard a deep chuckle.

We were back in the tunnel and the smell was worse. Another dim light lay far ahead of us, sending feeble illumination through the fleshy tube of the tunnel. "You okay, Graham?" Richard asked.

I couldn't meet his eyes; that would have told him the truth. "Yeah, sure," I said. I was shaken up, as much by what that imitation polecat had said as by what had happened right after. Well, that's almost true; it's what *should* be true. Yet I knew I had just come much closer to death than I had on Kendall Point. I could still see that huge grinning red face floating up above mine, and I knew how scared I'd been—too scared to move, if Richard had not intervened. The hand that creature had lightly touched still felt as though a tank had run over it.

"Are you?" Patsy asked.

"I never abandoned anyone," I said. "Jesus, I never did that. Someday I'll tell you the story of my marriages." But even as I said this I was seeing the grotesque red face hovering so close to mine, and feeling again that primitive terror. A devil! Devils did not exist, except as metaphors.

Then I remembered things I had said in London. *That devil is contaminating wells all over America.*

Oh, yes: I saw. I felt as though I could almost sort of move again.

"What the hell do you suppose is up ahead there?" I asked them.

"I wish I didn't have to find out," Richard said. We started forward again. I painfully revolved my right hand in the murk of the tunnel, and saw that it was completely unmarked.

This time we did not come around a loop in the tunnel to be blinded by a sudden barrage of light; that was what we expected. Instead the tunnel gradually became wider still and the light more pervasive. We seemed to be going down a slight incline. This too gradually became more pronounced, and as the light ahead grew brighter by degrees, the floor of the tunnel began to dip so markedly that the three of us had to move more slowly, using our knees to check the pull of gravity. When the tunnel began to level off again the walls and ceiling pulled away. Just when I was thinking that our tunnel was getting to look like a vaulted chamber we saw the first dead people.

They were fat and naked, standing at the side of the by now enormous tunnel; an old man and an old woman, motionless as department-store mannequins. Their eyes were closed, their skin chalk-white. They were just bulky old bags of flesh. Then I saw that they were my old friends from the beach, Harry and Babe Zimmer. I looked down in a hurry. As we went past, I felt as much as saw them turning toward us with an awful slowness.

"Oh, no," I said, seeing what was ahead. The tunnel walls swung out another step, creating a huge space that seemed hundreds of feet wide and as high as a cathedral. Dr. Norm Hughardt, as white and dead as the Zimmers, was turning to face us at the entrance to this enormous chamber. His little Lenin beard had overgrown its boundaries and now looked woolly and derelict. Like the Zimmers, he moved as if through a vat of glue. A thick white worm was working its way across Norm's substantial potbelly. Norm raised one of his hands in a gesture of almost witless entreaty.

Behind him hundreds of others trudged with that painful slowness through the vast chamber.

We walked past Norm Hughardt into this hopeless way station for the dead. My nerves were shot—I didn't want to see anybody, I didn't want to look at their faces, I just wanted to get through this horrible place. I felt pushing toward us the numb misery of all those dead, that stricken imploring wretchedness they could not help sending out.

At least we did not seem to be in any real danger—the dead moved so slowly and questioningly that even I could outmaneuver them. I thought this was an exercise in disheartening us, in softening us up. The hundreds of dead were beseeching us to rescue them: to bring them back with us to the surface of the earth: and we could not help but feel the drag and pull of that plea. Gideon Winter would weaken us with pity—weaken Patsy and Richard with it, anyhow, for already he had pretty well cut *my* strings—and then come in for the kill. Certainly we had to pity these poor creatures. I saw the people reaching out in such numbers that their arms interlaced.

And then I thought I saw the proof of this theory. In the center of the vast chamber lay a bubbling pool of gray lathery liquid; it belched out acrid fumes. Richard began to lead us around the edges of this sulfurous pond, at the same time trying to make sure that none of those reaching out toward us could actually get near enough to touch us. I was just trying to keep my feet moving. Part of me was tired enough to lie down and give up. Then Patsy went electrically taut at my side; and a few feet ahead, Richard Allbee stopped walking.

"No, no, no," Richard said. "That's not true": as if he were rebutting an argument.

I looked reluctantly toward the bubbling pool. A body labored at its far edge, struggling with that slow patient hopelessness to get itself out onto the floor. The body was slight, young, boyish. Beneath the streaks of gray scum from the pool, it was chalky white, like the others. After the boy's body had managed to get itself out of the pool, another head broke the surface. A man's corpse began trying to lift itself onto the ground, and as soon as it was halfway out of the pool I recognized it. I had just seen Les McCloud in the doorway of Bates Krell's kitchen, so the identification of his body was an easy task. Then I had to look back at the body of the boy and face what I had seen in the first microseconds of its appearance—seen with my heart as well as my eyes. The dead boy was Tabby Smithfield. The big worms had found him already and were sliding across his legs.

He could take us one by one, I couldn't see how we would have the heart to fight him, we might as well lie down in the chamber of the dead and get used to being there.

A little knot of flies had fastened on Tabby's neck.

At last I accepted the possibility—no, the likelihood—that Tabby was dead. That pitiful slight body on the far side of the pool rolled on its side with a horrible slowness.

I groaned, and the dim light filling the enormous chamber shifted to red. On the bodies still painfully limping toward us the white worms began to swell and bloat, now as red as the light. All around us the dead began to wail.

Two of them thrust their way through to the front of the pleading mob before us. I saw stringy red hair, and then recognized the face of the woman reporter who had stood over Johnny Sayre's body with me. Sarah Spry. She had managed to force one of her eyes open, giving her face a squinting and piratical appearance. "Go, give up," she said. Her voice was a rusty whisper. "You're gone now, you have to give up. Graham, you're dead."

The man woozily standing beside Sarah Spry popped open both of his eyes and screeched, *"Dead! Dead!"*

Something fat and white fell on Patsy from above, knocking her down flat to the floor. Richard and I were so startled by this sudden assault that we were frozen in our postures for what seemed like whole minutes.

I was just working out that what had fallen on Patsy was the body of a man, not one of the bloated worms, when she started to scream. Patsy was trying to get to her feet, and the dead man lying over her raised his fists and clubbed her back down. His body had been gnawed and chewed about the middle, and his buttocks were only shreds of white tissue. Patsy screamed again. I tried to pull him off by yanking back on his shoulders, but it was like trying to move a concrete statue. He turned his head and grinned, and I recognized him as Archie Monaghan, a lawyer who had been hot stuff on the golf course. He was trying to kill Patsy, and I could not stop him. I grabbed his ears and tried again to force him off. I started to hit him in the side of the head. Patsy bucked frantically on the floor.

"Move it, Graham," Richard shouted. "How many times do I have to tell you?"

"Huh?" I finally saw that Richard was pointing the shotgun at the same point on Archie Monaghan's head that I had been trying to turn into pulp.

"Get *away!*" he screamed, and I threw myself backward.

Richard put the Purdy right up to Archie's temple and pulled both triggers.

Archie's head blew apart. Gray tissues and flecks of white bone sprayed out over the bubbling surface of the pool. The rest of Archie Monaghan remained upright for less time than it took for the echoing blast to die away. Then it dropped sideways off Patsy like a dead crab. The shotgun in Richard's hand flickered feebly.

Both of us reached forward to help Patsy and she took our two outstretched hands. Around us the light was dimming, becoming only a red darkness.

Patsy came up on her feet and put her arms around both of us for a second.

"We have to run," Richard said.

In minutes we were back in a narrower space, then the

walls closed in even closer about us, and Patsy and Richard walked on ahead of me. Patsy's step was quick and firm, but I could see her hands trembling. The smells of the tunnel were even worse now, and here and there a small fire flared out, feeding on the gases. This was the world's bowel we had entered from the door in Krell's basement—the mirror's bowel, too. I knew it would bring us to Gideon Winter eventually; and all three of us must have known that Richard's turn was next.

6

Kendall Point

1

Richard Allbee's sense of direction, always dependable, had surprised its owner by functioning underground. When they had left Bates Krell's basement they had gone through the north wall and started angling east, and northeast was still the direction in which they were going. They were being led, he thought, to Kendall Point: Gideon Winter's burial ground seemed the inevitable place for their final confrontation. Richard did not want to show it in any way, but he was worried about his friends' readiness for this encounter.

Both Graham Williams and Patsy McCloud seemed half-stunned by what had happened to them—a large part of their stupor would have been caused by the sight of Tabby, so obviously dead, emerging from that stinking pool. Neither Graham nor Patsy would have survived the tunnel without action Richard had taken: after that pallid corpse had fallen on Patsy, Graham had seemed too stunned to do anything but strike it on the head. Obviously Winter was reserving some special torture for him, Richard thought, some sideshow worse than the Grand Central of the Dead they had just escaped; and he wondered if Patsy in particular were capable of acting quickly and rationally. Walking along beside him, keeping pace, she looked to Richard as if she needed most of her energy just to keep herself from fainting.

Whatever was going to happen, Richard thought, he would have to save himself. At the same time, he'd have to protect Patsy and Graham, to see that they also were not caught.

Ahead of them a dim light had appeared, and Richard felt all his muscles involuntarily tense themselves. His test, whatever it would be, was up there, and Richard was torn between bolting back the way they had come and breaking into a run—just to get it over with as quickly as he could. He kept walking, and the light playfully receded.

His testicles seemed to have frozen down to the size of a baby's. Patsy slipped her hand over his arm.

With every step he took, the light backed away, never altering its intensity, which was no stronger than that of a child's night-light. Richard gripped Patsy's arm close to his body with his own; his heart felt as though it were tripping on itself.

He took another step, and the dim light backed away from him again. He wondered what would happen if he shot at it. He and Patsy took another step together, and the fuzzy light once again retreated.

Then all at once the light was no closer, but it was familiar. He knew it. He had seen it somewhere, but without taking any notice of it: it was just a domestic workhorse, a bit of stage-setting.

Exactly.

He knew what it was, and as he and Patsy moved forward again the light did not retreat. They took another step forward, and Graham followed them into the unobtrusively altered space. *Stage-setting,* Richard thought. *What else?* The walls of the tunnel had widened, become more detailed. Shadowy objects loomed all about them. A few feet from the dim light, which in fact was a child's night-light, a triangular pennant cheered ARHOOLIE.

He saw his tall skis propped against the wall next to the closet.

Light came seeping into the bedroom, bringing its boyish clutter up into unchallengeable reality. If he kicked that chair, he would bruise his foot. If he threw the skis at the window, they would clatter down onto an actual front lawn. Richard heard noises from downstairs, the propmen and stagehands and cameramen moving about, all those who had been his true family during those years. From somewhere closer came the idle summery buzzing of a couple of flies.

A moment or two before the others, Richard saw the bodies on Spunky Jameson's bed. The flies he had heard were wandering up and down on them, lifting off and landing again. Tabby and Laura were only just recognizable. Naked, sprawled on their sides like lovers turned to each other, his wife and the boy were crosshatched with cuts and wounds,

strip-mined, trampled, pulped. Could Graham and Patsy take
it, seeing Tabby this bad? Richard turned from the bed, thinking almost that he should put a hand over each of their pairs
of eyes—but they had seen it, and were wondering the same
about him.

"Oh, Richard," Patsy said: he saw that she was more concerned for him than for herself.

Then a gray cat came padding toward them across the carpet, and Richard felt all his muscles tense themselves again.
The cat came to within two or three feet of Richard and Patsy
and sat on its haunches, looking at them with wide unblinking
eyes. A second later Billy Bentley strolled in from the same
nowhere.

2

Richard stepped away from Patsy and challenged Billy's pitted, mocking face. "You're Gideon Winter," he said.

Billy's shadowy face admitted another sharp slice of amusement. "Not yet I'm not. You'll see, bro."

"We want Tabby Smithfield," Richard said. "I don't care
who or what you are, but I do want you to get Tabby out of
whatever foul hole he's in and bring him to us."

Billy lifted his eyebrows.

"Alive or dead," Richard said. "Just give him back to
us."

"The way I gave your sexy wife back to you?" Billy
asked. "I guess you liked that." His cat opened its mouth
and laughed with a woman's voice.

Something struck the floor in front of Billy, the cat bunched
itself up and shot away, and a model airplane rolled over once
more before coming to rest. Graham thrust himself up beside
Richard, his eyes snapping. In Richard's hand, the old Purdy
shotgun flickered once.

Billy Bentley threw up his hands in comic horror. "Mercy!
Violence!"

"We want Tabby's body," Richard said.

"Well, take it. You get two for the price of one, Spunks,
best deal all day." He cocked his head and waved generously
at the corpses on the bed. "Before you go, though, there's
someone we want you to meet. Someone you *want* to meet,
Spunks—no lie, man. Really."

"I don't—" Richard began, but the space around him was changing in a manner by now familiar, opening up and elongating, and he understood that what he did or did not want was an irrelevance.

Far off to his side in a theatrical pool of light a man and a woman were seated at the Jameson dinner table. Both were looking at him warmly: and though he resisted it, Richard felt the honesty of that warmth touch him. The emotion was real, although nothing else may have been. Ruth Branden, the woman at the table, had genuinely loved him. For a time Richard let himself take her in—this was the first time he had seen a living Ruth Branden since he'd been fourteen or fifteen. Her early death had deprived him of knowing his "mother" as an adult. At fourteen Richard had been infatuated with Ruth Branden, and now he fully saw why; she was a beautiful woman, and half of her beauty was the intelligence and generosity that shone in her face. It was a beauty of soul, incapable of being cheapened. The Dragon had done his homework.

The man across from Ruth Branden was a stranger to Richard, but he proved the same point: proved it more conclusively, for this stocky short man with thick gray hair was a stranger only in the most technical sense. Richard knew instinctively—in his spine, in the pit of his stomach, in his cells—that this was Michael Allbee, who had fathered him. Michael Allbee had kindly though rather blurry features, and looked like a merchant seaman or a bohemian poet with a lot of bottles behind him.

His father was looking at him with precisely the right mixture of curiosity, sympathy, amusement, and wariness. Oh yes, the Dragon had done his homework perfectly: so perfectly that this twinkling figure before Richard had an immediate and unreasonable power over his emotions. Richard fought it, he understood exactly what was happening to him, but the sight of that raffish gray-haired man across from Ruth Branden hit him like a blow.

He even understood what the man's first words would be— these were preordained—but they too rocked him.

His father stood up and moved around the table. Richard saw that the man was precisely his own height. "Daddy's here, Richard," he said. "Daddy's here now and everything's all right. I'd like you to put down that silly gun. Empty anyhow, isn't it?"

Feeling boiled through Richard, with such immediate force that until he heard himself shouting he had not realized that he was angry or that he was going to say anything. *"You left me!"* he shouted. "You walked out! *Damn you!"* And once the words were out, he could not regret them—that rage was still pounding through his system.

His father smiled and said, "You have my genes, kid, you're carrying most of me around inside you. That's what counts." His eyes sparkled. "And anyhow, we're together again now."

Richard looked away from the twinkling wary face and saw that Ruth Branden was still sitting up and smiling at him in her chair; that she was only a skeleton in a frilly apron and housedress. Her lustrous dark hair had spilled down onto her shoulders and into her lap. Clumps of it lay like punctuation on the floor—commas and apostrophes of dark brown hair.

Both his father and Billy Bentley were coming slowly toward him. He was only ten years old, Richard realized. His arms and legs were stick-thin and he had to look up to see his father's face.

"Put that heavy thing down, Spunks," Billy was saying. "Hey, kid, don't you get it? We're back now—Jesus, we're *back*. We can go on forever now."

Richard could feel Patsy and Graham plucking at him, trying to pull him away . . . to get him to wake up. "I want Tabby," he said, but the sentence came out in his high-pitched ten-year-old's voice and was weightless.

He tried to raise and aim the gun, but it was too heavy for him—the barrels wavered and dipped. Was it really empty? He looked up and saw his father advancing toward him, beaming as if he were suddenly proud of his little boy.

"Oh hell, Spunks," Billy was whispering, "you know what happened to that kid, you saw him on the bed."

Tabby really was gone, Richard knew; Tabby was gone and everything was lost. His arms were too short to hold the shotgun the right way, and the recoil would break his shoulder.

"And you know something else, ol' Spunks?" Billy was saying to him. "Just what you saw there—that's what should have happened to you, up in Providence. But you got away, and I had to work on your wife instead. *Damn* old shame, Spunks."

The room lurched and spun, and the small boy who was Richard Allbee tottered with the shift in balance: the weight in his arms had doubled. The axis it made with his body, the resistance it gave his muscles, its density, all these had swum imperceptibly into a new dimension, and as the room swung upward and around him he nearly fell over.

"Didn't you think?" Billy Bentley whispered, leaning close over Richard with his wised-up face.

Richard tried to push his sword right through Billy's pitted cheek, but Billy ducked back.

It was a sword: he was holding a gleaming double-edged sword twice the weight of the Purdy, and he had somehow understood that before he had known it.

"Oh, you don't need that," his father said in a level kindly voice, "not that heavy old thing," bending over him. Michael Allbee's face seemed to be lengthening, and his chest too grew longer and thinner. "Too heavy for a boy, I'm thinking, that old thing."

The heavy metal was like ice in Richard's hand, so cold that it burned into his fingers, seared the skin that touched it. Richard groaned as the sword fell from his hands and thunked onto the floor. Michael Allbee, in the midst of a joyful transformation, reached toward him.

Richard cried out inarticulately, and Patsy McCloud's little .22 pistol, in Patsy McCloud's hand, appeared next to his head. Richard took in, as though he were seeing it in slow motion, that Patsy was going to shoot at his father. Could that really work? He saw Patsy's index finger slowly depress the trigger.

The explosion felt as though it took place inside his head.

A sudden hole had opened out in the middle of Michael Allbee's chest. Richard knew that Patsy had saved him, and as he saw a curl of smoke and a lick of flame push out of the hole he knew also that he had become an adult again. He was his proper size. A knot of angry flies belched from his father's chest. Another black curl of smoke pursued them.

His father screeched in pain and fury. Richard bent down to pick up the sword. As he got his hand around the grip he saw that Michael Allbee had become a towering column of blood, for a moment intact in the air above them. Then the tower of blood shattered down over them, instantly plastering their clothes to their skin, sliding down their necks, burning sourly in their eyes and mouths . . .

3

. . . sensations which ceased almost as soon as they began.
When Richard opened his eyes he saw Patsy McCloud staring
wildly back at him, just lowering her hand from her eyes.
Behind Patsy a dozen white spruces dipped long feathery
branches down through gray air. The sea hissed against a stony
beach almost visible behind the trees; an incoming tide.
Richard stood half on an immense gray rock, half on a scurf of
yellow weeds. He stepped down off the rock. Patsy now was
numbly staring at the pistol in her hand; then she flipped it onto
a stony bulge of land, and the little .22 bounced under a thick
gathering of nettles and burdock. Richard turned around—
against his skin the fresh air was blessedly alive, in motion,
perfumed with salt water and green growing things. Burs and
damp weeds adhered to his trousers; headless stems drooped
from his shoelaces.

As he turned he saw that behind him lay a deep cut in the
earth, too deep for him to see what lay at the bottom of the
overgrown slopes. So far back it must have been on the land
that led to this promontory, a long white building with an
oversize bar window blankly faced them. A beer sign twin-
kled in an upstairs window.

Graham Williams was sitting down with his back against a
taxicab-sized root which had rucked its way up out of the
ground and then dived back under again. Graham's gaudy
clothes had been smeared with dirt, and water had darkened
the cuffs of his trousers.

Richard looked back past Patsy at the white spruces letting their arms gently fall as if in defeat toward the earth.
Through them the Sound glinted as it beat toward the stony
beach.

"We're on Kendall Point," he said.

"A plus," Graham said, wheezing. "Right on the money.
And he's here. Can't you *feel* that? Gideon Winter has
Tabby, and he's here. Waiting for us."

Patsy tonelessly said, "Tabby's dead."

"I can't believe that," Graham said. "Winter wants all
four of us to die together—I think he'd really have everything
if he did that. That's why we're here, right?"

"Yes," Richard said. "I suppose."

Graham settled his shoulders against the monstrous root behind him. "Well, I wish he'd come out and do his stuff." He

looked from side to side as if he expected Gideon Winter to come walking toward him out of the Sound. "I have a little less respect for him than I did once. He only uses what we give him, have you noticed that? He doesn't know anything except what we tell him. HUAC. Patsy sees dead people, so he shows her a sort of Waldorf-Astoria of dead people. You and *Daddy's Here*. For all his power, he still seems limited, doesn't he?"

"Limited? Is that what you think?" The voice came from behind Patsy, from under the tall spruces. It was not a human voice, Richard thought, not at all. Too thick, too oily; and so resonant it might have been fed by a microphone to a loudspeaker. "My dear children."

Graham had struggled to his feet as soon as he heard the first words, and he and Patsy and Richard were all looking now at a big dark form lazing quietly in the shade of the tallest spruce. Then the form shifted itself, and they saw what sort of being had spoken to them.

Did this happen? *Could* this have happened? It was as impossible as everything else that had happened to them: but the three of them were now in a real landscape, in the middle of a real day. First they saw its face, at least twice the size of a human face and grotesquely exaggerated in its features—on the human scale, the features would almost have suggested handsomeness. So large, they looked like a roadmap to vice. The ears were long and drooping, the eyes brilliantly black; the creature's nose was strong and hooked, its chin thick and pointed. A long meaty tongue licked out of the curling lips.

The creature shifted itself forward, and an odor of shit and sweat and filthy skin drifted off it. At its waist began muscular goat legs and hindquarters. Tabby Smithfield was slung over this monster's shoulder. It laughed at the expressions on their faces, stood up, and cocked one of its legs. A ropy jet of steaming liquid shot onto the ground, where it began running in rivulets down the dry grass. A lot of little active things were swimming in the creature's urine, but Richard did not want to look at them—he could not take his eyes off Tabby's body, in any case.

At Richard's side Patsy McCloud despairingly sent out *(Tabby? Tabby?)* and met only the dead cold emptiness she had both expected and feared.

"*Give him to us!*" Graham suddenly roared out.

The devil-creature leered at Graham, hitched Tabby's body

off his shoulder, and needed only one hand to toss the limp
boy onto a brown little hill at their side. "Whatever you
say." The devil smirked, and started to walk toward them.

Instantly it was dark again, just as when they had set their
feet on Poor Fox Road. The creature moving toward them
chuckled, and Graham and Patsy and Richard scrambled
away toward inert Tabby. Off to their side, the water rose up
in tall waves and breakers and hurled itself at Kendall Point's
rocky beach. The devil's huge misshapen form slouched past
them, outlined in the moonlight descending everywhere.
Richard checked in his jacket pockets for shotgun shells, but
found he had none left: the shells must have fallen out somewhere in the tunnel. Hoping for magic, for whatever had happened to him in front of Billy Bentley, he held up the Purdy.
The Purdy stubbornly refused to turn into a Boy Scout knife,
much less a sword.

Patsy and Graham knelt on either side of Tabby. Delicately
Graham rolled the boy onto his back.

When Patsy probed again she met a faint

(. . . . .)

"Oh my God, he's alive," Patsy uttered so rapidly it
sounded like one long word, and then sobbed wetly, gracelessly—a sound made up wholly of emotion.

"'Course he is," Graham said, but his eyes looked wet
too.

"Look," Richard said urgently. "Look at what's happening."

The clumsy silhouette of the creature was changing in the
moonlight. The goatish body was growing, stretching out; the
suggestion of a massive tail lashed through the dark weeds.
Even Patsy looked up, having had another small flare of life
from Tabby, and momentarily saw the creature in clear moonlight as it began to descend into the deep slash in the land at
the inland edge of the Point. A head with a long lethal jaw,
pointed spikes down the length of the reptilian snout, malevolent eyes encased in bone . . . she had seen that head lift up
out of Dorothy Bach's *History of Patchin* in Graham's living
room.

dragon? what . . . dragon? Patsy?

Tabby's chest expanded as the boy took in air, and his eyes
opened a crack so tiny that only Patsy noticed.

whatwhat?

"A dragon," Richard said, as if he had heard the messages flying toward Patsy McCloud. "What the hell . . ."

One of the great spruces behind them fell over—the trunk splintered as if the hand of an invisible giant had broken it. When the tree struck the ground, the earth seemed to bounce.

"Let's move," Richard said. The earth trembled as another of the spruces crashed down. He knelt and got his arms beneath Tabby; braced himself; picked the boy up.

Tabby said, "Uh."

A wide slash came ripping through the land, announcing itself first in the whispery sound of loose earth falling into its crevice, then in the bone-snapping roots. Richard Allbee saw a big round-headed wild rhododendron bush fifteen feet from him heel over sideways and go rattling down a precipitous slope . . . *"Jump!"* Graham bellowed at him, and he finally understood what was happening just before the ground opened up beneath him. Holding Tabby in his arms, Richard crouched down and took the longest standing broad jump of his life.

His feet connected with solid ground, but his balance was still back where he had taken off. Richard staggered, then sprawled forward, dumping both himself and Tabby onto a rocky tuft of land. He turned his head and saw the jagged scar in the earth take both of the fallen spruces. A huge root-ball thumped down after the severed trunks.

Tabby whispered, "You trying to kill me, Richard?"

Richard hugged him close.

From the deep slash in the earth ahead of them a long arrow of flame ripped through the tall grasses, incinerating whatever it touched. Tabby's eyes were closed again, but he drew up his body like a child in a crib, resting his head on Richard's chest.

He heard noises rustling toward him, then saw Patsy and Graham slipping through the dark, skirting the multiple little fires which had sprung up after the withdrawal of the dragon's breath. Graham sat down next to him, and Patsy eased Tabby out of his arms and into her own. Something cold and hard fitted into the palm of Richard's hand, and he took his eyes off Tabby's slack face and saw that Graham had given him the Purdy shotgun again.

"I don't know what to tell you," the old man said. "But you know what we have to do if we ever want to get out of here."

"Yeah, I know," Richard said, feeling not at all adequate. "We have to kill that thing. We have to go down into that valley and destroy it. But how the hell do we do that?"

"I thought I asked you for an easy one," Graham said.

Richard thought of standing up and walking toward the dragon's little valley; of brandishing the shotgun. He would not live more than five seconds. The dragon would breathe on him, and first his skin would turn red and then it would turn black and all his hair would be gone and his eyes would burst. And then the dragon would emerge and do the same thing to Patsy and Graham and Tabby. It would provide interesting obituaries in the *New York Times*, Richard thought, except that if we're killed nobody on the *Times* will ever know it.

"I don't mind doing it, I just want to know how," Richard said.

Graham nodded.

"Damn," Richard said. At last he said, "How is Tabby?"

Patsy had been rocking him back and forth against her. "He's getting better." Richard saw a smile illuminate her face, and for a second was jealous of Tabby Smithfield—he would not have minded being in those arms himself, nor having caused that smile. Patsy's eyes flicked at him, and he sensed a complicated mixture of amusement and annoyance and pleasure and wondered if she had heard his thoughts in the way she could hear the boy's. Patsy had returned her glance back to Tabby with an almost deliberate lack of haste.

"Well, what do we do?" Richard asked.

The fire-bat sailed overhead again, igniting another of the spruces.

"I think it's no good if Tabby is asleep," Richard said.

"I'm going to try something," Patsy said. "I think I'll ask him to sing."

"Sing? Sing what?" Graham asked.

"Anything he thinks of."

The burning spruce popped and sizzled behind them. Richard could almost catch an unheard familiar song.

"Why not?" he said: and for a moment inexplicably felt the heaviness of that double-edged sword pulling against his muscles. "Yes, try it," he said. "Try it, Patsy."

Patsy bent her mouth to Tabby's ear and whispered, "Sing to us, Tabby. Sing us the first song you think of—and we'll help you sing it."

"God help us if it's some rock-'n'-roll thing," Graham said.

"Won't matter," Richard said. The image of Tabby Smithfield singing, and then of the rest of them joining his song, was still echoing in his mind with the mysterious rightness he had felt a moment before. Graham looked at him oddly, but said nothing more.

"Sing us a song, Tabby," Patsy whispered again.

Then, as Tabby told them later, the boy reached back into his memory and found something—an old childish song from the house on Mount Avenue. It was a song his mother had used to sing to him, back before anything bad happened and Tabby Smithfield was a small boy with a pretty mommy and a daddy who played tennis and a grandfather who loved him. That the song would have its own associations for Richard Allbee never occurred to him. He was back in his grandfather's house.

Weakly at first, and then with a little more strength, Tabby sang: *"When the red, red robin goes bob, bob, bobbin' along, along. . ."*

Richard gaped at the boy; this was the unheard song.

"There'll be no more sobbin' when he starts throbbin' his old sweet song," Graham Williams surprisingly bawled out in an off-key bass.

The shotgun resting in Richard's arms suddenly trembled with the urgency of a pheasant taking off out of a cover, and he closed his fingers around it to keep it still. Patsy sang out, joining the other two, *"Wake up, wake up, you sleepyhead."*

Richard had never heard the lyrics of the song during all his years in *Daddy's Here*. So when he chimed in, it was with *"Cheer up, cheer up, cheer up, the sun is red,"* making an unconscious allusion to Poor Fox Road.

The shotgun suddenly flared with white light.

"You're a genius," Richard said to Patsy. "What made you think—"

"It could have been anything, *anything*," Graham said. "It's that we're doing it together, all four of us."

"Well, don't stop now," Patsy said. "Tabby! Louder this time."

And the four of them huddling together sang that verse all over again, this time remembering to add the forgotten line:

When the red, red robin goes bob, bob,

> *bobbin' along, along;*
> *There'll be no more sobbin' when he starts*
> *throbbin' his old, sweet song.*
> *Wake up, wake up, you sleepyhead*
> *Get up, get up, get out of bed*
> *Cheer up, cheer up, cheer up, the sun is*
> *red . . .*

Richard stood up, still hearing the words sing in his mind. He was holding a long double-edged sword, though he had not been conscious of any transformation, nor of any specific moment when the object in his hands had ceased to be a shotgun. His mouth was very dry. "Sleepyhead," he said aloud but to himself, not knowing why. The voices of the others stuttered into the song again, then failed. An immense heavy body pushed itself back and forth down there, restlessly pacing like the giant black dog in Graham's backyard . . . Richard stepped toward it, imitating a much braver man.

Behind him Patsy alone sang: *"Dum da dum de dum, Now I'm walking through, Field of flowers: Rain may glisten, But still I listen, For hours and hours . . ."*

The little valley itself had altered, and where the dragon was so deeply hidden now resembled an arch into the earth, a leafy cave. Some of them, Richard hoped, would get off Kendall Point alive.

"I'm just a kid again," Patsy and Tabby sang, *"Doin' what I did again, Singin' a song."*

4

Singing, Patsy stood up and watched Richard approach the cut in the earth which had become the dragon's cave. He was walking with a kind of matter-of-fact assurance that Patsy found very moving—he could have been going out to check the bird feeder. If Richard Allbee had to walk to the gallows, it would be with that same apparent and unconscious confidence. She knew that he would not look back when he passed between the two large boulders that stood at the rim of the gorge and seemed to mark the entrance to the cave, and he did not. Richard walked between the man-sized boulders as if he did not see them and began to edge down the slope. Unexpectedly,

Patsy *heard* Richard's mind speaking in hers—as she thought she had heard it earlier, when she had been rocking Tabby in her arms. He wanted to turn and look at them again: that was what she heard, and only Tabby's presence beside her kept her from crying.

She concentrated on the song: Patsy was so afraid for Richard, so afraid for all of them, that singing now was a necessary therapy. She had kept herself from breaking down in tears, but she could not stop herself from shaking. Her mind too seemed no longer in control. Since she had brushed against Richard's thoughts, Patsy had felt her mind alarmingly flex itself—it was as though a new color ran through it, and Patsy did not trust this sensation.

She put her arm around Tabby's shoulder. The sword in Richard's hand gleamed as he took it down into that deep leafy darkness. She could hear Graham Williams rasping out *"Get up, get up, get out of bed"* in a toneless voice that was half whisper and half mere thought. Patsy trembled violently, feeling goosebumps raise all down her arms.

. . . *the sun is red* . . .

(the sun is red)

"I can't stand this," Tabby said.

She looked up and realized that what she had taken for two moons were really the sun and moon—one red, one white. That big red open mouth wanted to swallow them down

(Live, love, laugh and be happy!)

and take them out of the world forever.

"I'm going with him," Tabby said. "I can't just stand here."

"Kid, you're still pretty weak," Graham said.

"I'm okay," Tabby said, and stepped out from under Patsy's arm. "I'm going down there with Richard." He went a few paces forward, then looked back at her.

have to

o Tabby

Tabby turned away and started toward the boulders. Growling, roaring noises came from within the cave. Hadn't the Dragon warned them, that first night in Graham's house, not to push it this far? Patsy gave Graham an agonized look. "I have to go with him," she said. She opened her mouth, then closed it again almost immediately—anything else would be just repetition. Patsy made herself move away from Graham's protective largeness. After the first step she was able to run.

"God damn, guess I'll join the party too," Graham said. "Just don't expect me to jog."

Tabby stopped walking, put his hands in his pockets, and waited for them. Patsy stopped running, and when Graham was beside her, the two of them walked up to Tabby's slight form in the darkness. "Good," Tabby said.

Heat blasted toward them as soon as they reached the boulders. Patsy put her hand on one of the standing rocks as they looked down the slope and felt warmth beating out of the stone. Half of the bank down to the black entrance of the cave was on fire. All the clumpy little bushes were burning, and the earth too blazed in random patches. Richard Allbee was dimly visible far down the slope, picking his way around the fires toward the bottom.

Pale smoke belched out of the cave. Patsy saw Richard hesitate for a second, then continue making his way to the flat boulders.

Tabby jumped down over the edge and slid five or six feet, sending a cascade of pebbles and loose dirt rolling into a wide belt of flames. Graham followed the boy immediately, moving much more slowly and making sure both feet were solidly set before taking another sideways step down.

Patsy turned sideways and took a careful step over the edge. Holding her arms out for balance, she dug her left foot into the bank and lowered her right another eight or nine inches. Loose stones rolled away under her shoe, and she tottered. Then she noticed that the cloud of smoke which had emerged from the cave was neither drifting away nor dissipating—it moved upward almost purposefully, as if it had a mind. When it reached the top of the cave, Patsy took another half-step down, trembling as though she stood in a freezing wind.

(damn!) she heard from Graham as he lost control of his footing for a second and slipped downward in a shower of dirt.

Within the stationary cloud something huge and many-armed stirred, pushing out bumps and angles of the pale smoke. The thing in the cloud whirred and rattled, impatient with its prison. As Patsy opened her mouth to call to the others, the cloud broke apart and another, darker cloud hung in its place: then it instantly exploded into movement. Particles the size of robins spun away, reformed, spun away again. Not one creature but many had been trapped in the cloud. Patsy saw leathery wings and flinched, thinking the creatures were bats. A rattling knot of them swirled over a flat boulder the size of a sheepdog, and rivery fire instantly flowed across the top of the boulder, forming a liquid yellow stream that sheeted down the side and began to trickle toward the bottom through the stones. As they swirled up the bank Patsy saw their tiny snouts, their long reptilian necks. Baby dragons—they were baby dragons, not bats.

we'll be all right Tabby sent her.

you'd better not die twice on me, buster

Part of her shaking, she realized, was not fear—it was the effect of her relief that Tabby had survived his kidnapping by Gideon Winter. Without quite being aware of it, she had been party to Tabby's thoughts ever since he had opened his eyes: not just the messages he had sent her, but all of his thoughts, every spark that flew across his mind. All of these birds of thought had fed her relief—though they had been quiet, almost in fact inaudible, their singing had pulled her closer to Tabby.

Instead of calling out a warning, she started to sing. All those birds of thought flexed again in her mind, adding another band of color (or so it felt) to the first. She started to sing softly, uncertain of herself: a part of Patsy was still capable of feeling foolish about singing out loud on a burning hillside leading down to a dragon's cave—a nonexistent cave, a nonexistent dragon.

And anyhow, didn't women in this situation just keep their mouths shut and wait to be rescued?

Wasn't that *exactly* what she had done during most of her marriage, month by month after Les had turned sour and insecure, poisoned by his own success? Kept her mouth shut and waited to be rescued?

A grumpy, frightened, but still tenacious sliver of thought flew toward her, and she recognized in it the texture, the color, the taste of Graham Williams; either it was wordless or she could not hear the words, but she did not need words to identify him.

"*When the red, red robin goes bob, bob, bobbin' along, along . . .*"

Her high, pure voice sailed up out of her, becoming stronger with every word. Five feet down the slope and trying to avoid being forced into doing the splits, Graham Williams looked back up at her in astonishment; initially, fury too. He had been taking pains to be as silent as he could, thinking that apart from the sword, surprise was their only weapon. Patsy's singing was like an announcement to Gideon Winter that all four of them waited outside the cave. *"There'll be no more sobbin' when he starts throbbin' his old sweet song."* Then, as Patsy's voice grew and strengthened, he felt it take hold of him: almost as if Patsy's voice had physically wrapped around him. He easily went down another four feet, his legs working like a twenty-year-old's. Graham started to mouth the words along with Patsy, suddenly sure that she could hear him even if he did not actually sing anywhere but in his mind.

Because in that instant he felt her right beside him: he felt all the barriers of age and sex, of homeliness and beauty, of all the differing lessons taught by experience, fall where they had stood.

Graham understood even before Patsy herself that no matter what Richard did with that sword, it was Patsy who could save their lives. He felt enlarged—in the midst of his real terror, whatever Patsy was sending toward him, whatever she was doing to him, increased him. Though he still only mouthed the words, he could hear his rusty rumbling voice singing in his mind.

And Patsy, up above him, knew all that Graham had just experienced.

sing, Tabby, sing! she poured out toward the boy:

and instantly heard his two voices, his inner voice and his physical voice, pick up her song.

Now she could hear all of them in her mind, Graham's unmusical chanting, Richard's rush of anxious thought which had picked up the rhythm of her singing, and Tabby. Tabby's mind was moving in perfect sympathy with her own. Just as she herself felt that sense of enlargement she had met in Graham, Tabby had it too.

A kite-shaped arrangement of the baby dragons skirled toward her, igniting a four-foot-long strip of hillside, then circled away.

The song didn't matter, she thought, the song was ridiculous, it was the fact of singing that was powerful, and she sent the absolutely inappropriate words *"Live, love, laugh and be happy"* sailing out into the air. Patsy took herself halfway down the hillside, watching Richard getting nearer the mouth of the cave and for a second felt herself begin to find the conclusion toward which her energies and gifts had been moving her. Her personality almost physically stretched and widened within her. Patsy felt blood rushing up into her face: her heart surged: whatever Graham Williams had thought he had seen in her—whatever had given him that feeling of increase—almost surfaced in her.

For an instant Patsy saw herself as a net suspended beneath her friends: a Patsy who was a giantess, hovering beneath their exploits to catch them if they fell. Their different voices rang through her. She felt herself blushing even more feverishly—then instead of the odors of fried weeds, burning dirt (which smelled the way ginseng tasted), and smoke, she smelled fish. That relentless inner movement ceased, as shockingly as if contractions were suddenly to cease during childbirth.

A burly naked man with a black beard was standing beside her. He smiled, not pleasantly. Patsy saw the long scar which ran from hip to hip across his belly. The concentrated odor of fish leaked from his skin, from his pores. Bates Krell stepped nearer Patsy. She felt a sick wave of passion, stronger than the fishy smell, emanating from him: passion gone black and twisted, more powerful because of its sickness.

Behind Bates Krell's threatening body Patsy saw the horned head of the dragon emerge from its cave.

Krell's smile became more genuine and even less pleasant. His eyes glittered blackly; they were the same eyes, shot with iridescent green threads and veins, she had seen following the peeling spike up from the pages of a book.

Then an unseen movement caused a huge displacement of air, a stream of fire three feet wide ripped across the ground before her, and the head of the dragon in the cave had swung toward her. Bates Krell had vanished into smoke, and the dragon coming out of the cave looked straight at Patsy with the fisherman's eyes.

"When the . . ." The words died in her mouth. Patsy was too terrified to sing, and the other voices in her mind, which seemed like aspects of a single voice, diminished. The dragon crawled another step nearer Patsy, suddenly seeming much larger.

"Red!" Tabby shouted. "Red red robin!"

Graham's booming monotone half-shouted, half-sang, *"goes bob, bob, bobbin' along—ALONG!"*

And she heard Richard singing it too—singing it desperately in her mind.

"ROBIN!" Tabby shouted. "ROBIN!"

The dragon's head swung away from her, and a small winged body fell out of the sky and landed at her feet. The dazed baby dragon hitched its wings under itself and scrabbled a few inches down the slope. It was no larger than a mouse. Revolted, Patsy stepped on it. Its wings squirmed. She raised her foot and stamped down on the little dragon, and felt it crack open like a beetle.

"There'll be no more *sobbin'*!" Tabby screamed. "When he starts *throbbin'*!"

All of their voices flooded back into her, and she saw that image of herself and Tabby on the road before the old Smithfield house—the image was not enigmatic. Patsy felt the stirring of a power within herself, and knew that it was this she had almost come to unreflectively before Bates Krell had appeared to frighten her out of her wits. Now one of the others would be in the danger from which they had rescued her, and when she twisted her hands together and looked for Richard Allbee she saw that he was only twenty feet from the dragon. "Sweet song!" he yelled—

—and that pushed her shamelessly over the edge. Patsy opened her mind to all of them: she spread her wings, and they went farther than the fire-bat's. It was like opening her body, her essence spilled out to each of them, and for a moment she was so physically responsive that she thought she could see the map of her arteries and veins printed on her skin. Once half in despair she had written a list of the men with whom she imagined she might want to make love; but as Patsy's mind accepted Tabby Smithfield and Graham Williams and Richard Allbee into itself, as her wings spread over them, they were the only men on the planet. They melted into her; this was unbearably strong and sensual, and the strength was hers.

All around Patsy, the baby dragons came tumbling out of the sky. She squashed as many as she could, and saw more of them falling to the ground, as the birds had at the end of May.

When she touched her foot to them now, they burst apart, leaking smoke and sparks.

She brushed her foot against another crawling mouse-sized

dragon, and it split down the ridge of the spine. A little puddle of fire poured out of the crack, and the creature's wings sizzled into gossamer, then into black lumps.

5

Richard stood twenty feet from the mouth of the cave and heard Patsy singing in his mind even more strongly than before. Her voice had gone beyond being only a voice, it was the very sound of his own body, the traveling of the blood through his veins, the hammering of his heart. The huge greenish-black head of the dragon dipped toward him almost in confusion; he felt as much as heard its children plopping down onto the rocks. Richard raised his sword, calculating that he might have about a fifty-fifty chance of getting close enough to its neck to use the sword before the monster recovered.

Richardrichard

Then he felt Patsy McCloud slam into him—into his head and into his body, his heart and his ribs and lungs and eyes and hands—with such force that he was almost pushed over. He could taste her: for a vivid moment, her voice swelling in his mind, the tastes in his mind were hers. Richard felt almost as if he were levitating—as if Patsy's presence inside him freed him from gravity.

Richard looked up and saw two of the little dragons tumbling out of the sky like dying bats.

He did not know if he saw with Patsy's eyes or his own.

His mind poured helplessly toward hers—that was how it felt, as though their different minds were two liquids mingling in the same jug. Instantly they had gone far past intimacy into a realm of utter knowledge and acceptance, some beating pink chamber where they were totally revealed: as if he and Patsy McCloud had been married for forty years, and each knew what toothpaste the other preferred, how they liked their eggs, their favorite jokes and favorite novels, which movies they cherished and which they loathed, which people they loved and hated. All of this knowledge was somehow sexual, dyed in sexual colors—Patsy's sexuality informed it all. It was as though she had turned herself inside out and impressed her nerves and bloodstream into his system.

A squirrel-sized baby dragon fell beside his feet with the noise of a crumpling paper bag; seconds after it struck, smoke poured out of its leathery skin.

Graham Williams and Tabby Smithfield stood at the bottom of the slope down to the cave, exposed to the dragon; Patsy was halfway down the hill, isolated, it seemed, by the act of spirit Richard had not yet even begun to understand. He could hear Graham and Tabby singing that crazy song. A thick cocoon of smoke now completely enveloped the little dragon at Richard's feet. Sounds of sizzling and frying came from the solid-looking package of smoke. Patsy was singing too, but her mouth was closed.

The sword in Richard's hand deepened in color; surged forward of itself, like a dowsing rod. Now it glowed a deep reddish gold, and the handle warmed him halfway up his arm. Patsy's breathing expanded Richard's lungs. Off to his side, Tabby and Graham were surrounded by flickering reddish-gold light, the same color as the sword.

Another tiny dragon dropped to the boulders and split into two burning sections.

Richard had time to think: *This can't be happening.*

And the massive old dragon lingering in the entrance of its cave moved its head and fixed him with its pupilless gaze. The long hinged mouth opened. Richard stepped sideways, his foot brushing something slippery and hot, and the dragon followed him with those stony eyes. Total frozen terror immobilized him for a moment. Patsy's breath stirred in his lungs again, and he yelled, "RED RED ROBIN! JUST KEEP SOBBIN'!" He was no longer sure of the words or of their order, but he *saw* Patsy in his mind, saw her standing naked in that pink chamber where they were still absolutely joined; and then he saw Laura standing naked behind her, Laura with her full beautiful belly.

Women's laughter fell toward him—from all around him it seemed, from everywhere, from the world itself.

Richard bellowed "SLEEPYHEAD!" and lifted his glowing sword.

Then his dream, their dream, was happening all around him, and he did not know if he was awake or asleep, and he shouted out "SLEEPYHEAD!" again and stepped forward.

The earth convulsed; black fluid leaked and spurted from between the boulders, and a fine spattering of pebbles and dirt rattled down the hillsides. Richard walked straight toward the waiting dragon and heard someone yelling "SLEEPYHEAD! SLEEPYHEAD!" Foul black liquid gouted onto the flat rocks, but Richard heard the laughter of women and knew that it had no power to harm him—nor even to touch him. He knew what it was, he thought: the black stuff that dripped from Emma Bovary's coffin. He and Laura had left that book unfinished, amid a million unfinished things. A thick wall of flames shot out toward him and enveloped him, but he knew he could walk right through the flames; they too had no power to hurt him.

What the other three saw was Richard Allbee striding toward the dragon and passing through the blowtorch flames as though they did not exist: Richard seemed encased in a silken steely armor. They saw him raise his sword in the midst of the flames; heard him yell "WAKE UP!" when he brought it down.

Richard could not hear what he was shouting and in fact was not conscious that he was shouting anything. The dragon's breath roared furiously, deafeningly about him. Its pointed teeth were the size of fenceposts. The smells of death and rot, the stench of the tunnel, blasted toward Richard with the harmless flames.

He darted in toward the dragon and brought the sword glancingly down on the long snout. The edge sliced into the dragon's flesh, then skittered off, removing a greenish-black divot. Liquid fire rolled from the little wound, and the dragon inched backward, roaring. When Richard approached again, the dragon lunged and nearly caught him in its jaws. Richard flicked out the sword and nicked its mouth. He threw himself back and twisted sideways as the dragon thrust its head forward again, lunging at him. This time he was able to thrust the sword straight into the bottom of the jaw.

A spattering jet of fire jumped from the wound, and the dragon screamed with pain and threw itself forward. The long head darted at Richard again, and instead of trying to dodge out of the way he raised the sword just as in his dream and brought it down with all his strength. The sword sank into the end of the snout. A river of fire streamed out into the dragon's mouth.

Infuriated, in pain, the dragon screeched and hoisted itself upward. The sword pulsed in Richard's hand, and he moved forward, putting himself beneath the long powerful curve of the creature's neck. Richard put both hands on the handle of the sword, felt his biceps and shoulder muscles gather themselves, and then brought the sword back up in the strongest backhand of his life. The blade slid through the thick skin and bit into bone. Richard thrust on the haft with all the force he had left and sawed right through the obstruction. Wet flame dripped down over Richard's hands: then the dragon exploded.

Richard staggered backward from the mountain of fire, seeing rags of flame fluttering down over the boulders. The sword fell out of his hands, no longer a sword. He said, *"Wake up,"* and collapsed to his knees.

6

Graham and Tabby slowly came forward across the boulders, their throats raw and their legs trembling. Richard was bent forward over his knees, his head nearly brushing his outstretched shadow on the rock. "Richard?" Graham said in a rasping voice. Richard shuddered. He could not, or he would not, look up at them. "Are you okay?" Tabby asked. "No," Richard answered. "You did it, Richard," Graham said quietly. "You tell me what I did," Richard said to the stone. "I'll do better than that," Graham said. "I'll show you. You won't even have to walk—all you have to do is look up."

Richard slowly lifted his head and what the other two saw on his haggard face was deep disorientation: he looked fifteen years older. Long creases divided his cheeks. He was still shaking, and was very pale. "It's daytime again," he said— Graham and Tabby had scarcely noticed the return of the sun. Richard saw the expressions on their faces and said, "I hope I don't look any worse than you two guys." He wiped trembling hands over his face. "What're you going to show me?"

"Here comes, ah, here she comes," Graham said, sounding suddenly nervous and shy. "Patsy."

Tabby revolved like a man in a hypnotic trance, and Richard grabbed Graham's arm and pulled himself to his feet. Patsy was just managing the last few feet of the sloping hillside, and came down onto the boulders in a little rattle of pebbles. She was blushing, but as she walked toward them this little woman had the aura of great achievement about her—it was the air of an almost epic significance, and it fit her as well as her clothes. If any of them had been alone with her then, he would have wept and embraced her; but they were each too conscious of the others to risk such a display.

"Oh, Patsy," Tabby said. "How did you—?"

She shook her head, walking toward them. Patsy's cheeks burned a hectic red.

Tabby tried to speak to her in the private way that had been only theirs, but his thoughts failed to travel in the way they had—he sent his message and knew that it met nothing. That dimension had left them.

The ground trembled beneath them, but they scarcely felt it.

"I want you to see—" Graham began to say, and his voice trembled too.

"Hold me," Patsy interrupted, and held out her arms as she rushed toward them. So all three put their own arms around Patsy and around themselves, standing in a circle—none of the men could escape the feeling that now he *belonged* to Patsy McCloud, that he was a part of her.

At last Patsy stepped backward, and their arms broke apart.

"You wanted me to see something, darling Graham," Patsy said.

Now Graham blushed. He pointed to the rocky slope where the dragon's cave had been. It, like all the little dragons, had disappeared. Lying propped against the hillside was a small skeleton. Its legs, each of them saw, were slightly deformed, twisted. The skull, almost arrogantly large and long, seemed to have been intended for another body. Four ragged holes the size of nickels penetrated the top and back of the massive skull.

Beneath their feet the boulders moved perceptibly to the left, then back again.

"They all got him—our ancestors. They killed him jointly. Or serially, or however the hell. But they killed him together." Graham stuffed his hands in his pockets and looked at the others with something like his old vehemence. "And we did even better than that. Dammit, I think that monster's gone for good."

The boulders shook beneath them once more, and from the far end of Kendall Point they heard a series of loud thuds and crashes followed by the sound of heavy objects smacking into the sea. Loose stones pattered down around them.

Patsy looked up in alarm; Richard took her arm and immediately set off up the hillside which led to the base of the Point. He trusted that the other two would follow. Richard got Patsy up on the flat land and walked her nearly to the road. "Stay here," he said, and turned around to go back and help Graham. When he looked out across the Point, he saw that a big section of the tip had simply sheared off and tumbled into the water. A huge fissure shot across the land five feet from the ragged edge, and more of the Point slid down into Long Island Sound. Richard skidded down the slope until he nearly collided with Tabby Smithfield, who was pulling Graham uphill. He took the old man's other arm, and together he and Tabby unceremoniously hauled Graham up over the edge. "Thanks, I guess," Graham said.

They joined Patsy against the low wall and watched as Kendall Point tore at itself. The ground rumbled; cracks jumped across the earth, webbed out and widened, joining other fissures and cracks. The boulders on which they had faced the Dragon were forced up in an upheaval that pushed another five feet of the Point into the water. The spruces left standing toppled crazily and sprawled across each other—seconds later they had disappeared, taken by another shuddering displacement. The skeleton of Gideon Winter heaved into their view momentarily, its arms and legs sawing as if it were alive, and rolled off the edge into the water. A falling cliff face immediately buried it.

Then a widening crack in the land angled toward them, and they hurried back over the wall and onto the blunt end of the road. "Oh my God," Tabby said, pointing to the long white bar that stood near to the beginning of the Point. The destruction was widening out, claiming more land. An enormous fissure sped toward the building as if it consciously wanted to devour it. The enclosed court outside the long window at the rear of the building noisily sank out of sight, the thick concrete walls and floor snapping like dry bread. The entire building skated several feet forward—more noises of snapping and shattering, of pipes breaking and plaster walls collapsing. They heard screams, and a door flew open, releasing three young women and four or five middle-aged men. Two of the men carried beer bottles. The frightened little crowd ran into the middle of the road and watched the bar waltz forward again, shake its hips, and tip into the crack. The side of the building unhinged itself and dropped away in one tall flat section, exposing a tile floor, a curving wooden bar; in an upstairs room a yellow paper globe around a hanging light swung wildly to and fro, as if a child had hit it with a bat. Then the building seemed to groan, a thousand wooden boards pulled free from their nails, and the whole structure fell in on itself and rattled down into the fissure.

The people who had escaped it dazedly turned toward the four friends. One of the women and two of the men tentatively stepped forward. This was the first time that Patsy, Richard, Tabby, and Graham saw that expression of doggy wonder with which they later became familiar. It made them uncomfortable. "Jesus *shit*," one of the other men said, and they all turned away. Graham had been sure that the three people now turning to watch a row of houses skid into the Sound had been going to stroke them.

The rotting houses in the precinct of the devastated bar were shuddering forward like mechanical toys. Bits of them snapped away as they traveled, sections of walls damply crumbled. The widening gap that had swallowed the bar pushed them inexorably across a section of sand too despairing to have ever been a beach and rolled them into the water. Then the strip of sand fell leadenly into the hole.

From the other side of the Point, the direction of Greenbank and Mount Avenue, came another series of the agonized sounds of a large building meeting an untidy death. Stone and wood and glass screamed out as they separated and fell. Joints and ligaments intended to last another hundred years pulled apart, tissues meant to be whole ripped in half. Falling lumber, falling bricks, falling iron and lead and porcelain.

After that the destruction ended. Perfect stunned silence echoed all about them and floated upward, displaced by the scrabble of a lizard through the sand, the thumping descent into a deep gorge of a last unsteady rock.

The group from the tavern was frankly staring at Richard and the others. The little band of men was taking in Patsy with what looked like undisguised awe—they too sensed that aura about her.

"Let's go home," Graham said.

Tabby asked if he thought Greenbank too had been destroyed.

"We'll find out soon enough. But let's stick together when we pass these people."

The three of them gathered around Patsy and went slowly

up the road. They did not look at the people from the bar,
who backed up to let them pass. Nobody moved or spoke, but
Richard and the others felt the people from the bar pushing
confused emotion at them.

When Bobo Farnsworth came panting out of the rocky
woods to their left, having evidently taken a shortcut from
Mount Avenue, our friends stopped moving. The people behind them had already begun to drift away.

7

Bobo stopped about six feet short of the road. The blue uniform was streaked with mud, and one of his trouser legs
clung wetly to his skin. He seemed afflicted with a sudden
and uncharacteristic shyness—as if he were no longer sure he
could approach these four people. Bobo looked at Patsy, then
at Richard Allbee, then back to Patsy. "Ah," he said. "I
wanted to see you."

His face tightened around some private misery, and he
moved uncertainly to the side; took an equally uncertain step
forward. Then he permitted himself to look at Patsy McCloud
again, and almost apologetically walked the rest of the way to
the road.

"What happened, Bobo?" Richard asked.

Now, it is a fact, though perhaps not an admirable one, that
all four of the people in front of tongue-tied Bobo wished that
he would explain himself and then take off. Each of them
genuinely liked the tall policeman, and at most other times
would have welcomed his company. Of course they were exhausted, how profoundly they still could not appreciate; and
they could no more detach themselves from everything they
had just undergone than they could have picked up Bobo
Farnsworth and thrown him over the cliff that had been Kendall Point. But the real reason Bobo was such an intrusion is
that they were as clannish as lovers. They needed one another
unreservedly, and also needed the time to work out what that
meant, what its dimensions were. All they really wanted was
to get in a room together and close the door. So sweet Bobo
was a distraction, and Richard's question an act of unalloyed
charity.

"My car ran out of gas," he said, not very helpfully.
"You can't get gas anywhere in town—my needle was so far

down it was almost out of sight, but I thought I could get up this far, anyway. I had to run half of Mount Avenue and then all the way through Hillhaven to get here." He peeked at Patsy again, still breathing hard. That private trouble tugged at his mouth and eyes. "Don't ask me how, but I knew you'd all be up here—I just sort of had to be with you. Things aren't . . . aren't . . ." He put his hands over his face, hiding himself like a child. "I think Ronnie's dying. She might even be dead. Last night I know she almost died." The words were muffled, and he lowered his hands. "She ordered me out this morning. She didn't want me there." Bobo inspected the gravel on the side of the road, struggling with both his misery and the sensations of expressing it. "I'm afraid to go back to her house. I couldn't stand it if I went in there and she was dead."

"I think you'll find that she's getting better," Graham told him. "In fact I'm sure of it. And I bet she'll be delighted to see you." This turned out to be only fifty percent true.

"You're sure of it?" Bobo said.

"I just said so."

The policeman nodded. Very seriously he said, "Thank you. Thank you for everything, I guess I mean."

None of them replied to that, and Bobo shuffled back and forth for a moment. "Well, I guess we're all walking back together."

"If you like," Richard said, charitable again, though a fraction less so.

They moved in silence up toward the Hillhaven end of Mount Avenue. Bobo wanted to walk faster than the others, and kept twitching ahead, then turning around to watch them catch up. "You can run on ahead of us, Bobo," Graham said. "We understand that you're anxious to get back to Ronnie."

"I'd rather go with you," Bobo said flatly.

By the time they had passed the Hillhaven beach, Richard was almost holding Tabby up. Graham and Patsy had their arms around each other and plodded toward Beach Trail with mechanical determination. None of them had responded to Bobo's distracted attempts at conversation, and they were doing their best to ignore his frequent and darting stares. "We're getting there, Patsy," Graham said. Bobo chimed in with "Sure are." Eventually they came to his patrol car, tucked under the trees by the side of the road. *"This* son of a bitch," Bobo said, hitting the roof with the side of his hand. They went another silent, painful twenty yards and Bobo said, "Oh my God. Will you look at that?"

Monty Smithfield's old house had thrown itself down the hill behind it and left an odd, busy gap in the landscape. Water jetted from broken pipes; stone pillars stuck up out of the foundation. Dust thick as smoke still hung in the air.

"Oh my God," Bobo repeated. "That terrific house. It must be down in the water, right? Those quakes or whatever they were shook it right off the hill. I didn't think a place that solid would ever . . ." He stepped over the myrtle to get to the fence. "I hope no more of these places went over like that."

"This would be the only one," Graham said.

"I really have to see what happened down there," Bobo said. "Maybe someone needs help." He twisted indecisively against the fence, not wanting to leave them. "You'll all get home all right, won't you?"

"More than likely," Graham said, and the four of them backed away to walk the last short distance to Beach Trail.

"Why would only this house go down like that?" Bobo asked.

"Good-bye, Bobo," Graham said. "You're a good fellow. Everything'll turn out all right."

"I saw you—I saw you on Kendall Point," Bobo blurted out, and it was obvious that he had been worrying at this revelation since he had first come upon them.

Even Patsy and Tabby looked at him now.

"I was up high enough to see almost all the way down into that, uh, gully." Bobo appeared almost ashamed, as if they might accuse him of spying. "What was that thing down there, anyhow? You were fighting it, right? What was it?"

"What did you see?" Richard asked. Tabby and Graham and Patsy had instinctively stepped closer to him.

"Some kind of animal, I guess," Bobo said. "Pretty big. Ah . . . I hate to even *say* this . . . but, like it had a kind of human face?"

"I wish I could tell you," Richard said. "Honest, Bobo—I wish I could."

"Yeah," Bobo said, "I wish you could too." He paused. "I guess I better take a look at what's left of this house." Still he hovered before the iron fence. "You take good care of that lady, now."

"See you later," Graham said, and pulled himself and Patsy around. The four of them did not hear Bobo move away from the fence until they had turned the corner into Beach Trail.

Graham pushed his door open and let the others in. Patsy got just past the door, then leaned against the wall. Her head drooped. "Sorry," she said. "I don't have any energy left. None at all."

Richard and Tabby jostled together in the narrow book-filled hallway, wanting to help. But it was Graham who put his shoulder under her arm and helped her into the living room. "I just have to lie down for a little bit," Patsy said.

Graham took her to the couch and eased her down on her side. Patsy's eyes were already closing. He moved her legs up on the couch and fetched a plaid blanket from beside his desk. This he shook out and placed over her. Even in sleep, Patsy's face was drawn and taut—almost angular, pulled so tightly over the bones. "You can sit down, Tabby," Graham said. "She isn't going anywhere for a couple of hours."

"Me too," Tabby said, walking away from the couch in the direction of Graham's desk chair. He paused before he reached it, looked back at Patsy and returned to the head of the couch. Richard too had been unable to go very far from Patsy, and stood facing her from the other side of the coffee table.

"You guys are like the lions at the library," Graham said. "Do me a favor and sit down. Nobody's going anywhere for quite a while—I agree with Tabby."

"Good," Richard said, and moved only as far as the worn leather chair.

Tabby sat down beside the couch. He was close enough to reach up and stroke her hair.

"I suppose that'll do," Graham said. "I'm going to have a drink. At some point I'm going to bed. I feel like I've been up for three days. But I trust you will both stay here until we work out other plans."

Richard said, "I don't want any other plans."

"Okay," Graham said, actually smiling. "There's a lot of room here—there are rooms upstairs I haven't seen in fifteen years. Okay. I'm glad."

"Am I staying here too?" Tabby asked, suddenly looking stricken.

"If you try to go anywhere else I'll chain you to my desk," Graham said. "Good. That's settled. Anybody else want a drink? I still have some of that gin Patsy liked so much."

All three of them looked at her softly breathing beneath the plaid blanket.

"Sure," Richard said.

"I want some too, please," Tabby said. "If, you know . . ."

"Today you get anything you want," Graham said. He moved slowly into the kitchen and began cracking ice into glasses.

Tabby remembered Berkeley Woodhouse chopping the ice tray against the sink at "Four Hearths," and pulled up his knees and wrapped his arms around them. "Richard?"

"Yes."

"It's all right to stay here for a while?"

"Yes."

"All together?"

"All together."

"I don't really want to be anywhere else."

"I know. We all feel that way, Tabby."

"Do you think that cop Bobo really saw an animal with a human face?"

Richard slumped back into the chair. "We're probably going to be talking about Kendall Point for the rest of our lives. Right now is too soon, Tabby. I don't even know what I think."

Graham came toward them with three glasses half-filled with ice and clear liquid. "That's right, Tabby. It's too early. I put some water in yours, by the way." He gave each of them a glass, then removed the one clamped against his chest and put it on the coffee table. "I'll be right back. There's something I have to do while I still have the courage."

Tabby sipped at his drink and made a face. "You guys think this is good?"

"We think it's among the better poisons."

Graham's slow heavy steps went up the stairs.

"What's he going to do?"

"Let's ask him when he gets back."

"I don't think I can ever leave Patsy," the boy said.

"Yeah," Richard said. "I don't even think I can ever leave this chair."

Graham thumped back down the stairs and reappeared carrying a stack of paper eight inches high. He wordlessly went past them and made his way into the kitchen. A few seconds later Richard and Tabby heard something weighty hit the bottom of a plastic garbage can.

Graham came back into the living room, a peculiarly lighthearted expression on his face. He limped to the coffee table, picked up his drink and swallowed a third of it, then limped over to his desk chair. "Blisters," he said. He smiled at his glass, then at sleeping Patsy. "I just set myself free. I spent so much time on that book I couldn't admit that it died about a year ago. All I was doing was spinning my wheels. I don't even want to look at it anymore."

"You threw your *book* out?" Tabby asked in amazement.

"I wrote thirteen novels," Graham said calmly. "I'll get to number fourteen before I check out." He took another big mouthful of the gin, and swished it around before he swallowed. "I think I won't do anything but help you two take care of Patsy for a while."

Then they said nothing for a long time—the silence stretched and stretched, filling up with their thoughts. They all three watched her inhale, exhale beneath the blanket.

Tabby dipped his head into his knees; his mouth had begun to tremble, and his eyes suddenly stung.

"That's okay," Graham said. "Go ahead."

Tabby lifted his face and had to look at her again. "She . . ." he began, and then could not continue. "She, ah . . ." He could not say it.

"I know," Richard said. "She married us."

Impulsively Tabby got to his knees and kissed Patsy McCloud's cheek. "Yes," Richard said, and set his glass on the floor and went around the low table and put his lips against her forehead. Then Graham limped across the room and kissed Patsy somewhere in the vicinity of her left eyebrow. It felt like a ritual; it felt like the sealing of a contract or the acknowledgment of a sacrament, and should have signified some important and immediate transformation. But they stood motionless above her, and Patsy slept on.

Graham grunted, and returned to his typing chair. Tabby sat back down on the floor. Richard leaned into the ancient leather chair. They did not speak. Graham finished his drink, revolved the cracked old glass in his hand, and was visited by a flawless joy. His chest hurt, his feet burned, five minutes ago he had junked as many years of work (and even now was thinking if some of those pages might not be rescued from the garbage), he was at the near edge of a hallucinatory fatigue, but for an unmeasurable time he was thoughtlessly, blessedly happy. Each one of the three people in his living room glowed with a unique and necessary essence—glowed like the sword in Richard's hand out on Kendall Point. Had that scene actually played itself out, in that place and in that way? It did not matter, not for these few seconds. He was happier than at any other time in his life; he had gone beyond happiness, he thought, and imagined that he sensed realms beyond realms—the sun-drenched worlds where gods played. His eyes started open and he rescued himself from dropping his glass. Richard and Tabby both slept, as innocently as Patsy McCloud. Graham pushed himself out of his chair, took his glass into the kitchen, and retrieved the most plausible chapters from the tall plastic garbage can. Then he went upstairs, leaving his living room filled with the breathing, the soft intakings and subtle relaxations, of his sleeping friends.

After the Moon

After the moon had risen and set a score of times, Hampstead had gone a long way toward emerging from its fevers and comas; the visions which had peeped out of closets, tapped at doors and finally run freely through the streets faded back into the mind's most tightly buttoned pockets; Hampstead began to add up its losses and mourn its dead—it was ready to rejoin the world. And the world, for better or worse, was not only willing to accept Hampstead back, it rushed to embrace the town with its dazzling, intrusive attentions. Hampstead, like all the affected towns, was pale and thin, but now it could walk: and its voice was sane again. It was not a threat, but a gallant victim. The roadblocks came down, and the reporters and feature writers and television cameras flocked in.

Eventually most people in Hampstead had either spoken to a reporter themselves or been standing next to someone who did, and the four people in Graham Williams' house were no exceptions. During this period when life seemed more to be imitating normality than actually to have attained it, Patsy and Richard and the old man and the boy often considered that what was happening to them was as strange as anything that had occurred earlier.

At first there was the matter of what Richard called their "stardom." For a period slightly longer than a week they could not leave Graham's house without picking up a little following. Most often the following was quiet and passive: if Richard stood on the corner of Main Street and waited for the light to change, the two or three other people waiting with him would begin to turn toward him. Depending on their temperaments, they would stare forthrightly or discreetly; they wanted to talk, but did not. They were not quite sure that they knew what to say. At least some of them would shyly dog him down Main Street, pretending to window-shop.

Once while Patsy shopped in the still-depleted Greenblatt's, an elderly woman with heavy gold bracelets tremblingly stroked her arm on the pretext of admiring her blouse. Another, younger woman hugged Tabby Smithfield in the municipal parking lot behind Anhalt's. Richard said, "I think I'm beginning to understand Frank Sinatra," but what he thought was that these people had a chip of the same talent Patsy and Tabby had: enough of it to put a kind of spotlight on the four of them. Even the press seemed to circle in toward these four whenever they could.

They did not like going out. All they really wanted was each other's company. But when they were forced to leave the house, someone with a notepad and a pen or someone with a microphone was likely to appear, asking questions. The difficulty was in giving answers that would not brand them as hopelessly insane. They could not allude to themselves and Gideon Winter, the only subject that occupied them in these days, and so tried to give responses as flat and banal as possible—everybody else was excited about the lawsuits and the court cases against the Telpro Corporation and the investigations into the Defense Department, but as yet Richard Allbee and the others had not moved so far out of themselves.

"Oh, I think this town is getting back on its feet," Richard told CBS. "It's funny, but most of us have trouble even remembering what went on here this summer."

"I'm afraid that I've just been concentrating on my own affairs, which I kind of neglected over the summer," Patsy told *Newsweek*. "I have no plans to sue anybody."

"We're a pretty spunky bunch," Graham said to NBC. "No *[bleep]* gas can slow us down for long."

"Did we have a summer this year?" Tabby asked *Eyewitness News*.

After a week, they noticed that the stares and questions had become fewer; after two weeks they were again anonymous citizens, and for that they were grateful.

The Conrail trains again stopped at the stations in Hillhaven and Greenbank and Hampstead. Greenblatt's and the other grocery stores gradually filled up with fresh produce and cuts of meat as the warehousers and dispatchers were informed that Hampstead no longer meant danger to their trucks. By the third week in September all of the windows along Main Street had been replaced. A week after that, while Graham and Richard worked outside repairing the broken window frame and fractured boards beneath it, Graham saw a sparrow dart out of the trees at the end of his lot. A few days after that, birds of every kind seemed to have returned to Hampstead—gulls, cardinals, robins, finches, thrushes, and big thuggish crows.

All sorts of wandering birds came back. One morning Graham and Patsy met Evelyn Hughardt as they were taking a walk down to the beach. She was getting out of her car, and when Graham said, "Hello, Evvy, it's nice to see you again," she looked at her watch, glanced at him and said, "Is it?" and walked up the path to her door. "Now I *know* things are getting back to normal," Graham said.

Charlie Antolini hired a painter and took out of his house all the furniture he had daubed pink and piled it next to the curb. The television set, two couches, a rack of chairs, a big dining-room table: all sizzled with Charlie's happy pink paint. Seeing that pathetic but somehow hopeful-looking furniture brought back to Graham the precise sensations of the summer. He remembered the smell of Norm Hughardt's mouthwash when he rolled his body over; he tasted the saltiness of sleeping Patsy's temple when he had kissed her. Twenty minutes later, a Goodwill truck drove the furniture away.

Sometimes—for long after—the sight of a misprint in the *Hampstead Gazette* could give Graham that sense of total recall of what it felt like to live through a time when all the rules and conventions were suspended; but in fact there were no more misprints now than ever before. The only difference between the *Gazette* in September and the same paper the preceding April or May was that it had no social and gossip column. Sarah Spry had not been a great writer, but she had proved to be an irreplaceable one.

Those who had been among the saddest victims of the summer, Dr. Chaney's patients, had all died by mid-October—by then they bore no resemblance any longer to human beings, and when one by one they ceased to register life signs, even Chaney was relieved. He had a book to write.

Five weeks after the night Graham Williams went up to bed and left his friends asleep in his living room, Richard and Tabby moved across the street to Richard's house. Part of the reason for this split—which they regretted only slightly less than they understood its necessity—was that Graham's house was not suitable for three or four adult inhabitants. The unused rooms upstairs baked in warm weather, froze in cold: Patsy spent every night on the couch, and Tabby eventually made a bed in a cramped little room next to the kitchen. If Graham had been willing to move out of his house, they would very likely have all gone across the street—and stayed together for another few weeks of increasing discomfort. Graham missed his solitude, Richard Allbee wanted either to attend to his house or to sell it; that obsessive need to be together always had diminished. Reality, the world of other people, called them to itself, and they had started to respond to the call. Tabby was back in school, and Richard wanted to make sure he had a quiet place to study; he also wanted to get back to work regularly and stop leaning on John Roehm. Maybe Graham was sometimes dictatorial, maybe Richard sometimes felt impatient. Fathers; sons.

The old man had never expected Richard to sell his house, and felt no disappointment when Richard told him he had decided after all to keep it. "Are you going to adopt Tabby?" Graham asked. "I'd like to do that," Richard said, for the first time acknowledging it consciously. "That's right," Graham said—he had no reason to ask the younger man about Patsy. They all loved her, but in a way that mysteriously but firmly forbade the physical expression of love. Graham did not understand why, but what Patsy had done for them on Kendall Point had sealed that door forever.

Like an eccentric parody of a suburban social life, the two households often ate dinner together, went on walks, laughed together over drinks, even went to movies. Richard found that there were no impediments to his adopting Tabby, and began the legal procedures in late October. Graham and Patsy messed along together comfortably for a time, as if they were father and daughter.

But eventually Graham recognized that their roles had reversed. Instead of his caring for her, Patsy now seemed to be protecting him, coddling him, almost nursing him! For Graham this was deeply disconcerting. He did not want to feel as old as that. Like Richard, he wanted to get back to his work. And eventually Patsy came to decisions of her own.

• • •

Richard Allbee helped Graham get started. They were having a drink together in Graham's living room just before Christmas. A foot-high plastic tree on a bookshelf was the room's only acknowledgment of the season. Graham lived alone now, and felt a small secret relief that the woman he loved most in all the world no longer tried to make him eat breakfast every morning. Richard also was alone: Tabby had persuaded him to let him go to Aspen with the family of a school friend. The two men were having their own defiant little Christmas. Richard was roasting a duck, and had brought over two bottles of a good Margaux to drink with it. "Hey, I'm an *ex*-alcoholic," Graham protested. "I can't have a whole bottle of this stuff." He had dolled himself up for this dinner—in his attic he had unearthed a green velvet smoking jacket with black satin lapels, and this wonderful garment covered a neatly pressed blue woolen shirt and framed a knit tie with wide irregular horizontal stripes. On his feet were heavy black shoes from which he had not bothered to wipe the dust.

"Then stop drinking that gin," Richard said.

"Oh, I lay off this stuff most of the time—save it for special occasions. You know."

For a moment Patsy McCloud was almost in the room with them, so clearly had the allusion evoked her.

Graham broke the silence. "Hear anything from Tabby lately?"

"He calls every other day—I talked to him just before I came over here. He's having a great time. I miss him, but I'm glad I let him go out there."

They each knew that the other was still thinking about Patsy.

"Graham," Richard said, "I still don't know what really happened."

"No," the old man said.

"I thought I would somehow understand it better as time went on. I thought I'd come around to thinking that the Telpro business was more important than we thought at the time."

"That Telpro installation was just out there in the world," Graham said. "I think Gideon Winter could grab it and use it because of the name—DRG. Or the other position is that the name was a coincidence, and the accident was a real accident, and Winter simply capitalized on it. There's one other possibility, but I don't like that one."

"That we are partly responsible for the so-called accident too," Richard said.

"That we helped send that poison bob, bob, bobbing through Patchin County." Graham made an expression of distaste. "I think it was what that research guy, Wise, said it was—a wild card. I think once he realized what had happened the Dragon couldn't believe his luck. Everything was helping him get stronger. He really could have caused another Black Summer. Hell, I guess he did." He cocked his head and regarded Richard almost cheerfully. "At least we know what caused the fire at Royal Cotton."

"You think it was a dragon? You really do?"

"You killed it, didn't you?"

"I think Patsy killed it," Richard said. "Whatever the hell it was." He was silent for a moment. "You ought to write the whole thing down, Graham—put it all down just the way it looked to us. Then at least we'd all have that much straight."

"I'd be too tempted to invent things," Graham said. "I'd make up dialogue. I'd speculate about what happened to certain people. Pretty soon I'd be writing a novel."

"That's okay too," Richard said. "That sort of fits."

Graham nodded. "But it's still impossible. As much as we've talked, I still don't know enough about what you and Patsy were doing in May and June. I'd have to make it up, and you'd be likely to get ticked off at what I wrote about you."

"I'll let you use my diaries," Richard said.

"I'll think about it."

"Patsy keeps a diary too." He was grinning.

"I *know*. I'll think about it."

The next morning Graham called Richard and asked him if he would mind bringing his diaries across the street.

Two years later, just before Graham Williams finished writing the excellent book called *Floating Dragon*, Richard Allbee took a new wife, a new baby, and Tabby Smithfield to France for a short vacation. He had completed two large restoration jobs in New England, and would soon begin another in Virginia. He had been invited by a French architectural association to speak at their general meeting, and Richard delightedly took the opportunity of bringing his new family to Paris. His wife, who was ten years younger than he and worked for the Museum of Modern Art, spoke nearly perfect French. They would return two days before Tabby had to register for his freshman year at the University of Connecticut; and the baby was three months old, untroubled by schedules, and eminently portable.

Richard took them all to museums and parks and restaurants; he gave his lecture in a French which his wife had drilled into him; Tabby and his wife beside him, he pushed the gurgling baby down random streets and was implausibly content. If some malevolent power had given him the summer of 1980, other forces had given him this.

Then two days before they were to return, an unaccompanied Richard pushed the baby's stroller through the ornate entrance of the Intercontinental Hotel and turned for no particular reason toward the Place Vendôme. His wife had taken Tabby off shopping for an hour, and Richard wanted to give his infant son some fresh air—also he could feel his time in Paris coming to a close, and did not want to waste the small amount left. He idled through the Vendôme, inspecting shop windows, and then just as aimlessly began working his way in the general direction of the Opéra. After five or six blocks he began to think about how pleasant it would be to have a beer, and looked around for an outdoor café.

Richard turned down a street he did not know and saw a small group of tables on the next corner. He pushed the baby to the café, seated himself at an outside table, and sat down. The baby made motorboat noises with his mouth and pumped his hands happily up and down. The waiter came and Richard placed his order with an accent his wife would have described as "Serbo-French." Richard looked over the nine or ten other patrons of the café, hoping that no baby-adoring woman would come up to coo at his son and trap him into exposing more Serbo-French. *Oui, madame, il est très beau.* He could not go much beyond that. Then he saw the thick gray-haired man seated facing him on the opposite side of the café, and he thought his mind had gone. The summer of 1980 sped back toward him with its full freight of madness. He knew that face, and for a moment it held him paralyzed. The Dragon had shown that face to him in an endless tunnel, and had tried to murder him with it.

Cold seconds later, he realized that the man who owned the

face was not likely to do any such thing. The man was what he looked like, not a lethal toy of Gideon Winter's. Richard saw the qualities he had seen in the tunnel, the air this elderly man had of being a merchant seaman or a bohemian poet, but saw also his utter ordinariness—he was a man who enjoyed looking like the middle-class conception of a poet. His father would be a good talker, a good drinker, at most times a good worker; his essential irresponsibility would only emerge under stress. He would always have many friends. Richard even saw his own resemblance to the man. In another twenty-five years he would not look so very different.

Richard plucked his son out of the stroller and walked through the maze to the other side of the café. He held the tiny boy in his arms and said, his heart beating, "Michael Allbee, meet Michael Allbee."

A stranger lifted a puzzled face to Richard. This was not his father; he no longer even resembled the figure of the tunnel. The man was a bourgeois Parisian—he looked startled and offended in equal measure. Richard and the baby retreated. The baby began to squall.

Mystery upon mystery. Richard hastily pushed little Michael in what he thought was the direction of the Intercontinental and almost immediately was lost. For almost the only time in his life, his sense of direction had failed. He gave up and hailed a cab when the baby, who was still nursing, started screeching for milk in an unearthly and domineering tone. He did not tell his capable, attractive, and aggressive second wife about his ludicrous encounter with his "father"—she had long ago assumed that both his parents were dead. Richard did not feel truly comfortable again until he and his family were on the big Air France jet to JFK airport.

Mystery upon mystery.

Patsy McCloud had vanished from their lives, though none of them had quite accepted the reality of this. During her weeks with Graham, Patsy had taken to going out alone at night. Graham Williams customarily went to sleep before ten o'clock, and he could not object to her unexplained departures if he was aware of them only because the sound of the garage door banging down woke him up at three in the morning. Whenever this happened, Patsy greeted him six hours later with fresh coffee and orders about breakfast: she was firm and chipper, she appeared rested, she wanted him really to think about eggs. Quantities of eggs.

At last she confided to Graham that she had met a man she liked. The man was a lawyer in Chappaqua, New York, a widower; he had first met Patsy years ago at the Club Med in Martinique, where she had spent ten days with Les and four other couples from the company. The man had seen her picture in *Newsweek,* learned her telephone number through Information; he had reached her during one of the rare hours she spent at the Charleston Road house. His name was Arthur Powers. He had remembered her, and what Patsy especially liked was that Arthur Powers did not quiz her about the events of the previous summer.

Patsy sold her house through Ronnie Riggley—Hampstead was still a big convenient bedroom for New York, and some chemical ugliness four months before could not keep people away for long; especially when real-estate values had dipped so far. Les had carried mortgage insurance and a big life policy. If she lost money on the sale of her house, she still was left with almost as much money as Clark Smithfield had ruinously inherited.

Patsy spent the Christmas of 1980 in Chappaqua with Arthur Powers.

By that time she was gone altogether. After five weeks with Graham, she had driven to Manhattan—to stay with a girlfriend, she had told him without being any more specific. "I love you so much," she said on the telephone, "I love you because I have to love you," and the words made him ache to have her back, pressuring him about breakfast.

Twelve days later, he got a postcard from some island. The postmark obliterated the legend on the card, and no matter how long he peered at those wavy black lines, they hid whatever was beneath them. The message read: *AP quite a find after all. I miss you all so much. Sand white, sun hot. Delicious. Have a Bombay martini and think of me. Much love, P.* The picture on the card showed a setting sun, palm trees, languid blue water. The brutal cancellation barely permitted him to identify a British stamp. British? Bermuda? Or did what he could see of the stamp merely look British?

Patsy telephoned him from New York, from Chappaqua. She was always rushed, always tender. She and Arthur Powers were thinking of buying a house together. "His place is too much like yours, Graham! I'm spoiled, I want insulation."

She sent a printed card with an address: The Birches, 28

Woodland Glen, Chappaqua, New York. *Married again but still Patsy McCloud, love you all always and forever,* read the handwritten note folded around the card.

She was gone; utterly gone. Richard met the woman he would marry at a party in New York and asked her if she had ever seen Hampstead. "London? Sure." "Connecticut." "Do people still live in Connecticut?" They survived this exchange. Tabby fell in love with a girl in his class, had no luck, then fell in love again. Graham labored over his puzzling book. Richard spent more and more time with the woman he had met, and finally brought her home to meet Tabby. Patsy was gone.

She was married to a lawyer named Arthur Powers and she lived in Chappaqua. Or she was not and did not. One night Graham tried to get her telephone number from Westchester County information and was told that neither an Arthur Powers nor a Patricia McCloud was listed in Chappaqua. Richard sent a letter to 28 Woodland Glen telling her that he planned to marry again, but the letter came back stamped ADDRESS UNKNOWN.

Each of them dreamed of her: Richard dreamed of Patsy McCloud standing on a sloping hill the night before he married again. She was smiling at him, and he understood at last that she wished him well.

His telephone rang at four in the morning the night his son was born; he had just arrived home from the hospital. "Did something nice happen to you tonight?" Patsy's dear voice asked him.

"Oh, Patsy," he said. "Something wonderful happened— I just had a baby. How on earth did you know?"

"We Tayler women have our secrets," she said. "I'm happy now. Are you?"

"Now? I'm about to bust, I'm so happy."

"Good," she said. "If you feel that way, I do too."

"I sent you a letter," he managed to say, but Patsy was talking again, and his words obscured hers.

I got it? I moved again? It could have been either.

"Sorry," they both said.

"I have to go now," Patsy's clear voice told Richard. "I'm glad you're a father at last."

"Patsy, what's your telephone number? We've tried to reach you . . ."

"We're changing it. I'll send you the new number as soon as I get it."

"Please do. I want to see you again, and Graham is pining for you, and Tabby wants to tell you all about his girlfriend."

She laughed. "Well, you've done a great thing!"

"*We* did a great thing once," he said, but the telephone was already dead.

> *And he laid hold on the dragon, that old serpent, which is the devil, and bound him a thousand years.*
> —Revelation 20:2

Peter Straub is the author of seventeen novels, which have been translated into more than twenty languages. They include *Ghost Story*, *Koko*, *Mr. X*, *In the Night Room*, and two collaborations with Stephen King, *The Talisman* and *Black House*. He has written two volumes of poetry and two collections of short fiction, and he edited the Library of America's edition of *H. P. Lovecraft: Tales* and the Library of America's two-volume anthology, *American Fantastic Tales*. He has won the British Fantasy Award, eight Bram Stoker Awards, three International Horror Guild Awards, and ten World Fantasy Awards. In 1997, he was named Grand Master at the World Horror Convention. In 2005, he was given the Horror Writers Association's Lifetime Achievement Award. At the World Fantasy Convention in 2010, he was given the WFC's Life Achievement Award.

CONNECT ONLINE

PeterStraub.net

🐦 PeterStraubNYC

📘 PeterStraubAuthor

Ready to find
your next great read?

Let us help.

Visit prh.com/nextread

ADDITIONAL PRAISE FOR *NOT WITHOUT PERIL*

"*Not Without Peril* is an outstanding addition to the literature of mountaineering. Howe's work gives us a masterful, riveting, and meticulously researched account of some of the most tragic encounters with the wrath of the White Mountains. These stories are made even more chilling because of the accessibility of these mountains to the recreational hiker."—Donna Urey, President, New England Booksellers Association

"This should be required reading for anyone who will be—or has already gone—hiking in the mountains."—Nelly Heitman, *Foreword Magazine*

"Howe tells the stories straightforwardly, deftly blending in the historical and geographical information needed to make them complete. *Not Without Peril* makes a memorable, informative, and ultimately sobering read about the high peaks of the Northeast."—*Sentinel & Enterprise*, Leominster, Mass.

"Between the excellent prose, the interesting historical details and the riveting accounts of misadventure, *Not Without Peril* will be appreciated by anyone with an interest in outdoor recreation or in the Presidential Mountains of New Hampshire. Reading about these mountains is gripping."—*The Bridgton News*, Bridgton, Maine

"Nick Howe has tramped virtually every inch of Mount Washington's surface, and with this book he becomes its preeminent historian. That he happens also to be a graceful and charming storyteller is pure bonus. *Not Without Peril* is a compulsively readable thriller—actually, a series of thrillers. It will hold equal fascination for mountain lovers and flatlanders and for anyone who enjoys a good read."—John Jerome, author of *On Turning Sixty-Five, The Elements of Effort, Stone Work,* and *The Sweet Spot in Time*

"In essays that preface each episode, Howe examines the odd circumstances that surround it and the occasional ripple effects of death in the mountains."—D. Quincy Whitney, *The Boston Globe*

"Fans of outdoor disaster and unpleasantry, as well as collectors of New England mountain lore, will find Howe a generally satisfying guide to New Hampshire's dark side."—*Kirkus Reviews*

NOT WITHOUT PERIL

NOT WITHOUT PERIL

150 Years of Misadventure
on the Presidential Range
of New Hampshire

Tenth Anniversary Edition

NICHOLAS HOWE

Appalachian Mountain Club Books
Boston, Massachusetts

The AMC is a nonprofit organization and sales of AMC books fund our mission of protecting the Northeast outdoors. If you appreciate our efforts and would like to make a donation to the AMC, contact us at Appalachian Mountain Club, 10 City Square, Boston, MA 02129

outdoors.org/books-maps

Book design by Eric Edstam
Front cover image © Jerry and Marcy Monkman, ecophotography.com
Maps by Louis F. Cutter. Excerpted from *Appalachian Mountain Club Map of Mount Washington Range*, copyright © 1992 Appalachian Mountain Club.

Library of Congress Cataloging-in-Publication Data

Howe, Nicholas S.
  Not without peril : 150 years of misadventure on the Presidential Range of New Hampshire / Nicholas Howe. — 10th anniversary ed.
    p. cm.
  ISBN 978-1-934028-32-2 (alk. paper)
  1. Mountaineering—New Hampshire—Presidential Range—History. 2. Presidential Range (N.H.)—History. I. Title.
  GV199.42.N42P744 2010
  796.52209742'1—dc22
                                        2009027665

The paper used in this publication meets the minimum requirements of the American National Standard for Information Sciences—Permanence of Paper for Printed Library Materials, ANSI Z39.48-1984. ∞

Interior pages and cover are printed on responsiby harvested paper stock certified by The Forest Stewardship Council®, and independent auditor of responsible forestry practices.
Printed in the United States of America, using vegetable-based inks.

FSC
www.fsc.org
MIX
Paper from
responsible sources
FSC® C005010

10 9 8 7 6 5 4   22 23 24 25 26 27 28 29

T here have been joys too great to be described in words, and there have been griefs upon which I have dared not to dwell, and with these in mind I must say, climb if you will, but remember that courage and strength are naught without prudence, and that a momentary negligence may destroy the happiness of a lifetime. Do nothing in haste, look well to each step, and from the beginning think what may be the end.

—EDWARD WHYMPER, who made the first ascent of the Matterhorn with six others in 1865. On the way down, four of his companions fell to their deaths.

Contents

Foreword

𝒜LMOST A DECADE HAS PASSED SINCE I FIRST READ NICK Howe's wonderful book, *Not Without Peril*. I had, for several years, been reading the accident reports in the mountaineering journal *Appalachia*, so I was quite familiar with the dangers that lurk in our mountains. But whereas the accident reports consist of a rather dry summary of the events, followed by an analysis of what went wrong, Nick's book tells a series of fascinating tales. In spite of the fatal outcome of almost every chapter, the tone of the book is never morbid.

For the last five years I have been writing the accident reports of *Appalachia*, and I have become even more familiar with the perils of the White Mountains in the process. Some aspects of people's misadventures there seem to have changed since the earlier years that Nick describes, but others seem to have remained constant.

The biggest changes are the disappearance of guides (and of summit accommodations), and the post-World War II embrace of winter hiking. More subtle is the widespread understanding, among the community of regular hikers, of the dangers in the mountains. I suspect that few hikers today would, like "Father" Bill Curtis in the late nineteenth century, write in their trip notices that "This outing will not be canceled or postponed due to inclement weather."

On the other hand, much has not changed. The mountain weather is as unpredictable as ever, and while those who hike regularly understand the dangers, many casual visitors do not. Too many people simply do not think; every year the New Hampshire Fish and Game Department "rescues" at least half a dozen hikers who started out late in the day with no lights. When the sun sets they use their cell phones to call for help.

You can see the similarities and differences by comparing the story of Frederick Strickland, the first recorded fatality on Mount Washington, with contemporary mishaps. Strickland was an Englishman who, at the age of 29, was visiting America. At the end of a long tour of the country he returned to Boston in October of 1849. According to the *Boston Transcript*, "... he was advised to visit the White Mountains by several gentlemen of science and taste in our community."

Strickland traveled to Crawford Notch, where Thomas Crawford strongly advised him against attempting to climb Mount Washington, as a severe early season storm had deposited deep snow on the mountain. He insisted, and Crawford ended up providing him with a guide and horses. Strickland claimed that he did not need any provisions for that long trip, but his host finally persuaded him to take a couple of crackers. He was, as was usual at the time, dressed in street clothes with an overcoat. On reaching the ridge, the guide decided to turn around, as the snow was too deep for the horses. He advised Strickland to return with them, but the latter insisted on continuing. He never did return, becoming the first fatality on Mount Washington. When he did not show up at his destination, a search party went out, and his body was found and brought down.

The first thing that is unchanged is the difference in weather between Boston and the mountains. The latter are farther north, farther inland, and much higher than the city, all of which lead to very different weather. Yet Boston-based outdoors enthusiasts often base their decisions on the weather in the city. The owners of New Hampshire ski resorts complain that, when there is no snow on the ground in Boston, skiers stay home, regardless of how much snow there may be on the mountains. This works the other way around for hikers, especially in the spring. At that time, hikers who have hibernated all winter see crocuses in their yards, head north, and wallow in deep soft snow a few hundred vertical feet up the trail.

Strickland's guide advised him to turn around, but he stubbornly continued. While guides have disappeared from the scene in the White Mountains, many accidents occur after other hikers have warned the victims to turn around. Unfortunately there is no way to fully understand the decision-making process of those who continue hiking under clearly adverse conditions after having been advised to turn around. Perhaps it is bravado, or simply inertia: We were planning to go to the summit so we will keep going. Hard

The Southern Presidentials, as seen from Mount Washington.

Mount Washington, with Tuckerman Ravine on the left and Huntington Ravine on the right.

The Northern Presidentials as seen from Mount Washington over Great Gulf: Mount Clay is on the left, Mount Jefferson is in the middle, and Mount Adams on the far right.

to tell, and there is little to be learned from the appearances of survivors on TV; they are usually more interested in justifying their decisions than in analyzing them carefully.

I do not know how much the lack of food contributed to the fatal outcome in Strickland's case. Many inexperienced hikers climb big mountains with inadequate provisions, though the most common resulting problem is dehydration on a hot day. Strickland certainly wore enough clothing, though I suspect that he must have been sweating substantially after the horses left and he hiked to the summit. His clothing eventually became a problem when he lost his way down the other side of the mountain and fell into a stream; his pants apparently froze to his legs. The idea of layering and the technology of wicking fabric are clearly much more recent developments!

When Strickland did not show up at the hotel to which Crawford had directed him, two search parties went out, one from each end of the route he had been planning to follow. Eventually his body was found and was returned for burial. This has been an unchanging pattern in our mountains: Whenever someone is believed to be in trouble in the mountains, the local community attempts to rescue him or her. Even today, with the New Hampshire Fish and Game Department overseeing rescue operations, the vast majority of the rescuers are local volunteers. Those who live in the mountains understand full well that, as Benjamin Franklin wrote long ago, "We must, indeed, all hang together, or most assuredly we shall all hang separately."

Yet while our modern rescue groups are top-notch, it is still best not to get into a situation where you require their assistance. Smart preparation before heading into the mountains and wise decision-making once there can help you get home safely. I wish more hikers would learn these lessons and leave mountain dangers for their armchair reading. *Not Without Peril* makes such stories a delight.

Mohamed Ellozy
June 2009

Chapter One

IN THE BEGINNING

*M*OUNTAINS WERE INVENTED IN THE 19TH CENTURY. There had always been high places, of course, but the ancients usually thought that the gods lived there and avoided them for fear of giving offense. More recently, settlers considered mountains to be a piece of bad luck, a barrier to travel, and a hindrance to farming. One of my forebears was named Jemima Tute and she lived on the western frontier when the frontier was at the Connecticut River. There were two mountain ranges within reach, but no one in her family went hiking. If their eyes were open they were working, and they held off all the Indian attacks except the last one.

The high mountains of New England were approached slowly. They were first reported by a coastwise navigator in 1524, and early news was a mixture of wonder, dread, and confusion. One account was "A Voyage into New England," published in London in 1628: "This River (sawco), as I am told by the Savages, cometh from a great mountain called the Cristall hill, being as they say 100 miles in the Country, yet it is to be seene at the sea side, and there is no ship ariuse in NEW ENGLAND, either to the West so farre as Cape Cod, or to the East so farre as Monhiggen, but they see this Mountaine the first land, if the weather be cleere."

The ecology of the new world was not yet subject to rigorous study and some seaborn observers wrapped themselves in the mantle of whatever science as was available, so they attributed the brightness of that inland "Mountaine" to white moss. Others heard the optimistic accounts of distant sightings and early speculators, and thought it might be the sheen of precious stones. One gazeteer of 1638 brought less promising news; he pushed northwards from the Massachusetts settlements, but the track became difficult and he reported that the regions ahead were "daunting terrible," so he turned back.

If he'd persevered, he would have learned that the Cristall hill was Agiocochook, the highest point in the northeastern quarter of the North American continent. This distinction loomed large in the Indian culture of the region, and those natives dared not tread the heights that were reserved for the gods. When the summit was finally reached, the attempt was not inspired by any sense of adventure or scientific inquiry, it was politics.

That climb was made by Darby Field. He'd been living in the Massachusetts colony, then in about 1638 he settled in Dover, near the bustling docks of Portsmouth in New Hampshire's short coastline. At that time, leaders in Massachusetts were looking northward with a view to extending their realm. Governor John Winthrop and Richard Saltenstall were willing servants of the spirit of expansion that would characterize America, but they had not forgotten the sense of religious propriety that brought them to the New World. This meant that they had to deal with the natives that they found there, but they had to do it properly, with conferences and deeds.

Darby Field was a quick study and he learned several Indian tongues. He also had his eye out for the main chance, and he became a translator for Messrs. Winthrop and Saltonstall in their dealings with the natives. In particular they had to deal with Passaconaway, the principal chief of the Abenaki in the north. It seemed important to impress upon the natives that these European newcomers were not to be trifled with, that they were not afraid of either nature or gods. Darby Field decided that the surest way to do this was to conquer the throne room of their gods. So, in June of 1642 and in the witnessing company of an Abenaki, he found the untrodden top of Agiocochook. The prize was far more valuable than precious stones—this ascent helped convince Passaconaway to treat with the white settlers and trade away his lands.

The expansionist element in the Massachusetts colony lost no time in executing an intricate series of deeds with the Indians living in New Hampshire, but this was not the end of their ambition. They knew that the lands east of New Hampshire were more amenable to farming and better provided with access to the sea, so they looked to the territory that would become Maine.

When the negotiations were held, the delegation from Maine may have been surprised to learn that the men from Massachusetts already had maps of their lands. Darby Field had made a second ascent of Agiocochook in October 1642 and brought back reports of what he saw and gave them to his patrons in Massachusetts. As far as can be determined, that was the extent of high climbing in colonial New England.

It takes security from physical and economic threat before people feel they can take time off; that is to say, it takes vacations to turn daunting high places into something to be enjoyed, into mountains. The first vacationer of record in the hinterlands of New Hampshire was a person who had every right to feel secure in person and purse. This was John Wentworth, the last colonial governor of New Hampshire and probably its first tourist.

When the Honorable Wentworth took office in July 1767 he promised "to preserve the honor of the crown and advance the prosperity of the district." He was also "surveyor of the King's Woods in North America," which meant that he should see to it that a plentiful supply of trees suitable for ships' masts was provided to the king's navy. Two months after the governor took office he provided a further insight into the prosperity business. Portsmouth was the capitol of the colony and a circular advised the people that "John Wentworth gives notice that the General Court having empowered him to receive in demand 10,000 gallons of West India rum from the several towns in the state in lieu of taxes, he is ready for it and requests delinquent towns to hand it over."

This was a wide-ranging job description, and Governor Wentworth sought to escape the burdens of office and the hubbub of city life by building a second home on the shore of Lake Winnipesaukee, which lay at the beginning of the mountain region in the north. He spent his summers there from 1770 through 1775, thereby becoming the first New Hampshire vacationer of record, and he also built a series of splendid roads in the state. His visits were cut short by the stirrings of revolutionary sentiment and in 1778 he fled

The Mount Washington Road

This splendidly hyperbolic view of the Presidential Range was published in 1872. The foreground shows the eight-mile carriage road to the summit of Mount Washington and the sunlight picks out "Camp House" in the lower right.

to a more comfortable situation among the Tories of Nova Scotia, never to reclaim either office or vacation home.

Agiocochook could be seen from the waters of Winnipesaukee and in 1784 it was renamed to honor the general who won the Revolutionary War: Mount Washington. Before long the stage drivers were persuaded to drive on for another day to reach the highlands and soon there were inns and hostelries to accommodate travelers. One prominent visitor was Anthony Trollope, the celebrated English writer who flourished in the years after the American Civil War. He wrote that he was amazed "that there was a district in New England containing mountain scenery superior to much that is yearly crowded by tourists in Europe."

Mr. Trollope spent a night in Jackson, ten miles southeast of Mount Washington, then he went through Crawford Notch at the southern end of the Mount Washington range and met Mr. Plaistead, who spoke in the simple patois of the yeoman farmer: "Sir! I have everything here that a man ought to want; air, sir, that ain't to be got better nowhere; trout, chicken, beef mutton, milk—and all for a dollar a day. A-top that hill, sir, there's a view that ain't to be beaten this side of the Atlantic, or I believe on the other. And echo, sir! We've an echo that come back to us six times, sir; floating on the light wind, and wafted about from rock to rock till you would think the angels were talking to you."

"That hill" was Mount Washington and the peaks and valleys in its range, once daunting terrible, were now stylish. New England was prosperous and this brought wealth, leisure, and rather unpleasant cities. All traffic was horse-drawn and calculations show that one million tons of manure fell in the streets of London each year, with proportional amounts in downtown America. Not only that, but when horses died on the job they were not always removed from the street very quickly. The heat of summer lent emphasis to these conditions and affluent families were easily persuaded to escape.

The security of empire and the leisure of aristocracy sent Englishmen into the high places of Switzerland in the 1830s, and those sons of privilege were the first great generation of mountaineers. Their fame became fashionable and was admired even by those who would not follow them, thus Queen Victoria's husband had a panoramic picture of the Mount Washington summit view on the wall of his study in Buckingham Palace.

The Edenic promise of Mr. Plaistead's oration was not a complete inventory of those echoing heights. He would have known that "the sheen of precious stones" reported by the coastwise navigators was actually rime ice or snow, which can accumulate on the Mount Washington range in every month of the year. Mr. Plaistead could see that, but he probably did not know why winter came to the range even in midsummer.

Mount Washington is 6,288 feet high, and the summit and its buttress ridges lie at the intersection of two jet streams in the upper air. These combine with the upslope on the windward side of the range and the high elevation of the crests to create local weather systems of sudden and extraordinary violence. In later years, scientists would occupy the summit of Mount Washington and measure temperatures of 60° below zero and winds of 231 mph, the highest ever recorded on the surface of the earth.

These lethal conditions would cause 140 deaths and uncounted desperate survivals in the years to come, but Anthony Trollope didn't know that. He followed Mr. Plaistead's suggestion and went to see the celebrated view for himself, and all he saw was the inside of a cloud. It was worse for Frederick Strickland.

FREDERICK STRICKLAND
OCTOBER 1849

Frederick Strickland was a gentleman of substance and good prospect, the son of Sir George Strickland of Bridlington, England, who was a baronet and a member of Parliament. Frederick graduated in 1843 from Cambridge University, the school that taught Charles Darwin in the previous decade.

There was a lot going on then. Queen Victoria was in the second decade of her reign and Darwin was in the first gestures of his ascendancy. He'd gone from college to his five-year voyage on the Beagle, and upon his return he began to publish the essays that would be collected as *Species and Speciation* and lead to an enthusiastic but mistaken reading of his ideas. Darwin didn't think evolution is teleological—it has no direction or goal or end, evolution is what comes out in the wash. But it was convenient for English gentlemen of that era to believe that the whole history of evolution ended at English gentlemen, destined as they were to achieve dominion over palm and pine and to know a good sherry when they tasted one.

Young Mr. Strickland was very keen on science; he would have been attuned to the Darwinian buzz at Cambridge and encouraged by the confident energy of his countrymen. In 1849, he went to see America. Frederick was twenty-nine years old when he sailed in the company of his brother Henry, and they spent several months touring the hinterland of the vast continent. Returning to civilization, the junior Stricklands reached Boston during the first week of October and took rooms at the Tremont House, whence Frederick's brother soon returned to England.

The travels of an English gentleman were dignified and the details were well-understood. Chief among them was the letter of introduction, a sort of pre-packaged reputation, and *The Boston Advertiser* reported that Frederick Strickland was "most respectably introduced (and) had become known to a considerable number of persons in this city and vicinity, by whom he was highly respected as a gentleman of amiable character, ardently devoted to literary and scientific pursuits." *The Boston Transcript* added, "He brought letters to some of our most distinguished citizens and was advised to visit the White Mountains by several gentlemen of science and taste in our community."

History is silent on the names of his new friends, but gentlemen of science and taste would certainly be found at Harvard College, where the faculty included geologist Louis Agassiz, geographer Arnold Guyot, and mapmaker George Bond. They had all been active in the White Mountains that summer, they left their names on the mountains they explored, and they might well have advised the young Englishman to visit the same region. Frederick stayed on in America after his brother went home, and in October 1849 he took the stagecoach north.

A measure of endurance was required to approach the mountains. A road had been built to provide a way for farmers in the upper reaches of the Connecticut River to trade in the markets of Portland, Maine, but it was not a trip that invited the casual tourist. The route led through what they called The Notch of the Mountains, soon renamed Crawford Notch, and the way was so difficult that the first person to make the trip had to lower his horse down one section with a block and tackle. Even after the road was improved, the spur of commerce was barely enough to force the passage; "It was," said one rump-sore hero, "like driving a wagon up a brook bed."

Once Frederick Strickland was in the shadow of the mountains, he stopped in Crawford Notch at Abel Crawford's inn named The Mount Crawford House just south of Mount Crawford, then he went on to The Notch House kept by Thomas Crawford. Frederick came to the mountains with the intention of climbing the Crawford Path, a density of nomenclature that must have persuaded him that he'd come to the right place. The surroundings would have added to the assurance. Five years earlier, a traveler wrote that "the cavernous descent into which you look from the road is so savagely torn & distracted, so to speak, by the confused mingling of black depths and contending masses of old and young trees, & scattered & monstrous rocks, while the heights above are perhaps higher than anywhere else, that the scene is more imposing than in any other part." Another few hundred yards led to Thomas Crawford's door.

Two generations of this protean family built their hostelries for the convenience of farmers and tradesmen with accommodations that were minimal, but sufficient. Winter was the easiest time to travel because the streams and muddy swales were frozen and the Crawford diaries report that in 1819, "Lucy would many times have to make a large bed on the floor for (the travelers) to lie down upon, with their clothes on, and I would build a large fire in a large rock or stone chimney that would keep them warm through the night. It was no uncommon thing to burn in that fire-place a cord of wood in twenty-four hours, and sometimes more."

The next summer some pleasure-seekers inquired about climbing the mountains and seven of them signed Ethan Allen Crawford's register. Alert to this new commercial opportunity, he and his father Abel "made a foot path from the Notch out through the woods, and it was advertised in the newspapers, and we soon began to have a few visitors." This trail building would have been a prodigy of labor, but the Crawfords were used to hard work and Ethan was a giant of a man. He was over 6'2" in a time that counted 5'6" as well grown and he could lift a 500-pound barrel of potash two feet to the bed of their carrier. In present terms, the Crawford's path led three miles up Mount Clinton and another 6.2 miles along the ridge to the summit of Mount Washington. Then in 1840 Thomas Crawford's crew widened and graded their path for horse travel, which was considered to be the most

Crawford Notch, circa 1860. Early settlers had no way through the major mountain ranges of northern New Hampshire until a narrow gap was found in 1771. Today the gap is U.S. Rte. 302. This picture shows the route at about the time Frederick Strickland stopped at Thomas Crawford's hostelry, just beyond the rocks on the right.

reasonable way to ascend a mountain and, for the owner of the stable and the toll gate, the most profitable.

Thomas Crawford was keeping the family's inn beside the small lake at the top of the notch when Frederick Strickland arrived and announced that he'd like to climb Mount Washington. The innkeeper replied that the season for such an undertaking was past, there had been an unusually severe early-season storm and the snow up on the range was too deep for his horses to negotiate. Frederick thought that this country cousin was trying to shake him down for more money.

Thomas Crawford's cautions were rooted in something that he understood even if he couldn't explain it. Mount Washington is 130 miles north of

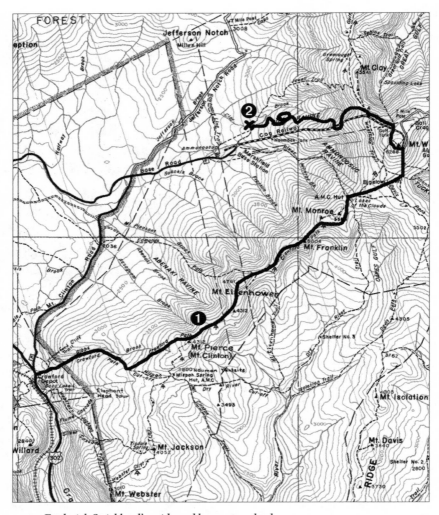

1. Frederick Strickland's guide and horses turn back
2. Body found below treeline

Boston and this puts the seasons as much as two months behind the down-country metropolis due to an indwelling global imperative. The summit of the mountain is more than 6,000 feet higher than Boston and each 100-foot gain in altitude is equivalent to moving ten miles north. By this formula, the summit is 500 miles north of Boston. Frederick Strickland would soon understand the effect of this rule, although he'd probably think that it didn't apply to him.

The English visitor came from a time and a culture that believed man could do anything, that triumph over nature was steady and inevitable and seemed to be confirmed by the recent propositions of the estimable Mr. Darwin. Thus strengthened, Frederick told Thomas Crawford that he was sure he could make the climb, he insisted that he could. Mr. Crawford agreed to provide a guide and horses and told him that if he did reach the top of Mount Washington he should not return by the Crawford Path, he should take the short route down by Horace Fabyan's bridle path, a three-mile route over the same terrain the cog railroad would follow twenty years later, then seven miles out along the Ammonoosuc River to Mr. Fabyan's hotel.

The English visitor seems to have been gaining in bravado, if not in wisdom. He said he didn't need any provisions for the long trip, but his host finally persuaded him to take a couple of crackers. Another Englishman was present, and he joined his countryman and the guide as they started up the Crawford Path on Friday morning, October 19.

Clothing is important here. Man is a tropical animal and nature does not protect him from cold. Darwin argued that the survival of a species depends on successful adaptation to a changing environment and the fittest among them survive best. Mr. Strickland would not have been worried. Consonant with the habits of his class while on a country outing, he would be wearing a shirt with high collar and floppy tie, a vest and hip-length jacket nipped at the waist, and tapered trousers. He'd been traveling with a large steamer trunk and here, facing the snowbound heights in North America, he put on his overcoat.

Ethan Allen had no education past his letters, but he was a natural civil engineer of the highest order and the location of his bridle path brought travelers to the crest of the Southern Peaks by steady and moderate grades. This is a delightful climb. The Crawfords' trail leads up the western slope of Clinton and as the prevailing winds carry moist air up the rising land it cools and the moisture is wrung out of it. This slope is a forest primeval, with moss carpeting the ground and draping every tree.

The same atmospheric laws wring snow out of October air and although the valley weather was fine this day, a storm had just blown through and, as Thomas Crawford anticipated, the snow up on the ridge was deep. The Crawford's trail reached the ridgeline just north of Clinton, a place with scrub spruce from a foot to about eight feet high and far too dense to push through, which means it provides good shelter from bad weather. The small party went on northward along the ridge. The terrain here is gently rolling and it's almost exactly at timberline—on the open rocks for a way, then dipping into the dense spruce, then rising into the open again. On this day, it was also clogged with snow and very heavy going for the horses.

The party got some little way along the ridge from Clinton, but the snow was getting too deep for the horses. The trail would soon leave timberline behind and the climbers would be wholly exposed to the elements. The guide decided they should turn back; he did not want to risk either his horses or his clients on a trip that obviously could not go very much farther. Frederick Strickland wanted to keep going and the guide refused. Mr. Strickland was adamant; he said he'd go on alone. The guide implored him to turn back, but he was unmoved. Then the guide and the other Englishman returned to the valley and Frederick Strickland went on alone, heading for the summit of Mount Washington five miles away over increasingly steep and exposed terrain. He did reach the summit, then he found the Fabyan Path and started down the west side of the mountain.

The amenities were being observed in the valley if not on the heights and Thomas Crawford, knowing that Frederick planned to come down the Fabyan Path, sent his trunk on to the hotel kept by Horace Fabyan, near the place where the old Bretton Woods railroad depot now stands. Thomas went over the next morning and learned that Mr. Strickland was not there. He immediately directed that a search be started on the Crawford Path while he and Mr. Fabyan gathered a few more men and started up the Fabyan Path. This second search party found footprints in the snow about a mile up the mountain, well below the last of the difficult terrain and, it seemed to them, safely below timberline. They followed the track and it led to a small brook. They came to a pool and in it they found a pair of trousers and underclothes which proved to belong to Frederick Strickland. By then it was getting dark, so the searchers repaired to the valley. The next morning Thomas Crawford and Horace Fabyan gathered a larger search party and they found the body about a mile from where they'd found the clothes; Frederick was lying face down in a pool of water with his head wedged between two rocks. His overcoat and his gloves were missing, and his torso and his legs were bruised and cut.

He had followed the Fabyan Path down the western slope of Mount Washington to timberline and then he lost the path among the trees. The searchers said that he'd circled around in the woods, crossing his own track and crossing the bridle path twice without realizing it. Finally he found a small stream which shows on modern maps as Clay Brook and leads to the larger Ammonoosuc River, which eventually reached Horace Fabyan's hotel in the valley.

Mr. Strickland was apparently still thinking clearly enough to follow the brook downstream, but blood in the snow indicated that injuries were slowing him until his final fall. The men in the rescue party were puzzled by the clothes they found in the pool. The body was examined by a physician and he suggested that when Frederick fell into the water his pants froze to his legs and he pulled them off so he could keep going, thus explaining the places where the flesh seemed to be stripped away. The doctor's education would not have included studies of hypothermia and the attendant drop in core temperature, but experience would have taught him that the combination of cold and water are lethal.

Frederick Strickland's body was taken back to Cambridge, Massachusetts, and he was buried near Green Briar Path in the Mount Auburn Cemetery, about a mile from the place where he first heard stories of the Presidential Range. He was the first person to climb Mount Washington in winter conditions, and he was the first to die there.

Chapter Two

GENTLEFOLK ESSAY THE HEIGHTS

*W*HEN GENTLEFOLK OF THE MID-NINETEENTH CENTURY
went climbing on the Presidential Range, it was widely assumed that horses
would do the work. The Crawford family converted their first trail up the
Southern Peaks to a bridle path in 1840 and Nathaniel Davis sought to cash
in on the Crawfords' success by building his own bridle path up the adjacent
Montalban Ridge to the summit of Mount Washington in 1844. Then the
Crawfords built a road to the base of a western ridge of Mount Washington,
which provided a shorter route to the summit by way of a bridle path managed by the Fabyan family. Finally the Thompson Bridle Path up the eastern
side of Mount Washington was built in 1851.

The Glen House was the only hotel on the eastern side of the Presidential
Range. It opened in 1852 and the bridle path already ran from the Glen to
the summit of Mount Washington. The path was named for the man who
kept the Glen House and it's worth noting that the Canadian Grand Trunk
Railroad paid the construction costs. This was an investment to draw tourists to the northern end of the Presidential Range and gain a share of the
revenue provided by customers of the popular Crawford Path leading up the
Southern Peaks of the range.

The first four miles of the Thompson Path were built on the same location as the auto road of today, then known as the carriage road, and the remainder of the bridle path was abandoned when the carriage road was completed to the summit in 1861. Most of the old location is very difficult to find today, but traces can still be discovered. As the old texts would put it, persevering effort by an attentive tramper will be rewarded.

Just before the present auto road rises above timberline, there's a wide clearing where the Halfway House used to stand. Soon the road starts a large bend of 180 degrees around a conspicuous outcropping of rock known as the Ledge in the early days and, more recently, Cape Horn. Sections of the summit road have always been identified by the markers along the way and the 4-Mile post is near the beginning of this turn. The last of the dwarf spruce are soon left behind, then the road begins a long traverse of the northeast side of the mountain, passing 5-Mile en route.

The bridle path turned sharply left at the Halfway House clearing and went into the woods at the back of what is a rocky gravel pit today. It went up the steep slope here, thus cutting off the loop of road around the Ledge, and met the present auto road again a short way above the point where the Chandler Brook Trail departs to drop steeply into Great Gulf. There are two paved parking lots at this point. The bridle path entered the back of the upper lot bearing slightly to the left, looking upslope. A conspicuous winter tractor route begins just above this point and heads upslope to cut off the long loop out to Cragway Turn on the auto road, then it rejoins the road just below the point where the Six Husbands Trail departs right and the Alpine Garden Trail departs left. This tractor route was roughed out directly on top of the bridle path, so no traces remain here.

The bridle path crossed the auto road location at 6-Mile and ran close to the Alpine Garden Trail up the slope toward the top of the ridge. This part of the old location is the easiest to see. The horses followed several switchbacks here to ease the grade and these are quite visible from the Alpine Garden Trail, then the bridle path turned sharply right just before the top of the ridge. The horses continued along a meandering and still quite obvious route up the shoulder of Chandler Ridge, then the path cut across the large right-angled loop the road makes around the flat area known as the Cow Pasture. The stone foundation of a structure used in that windswept animal husbandry can be found in the cow pasture, and a few steps away to the

Nineteenth-century gentlefolk liked to climb their mountains sitting down, as in this Winslow Homer view on the Crawford Path up Mount Washington.

Specialized clothing for recreation is a very recent innovation as the mountains count time. In 1915, Sheldon Howe, the author's father, leads the way in white shirt and tie, with his sisters Louise and Harriet, dressed in bloomers, following him. Few people had rucksacks in those days, so Harriet has dropped her sandwiches down her bloomers and they're visible at her knee.

northwest, toward Mount Madison, there's the old spring and the fragile remains of its wooden framing.

The bridle path ran diagonally up the slope below the road and, from this viewpoint, it disappeared around the horizon just below 7-Mile. It crossed the road location again to cut off the more moderate last bend below the summit, but at this point the terrain was very much modified for the research buildings built in the 1950s and now razed, so the old route is impossible to find. The bridle path crossed the present auto road for the last time and passed under the cog railway trestle near three large fuel tanks of the summit establishment, then climbed the last few yards to the summit.

Seen on a larger scale, the bridle path followed a nearly straight line up the crest of Chandler Ridge from 4-Mile to the summit. Seen on the closest scale, it quickly becomes obvious that a horse could step higher and manage more difficult terrain than we of the post-horse age would probably imagine.

By the same token, Americans were expected to negotiate more difficult terrain than the dress of the mid-nineteenth century would suggest. Most Americans' clothing was not yet diversified according to activity and a gentleman's turnout would not have been very different from what he wore to work: shirt and tie, vest, jacket, trousers, and probably a bowler hat.

Well-placed young ladies would have large wardrobes, but they would not have many choices. Their dresses would be older or newer, or plainer or fancier, or made for summer or winter, but they would all be dresses—a woman could not decide among a skirt or pants or shorts. This was flood-tide ante-bellum America and young women would look very much like Scarlett O'Hara, lacking only Rhett Butler on the stairway. The dresses of the time were extraordinarily complicated and a stylish lady aspired to the shape of an elaborately-draped bell. Her outfit would be close-fitted down to the high waistline, then widen steadily to her toes over a skirt stiffened by several petticoats, one of which would have been a crinoline stiffened with horsehair, the whole decorated by flounces and ruffles to taste and worn over ruffled pantaloons and high stockings. Thus prepared, she would deflect any untoward meteorological effects with a shawl as wide as she could reach and a bonnet.

The workload of such an outfit would be considerable, but fashions of the late twentieth century are so distant from those days that an exact appreciation is difficult. So, in the interests of White Mountain studies, I brought illustrations from the 1855 section of a fashion encyclopedia to a dressmaker of my acquaintance for a comparison in real-world terms. She said that a woman of today who went out wearing a blouse and a comfortable skirt would be carrying between a yard and a half and two yards of material. Then, using a bridal gown she'd just made for dimensions, the dressmaker studied the 1855 illustrations and calculated that a stylish young woman ascending the heights in that year would be wearing at least 45 yards of material. Depending on the fabric, this could weigh as much as a well-provided overnight pack of our times, and the amount of moisture it would absorb on a wet day could make it a truly significant factor on a hike. But it would preserve a lady's modesty from throat to toes and, not incidentally, make anything unladylike not just unthinkable but practically impossible.

LIZZIE BOURNE
SEPTEMBER 1855

On the morning of September 13, 1855, Lizzie Bourne bowled a string of tenpins at the Glen House. The other guests were impressed. In those years a young woman was expected to be, at the most, demure. Here was a game girl, and the guests remarked on her vigor and vivacity.

Lizzie was the daughter of the Honorable Edward Emerson Bourne, judge of probate for York County, Maine, which included the large mercantile city of Portland. She was twenty years old in the summer of 1855 and she'd always wanted to spend a night in the hotel on top of Mount Washington. Her uncle George was a principal in the shipbuilding firm of Bourne & Kingsbury in Kennebunk, and he agreed to go with her on such a trip, then his daughter Lucy persuaded him that she could come, too.

Those three, together with George's wife and another couple, arrived at the Glen House on September 12, a day of damp and glowering weather in the valleys surrounding the Presidential Range. The next morning brought steady rain and no promise of better skies, so they engaged horses for a ride up the mountain the next day. Then shortly before noon the sky showed promise of clearing and while the 1:00 P.M. dinner was being served, Lizzie launched a campaign to walk for a way up the road on foot that afternoon. In fact, she and her cousin wanted to go to the summit and spend that very night, which would surprise the party they'd left behind. She prevailed, and George Bourne and his daughter and niece stepped off the veranda of the Glen House at 2:00. Lizzie waved goodbye to those who remained behind and she kept turning to wave until she was lost from sight. In the words of another guest, "Sunshine was around their steps as they walked cheerfully up this new road."

Lucy and Lizzie Bourne were very excited at the prospects of a night in the summit hotel and even more so when they crossed the Peabody River bridge in the meadow fronting the hotel and met Mr. Myers, a particularly courteous gentleman who was supervising construction higher up on the mountain road. George Bourne glanced at his watch just then, and it showed 2:15 P.M.

Mr. Myers was going up the road himself, and he walked along with the Bournes for about two and a half miles, pointing out notable views and other objects of interest as they went along and describing the difficulties of building a carriage road under the unfavorable circumstances found on Mount Washington. At some point Mr. Myers was detained by his duties and the Bournes went on alone.

Only the first four miles of carriage road were built at that time, half of the eventual route, and the Bournes paused at the end of the prepared track. They'd risen 2,437 feet above the valley and there were 2,288 ahead of them.

The way ahead, however, bore no resemblance to what they'd just passed over. The first four miles led by steady but moderate grades through a mixed forest of hardwoods and evergreens and the shelter was about the same as they'd find in any forest lane at home. At the farthest advance of the carriage road there was a building known as Camp House, mainly used by guides on the bridle path and workers on the carriage road. The bridle path led on from here and soon rose above the tree line, and from there to the summit the Bournes would face a wasteland of jumbled broken rocks, sharp-edged, rough-faced, and often in precarious balance underfoot. Worse than that, they'd find no shelter at all from the violent weather that threatens at every season of the year: gale-force winds, rain and snow, and impenetrable cloud banks clinging to the ground.

In the summer of Lizzie's climb, many visitors would engage a guide to ensure their way to the summit. Mr. Bourne knew this but he decided that he

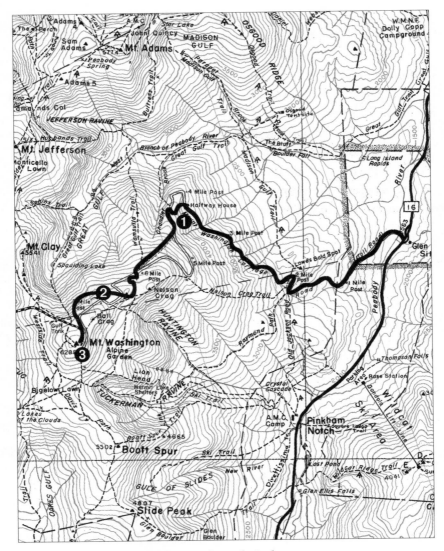

1. Lizzie Bourne first hit severe weather at the Ledge
2. Admired sunset from Cow Pasture
3. Sought shelter just short of summit

did not need a guide; the carriage road was unmistakable and he knew that the bridle path was easy to follow, too. When the three Bournes reached the end of the road they met a construction crew and asked about conditions up ahead. The men replied that the path was clear and the weather seemed favorable, and the family started on to the summit. George was a meticulous person and he again glanced at his watch; it was exactly 4:00 P.M.

They made the short steep climb to the crest of a prominent ledge above the tree line—in the manner of the day, Mr. Bourne described this ledge as "a mountain." When they topped the crest they were immediately struck by a much stronger wind than they expected, so strong that the ladies had to sit down until there was a lull that let them start moving again. They were not dismayed; in fact, they seemed to relish the blast and Mr. Bourne thought that the ladies went on with renewed vigor.

They found another "mountain" up ahead, then another. They pushed on to the top of each one, every time expecting it to be the last. They were going more slowly now, because the ladies had to sit down frequently to catch their breath. Then they climbed what they expected was the last mountain and walked out onto the conspicuous flats of the Cow Pasture. There in the west was the setting sun that, as George Bourne wrote later, "enrobed in his mantle of gold and crimson, bade us adieu."

The three Bournes sat there for a few minutes, admiring the grand spectacle of the departing day. They got up to climb onward and suddenly the clouds dropped onto them. Two members of the Spaulding family emerged from the gloom; they were keepers of the hotel on the summit and they thought these late-afternoon climbers were in good spirits.

George Bourne, however, thought that Lizzie seemed to be tired—she needed to be helped over the rougher steps. They thought the next pitch was the last mountain they'd have to climb, so they gathered their strength and, as George wrote, "We at last reached the Summit. It was now late in the twilight and the shadows of night were fast creeping upon us; but to our sorrow another mountain stood before us, whose summit was far above the clouds."

The Bournes kept going as long as they could see well enough to find the bridle path, but Lizzie was weakening and they had to stop often so she could rest. Finally they could see no longer and they stopped. In George's

The only known photograph of Lizzie Bourne.

words, "It was very cold and the wind blowing a gale, the night dark and fearful, and we were upon the bleak mountain without a shrub, rock or tree under which to find shelter. What was to be done? To lie down and commit our souls to the keeping of a merciful Father, probably to sleep that sleep that knows no waking?"

George Bourne decided not to sleep that sleep. He was very tired himself, but he realized that something had to be done and he was the only one to do it. Each of the ladies had a shawl, but Lizzie had lost her bonnet in the wind. They were still on the path, so the ladies lay down in the treadway and George went to work gathering stones and building up a wall to protect them from the wind. This was difficult work. It was full dark now, the wind was blowing a gale, the clouds were right down on the ground, and he had no light and no clear idea of what was around him. He'd work until he was tired, then he'd lie down next to the ladies to rest himself and give them a little warmth and a bit more protection against the terrible blast.

George Bourne made a routine of this: he'd gather stones, lie down, get up and, as he put it, "thrash around" to warm himself, gather more stones and for his windbreak, and lie down to warm the ladies again. This worked rather well. They seemed comfortable and George believed they'd survive the night. At 10:00 P.M. he finished a stint of thrashing and wall-building and lay down to warm the ladies again. He took Lizzie's hand to encourage her and found that it was cold: "Her spirit had winged its way to that better land where the black mountain chill could not reach her. She was dead—had uttered no complaint, expressed no regret or fear, but passed silently away."

Now there was only Lucy to keep warm, so George kept up the thrashing for himself and the warming for his daughter, "And thus passed the long, long weary night. Oh, how anxiously did we watch for the first gleam of morning." At that first light, the two of them got up, walked a few steps, and saw the Tip-Top House right in front of them.

George knocked on the door and, as he said, "aroused the inmates," who were keeper Spaulding and his family. They knew that the temperature had dropped below freezing during the night, so two ladies and two gentlemen left straightway and soon returned with Lizzie's body. A boy was sent to run down the mountain with word of the trouble while the others tried to help Lizzie. "Hoping against hope, for four hours they labored with hot rocks, hot baths, and used every exertion to call back her spirit, but all in vain."

Mr. Joseph Hall was stopping at the Glen House, a right-hand man for the Crawfords in their trail-building and a guide of deep experience in these mountains. He'd started up the carriage road that morning and had passed Mr. Myers' Camp House, then he met the boy near the Ledge. He returned to Camp House and directed the workers to make a long shallow box while he cut a stout pole in the woods. Then he took some straps from a horse's pack saddle and he and another man went on to the summit.

The Spaulding women prepared Lizzie's body and placed it in Mr. Hall's box and packed it carefully with bed linen. Then Mr. Hall used the pack

Lizzie Bourne's final resting spot years after her death, just yards from the safety of the Tip-Top House.

saddle straps to hang the box from the pole he'd cut, and he and Mr. Davis and another man shouldered the load, tallest man in front, and they started down the road. It took them three hours to reach the Glen House. The news had preceded them and George Bourne's wife met them crying, "Oh! Lizzie—Lizzie!" The Bournes and their friends returned with her to Portland, "And," wrote her uncle, "though the angel of death had set his seal upon her brow, yet a sweet smile still lingered and she seemed as one lying in angelic slumber."

A little later, Mr. Hall received a letter from Judge Bourne. "Moses was taken up from Mount Pisgah, Aaron from Mount Hor, and Lizzie, frail child of earth, to heaven from Mount Washington. Knowing her as I did, I am sure she would have chosen Mount Washington as the place to pass from earth to heaven."

FRIENDS SAID THAT THE BOURNE FAMILY NEVER RECOVERED from the loss of their beloved Lizzie. Curiously, though, several newspaper accounts and the marker on Mount Washington and her elaborate tombstone in the family burying ground give her age as twenty-three, not twenty.

George Bourne wrote several sharp notes to local newspapers correcting the error, but the memorials were not changed.

Mr. Hall returned to the summit and built a tall pile of stones on the place where Lizzie died, and when he was done he topped it with a block of rose quartz. After his long life in service of the mountains, he never went back.

Chapter Three

THE MAN WHO COLLECTED VIEWS

*P*OOR JUDGMENT TENDS TO MULTIPLY; ONCE AN OUTING begins to go wrong, the participants make one mistake after another in a sort of fatal contagion. One exception came the month after Lizzie Bourne's death. Against advice and with his eyes wide open, Dr. Benjamin Lincoln Ball walked straight into a lethal situation, but that was the last mistake he made.

Not only did the weather turn violently against Dr. Ball on the high slopes of Mount Washington, but he had no map because the mountains had not yet been mapped, he had no trail guide because no trails had yet been made north of the summit, he'd never been in the White Mountains before, and he had no idea at all of either the large or the small features of the terrain around him because the clouds were right down on the ground until his last day.

Dr. Ball's story looms large in the annals of these mountains and his name remains on Ball Crag, just below the summit of Mount Washington. Part of this fame was certainly due to his association with Lizzie Bourne, who died on the mountain a month earlier, and it was amplified by the book he wrote the next year: "Three Days on The White Mountains, being The Perilous Adventure of Dr. B. L. Ball On Mount Washington. Written by Himself."

The doctor was almost continuously mystified by his surroundings, but he was a precise chronicler of his attempt to negotiate them and his perilous adventure can be followed almost step by step.

DR. BENJAMIN LINCOLN BALL
OCTOBER 1855

Dr. Ball was serious about views; he collected views the way other connoisseurs collect paintings. He graduated from the Harvard Medical School in 1844, but if he ever did practice, his infirmary days must have been short indeed, fitted into the space between extended trips to the Alps, to Java, to the Philippines, and through Asia.

In the summer of 1855, Dr. Ball was in Boston attending to the publication of his book *Rambles in East Asia* and thinking he ought to make a trip to the White Mountains of New Hampshire, a place that was so close he'd never been there. He was thirty-five years old and he thought it was time to make up that deficit, but preparing the text of his book took more time than he anticipated and it was October before he was finished. It was too late, he thought, to travel to the northern mountains.

One day he met Starr King, who was working on *The White Hills*, his monumental account of rambles in the White Mountains. Starr King was to writing what Albert Bierstadt was to painting, he was the prose laureate of the sublime acclivity and the dreadful abyss, the man who found forty-three adjectives to describe Mount Chocorua, and he told Dr. Ball that he hadn't seen anything until he'd seen the views from Mount Washington. In fact, he'd always wanted to make a late-season trip himself, he'd never been there after the leaves had fallen and, no, October wasn't too late.

So Dr. Ball turned his face northward from Boston. He arrived in Gorham on the morning of Wednesday, October 25, and was dismayed to find that it was raining and no mountains could be seen. He engaged a horse at the local livery and rode nine miles to the Glen House, protected only by his umbrella. It was raining at the Glen House, too, and he could see nothing but clouds. Dr. Ball was determined to see what he described as The Mountain, to compare the sight with famous views he'd found around the world, so he took counsel with Mr. Thompson, the keeper of the Glen House.

Dr. Benjamin Lincoln Ball.

Hotel keepers were an essential part of the White Mountain economy of the day. They not only provided food and shelter, they explored the hinterlands, they built trails, provided advice, guided visitors, and searched for lost trampers who had not partaken of their services. Mr. Thompson told his visitor that he might walk a way up the new road on Mount Washington and see what he could see.

This came as news to Dr. Ball—he hadn't heard of such an innovation. Mr. Thompson told him that four miles of the road were passable ending at the Camp House, a place just below timberline where workers were sheltered, though work had been suspended and only a few men would be there. Mr. Thompson said it was not a difficult walk that far, but above the Camp House the weather would be worse and the exposed terrain much more difficult, and it would not be wise to go up there on a day like this.

Dr. Ball decided to start up the road straightway, so he exchanged his hat for a cap he saw hanging on a rack in the hotel lobby, opened his umbrella, and set out in a chilly drizzle.

Dr. Ball reached the Camp House in two hours, sooner than he expected. The weather had not grown worse, in fact, he could manage without his umbrella and he thought of leaving it behind, but didn't. He could see a promontory called the Ledge above the Camp House and reasoned that the view might be better up there. "Casting my eyes to the top of the Ledge, and reflecting a few moments, I concluded, as it was not very high, that I should not be violating very much the advice of Mr. Thompson if I went to the top."

Soon Dr. Ball was above the trees and a freezing rain was crusting his clothes and his umbrella and the foot-deep snow. He kept going until he realized that darkness was falling, then he turned back but it was a near thing, he could find his way only by feeling for his ascending footprints. He found the Camp House with three men resident, they made him coffee and supper and he spent Wednesday night there, but he did not sleep.

Mr. Myers was the foreman at the Camp House, the same man who had accompanied Lizzie Bourne on the start of her trip, and he cautioned Dr. Ball not to tempt the fate that befell the young lady who went by the Camp House last month. He told her party that it was too late in the day to continue, but they disregarded his advice. Dr. Ball borrowed Mr. Myers' boots and accepted the gift of his walking stick and set out, but not before being warned about bears. The boots were much too big for him, but that couldn't be helped. He followed the tracks he made above the Ledge on the previous day and saw bear tracks covering his own. At least Mr. Myers was right about that.

Dr. Ball climbed up the bridle path until the snow became too deep and he lost the track, but he kept going; he'd been told there would be four Mountains on the ridge, the last being Mount Washington, and he was sure he could find his way. At this point, the sleet and freezing drizzle had turned entirely to snow and he folded his umbrella. Conditions were not improving, but he hadn't yet taken a view, so he decided to keep going, he could always follow his footprints back. As a precaution against deeper snow, he made small cairns on prominent rocks to lead him down.

The footing and the terrain got more difficult as he climbed the ridge and several times Dr. Ball thought of turning back, but each time he remembered the many times he'd pressed on against both weather and advice only to be richly rewarded. Twice in Switzerland, he ignored the advice of guides and made his own way to majestic views. In Java, the natives told him that not even birds could survive the ascent to the top of the smoking mountain, but

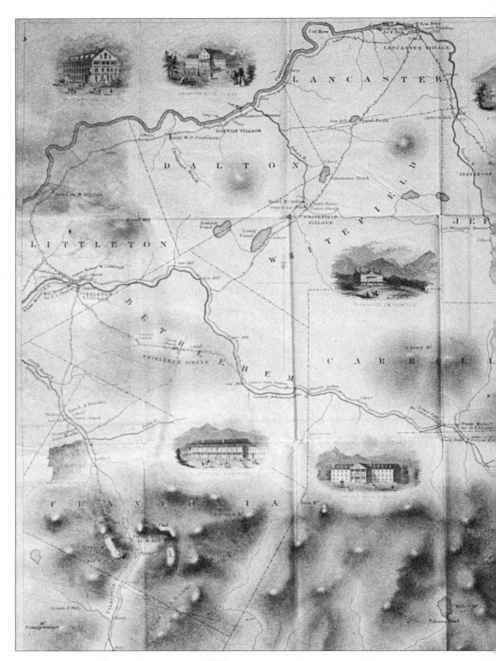

Mid-nineteenth-century maps provided detailed pictures of the hotels while vague humps stood for the Presidential Range. Dr. Ball had no map at all when he started to climb Mount Washington in October 1855.

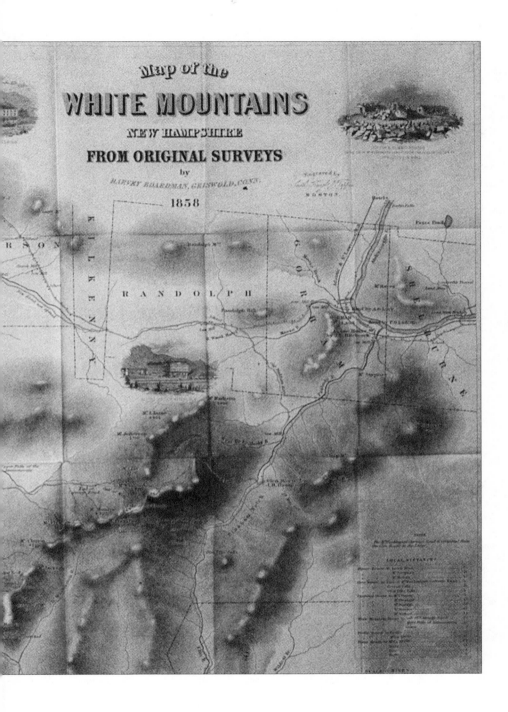

Less than two months apart in 1855, Benjamin Ball and Lizzie Bourne both took shelter in the Camp House, which housed workers. It later became known as the Halfway House.

he pressed on and found "the grandest specimen of volcanic scenes." Besides, he'd been assured that snug lodgings awaited him in the Summit House on Mount Washington, provided with the makings of fire and light, with food and drink, and beds and bedclothes.

The storm grew severe, the worst he'd ever encountered in all his travels; he ached with cold and he fell more and more often. He lost his way completely and was just taking whatever upward direction that seemed to offer good footing. Toiling on, he felt an unusual pain in his face; putting up his hand, he found that it was completely encased in ice: cap, beard, even eyelashes, were all ice. "I considered the aspect of affairs to be somewhat desperate, and looked back. But no, thought I, the summit must be near, and, after so long a time and so much labor, I will not turn yet. At the Summit House I can make myself comfortable; and the storm is too violent to continue long, especially so early in the season as October. Thoughts of this nature passed through my mind, and, holding to my resolve, I said to myself—I will still try for the Summit House!"

Finally, after a terrible battering, Dr. Ball reached a flat place he believed to be the summit, but he could not find the Summit House. "The storm pours down as if I was the only object of its wrath, as if avenging itself for some unknown offence. Blasts of the confused elements grapple each other, in rapid succession, and envelop me in commingled sheets of impenetrable snow. The wind, encircling me with its powerful folds, presses the cold to my very vitals, colder than the coldest robe of ice. Now it wrests me from my feet; again, it carries me furiously before it, and I sink down in fear that it will hurl me over an unseen precipice. For a few moments I remain to breathe and to rest. Shall I retreat, or shall I persevere? For I am freezing." He persevered. He persuaded himself that he lost count, that he'd climbed only three Mountains, not four. Then, seeing his situation more clearly, he realized that he must go down.

Again the plunging and falling, again the battering wind and his freezing hands and feet. Then Dr. Ball found a line of stakes, which he supposed were survey markers for the road builders. He followed these downslope, but with increasing difficulty. Then he lost the line altogether and he suddenly realized that the light was failing. "'My God!' exclaimed I, 'am I to pass the night here?' Much exhausted in strength, my whole body was trembling with cold. Darkness was closing in. A snowy bed, unsheltered from the piercing blasts, my only couch, awaited me. Is it possible to survive this?"

Dr. Ball found a flat rock and a patch of scrub spruce, with a little space in between. He'd saved a piece of string from some small duty the day before, so he used this to anchor his umbrella in a root, then he pulled up scrub growth and broke out slabs of snow and cut the twisted limbs around him with his penknife and piled them all around his umbrella, making himself a fortress against the coming ordeal. He worked himself to a frenzy here, "with the view to quicken the circulation of the blood and restore warmth to my body. But the cold, by the force of the wind, penetrated like water, and conducted off the heat as rapidly as it was generated." His small shelter perfected, he tried to light a fire; he burned almost all his matches, almost all his papers, even his money, but it was no use. "Here, shivering and chattering, I went to my dreary covert, not to sleep, not to rest, but to await in suspense the coming of another day.

"Sleep! Ah, that which now is most desirous of all, and which forces itself upon me with such power, must be averted. I know too well its fatal

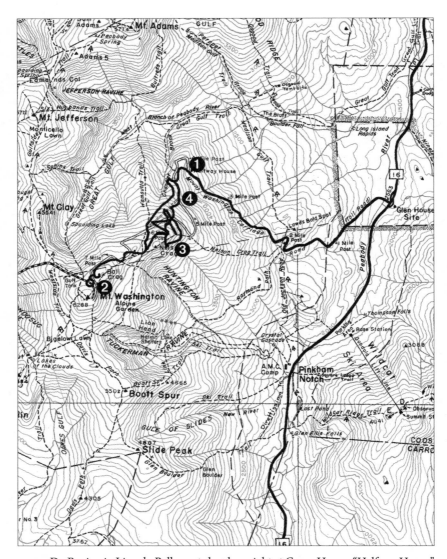

1. Dr. Benjamin Lincoln Ball spent sleepless night at Camp House, "Halfway House"
2. Looked for summit hotel on flats near Ball Crag
3. Umbrella camp was just above Cragway Turn
4. Basin rock

consequences. A few minutes' indulgence, and I never should awake, except in another world. But can I prevent it? Food I require, and thirst presses me hard. These I can endure. I can, at least, palliate their gnawings by the snow around me. But can I prevent this sleep? Have I sufficient vital force left to resist its influences? There I do not know myself. The ordeal I have never experienced. But it will be put to the test, and I can but try."

First, Dr. Ball avoided comfort. He twisted himself into one painful position after another, he invented difficulties every way he could, anything to avoid comfort. He thought of all the people he knew that were more comfortable than he was, all his friends, all his family. Then he thought of what few there could be who were in worse circumstances: soldiers dying in the Crimea, and an explorer he knew facing his ordeal in the polar sea.

Joseph Hall, the same guide who had been active in the unfortunate Bourne episode in September, was again stopping at the Glen House on Thursday evening. Given his reputation, word came to him that that a gentleman had stayed with Mr. Myers at Camp House the night before and it was assumed that he'd return to the Glen House sometime Thursday, but he had not appeared. This did not seem alarming; people in the Glen could see that the weather was very bad on the heights and they assumed that he was staying with Mr. Myers for another night. This seemed prudent; Mr. Myers was as familiar as anyone with the mountain, and he'd see to it that the visitor came to no harm.

In fact, Dr. Ball had not returned to Camp House to spend a second night with Mr. Myers; he spent the night in his umbrella camp. Day did come to his wretched shelter, and with it clearer air but no less wind. Dr. Ball was above the trees but he had no idea at all of where he was, there was only rock and snow and off to his right a sharp peak towering above everything. He assumed this to be Mount Washington, but he'd lost all his desire to go to the top and take the views and compare them to all other views he had known. Staying alive would now be sufficient reward.

He had no idea which way to go. "All was alike to me; there was no reason why I should go one way rather than another; and I could have no prejudices to bias me in favor for or against any particular way. If one thing, however, in my dilemma, seemed to be worse than the others, it was that there did not appear to be anything from which to form an opinion."

Lacking any hint or guidance, he decided to circle the summit cone of the mountain. This way, he'd be sure to cross the line of stakes or his track from the day before, or at the very least he'd see the Camp House or the Glen House far below and be able to chart a course.

Down at the Glen House, Mr. Thompson was told that a man had departed from the Camp House on the morning of the previous day and had not been seen since, so he sent Francis Smith and another man up the bridle path to look for him at the Summit House.

While those two were making their way directly up the mountain, Dr. Ball was struggling across the open slope of the mountain, heading for a promontory which he thought would have a path, or at least an orienting outlook. It took four times longer than he thought to cover the distance, and when he got there he could see only a long ridge dropping out of the clouds above and plunging into a vast chasm below, a place he thought was called the Gulf of Mexico, which was an old name for Great Gulf. All he could do was retrace his steps.

When he was almost back to the place he'd spent the night, the clouds thinned and he could see the valley, but there was nothing there, no road, no clearing, no twist of smoke, only the endless forest, and he realized that he could not possibly push his way through the dense interlaced growth below him. Then he heard a sound, as of steel upon stone. Turning that way, he saw two men on the bluff a little way off. The sound continued and he thought they must be workmen on the new road and he called to them over and over, but they took no notice. He decided they must be stones, and turned again to retracing his steps.

Now he realized that the light was fading again, he'd spent the whole day on that traverse. "I sat down to rest and to reflect. What can I do? What is best to be done? What ought I to do? for I am yet free to move and act. There is no reason why I should act impulsively or without thought, but rather from sober judgement. What is the best course under the circumstances? Shall I push ahead with all my strength around the mountain, taking the course opposite that of today? Or shall I risk my chance in recklessly plunging through the brush among the rocks, precipices, or anything that presents down the mountain side?"

Snow was in the air again and the wind had not slackened, and he was wracked with intolerable thirst. He collected slabs of ice and crusted snow but the scrub growth was too thick to walk through, so he tried to crawl under the tearing branches, pushing his ice and snow toward the place he spent the night. With a heavy heart he again rigged his umbrella and piled on scrub branches and slabs of snow and ice, and he tried to smooth out the place where he lay inside and put some spruce branches on it for a bed, but it didn't help much.

Late that evening, Mr. Smith and the other man reached the Glen House with news that the visitor had not been seen at the Summit House, and that they'd seen his tracks at several places along the bridle path. They hadn't see any trace of the man, though, and Mr. Smith thought that he'd either perished on the heights or found his way down into the woods.

Dr. Ball was neither dead on the heights nor safe in the woods, he was settling himself for another night in his umbrella camp and he turned again to thought. This time he composed his own ironic epitaph. "How singular, that so immediately after the publishing of *Rambles in Eastern Asia*, this last and shortest of all my rambles, and within my own country, should be the winding up!—the thread caught and broken on Mount Washington, almost in sight of my own home. Terminated in such a manner, no one could know the circumstances. Different reports, if any, would be circulated. Some, perhaps, would have it that I was insane; others that I wished to commit suicide; and the most charitable might allow that I was lost in the fog. Of course there would be no one to say to the contrary of any of them."

The weather was, if anything, worse. The wind howled and the snow blew in through the front of Dr. Ball's shelter and the ice-laden blast threatened to tear his umbrella to shreds. This was his third night without sleep and he shook uncontrollably all through the dark hours. He was tormented by thirst and he sucked his ice supply, but his mouth was so cold the ice would not melt. In the midst of it all, he formulated a plan. If his umbrella is torn away, he'll head downhill, whichever way that might be. He'll keep going as long as he can, and when he reaches the end of his endurance he'll fasten his handkerchief in some conspicuous place and write an account of his perils on his remaining scraps of paper for the satisfaction of anyone who might remember him.

Then, a doctor again, he noticed that his lungs were not working properly. It seemed he could only half inflate them, and he studied this effect and formulated an explanation. He considered the condition of his heart and, as during the night before, he took his pulse often. Now, though, he could not feel it with his fingers, so he used the palm of his hand. The heart rate was accelerated, but reduced in force by about a third, and somewhat irregular. Dr. Ball concluded that he would live through the night, if only he could stay awake. Indeed, his assessment led him to the thought that, if need be, he could stay out like this for a third night, his fourth without sleep, "And I was glad I could think so, for I much preferred to have my hopes leading ahead of my actual powers, than to have them following behind short of reality."

Now Dr. Ball turned again to the only part of his situation he could control. He took refuge in his thoughts, he followed every thought to its end, and he chose successions of topics as different from each other as he could devise. He thought of the people he had known around the world, and as the hours passed it seemed to him that he reviewed every acquaintance he'd ever had. Then he wondered if the people he met in Gorham and the Glen House and the Camp House will ever think of him again. They probably won't, except for the liveryman in Gorham who will wonder why his horse is away so long. He thought of his umbrella, and how he would not have brought it if not for the sprinkle as he started up the road, and how he would surely have died during the first night without it, and how he'd almost set it aside when the rain eased soon after he'd started up the road, and how many times the first day he'd been tempted to throw it away as a nuisance and an impedance.

This night Dr. Ball never tried to stay awake simply by trying to stay awake, for he knew if he did that he would quickly fall asleep and that would be the end of him. Still, though, he was not sure his thoughts would last the night, he was not sure if he had enough of them. So he placed one elbow on a pointed stone and rested his head on the palm of that hand. This way, if he fell asleep the pain would waken him. Lacking that, his head would fall off his hand, it would, as he wrote, "recall the notice of my mind." Then he surrendered himself to that saving mind and let whatever impressions it might have come flooding in upon him.

It didn't work, no thoughts came. "The sensation of cold was succeeded by a kind of soothing glow stealing along through every nerve and fiber, filling the whole system as if with an invisible ethereal fluid. My body soon seemed like a mass of cold clay, over which I had no control, and in which my own self was dwelling as a mere tenant, and from which I was about to escape, leaving it behind me. My mind became perfectly composed and quiet, as if absorbing some balmy and mysterious influence that floated gently over and around me. I did not wish to move or make the least effort. I felt resigned and reconciled to whatever situation I might be in. The world seemed nothing to me, and life not worth living for. What tie could the world possess against the fascinating spell which was now riveting its bonds upon me! I would willingly and gladly give up all for a half hour of this delightful indulgence. I would not if I could stay its procedure. It comes—I am happy—and let it continue, was the thought or the sum of my sensations; and I believe I was fast sinking, as in a charmed and unresisting state, into the soft folds of that insidious enemy—SLEEP!"

Dr. Ball let himself drift thus for, he thought, ten minutes. Then he began to reflect on this sensation, he concentrated on it, he made it into an experiment. He realized that he was not directing the experiment, and this was not sound scientific practice. So, as a good clinician, he decided to pursue the course he would take if he was not subject to such languid temptations, to regain the control which he always brought to laboratories and to emergencies. So he woke up.

His third day on the mountain dawned and, looking out of his shelter, Dr. Ball saw a house far below him and a peak above it domed with white. He was profoundly puzzled by this. He thought the snow-capped mountain must be Mount Washington and the buildings the Glen House, but how can that be? He is on Mount Washington. Or is Mount Washington that pyramid across the Gulf of Mexico? He could go straight toward it, straight down the slope, but this would soon bring him to the impenetrable forest and he did not think he had the strength to push through its tangles and hazards. So, still hoping to find the bridle path or the line of stakes or his own track, he resolved to circle the mountain in the opposite direction than the one he took the previous day.

The men down there in the valley were thinking that the visitor had very little chance now. Even if he was alive at the beginning of this day, he'd certainly be dead by the time they could reach him. Nevertheless, they made an early start up the mountain to see what they could find. Mr. Hall was thinking that if they found their man at all, they'd find him "in the cold embrace of death," and the kit they brought was not chosen to help an invalid, but to carry down a dead man.

Mr. Hall, J. J. Davis, and Francis Smith started up the carriage road and they recruited another man at Camp House. When they had almost reached the summit they found footprints they assumed were made by the visitor and they crossed the bridle path from east to west, heading for the top of Great Gulf. They followed the track without much difficulty and before long it lost its heading and wandered for a while, then the maker turned toward the northeast with apparent resolution, a line that seemed to follow the surveyed route of the carriage road that Mr. Myers was building up from Camp House. They followed this track down the ridge for about half a mile and it crossed the old bridle path heading almost directly east toward the Glen House in the Valley.

At about this point they met the Culhane brothers, Patrick and Thomas, and the six of them pushed on along the easterly track. If they continued on this heading for very much longer, they'd come to the edge of the great ravine on the opposite side of the ridge from the Gulf of Mexico. The men were able to stay on this track for a mile and its purposive nature raised hopes in Mr. Hall, he thought the man might reach the woods after all and they'd find him alive. Unfortunately, they came to a thick patch of stunted spruce where new snow had drifted in, and they lost the track.

With renewed hope, the men stopped to consider their situation. Then Mr. Hall divided his group and spread three to the left, three to the right. They'd make a close search for signs of a camp or any other sign of survival they could find, and they worked their way almost to the end of this large growth of stunted spruce.

Dr. Ball was very weak now. He was no longer hungry and thought he would not eat if food was put before him, but his thirst was terrible. He could not hold both the cane and his umbrella, so he hooked the handle of his umbrella into his jacket against future need. He could move only in a stooped posture, supporting himself with his cane on one side and leaning against the uphill rocks. He pressed on, now resolving to circle the mountain a hundred feet higher to be able to see into the valley over the bulge of the terrain.

At about noon, as he counted the hours, he looked up and saw a line of men approaching. "They had long sticks or poles, and were advancing in a line a little distance from each other. They appeared to be looking around on the ground, as if for some object in the snow. With not the shadow of a thought that I could be the object they were in quest of, I cried out to them in a loud voice. All stopped short, and looked at me with a steady gaze. Why do they stare at me so? I wondered. They seem astonished and amazed. Perhaps they are surprised in meeting with any one on this side of the Mountain. But I am most happy to fall in with them. I shall soon know whether I am on the right course or not."

One of the searchers walked straight up to the haggard wanderer and said, "Is this Dr. Ball?" Dr. Ball said that he was that very person.

Joseph Hall said, "Are you the person who left the Glen House Wednesday afternoon to walk up on the new road?" Dr. Ball assured his interlocutor that he was still on the right track.

Joseph Hall said, "And you have been out on the Mountain since that time?" Dr. Ball replied that this was indeed the case.

Then Joseph Hall said, "It is indeed wonderful! How could you preserve yourself all this time? You had nothing to eat, nothing to drink! And you can still stand?" Dr. Ball asked for something to drink. They had nothing to drink, but they gave him a piece of gingerbread. He could not eat it.

The men said that they were searching yesterday as well. They said they'd gone to the summit and they were the people he saw making the metallic sound. Mr. Hall saw that Dr. Ball was in good spirits, but his hands were very much swollen and he seemed hardly able to stand on his legs. By now, Dr. Ball had again reverted to his professional training and he noticed that he felt less strong than before he was discovered, so he put his arms around the necks of two of the men and they started back along the way he had just come. "And I shall not forget the thrills of emotion I experienced, from their hearty goodwill, readiness, and earnestness, in affording me their assistance, each anxious to render me some aid. But I could not but notice, from the implements they brought, that the party had no expectation of finding me alive."

He was perplexed by their course toward Mount Washington up ahead; shouldn't they be going away from it? They told him his idea of the mountain was turned around, that the peak was Mount Jefferson, the place he thought was the Gulf of Mexico was Huntington Ravine. They might also have told him that the domed summit looming above the hotel was Carter Dome rising above the Glen House.

Dr. Ball was still wracked by a thirst no handful of snow could slake and soon they came upon a rock standing up out of the snow as if put there by Providence. There was a large bowl cut into one side, "Which," Mr. Hall

His mouth too cold to melt snow, Dr. Ball drank from water collected in these glacial basins.

thought, "like the rock that Moses smote, and water gushed out to slake the thirst of the children of Isreal, afforded the greatest luxury that could be administered." After his saviors had broken away the lid of ice, Dr. Ball finally drank his fill.

Thus refreshed, Dr. Ball regained the shelter of the Camp House, where Mr. Myers told of his own vigil on the Ledge that first night, how he stayed there so long his heels froze, how he couldn't sleep for worrying about what had become of the doctor. The rescue party warmed Dr. Ball and gave him warm tea, which he could not hold down. Then they gave him ice water, which he could. They found his feet were frozen, so they put them in cold water to draw the frost. Then they wrapped him up and put him astride a horse belonging to the bridle path company. The animal was named Tom and he was accustomed to carrying rather inert riders, so he went gently and without guidance down the carriage road. As they began to descend from the Camp House, snow began falling again on the heights behind them, so heavy that it quickly obscured all signs of human passage on the mountain.

Before long they met Mr. Thompson from the Glen House, upward bound with a horse and carriage. He'd arranged for the searchers to alert him with signal flags when they found Dr. Ball's body, and he was watching with a telescope as they made their way across the flank of the mountain toward the place they found Dr. Ball.

By now the rain had started again and the rescuers put Dr. Ball in the wagon and covered him with blankets, and as one of the men steadied his head, he descended comfortably enough. They arrived at the Glen House amidst cries of astonishment and joy; Dr. Ball was taken inside, warmed up, and asked what he would like first. He said he'd like a hot toddy, which agreed very well. Then, mindful that a starving man should not eat too much, he took part of a cup of gruel with warm milk. He took a little more gruel each hour, along with cups of water. His feet were blackened and without feeling, "like masses of cold clay attached to the extremities, with heavy dragging sensations." He feared for their vitality and also for his hands, which were numb and useless.

Dr. Ball thought that a poultice of flaxseed meal mixed with oil and charcoal would be the best restorative for his frozen limbs, but he gave way to the suggestion of a Mr. Hall, who seemed to have long experience with these conditions. So they made a poultice of charred hickory leaves, pulverized and simmered in fresh lard. This was applied to his hands and feet and wrapped in cloths and he gratefully took to a warm soft bed. He'd been out in the arctic storm for sixty hours, and without sleep for eighty.

"Toward nine o'clock in the evening I began to experience for the first time since my return, a strong desire to sleep. In this I was very soon able to indulge, happy with the thought that there was now no fear—that I might give myself up entirely to rest with no anxiety for the morrow." Mr. Hall stayed in the room with him and awakened him at intervals, lest he sleep too deeply.

Difficult times followed. "Slight chills, commencing at my feet, frequently ran though my body, causing the whole nervous system to vibrate. My feet, as if dead, were without feeling or sensation, distorted by swelling, and covered with water-blisters. About the ankles, and above the injuries, the pain was severe, with piercing and racking sensations, as if pointed sticks and nails were thrust into the flesh, and wrenched back and forth among the bones, tendons, and nerves; and, when cramp set in, the pain for a few minutes was excruciating. My hands ached and burned day and night, quite as if freshly immersed in scalding water; but, with no other frozen parts, I only experienced a general soreness and tenderness, and I thought my self under the circumstances comfortably well off."

Dr. Ball stayed at the Glen House for a week, then returned to Boston, where his brother and two other men, doctors all, supervised his recovery. He continued to study his situation, a habit that had already been his salvation. During the winter he read of a more recent climb to the summit of Mount Washington and realized that three climbs were made in successive months: Miss Bourne died in September, he nearly perished in October, and the climb made latest in the season was the only one that succeeded. He concluded that his own misfortunes were not the result of bad judgment, only of bad luck.

Four months later, Dr. Ball wrote a letter of advice for others who might want to try the hazards of Mount Washington. He urged the employment of a guide, or going with others, "It is true many prefer to go alone and independently, to the risk of an uncompanionable and unintelligent associate; but safety here demands more than the gratification of minor wishes."

He expanded on the matter of clothing. "I was informed at the Glen House that in the majority of cases it is very difficult to convince visitors that they will absolutely require warmer garments at the summit than at the base of the Mountain. When the weather below is very warm, they expect to find the same above; but in reality there is a difference of several degrees. In July and August the thermometer shows frequently a sinking to below the freezing-point; and in general overcoats and shawls are necessary for comfort, even in the warmest part of the day.

"Visitors arrive at the summit in a considerable glow and perspiration; they remain looking at the Mountain, absorbed with the beauty of the prospect, and forget the cold wind which is blowing upon them. Too late they think of their shawls or cloaks, that they might have brought with them, which would have obviated all difficulties. The result frequently is a cold and cough; perspiration has received a sudden check; pains in the chest, irritation or inflammation of the lungs follow, and ill health is often a consequence."

DR. BALL'S AGGRESSIVE SELF-PROMOTION LEAVES FEW MYSTERIES and his route can be followed easily on a trail map of today. He followed the bridle path to the Camp House just as the Bourne party did a month earlier.

The completed carriage road reached the summit in eight miles, so this name was changed to the Halfway House and all that remains of the historic building is a large clearing on the right side of the auto road just short of 4-Mile. The road goes straight past this site to make the sharp left turn around Cape Horn, but the bridle path turned left at the Camp House and climbed the amphitheater of loose rock directly across the road. Dr. Ball scrambled up the steep bridle path here and then on to the mass of rock just above timberline that he called the Ledge. This is still the most conspicuous feature of the area; it's the pivot of the large U-turn the auto road makes just above 4-Mile. There's a parking space at this point and the remains of an army Signal Corps installation built during the 1950s.

The carriage road company had just gone bankrupt when Dr. Ball made his climb and their work ended at the Camp House, though the route had been staked out for some distance above the Ledge. Dr. Ball knew this but he lost the track almost immediately. Accustomed as he was to trackless wastes, he pushed on. He knew there were four "Mountains" on the ridge, so he apparently kept to the highest ground he could find and this led him up the ridge on about the line taken by the present-day Nelson Crag Trail. His high point was almost certainly the flat area just below the summit now marked by the foundations of test facilities built in the 1950s.

Dr. Ball turned back there and the place where he made his camp can be located from the evidence he provides. When the weather cleared he was at the top edge of a thick patch of dwarf spruce, he saw an unbroken forest below him, a conspicuous pointed peak off to his left, and the Glen House in the distant valley, but he cannot see the Camp House. Only one place on the ridge matches all five of these conditions.

"Cragway Turn" is a sharp bend in the auto road where the Nelson Crag Trail meets the road and departs again at the apex of the turn. Above the turn the road enters a large patch of dwarf spruce and it was this barrier which stopped Dr. Ball as he tried to find his way down. The Nelson Crag trail ascends along one side of this patch and the site of his umbrella camp can be found by climbing a short way up the trail and then turning at the upper edge of the spruce patch. From this point he made his embattled way back and forth across the broad shoulder of Chandler Ridge, coming almost to the edge of Huntington Ravine to the south and back toward Great Gulf at the other limit of his swing.

All this is obvious from his chronicle and only one landmark remained to be found in the soft summer days I spent retracing his steps. This last one was the basin-shaped rock where he finally drank his fill of water and this detail seemed improbable—the rock on this part of the mountain is harsh and jagged and does not lend itself to basin shapes. Nevertheless, I found the traces of the old bridle path and started down the slope.

The footing was mild and the August day was sweet, and it was easy to let Dr. Ball's fierce ordeal drift out of mind. Then the corner of my eye caught a section of ledge rising about four feet above the grade. As the ice of the Laurentide glacier was melting, a stone got caught in an eddy of meltwater at just this place and began to spin on the bedrock. This tiny scrubbing went on for centuries, for a whole geologic age, until the ice drew back from our part of the continent. And there it was in front of me, the basin-shaped rock just as the glacial melt and Dr. Ball had left it.

Our monuments usually remind us of death. Lizzie Bourne is remembered by a conspicuous marker next to the railway tracks and just below the large bay window in the tourists' building on the summit, and thousands of people see it every summer season. Dr. Ball's persistent defense of life goes unmarked except at the hidden place where that ancient spinning stone cut a basin to catch a saving drink for him.

That is the only souvenir of his passing. Dr. Ball never found his view from Mount Washington and four years later he died in some unknown place and clime, still adding new prospects to his collection.

Chapter Four

CALAMITY IN THE UNROOFED TEMPLE

*E*VER SINCE I CAN REMEMBER, A REMOTE CLOSET IN OUR house has held essential things that have outlived their need. There's an ornate sword in there, the one great-grandfather Jenckes wore while parading with the Providence First Light Infantry. There's also a complex device made of tin; it has a small tank with a filler and three lamp wicks, each of which can be adjusted with a knurled brass wheel smaller than a dime. It's the power supply for what my grandfather's generation called a magic lantern, a kerosene-burning slide projector. Camera lenses of the day sometimes made an image that was brighter at the center than at the edges, so the three wicks would be adjusted to burn at different intensities and the magic lantern projected an evenly-illuminated image against a bed sheet stretched across the living room wall. If the room was large enough, the guests were in front of the sheet and the magic lantern behind it; this was called a shadow play.

Those generations did not require the elaborate distractions that fill our early twenty-first-century days, there was not as much noise then, and one or two magic lantern shows in the course of a summer would be remembered all winter long. The outdoor equivalent of a magic lantern show was a hike up to the snow arch in Tuckerman Ravine.

For a geologist, Tuckerman Ravine is easy to describe: it's a cirque cut by a local glacier that remained after the continental ice sheet melted. It was more than that for Starr King. He published *The White Hills* in 1859, and tells us that when he saw Tuckerman Ravine, "One might easily fancy it the Stonehenge of a Preadamitic race, the unroofed ruins of a temple reared by ancient Anaks long before the birth of man, for which the dome of Mount Washington was piled as the western tower." The public preferred Starr King's version.

The ridges on three sides of the unroofed temple act as snow fences and break the force of the winter winds. As with snow fences of every kind, the snow falls to the ground on the downwind side; in this case, into the ravine. The snow piles in from October until May, not just the ravine's own allotment but also the accumulation that's swept from the treeless uplands on three sides. By the middle of spring the drift piled against the headwall of the ravine may be more than 100 feet deep and compacted to the consistency of glacial ice. There comes a time in early summer when that headwall snowbank is all that's left. Now meltwater from higher up cascades down behind it and tunnels through the icy mass, and the snow arch is formed.

Ethan Allan Crawford discovered the arch in the summer of 1829 and he was deeply impressed: "Such was the size of this empty space that a coach with six horses attached, might be driven into it. It was a very hot day, and not far from this place, the little delicate mountain flowers were in bloom. There seemed to be a contrast—snow in great quantities and flowers just by—which wonderfully displays the presence and powers of an all-seeing and overruling God, who takes care of these little plants and causes them to put forth in good season."

Major Curtis Raymond was also impressed. He spent his summers at the Glen House and he thought there should be a way to hike from the Glen up to the ravine to view the snow arch. In 1863, Mr. Raymond began to build a trail extending 3.3 miles from the carriage road to the snow arch and he maintained it until his death in 1893. By that time, the snow arch was drawing admirers from near and far; there was something about the dreadful grandeur of Tuckerman Ravine and the graceful relic of winter still there in mid-summer that people found irresistible. By that time, the snow arch had killed Sewall Faunce.

C. E. Philbrook kept lodgings in Shelburne, New Hampshire. His place was called Grove Cottage, and on the morning of July 24, 1886, a group of eleven guests climbed aboard his mountain wagon and rode to Osgood's Castle, a picturesque creation built in Pinkham Notch where the Cutler River crossed the road. This was the start of the trail up to Tuckerman Ravine, where Mr. Philbrook's guests would view the snow arch. It was a bright and lovely day and they reached the ravine at two o'clock. Edwin Horne was the most experienced hiker in the party and he was accompanied by his wife, three other men, five other ladies, and young Sewall Faunce. The boy had just turned fifteen and his parents back at Grove Cottage had entrusted him to the care of Mr. Horne.

The hikers were in high spirits when they reached the snow arch and the weather, always uncertain on Mount Washington, was so fine that Mr. Horne decided to climb on up to the summit of the mountain and walk down by the carriage road. When his party reached the ravine they saw the snow arch at the right side and he knew the trail led up the headwall still farther to the right. Apparently not fatigued at all by the climb up from the valley, Mr. Horne quickly scrambled up the trail above the rest of his party.

Everyone in the group knew that the snow arch melted gradually until the span could not sustain its own weight, then it would fall and drop tons of ice on anyone underneath it. Accordingly, they did not climb up on top of the snow mass, but they did scamper into that space which Ethan Allen Crawford thought might hold a coach and six. Even the most hesitant visitors are tempted to do this; there's the deep cavern, the dashing water, and the twin contrasts between the cathedral darkness inside and the high blue sky at their backs, and between the frigid air in the cavern and the heat of the day outside. Returning to that new summer, the group found convenient rocks to sit upon while they contemplated the majesties on every hand.

Meanwhile, R. J. Beach and F. D. Peletier were just leaving Hermit Lake, the glacial tarn half a mile back along the trail. They were both from Hartford, Connecticut, and Mr. Beach was a cadet at West Point. They'd arrived by the Raymond Path, eaten their lunch at Hermit Lake, and started on up to the

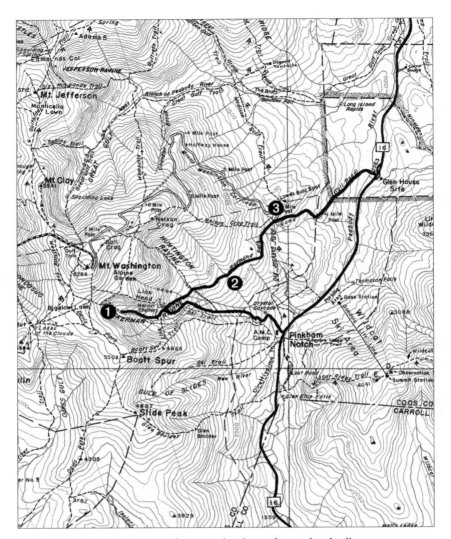

1. Sewall Faunce encountered snow arch at base of ravine headwall
2. Miss Pierce carried out by way of Raymond Path
3. Met wagon at 2-Mile on Carriage Road

floor of the ravine. They planned to view the snow arch, then climb to the summit of the mountain.

Mr. Lathrop, one of the single men, was standing next to Miss Pierce, one of the single women. Sewall Faunce was standing farther away in front of them. Mr. Lathrop said a few words to Sewall and a moment later he found himself thrown forward as if by the hand of an unseen giant and someone cried out, *"We are killed! We are killed!"* The snow arch had not collapsed, it had not fallen down into the cavern; it had tipped over frontwards, toward the hikers Mr. Horne had brought to the ravine.

Mr. Horne was about 400 feet up the trail on the headwall when he heard the crash and looked down into a cloud of snow and flying ice. At that moment, as one of the men later put it, "We looked around us to see who were lost and who were saved." Mr. Horne rushed back to his friends and found Miss Pierce trapped by several blocks of ice and he heard his wife cry out, "Where's Sewall?" Mr. Horne answered, "My god! Think of his father and mother!" One of the other men remembered, "We did not dare to think, we must *do*!"

Miss Pierce was upright, but buried to her waist in ice and snow and unable to move. The men extricated her without much difficulty, but she was shaken and in pain and they laid her out on a nearby rock. Then they turned back to the enormous pile of snow and broken ice, tons and tons of it, and began picking and prying at it with their walking sticks, trying to find Sewall. They could make no headway at all, so after a brief discussion Mr. Horne decided to try to find help on the summit.

R. J. Beach and F. D. Peletier were just topping the rise above Hermit Lake known as the Little Headwall. They were hurrying to reach the summit but they were not sure of the way, so they were glad when they met several ladies coming down and asked them about the trail. The ladies, however, were not much help. They seemed distracted, they said they had to get to the bottom of the mountain as fast as they could and they said something about an accident. The two young men hurried up to the huddle of people at the snowbank and quickly added their efforts to those helping Miss Pierce.

Mr. Beach, the West Point cadet, asked her if she was hurt and she said she was; he asked her to describe the pain and she said it was in her back and she could not walk. Satisfied that her arms and legs were not injured, the two young men took off their belts and looped one under her arms and

The immensely popular "snow arch" in Tuckerman Ravine killed Sewall Faunce in 1866.

the other around her legs and, hoisting her with this crude sling, they started for the valley.

Mr. Horne reached the summit in forty-five minutes, about half the time usually needed for the steep rough hike. The summertime population of the top of Mount Washington was considerable. The U.S. Army Signal Service acted as the national weather bureau in those days and their observers occupied one summit building. The Summit House was a full-service hotel with a large roster of guests and help, some of whom stayed in the original Tip-Top House. The cog railway and the carriage road kept employees on the summit, and another building was occupied by the publisher, editor, reporters, and pressmen of *Among the Clouds*, the twice-daily newspaper published up there during the summer season.

Mr. Horne went straight to the Summit House with his terrible news and, as a guest said later, "It needed but the intimation of human suffering and death to start a sympathetic and willing company to the rescue." The signal service men, employees of the hotel, the railway and the road, and the entire staff of the newspaper all turned out and started down the mountain with axes, shovels, blankets, and "restoratives," which in the language of the day usually meant brandy.

The rescue party from the summit reached the trouble at 4:00 P.M., just as four other men were leaving with Miss Pierce. Hope for Sewall's life still ruled and the summit group began chopping and digging above the point where they were told he was entombed, but it quickly became obvious that their tools and forces were inadequate. Someone suggested a tunnel and in about four minutes one of the men uncovered Sewall's head, pressed against a rock. As they continued to dig they realized that he'd been standing on top of a rock and was still in the same position, but jammed hard against another rock. There was, as one of the men put it, no breath in his body.

Seven men started back up the headwall with the body, but the going was so difficult that one of them soon hurried on to the summit to find a stretcher and recruit three more men. They rejoined the others just above the headwall of the ravine and regained the summit at 6:15. A doctor staying at Horace Fabyan's hotel had taken the late cog train to the summit and he was puzzled to find scarcely a sign of injury anywhere on the boy's body, though the sole of one shoe was partly torn off.

The women who started for the valley immediately after the accident brought the alarm to the Glen House and Mr. Milliken, the keeper, organized a six-horse mountain wagon with fourteen men and a doctor who would go two miles up the carriage road to the point where the Raymond Path departed for the ravine.

Meanwhile, the West Point cadet, his hiking partner, and two other men were making their way down with Miss Pierce, but they found the carry exceedingly difficult. It could be worse, she reminded them, and pointed out that she weighed only 112 pounds. Thus encouraged, they struggled on down the Little Headwall with the belt arrangement, but this proved so awkward for them and, they feared, so painful for the plucky Miss Pierce, that they decided they could get only as far as Hermit Lake by nightfall. Three of them would stay there and one would go to the valley and return with provisions for the night, then they'd start out again in the morning.

To their surprise, a relief party from the valley met them at Hermit Lake. There was a new telegraph connection from the summit to the Glen House and word of the accident reached the valley immediately after Mr. Horne reached the summit, a factorial advance in the speed of communications. Now they determined to improve the carry and press on through the evening. Having no axe, they hacked down two birch trees with a shovel and improvised a litter with their raincoats, their belts, and what the West Point cadet gallantly described as "the lady's gossamers." These would have been her stockings, though no gentleman would use that word lest he reveal too great a familiarity with a lady's legs.

Major Raymond's path left the carriage road at the two-mile mark and gained 1,900 feet in 2.7 miles to reach the ravine, a rather moderate grade by local standards. The way was complicated, however, by four stream crossings, two of them twenty feet wide and all filled to the top of their banks this evening with the runoff of waning snows higher up. The rescue party's birch poles cracked twice and they stopped to cut new ones.

A giant of a man joined them and he held back branches and lifted blowdown trees out of the way that four other men together couldn't move. A large stone rolled onto the foot of one of the crew and he was lost to the carry, but after three hours on the Raymond Path, R. J. Beach heard a shout from somewhere in the darkness ahead of them.

"Come and give us a lift," he called, and the answer came back, "I will if you'll hold my horse." It was the Glen House crew with the mountain wagon on the carriage road and in a few more minutes they had Miss Pierce eased onto a mattress in the wagon and they reached the Glen House at 9:15 P.M., just seven hours after the accident.

Two hours later, the body of Sewall Faunce arrived at the Glen House; it had been brought down the carriage road by mountain wagon. The next day, the grieving party gathered once more at Grove Cottage and composed a formal resolution of thanks to the many people who had helped them. Then they passed it by unanimous vote.

Chapter Five

A PRESIDENTIAL BRAIN TRUST

*T*HE CANADIAN GRAND TRUNK RAILROAD RAN PAST THE north end of the Presidential Range and on July 1, 1900, the company's engineers undertook an experiment to see if an electric light would be more effective than a kerosene lamp to illuminate the track ahead of their locomotives. That same day, more than seventy-five members of the Appalachian Mountain Club gathered at the hotel on the summit of Mount Washington for their thirty-fifth field meeting.

The principal impetus for the AMC came from the faculty at the Massachusetts Institute of Technology in Cambridge, Massachusetts. That was in 1876, but the heart of the club was already deeply rooted in New England sensibilities.

Inside every Massachusetts Bay Puritan there was a Calvinist trying to get out, a person devoted to the sturdy conviction that the virtue of any undertaking is directly proportional to its difficulty. This tenet did the heavy lifting, it cut down the forests and pried the boulders out of the fields and built all those hundreds of miles of stone walls.

By the middle of the nineteenth-century, the calluses had gone west and a new salvation took hold on the roads between Cambridge and Concord. The first generation of priests were the Transcendentalists; for them, landscape was a moral category, they spelled nature with a capital N and they believed that there were lessons to be learned in the wilderness that would make us better. Starr King found their gospel in the White Mountains: "Nature is hieroglyphic," he wrote. "Each prominent fact in it is like a type; it's final use is to set up one letter of the infinite alphabet, and help us, by its connections, to read some statement or statute applicable to the conscious world."

The members of the AMC were drawn by their own nature and by New England geography to the White Mountains and they got to work quickly. In 1877, Jonathan Davis laid out an AMC path from the town of Jackson, New Hampshire, north to Carter Notch. Beginning in 1879, the AMC maintained the Crystal Cascades Trail from the Pinkham Notch road up toward Tuckerman Ravine. The club built the Hermit Lake shelter at the entrance to the ravine in the early 1880s, they built the Imp Shelter on the mountain range across Pinkham Notch from Mount Washington in 1885, and the first high-altitude hut at Madison Springs on the Presidential Range in 1888.

At intervals the club would hold a field meeting in some suitably rusticated upland site where they would discuss club business, listen to papers read by their peers, and stride vigorously into the landscape. These meetings were not easy, as witnessed by an address by AMC president Charles Fay. He took his text from *Mind*, a quarterly review of psychology and philosophy, and the article he chose was titled "The Aesthetic Evolution of Man." "We must never forget," he began, "that the taste for scenery on a large scale is confined to comparatively few races and comparatively few persons among them. Thus the Chinese, according to Captain Gill, in spite of their high artistic skill, 'the beauties of nature have no charm, and in the most lovely scenery the houses are so placed that no enjoyment can be derived from it.' The Hindus, 'though devoted to art, care but little, if at all, for landscape or natural beauty.' The Russians 'run through Europe with their carriage windows shut.' Even the Americans in many cases seem to care little for wild or beautiful scenery. They are more attracted by smiling landscape gardening, and, it seems to us, flat or dull civilization. I have heard an American just arrived in Europe go into unfeigned ecstasies over the fields and hedges in the flattest parts of the Midlands." This opening is extended through twelve pages of rumination. That is to say, the field meetings of the AMC had elevation, and they also had loft.

By the closing years of the nineteenth century, the really important values in the academic community of Boston had to be faced. The Harvard-Yale game loomed on the fall horizon of 1897, a situation that called for the best the temples of fortitude could muster, so Harvard planned to send its team up to the Presidential Range for a pre-season hike. *The Harvard Crimson* student newspaper did not fail to note the gravity of the situation and its proper response: "We know little of football, but we have great faith in White Mountain air and exercise to make hardy and resolute men."

William Curtis was the referee for thirteen Harvard-Yale games, he was himself a celebrated athlete and the very image of a hardy and resolute man, but in July of 1900, he and his friend Allan Ormsbee lost their game in the White Mountain air.

WILLIAM CURTIS AND ALLAN ORMSBEE
JULY 1900

The thirty-fifth field meeting of the Appalachian Mountain Club was announced for the summit of Mount Washington and more than seventy-five members gathered there on Saturday, June 30, 1900. By this time, the summit had achieved a very considerable degree of civilization. There was the Summit House hotel, a large observation tower, the old Tip-Top House hotel, the editorial and printing office of *Among the Clouds*, the office of the carriage road, the observatory of the U.S. Army Signal Service, the engine house of the railway, a garage for the carriage road, and two stables.

Reverend Harry Nichols did not favor such latter-day novelties. He and his sixteen-year-old son Donaldson planned to approach the summit by way of an overnight hike up the Davis Path on Montalban Ridge. William Curtis and Allan Ormsbee were of a similar mind, they'd make the meeting the last stop on a lengthy tour of the White Mountains.

William Curtis lived in New York and he was noted for his physical prowess. He was affectionately called "Father Bill" in recognition of his leading role in the establishment of the Amateur Athletic Club and the Fresh Air Club in New York, he was an admired writer for *The Spirit of the Times*, and he was nothing short of a sporting prodigy. In 1868 he set the record for harness lift at 3,230 pounds, and he set records in the 60- and 100-yard dashes, the hammer, shot put, and tug-of-war. He set rowing records in single, double, and four-man sculls, and he won in the 100-yard hurdles, 200-yard and quarter-mile runs, the mile walk, the high jump, swimming, skating, and gymnastics. He was sixty-three years old in 1900 and described as a splendid figure of a man, deep-chested and vigorous, a man who did not wear an overcoat even in the harshest winter weather. He often led hikes and his circulars of notification were apt to include notes such as, "This outing will not be cancelled or post-poned due to inclement weather." His friend Allan Ormsbee was thirty years old and he too was from New York, a trained athlete and a man of notable physical prowess.

The two friends had come north a week before the AMC meeting and climbed Mounts Lafayette, Whiteface, Passaconaway, and Sandwich Dome with another friend, Fred Ilgen. The three of them spent Friday night at the Pleasant View Cottage in Twin Mountain, the first town north of Crawford Notch, and they separated on Saturday morning. Mr. Ilgen wanted to climb Twin Mountain, then he'd take the train to Fabyans and go to the summit on the cog railway. Messrs. Curtis and Ormsbee had a slightly odd day in view: they'd take the train to the head of Crawford Notch and climb Mount Willard, then come down and climb the Crawford Path up the Southern Peaks to the meeting on the summit.

Reverend Nichols took the longest and most difficult approach to the meeting. In the large topographical view, the Presidential Range is more than Mount Washington joining the Northern and Southern Peaks; the lower but longer Montalban Ridge lies just east of the Southern Peaks, and the long and largely untracked Rocky Branch Ridge is still farther to the east. The Davis Bridle Path up the Montalban Ridge bumped along in the woods for an interminable twelve miles before it broke into the open on the shoulder of Mount Washington and this dreary prospect found no favor among the stylish gentry who did their mountain climbing on horseback. Mr. Davis lost his shirt, his trail was abandoned in 1854, and when Reverend Nichols started up to join the 1900 field meeting, no less an authority than Professor Frederick Tuckerman had long since declared that the Davis Path was "in a state of innocuous desuetude."

Reverend Nichols was not deterred. He'd made the same trip six years earlier and this time he added several miles by bushwhacking up Razor Brook from the town of Bartlett, at the south end of Crawford Notch. The rever-

William Curtis and Allan Ormsbee approached the AMC meeting on the summit by way of the 8.2-mile Crawford Path. They encountered a fierce storm and took shelter by burrowing into this clump of dwarf spruce.

end and his son were accompanied by Walter Parker and Charles Allen, two experienced woodsmen from Bartlett hired to serve as guides, packers, and aides-de-camp. It did turn out to be tough going, but it was a fine summer day and the four of them reached Mount Isolation, about two-thirds of the way along their route. They built a lean-to shelter here, had a good supper, and lay down to sleep on beds of fresh balsam boughs.

A sharp thunderstorm broke over them in the middle of the night and a strong north wind pushed it on past them, then Saturday dawned with dark skies and heavy gusts of drizzle blowing through the woods. The next four miles were a struggle through the undergrowth of the abandoned trail and seemingly endless blowdowns; later Reverend Nichols wrote, "By eleven o'clock, after a final hour of toilsome crawling under, over, and through gnarled and unyielding and water-soaked scrub, we stepped out, presumably on Boott Spur, into the full fury of the storm." The fog was so dense they could hardly see each other at shouting distance, the mist soon turned to sleet, and the ferocious wind knocked them down again and again.

At about that time, a driver was approaching the Cow Pasture on the carriage road, a place two miles straight across the Alpine Garden from the crest on Boott Spur that the Nichols party had reached. This was Nathan Larabee and he'd started his four-horse mountain wagon up from the Glen in bright sunshine, then he hit rain at the Halfway House and at 6-Mile he came to ice and such a strong north wind that he had to pile heavy rocks in the windward side of his wagon to keep it from tipping over.

Reverend Nichols was familiar with the terrain and the hazards of the weather, and he realized that the wisest course was to get down to the valley by the shortest route available. But, as he wrote later, "Who would have done so on such an expedition—what climber, what explorer? You say, "'Keep straight up—on and up steadily, resolvedly, bucking the wind.'"

So the Nichols party plunged on across the long and completely exposed crest of Boott Spur. There were places where the trail was almost lost in the ice and the abyss of Tuckerman Ravine was at their elbows, but they kept on and up, steadily, resolvedly. Soon they could make their way only in short rushing bursts, crouching behind rocks when a gust hit, then rushing again, sometimes falling flat if no large rock was nearby to shelter them. "It seemed," said Mr. Allen, "as if the hail would take the hide off."

In normal weather, this part of the trail is a pleasant stroll, the terrain is virtually flat and the footing is no more difficult than a garden walk. The Nichols party required two hours to make a mile of this walk against the fierce barrier of storm. As agreed, their guides left them where the Davis Path joined the Crawford Path and those two men found their own way down the Southern Peaks with the camping gear. Reverend Nichols and Donaldson pushed on toward the summit cone. The reverend tied blankets around his son's head and around his own, partly for warmth, partly as helmets to ward off the rocks when they fell, and so they kept on, the blankets blowing wildly in the gale.

The reverend's diary recounted the harrowing trip: "Suddenly I stumbled on a cairn, a stoneman one and one-half feet high, with another just beyond in sight even through that driven rime; they were cairns built the day before by the Lowes for the Appalachian Meet. I knew at once that we were safe. We had only to follow those cairns to the summit. I bade my son crouch behind me, await a lull in the wind at each cairn, then make a rush on hands and knees for the next—making least resistance, yielding full subservience, to the storm's blast. And so we made port, reaching the summit about two-thirty P.M."

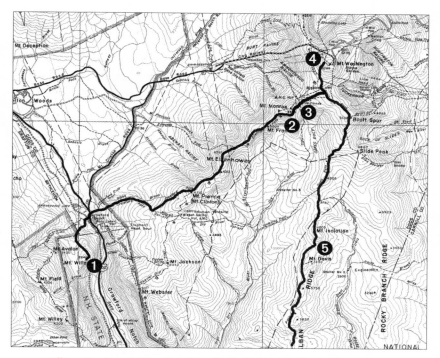

1. William Curtis and Allan Ormsbee climbed Mount Willard in the morning
2. Took shelter in stunted spruce
3. Curtis died on Bigelow Lawn
4. Ormsbee died just below summit
5. Reverend Nichols and party came up Davis Path and spent their first night near Mount Isolation, a trip made longer by bushwhacking up Razor Brook from Bartlett

Among the Clouds reported, "The thermometer had fallen from 48 on Friday evening to 25 on Saturday morning, and so rapid had been the formation of the ice, and so fierce the velocity of the wind, that even small particles, driven like from a gun, broke dozens of panes of glass on the Summit House." Inside, bellboys hastened to each new break and replaced the broken glass with wooden panels while the Appalachians had lunch and began their scheduled events with the reading of papers and following discussion. Reverend Nichols and Donaldson joined them and, as the minister wrote later, "Along toward supper-time the chairman remarked, "It surely is time for our two friends to come in.' 'What friends?' said I. The chairman replied, 'Two of our party, Mr. Curtis and Mr. Ormsbee, who kept around by the Crawford House to walk up the trail.'"

At this time, William Curtis and Allan Ormsbee were some four miles away down the Southern Peaks, pressing on toward the AMC meeting. Father Bill was familiar with the area and when he was on top of Mount Willard he could have looked up the range and seen the heavy cloud cover on Mount Washington. He could also have stopped in at the Crawford House earlier in the day and inquired about conditions on Mount Washington; the Crawford House was connected to the summit by telephone and they were in the habit of warning hikers of threatening conditions. Instead, Father Bill and his friend descended from Willard, crossed the road to the beginning of the Crawford Path without talking to anyone inside the lodgings, and started right up toward the summit of Mount Washington more than eight miles away.

They reached timberline on Clinton and turned south, against their line of travel, to sign the weatherproof register the AMC kept at the top of that mountain. Turning north again, they reached Pleasant Dome and, rather than take the level bypass trail that avoided the climb up the dome, they took the higher trail. Two workmen were cutting overgrown brush on the bypass at about 1:30 P.M. and, since there was already a high wind and blowing sleet, they tried to overtake the two hikers and warn them not to go on. Failing that, they called after them but could not get a response.

By 3:00, the trail workers decided that the storm was rising past endurance, so they packed up their tools. The Bartlett guides appeared just then and reported that they'd passed two hikers, headed uphill and into the storm. Guide Charles Allen said that he'd greeted the younger hiker but got only a grunt in reply. Mr. Allen told him that it was very bad up ahead, so bad that they'd had difficulty getting down and out of it themselves and it was unlikely that anyone could climb upward against such a storm. This caution drew no response, and the two parties continued on their opposite courses.

In the interval between passing the workmen and passing the guides, Father Bill and Mr. Ormsbee had climbed Pleasant Dome and again left their names in the AMC weatherproof register. They added, "Rain clouds and wind sixty miles—Cold."

By this time, most of the AMC members had reached the summit by way of the cog railway. As they neared the summit they admired the delicate tracery of rime ice collecting on every surface and they were inconvenienced by the wind as they hurried from the cog trains across the platform into the hotel, but this was, after all, Mount Washington—vigorous conditions were the reason they'd chosen the summit for their meeting. They settled themselves, had dinner, and then gathered to hear the schedule for the coming week. The AMC had written a full menu of activities and this introductory evening began with remarks by John Ritchie. He was one of the two secretaries of the club and he took as his theme, "Simple Rules Which Will Insure Safety to all on Any Mountain Walk."

"A high mountain range," he began, "introduces into a country certain elements of uncertainty so far as the weather is concerned." He went on to urge the members to make a good hiking plan and keep to it, to stay close together, to wear strong clothing, to avoid high-spirited shouting which might be interpreted as a distress call, to avoid the temptation to roll rocks down steep slopes, and to avoid touching the streamside plant known as hellebore. As Mr. Ritchie spoke, the most dangerous summer storm in living memory was still gaining strength on the other side of the walls.

The Appalachians were expecting Messrs. Curtis and Ormsbee. Fred Ilgen came up on the cog train that afternoon and he put word around that his two companions would be along presently, but when they did not appear a telephone call was made to the Crawford House. The people there said they had not seen anyone meeting that description and as far as they knew no hikers had started up the Crawford Path that day.

The Appalachian Mountain Club had gathered a notable group on the summit. J. Rayner Edmands was there, the greatest trailbuilder in the history of the Presidential Range, the man who built the Gulfside Trail, the

Randolph Path, the Link, the Israel Ridge Path, and the Edmands Path, to name but a few. Louis Fayerweather Cutter was there, the man who drew the definitive White Mountain maps for fifty years. Vyron and Thaddeus Lowe were there, the renowned trailbuilders and guides from Randolph, as strong, as experienced, and as reliable mountain men as any in the region. It was little short of a Presidential brain trust, and now the chairman of the AMC program took counsel with the Lowes and they were uneasy; there were summit loops and bypasses on two of the Southern Peaks, and if Father Bill and Allan Ormsbee were living up to their reputation for vigor and determination, they might well have taken a summit loop while the two Bartlett guides were on the more prudent bypass.

Accordingly, the two Lowes lit their lanterns and started out the door to see what they could find on the Crawford Path. They'd barely stepped onto the platform when their lanterns blew out. More ominously, the platform was heavy with ice and it wasn't the light and crumbly rime that often comes with an off-season storm, it was clear solid ice. The Lowes had all they could do to get back to the door of the hotel.

Inside, however, fears were being allayed. Reverend Nichols told of the severe weather his group met and how their two guides had turned back at the Davis Path junction and gone down the Crawford Path. Surely they'd meet Father Bill and Allan Ormsbee and tell them not to go any farther up the ridge, to come down to the valley with them. Surely Messrs. Curtis and Ormsbee were safely down in some valley lodgings by this time in the evening, and they'd join the Appalachians' field meeting as soon as the weather cleared.

Father Bill and Allan Ormsbee were not safely lodged in the valley. They passed the Bartlett guides and the trail workers between two and three o'clock, then they pushed on up the rising and entirely exposed trail over the crests of Franklin and Monroe. This section of the Crawford Path is about a mile long and the terrain is very similar to the ridge of Boott Spur, where Reverend Nichols and Donaldson were taking two hours to cover the same distance that storm-lashed afternoon. Those two were able to reach the safety of the summit hotel before Saturday nightfall. Father Bill Curtis and Allan Ormsbee were not.

Sunday was impossible for any outdoor purposes on the AMC schedule, but there was inside work to do, there were papers to read and proposals to be heard. One proposal asked if the Appalachian Mountain Club would accept the gift of a house and land on Three-Mile Island in Lake Winnipesaukee and, if so, would it also buy the rest of the land on the island for a club reservation? Both proposals were approved.

Outside, the wind remained at gale force and the temperatures dropped into the 20-degree range, but, curiously, the precipitation did not turn to sleet or snow, it was rain and it froze on every surface as solid ice. Frank Burt, publisher of *Among the Clouds*, wrote, "At the end of the turntable lever, whose dimensions are three by four inches, there projected on Sunday morning a solid block of ice in the teeth of the wind a foot and a half in length."

The storm blew itself out on Monday morning, the summer sun warmed the ice-clad summit buildings, and soon whole walls of ice were falling to the ground. Several parties of Appalachians set out to make up the planned hikes they'd lost to the storm on Sunday while others remaining on the summit looked out for the arrival of Father Bill and Allan Ormsbee.

Mapmaker Louis F. Cutter started down the Crawford Path to meet the missing hikers or, failing that, to see if he could find any trace of them. He reached the bottom of the cone and started toward the twin peaks of Monroe about three-quarters of a mile away across Bigelow Lawn. This is a remnant of the ancient upland peneplane; the summit cones of the peaks rise above it, the ravines cut into its sides, and the ice sheet scrubbed its surface to leave a gently rolling place of ledge, tundra-like grass, and broken rock. Mr. Cutter stayed on the Crawford Path until the trail up Monroe was only 300 yards ahead and the Lakes of the Clouds were just to the west; then he came to a place where the path ran between two sections of ledge. The floor of this slot was barely wide enough for the path and there, face down with his head resting on a rock, lay Father Bill Curtis. He was wearing strong hiking boots, a medium-weight woolen coat, a shirt made of shoddy, and long pants; a light cap was near his head.

Mr. Cutter determined that he was dead, then he went looking for Allan Ormsbee. A few hundred paces south on the Crawford Path, not far beyond the beginning of the trail up to the summit ridge of Monroe, he found a camera and a milk bottle lying in the Crawford Path. Just downslope on the left, there was a patch of dense scrub that seemed to have been modified in a curious fashion; it seemed like a sort of shelter, but a quick glance revealed no trace of Allan Ormsbee. Mr. Cutter continued down the Crawford Path almost as far as Pleasant Dome, where he met a group of upward-bound hikers. They said they hadn't seen anyone else on the trail, so he turned back toward Mount Washington. At the junction of the Davis Path he met three Appalachians who were starting for Boott Spur; these were Messrs. Coffin, Parker, and Weed. Mr. Cutter told them of his discoveries and went on up to the summit where he alerted several more Appalachians. Two members of that cadre started down the Tuckerman Ravine Trail to intercept a group of clubmen returning from a hike to the edge of the celebrated chasm and they were added to the work force.

While these excursions were afoot, the Coffin, Parker, Weed group went on toward Monroe to make a more thorough study of the shelter in the scrub patch that had caught Louis Cutter's eye. These patches are impenetrably dense on top, but there is often some space among the lower stems and it looked as if someone had cut away several pieces of the tangled mass and used them to close up an opening on the exposed north side and at the same time make more room inside. Crawling into the opening, they found three slices of bread wrapped in waxed paper with one of them partly eaten, and, in the deepest and most protected corner of the shelter, they found another camera. Mr. Parker knew Allan Ormsbee and he recognized the camera in the path as belonging to him. It seemed reasonable to assume that the camera inside the shelter belonged to Father Bill. This precipitated a close search of the area in hopes of finding Mr. Ormsbee, but there were no further traces.

Now the three men returned to thought. They reasoned that Allan Ormsbee was less than half the age of Father Bill and, since both were heading for the summit and seemed determined to get there through Saturday's storm, the younger man would probably have gone farther. And, since Father Bill was found lying right in the Crawford Path, it seemed likely that they were trying to stay on the trail come what may. They would be crossing the same terrain that the Nichols group had needed two hours to negotiate a little earlier on the same day and, calculating the daylight available, the searchers decided that if Allan Ormsbee survived a reasonable length of time, he would have made his way some considerable distance up the cone of Mount Washington. Offsetting this calculation, they realized that the moss inside the shelter was noticeably worn down. How long had the men stayed there? Had they both stayed the same length of time, or had the younger and presumably stronger Allan Ormsbee gone ahead for help? Had Father Bill rested

Until it was stolen by vandals, a brass plaque marked William Curtis's final resting place.

in the shelter and started out again Saturday afternoon, or had he stayed in the shelter and then started up on Sunday when his companion did not return? Had one or the other of the men left the camera and the milk bottle in the path to serve as a signal?

Bearing these imponderables in mind, Messrs. Coffin, Porter, and Weed divided their three-man force; one stayed on the Crawford Path while the other two moved out on either side, Mr. Weed on the right, Mr. Coffin in the center, and Mr. Parker on the left. Thus arrayed, they went along the Crawford Path to the Davis Path junction and then followed the Davis Path out toward Boott Spur for a distance before deciding that such a divergence was unlikely. Returning to the Crawford Path, they paused again to think.

Mr. Parker was the only one among the Appalachians who knew Allan Ormsbee personally. He made the point that his friend was a strong and resourceful man who favored a direct approach to problems. Given this nature, Mr. Parker suggested that he might have left the wandering Crawford Path and taken a direct line to the summit, which would have the added advantage of moving him somewhat toward the lee side of the cone. Accordingly, the three men altered their course and made straight for the summit while keeping their spread pattern for greater efficiency.

Their progress was slow and difficult because their new route was almost entirely over the large, angular, and unstable rocks that make up most of the cone, and this day they were further slowed by the ice remaining from the storm. Pausing to rest, they decided that if they were having so much trouble, Allan Ormsbee must have had a great deal more. Taking this into account, they changed their route to the staggering zig-zag pattern they thought a man *in extremis* would have taken. Mr. Weed, farthest to the right, passed the pile of stones marking the place where Harry Hunter gave up the ghost twenty-six years earlier. Mr. Parker was farthest to the left and at 4:30 in the afternoon he found the body of his friend Allan Ormsbee. He was about fifteen paces west of the Crawford path and within sight of the back wall of the signal station on the summit.

Mr. Parker could see some ladies of the Appalachian group near the signal station and he called to them, they passed the word to the AMC men, and a group quickly formed to carry Mr. Ormsbee's body the little way remaining to the mountain-top settlement. The other body lay a mile and a half distant, so a stretcher was improvised and a group set out at 6:00 P.M., then when more Appalachians returned to the summit from their days' excursions they went down the Crawford Path as reinforcements. This made twenty carriers in all, and even with this considerable strength the remains of William Curtis did not reach the summit until the middle of the evening. Colonel O. G. Barron, keeper of the Fabyan House, made the necessary arrangements in the valley; he called on two undertakers in Littleton, brought them to the base station of the cog in his carriage, and ordered two caskets to be sent up by a special train. Another special train brought the bodies down that evening and Fred Ilgen accompanied them to New York the next day.

That was the end of the sad affair for Father Bill Curtis and Allan Ormsbee, but not for the Appalachian Mountain Club. Given the strength of their numbers on the scene, the concern any deaths on the Presidential Range would cause, and the many prominent members of the club who were present, the accident that opened their field meeting had several consequences.

The cause of the deaths was the first matter to be settled. Dr. George Gove of Whitefield was the medical examiner and he made the rulings. Mr. Curtis was discovered with his head resting on a stone and Dr. Gove found a large bruise at that point on his forehead. The depth of the bruise indicated that

This cross marked the spot where Allan Ormsbee perished.

Mr. Curtis was rendered unconscious by the blow, the position of his head on the rock proved that he did not regain consciousness, and the maturity of the bruise showed that he did not die for several hours after he fell.

Allan Ormsbee's body was covered with bruises and lacerations that testified to the battering he sustained as he tried to reach the summit. If a strong hiker such as Reverend Nichols could not stay on his feet in daylight, much earlier in the storm, and with far less ice to contend with, it was obvious that Allan Ormsbee's night must have been terrible indeed, and that he gave everything he had to give in his effort to find help for his friend before he himself died at the place of his last fall.

This episode involved many prominent people in the Boston community and, needless to say, the press was not slow to react. As so often happens at times like this, the more distant the reporter, the more lurid the report. Thus the Wednesday edition of *The Boston Globe* included the news that during the course of his ordeal Allan Ormsbee broke his leg and tore loose the branch of a tree to make a splint. Dr. Gove did not agree.

More substantial studies were undertaken by the Appalachian Mountain Club. During the week of the field meeting they agreed that Mr. Ormsbee would not have left Mr. Curtis unless the older man could not go on. Following on this, three theories emerged. One was that the two men reached Mount Monroe and improvised the shelter in the scrub, Mr. Curtis remained there while Mr. Ormsbee went for help after leaving his camera and the milk bottle as a sign, then Mr. Curtis revived himself and pushed on alone. The second theory was that both men rested in the shelter and then went on together, but became separated and were not able to find each other in the storm. The third theory was that they rested in the shelter and went on together until Mr. Curtis fell, then Mr. Ormsbee went on alone.

As reported in *Among the Clouds*, "Those who advocated the first theory are divided as to whether Curtis followed Ormsbee on Saturday night or on Sunday morning. Against the Saturday night theory it is argued that he would be more likely to stay overnight in comparative shelter than to set out in darkness, which must have come on soon after Ormsbee left. Against the Sunday theory it is argued that he possibly could not have lived through the night, and if he had, why was the bread left uneaten? As to the theory of their both leaving the shelter together, it is asked why did they leave their cameras behind?" The editor of the paper further wondered about the milk bottle: If the men understood the seriousness of their situation, why didn't they leave a note in the bottle?

By Thursday, another theory had emerged. T. O. Fuller was a member of the Appalachian gathering and he had gone down to the cleft ledge where Father Bill died. The exact situation was well known by this time, and as Mr. Fuller was studying the place he found a deep hole among the rocks. He saw something down there that caught the light and, reaching in, he pulled out a pair of gold-rimmed bifocal spectacles.

Mr. Fuller and two others studied the rock upon which Mr. Curtis was reported to have hit his head and they decided that this rock and two others had been placed there recently. Father Bill, they decided, had not fallen and hit his head, he fell and then those three rocks were put there so he could rest his head. Furthermore, Mr. Fuller's group thought, the ground where he lay had been newly formed into a slight hollow. His spectacles, presumably, fell off as he rested there and they dropped down into the hole.

All this suggested that the two men rested together in the scrub shelter and then went on together to try for the summit. There was a large rock in the trail near the spot where Father Bill was found, and Mr. Fuller's theory was that he had tripped on this rock and fallen. Then, this theory held, the two men decided that in light of Father Bill's weakened condition he should stay in the shelter provided by the trough of ledge while Allan Ormsbee went for help. The younger man improved the hollow and made the rough rock pillow to ease Father Bill's suffering, then set out for the summit.

Before the field meeting was over, a committee was appointed to study the deaths and write a report to settle the matter: Albion Perry, John Ritchie Jr, and J. Rayner Edmands. They reviewed and considered the experience of Reverend Nichols and Donaldson, their two guides, the trail workers, and Messrs. Ormsbee and Curtis, and they reconstructed the distance and timing of those four parties, and the progression of the storm.

The study committee decided that the bread, the cameras, and the milk bottle were moot points, they were silent witnesses and nothing important could be learned from them. The committee deputized Mr. C. F. Mathewson to study the place where Mr. Curtis was found and he concluded that the body fell where it was found and the weight was too great for Allan Ormsbee to move it very far, if any distance at all. The study group also concluded that Mr. Curtis had not fallen at some other place, then gotten up and walked to the place where he was found. They discounted the report that Mr. Curtis had experienced some slight heart problem a few years earlier and had now suffered a major attack. Dr. Gove certified that death did not occur for some time after the fall and the accumulation of blood in the bruise indicated that Mr. Curtis' circulation was not impaired. The committee approved Professor Parker's written report that Mr. Curtis fell from exhaustion and that the position of the head did not lead to any helpful conclusion.

The committee considered the layout of the Crawford Path, noting that the air-line distance from the fatal site to the summit was about a mile, but the wandering route of the bridle path covered a mile and a half. Since Mr. Ormsbee had never been to the area before, it was not likely that he was able to follow the path. Rather, he had gone straight for the summit and had fallen repeatedly in the chaos of broken rock.

Here they cited Reverend Nichols' written report: "The wind increased in force. It blew us over on the sharp rocks. It blew the breath out of our bodies. Our progress was by a series of dashes—a few rods, then a rest, then a dash again for shelter. The rest must be but for a moment, lest the fatal chilliness come on. I could feel it creeping over me, I could see it in my boy's chattering teeth. The fog had become sleet, cutting like a knife, it gathered on the rocks, every step meant danger of a slip, a fall, a jagged cut. Whether the wind, or the sleet, or the ice under foot, were the greatest element of danger is hard to say. I lost my hat, though it was tied down; my alert boy found it, he shouted its safety to me from three feet away, but I heard nothing save the howling wind." The committee pointed out that the ordeal of the Nichols party probably fell short of the conditions Mr. Ormsbee faced, that the effect of higher wind and the onset of darkness could be judged by at least fifty severe bruises and lacerations on his body.

The makeshift shelter was puzzling. The men were probably in good shape when they came over the low crest of Franklin; they were in good physical condition when they started and, although there had been warnings, the severe conditions were still up ahead. So why had they taken the time to make the shelter and, once made, why had they left it before conditions moderated? Was it made because one of them was already exhausted or injured, or was it abandoned because one of them was in need of attention, or because the conditions were already so difficult at the shelter that they decided they might as well push on? Was Mr. Curtis already in such bad condition that they couldn't descend to the greater safety of the woods so Mr. Curtis could rest while his companion went down to the valley for help?

If the shelter was not vitally needed, there must have been some vitally important reason for the two men to separate farther on. The committee decided that if for some reason the two men could not go back, they both should have gone down to the woods rather than one or both going toward the summit. They urged any readers of the report to remember this point, but at the same time they recognized that most people would try to keep going onward toward their original destination and, in this case, the safety and comforts of the summit hotel.

The committee again cited Reverend Nichols' writing on this point: "Coming out from the scrub into the wind, just one step back means safety; that is surely the step to take, though the way down by ravines and brook beds be long and tedious. All pushing on makes return less possible and develops new elements of danger. The only safety on finding such a wind above tree level is to turn back at once. There is always protection under the trees and a chance to work one's way out, however toilsome." On this point, however, the reverend did not follow his own advice.

The committee continued to ask questions. Did Mr. Curtis push on alone after he was left at the shelter? Did Mr. Ormsbee go on alone after being with the older man when he fell? Did he know that his companion had fallen? These and many other conjectures occupied the select committee for eleven published pages, but they had no further evidence beyond the injuries and the artifacts and they reached no conclusion.

At the end, they returned to the manuscript of Reverend Nichols: "The one essential is to retain hope. To have missed the line of cairns across the Lawn, to have got out of the trail, to have left the old corral of the Bridle Path just on one side, or not to have known that it was but a short distance from the Summit House—for one moment not to have known where we were, would have meant discouragement, despair, exhaustion, death."

THE CURTIS-ORMSBEE ACCIDENT PRECIPITATED WELL-ORGANIZED searches and engaged several elements of the valley population, it was intimately studied and widely debated, and it was the object of a scholarly report. As such, it can stand as the beginning of the modern age of misadventure on the Presidential Range.

More concretely, it resulted in immediate planning for a refuge shelter on Bigelow Lawn, the saddle connecting Monroe and Mount Washington. This was in service by the next year, 1901, a minimalist structure accommodating six or eight hikers in distinctly minimal comfort. (The AMC guidebook warned, "It is far too uncomfortable to attract campers.") It seemed obvious that a similar provision on the Northern Peaks would make sense, and in 1901 Guy Shorey and Burge Bickford spent two nights at Madison Spring Hut while scouting for a refuge location along the Gulfside Trail. That shelter would not be built until 1958, in Edmands Col, but both of the men would go on to wider and more immediate fame, Guy as one of the greatest of all White Mountain photographers and an indefatigable North Country promoter, Burge as the most famous of the guides working from Gorham.

The deaths of William Curtis and Allan Ormsbee led the AMC to create the first hiker's shelter on the upper slopes of Mount Washington in time for the 1902 summer season. It was purposely made too oddly-shaped and uncomfortable to appeal to anyone not in dire straits.

The presence of the Bigelow Lawn refuge shelter provided a strong impetus to the construction of the nearby Lakes of the Clouds Hut in 1915 and, by extension, the rest of the AMC hut system.

The landmarks of this episode can still be found 100 years later. The Camel Trail starts at the three-way junction with the Crawford Path and Tuckerman Crossover, just a few minutes' walk above the Lakes of the Clouds Hut. Near the height-of-land on the Camel Trail, two iron bolts rise from the ledge a few paces south of the trail, and the stubs of two more bolts are broken off level with the rock. These bolts anchored the refuge hut. The old Crawford Bridle Path can be found here, too; its visible relics are a narrow but distinct depression in the ground, thin grass cover or none at all, and rocks that have been moved to make easier footing for the horses.

Unlike most modern trails, this trace does not run straight at all, it turns and meanders as a horse would prefer to go. Heading south, the Lakes of the Clouds and the hut can be seen on the right and before long the old bridle path passes between two slabs of ledge rising opposite one another to make a narrow trough. This is the place where William Curtis died, and the hole where the gold-rimmed glasses were found is still there. The bridle path meandered on toward Monroe, and numerous traces of the old location can be seen as the Crawford Path climbs the summit cone of Mount Washington; they're easily recognized by the hollow made by the horses' hooves among the rocks and grasses and by the large shifting of rocks to make the horses' way easier. The place where Allan Ormsbee died is on the Crawford Path just below the summit and twenty yards off the trail to the west, marked by a plain wooden cross.

It is probable that the clump of scrub spruce that so vexed the AMC study group still exists. This scrub is found all along the range at timberline; in fact, it *is* the timberline. The spruce trees of the valley diminish in stature as they gain in altitude until they form very dense clumps that may be only a foot or so high, full-grown trees that never grew up, nature's own bonsai.

Nature's metabolism in the subarctic conditions at timberline is very slow, and it's likely that the scrub patches have not changed very much since William Curtis and Allan Ormsbee passed by. The scrub cave they fashioned was on the eastern side of Monroe and described as close to the Crawford Path in a place with a short downward slope.

The scrub on the eastern side of Monroe shows two patterns. Heading north from Franklin, as they did, a hiker first finds a wide and unbroken mass of scrub that is continuous from above the trail all the way down to the full-grown trees on the floor of Oakes Gulf. This does not meet the "scrub patch" definition from 1900 and it is unlikely that it ever did.

That continuous mass of scrub ends about halfway along the flank of Monroe. From this point on, the surface is either the grasses typical of Bigelow Lawn or scattered patches of scrub. There is only one patch that's on a short slope below the trail, and this is also the largest in both area and height. It is L-shaped and there's enough room for several adults to crawl in among the stems under the greenery; in fact, the presence of old tin can fragments shows that others have had the same idea. There is one thin place in this patch of scrub, it's at the inside angle of the L and it faces north; this matches the Curtis-Ormsbee effort to cut branches and put them in the north-facing opening of their shelter. This patch is 400 paces south of the place where the body of Father Bill Curtis was found lying in the old bridle path.

Chapter Six

THE GRAND SCHEME

*L*IFE WAS GOOD IN 1912. THERE HAD BEEN NO EUROPEAN wars since 1871, it was *la belle epoque*, and the last generation had brought a dizzying profusion of wonders: electricity, telephones, automobiles, airplanes, moving pictures, pneumatic tires, phonographs, diesel engines, and Woolworth five-and-dime stores. The germ theory of disease, chromosomes, and X-rays were discovered, and the Hague Conventions were established to replace war with arbitration. The North and South Poles were reached, the oceans were being joined in Panama, and Chester Beach invented the first electric motor for use in home appliances. On top of all that, there was a plan to build a new railway to the summit of Mount Washington.

The famous cog railway had been finished in 1869, but by 1912 the pages of *Among the Clouds* announced that "it is safe to say that the little engines and closed cars are becoming insufficient to handle the growing traffic." Further increases in that traffic could be expected because of developments in hotel accommodation on the summit. The great fire of 1908 had destroyed everything but the old Tip-Top House, and the business boom and buoyant optimism of the day made it obvious that a new hotel would be built, grander and more modern than anything previously known or even imagined.

The hotel would be three stories high, it would be star-shaped and made of stone and steel and plate glass, there would be 100 guest rooms and many would have private baths, and there would be a dining room seating 400. There would be a wine cellar, a barbershop, a billiard room, a grand lobby, and a rotunda 150 feet in diameter. There would be an observatory with a circular walkway on the roof, and above that there would be a searchlight so powerful that it could be seen from the ocean. Most remarkable of all, the summit of Mount Washington itself would rise up through the floor of the grand lobby so guests could climb to the top of the mountain without first climbing almost to the top of the mountain.

All of this, however, seemed modest when compared with the new railway that would bring up the guests. The cog railway ran three and a half miles straight up a west ridge of the mountain, but it was small and noisy, it shook in every joint, and it trailed clouds of smoke. Work had started before the Civil War and the train looked old-fashioned even when it was new; now it seemed faintly silly. Clearly, it was time for a conveyance befitting the new century and the new age.

Mr. Charles S. Mellen was ready. *La belle epoque* was an age of unrestrained commercial expansion and Mr. Mellen began his climb by taking over the New York, New Haven & Hartford Railroad. He found a willing ally in J. P. Morgan and expanded his influence throughout southern New England, then gained control of the Boston & Maine Railroad and, through that, of the cog railway. Now Mr. Mellen had just the ticket for the new age: he would build an electric trolley line to the summit of Mount Washington.

The power would be carried on overhead wires suspended from poles set in pairs about every 100 feet along the track and the traction drive meant that the gradient could not exceed six percent, so several routes were considered. The most dramatic climbed the walls of Great Gulf from Pinkham Notch, but on reflection this seemed to promise more drama than most passengers could probably endure.

The terrain on the west side of the mountain was more suitable, and it was also available. This area was largely owned by timber companies in Berlin and Conway, New Hampshire, and, since they both depended on the Boston & Maine to move their lumber, they would not be likely to oppose Mr. Mellen's plan.

The land rose 4,200 feet from the Boston & Maine connection in Fabyans to the summit; given the limits of gradient, this dictated a rail line of 19.8 miles. It would follow the Ammonoosuc River up to the base station of the cog railroad, then swing left up the flank of Jefferson Notch to cross the lower slope of the Ridge of the Caps and rise across the western slope of Mount Jefferson toward Castellated Ridge. The railroad would tunnel under the ridge, swing back and pass over itself below the lowest Castle, then climb the side of Jefferson again to a switchback, upward to a higher point on Castellated Ridge and another switchback, then across the flank of Jefferson for a fourth time. It crossed Mount Clay below its summit ridge, then circled the summit cone of Mount Washington two and a half times to end at the door of the new hotel. It was an audacious plan, even fantastic, but it suited the age and survey work began, fittingly, on the Fourth of July, 1911. "Soon," the planners said, "Mount Washington will have an electric necklace and a crown of cement."

JOHN KEENAN
SEPTEMBER 1912

In 1912, John Keenan was preparing to make his way in the world. He finished high school in Charlestown, Massachusetts, and secured a position as an elevator operator. Then, in the third week of September, he went north to take a job with the survey crew on the Mount Washington trolley job.

John was an unlikely candidate for such heroic enterprise; he was afraid of darkness and easily frightened by animals and other woodland hazards, and he reported for his first day of work on Mount Washington wearing fashionable street shoes and a pink-and-white striped shirt better suited to a lawn party. That was Friday, September 13, and he was assigned to odd jobs around the base of the cog track. The next Wednesday he was sent up the mountain with the surveyors.

Mr. H. S. Jewell was in charge of twenty-one men, and it was a rough and ready crew. They lived at the base and after dinner they played poker with such passion that Mr. Jewell often had to step in and restore a measure of order by redistributing lopsided pots. The men carried guns all the time and shot at almost anything that moved. One got a huge deer, but, as a thankless beneficiary put it, "You might just as well try to eat your shoes." If live game

In 1908 a fire destroyed most of the summit buildings atop Mount Washington. An astonishing new hotel was planned, shown in this prospectus, to be served by an electric trolley. Survey work for the trolley began in 1911 but was stopped in 1912. On one of the last days of work, John Keenan disappeared in a cloud near the summit and was never seen again.

was not in sight, they'd shoot at improvised targets and bet on their hits. They found the slide boards the cog railway company had confiscated a generation earlier and survived every ride down the mountain on them, and they found a huge but rickety Winton automobile that was rigged with railroad wheels and for a nightcap they'd get this started and drive seventy miles an hour down the Boston & Maine track, no lights. The fresh-faced elevator operator from Boston didn't fit in, and they teased him about his fears.

The valleys around Mount Washington had been unusually warm for September and on the day John went up for his first day of work it touched 81° in the valley, the leading edge of a cell of hot air that would push temperatures into the 90s later in the week. At times like this, the prevailing westerlies drive warm damp air up the windward flank of the Presidential Range, orographic cooling condenses the moisture, and clouds as dense as milk can envelop the rocks with startling speed.

John was to serve as the back-flag man, the one who stands at the last point fixed by the transit party to give them the base for the next angle. The crew was working on the south side of the summit cone and not far from the summit; the place where William Ormsbee died was just below them and the place where Harry Hunter died in 1874 was further down the cone and a bit to the east. Lifting their eyes, they could see the broad and lovely expanse of Bigelow Lawn and the place where Father Bill Curtis died.

John Keenan's first day on the heights was not pleasant. The wind on the summit was blowing more than 50 miles an hour, the sky was overcast, and the temperature was about 40°. This was not uncommon for September and the survey crew went to work, first warning their new man that the clouds could close in very quickly and if this happened he should stay where he was and they'd come to get him. By mid-morning the transit crew was near the Ormsbee marker and facing the Lakes of the Clouds, and John had the back flag about 100 feet away. At ten o'clock a sudden cloud enveloped them and he disappeared.

The crew waited half an hour for the cloud to lift. It didn't lift, it grew thicker. The crew yelled for John to come in, but he didn't. One of the men went to the place where they'd left him and he wasn't there. They all fired their guns, still with no result. Then one of them went to the summit and telephoned the base. "Jewell," he said, "that new fellow you sent up here, we lost him." Mr. Jewell said, "Well, stay up there until you find him."

The survey crew searched the area until nightfall and found no trace of him. There was a large bell on the summit and that was rung steadily all night, there was a steam plant at the base station of the cog railway and Mr. Jewell arranged to have a whistle blast sounded every minute all night long, and the base crew strung lanterns all around their dormitory by the river in case young Keenan used his head and followed the Ammonoosuc stream down. Mr. Jewell sent a telegram to the B&M headquarters in Boston and the reply came back, "Spare no expense. Find the boy."

That evening calls went out to the principal hotels in Fabyans, Randolph, Gorham, and Bretton Woods, the four tourist centers around the Presidential Range. A strong wind continued to blow all night on the heights, but by the next morning the air was almost calm, with the same chill.

High-elevation weather continued bad on Thursday, but Mr. Jewell lead a search party of survey workers, cog railway crews, and the staff of *Among the Clouds*. They spent the whole day groping through the dense clouds above timberline and found no sign of their back-flag man. The weather turned

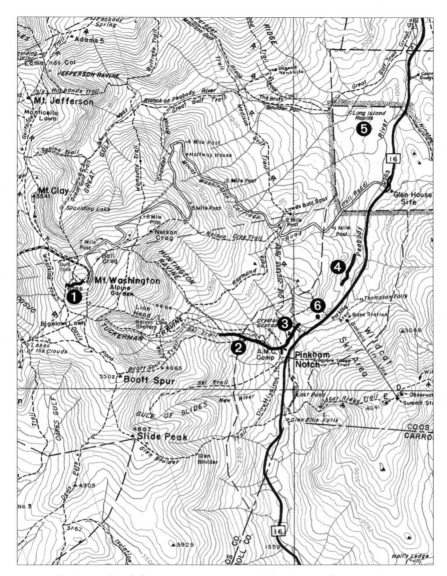

1. John Keenan's only known time on Mount Washington was here
2. Probably reached road by lower Cutler River
3, 4. Seen twice on road
5. Milliken's Pond drained
6. The Darby Field

sharply colder on Friday and the enveloping fog was glazing the rocks with ice. Search parties widened their scope and still found nothing. Mr. Jewell called Burge Bickford, the famous one-armed guide in Gorham, and asked him to gather a crew of all the woodsmen he could find and head for the Glen House. Mr. Jewell said, "I saw fifty men go into the woods and I saw fifty come out." Burge Bickford's men had searched far and wide and had no words of hope.

Friday was marked by one of the weather contrasts which so often complicate hiking on the Presidential Range; the surrounding valleys enjoyed what residents thought was one of the finest days of the season, with bright sun and sweet warm airs, while fog and ice beset the searchers on the heights.

At about 11:00 that morning, Fire Warden Briggs was making a tour of some of the skid roads left by the many logging operations that had been pursued in the White Mountains. This one led to the Pinkham Notch road near the Darby Field, a clearing around a lodging house two miles south of the Glen House. Warden Briggs heard a noise in a thicket of spruce slash and stopped to listen. Then he saw a man and they both said hello. The stranger climbed up to Warden Briggs and asked what day it was. Learning that it was Friday, he said that he'd been out for two days, that he was lost, and that he was looking for the Keenan farm.

Then he said that he'd been working for a survey party on Mount Washington and his boss was Mr. Jewell and he had fallen down a ravine thirty feet deep, but he did not say that he was hungry, he just asked for a piece of spearmint gum. Warden Briggs thought it was an unsatisfactory exchange; the man's talk was rambling and incoherent, the clearest part having to do with his search for the Keenan farm. Warden Briggs had further doubts. For one thing, the man was wearing a fancy pink-and-white striped shirt. Beyond that, the warden did not believe the account of Mr. Jewell's survey party because he knew that Mr. Jewell ran a livery stable in Gorham. He thought the stranger could not be a surveyor or have any other kind of work on the mountain because no person would go to the heights wearing the clothes this fellow had on.

Warden Briggs knew the territory as well as anyone could and he knew that there was no family named Keenan anywhere in the Glen, so he decided that the stranger was sound of limb, but failing in his mind. Warden Briggs brought him out to the road and directed him to the Glen House two miles north along the road, then he went to his own camp half a mile away in the opposite direction to attend to other duties. The incident was certainly unusual, but Warden Briggs was a man of experience and he took unusual incidents in stride.

That day, Honorable George Turner and Dr. Gile were driving the roads around the Presidential Range. Mr. Turner was familiar with the area; he lived in Bethlehem, just west of Mount Washington. Now he was a representative to the state government in Concord and a member of the Governor's Council. Dr. Gile was a representative from Hanover, and on Friday he and Mr. Turner were inspecting the state roads in the north country, roads which at this time were little more than one-lane rocky tracks.

Shortly before noon, they were on the Pinkham Notch road and they passed a young man who made an odd impression on them. They were driving slowly in their open car, but he did not call out to them; he seemed to have a vacant expression on his face and he waved his arms and pointed up at Mount Washington looming above them. The two inspectors did not know that a man was missing, so they continued their drive along the road.

There was a second car in the inspection party that day. It was driven by a Bethlehem chauffeur named Howard Lightfoot, who had been engaged to carry the luggage of Honorable Turner and Dr. Gile. Mr. Lightfoot had fallen some ways behind them, and later in the day he reported that about noon he was flagged down by a young man who asked for a ride. This was on Darby Field hill, a little less than two miles south of the Glen House, but the story was soon contradicted by men in more authority than the chauffeur.

The inspectors were lodging at Fabyans, fifty miles away on the opposite side of the mountain, and when they arrived that evening they learned that a man was lost and that his description matched the apparition they'd seen in Pinkham Notch. Honorable Turner called the base station of the cog railway with the news.

This was the day of heavy clouds and ice on the upper elevations and the search party was going to spend the night in one of the summit buildings. Word was passed along that they should go down to the Glen House early the next morning, Saturday, and join Mr. Bickford's men.

Reporters from the Boston newspapers had gotten wind of the story and soon they were everywhere. There was no news to report, so they began making up their own. One of them offered Mr. Jewell a large sum of money to go off for a week so he could write that even Mr. Jewell had gotten lost and came struggling out of the wilderness a week later. One of them made himself the hero of his own news story, saying he'd joined the search party and been attacked by a wildcat.

Saturday was a day of mixed weather in the Glen, by turns sunny and gray with temperatures in the 70s and afternoon showers. The newly formed search party at the Glen House soon found Warden Briggs. The searchers told him that a man was missing from the heights; they described John Keenan, and asked the warden if he'd seen anything out of the ordinary.

He had indeed. Warden Briggs said that the previous morning he'd met a crazy man coming down the old logging road at the Darby Field, very near the place on the state road where the inspectors had seen a person of the same description, and Mr. Briggs provided so many details that the searchers knew it was John Keenan. Now they knew that John had been started along the road toward the Glen House the previous morning and that Warden Briggs thought he was in good physical condition, so they decided that he must have gotten most of the way to the hotel before nightfall. On the basis of these assumptions, they spent all of Saturday searching the area between the Glen House and the Darby Field, but they found no sign of hope.

This day, Lawrence Keenan took the train north from Charlestown to attend the search for his son. He went to the base station of the cog railway and spent the night at the surveyors' camp, then on Sunday morning he took the train to the summit and rode down the carriage road to the Glen House and joined the search party there.

This was September 22, and the first stretch of tolerable weather since John disappeared four days earlier; it was almost 20° warmer, but steady rain began in the afternoon. By now, more than 100 searchers had gathered at the Glen House, including photographer Guy Shorey. They made a detailed search of the land between there and the Darby Field, they pushed into the woods for a mile on either side of the road, they waded through the Peabody River running beside the road, and they even drained Milliken's Pond, still without effect.

Mr. Keenan pronounced himself satisfied with the effort and that night he went back to Charlestown, stating that he had given up all hope of seeing his son again. The next day the search party was disbanded, though a small group of guides and surveyors continued to look for difficult places they might have missed.

Later that week, Howard Lightfoot returned to the Glen and pressed his story on whoever would listen. He said that on Friday he was driving through Pinkham Notch with the inspectors' luggage and about noontime he was half a mile from the Glen House and he came upon a man waving his arms wildly, as if to stop the car. Then the man got in with the chauffeur.

Mr. Lightfoot said that his passenger was about twenty years old and was wearing a pink-and-white shirt with attached cuffs from which the cuff links had been lost. He said that he remembered this in particular because it was not something he'd expect to see on a tramp or a mountain boy, and because the fellow was not wearing a coat or an undershirt despite the inclement weather.

The chauffeur carried this strange person about two miles along the road and when they reached the old lumber camps near the Darby Field the stranger said, "I think I want to get out here. Yes, this is the place I want to get out." Then he asked where the Keenan farm was and how far it was to Charlestown and how far it was to Franklin. Learning that it was more than 150 miles to Charlestown, he said, "Yes, I guess it is quite a ways." Mr. Lightfoot was struck by his rambling talk and how he didn't seem to be much bothered by his situation even though it was cold and raining hard. But time was wasting and Mr. Lightfoot was anxious to catch up with the inspectors, so he drove away down the road without even looking to see where the fellow went.

In fact, Mr. Lightfoot already knew that a man was missing from a survey crew on Mount Washington, but he did not believe he'd met that person because, as he put it, "I would have looked for a bright-looking fellow dressed as you might have expected a surveyor would. This fellow was not bright looking. He had a slightly receding chin and, if I remember right, his nose was a little larger than the average man. He drooled at the mouth, which might have been due to his being cold and wet, although he was apparently suffering from neither cold nor hunger."

When the chauffeur got home the next day he was shown a copy of *The Boston Post* with a picture of the lost man, but it did not seem to be the person he'd met on the road. Then he was shown a picture in *The Boston Herald*, and he decided at once that it was Keenan who had been his passenger.

This new account reached the Glen House after the 100-man search party had been disbanded, but it was quickly understood that at the time of the great effort on Sunday none of the searchers knew that John Keenan had been taken two miles back to the Darby Field, so their search had not covered some likely terrain. Another group was organized to cover the territory around the Darby Field and the old logging camps, but they found nothing.

A week after the disappearance on Mount Washington, strange nighttime noises were heard near the Glen House, it was as if someone was shouting or crying out. A new search was organized the next morning and concluded before dark. The same week, Mrs. Keenan came up from Boston and visited the spot where her son was last seen, then she went home. A call came to the Glen House one night that week to say that John had been found, but the source of the call was never learned, nor the place of the sighting. Another sighting was reported in Woodstock, nearly 100 miles away at the south end of Franconia Notch, but nothing came of that report, either.

Ten days after the cloud settled over John, his mother had new word for a reporter with *The Boston Journal*: "My son is alive," she said, "and confined in a hospital alongside a river in the west." Pressed for an explanation, Mrs. Keenan said that he'd been picked up by an automobile driver and taken there. Then she began to sob and said, "The lad is in an unconscious condition, and if I only knew the hospital where he is located I would go there immediately." The reporter could not learn where she'd gotten this news, but she said that her in-laws had gotten the same report. Some said that the source was a clairvoyant. By this time, skeptics were denying that John had been seen by anyone at all since he disappeared in the fog.

Two weeks after the disappearance, *The Littleton Courier*, published twenty miles west of Mount Washington, had more plausible news. According to the *Courier*, Mr. O. A. Wood, a guest at Pleasant View Cottage in Twin Mountain, had found a water dipper and a knapsack while hiking on Mount Washington, and it was presumed that John was carrying just such items as these when he disappeared. Closer study showed that it was not a knapsack but a particular type of double-closure bag used only by surveyors, but Mr. Jewell's men said that John did not have one of these on his first day of work. John was wearing a coat and a hat and carrying his back-flag staff when he disappeared, but the man seen by Honorable Turner and Dr. Gile, by Warden

Briggs, and by Howard Lightfoot did not have any of these things and none of them was ever found.

The Keenan family had not entirely given up. They'd been writing to hospitals in the United States and Canada, and on November 26 *The Boston Post* carried a story that a person answering John's description had been found in the hospital of St. Jean de Dieu in Montreal, an asylum for the insane. George Villeneuve was the superintendent at St. Jean and he'd written to the Keenans: "In answer to your letter of November 23 I beg to inform you that the person answering the description you give in this letter has been admitted into this hospital since September. All those admitted since that date are known."

Hope surged, and the Boston & Maine Railroad sent Mr. Jewell to investigate. He was met in Montreal by a driver in a handsome sleigh with a luxurious robe, but he found no basis for the report. Then it was discovered that one word in the letter had been miscopied by the doctor's secretary. "I beg to inform you that the person answering the description you give . . ." should have read, "I beg to inform you that *no* person answering the description you give . . ."

That was the last entry in the story of young John Keenan, but the mystery continued to occupy the citizens of the North Country. Many of them were guides or hunters, or they worked on the carriage road or on the cog railway, and they knew how frightening and disorienting the sudden cloud-bank whiteouts can be even for someone perfectly familiar with the trails and the lay of the land above timberline.

John Keenan knew nothing at all of that world, he was in his first hours on Mount Washington, and he was not on a trail when the cloud covered him. Indeed, he might not even have known that the piled-up rocks marked a trail, and the white paint marks along the trail might have looked like the lichens that grew everywhere above timberline.

That day, rain was being driven by a cold wind at a steady 50 miles an hour from the west, and those familiar with such situations knew that there's an almost irresistible impulse to walk downwind: it avoids a cold face, it takes less effort, and there seems to be a subtle prompting from nature itself that this is the right direction to go.

That wind would have pushed John eastward around the summit cone and toward the terrain funnel leading into Tuckerman Ravine, but the precipices ahead of him would have been intimidating. The ridges of Lion Head and Boott Spur on his left and right would have been easier going, but he might not have been able to see them in the fog and they would have kept him in the wind for much longer, so the chances were good that John had scrambled down through the ravine. He could have picked up the trail on the floor of the ravine or he could have followed the watercourse of the Cutler River which drains the ravine; in either case he would have come out on the Pinkham Notch road in the near vicinity of the place Warden Briggs had seen the demented stranger.

As it happened, he'd been seen by Warden Briggs at about 11:00 A.M., by the road inspectors between 11:30 and noon, and by Howard Lightfoot perhaps fifteen minutes after noon. Warden Briggs was in the best position to help him, but his doubts about the story were confirmed when he heard that the survey party was led by Mr. Jewell. He knew that Mr. Jewell was not a surveyor, he kept a livery stable in Gorham. Warden Briggs did not know that there were two men named Jewell: H. S. led the survey party, W. W. kept the livery stable.

In addition to these many missed connections, there was the condition of John Keenan. By the time he met Warden Briggs he was already in such a distressed state that he did not recognize help when it appeared, nor perhaps even his own need for help. Instead, he tried again and again to make his way back into the perils that had already cost him so much. No trace of John was ever found and no cause of death ever assigned, but a coroner's jury might rule that he died of complications attending the sudden onset of dread.

THERE IS NO MARKER ANYWHERE TO REMEMBER THE DEATH OF John Keenan, and even the tokens of his difficulties are almost gone. There is no water today that could be Milliken's Pond and the name does not register in local memory. Mr. C. R. Milliken built and managed the second edition of the Glen House, 1887–1903, so the pond must have been in the near vicinity of the Glen House and it must have been large enough and deep enough that draining was both necessary and possible. The Peabody River is not a large stream here and its bed near the Glen House does show the footings of an old dam about 100 yards upstream from the crossing of the Mount Washington auto road. But the channel is very narrow and, given the terrain, any ponded water would have been so shallow as to be transparent to the bottom, not anything that would require draining.

This puzzled me. Then, while looking through an old family trunk for a mid-nineteenth century property deed, I found a panoramic photograph I'd never seen before. Given family habits, it must have been taken by my grandfather in about 1910, and the view was straight up Great Gulf, with Mount Washington on the left, the Northern Peaks on the right, and a lake in the foreground. An hour of bushwhacking established the place where grandfather must have stood, then I walked straight into the picture.

The terrain drops to Route 16 and runs level for about seventy yards beyond the road, then there's a steep drop twenty feet down to a broad flat swale which, by the evidence, is a favorite with moose. Then there's the Peabody River. Not far downstream the stubs of heavy planking rise up through the shallow water and for another 100 feet the rocky bottom is laced from shore to shore with immense square-cut timbers fastened with wrought-iron spikes, all bracing the planks against the pressures of long-gone freshets. This was the dam which formed Milliken's Pond, with a spillway for draining.

Then, in one of the converging surprises that can accompany even the most obscure studies, I came across a framed picture in our house which I'd been looking at for many years without ever really seeing. The back shows that it came from the Cummings & Son art shop in Oberlin, Ohio, and it shows the long prospect up Great Gulf from a point somewhat south of the panorama. There's quiet water in the foreground; it's only a few inches deep and it reflects the tree-framed mountains. This can only be the far upstream end of Milliken's Pond, there's no other flat water in the Peabody River until several miles farther along toward Gorham.

My aunt Harriet was born in 1900, and her first job after college was in Oberlin. So Milliken's Pond provided no help in the search for John Keenan and its very existence was ephemeral, but it gained a much longer life as foreground for our family pictures. My grandfather probably took this one on the same day as the panorama and when aunt Harriet set out to make a career far from home she put the picture in her suitcase; when she reached Oberlin she went to Cummings & Son and had it framed to remind her of the mountains she loved so much.

There's another landmark in the Keenan story. The search parties kept passing what they called The Darby Field and contemporary texts suggest that they did well not to stop there: it was a large but ramshackle hostelry serving hunters, fishermen, and other travelers and run by "Hod" Reed, a man well known for his close association with Demon Rum. This, the old accounts say, was just past The Darby Field hill. Now the Wildcat Ski Area is at the crest of a long hill and a little farther along is the state road camp, the place where snowplows and sand are kept waiting for winter storms. Mr. Reed's establishment stood on this spot in the days before snowplows and even before most automobiles, excepting the small caravan of road agents who narrowly missed saving John Keenan. Today, a metal sign stands across the road from the state camp announcing that it was near this spot that Mr. Darby Field began his historic first ascent of Mount Washington in 1642. Denizens of the notch must have chuckled at the tidy little play on words that let them call this mountain pasture The Darby Field.

The many missed connections in this episode contrast with a step into the future that had been made at Madison Spring Hut, less than six miles across the Northern Peaks from the place where John Keenan disappeared. The Ravine House was a large hotel and highly favored by the hiking community that animated the town of Randolph. That summer the hotel contracted with the Coos County Telephone Company and a telephone line was strung 3.7 miles from the Ravine House up the Valley Way trail to Madison Spring Hut above timberline. This was for the convenience of hikers who might want to send messages in either direction and it earned $7.60 in tolls the first summer and $13.00 the next year. It was disconnected soon after that, but some of the white china insulators that carried the wire can still be seen screwed into the trees along the Valley Way.

Mr. Mellen's enterprise fared no better than John Keenan. The Boston & Maine Railroad collapsed under his management, and although he spoke vaguely of reorganization, the lumber companies had other straws in the wind. The Weeks Act had just passed and the national forest was being established. Perhaps sensing that the United States was a more substantial partner than Charles Mellen and his amazing schemes, the lumbermen sold their land and the trolley's right of way to the government.

Still, though, it seemed that the survey marks left by Mr. Jewell's rowdy crew must still be in the rocks—it is in their nature to endure. The crew used a ⅜-inch drill to make some 6,300 holes about half an inch deep in the rock;

they ran along the center line of the right of way the crew pushed through the woods of the lower elevations, through the almost impenetrable thickets approaching timberline, and across the rocks and ledges of the alpine zone.

The trolley plan called for a double row of utility poles to carry the many miles of electric lines, but the organizers didn't say how and for how long they thought these would withstand the violent weather on the heights of the Presidential Range. Now, eighty-six years and perhaps 20,000 cycles of melt and freeze have passed and even the drill holes seem to have been smudged beyond discovery.

The work of many patient summer days, however, found three sets of marks that do not match the scallop-shaped weathering on the mica schist rocks above timberline on the range. The first to catch my eye was below the point where the Caps Ridge Trail crosses the Cornice Trail on Mount Jefferson; they're aligned in the right direction and they're at the right elevation for the trolley route between its upper switchback at Castellated Ridge and its passage along the col between Mounts Jefferson and Clay. But they weren't neat ⅜-inch drill holes half an inch deep, they were rounded squares half an inch deep and I regarded them with caution. I found a pair of similar marks just above the location of the old Gulfside tank beside the cog railway track on the side toward the Great Gulf headwall and these, too, were aligned as logic and terrain suggests they would be. But they still didn't look like the holes I was expecting, two holes do not a survey make, and I rejected them for lack of confirming evidence.

Then I found a contemporary citation indicating an exact spot the trolley would pass on the lower of its two circuits around the summit cone, so I bore down on this area, I studied it on my hands and knees. An alpine meadow starts here and it rises with a moderate grade, just the sort of natural aid a prudent survey crew would favor.

As on the Northern Peaks, the rock of the Mount Washington summit cone is a grainy mica schist and the surface weathers into myriad small dishes overlapping each other on every upturned side. At a point near a corner of the meadow I found a change in the pattern; instead of another scallop, there was a rounded hole half an inch deep and about the size of a small postage stamp, and very much like the holes on Jefferson and on the north side of the summit cone. I'd been looking for ⅜-inch holes for six days, but I found none. So perhaps the work of those 20,000 cycles of melt and freeze did not leave the rock untouched, perhaps the grainy schist flaked away around the small round drill hole and left this larger rounded shape as its descendant.

Seventy rising paces across the meadow there's another one of these marks, and seventy rising paces farther along there's another one. That convinced me. These must be all that's left of the electric necklace that lifted those boardroom hearts at the floodtide of *la belle epoque*. Now they reward the attentive eye with a tiny variant in the patterns of ancient weathered rock, and Sylvester Marsh's cog trains still pant and chuff up the western flank of the mountain, neither train nor terrain substantially changed since 1869.

Chapter Seven

THE MAYOR OF PORKY GULCH
TAKES OFFICE

*T*HE SHAPE OF THE PRESIDENTIAL RANGE IS VERY LARGELY the work of the Laurentide ice sheet, which arrived in 23,000 B.C. The character of the Presidential Range is very largely the work of Joe Dodge, who arrived in 1922 A.D.

The Dodge family arrived on the American shore in 1638. They settled in Salem, Massachusetts, and in the next 260 years they moved only a few miles north to Manchester-by-the-Sea, where they pursued the woodcrafter's trades. Joseph Brooks Dodge made his first appearance on December 26, 1898; as he liked to put it, "I was a great Christmas present." When Joe was a boy the family was still engaged in the furniture business; his own interests, however, had already turned elsewhere.

A strong nor'easter blew up the New England coast a month before he was born and the *City of Portland* sank with all hands off Provincetown, Massachusetts. Disasters always make good story-telling, Joe heard this account over and over again, and it pulled his young attentions toward the sea and also toward the weather. Joe wanted to be a locomotive engineer when he grew up, an urge that is widespread in young boys. He also wanted to go to sea, an urge that is widespread in shore-dwellers.

This second calling was more easily tested, and the summer Joe was twelve he managed to secure an entry-level position on a fishing smack and went as far as the Grand Banks before he was required to resume his career in grammar school. All was not lost, though. There was a great fire in Salem when he was fifteen, and, noting that one of the firemen had not come to work, Joe alertly stepped forward and filled in for him stoking Manchester's steam-powered fire engine. This did not lead to a job driving locomotives, so Joe turned to another chance at the future.

One of the central events in every imagination was the loss of the *Titanic* in 1912. Joe had become interested in radio two years earlier and now he was absorbed by the stories of the radio messages that might have averted the disaster, but did not. The first transmissions from the doomed ship had been picked up by a teenager on a rooftop in New York and Joe learned that there was a Marconi wireless station in Wellfleet, out on Cape Cod, so he built a small radio and taught himself Morse code by listening to the Wellfleet traffic.

The first adventure in radio was played out in the Dodges' kitchen. Early radios looked complex, even mysterious, and Joe strung the antenna wires across the ceiling, which was not what most people expected. The very idea of radio was new to most people, and one winter day a relative came to visit and quickly inquired about the unusual utensils in there with the pots and pans. Joe provided a first lesson in the propagation of radio waves and said that the wires would intercept the waves when they came in. The relative, not fully in touch with the new world of electronics, said, "You'll freeze us out when you open the window to let in the waves."

Joe moved on to more powerful radio sets and news of this novelty did not escape wider notice. The Manchester Cricket sent a reporter to inquire and his story ran in the next issue: "Joseph Dodge, who has one of the most complete amateur radio outfits in the country, has achieved some wonderful results of late, and one evening this week gave a startling demonstration in reproducing the voice of a lady as she sang 'solos' in Chicago. The fact of her voice coming from a distance of nearly a thousand miles without the aid of wires and heard perfectly, is almost beyond comprehension. The sound is caught from an antenna and amplified by means of a gramophone horn."

The relative's fears about snowstorms coming through the open window with the radio waves proved unfounded and Joe kept moving. He got his first commercial license when he was sixteen and quickly gained employment on the *SS Bay State* for the Boston–Portland run, a position that required him to wear his first long pants. Joe telephoned his father to tell of his advancing station in life and was told to come home at once. He didn't. He went on board and told the captain that he was a radio operator. The captain cast off and two days later tied up again at the Portland dock. The senior Dodge met the ship, asked Joe how he'd liked it, and took him home. Nothing more was ever said.

Two years later the United States was being drawn into the World War; Joe quit high school the day war was declared and joined the navy on February 14, 1917. He was assigned as instructor in the radio service at Harvard, then in January of 1918 he was reassigned to the Western Electric laboratories in New York to learn radio telephone and this led to the navy base in New London, where he set up a radio telephone school and research laboratory. One day he was put aboard a submarine for a training mission and, once at sea, the vessel sank. No one on board could find a way to bring it back to the surface and the situation looked grave indeed; then the young radioman stepped forward and, with only a pair of pliers, he found the trouble and effected the repair. The engines were restarted and the ballast blown, and the submarine was soon back on the surface.

Joe mustered out of the navy in 1920 with the rating of Chief Electrician (Radio) and quickly joined the merchant marine. He signed onto the *J. M. Danziger*, an oil tanker under Mexican flag, and made port in Tampico just as Alvaro Obregon's revolution was breaking out. The rebels attacked the ship with machine guns and Joe returned fire by throwing rocks at them. That proved sufficient and the *Danziger* eventually headed into harbor in Newport, Rhode Island. The captain had not picked up a pilot, though, and first they hit a sewer line and then they took thirty feet off the end of the dock. The skipper leaned over the rail of the bridge, spit a cud of tobacco past Joe's ear, and said, "Well, Sparks, I guess we made a grandstand finish."

Thus ended Joe's ocean-going career, but another stone had already been cast. In 1909, he and his father headed north toward the mountains. They followed the usual route of the day: a steamer from Boston to Portland, Maine, a train from Portland to Glen, New Hampshire, and a buckboard from there up the narrow rocky road through Pinkham Notch to take lodgings in the Glen House, the famous hotel at the foot of the carriage road that led to the summit of Mount Washington.

The senior and junior Dodges did not take a carriage. They hiked up the road to 2-Mile, then turned off on the Raymond Path that led to the floor of Tuckerman Ravine. They climbed up through the ravine and spent the night in the old Tip-Top House, hiked down the Southern Peaks on the Crawford Path, found the station in Fabyans and took the train back to Portland, thence home by steamer.

In those days young men were expected to take their place in the family business, and when Joe left the good ship *Danziger* he made a try at the furniture trades, but it didn't work out. He odd-jobbed his way around Maine for a year or so, then in 1922 he learned that an organization called the Appalachian Mountain Club had a small encampment in Pinkham Notch, at the foot of Mount Washington. He remembered that the hiking trip he'd taken with his father had gone right past that place, so he made inquiries. The club had one employee at their office in Boston and he offered Joe a bunk at Pinkham Notch.

That was June 9, 1922, there were two log cabins and several army surplus pyramid tents at Pinkham, and Joe went to work. His first job was to fasten a roof over the outdoor washstand, the better to shelter guests against inclement weather.

Other visitors were both better adapted to the elements and more frequent in their visits: porcupines. These natives were so numerous, and so attentive to the buildings and supplies, that Joe and his partner would kill as many as a dozen in one night. The state game wardens paid a bounty on porcupines, so the noses would be taken to Gorham and redeemed at the rate of twenty-five cents per. Then the hutmen would redeem the coins for strawberries and cream, which they'd take back to the notch and make what they called porcupine shortcake. The recipe for that staple is lost to history, but the name that summer inspired is not—Joe called his new lodgings Porky Gulch.

Bears were also frequent visitors and they, too, were convertible assets. The Cutler River flows out of Tuckerman Ravine and eventually drops into Crystal Cascade just above the AMC settlement beside the Pinkham Notch road. There's a deep pool below the cascade and one day Joe found a dead bear in the water there; as he told a visitor, "Committed suicide, I guess." The late bear was many days gone and quite smelly, and Joe thought that no game warden would want to give him even temporary accommodations, so

Joe Dodge found his life's work when he arrived at the AMC base camp in Pinkham Notch in 1922. Over the next 36 years he'd change the lives of countless hikers and save the lives of many.

he took the bear around the circuit of game wardens and collected the five-dollar bounty in four different towns.

The AMC camp in Pinkham Notch was open for summer use only and Joe kept coming back. In 1925 and 1926 he was chief carpenter in building the "portables," which were bunkhouses to extend the lodging capacity. As the summer of 1926 drew to a close he proposed a plan that would keep him at the AMC settlement over the winter: he'd care for the cabins there, attend to the needs of what few climbers as might come by, and make occasional trips to the huts at Lakes of the Clouds, Carter Notch, and Madison Springs to see that they were holding out the elements and other intruders who might have designs on them. Joe did not have to wait long for the first real test in the thirty-six years he would spend in Porky Gulch.

MAX ENGELHART
OCTOBER 1926

No warm season ever matched 1926 for cold. The snow arch in Tuckerman Ravine did not fall until September 3, the last snow in the ravine disappeared on September 23, and five inches of new snow fell the next day. The last of the old winter's snow melted on October 4; then on the evening of Friday, October 9, a great storm broke over New England and by morning ten inches of snow had fallen on the AMC encampment in Pinkham Notch and it was still coming down hard. After breakfast the temperature suddenly dropped and a strong wind began to drift the snow. By noon, it was worse.

Joe Dodge was not yet fully rigged for winter and Pinkham froze up. The storm continued; indeed, it seemed to intensify. The AMC had a Model T Ford truck called Ringtail and Saturday afternoon Joe drove fifteen miles down the notch road to Intervale to meet the train. On the way back he rescued a dozen vehicles on the steep northbound grade of Spruce Hill, which had not yet reached the standards of a gravel road; in fact, it wasn't much more than a rocky one-lane track. By Sunday afternoon the weather had broken in the valleys, but Joe could see the cloud base racing across the ridges above Pinkham and he knew that was a sure sign of desperate conditions on the heights.

On Monday afternoon, Joe drove ten miles north to Gorham to borrow blowtorches so he could thaw the water pipes of Porky Gulch. On the way back, he stopped at the Glen House to get some milk and they told him that Max Engelhart was missing.

The two hotels on the summit of Mount Washington had closed in the third week of September, but there were still hikers on the range and if they

"The Stage Office" on Mount Washington housed the first year-round weather observatory in the 1870s. It was used again when observers re-occupied the summit in 1933. Max Engelhart was serving snacks here when a storm overtook him in October 1926.

wanted shelter and found a closed building, they tended to break in. The auto road company had a small building on the summit known as the stage office, so the plan was to keep it open until October 15 in hopes of deflecting people who might otherwise break into the Summit House and the Tip-Top House.

Max Engelhart had been the cookee at the Glen House, the second cook, and he'd been sent up to the stage office. Max was to provide sandwiches and small provisions as needed for hikers or others who might come up by the road. He was supplied with food, water, and firewood, and he was there at the onset of the great storm on Thursday evening.

Two hikers had taken lodgings at the Glen House in hopes of climbing to the summit. They'd arrived with the storm and waited four days for the weather to moderate, then on Monday they started up the auto road. They'd been told that Max Engelhart was living in the stage office and they should tell him to come down with them.

This sentiment was widespread. Dennis Pelquark worked for the summit road company and he wrote, "Much concern had been held out for the man, cast alone on the wind- and storm-swept mountain for two days. The gist of the talk in mountain camps, hotels and the country-side was about the keeper's danger." The wind was still strong, but the two Glen House guests pushed through the drifts and blowing snow and reached the summit, then they went to the stage office for shelter and found a room full of snow. Max Engelhart was not there.

The hikers brought this news down to the Glen House and Joe stopped by on his way back from Gorham with the blowtorches. The clerk asked Joe if there was a stranger with him at the AMC camp. There wasn't, but Joe knew Max was an old woodsman and trapper from Quebec and his friendly salute was more direct than the road worker's elevated words. Max was, Joe said, "A goddam wild Frenchman."

He also knew that Max was fifty-eight years old and although he was very much at home in the woods, he was not accustomed to the rigors of life above timberline on Mount Washington, much less was he equipped for surviving an assault such as the storm just ending. Joe also knew that Max was smart. If life in the stage office became too difficult, Max would surely move a few yards to Camden Cottage, a sturdier building and a well-known fortress against the wintry blast.

The two climbers brought down a note from the stage office: "Laf at 12 for Tocmans Arien—no wood." The Glen House crew thought it might be some kind of code. Joe asked to talk to the climbers and they said there wasn't any firewood in the stage office and there was a six-foot drift of snow that blew in through the cracks. They also reported footprints in the hard packed snow of the auto road about a half-mile above the Halfway House, as the old "Camp House" was now called. They said the track led downhill and they thought it was made by Max, nearing the safety of the woods.

No one could make much sense of this—if Max had gotten that far, why hadn't he come the last, easy sheltered miles? Plans were made to send a search party up the road early the next day. Joe said, "You can count on two of us in the morning." He meant himself and Arthur Whitehead, his partner at the AMC camp, and always called Whitey. The two of them talked it over and, as Dennis Pelquark put it, "they, being of the character of real mountaineers, God-fearing and healthy strong youths, brought to light all their theories."

Other theories were brought to light during Monday evening at the Glen House. Someone remembered that a carpenter named Paul LeClair had been

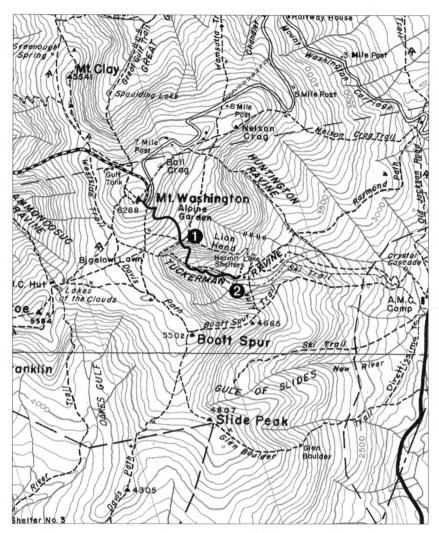

1. Max Engelhart probably went down Right Gulley in Tuckerman Ravine
2. Found in brook near base of Little Headwall

working on the summit the previous week and he came down a few hours before the storm started on the ninth. His boots had probably cut into old snow and the prints were bared by the wind after the four-day snowfall just ended. That would account for the tracks the climbers saw. The puzzling note from Max could be read: "Left at noon for Tuckerman Ravine."

Joe and Whitey returned to the Glen House the next morning with heavy clothing, a hatchet, a hunting knife, a long coil of rope, a flashlight, food, hot coffee in Thermos bottles, and binoculars. They were joined by five men from the Glen House: Fred Pike, Elliott Libby, Dennis Pelquark, and two others. The news of the missing man was already in the state and national press, but no men came from Gorham, as they had hoped, much less from farther away.

The rescue party started up the auto road in one of the vehicles that were used for the summer trade. These were monumental seven-passenger 1917 Pierce Arrow touring cars with the high sweeping lines of a steel-and-leather prairie schooner. The men put tire chains on the Pierce and got almost three miles up the road before it foundered in the new snow. They knew there was a crew closing up the Halfway House for the winter and they expected them to join the search effort, but those men declined the chance to help, which struck Joe and Whitey as rather callous.

The Halfway House was just below timberline, and a mile farther up the road the rescue party ran into the full force of the storm. They could see only about thirty feet and rime quickly built up on their clothes and hair as they pushed on to the summit through waist-deep drifts and stinging blowing ice. Joe and Whitey and Dennis realized they were stronger climbers than the other four and they went on ahead, taking care to look for places along the road where Max might have tried to find shelter. The stage office was, as Dennis wrote, "a grotto of frost, snow, and emptiness, the remaining coffee in the pot frozen solid, indicating very severe temperatures." Max was indeed missing.

The bed in the stage office was in good order and there was a considerable amount of food on the shelves, but as the men looked through the other effects they realized that there were heavy clothes hanging on the wall. One of the men thought he remembered another bed in the stage office and found its splintered remains in the large airtight stove, charred but not burned. They also noticed that there was no money in the box where Max kept the coins

An observatory crewman climbs the section of the auto road known as Five-Mile Drift in 1935.

he collected for sandwiches and they knew that the keeper had not brought much of a wardrobe up to the summit, so they gathered from the missing money, the failed fire, and the clothes on the wall that Max had probably departed quickly, without intention of returning and without much thought of what lay ahead.

The slower members of the party appeared twenty minutes later and joined in a tour of the summit buildings. Nothing seemed amiss and Camden Cottage had not been used. Back in the stage office, Joe spotted what appeared to be writing on the wall, mostly covered with rime. He brushed it clear and found: "*Je pars, date Oct 11 1925. Poudre de neige; le vent souffle d'une force de 100 miles à l'heure; maisante, temperature trés mugir. Max*" (Snowing, wind blows 100 miles an hour, temperature very low.) The caretaker had left the building two days ago.

Joe knew of several non-standard ways of getting into the Summit House and the Tip-Top House, and, thinking that Max might know of them too, he and Whitey looked into those possibilities and also into Camden Cottage, but there was no sign of Max. They considered the situation and reasoned that when Max left the summit there was a very strong northwest wind blowing, so he would almost certainly have gone downwind, to the southeast. Joe and Whitey decided to continue their search and returned to the stage office to prepare their kit.

During these summit perambulations Joe had been kicking at the frost feathers that formed during the storm, those friable horizontal icicles which build out into the wind and give a sure index of its direction and a good indication of its strength. One fell more heavily than Joe thought it should, so he broke it apart and found a stone inside. Then he knocked loose some of the frost coating the windward side of the stage office and found many small rocks embedded there; the wind had swept them up from the flat graveled area near the cog trestle and hurled them into the ice accumulating on Max's fragile shelter. Now someone remembered that a storm door had been hung on the outside of the door frame and this was gone, evidently torn from its hinges and blown to some distant place. The reasons for his hasty retreat were becoming more clear.

It was now about eleven o'clock in the morning, no sign of Max had been found in the valley, and all the evidence suggested a panicky flight from the summit. Since bewildered hikers tend to go downwind, Max would have gone down the steeper side of the summit cone toward the greater hazards of Tuckerman Ravine. Joe took charge and said that Whitey and Dennis Pelquark should come with him. The others, less experienced, not so well equipped, and apparently more fatigued, should stay in Camden Cottage.

Those four men argued that Joe, Whitey, and Dennis should not continue; they said it was too dangerous to go out onto the unmarked and wind-blasted slopes, and that if Max was still on the higher terrain he was certainly dead. Joe said they were going to do it anyway, and the four announced that they would go back down the road to the valley.

The weather was still severe, with scudding clouds and a strong lashing wind, and Joe and Whitey realized that they were probably searching for a dead man. They stayed thirty or forty feet apart, which was as far as they could see, and as they made their way downslope one or another of them spotted what seemed to be tracks, but each time it turned out to be a trick of the wind-carved snow. They'd see what they thought was a body, but each time it was an oddly-shaped rock. At times they lost their footing and took battering slides down the slope; other times they sank armpit-deep between windbreak rocks.

"Shelter" must be understood conditionally on the heights of the Presidential Range. Here snow blows in through a stoutly sheathed wall. Such conditions drove Max Engelhart out the door and into a ferocious three-day ordeal.

They crawled on all fours to stay on top of the snow and eventually they reached the dwarf spruce near the tops of the ravines. They hoped to find a viewpoint down into Tuckerman Ravine but the going was all but impossible; there were windslab drifts covering the dense scrub growth and they could neither push through the snow nor stay on top of the limbs, so they huddled together for their first rest of the day and considered the situation.

It seemed likely that they'd moved too far to the south, so Joe decided to make a climbing traverse northward across the east side of the summit cone, above the Alpine Garden. It was terribly difficult going; this was the lee side of the mountain and heavily drifted, so again and again they'd break through the windslab surface and sink into shoulder-deep drifts and have to pull themselves out of their sudden prison. Still reasoning that Max would have kept the wind to his back, the three of them pushed on until they'd passed the point at which no downwind line could be drawn from the summit. It occurred to them that, since Max must have had some sense of the shape of the mountain, he might have continued along the lee slope to intercept the auto road above 6-Mile, but still there was no sign of him. They found shelter behind a rock here and took a few minutes for sandwiches, some still-warm coffee, and an eggnog that Joe favored. Then they climbed back to the stage office. It had taken four hours to equal the span of a pleasant summertime hour.

Still not satisfied with the job they'd done, Joe and the other two made another line of search, this time descending to the west of their first track. Max would probably know that there was shelter at the Lakes of the Clouds Hut about a mile away on this heading, and he might have tried for that.

Almost immediately, Dennis found a line of distinct footprints and they followed them with their highest hopes of the day, but the track soon disappeared in a tremendous drift of snow. They struggled back and forth and back and forth over this snowbank, but found no sign of Max. They also noticed that their own tracks, made only a few minutes before, were quickly obliterated by the wind. This meant that there was little chance of finding any tracks Max might have made two days earlier. Now the storm was picking up again, darkness was coming on, and, as Whitey put it later, "the cold came down with almost a crash."

Joe and his two mates hurried back up to the top, had a sip of chilly coffee from their Thermos, and started down the auto road. The wind had risen to such a blast that they had to hold onto each other and push ahead in a kind of stiff troika; they saw white spots on each other's faces where the flesh was freezing and they took off their mitts to wrap on silk handkerchiefs. They hoped to find relief at the Halfway House, and perhaps a little warmth, but when they got there no smoke was coming from chimney and the shutters were all nailed up. At last they found the normal warmth of October and went slipping and sliding in mud on the lower stretches of the auto road.

They had supper at the Glen House and returned to thought. Joe felt that there was no point in spending more time on the summit cone until the air cleared and the wind abated, but Max might have been able to get down into one of the ravines. They had no snowshoes, but if they could borrow some from the Glen House they'd go up and search Tuckerman and Huntington ravines and the adjacent ridges of Boott Spur and Lion Head. The others thought they were crazy, Max was surely dead by now, but Mr. Libby of the Glen House was persuaded to bring some snowshoes to the AMC camp in the morning, so Joe and Whitey drove Ringtail back home, hung their wet clothes out to dry in the cold kitchen, fed the cats, and went to bed. It had been a dispiriting day, nearly twenty-five miles of hard going to learn that they'd do it all again the next day.

Joe and Whitey were almost numb with fatigue, but their minds kept running away from sleep and they were not much rested when they got up on Wednesday. Mr. Libby did not arrive with the snowshoes until 11:30 that morning; he explained that he'd been on the telephone for several hours, talking to Boston newspapers.

This day's climbing was terribly difficult. The snow line was at Crystal Cascade, only a few minutes above the AMC camp, and they had to put on the snowshoes about a mile up the trail. The improved equipment was not a success. The webbing was good, but neither Joe nor Whitey could get their bindings tight enough and the snowshoes flopped about in the snow and snagged on every twig, so the men plunged this way and that trying to keep from falling. Whitey's binding soon broke, and they had to stop while he made a jury-rig from his moccasin laces.

The snow was drifted thigh-deep on the Tuckerman Ravine Trail but they reached Hermit Lake, two and a half miles above the valley, in a time most people couldn't match on a fine summer day. Now they were within the extended arms of the ravine and there was a Forest Service register at Hermit Lake, so while they were resting Joe improved the time by looking over the entries to see when the last hiker had come through.

It was at just this moment that they heard an unexpected sound. Perhaps not trusting their own ears, neither Joe nor Whitey said anything about it.

Then they heard it again. Then they heard it a third time. Their first thought was that it came from a steam engine; the air was still, trains ran frequently through Gorham, and the sound of a whistle could certainly carry eleven miles up to Hermit Lake. It might also be a cry from some other search party; given the fair weather and the anxiety for Max's safety, another group might have started up the mountain without the AMC men knowing about it.

Realizing that they'd both heard the strange wail, Joe and Whitey yelled as loudly as they could. Several echoes come off the walls of the ravine here, but mixed in with their own resounding voices there seemed to be one that did not belong to them, one that sounded like a long tenuous . . . "Help!" Still not trusting their ears, neither Joe nor Whitey said anything hopeful. Instead, they yelled again. When the echoes died away, they still heard the other sound, weak, but unmistakable.

The sound seemed to come from Boott Spur, which forms the south wall of the ravine. Max could certainly be up there. Given the mindless, wind-driven track they imagined for him, he could certainly be up there on the wall of Boott Spur, but Joe and Whitey both privately hoped he wasn't; bringing him down from those steep and rocky heights would be difficult. By now they were rushing toward the sound as fast as they could on their flopping snowshoes and exchanging calls with the undiscovered voice and suddenly Whitey saw a head through the scrubby spruce and birch. It seemed to be disembodied, just a head low down on the snow. Joe said, "Do you see him?" And there he was.

This was just at the place where the Tuckerman Ravine Trail crosses the newborn Cutler River below the steep pitch known as the Little Headwall of the ravine. The stream had not frozen, so there was open water flowing past a large boulder between high banks of drifted new snow. Max was down on the edge of the channel, clinging to a sort of shelf he'd either made or found. It was 1:00 P.M. on Wednesday, October 14, and he had been out in the weather for seventy-three hours.

Max had no hat and what parts of his clothes that were not frozen solid were soaking wet. He was wild-eyed and his face was mottled with frostbite, his lips were black, his tongue was swollen, and his arms and legs were so stiff that Joe and Whitey could hardly bend them at all as they lifted and dragged him out of the Cutler River channel.

Joe Dodge's search for Max Englehart was greatly hampered by the snow drifts that form on the heights of the Presidential Range.

Max seemed almost incoherent, then he saw that Joe and Whitey were stripped down to their shirts and steaming with effort and he said, "Oh, my dears, put on some clothes before you freeze!" Joe and Whitey arranged their snowshoes to make a sort of bed for him and laid him down; they took off his wet clothes and wrapped him in their own spare clothes, and they gave him some food and coffee with brandy mixed in. These attentions revived Max somewhat and he told them to be careful of his jacket because he had the money from his trade at the stage office, it wasn't really his, and he didn't want it to be lost. Then Joe and Whitey lay down close beside him in hopes of giving him some of their body heat and Max did what he could to make them understand his two nights above timberline on the mountain, then a terrifying slide down Tuckerman Ravine and the twenty-four hours he'd been in the stream channel.

Suddenly the three of them were in shadow. The sun had dropped below the barrier of Boott Spur, the temperature dropped abruptly, and they realized they had to get a move on. They'd found Max about halfway out the long floor of the ravine where the terrain is thick with stunted birch and spruce. Joe tried to carry Max on his back while he pushed through the scrub to the trail on his snowshoes, but Max weighed fifty pounds more than Joe did, he was an awkward load, and the snowshoes still flopped uncontrollably. Joe fell almost immediately, then he fell again. This kind of carry was also very painful for Max and, to complicate matters, he couldn't keep anything in his stomach.

Joe and Whitey decided to try a litter carry, so they cut two birch poles and rigged a stretcher with their extra shirts and jackets, but their snowshoes kept jamming between boulders or snagging on the broken branches of the stunted trees and the two men couldn't keep in step with each other. Their progress was so slow and tormented that they gave it up after about three-hundred feet and decided to try a drag carry, what woodsmen call a travois.

They'd need to cut a pair of fir trees for this, so they went down the trail to where the growth was larger and Max became terribly agitated, he thought they were leaving him behind. So Joe and Whitey made as much noise as they could and talked loudly to cheer him up. They came back with two fir poles and this seemed to bring Max back to his old self and his better nature. He told them that in his days as a woodsman he'd always found that it helped to shave the bark off the lower ends of an improvised drag to reduce friction, and he showed them how to rig their ropes to best advantage.

Now they'd brought their tools and devices to as great a perfection as they thought possible and they pushed off again. The terrain here is flat, gravity was not helping at all, and it took almost three hours to go a third of a mile through the deep snow with one man between the poles pulling and the other in back pushing. There were places where they couldn't move the drag at all, so they changed Max's position, but that didn't help much. They plunged and staggered along on their snowshoes, then they lifted Max off the drag and helped him crawl along on all fours. This was more difficult and more time consuming than anything else they'd tried, so Max told them how to rig tump lines and hitch themselves in tandem like a yoke of oxen and they struggled on through the snow, lurching and falling every few steps.

By now they were on the summer trail. Or, more properly, over it. The trees grow very densely at this elevation and they could make out the route of the trail by following the hall-like opening through the trees, but they were past the flats now and the trail twisted and dipped and rose again as it followed the lay of the land. There were places where the turns were sharper than the length of their drag could negotiate and Max rolled off and crawled so they could move the poles around the corner. The snowshoes were a continual agony and Max joined in the volleys of curses directed at them, so they concluded that he was feeling better.

Darkness began to overtake the embattled trio by the time they'd made a half-mile to the good, and there was still a quarter-mile to go before they reached the upper crossing of the Cutler River. By this point the stream was no easy hop-across, it was a full mountain torrent and they'd been dreading the ordeal of crossing even as they tried to imagine a way they could do it. They also realized that their progress with the drag was becoming prohibitively slow, so they left it near the junction of the Raymond Path; one of the men carried all their equipment and the other slung Max over his shoulder and carried him, or half-pushed him and half-dragged him along on the ground.

The stream crossing was worse than they'd feared. They'd gotten across only with difficulty on their way up, and now the warmer weather of the day had added more meltwater to the stream and they faced a flood of freezing water and ice. The summer crossing is a matter of hopping from one rock to the next, but that was out of the question; the snow and ice made the footing far too uncertain and they were burdened with their awkward packs and with the almost helpless body of Max. The only solution was also the most drastic: Joe and Whitey filled in the gaps as well as they could with blocks of ice, then they lay down in the rocks and rushing water and made a bridge of themselves that Max could crawl across.

It was full dark now and, with the crossing behind them and less snow to slow them, they turned on their flashlights and made good time. This also encouraged Max, and he told them his story.

He said that the carpenter Paul LeClair looked in on him just before the weather broke and then hurried on down the mountain. The force of the storm rose quickly and reached a pitch of fury Max had never imagined, and he feared that his shelter would break its bonds of chain and blow right off the mountain. His firewood was soon gone, so he tried to get to Camden Cottage but the storm blew him off his feet and he couldn't even crawl across against the wind, so he broke up what little furniture he had and burned that. By Sunday he was thinking that this must be the onset of winter and, fearing that he'd be marooned, he decided to make a break for the valley. So, taking only a handful of raisins, he started down at noon.

His hat blew off immediately, then he went slipping and floundering down the lee side of the summit cone until he found the edge of Tuckerman Ravine, but he couldn't find a way down that seemed safe enough to try. He dug a snow cave and let the blowing snow fill in on top of him, then on Monday he broke out and tried again to find a way down, again without success. By this time the uncertain shelter of the stage office seemed more desirable than a snow cave and he tried to climb back up to the summit, but with the storm and the slope against him it was beyond his strength. He hadn't had anything to eat since the raisins the previous afternoon and he believed that eating snow would kill a dying man, so hadn't had anything to drink, either. Thus reduced, he dug in for a second night of full storm above Tuckerman Ravine.

On Tuesday morning Max believed he was close to death, so anything else that happened would not be much lost. He found the edge of the ravine, pitched over into his final effort, and fell until he stopped sliding about seven-hundred feet down the precipitous slope. Finding himself battered but still alive, he set out to find water and reached the place in the brook bed where they found him after his third night in the open.

This halting account filled the time as Joe and Whitey half-carried him down the trail, still carrying their own packs which added eighty pounds to Max's very considerable heft. They'd turned on their flashlights and, stopping to rest at a spot called Windy Pitch, they saw the lights of a car at what they knew was the Darby Field. They signaled with their flashlights, but got no response.

The trail was steeper and rougher now, and they had to be careful not to hurt Max. To complicate matters, his mind was drifting; he thought they told him it was two miles to camp, but he was sure they'd gone sixteen, which meant they'd lost their way.

The last landmark was the lower bridge over the Cutler River, and as they grew near they finally indulged the luxury of planning ahead. Joe would hurry on from the bridge and start a fire in their cabin, then fill the radiator in Ringtail and let it warm up while he heated some broth to reinforce Max before the long jolting ride to the hospital. Accordingly, Joe took both their packs at the bridge and started running the last quarter-mile. He fell and broke his flashlight almost immediately and kept running without it.

The parking lot at the AMC cabins was a blaze of light; it was filled with the cars of reporters and curious citizens. Joe said he and Whitey had found Max Engelhart, and they wouldn't believe him. Then, persuaded, they asked what had taken them so long. Then they asked if Max was all right. Joe decided not to pursue this interrogatory any further.

He sent a reporter to the Glen House to call Dr. Bryant in Gorham, then he opened the cabin and began preparations for Max. The reporters kept asking questions and Joe did not fail to note than no one offered to go up and help Whitey. Soon his mate came in with Max slung over his shoulder and they noticed that it had taken seven and a half hours to bring him down from his small refuge in the bank of the stream.

Joe and Whitey got Max out of his frozen clothes, but he was very much concerned about the knife he'd lost during his ordeal. They found it in his boot, which helped. They put him into warm dry clothes, wrapped him in blankets, and got some hot broth into him before Dr. Bryant arrived and started Max on his way to the hospital.

Now, in the first time they'd had to themselves in three days, Joe and Whitey began wondering why no one had come up to help them; even the people parked at The Darby Field had known it was their flashlights moving so slowly on the trail and had not come to help. Not finding any answer, they fed the cats and made a sign saying "Don't bother us, we're asleep!" Then, too exhausted to eat, they went to bed.

They were also too exhausted to sleep. They rolled to and fro in their blankets, but they were still awake when the sky began to lighten so they made breakfast at 6:00 A.M., but they still couldn't eat. They cleaned up the cabin and as they worked they thought how nice it would be to have somebody else do the work. This idea took hold, so they put on their best clothes, fired up Ringtail, and drove twenty miles north to the Berlin YMCA. They took showers there and went on to the Ravine House in Randolph, where the faithful Mr. and Mrs. Bradstreet cooked steaks and vegetables and biscuits for them.

Joe and Whitey read the Boston papers and learned of their adventures and then they went upstairs for a long sleep in a proper room, stayed on for breakfast and noontime dinner, and stopped in Gorham to have supper with photographer Guy Shorey and the honored guide Burge Bickford to talk over the storm and its consequences. Then they went to Berlin to see how Max was getting along. The toes and heel of one foot had been amputated, and the toes on the other foot, but he wasn't much bothered by this. He told them many stories of the days just past, including how he'd discovered gold in the Cutler River while he huddled by the rock and how he was just about to make some snowshoes out of twigs and branches when they found him, and then he proposed that they come up to his place in Canada and go trapping with him.

Max was kept in the hospital for almost five months. He went home and there was no news of him for many years, then two young women stopped by the AMC cabins in Pinkham Notch. They found Joe and told him that they'd talked to an elderly man in Canada who said that if they ever met Joe Dodge they should tell him that Max Engelhart had a job cooking for the railroad. Nothing more was ever heard of him.

Chapter Eight

THE WRECK OF OLD NO. 1

SYLVESTER MARSH WAS BORN IN 1803 IN CAMPTON, NEW Hampshire, at the southern end of Franconia Notch. He was the ninth of eleven children, a situation which latter-day psychologists say fosters a certain competitive push, and when he was nineteen years old he set out to make his fortune. He had three dollars and he headed for Boston, 150 miles away. It took young Sylvester three days to walk there and he found employment on a farm in Newton, west of the city. Soon he had a stall in the original Quincy Market in Boston and he was a passenger when the DeWitt Clinton pulled the first steam train on the Albany/Schenectady run.

By 1833, he was in Chicago, a place of 300 souls that Sylvester thought had a bright future. Fortune seemed to hitch Sylvester to this star and the first railroad to operate out of Chicago ended just behind his property. He alertly went into the meat packing business and built a large plant to abut the railroad terminus. Then he developed a revolutionary method of preserving corn. All this earned a very considerable fortune, familiarity with the many uses of steam, and a fulsome salute from *The Chicago Press and Tribune*: This "enterprising, ingenious inventor will live in history as one of the benefactors of his species."

Sylvester Marsh retired from his several businesses in the mid-1850s and moved to West Roxbury, Massachusetts. Inactivity did not suit him; in fact, it brought on a sinking spell that was diagnosed as dyspepsia. Seeking more salutary air, as the fashion of the day indicated, he returned to his old neighborhood in the White Mountains. Further obedient to the fashion of the day, he sought to climb Mount Washington by way of the Crawford's Bridle Path. The weather turned against him and he barely reached the Tip-Top House.

Characteristically, Sylvester resolved to improve the condition of suffering mankind, in this case, to find a better way to reach the heights. Three years later, he approached the New Hampshire state legislature with a model of a mountain-climbing railway. A charter was granted, sort of—one generous voice in the debate said that Sylvester Marsh could build his railway to the moon if he wanted to. The tone suggested skepticism.

Work began in 1866, the rail line was built up a western ridge of the mountain, and on the Fourth of July, 1869, word went forth that the railway to the moon had reached the top of Mount Washington. The train was driven by a rack and pinion system under the engine, which was itself one of the oldest designs in the whole inventory of steam power, a firebox with a vertical boiler on top of it and a smokestack on top of that. Engine № 1 was officially named "Hero," but the look was familiar: people thought it resembled the bottle used for a popular condiment called pepper sauce. It didn't take long for the north-country tongue to sharpen the word and Engine № 1 entered history as Peppersass.

This pilot model retired from active duty in 1878. It went west for display at the World's Columbian Exposition of 1893, more widely known as the Chicago World's Fair, then it was at Chicago's Museum of Natural History, and in 1904 it went to the Louisiana Purchase Exposition, popularly known as the St. Louis World's Fair. Then it disappeared.

Reverend Guy Roberts lived in Whitefield, New Hampshire, at the northwestern edge of the great mountain ranges, and he developed a consuming interest in finding the well-loved Mount Washington native. He followed the engine's trail to Baltimore and through heroic personal efforts he managed to have it returned to the place of its first fame, where it was reconditioned and pronounced sound in June 1929. The annual Conference of New England Governors was scheduled for the Bretton Woods Hotel in July, the base station of the cog railway was just up the road, and it seemed like a fine thing to send the official parties up Mount Washington to see the ceremonial return of Old Peppersass.

DANIEL ROSSITER
JULY 1929

Even today, the base station of the Mount Washington cog railway is like any other train yard in the elder days of steam, only smaller; there are whistles tooting and cinders underfoot and smoke and steam swirling overhead. On the morning of July 20, 1929, however, the party clothes were out of the closet; there were grandstands and flags and banners and bunting and a grand patriotic display to greet the double holiday proclaimed for the arrival of the six New England governors and the return of Old Peppersass.

In the language of the cog railway, a train is one engine pushing one passenger car up the mountain. The engine is not connected to the car and there is no turnaround for the return trip: the engine backs down the track with the passenger car resting against it in front. The engine and the car both have primary brakes and back-up brakes and either unit can stop itself independent of the other.

The program for this festive day was elaborate. The governors and the other invited guests were served a grand breakfast at the very grand Bretton Woods Hotel, then the governors and Reverend Roberts climbed aboard an original and bunting-bedecked Concord stagecoach drawn by six prancing horses which took them to the Boston & Maine Railroad station. Two special trains, also draped in red, white, and blue for the day, took those distinguished gentlemen and more than 900 other guests the few miles to the base station of the cog railway. The two trains proved insufficient for the multitude, and those who had to wait for a second run were entertained with selections by a brass band and a splendid tenor soloist.

Once everyone was at the base station of the cog and seated for the ceremonies, the president of the Baltimore & Ohio Railroad officially returned ownership of Old Peppersass to the president of the Boston & Maine, who in turn presented the relic to the governor of New Hampshire. Then the governors, their entourages, and other invited guests boarded six cog trains

Sylvester Marsh's cog railway reached the summit on July 4, 1869. The first engine was officially called "Hero № 1," but was known as "Peppersass" (seen behind several newer models on the summit). In 1929 Peppersass was brought out of deep retirement for one more ceremonial climb, which would prove fatal for Daniel Rossiter.

that would take them to the top of the mountain, trailing yet more bunting and flags as they climbed.

After those trains were well-started up the track, Old Peppersass began a ceremonial final climb up to the trestle called Jacob's Ladder, two-thirds of the way to the summit and the steepest, highest, and most spectacular section of the whole route. This would prove that even after seventy years, the old campaigner still had what it takes to climb Mount Washington. The program called for the erstwhile Engine № 1 to descend for the last time and, filled with honors and achievement, go to an honored retirement and permanent display in the valley.

When the presentation ceremonies were over, fireman William Newsham topped off the firebox, engineer Edward Frost opened the valves, and Peppersass headed up the mountain. The antique climbed slowly but it climbed well, and when it reached Jacob's Ladder the fine performance and the spirit of the day inspired the crew to change the original plan and keep going to the summit, so they kept going. Then they changed their plan again. Peppersass moved so slowly that a complete climb would delay the six trains on top beyond the departure time needed to get them all back to the base at a prudent hour. Engineer Frost engaged the reverse gear and began to back the engine down the track. Then he heard a sort of snap; it seemed to come from the front of the engine. A tooth in the cog driving wheel had broken.

Almost every steam engine in the history of railroading towed its fuel tender as a separate element. Peppersass did not. The boiler and the tender were on a single frame and the engineer and fireman stood out in the weather as they did their work. This day three extra people started up the mountain on Peppersass, riding on the fuel bunker any way they could. One was the engineer's sixteen-year-old son Caleb; the two others were photographers Daniel Rossiter and Winston Pote.

Reverend Guy Roberts, the man who led the recovery of Old Peppersass, rode on the last of the six trains sent up ahead of the day's honoree. No cog train ever moved very fast, and the reverend stepped off the platform of his train just above Jacob's Ladder. He thought this was the right thing to do; he'd hike along beside Peppersass as it made its last climb. He stopped at Jacob's Ladder, the better to savor the noble sight as the engine climbed the trestle for this last time, the crown of his twenty-three year effort on behalf of history. Then he thought he'd walk beside the train, or perhaps catch a ride, all the way back down to its final rest at the bottom of the mountain.

The reverend was somewhat surprised to see the engine continue on above Jacob's Ladder and then out of sight over the skyline. He waited forty minutes before he heard a rumbling in the tracks that signaled the return of the train. Then, he wrote later, "Glancing up the track I saw steam or smoke as from her stack, the engine was being concealed by a brow of the mountain. But in an instant she was in sight and I thought, 'Here she comes.' Then I realized that her speed was very fast and the next instant I thought, 'Why, she is running away!' On she rushed, careening and tottering, when with a sudden lurch, off toppled her smokestack, crashing onto the rocks at my right. Then I noticed that a man was hanging to the flaring top of its tender, swaying as it careened! The terrible outfit flashed past, showering me with its cinders, as on it dashed in its mad rush to death down Jacob's Ladder, tearing and crashing. When but some fifteen feet beyond me the man dropped from his hold on the tender and was shot down some forty feet through space outside the upper side of Jacob's Ladder, where he crashed to death on the sharp jagged rocks and huge timbers at the foot of the trestle and about midway its length.

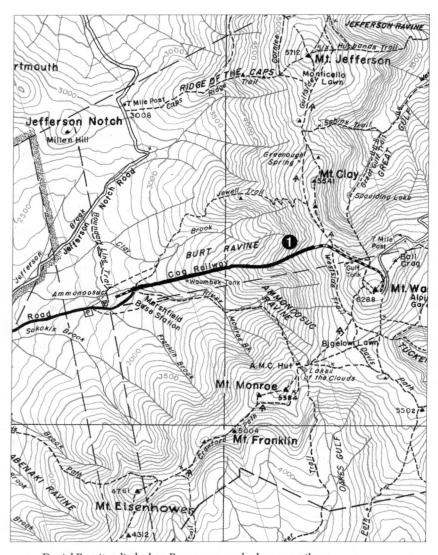

1. Daniel Rossiter died when Peppersass crashed on cog railway

"Watching Old Peppersass as she shrieked out her swan song, she continued tearing down the Ladder until coming to the reverse curve at its foot. Being unable to make the curve she leaped from the rails into space over the brink of Burt's Ravine, where with a thunder-like report the boiler exploded amid a great puff of steam, landing her some thirty feet from the rack and with pieces of metal and debris flying in all directions, at last burying her shattered and scattered self amid the rotten wood, stunted spruce and birches that there were growing."

The engineer, the fireman, one photographer, and the boy all jumped clear of Peppersass while it was still going fairly slowly. They were all considerably battered and some were broken in minor ways, but their lives were not threatened. Daniel Rossiter was the other photographer and he had the same chance to escape the mad plunge as the others did, but for some reason he hung on to the tender. Some say he seemed to be reaching for his camera, as if to save it from the wreck that must occur.

The enormous explosion of the boiler hurled fragments of the engine more than 900 feet down the mountain and Reverend Roberts hurried to the wreck, putting out small fires beside the trestle as he went. Just below Jacob's Ladder he found "the bruised and broken body of what proved to be that of my friend, Daniel Rossiter, lying on the jagged rocks below and in such a broken position as to not in the least resemble a man as seen from above." A caddy had hiked to a vantage point a little farther up the trestle and he ran to help Reverend Roberts. As the savior of Peppersass put it, "We lifted Dan and placed his head and shoulders in a less terrible position and thus was he found by those who removed his body."

The caddy slipped when he climbed down from the trestle and a large splinter was driven into his thigh, but after he'd helped the reverend with Mr. Rossiter's body, the caddy hobbled and ran all the way down to the place he called Kro Flite, the name applied to the settlement at the base of the cog railroad in 1925 and 1926. As a reporter wrote, "He gave the first news of the disaster, just before he fainted."

The situation was difficult. Old Peppersass was destroyed, five people were injured and one was dead, and, since a section of track on Jacob's Ladder had been damaged by the crash, six trainloads of guests were stranded at the top of the mountain. There was one spare engine at the base and a fire was lit under the boiler, but no engineer could be found. The first of the six trains had started down from the top with a full load of passengers, then it stopped when the first damage to Jacob's Ladder came into view.

Joe Dodge had been engaged as a guest lecturer for the ceremonies and he knew how to dress for celebrations like the return of Old Peppersass: he was wearing plus-four knickers from a golfer's outfit and a bright red Hudson Bay jacket. Joe was on the first train to start down from the summit, but it stopped some way above Jacob's Ladder and out of sight of the wreck. The train was also below the Gulfside Tank, the place where upward-bound engines took on water to finish the trip to the top. Joe knew this meant trouble for the guests; the train apparently could not go on down the mountain and, not having enough water to make sufficient steam, it could not get back to the top.

Soon the passengers knew there was trouble, too. Nightfall was approaching and they were stranded above timberline with no news of their future. As Joe remembered, "It was getting dark and sort of cool and I had about twenty-five men and women to look after, all of them complaining. One woman on the train got hysterical. Her husband wasn't much help, so I picked her up piggy-back, and I said to her, 'Come on, sis. You'll have to get going if you want to get down the mountain.' Well, sir, she clawed at me, she screamed, and she talked baby talk all the way down. It was rough going along those tracks, but I kept my footing. When we finally got to a path, I gave her a shove and said, 'Get going, sister.'"

The reserve engine at the base was kept hot while an engineer walked the three miles down from the summit, and as dusk was falling he started the engine back up to Jacob's Ladder pushing a flatcar loaded with timbers and tools and a work crew to study the damage.

The men were able to make the trestle marginally passable, and at 10:00 P.M. the work train returned with the engineer of Old Peppersass, his fireman, and the others injured in the crash. Before long, Joe's group reached the base station. He'd led them down in the dark and there were no injuries, but they noticed that someone had taken down all the flags and bunting from the morning's ceremonies.

Five trains and the guests riding on them remained on top long after nightfall; as one of the passengers said, it was like being shipwrecked at sea, families were separated and not to be rejoined until the small hours of Sunday morning. They were eventually taken down the mountain on the auto road and, true to the spirit of shipwreck, Governor Tobey of New Hampshire was the last to leave the summit. They all finally gathered at the Bretton Woods Hotel, the place they'd left with such fanfare less than twenty-four hours earlier. Colonel Barron owned the hotel, and he and Senator George Moses served sandwiches and coffee until Governor Tobey arrived at 4:15 A.M. with the last of the guests that were stranded on the summit.

Mr. Rossiter's camera was smashed beyond repair, but the first three pictures he took that day survived and they lived on for their posterity in the archival memory of Old Peppersass. His spectacles and his monogrammed gold watch, now dented and stopped at the moment of his death, were found near the trestle of Jacob's Ladder and returned to his family. More than anything else, the broken watch told of changing times. On Friday of that week, July 25, 1929, the White Mountains Air Line began daily service to Boston and New York from the new airport in the hometown of Reverend Guy Roberts, ten miles from the cog railway for which he'd worked so hard. The plane carried five passengers in addition to the pilot, and the cabin was enclosed for greater comfort.

Chapter Nine

SUMMER PEOPLE GO NORTH

*F*AMILY STORIES MADE IT SEEM AS IF MY FOREBEARS HAD lived in Providence forever. There was no shortage of stories because, by an unlikely but verifiable coincidence, both of my parents' families arrived in the New World on the same boat, the good ship *Mayflower*. Life was not perfectly harmonious in the Plymouth Rock neighborhood and in 1630 family member Roger Williams left the Massachusetts Bay Colony and crossed Narragansett Bay to make a new start in a place he called Providence. By the 1870s, the family was headed by John Howe. He was an actor in a troupe led by Edwin Booth, and they were occasionally joined on stage by Mr. Booth's brother, John Wilkes Booth.

In 1872, the mail brought news from a forgotten past. It concerned the French Spoiliation Claims which, though obscure, would loom large in the future. The notice was addressed to Seth Russell & Son, forebears of John's wife, Louise Russell Howe, familiarly known as "Gubba." Her family had been in the shipping trades after the American Revolution, but those were unsettled times. The long run of royalty and absentee rule was destabilized by the American revolution against George III and then by the rising of the French proletariat against Louis XVI, and these shocks left things at loose ends on several fronts. One popular approach to knitting up loose ends is conflict and the War of 1812 was launched, a curious affair in which the most important battle was held three weeks after the war was over.

Then the several parties to the war gathered for the really useful part, the peace conference. This resulted in the Treaty of Ghent, written in the Belgian city of that name. The first job in any treaty gathering was a sort of bluffing game in which the diplomats put their claims on the table, so our man entered a claim asserting that American shipowners who had lost value to the British should be indemnified by the French.

This is known as spoiliation, and the improbable claim survived the scrutineering phase at Ghent and it was written into the treaty. The mills of the gods may grind slow, but the mills of the nations grind slower. Seth Russell & Son had owned a ship that was put at risk by British raiders after the Revolution, and somewhat more than 100 years later Gubba received a check for damages suffered by a long-forgotten ship named the *Fox*.

The family was already spending summers with Providence friends who had a place in Jackson, New Hampshire. Now Gubba applied the *Fox* money to the purchase of the old Moody property in Jackson so her family could have a summer place of their own. There was a farmhouse with a carriage shed and a large barn and several outbuildings, and it wasn't long before Gubba's family began inviting friends up for summer visits. These friends were from Providence at first, then they began coming from Boston and other outlying districts. This was very much in the summer fashion; for an urban world with no air conditioning in the houses and many horses in the streets, summer in the mountain breezes was irresistible.

The Jackson house was enlarged a bit, then the carriage shed was made livable, then the house was enlarged again. They called it "Overlook" and friends began bringing along their own friends, and the house grew larger. Gubba's older daughter was named Fannie, she was first in line as matriarch presumptive and her first child was born in 1887. This was my father, and before long he had a brother and two sisters, and by the time they were in school they began bringing up their friends. They'd pitch tents in the meadows, and then my uncle dragged some cots out into the field and built a sort of cabin over them for the boys to stay in. The girls soon asked him to exercise his teenage carpentry skills on their behalf, and then regular guests began asking for their own cabins.

By the time I was a child there were nine cabins ringing the property and the barn was partly converted for rudimentary summer living and the old farmhouse had a great many rooms. Once, in the grips of summer *ennui*, I took stock. There were forty-nine spaces I identified as rooms in the main house, but that included bathrooms. Even so, upwards of sixty people could be accommodated in the house and the cabins and the barn, and the stories of four generations of family, friends of family, and friends of friends had grown so numerous and so complexly entwined that I was never exactly sure who was kin and who was not. There was, for instance, a recurring class of guests who were called "loose connections," and to this day I don't know if they were relatives or not.

It didn't matter, because the elders and their heroics were recorded in a pile of black photograph albums in what we called The Big Living Room. The pictures showed gentlemen in suits and ladies in skirts that swept the ground and boys in white shirts and ties and girls in middy blouses and bloomers and black stockings, all of them up there on the mountain heights with blanket roles over their shoulders. Those of us in the rising generation would study those pictures through many a rainy afternoon, and we understood that, as it is said in Genesis, there were indeed giants in the earth in those days.

The Big Living Room had a large bay window that faced the north meadow. A sofa faced the window and that's where we sat to look at the photograph albums and when we looked up we saw Mount Washington rising at the end of the meadow, and even as children we knew that people died up there. We thought about them and we thought most about Lizzie Bourne; she reminded us of the ladies in the photograph albums as they went striding across the heights in skirts that swept the ground. Closer to the moment, we thought about Jessie Whitehead.

JESSIE WHITEHEAD
JANUARY 1933

Jessie Whitehead was a notable person. We knew that, because she was at the head of the list of notable persons who stayed at Overlook. Charles Evans Hughes stayed with us, he was Chief Justice of the Supreme Court; there were Rockefellers; there was Curt Chase, commanding general of the First

Jessie Whitehead was a scholar, early champion of high-achieving women, and an ardent mountaineer. In January 1933 she fell 800 feet down Huntington Ravine and lived, which did not surprise people who knew her.

Light Cavalry Division, and there was a large and energetic family from Boston named Kennedy whose father was the ambassador to the Court of Saint James. But my father always told us most particularly of Jessie Whitehead and her terrible fall in Huntington Ravine.

We knew Jessie because of her stutter. It wasn't that she had an occasional stammer, that she stumbled over a word now and then—Jessie could hardly talk at all. Father said she'd broken her neck in the fall, and that was why she stuttered. Grandmother Howe ran Overlook in the summer and she took it for granted that children should not be heard. She believed that we shouldn't be seen very often, either, and the children of my generation stayed in our various families' cottages at the perimeter of the property. This reduced our contact with the notable people to zero, but we did know one way we could see Jessie Whitehead.

Overlook had a back porch that had been made into a room. It was called the Trough, and this was where employees, disreputable relatives, and children of my generation were fed at a long trestle table. The Trough had windows on the outside wall and also the old windows on the inside wall. One day Jessie sat down for dinner at the end seat of the biggest of the dining room tables and we could see her through the inside windows of the Trough.

At the beginning of a meal the waitresses always went around their tables saying, "Tea, coffee, or milk?" and they'd take the orders on their fingers. They'd hold their hands behind them and count on one hand for tea and the other hand for coffee. Back in the kitchen, they'd subtract the total number of fingers from the total places at the table and the remainder would be milk.

We could see the waitress's fingers when she took Jessie's order, and as the choking, gasping sounds began to sound like "Tea," one finger began to record the message; then as the sounds veered away toward "Coffee," a finger on the other hand would move. We watched through the back windows and we were fascinated. We understood that Jessie's fall in Huntington Ravine must have been terrible indeed.

We knew about Huntington Ravine. When we looked out past our croquet lawn, Mount Washington rose directly in front of us: Tuckerman Ravine was hidden behind Boott Spur, but we could see straight into Huntington Ravine. There was a huge boulder at the corner of the croquet lawn that we called Mount Washington Rock. It had the same general shape we could see on the skyline and there was a deep cleft for Huntington Ravine. We'd look at that and think of Jessie Whitehead.

Jessie had a wider fame. She was the daughter of Alfred North Whitehead, a leading member of the last generation of great philosophers, the last generation of scholars whose ideas were on the front pages of newspapers. He was British by birth, but he made his career at Harvard and Jessie had an elevated childhood, she'd say, "I grew up in a cloud of Huxleys," meaning the most powerful family of intellectuals of the age.

Jessie lived in an apartment near Harvard Square and she almost always had one or two cockatiels with her. They're small parrots from Australia and during the harshest winter storms she'd be out there striding along the sidewalks of the Square and smoking a pipe, with her birds sitting on her shoulder and ruffled out to twice their normal size to hold off icy blasts their homeland never knew. She liked to take her meals at the popular and economical Hayes-Bickford restaurant on Harvard Square and the Bick did not allow animals to mingle with the diners, but Jessie was a person of character and of consequence, and the management of the Bick let her bring the birds to her regular place at one of their front window tables. Jessie was a scholar in ancient Arabic languages and she worked at Harvard's Widener Library in her academic specialty. One day the hushed precincts of Widener were suddenly rent by a great cry: "Oh God, if there is a God, what does it all *mean*?" It was Jessie, whose own long silences were occasionally broken by questions like that.

Perhaps it was those silences that had made Jessie a devoted hiker and a serious rock climber long before anyone thought such a calling would include women, and she was not afraid of anything. She and three men made the first ascent of the northeast ridge of the Pinnacle in Huntington Ravine, considered unclimbable until her group climbed it in October 1928. She was a relentless champion of what she called "manless climbing," and she and three other women spent the summer of 1931 on the major peaks of the Alps. Inevitably, they went to the Matterhorn. The weather was bad, but they reached the highest hut on the mountain and found it filled to the rafters with hikers from every point of the compass, an alpine Tower of Babel. Jessie couldn't make out any of the tongues, so she stood up and called for attention, then she addressed the multitude in Latin. Two climbers answered and those were her friends for the evening. The bad weather persisted and they were turned back from the top of the Matterhorn four times, so they went to Africa and took a fleet of camels into the desert.

Jessie was an early skier and a literate reporter of her outings. "In nothing is Katahdin more praiseworthy," she wrote, "than for the enjoyment it affords to bad skiers." She had a hike-to cabin on the slope of Mount Chocorua and she was a year-round habitué of Pinkham Notch, where Joe Dodge regarded her with affection and respect. Jessie was thirty-eight years old in 1932 and she went to Pinkham to spend the Christmas season with Joe and his family.

Winter had not taken hold in Pinkham. There was only four inches of snow on the ground and it had been raining for several days, but on December 31 the temperature was dropping from 51° to 8°, the wind was gusting up to 40 miles an hour, and late in the afternoon the drizzly rain turned to snow flurries. Undaunted, Jessie left Pinkham by the trail called the Old Jackson Road, reached the Mount Washington auto road after two miles, hiked six more miles up the auto road to the summit, and spent the night in the frigid shelter of Camden Cottage.

During the night, the wind veered from the southeast into the northwest, the sky cleared, and the temperature dropped below zero. The next morning, New Year's Day, Jessie descended by way of Boott Spur to the AMC cabins in Pinkham Notch. Later she wrote, "Nowhere had I seen snow conditions that seemed to make solitary skiing a desirable proposition for the next day. I had worn crampons the whole time and did not feel that an elementary acquaintance with stem turns would avail me very much on the hard crust of the trails."

The AMC encampment included the house Joe built for his family in 1928 and the two log cabins that were not yet rearranged and joined to form the Trading Post of later years. Jessie had supper with Joe and his family, then she walked three miles down the road to the Glen House; the caretaker kept a few rooms open for winter hikers and she knew that a group from the Harvard Mountaineering Club was there. Jessie hoped to find some Harvards to accompany her up to Huntington Ravine the next day and have a look at the gullies, and Walter Sturges agreed to go with her. After breakfast the next morning they started up with crampons, ice axes, carabiners, two ice pitons, and 120 feet of rope. There are seven climbing gullies in the ravine: Escape, South, Odell, Pinnacle, Central, Yale, and Damnation. Jessie and Walter decided that Odell Gully offered, as she put it, "a tolerable problem."

The first winter ascent of the gully was less than four years past. It was led in March 1929 by Noel Odell of the Harvard Mountaineering Club, who had already earned his place in mountaineering history: he'd been on the epochal British Everest Expedition of 1924 in which Mallory and Irvine disappeared in the mists just below the summit and were never seen again. Odell Gully in Huntington Ravine had been the goal of AMC groups since 1929, and Jessie had been a member of two of them. All those trips had been in March or April, when there was better snow and more tolerant weather.

Odell Gully is on the left side of the ravine and the approach rises over a broad scree slope, then winter climbers find a steep narrow ascent with several frozen waterfalls. A three-man rope from Yale had climbed here the day before and they did not like what they found; the ice was brittle and they thought the snow was dangerously unstable. Now Jessie and Walter agreed that they would not force the issue. This policy was further recommended by the fact that they had never climbed together and neither knew the habits or capacities of the other.

They climbed the snow-covered scree to a prominent rock just at the beginning of the serious terrain. They had lunch and then roped up. They decided that Jessie would select the route on the basis of her greater experience,

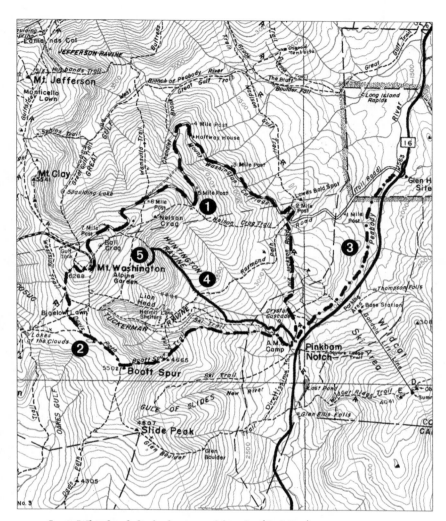

1. Jessie Whitehead climbed auto road first day (dash line)
2. Descended by Boott Spur second day (dash-dot-dash)
3. Walked to Glen House after supper (dash-dot-dash)
4. Up Huntington Ravine third day
5. Fell in Odell Gulley

and her first decision was that they should change leads often because the day was cold and a strong wind was blowing down the gully. Jessie knew from experience that a person standing on belay would get chilled quickly. She also felt that this would allow each of them to become familiar with the way the other one moved.

The first pitch resembled the frozen snowpack that Jessie had found in previous late-winter climbs up here. She thought she'd be all right on crampons, but approaching the first steep pitch she chopped a few steps as a test. Walter Sturges led up to the first frozen waterfall. He kicked steps to a rock at the extreme right side of the steep ice, then as he moved to his left Jessie drove her ice axe into the snow to see if there was underlying ice which might increase the danger of a slide.

Walter cut handholds and footholds across the ice, and when Jessie followed him she cut some of the holds deeper and was surprised to find hard water-ice. She set a piton here, then led over the next pitch of ice. This was hard work and complicated by a bitter wind sweeping down the gully, but she reached a sloping shelf of glare ice and stopped to consider their situation. She was a rather small woman, she didn't consider herself to be very strong, and she realized that she could not hold Walter from the stance she had, so she drove in a piton before he started up.

Odell Gully forks at this point, and they started up the right side on a rather easy ice slope to the second frozen waterfall. This was not as steep as the first one but it looked higher and more complicated. Jessie was surprised by this, too, she'd never seen ice here nor had she ever heard of any. Wisps of cloud were blowing down the gully and she wondered if she and Walter would be able to see each other if the clouds got much thicker. Nevertheless, she wanted to get to the second pitch of ice because she thought it might be wiser to move to the right at that point and go up the rocks, even though this route would not be much easier on the glaze that covered them.

While she was considering these factors and the time they had taken so far, she chopped a stance for Walter and called down to him to knock out their lower piton and bring it up. Still thinking of the difference in their size, she decided he should drive that piton at the stance she was cutting and she'd set the next one when she was out on the severe section of ice, or near the rocks if she decided to go up that way. Then, she thought, they'd be secure even if the clouds thickened and they lost sight of each other.

The lower piton was about halfway across the ice toward Jessie's stance and Walter reached to take it out. He hit it quite hard, and it came out easily. The disparity between his large effort and the piton's small resistance threw him off balance and he slipped out of his step and slid down the ice on his face. Up above, Jessie saw the rope begin to run out and she realized that something had happened at the other end.

She dropped her ice axe and lunged for the rope, hoping at the same time that he hadn't pulled out the lower piton. Walter felt a slight pop in the rope as Jessie took the strain. It seemed for a moment that his fall had stopped, then Jessie was torn off her stance. In the slow motion of a dream she felt herself sailing down the 50-degree face, never touching anything until she hit the lower pitch of ice about 140 feet below the shelf she'd been standing on. Jessie hit the ice upside down, taking the force of the blow on her head and shoulder.

Moments like this divide us into two camps. It's a matter of time: some will say later that everything seemed to happen at once, others find that time slowed down, everything appeared in bright detail and the mind provided extended observations. As Jessie hurtled headfirst down the gully, she thought, "This is grotesque, if true." Then she took inventory of her physical sensations and thought, "It probably is true." In fact, her neck and shoulder were broken, there were five fractures in her jaw, and severe lacerations in her neck and head.

Then Jessie concentrated on slowing down. She was falling headfirst and on her back and she found it difficult to get much traction with her elbows and crampons, but she tried. Then she was swept with anger and humiliation at the thought that she'd dropped her ice axe and could not remember where it was. As she wrote later, "I also knew that my subsequent moments of consciousness were to be quite limited. In fact, I rather hoped they were."

She thought of Walter and decided that he was dead, forgetting at the moment that he hadn't necessarily taken the same fall as she had. Then she thought that a body making such a strong pull on the rope could not be lifeless and she decided that he was alive and he probably had his ice axe, and if this was true, he could probably start slowing their fall when he got to the snow-covered scree slope. She wanted to tell Walter that the rest was up to him, though she wasn't sure if he could do anything to stop their fall. "Still, I longed to tell him that he could no longer count on any cooperation from me. I thought he ought to be told, I longed inexpressibly to tell him, but as I reached the fan I passed out." As Jessie feared, Walter did lose his ice axe and they both were finally stopped by the bushes at the bottom of the scree slope. They had fallen 800 feet.

At about eleven o'clock that morning "Stitch" Callender and John Howell had crossed the floor of Huntington Ravine, and as they put on their crampons near the lower edge of the fan they saw two other climbers coming into view behind them. Stitch and John were headed for Central Gully, and as they started their own climb they saw the other people putting on their crampons. Stitch and John spent two hours cutting steps up the ice in Central before they moved onto the milder slope above and headed toward the rocks on their right. It was just at that point, about one o'clock, that they heard someone calling for help.

Stitch called back, and although he could not see where the trouble was, he and John immediately started down. It took them about half an hour to reach the two people on the snow slope below Odell Gully.

Jessie slid 100 feet farther than her companion, but Walter was still conscious and he heard voices somewhere in the ravine. This was the moment when he shouted, then he began to move down toward Jessie. He could hear her moaning, but at first he didn't realize how badly either of them was hurt. Just as he reached her, two men appeared through the mist and Walter saw that it was his friend Stitch Callender with a companion. Stitch untangled their packs and rope and saw that Jessie was badly hurt. Stitch and John tried to make Jessie comfortable with their extra clothes, but they quickly realized that more help was needed than they could provide, so Stitch started down the ravine at a run, heading for the highway three miles away. Walter Sturges followed, making his way through the rocks on the floor of the ravine, moving very slowly.

The Huntington Ravine Trail soon crossed the Raymond Path and continued downslope until it met the Tuckerman Ravine Trail a mile and a quarter above the highway. These paths were narrow and they had all the humps and twists that the terrain dictated, but travel habits on Mount Washington had just been dramatically changed. The Forest Service had built a new trail from Hermit Lake down to the AMC camp at the highway. Work began in 1930 and now it was a smoothly-graded route, 15-feet wide, a main street in a land of goat paths.

Stitch reached the junction of the Huntington Trail and the new trail and kept running. Three hundred yards later he came upon Bradford Washburn and a group of six other men from the Harvard Mountaineering Club.

Few people knew the area better than Brad. He'd been fascinated by the mountain ever since he was a boy and while he was still in prep school he wrote *Bradford on Mount Washington*, the story of a 1928 climb he and two friends made during their March vacation. Now Brad was twenty-two years old and president of the Harvard Mountaineering Club, and he'd spent the holiday season with six other Harvards working on the cabin the club was building a mile and a half below Hermit Lake.

Brad climbed to the summit the day before and this morning he'd come down over Lion Head in a 60-mph wind, noticing as he descended that the clouds that settled on the summit at sunset were now down to the 4,500-foot level, near the floor of both Tuckerman and Huntington Ravines. He went on to the Harvard cabin to meet his mates and a little after two o'clock they gathered up their gear and started for Boston. Each of them had a Yukon packboard with 30 feet of rope and they also had a dull axe they'd have sharpened in Boston. A Yukon packboard is a wooden frame with two vertical slats and four cross braces, and remarkably heavy loads can be tied on and carried quite easily. They'd just passed the Forest Service work camp at the junction of the new Tuckerman Trail and the Huntington Ravine Trail when they heard Stitch Callender yelling at them from behind.

If Stitch had been just a few minutes earlier or later he would have missed Brad's crew, but now he told them that Jessie Whitehead and Walter Sturges had fallen in Odell Gulley, that Jessie was badly hurt and still in the ravine, and Walter was also in bad shape but making his slow way down the trail. He said that Brad's group should get back up to the ravine and try to find Jessie because Walter had told him she probably wouldn't survive the coming night without help. They huddled briefly and realized that their strengthened party still wasn't enough, so Stitch ran on down to Pinkham for more help while Brad and his crew headed back up to the accident. There's a level stretch on the Huntington Ravine Trail just before it starts through the boulder field on the floor of the ravine and they found Walter Sturges there. By now he was only semi-conscious and not able to tell them exactly where Jessie was, but he was still moving, so Brad left three of his crew to help Walter down toward Pinkham. The three Harvards remaining with Brad still had their Yukons and ropes and the dull axe, so they cut two slender spruce trees and rigged the trees with their packboards for a lash-up stretcher and started out to find Jessie.

Conditions were not good. After a week of rain the weather had cooled, the rocks were glazed with ice, and new snow had fallen to hide almost everything underfoot. It was this uncertain combination that had persuaded Jessie not to go skiing two days earlier, and Brad found the going more treacherous than even his own large experience would have liked.

Brad's crew found Jessie huddled in the middle of the trail about a hundred yards above the boulder field. In fact, they almost stepped on her, because the wind-driven snow had nearly covered her already. They brushed away the snow and discovered a sight that is still vivid in Brad's memory after sixty-six years: "All the front part of her scalp was bare bone, with her hair upside-down on the back of her skull—a dreadful sight. She shrieked in pain as we untangled her and got her onto our little stretcher, to which we tied her with another of our packboard ropes."

They made Jessie as secure as they could and started down over the boulders and the ice and the snow. Jessie was conscious and in terrible pain, so they were as careful as they could be, but it was very tough going through the boulders. The shortest day of the year was only just past, the sun was long gone behind the ridge above them, and they'd only gotten as far as the trees on the floor of the ravine when night began to fall. They had almost three miles to go.

When Stitch Callender got to Pinkham, "Itchy" Mills and Wendell Lees were just driving out of the parking lot with the AMC truck, headed down the notch to meet the train in Glen. Stitch yelled and they turned around to join Joe Dodge and Johnny Hall in a dash up the mountain. They met Brad and his crew just below Huntington Ravine, moving slowly. Jessie recognized Joe and she said, very clearly, "Joe, give me a drink of milk and take me to the hospital. I'm sick."

The combined forces shifted Jessie to the stretcher that Joe's crew had with them, but the carry didn't get much easier; the terrain was rough, the dense spruce growth was only cleared for single-file hikers, and their wide carry kept crowding them off the trail.

Johnny Hall was coming up behind Joe's group and he had blankets and another stretcher, and when he caught up with Joe and Brad he realized that they had the situation in hand. He'd passed Walter Sturges on his way up and he decided that his equipment could be put to better use by the three Harvards helping Walter, so he turned around to find them. This left Brad and Joe Dodge and seven other men, enough to shift off as they carried Jessie. Joe's group had flashlights and with this improvement they decided to cut across to the new Tuckerman Trail; it would be somewhat longer but certainly faster than continuing down the old Huntington Trail to the lower junction. As they were working their way through the woods the deep laceration on Jessie's neck hemorrhaged, so Joe stuffed handfuls of snow into the wound and stopped the bleeding. Most of the men knew Jessie and now they were dumbfounded. All through the jolting carry down the mountain, Jessie cursed volubly and loudly, with nary a stammer or a stutter anywhere in her litany of pain.

By now they were out of the wind vortex churning down from the ravine and even though the temperature was approaching zero they felt warm enough to strip to their shirt sleeves. They'd left most of the clouds behind, too, and a quarter moon was showing through. They reached the wide avenue of the new Tuckerman Trail at about 8:30, and now their progress over the thin firm snow was as rapid as anyone could hope for. They reached the lower junction of the Huntington Trail in twenty minutes and found the toboggan and some blankets that Joe's party had left on the way up, so they put Jessie's improvised litter on the toboggan and reached Pinkham at 9:25.

Meanwhile, Walter Sturges had used up the last of his strength, so Johnny Hall and three Harvards carried him more than a mile and a half from the crossing of the Raymond Path down to Pinkham. Teen Dodge, Joe's wife, gave him hot tea and turkey soup and put a hot-water bottle under his feet; then, just as Jessie was brought in, Walter was started down the road to the hospital seventeen miles away in North Conway.

Jessie's injuries dictated all possible speed to the hospital. By this time she was struggling against her pain and her restraints, so the rescue party swaddled her in blankets for both warmth and bracing and put her in the back of the AMC truck. Wendell Lees climbed in with her and held her head steady while Joe drove the truck as fast as he could down the Pinkham road, but with the winter conditions, the primitive surface and marginal maintenance, it was about like driving crossways over a farmer's plowed field. Later

Mountain rescues used to be simple. Here an injured woman is being carried in the Great Gulf, circa 1910.

Joe said, "I can't understand it. We were rougher than a son of a bitch with her—had to be. But she lived."

The AMC had no telephone in Pinkham Notch, so someone had gone to the Glen House to call Harold Shedd, the principal doctor in the North Conway hospital. He heard the ring just as he was walking down the steps of his house on his way to visit his wife in Boston.

Dr. Shedd was typical of the medical arts in his day: no matter what the occasion or the details, if care was needed he provided it. After he'd treated Jessie's most threatening injuries he called her family in Cambridge and told them that she was out of danger, but there was one disturbing consequence: when she came out of the anesthesia there was a neurological problem he had not expected: she had a severe stutter. Jessie's family told Dr. Shedd not to worry about it, she'd stuttered all her life.

Jessie was admitted to the North Conway hospital shortly before midnight on January 2 and she was discharged on May 16, a stay of 136 days. The hospital charge was one dollar a day, with home-cooked meals; surgery and various other attentions added about $100 more.

Joe Dodge carries an injured hiker off Mount Washington. He's just passing "Lunch Rocks" in Tuckerman Ravine and has almost three tough miles to go before reaching the AMC base camp at the highway.

Over time, rescue operations evolved. In this particular operation, in which a team of rescuers carries a victim in a Stokes litter, six carriers are required in a shift, with two or three shifts waiting to relieve them.

TWO MONTHS AFTER JESSIE WAS RELEASED FROM THE HOSPITAL she was back up on Mount Washington, looking for her ice axe and anything else she might have lost. She continued to work at Widener Library and she continued her year-round trips to the mountains, sometimes staying in her cabin on Chocorua, sometimes with Joe Dodge in Pinkham Notch, and sometimes with us in Jackson.

When father finished telling us the story of Jessie and her terrible fall in Huntington Ravine, he'd tell about Jessie and the King's Broad Arrow Pine.

The King's Pines were the trees that the quartermasters of George III marked in colonial days. Europe had used up its supply of trees suitable for the masts of ocean-going ships, so the virgin forests of the New World were a critical military and commercial resource. The mast trees were marked with a broad arrow cut into the bark, and if any colonial yeoman used such a tree for his own purposes he was severely punished. It was known that some of these trees survived the age of sail, and it was rumored that even 150 years later they were sometimes found by determined explorers of the deep woods. Jessie was just such an explorer, but she'd never yet found one of the King's Pines in her many lonely hikes. Still, though, she kept trying.

Then the great hurricane of 1938 struck New England. It came ashore on Long Island, it went straight up the Connecticut River, and when it reached Jackson it was still so strong that it lifted our four-car garage off its foundations. Vast tracts of the mountain forests were knocked flat and Jessie was heartbroken; she was certain that there must be a few of the King's Pines still standing in some undiscovered glen and she was determined to find one. Now it seemed obvious that she had lost her last chance.

It was not obvious to Jessie. She was sure that a certain distant corner of the forest still had a colonial relic and the summer after the hurricane she went there and was unreported for many days. The destruction was terrible and one day she was crawling on her hands and knees, trying to get through an endless blowdown. Jessie's sweater snagged on a broken branch and she twisted around to attend to it. As she looked up, she saw above her head the mark of the King's broad arrow.

Chapter Ten

WRONG-HEADED FROM THE BEGINNING

*T*HERE WAS A TIME WHEN THE SOURCE OF MISFORTUNE LAY outside of ourselves; it might be the result of a curse, or a poison philtre, or a misalignment of the stars, which is the origin of the word disaster, but it was not of our own doing. My father did not believe in such fancies; he always said that people got into trouble because they didn't use their heads.

Father was certainly right when it came to Simon Joseph and his two friends in 1933. Their plans for a Mount Washington climb were wrong-headed from the beginning, a textbook of accumulating errors; the inevitable misfortune created a great stir among New England climbers, and its many consequences still mark the Presidential Range. All this, however, came too late for Simon Joseph.

SIMON JOSEPH
JUNE 1933

On Friday, June 17, 1933, Simon Joseph, Gerald Golden, and Charles Robbins took the train from Boston north to the station at the top of Crawford

Notch. They were all college age; Simon was nineteen and a sophomore at Harvard. They planned to sleep in the woods near the Crawford House that night, get food at the hotel, and then hike across the Southern Peaks to the Lakes of the Clouds Hut.

The site of the Crawford House had deep memories of hikers; the patronymic Crawfords built the first trail to the summit of Mount Washington in 1819 and it began here, and Frederick Strickland started his 1849 climb from the family's inn here. In 1933, the most recent edition of the hotel loomed like a great white ocean liner anchored at the top of the notch and it had become a rather starchy place that sheltered five presidents, assorted captains of industry, and P. T. Barnum.

The three boys from Boston were intent on saving money and they were not provided with starchy clothing. History is silent on this point, but it seems likely that they hoped to get something to eat in the help's dining room next to the kitchen. The hoteliers thought otherwise and told the boys that they could find food at the store maintained by the proprietor of the Willey House, at the site of the disaster celebrated by Nathaniel Hawthorne in *The Ambitious Guest*. This was a three-mile walk down the steep Crawford Notch road and then back again, and the trio decided they didn't want to make the effort. They each had two blankets, so they curled up to sleep in the woods, though it wasn't a very comfortable night: the temperature was down near 40° and there were fairly heavy spatterings of rain. The next morning they again tried for some food at the hotel and they were again turned away. Thus prepared, they started the hike of 6.8 miles along the Southern Peaks to the Lakes of the Clouds.

The Crawford Path is one of the most delightful outings in the White Mountains and the terrain is easy. The Northern Peaks were sharply cut by the glaciers and they're jagged pyramids above the main ridge. The ice sheet slid over the first five of the Southern Peaks, so they have rounded summits joined by moderate depressions in the ridge; only Monroe has a jagged outline. The Crawford Path was graded for horse travel. It rises by easy grades to Clinton, then turns north along the ridge to Pleasant Dome, which may be avoided by following a bypass. Franklin has so small a rise that it hardly seems like a separate summit at all, and there's another bypass around the sharper summit of Monroe.

Simon Joseph.

The Southern Peaks are generally lower than the Northern Peaks and the Crawford Path flirts with timberline for almost its whole length as it climbs toward Mount Washington. The easy grades and long views, the quick access to the shelter of dense spruce, and the connecting trails back to the valley, all make it an excellent climb for a day of dubious weather.

Sunday, June 18, was a day of dubious weather. Simon Joseph and his two friends left warm early-summer days in Boston and they did not anticipate the climatic difference their northerly trip would create. This morning the temperature at the Crawford House was still in the 40s, wind-driven rain was falling when they started up the trail, and they had not brought anything beyond the clothes they'd need for a summer evening.

The trio had no food with them and they knew the Lakes of the Clouds Hut was not yet open for the season, but they thought there would probably be some other hikers staying in the off-season refuge room at the hut who would probably have some extra food they'd pass around to new arrivals. If that didn't work out, Joseph and his friends planned to break into the closed part of the hut; surely there would be some nonperishable food left from the previous summer.

The hikers were in the clouds long before they reached timberline on Mount Clinton. Charles Robbins was getting along better than the other two, so at some point after they reached the crest of the ridge he hurried on toward the Lakes of the Clouds Hut. The conditions up ahead would not improve: the 8:00 A.M. readings at the Mount Washington Observatory showed a temperature of 33° with a northwest wind gusting to 75 mph and carrying sleet and snow.

There was indeed a party of hikers in the refuge room at the hut. Five youngsters from Massachusetts had come in Saturday night and stayed on through Sunday, pinned down by the weather. Several other hikers came in during the morning and ten more came by at about noon, heading down the Ammonoosuc Ravine Trail and the quick shelter they'd find there, but first they left a note in the logbook saying that conditions up on the summit cone were very unpleasant. Their retreat was wise and time-honored; the original name for the Ammonoosuc Ravine was Escape Ravine.

The next entry in the logbook shows that Charles Robbins came in at about three in the afternoon, very much reduced by the weather and by the lack of any food since early in the previous day in Boston. The group waiting out the storm in the Lakes refuge room spent twenty minutes getting him warmed up, then John Ellsworth and Don Plympton started out to find Simon Joseph and Gerald Golden. They headed south along the Crawford Path and found Gerald on the bare, rocky terrain between Monroe and Franklin, about a mile from the hut. He seemed lethargic, but he was on his feet and moving in the right direction and they asked him where the other fellow was, meaning Simon. Gerald said that his friend was ahead of him on the trail, so the two rescuers turned in that direction, back toward the hut.

The Lakes of the Clouds Hut did not exist when the Crawford Path was laid out, so the bridle path followed the height-of-land along the rounded ridge that leads from Mount Monroe to the beginning of the summit cone of Mount Washington. The lakes are west of the height-of-land and about 150 feet lower, so when the hut was built in 1915 the Crawford Path was redirected toward the lakes. The new trail turned sharply west on the flats at the northeast edge of Monroe and the original location was abandoned. The old path was still visible, though; rocks were rearranged to make a better footway, conspicuous depressions were worn into the terrain in many places, and grass and moss had not yet covered the wear of eighty years. The two rescuers were hurrying to find Simon and in their haste they missed the abrupt turn and

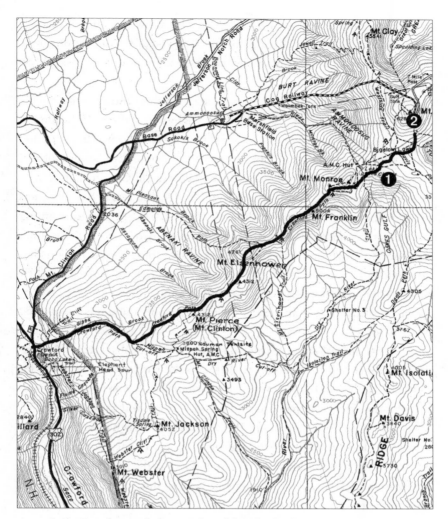

1. Simon Joseph missed turn to Lakes of the Clouds Hut
2. Died just short of Southside Trail

continued straight on along the old path. John Ellsworth quickly realized the mistake and they went back to the junction and down to the hut, where they reported that they'd found Gerald Golden, but not Simon Joseph. So ended Sunday.

Monday brought somewhat more tolerable weather and a group from the refuge room finished their trip and went down by way of the AMC headquarters in Pinkham Notch, which did not yet have a telephone. They reported that a fellow seemed to be missing up near the Lakes of the Clouds Hut, but they were not good on the details. Meanwhile, Gerald Golden and Charles Robbins had recovered some strength and they joined two of the stay-overs and went looking for Simon. The hut was scheduled to open for the summer season that day, and at about 4:30 in the afternoon AMC hutmen Ellis Jump and Don McNaughton arrived and started putting things in order. Soon Gerald and Charles returned with the two other searchers and no news of their missing friend, so they went up to the summit and found Alex McKenzie at the weather observatory and told him that their companion was unreported for a whole day.

Alex was a member of the crew that established the observatory the previous October and he'd been there through the winter. Now he was a bit skeptical. He remembered several times when winter hikers came in with dire reports of lost companions and each alarm proved to be unfounded. Nevertheless, he took two steps. The observatory crew had improved the time during their long winter isolation by building a twenty-pound two-way radio and they sent this breakthrough unit down to the hut to see if it would help with the search. Alex also opened the radio link to the Forest Service office in the town of Twin Mountain, twelve miles west of the summit, and the district ranger said he'd organize a search party and come up to the hut the next day, which was Tuesday.

Tuesday was election day in Twin Mountain and the district ranger could find only one person who wanted to climb the Southern Peaks on the chance that someone was missing. The two of them searched the middle section of the trail the boys had taken and found nothing. They returned to their office in Twin Mountain that evening and called the district supervisor in Laconia, who authorized funds for a ten-man search party. While this was going on, the two hiking partners of Simon Joseph also went down to the valley and hitched rides another eighteen miles to the Willey House in Crawford Notch, where they made a telephone call to Simon's parents. Their son had now been missing for two days and this was the first time they'd heard about it. Mr. Joseph immediately called the governor of Massachusetts, who organized a search party and dispatched it to the northern mountains.

On Wednesday, these two groups converged on the Lakes of the Clouds with a total of nineteen men. One group was led by District Ranger Spinney of the Forest Service and New Hampshire State Fire Chief Boomer. They took the Edmands Path up the west flank of the ridge to join the Crawford Path between Pleasant Dome and Franklin, then turned north and searched the middle section of the Crawford Path. The other group was led by District Ranger Van Alstine; they climbed the Ammonoosuc Ravine Trail to the Lakes of the Clouds Hut and searched southward toward the other group. No one found any trace of Simon Joseph.

On Thursday, Assistant State Forester Hale reached the hut with a third search party, but the morning brought thickening weather and the searchers stayed inside the hut. The air cleared later in the day and all three groups renewed their work. At the same time an airplane made repeated low passes along the length of the Southern Peaks and over the slopes at the head of Oakes Gulf, which runs the length of the ridge on the east side. Mr. Spinney and Mr. Boomer led their groups back to the areas they'd been searching on Wednesday, while Mr. Hale's group went out along the Camel Trail leading from the hut eastward across the head of Oakes Gulf.

At 4:00 Thursday afternoon, Mr. Hale's group found the body of Simon Joseph near the old Crawford Path. He had indeed been ahead of Gerald Golden and he'd gotten to the place where the new section of the Crawford Path turned left toward the hut, the place where John Ellsworth and Don Plympton had briefly followed the old path, then corrected their mistake.

Simon Joseph followed the old path, too, and he did not correct his mistake. The bridle path ran fairly straight along the crest of the Southern Peaks, in fact, today's trail is hardly changed at all from the first location. The old path continued straight at the junction by Monroe and ran about twenty yards across a pebbly flat, then it wandered and curled across the broad saddle for more than half a mile until it reached the Davis Path. This route makes no sense except for horses; the Crawford family liked to keep their animals on the soft tundra-like soil as much as possible, and they stayed away from ledge and areas of loose or rough rock.

Simon Joseph ran out of strength here. If he'd turned to the left he would have seen the AMC's Lakes of the Clouds Hut, but the wind was blowing from that direction and exhausted hikers rarely turn into the wind.

That old location had been officially abandoned after the new trail was built to the Lakes of the Clouds Hut, but the old footway made by the horses was still much more obvious than the new route. Simon must have been well aware of his surroundings at this point because he kept on the crooked path, stepping on the very place where Father Bill Curtis died thirty-three years earlier, but he finally ran out of strength forty paces short of the anchor bolts remaining from the refuge built after the Curtis-Ormsbee episode. At this point the strong northwest wind would have been hitting Simon on the left side of his face, so he turned away from the icy blast and made his way twenty paces across a grassy patch to an outcropping of rocks on the lee side of the ridge. There's a high-walled split in the rocks here; it's floored with grass, a soft and well-sheltered spot, and Simon lay down to rest on this bed.

After two days of uninterrupted bad judgment, Simon had finally done something right in finding this shelter. But those who believe in star-crossed enterprise would note that if Simon had looked left instead of right as he stood on the Crawford Path he would have seen the Lakes of the Clouds Hut only a few easy minutes away. Moreover, if he'd kept going for a few moments longer he would have found the Camel Path just beyond the iron

Simon Joseph lay down to rest on this patch of grass, where he died without unrolling the blankets he was carrying. Mount Washington is in the background.

bolts and a sign there directing him to the hut a quarter of a mile away. Simon did not get up from his rest, though, and he died on that grassy bed with his blankets still rolled up.

NEWS OF THE COMPLEX SITUATION SURROUNDING SIMON JOSEPH'S death spread quickly, and the results were both immediate and long lasting.

The first concerned radio. As the nineteenth century turned, virtually nothing of what we think of as modern times had emerged. One of the first hints of the world we now take for granted was the amazing device put together by a young Italian named Guglielmo Marconi, who successfully transmitted a wireless telegraph signal for about a mile in 1896, what would become known as radio. But Marconi was not a disinterested scientist; he was more like an electronic entrepreneur and he had his eye out for the main chance. This came in the fall of 1899, when that year's edition of the America's Cup yacht races were scheduled for the ocean off Sandy Hook, at the northeast corner of New Jersey. James Gordon Bennett was the editor of *The New York Herald* and he thought it would be a splendid thing if up-to-the-minute news of the races could be flashed from the off-shore excitement to his downtown editorial offices. So he sent the proposition and an offer of $5,000 to Signor Marconi, who came to America to cash in both the check and the publicity and create the world's first ship-to-shore radio contact.

It was an important moment. From the wine-dark seas of Homeric legend until that day, ships at sea had always been alone. Ocean communications were limited to line of sight with flags or lanterns; beyond that they were at the mercy of the many gods of the sky and the deeps. Now they could send messages over the horizon, but, perhaps following Marconi's commercial impulse, ship-to-shore telegraph was seen as a novelty, a way to send birthday greetings and other such trifles, and operators were licensed by the Marconi Company as if the Italian meant to keep radio as a proprietary account.

One licensee was Jack Irwin, at the Marconi station at Siasconset on the eastern shore of Nantucket. Another was Jack Binns, the Marconi operator on the White Star liner *Republic*. On the night of January 23, 1909, the *Republic* collided with the *Florida*, inbound from Italy, and received a mortal wound. Marconi operators did know of a distress call, but it had never been used; it was CQD, standing for "Seek You—Danger." Now Jack Binns sent that code and Jack Irwin picked it up, and for the rest of the day the rescue of the *Republic*'s crew and its 1,500 passengers was directed by radio. This proved the true usefulness of Marconi's novelty, but CQD was an awkward series in Morse code, it was (−·−· −−·− −··). So it was changed to the simpler (··· −−− ···), which was SOS, a letter-clump standing for no words but easier to transmit under stress.

The rescue of the *Republic*'s passengers created an enormous sensation and Jack Binns was the unwilling hero of autograph seekers, tabloids, popular songs, and a fictionalized film by Vitagraph. Jack fled home to England and grateful White Star executives offered him the most prestigious Marconi job they had, but at the last moment he fell in love and asked for a later posting. This cost Jack Binns his chance to sail with the *Titanic*.

In the coming years Guglielmo Marconi continued to devote more time to his reputation than to his laboratory, and the effect was to freeze the official dogmas of radio at the rather primitive stage represented by his low-frequency transmissions. It wasn't that higher frequencies were not known or the necessary equipment was too difficult to make, the problem was that the sainted Marconi had not gone in that direction.

This led to a curious situation in which eager youngsters building high-frequency radio sets at their kitchen tables were often considerably ahead of the industry. They formed a loose sort of juvenile federation which they named the Radio Club of America, or RCA, and Joe Dodge was in that loop, reassuring his aunt that he didn't have to open the window to let in the radio waves.

Alex McKenzie was another of those inventive youngsters, and he and Joe stayed with it. By the early 1930s, they were leading spirits in establishing the weather observatory on the summit of Mount Washington, a place with something very much like the old isolation of the silent ships at sea. The observers rarely came down the mountain, Joe Dodge and the AMC camp in Pinkham Notch was their nearest contact with the outside world, and there was only fitful highway traffic and no telephone in Pinkham.

Joe had been one of the first few Americans to contact Europe with short-wave radio; he'd been working a short-wave set in Pinkham Notch since his summer-only tenure before 1926, and when the summit observatory opened he had a line-of-sight link to the summit. Now the plan called for the observatory to make radio contact with the Blue Hill Observatory four times a day and transmit weather data on the same schedule.

Radio traffic from Marconi sets traveled in relatively long waves and, given the practice of the day, the antennas were correspondingly long. Ocean-going ships in the days of the *Republic* and the *Titanic* usually transmitted on the 100-meter band with antennas that stretched most of the length of the ship. This was still the model in 1933, and it presented an immediate and obvious problem for operations on the summit of Mount Washington: the antenna wire would be too long to mount inside the observatory building and an outdoor antenna would be destroyed by the very reason for its existence, the violent summit weather.

The observatory crew decided to try a higher frequency and they put the shorter antenna in a stout wooden box bolted to the summer water tank on the highest point of the summit settlement. Accepted Marconi practice indicated that the higher frequencies could be used only in line-of-sight transmission and Blue Hill was over the horizon, but Joe and Alex were right: the Blue Hill transmissions were successful and a page was turned in the theory and practice of radio. Closer to home, Joe Dodge maintained daily radio contact with the summit station from opening in the fall of 1932 until wartime restrictions were imposed in 1942, then he resumed the contacts until the hour he left Pinkham Notch in 1959.

Many years later, Alex McKenzie thought back to those times. He realized that the scatter effect and bending capacity of the troposphere had been greatly under-estimated in 1933, and the success of the summit transmissions forced an important reconsideration in this area. Furthermore, the position of the antenna box on the tank was fortuitous; they'd faced it toward Blue Hill, which seemed obvious, but they didn't realize that the steel hoops and curved back wall of the water tank might work as reflectors and reinforce the signal. Furthermore, their Blue Hill schedule gave them a self-contained index to the effect of weather on the propagation of radio waves. In further contradiction of prevailing electronic wisdom, the summit crew discovered that their signal could reach New York City on certain days. This was much farther down the curve of the earth than Blue Hill and, putting this together with their weather maps, they realized that high-frequency signals were reinforced by traveling along a weather front and were also boosted by traveling through bands of certain temperatures, a method whales use to send their sonic messages across thousands of miles of ocean water.

The more immediate result of the Simon Joseph episode was the success of the twenty-pound portable unit the summit crew sent down to the Lakes of the Clouds Hut to help coordinate the search.

Radios of those early days were imposing. They had heavy metal frames and coiling cables and ranks of glowing vacuum tubes and black boxes, with numerous separate elements ranged along the shelf; this is why a complete radio was called a "set," a term that survives in today's television market. So when the observatory crew of 1933 made a twenty-pound portable, they achieved an important breakthrough.

The AMC was so impressed by reports of the Joseph episode that their high-elevation huts—Lakes, Madison, and Greenleaf—were equipped with portable two-way radios against the needs of search and rescue. Word spread, and by 1938 the Swiss were equipping their mountain refuges with thirty-pound portables.

The most immediate and visible result of Simon Joseph's death was the project to rebuild all the cairns marking the trails above timberline on the Presidential Range: the cairns on the more popular trails were raised to a height of four feet and the interval was tightened to fifty feet. This enormous job was done by members of the Civilian Conservation Corps, "CCC boys" as they were always called.

The CCC was one of the earliest of President Franklin Roosevelt's New Deal initiatives. Roosevelt took office on March 4, 1933 and on March 5 he convened a meeting of the secretaries of labor, agriculture, interior, and war, the director of the bureau of the budget, the judge advocate general of the army, and the solicitor of the department of the interior. They roughed out the plan for the CCC, the enabling legislation went to Congress on March 21, it passed on March 31, and on April 7 the first of four-million CCC boys signed up.

About two months later, a troop of CCC boys was assigned to work on the cairns of the Presidential Range. They were bunked three apiece in the AMC huts at Madison Springs on the Northern Peaks and at the Lakes of the Clouds, and two or three of them stayed in the summit hotel on Mount Washington. This caused some concern. The CCC was organized along distinctly military principles and soon after the CCC boys were on station, an army captain blustered into Joe's office in Pinkham Notch and inquired, with some heat, if there was enough air for the boys to breathe up there above timberline. Joe assured him that air was supplied in pretty generous quantities up there.

That summer the U.S. Forest Service put up the first generation of yellow metal signs on all trails that led above timberline: "STOP: This is a fine trail for hiking, but be sure you are in good physical condition, well rested and fed, have sufficient clothing, emergency food and equipment. Travel above timberline is hazardous. Climatic changes are sudden and severe at all seasons."

There were further consequences. Simon Joseph was the thirteenth person to die on the Presidential Range, and the New Hampshire State Development Commission launched an initiative designed to prevent further deaths. They sent word to the Appalachian Mountain Club, the Dartmouth Outing Club, and the Mountain Hotel Proprietors Association asking for their help in a crusade to educate hikers. One of the leading elements in this idea was that all people planning to climb Mount Washington should be examined by an official who was competent to judge the state of their clothing, their boots, and their health, and to test their knowledge of the mountain. A similar proposal went to the New Hampshire legislature, but it did not gain enough support to merit a vote. Neither of these precautionary measures was ever heard from again.

The CCC boys did their work so well that the cairns they built have lasted to the present day with very little additional maintenance, and the yellow signs still guard trails leading above timberline.

Chapter Eleven

A DEADLY CROSSING IN
GREAT GULF

*S*EPTEMBER OF 1934 WAS NOT A GOOD TIME TO BE STARTING college. The Great Depression was five years old and its grip was still growing tighter on the land; President Roosevelt's myriad New Deal agencies were everywhere, but they had not lifted the stock market out of the low 40s. On the other hand, more Americans were going hiking than ever before.

Several factors were at work. For one thing, the growing number of good roads in North America and increasingly reliable automobiles made backwoods outposts more accessible. Beyond that, the Depression did not close schools. Indeed, this was a period of large growth in private schools and the faculty had secure jobs, a relatively high income, and more than three months of vacation every summer. The hidden lesson here is that the more comfortably fixed American families kept their money. Finally, there was an unprecedented burst of exploration and mountaineering in North America that was discovering new mountains in the high ranges of Canada and Alaska and making first ascents that loomed large in the pages of publications such as the AMC's semi-annual *Appalachia*. Bradford Washburn led many of these expeditions, and for entry-level excursionists there were the more familiar reaches of the White Mountains with the AMC huts and dozens of lean-to shelters to welcome them.

My father taught at Deerfield Academy in Massachusetts, and he was the resident faculty member in the Saxton House, which was an academy dormitory with our family on the first floor and students on the second floor. In 1933, one of the students was John Pierce, conspicuous because his fine and enthusiastic singing voice could be heard all over the house. The Saxton House was not very large and my bedroom was a space under the stairs just large enough for a cot bed, and I was too young to remember John's singing.

In the fall of 1954, I was visiting Goddard College in northern Vermont as a prospective student, and when the tour was over I was deciding that I didn't like it very much. My mother had driven up with me, and while I was making the official tour she was making herself politely scarce in a far reach of the campus. She heard singing and followed the sound until she saw a man weeding a flower garden. He was on his knees in the corner of an L-shaped building, facing inwards, and my mother came up behind him and said, "John Pierce?"

It was. He was on the faculty at the college and he kept this garden in order because he could see it from his office, so he took me in hand and told me about the real Goddard. Mother and I returned to Deerfield and I packed a supply of clothes and went straight back to Goddard. I stayed there in one connection or another for eight years.

John Pierce became my closest friend on the faculty, and he and I and some other students often went hiking together. There was a chip in one of his front teeth and after I'd known him for a decent interval I asked what happened to it. He said that happened years earlier during a camping trip in Great Gulf, over on the Presidential Range. He said he'd been diving in the river and hit an underwater rock, and he never had the tooth fixed because it was a reminder. John never told me any more than that, and forty-four years would pass before I learned what happened in Great Gulf.

JEROME PIERCE
SEPTEMBER 1934

The Intercollegiate Outing Club Association was a vigorous force a generation or two ago and they published a song book, actually, *the* songbook, what everyone called the IOCA book. This was the collection that had all the verses of all the songs—*Abdulah Bulbul Amir, The Eddystone Light, Oola Ski Yumper from Norway, Juanita, Who Threw the Overhauls in Mrs. Murphy's Chowder*—and all the other favorites in the days when skiers and hikers actually did gather around the fire to sing. It was an institution and the catch was that no one wanted to be seen using the IOCA book; it was a point of honor to know all the words without it.

In September 1934, the IOCA had their annual College Weekend. This year there would be hiking on the Presidential Range; forty-two people signed up for the outing and fifteen of them were staying at the Great Gulf Shelter, which was also an institution. The first small refuge on the site was built in 1909, then replaced in 1927 with a new one rated at twenty-two hikers.

This shelter was a sort of grand central station for Mount Washington and the Northern Peaks. It was on the Great Gulf Trail, which is most conveniently entered from the Glen House or the AMC camp. The trail leads uphill from the shelter to the summit of Mount Washington and downhill to the highway, and the shelter was a quarter of a mile from the spot where the Wamsutta Trail led up Mount Washington on one side of the Gulf and the Six Husbands Trail led up Mount Jefferson on the opposite side. Two other trails branched off Six Husbands soon after it left the floor of the gulf, one was the Adams Slide Trail up Mount Adams and the other was the Buttress Trail to Mount Madison and the hut there.

Spaulding Lake lies high up in Great Gulf, a glacial tarn named for the first keepers of the Summit House, the family who tried to restore life in Lizzie Bourne. The West Branch of the Peabody River starts at the lake and flows 6.8 miles out to the main river in Pinkham Notch, running close to the Great Gulf Trail all the way down. The sides of the gulf are uniformly steep and they hold very little soil, the terrain is mostly ledge with an overburden of rough rock broken loose by millions of cycles of frost and thaw, and there's a thin mantle of soil and moss. This combination does not absorb much water and after a rainstorm the many streams running down the sides of the gulf quickly swell the West Branch to a torrent.

The IOCA group reached the Great Gulf Shelter Friday afternoon and found a considerable number of hikers already in residence. Nothing daunted, John Pierce and Hartness Beardsley built a snug little hemlock lean-to for Harty's sisters Mary and Connie and three other IOCA girls, and they

The Intercollegiate Outing Club Association chose the Great Gulf Shelter as their camp for their annual September hike in 1934. After a torrential rainstorm the tiny stream in the foreground flooded the shelter. A nearby river rose correspondingly and took Jerome Pierce's life.

improvised poncho shelters for themselves. The Pierces and the Beardsleys were neighbors back home in Springfield, Vermont, and they all knew each other very well.

An easterly wind had been blowing all day, which is an alarm bell for veterans of the Presidential Range. It brought intermittent rain on Friday, then during the night the wind moved into the southeast and a torrential downpour commenced in the hours before dawn. John and Harty kept getting up during the night to keep their campfire going, but the rain soaked everything else. A small stream runs down off Mount Washington and passes a few steps from the shelter, so small a stream that it would more properly be called a rill—two or three people with pails could move as much water. On Saturday morning, it had risen two and a half feet and threatened to flood the IOCA campsite.

The college crew decided to stay with their plans; this was, after all, the last weekend before the semester began. The Beardsley-Pierce group, along with a few friends, was going to start by climbing Mount Adams by way of the Adams Slide Trail, which meant that they'd have to cross the West Branch immediately.

The course of the river is steep all the way down the gulf, mile after mile of rapids and falls studded with rocks ranging from the size of a plum to the size of a cottage. There are many trails and many streams in the gulf and the crossings are not difficult, most of them are a matter of hopping from one rock to another. The usual crossing from the Great Gulf Trail to the Adams Slide Trail requires from three to six hops, depending on length of leg and zest of hop, but the river is quite flat here and in normal times a dry crossing is routine.

The morning of September 9 was not normal times. The air had cleared by 10:00 A.M., but the West Branch had risen far above its normal level and the crossing to the Adams Slide Trail had no stepping stones showing at all, just a flood of churning water. Some other place to cross would have to be found if the IOCA crew was going to make the climb they'd planned for that day.

It probably would have been a better idea to change their plan. If they turned right instead of left at the Adams Slide junction they could go 1.6 miles up the Wamsutta Trail to 6-Mile on the auto road, a wonderful hike that gets above timberline quickly and opens spectacular views of Great Gulf and the Northern Peaks. If they wanted to go farther, they could connect there with the Alpine Garden Trail across the head of the ravines or up the Nelson Crag Trail to the summit of Mount Washington. Alternatively, they could continue along the Great Gulf Trail and on up the headwall to the Gulfside Trail, then follow this route two miles along the ridge to the Sphinx Trail down into the gulf and thence back to the shelter. Any of these choices would be easier and more interesting than the relentlessly steep Adams Slide Trail and would not involve major water crossings. Instead, the IOCA group stuck with their original plan.

Jerome Pierce had just graduated from high school in Springfield and at seventeen he was the youngest fellow on the trip. Also called "Jerry," he'd come along with his older brother John, who was going into his junior year at Middlebury College in Vermont, and Jerry would follow John to Middlebury the week after the trip was over.

John and Jerry both had strong personalities. John was assertive and apt to think that his view of any situation was the correct one, a quality which

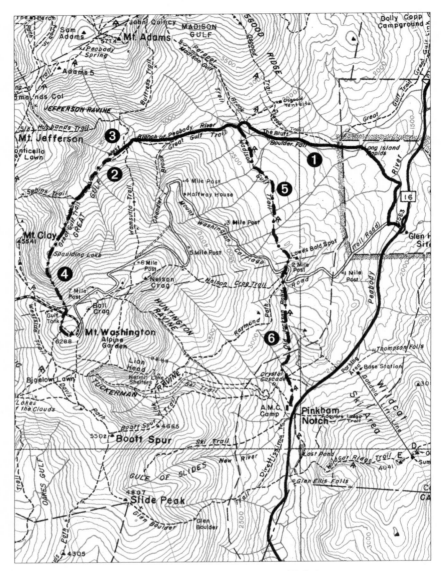

1, 2. Jerome Pierce went up Great Gulf Trail to Great Gulf Shelter

3. Fell just above crossing

4. Friend ran for help up Great Gulf headwall to summit

5, 6. Mary Beardsley and companion continue to Pinkham for help via Madison Gulf Trail and Old Jackson Road

gained emphasis by the discovery that he usually turned out to be right. Jerry shared the assertive part but the edge was softened by his friendly and engaging character, and he was very popular with everyone who knew him.

Jerry was a good friend of Mary Beardsley. She was sixteen years old and an ardent hiker, and she liked to go on long walks with the Pierce boys or anyone else who shared her enthusiasms. People underestimated Mary at their peril and whenever she was out hiking it wouldn't be long before the others would be yelling, "Slow her down!" Mary and her family hiked the whole length of the Long Trail in Vermont, one section at a time, the ridgeline traverse of the Green Mountain from Quebec to Massachusetts. Mary was only partway through the Dana Hall School in Wellesley, Massachusetts, but her family let her come on the IOCA trip with her brother Harty because, it seemed to her, they'd let her go anywhere with her older brother.

The first day in Great Gulf certainly wasn't what the IOCA crowd had hoped for, but after cooking the best breakfast they could under the circumstances, John and Harty started working on the problem of high water in the West Branch. They thought they could build a bridge across the stream, so they took an axe and went looking for spruce trees that would be suitable for civil engineering.

Jerry Pierce had other ideas and, perhaps eager to prove his mettle to the college men he'd soon join, he went looking for his own place to cross the West Branch. The stream is quite flat below the trail crossing and all possible stepping stones were deep under the flood. There wasn't any possible footing just upstream, either, but about forty yards farther up he spotted a large pool with a curious waterfall above it. A room-size boulder jutted out from each bank and just above them a third boulder was securely lodged. The whole content of the river divided around the upper boulder and the two lower boulders forced the streams together again in two falls that met in a 45° angle. This appeared to be the only place to cross, because the river widened and flattened again just above this barrier and all the low rocks were covered.

These three boulders were so large that they rose above the flood and the space between them seemed a reasonable two-jump way to cross the river, so Jerry tried it. He missed his footing on the first jump and fell into one of the angled waterfalls. Two of the boulders, the center one and the far one, sloped inward on their downstream side and the massive force of the two opposing falls pushed him back into that undercut.

The IOCA boys immediately formed a human chain and on one try they got close enough to feel Jerry's head about three feet below the surface, but they could not pull him free, he seemed to be caught in the rocks and an old log under the waterfall. They found a slender spruce tree and quickly trimmed it and tried to use that to get Jerry free. They tried again and again, but the pool below the boulders was eight feet deep, the force of the stream swept them away again and again, and the full-body push of the water quickly stole their strength. They kept trying until they were exhausted, and then John kept diving and diving, trying to reach his brother at the base of the falls. John was being badly battered by the crushing falls and the underwater rocks but he kept trying and trying until at last he, too, had gone beyond his strength and his friends pulled him to shore.

Meanwhile, Mary Beardsley and one of the Middlebury students ran down the Great Gulf Trail and turned off on the Madison Gulf Trail and then the Old Jackson Road to find Joe Dodge at the AMC headquarters, an urgent dash of four and a half miles. As always, Joe dropped everything, gathered a crew at Pinkham, and headed for the trouble.

One of the other IOCA boys climbed 3.3 miles and 3,038 feet up the headwall of Great Gulf to get help from the summit of Mount Washington. CCC boys were billeted on the summit and at the Lakes of the Clouds and Madison Springs Huts and they'd been put to work at useful jobs on the range. Now they were back for their second summer and they'd become used to pitching in on unexpected jobs. The IOCA call was answered by three CCC boys, two men on the hotel staff who had worked in the AMC huts, and several other volunteers, and they all headed down into the Gulf.

The summit group got there first. Some of them cut several long poles in the woods while the rest of the hands piled rocks in the channel of one of the facing waterfalls to divert the flow into the other channel and take the criss-cross pressure off the rocks down below. They jammed the pole under the waterfall and anchored it on shore, and then they worked their way down the pole and groped around under the fall and in the whiteout of the foam.

They found that Jerry's feet were wedged between two rocks so his head was held underwater, and it was obvious that the IOCA group never had any chance of pulling him free. Now the group from the summit retrieved his body and they'd just started down the trail when they met Joe Dodge and his group coming up with a stretcher to complete the carry to the Glen House.

Mr. and Mrs. Pierce had been notified and they drove up to the Glen House. Many of the others on the IOCA trip were there, and Harty Beardsley went to the train station in Gorham and took his friend's body home to Springfield. John was at the Glen House, too, and didn't want much company. Instead, he found a piano and sat there for a long time improvising quiet laments in all the minor keys he knew.

NOT LONG BEFORE THE TRIP TO GREAT GULF, JERRY PIERCE GAVE his mother subscriptions to all her favorite magazines. That way, he thought, she wouldn't be so lonely when both her sons were away at Middlebury College. After the news from Great Gulf, she never let the subscriptions lapse.

The two Beardsley girls returned to school the week after the trip, Mary to Dana Hall and Connie to nearby Wellesley College. Church attendance was required and Dana Hall did not have its own chapel, so on Sunday the girls went to the services at Wellesley. The minister was Boynton Merrill, and when he rose for his sermon on the first Sunday of the new term he chose the Great Gulf accident as his text. Mary was stunned, and her sister was so upset that she had to be taken back to her dormitory.

The Great Gulf Shelter was the place of my own first overnight hike, in 1947. Later on, smaller companion shelter was built nearby and then another one further down the Gulf, then all three were demolished when the Great Gulf was designated a Wilderness Area and all human additions were removed except for the trail signs and the trails. The old clearing is still there beside the small brook, and it's still used by campers as a tent site.

John Pierce carried the memory of the IOCA trip for the rest of his life; he was haunted by the thought that the bruise on Jerry's head was from the pole he used when he tried to free him from the waterfall, and that was the cause of his brother's death. John named his first son Jerome, and he died before I found the doctor's report showing that the bruise came from a fatal impact on the rock before Jerry went into the water.

Chapter Twelve

THE CHOICE OF PRESIDENTS

*T*HE NORTHERN PEAKS AND THE SOUTHERN PEAKS OF THE Presidential Range are joined by Mount Washington, but that's about the only thing they have in common.

The Southern Peaks begin with Webster, which is more like one wall of Crawford Notch. Daniel Webster wasn't a president, but he was a son of New Hampshire who went on to debate Lincoln and climb Mount Washington in conditions he did not enjoy.

Next comes Jackson. Some believe it was named for the hugely popular sixth president, the first one who didn't seem vaguely like a king, the first one who shook hands with people. It was in fact named for Charles T. Jackson, the man who conducted New Hampshire's first geological survey, a study reflecting its author's primitive understanding of geology. Jackson's summit has a lovely all-around view and, although there's a steep scramble up the south side, the trail goes on through a swamp just past the summit on the north side, which isn't what one expects on a mountain ridge.

Then there's Pierce; it's a brisk 500 foot rise up the south side but there's no summit, just the end of a ridge leading north.

Next comes what we always called Pleasant Dome, and so did everyone else for most of its history, and it's the only one of the Southern Peaks that really stands up from the ridge. Then, without warning, the name was changed to Mount Eisenhower. This was because the military hero started toward the White House in the New Hampshire primary and, being a military man, he was the first president who had a chief of staff. This was Sherman Adams of New Hampshire, a peppery little wood chopper turned governor who quickly became known as the president's No man and brought his edibles to the White House in an old-fashioned woodsman's lunch pail, then patrolled the dining room to see how much time the rest of the staff were taking off for lunch.

Next past Pleasant Dome/Eisenhower there's what we always called Franklin Pierce; we thought it was actually named Franklin, but the venerable kite-flyer was never president, so we called it Franklin Pierce. Most people don't recognize that as a presidential name, but we knew he was the only president who came from New Hampshire. At any rate, this presumptive summit is so low it's easy to miss as you hike over it.

Finally there's Monroe, a crest that we admired because we all learned the Marine Corps Hymn during World War II, the service song that told about the halls of Montezuma and the shores of Tripoli, and it was president Monroe who sent the marines to the shores of Tripoli to smite the Barbary Pirates.

The sun always seems to be shining on the Southern Peaks, the trail along the crest flirts with the sweet shrubs and moss of timberline all the way, and the quirky elements of their topography and nomenclature and the pleasant trails that reach the crest of the ridge have always been the signals of a friendly nature.

The Northern Peaks seemed serious to me right from the beginning. There is no easy way up Madison and Adams and Jefferson, they leave timberline far below them and they drop straight from their sharp summits into the Great Gulf. This is what the nineteenth century artists had in mind when they contemplated the sublime acclivities and the dreadful abyss, and even the fairest days up there are tinged with threat.

In 1938, three friends were already weak when they began their climb up the Northern Peaks and they chose one of the most difficult routes to reach the heights. They made it through their traverse to the Southern Peaks, but not by much. Then things got worse.

JOE CAGGIANO
AUGUST 1938

Joe Caggiano and Frank Carnese lived near each other on Long Island, New York, Phillip Turner lived near Boston, and when the three friends left for a week of hiking in the White Mountains they were thinking of ways to save money. The stock market hit bottom at 33.10 in 1932, when they left for their trip six years later it had climbed 14.8 points to 47.90, and during their four days in the mountains there was good news from the railroads, which led a strong advance of 0.7. But still, the three friends didn't have much money and they decided to economize on food and accommodations during the trip they planned.

There was some hiking experience in the group, but not much. Joe was seventeen years old and he'd hiked on the Long Trail in Vermont. Frank was twenty and he'd done some hiking on Bear Mountain, north of New York City. Phillip was twenty-two, he was a student at the New England Conservatory of Music near Boston, and had a job at Jordan Marsh in that city. He and Joe had met two years earlier on the Long Trail. Phillip was born in New Hampshire and he'd climbed Chocorua several times and had hiked a little further north once. None of them had any experience with conditions above timberline.

This trip would be a climb on the Presidential Range during the last week of August and the boys decided to travel light, so they saved weight by bringing a minimum of clothing. Sleeping bags were not yet widespread among hikers and the few types in the market were very expensive, so all three boys were using blanket rolls with rubberized ground cloths tied to their rucksacks, clumsy and inefficient loads that ranged from forty to sixty pounds.

The trio boarded the train on the afternoon of Saturday, August 20. Their first stop was Mount Chocorua, where they'd make a sort of shakedown hike to test their kit and their condition. Chocorua is thirty-five miles south of Pinkham Notch and it's one of the most popular mountains in the Northeast.

It has a rich Indian legend, it's right beside the main road, and the towering summit ridge of bare rock is framed by a stand of birch trees and reflected in a lake, a favorite with artists and calendar-makers everywhere.

The three friends reached Chocorua late Saturday evening and climbed three miles to a shelter on the upper shoulder of the mountain, where they camped for a rather short night. On Sunday morning they climbed another mile to the summit, then came down and got a ride to the AMC headquarters in Pinkham Notch. They hardly paused at Pinkham, though; their plan was to spend the night at Crag Camp, on the northwest side of Mount Adams and eight miles of stiff climbing from Pinkham. So they started out on the trail called the Old Jackson Road, connected with the Madison Gulf Trail into Great Gulf, and climbed on up the headwall of Madison Gulf.

This made a very long day, little less than a hiking frenzy. Each of the boys had been working at sedentary in-town occupations and Joe was just getting over a lingering illness; he weighed only 123 pounds and he was in reduced condition. The headwall of Madison Gulf is forbiddingly steep, all three of them had been feeling a bit ill since morning, and they'd eaten very little. So they gave up on their plans for Crag Camp and slept in the open at the top of Madison Gulf.

Hikers on the Presidential Range had enjoyed fair weather for the previous three days, with moderate wind and mild temperatures, but that was changing as Joe and his friends climbed the headwall of Madison Gulf. The Mount Washington Observatory is four air-line miles from the place the hikers slept, with the chasm of Great Gulf intervening, and the observatory records show that the wind was shifting from the northwest around into the south with a rise in humidity to 91 percent at midnight, sure signs of less pleasant things to come.

On Monday, Joe and his friends packed up their overnight gear and crossed the plateau to Madison Springs Hut, but in keeping with their economies they didn't partake of its comforts and services. They "hovered about," as one of the hutmen put it, then they climbed up the rocky slide on the shoulder of Adams and continued along the Gulfside Trail to Thunderstorm Junction at 5,500 feet before descending to Crag Camp, perched on the very edge of King Ravine at about 4,300 feet. The portents of the evening before had come to pass, and they'd been in clouds almost all day with temperatures in the low 50s and dropping into the 40s.

The Presidential Range makes its own weather, a result of the convergence of two jet stream tracks over the area and the sweep of prevailing winds driving warm valley air upslope into the cold air on the heights. This can create sudden and completely unexpected fog that has brought many hikers into serious trouble.

They'd been above timberline and fully exposed to a cold wind for all of this day, so the boys finally got comfortable at Crag Camp, their first good rest since leaving home three days earlier. Indeed, Crag Camp was very much like home. It was one of the private cabins built in the golden age of the Randolph Mountain Club, a quite improbable house pinned to a ledge overlooking King Ravine and fitted with a kitchen and bunk rooms, a fieldstone fireplace, a cast-iron kitchen stove, a library, and a parlor organ.

The weather broke in the hours surrounding midnight and a brilliant aurora borealis lit the sky, but the fair promise of morning faded and the fog closed in again as they climbed back to the crest of the ridge. The Gulfside Trail stretched 5.5 miles across the Northern Peaks to the summit of Mount Washington and the temperature was in the 40s all day long and the wind rose into the 50-mph range. The observatory calculates wind in two ways: momentary velocity and total miles passing the instrument in twenty-four hours. During the previous day there were 337 miles of wind, this day there were 1,058. Conditions were so unpleasant that the boys spent the afternoon in the Summit House, then at about 5:00 P.M. they started down the Crawford Path to the Lakes of the Clouds Hut, 1.4 miles away and still above timberline.

They didn't stop there long, however, they went on another mile or so along the Crawford Path and made camp in the scrub growth just above timberline on the Southern Peaks, near the place Father Bill Curtis and Allan Ormsbee took refuge. They were not abundantly provided for this, but they found a soft place on the stony ground and made what Phil described as "a good supper," then they spread their blanket rolls on their ground cloths and lay down.

About midnight, it began to rain. They huddled under their ground cloths for two hours and waited for it to end, but it didn't end and at 2:00 A.M. they gave up. They left all their gear where it was and groped their way a mile back up the ridge to the hut. One of the hutmen heard them, so he got up and gave them some blankets and they lay down on the floor.

It was a short night and an uncertain start for the next day. The rain had broken into their first sleep, and the hutmen and early-rising hikers began moving around at first light. Phil Turner hiked back to their camping place and brought in their sodden gear, and when he returned Joe Caggiano realized that he'd left his knife where they'd camped, so he and Phil went back to look for it, without success. When they were all back at the hut the crew offered to fix a late breakfast for them, but the boys declined the chance. They each had a cup of coffee and a piece of leftover corn bread and started back across the range, retracing their ridge-top steps of the day before, but under far worse weather conditions.

This was a curious plan. If they'd kept going down the Crawford Path past the Lakes of the Clouds, they would have been hiking on new and much easier terrain and seeing new views on the Southern Peaks, and they would not have had large verticals to deal with. If the weather continued wet and windy they'd have the shelter of thick spruce trees for a large part of the way, and they could look forward to the snug comforts of Mizpah Springs shelter at the end of a moderate day's hike.

Instead, they turned north again, and it was not a good start. The only dry clothes they had were at the bottom of their packs—shorts, sweaters, and low socks—and that was not what was needed for this day. The rain turned heavy at 8:00 A.M. but the boys persisted and got on the trail two hours later, still in heavy rain with the temperature dropping into the 30s and winds gusting to more than 50 miles an hour on the summit just above them.

The Westside Trail skirts the summit cone of Mount Washington, then meets the Gulfside Trail to cross the Northern Peaks to Madison Spring Hut. As before, the boys planned to turn off at Thunderstorm Junction and go down to Crag Camp. They were virtually retracing their steps, but this day was cold, wet, and windy, with dense fog settling onto the range early in the afternoon, so it was slow and treacherous going over the slippery rocks.

The embattled hikers fell again and again, but they kept going. In fact, they tried to go as fast as they could on the theory that the exercise would keep them warm. It didn't, it made them more tired and more unsteady on their feet. Now there was sleet mixing with the rain as they crossed the saddle between Clay and Jefferson. Here the trail starts to climb toward Monticello Lawn below the summit cone of Jefferson. In fair weather this is one of the sweetest places in the mountains, so level and grassy that in earlier years there had been a croquet set for the pleasure of passing hikers.

This was not a day for croquet. Joe and his friends met two other hikers on Monticello Lawn, hurrying to get out of the storm. They saw that Joe Caggiano was, as one of them said, "blue from the knees down," and they urged the boys to turn around and come with them down the Sphinx Trail, a quick and well-protected one-mile descent to the floor of Great Gulf, then an easy 0.6 to Great Gulf Shelter. They boys said they were getting along all right and they'd get warmed up and dried out when they reached Crag Camp.

Joe and Phillip and Frank stayed together until they were skirting the summit of Jefferson and heading for Edmands Col. They'd been exposed to cold, wet weather and the full force of the wind ever since they left the Lakes of the Clouds Hut, they'd been sleeping in unfamiliar outdoor beds for four nights, they did not have warm clothes, and they hadn't had anything to eat since the coffee and corn bread at the hut.

The Gulfside Trail is steep and rough as it pitches down into Edmands Col, difficult footing even in good weather. Somewhere on this stretch, one of the straps on Joe's pack broke. Frank stopped to help him, but Phillip Turner didn't realize what had happened and he kept going. He wrote later, "The wind was so bad, the fog was so thick and the wind so heavy, biting

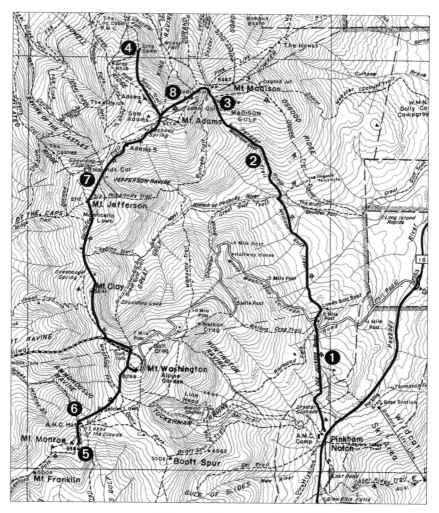

1, 2. Joe Caggiano went up Old Jackson Road and Madison Gulf Trail
   3. Spent first night near Madison Spring Hut
   4. Spent second night at Crag Camp
   5. Across Gulfside Trail and Crawford Path to start third night near trail below Mount Monroe
   6. Forced to Lakes of the Clouds Hut by rain in middle of night
   7. Caggiano began faltering near Edmands Col and Frank Carnese went for help
   8. Caggiano collapsed near Gulfside Trail above King Ravine

into us with a chill that turned us limp and weak, that we couldn't see more than ten or fifteen feet and, somehow, despite our best efforts, we lost sight of one another."

This is a terrifying situation. Everything turns gray and even a person who grew up on these trails, someone who knows exactly where he is and where the next trail junction is and which is the quickest way to shelter, someone who is *at home* on the Northern Peaks, even someone like that will feel a kind of sudden dread.

These three flatlanders had none of those advantages but all of the dread. Later, Phillip wrote, "Joe and Frank were walking ahead of me near Edmonds Col, picking their way slowly and carefully—and then they were not there. The wind was so terrific and the rain and sleet were so weakening that I was nearly all in. A great terror came over me, I didn't know which way to search for Joe and Frank. Again and again I shouted their names. All I heard in answer was the fearful howl of the gale. Whenever I stopped to get my bearings, I nearly froze. My feet were so heavy they were like lead, my head was pounding terribly, and I began to wonder if I'd ever make shelter. I kept struggling along, half in a coma, and every step took all of my will power." Phillip was ahead of his companions as he descended into the wind tunnel of Edmands Col, but he didn't know it. He went on through the col and followed the Gulfside Trail up the long shoulder of Adams toward Thunderstorm Junction.

As badly as Phillip's day was, it was worse for Joe and Frank. Of those two, Joe was in greater difficulty. Slight of frame and weakened before the trip began, he did not have much reserve strength to call on. Joe's pack was the heavier of the two, so Frank took it and they reached the bottom of Edmands Col and headed up the south slope of Adams, still facing into the worst of the storm. Their packs were very difficult to manage and seemed to contribute to their frequent falls, so when they reached Peabody Spring, about a mile and a quarter from Madison Spring Hut, they dropped their packs and their extra clothing and their blanket rolls.

Half a mile farther on Joe fell and cut his knee badly. Frank was not doing much better, but he managed to get his friend back to his feet, then after a few more steps Joe staggered and fell again and this time he couldn't get up. Frank decided that the best thing to do was leave Joe and go on to Madison

Spring Hut for help, so he found a grassy place between two rocks and put Joe in that meager refuge and headed for the hut.

Phillip Turner had already reached the refuge: "Even when by good fortune I found the Madison Springs Hut looming before me, I had all I could do to finish the last few yards. I couldn't have gone another ten feet. They told me that at the hut, and I knew it. I managed to stammer out that my two companions were up on the trail."

It was now mid-afternoon and the hut was full of hikers waiting out the storm, with hutmen Bob Ohler, Fred "Mac" Stott, and Ernie Files keeping an eye on things. One of them put Phillip in a bunk, wrapped him in blankets, and gave him something hot to drink, but Mac Stott had an uneasy feeling. It seemed to him that Phillip was in pretty good shape and not saying much about his friends, and Mac wondered if he'd become separated from them by accident or if he'd left his friends behind.

There was no time to extend these thoughts now, though, so Mac and Ernie recruited one of the weather-bound hikers, gathered up their emergency gear, and made ready to start up the Gulfside to find Phillip's companions. Just as they were leaving the hut, Frank Carnese staggered out of the wind-driven fog and collapsed in the dooryard of the hut. The crew carried him in and, with the last of his strength, Frank told them that Joe Caggiano had fallen, that he couldn't go on, and that he'd left him in the lee of a rock about half a mile up the trail.

Mac Stott and Ernie Files and their recruit took off up the Gulfside at a fast trot. This left only crewman Bob Ohler at the hut, but "The Red Shirts" were there, a hiking club of twenty ministers from Massachusetts, and they had a helpful and steadying effect in a situation that was becoming difficult. Addison Gulick was another guest, he was a professor in the geology department of the University of Missouri and he asked what he could do to help, then he started down the Valley Way to the Ravine House, where he called Joe Dodge at the AMC headquarters in Pinkham Notch.

As the Gulfside Trail leaves Madison Spring Hut it crosses a patch of stunted spruce, then rises sharply up a stretch of loose rocks to the ridge and begins a long rising traverse across the northwest side of Adams to Thunderstorm Junction, a mile from the hut. Mac and Ernie and their volunteer went all the way to the junction and found no sign of the fallen hiker, so they turned around and spread their forces: the volunteer stayed on the trail, Ernie went upslope about thirty yards and Mac went downslope the same distance, as far as they could go without losing sight of the man in the middle. Then they started back toward the hut.

They found Joe Caggiano at 3:30 in the afternoon. He was about half a mile along the Gulfside from the hut and 150 feet north of the trail and he was wearing only shorts and a light sweater with his boots. He was not in the sheltered place Frank had described; he'd used the last of his strength to get a few yards farther along toward the hut, and then he died.

Just as they found the body, Sumner Hamburger came running by on the Gulfside. He was on the crew at the hut and he was coming back from days off. He kept running and brought news of Joe's death to the hut and said they needed a stretcher up on the ridge. Madison Spring Hut was provided with tiers of fold-up pipe-frame bunks, so one of these was unbolted and a crew of volunteers went up to retrieve Joe's body.

They took the body into the kitchen by the back door. Bob Ohler was a medical student at Harvard and he said they should prepare Joe's body for the carry down to the valley before it began to stiffen up, so they tied a prune crate to a packboard, put Joe's body on this makeshift seat, wrapped it in blankets, and tied it to the packboard. "Then," as Mac Stott remembers, "in absolute silence, we carried him through the main room and out the front door. Four of us alternated in the carry and halfway down the Valley Way we met Joe Dodge leading a dozen rescuers. The next morning's *Boston Herald* carried it on page one."

Frank Carnese and Phillip Turner rested overnight at the hut. During those hours the wind veered into the northwest; it was the classic pattern for a northwest clear-off on the range, and the next day dawned so brilliantly fair that the ocean was visible from the summit of Mount Washington. This weather had come too late for Joe and his friends, so the survivors went down the Valley Way to the Ravine House in Randolph. Phillip's two brothers drove up from Boston and started them on their way home. They were still traveling as economically as they could, with severe costs.

AS OFTEN HAPPENS, THIS ACCIDENT LED TO COUNSELS AND PLANS in the AMC and the Forest Service. The AMC's Committee on Trail, Hut and Camp Extensions took up the questions left by Joe Caggiano's death and their report was published in June 1941.

"In view of the number of diverging trails which lead to shelters," they wrote, "it is obvious that there would be little danger if trampers would only use reasonable judgement and descend one of these trails in case of trouble. The Committee felt, however, that they could not ignore the safety of the many trampers who will not use such judgement." As a result of this reading of topographic and human nature, "public safety makes a refuge of some sort desirable." Given the length of the Gulfside and the layout of trails on the Northern Peaks, it was persuasively obvious that such a shelter should be in Edmands Col on the Gulfside, just above timberline on the crest of the ridge and equidistant from almost everything.

All the AMC huts had a refuge room left open in the off-season, but despite this convenience, hikers repeatedly burned everything flammable in the place and stole the few utensils left for their convenience, and sometimes they broke through stout defenses and got into the main hut to do more damage there. So the committee decided on a minimalist approach and recommended that, "Unless such a refuge could be in charge of a caretaker, it should be so constructed as to discourage camping and any use except in case of emergency. It should be built of stone with a non-combustible roof supported on steel rafters. No wood should be used in its construction, and it should contain no equipment whatsoever.

"Regardless of the erection of a refuge, conspicuous signs should be placed at important junctions on the Gulfside Trail indicating the direction and distance of the nearest or best shelter in case of emergency."

For most of remembered history, the nearest refuge to Edmands Col was the Perch, 1.2 miles down the Randolph Path from the col. J. Rayner Edmands himself built it for his own convenience in 1892, a curiously elaborate shelter tucked in well below timberline and next to an unfailing stream. The Randolph Mountain Club took it over and it had been a great favorite of hikers ever since. But the Perch eventually fell into disrepair and the RMC announced that it would be abandoned. In light of this development, the AMC committee recommended that if a new refuge was not approved for Edmands Col, a standard lean-to shelter should be built on the site of the Perch. The report was approved by the club and a copy was sent to the Forest Service.

The United States entered World War II six months after the report appeared, all work on the range was suspended, and the 6.3-mile span of exposed ridge between Madison Spring Hut and relief on the summit of Mount Washington or at the Lakes of the Clouds Hut remained without any shelter until 1956, when a refuge was built in Edmands Col.

This was Spartan beyond anything the committee could probably have imagined, and if the 1901 refuge on Bigelow Lawn was "far too uncomfortable to attract campers," the refuge in Edmands Col positively repelled such visits. It looked like half of a large corrugated steel pipe bolted to a concrete pad, there was a crawl-in entrance and the dark interior dripped moisture and rattled with metallic echoes. But hiker traffic on the range was rising sharply in the 1960s and '70s and the Edmands Col refuge became an overnight destination despite its uninviting characteristics. The Forest Service decided that this non-emergency use was blighting the grand setting and delicate environment, and every trace of the refuge was removed about 20 years after it was built. The high Northern Peaks traverse has been pristine ever since, but, happily, the RMC had succumbed to the pressure of its own history and the Perch was rebuilt in 1948.

Chapter Thirteen

DEATH COMES IN SMALL PARTS

*A*S MY GENERATION OF OVERLOOK COUSINS GREW UP, our summer hikes grew also. The greatest trips were on the Presidential Range and we'd watch as the trees got smaller and smaller as we climbed until the last of them were squashed into moss and there was only rock and sky in front of us. There was a metal sign about here on every trail, bright yellow with black lettering: STOP: *Weather changes above timberline are sudden and severe. Do not attempt this trail unless you are in good physical condition, well rested and fed, and have extra food and clothing. Turn back at the first sign of bad weather.*

This meant that we were getting into serious territory. We'd always known that people died up on the heights, and now we were up on the heights ourselves. My brother had worked for Joe Dodge for many years; he was on the crew at Madison Spring Hut and I could think of no higher aspiration than to follow in his footsteps. Finally I was old enough to work for Joe myself and there was no doubt in my mind where—I'd work at Madison.

The Gulfside Trail began at the hut and not long after it topped the first crest there was a brass plaque beside the trail. It marked the place where Joe Caggiano died in 1938 and this brought an immediacy to the times of peril and heroics that I'd never felt before. Up until now, those stories had been stories that someone told and the names were places on the list of fatalities on the wall down in Porky Gulch. Ever since our earliest visits, we'd go over to that list and read all the names again and feel a distant surge of danger, but standing by Joe Caggiano's marker was standing on the very rocks that were in those stories, this death was the closest in both time and distance to our bunks at Madison and we thought about it without really knowing what we were thinking. It would not be long before we became one of the stories ourselves.

RAYMOND DAVIS
AUGUST 1952

August 23 was a major event in the hutman's calendar. This was a celebration established three years earlier at Lakes of the Clouds Hut when the crew laid on a particularly memorable dinner. It evolved, as social functions tend to do, and by this time it was a sort of moveable feast and provided a convenient occasion for a party to mark the end of the summer season.

That August week in 1952 brought very severe weather. On the twenty-first, clouds thickened steadily on the heights, the wind backed into the southwest and, curiously for that heading, the temperature on the summit of Mount Washington did not rise out of the 40s all day. The upper reaches of the range remained in the clouds all the next day and the wind veered into the northwest and rose from the 20-mph range in the morning to a peak of 71. The temperature settled from a morning high of 46° down to 32°.

Early the next day the trails on Mount Washington and the Northern Peaks were closed to hikers, so extreme a measure than no one could remember such a step being taken before. The wind was out of the west and blew steadily in the 40–60 mph range all day at the observatory and rose to 76 after supper. The summit temperature was nailed at 30° all day, with snow and sleet collecting on the ground.

Bad weather or not, about twenty-five hutmen got to the party in Pinkham Notch. It was always a spaghetti and beer bust, and momentum gathered quickly. Suddenly a young woman appeared. She was wet, muddy, and out of

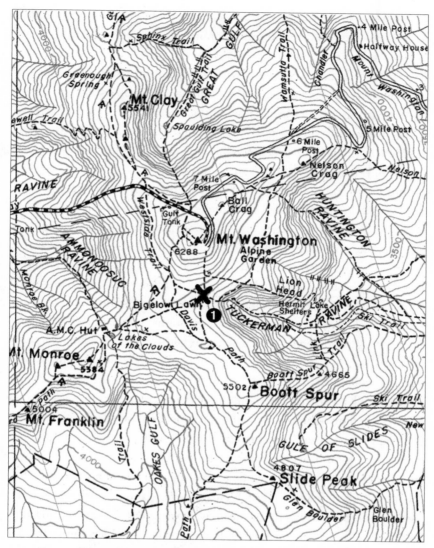

1. Raymond Davis's route of hike unknown; he died at Tuckerman Junction

breath; she said she was a nurse and a man had collapsed up above Tucker-man Ravine. Her companion, another nurse, had stayed with him.

Joe Dodge's example taught us that there was never a moment of hesitation at times like this, so we put down the spaghetti and the beer and took off up Mount Washington at a trot. The clouds closed in on us, the rain turned to sleet partway up Tuckerman Ravine, then ice was gathering on the rocks. It was the weather those signs warned about and it was tough going, but at nineteen you are not only invincible, you are immortal, and we were all nineteen. When we got to the man, he was dead.

Most of us had never seen death so close and many had never seen death at all, we hadn't learned that when lifeless flesh is pressed, it does not rebound, it does not press back. This man seemed extraordinarily large, too heavy to lift, and we learned the meaning of "dead weight," a weight that doesn't help you at all. We could barely keep our feet as we headed down over the headwall of Tuckerman Ravine; we half-dropped our burden several times and we did drop it several times. Some laughed, saying we should just let him slide down the dizzying slope, he wouldn't mind, and we'd catch up later; others wondered if the spaghetti was getting cold. That, apparently, is what you do when you're at the height of your powers and carrying a dead man you can hardly lift.

Being tall, I was at the downhill end of the load. One of the man's booted feet was flopping right beside my shoulder, just flopping there with an absolute limpness I'd never seen. The nurse who stayed behind said she'd found a prescription for heart medicine in the man's pocket and I kept wondering what he was thinking when he passed the sign telling how the weather changes above timberline are sudden and severe, and how the upper trails are now closed. I wondered if he meant what was going to happen, and I kept looking at the boot laces on the foot flopping on my shoulder. They were tied with a double bow knot and I kept thinking the same thing over and over, that when he tied that bow this morning he was looking forward to the day.

They were beautiful boots, carefully greased for waterproofing and flexibility. All our boots were leather and they were part of us, our link to the ground. Now here was this man's beautiful boot, flopping at my shoulder. Like us, he'd taken out the cloth laces and replaced them with leather, also greased for strength and longevity. I kept looking at the bow knot, thinking how carefully he'd tied it that morning, so it wouldn't come undone. As it turned out, that was not the weak link.

My friend Chan Murdoch was level with the man's arm and he told me later that all the way down he could only think of how the man's limp elbow kept nudging him as he struggled with the carry, just that persistent mindless nudge. When Chan said that, I realized that we'd both seen our first death in very small parts.

For Joe Dodge, there was other business to attend to. He lived with emergency like his own shadow and he'd led the charge uncounted times. So when we got to the AMC headquarters at the bottom of the trail, Joe made the call. It appeared, however, that the person at the other end of the line insisted on hope. Finally Joe said, "Hell no, lady, it's worse than that. The poor son of a bitch is dead."

Chapter Fourteen

THE SUMMIT AS HOME

*T*HE PRESIDENTIAL RANGE IS UNIQUE AMONG THE MAJOR mountains because the highest point has been an outpost of civilization from the earliest days. The first party to climb to the summit of Mount Washington went up in July 1784 and the mountain they climbed had been called, variously, Agiococook, Waumbekket-methna, Christall Hill, and Trinity Height. When they came down it was called Mount Washington, because the six climbers had gone up for a christening to honor the man who would soon lead the new nation. In the same festive vein, five of the men named the river flowing out of the great eastern ravine after their companion Dr. Cutler.

The first shelter on the summit was a primitive stone hut built by Ethan Allen Crawford. That was in 1823 and, pleased with his work, he immediately built two more. Always alert to a commercial future, the epochal mountain pioneer installed a sheet of lead upon which visitors could scratch their names. Needless to say, they often scratched more than that. Samuel Cowles, of Farmington, Connecticut, started toward the summit with Thomas Crawford on June 10, 1823, and reached the top the next day. He was the first to leave his trace on the register, but he saw very little beyond that, an experience that would be repeated many times over in the years to come. "The

Creator," he wrote, "had spread a veil over the grandeur and beauty of His works."

The summit of Mount Washington proved to be a dependable source of inspiration. Many American citizens never went beyond their letters and numbers, but those who did often became intimates of the classics. Not only could they explain without hesitation the distinctions separating elocution and rhetoric and oratory and declamation, but if surviving diaries are to be believed, outbursts of eloquence threatened to overtake them at every pleasing prospect. On July 8 of the same summer, a visitor spent an uncomfortable night in one of the Crawfords' stone huts, but found that the morning made up for it:

> The Muses' most inspired draught,
> From Helicon's pure fountain quaff'd—
> What is it to the rising sun,
> Seen from the top of Washington!
> Canst thou bear a dreary night?
> Stranger! go enjoy the sight.

Spiritually rewarding as the heights might be, the Crawfords' stone tourist court was a financial failure because the huts did not keep out very much weather and visitors soon discovered that the summit of Mount Washington had a variety and a force of weather entirely beyond the experience of most mortals.

Mr. Crawford already knew about that. An early commentator wrote that his stone cabin "was ever by the winter's storms rendered a most desolate object, though sheltered behind a bold crag. The shingle roof, split down in the woods on the mountain side and packed up on the backs of men, was scattered to the four winds. The levers of the frost, and the wild hurricane, tumbled down the thick stone walls; and every spring a roofless heap of ruins, with a rusty old stove, and the iron chest, was left to tell a sad story of the invisible power that over these towering summits stretches the arm of destruction."

Undeterred by these elemental setbacks, Mr. Crawford abandoned his stone cabins and put up a tent, thoughtfully equipped with a wood stove to keep out the damp. This innovation brought the windy nature of life on the summit into sharp focus, and the first good blow ended the era of canvas on Mount Washington forever. Ontogeny recapitulates phylogeny, it always does, so the Crawfords continued to compress the whole history of lodgings into this short time and small span and they built a tiny shelter made of wood. This proved inadequate to vacationers, so in 1852 Lucius M. Rosebrook and Joseph Hall of Lancaster and Nathan Perkins of Jefferson built a handsome and substantial building of wood, masonry, anchor bolts, and steel cables. This new hostelry promised so much that they named it the Summit House.

Nothing succeeds like success and that same year Samuel Spaulding built a larger hotel called the Tip-Top House. A contemporary guide wrote that "cement and iron hold this monument of daring enterprise, in proud defiance of wind and storm, to the most bleak top crag of Mount Washington." The new hotel measured twenty-eight by eighty-four feet, and it was provided with a telescope on the roof and fresh dairy goods in the kitchen, the latter supplied by hardscrabble cows tethered about a mile below the summit in the Cow Pasture. Many lodgers rode to the summit on horseback, using the four bridle paths that had been built by then. Work on a carriage road up the eastern flank was begun in 1855 and then the cog railway on the western flank reached the top in 1869, and the larger throngs they brought required a larger hotel. This was an even grander Summit House, a full-service installation to meet every need for 150 summer lodgers. By now there were also buildings to serve the needs of patrons of the carriage road and the railroad, a large three-story observation tower, a building for the U.S. Army Signal Service, and a building for the editorial staff and press gang of *Among the Clouds*.

Everything except the Tip-Top House burned in 1908. By 1915, the third-generation Summit House was open, a lovely heavy-timbered place with twenty-two double guest rooms and every amenity the stylish traveler could desire. In 1924 a small cabin was built near the Summit House and named Camden Cottage to salute an admired employee of the cog railway who slid down the 3.25-mile track on a board in only three minutes. This refuge was for climbers and it was left open all year round, partly to deflect the attention of cold-weather visitors who might otherwise break into the hotel.

The U.S. Army Signal Service served as the national weather bureau and a detachment of soldiers set up an observatory on the summit of Mount

Washington in November 1870, using a building with two heavy chains run up over the roof and anchored to bedrock.

Heavy and reassuring as the construction was, there were times when the men thought it might not be enough. Consider, for instance, the experience of Private Doyle in January 1877. As the account of that year describes it, "Anticipating, from the aspect of the heavens in the afternoon preceding the gale, when the clouds spread for miles around—an ocean of frozen vapor—and became, late in the day, so dense as to reflect the colors of the spectrum, that some great atmospheric disturbance was impending, the observers made everything snug for a storm."

Night came on and the wind rose to 100 mph, driving sleet so thick the men dared not make their outside observations. At midnight they recorded winds of 120 and the thermometer stood at −24°. The small building was heated with a coal stove and this night they stoked it until it was red hot, but water froze less than three feet from its glowing sides.

By one o'clock in the morning the wind touched 150 and blew through the sturdy building so freely that the carpet floated a foot above the floorboards. Soon one of the windows collapsed. There were only two observers on summit duty and they struggled mightily to close the inside shutters, but the repair held for only a few moments before the wind burst through again. As described in the account of that year, "After a hard tussle, they again secured the windows by nailing a cleat to the floor and using a board as a lever. 'Even then,' said Private Doyle, 'it was all we could do to force the shutters back into place. But we did it. We had to do it.'

"The remainder of the night was spent in an anxious and alarmed state of mind, as was but natural when they did not know but that at any moment the building would be carried over into Tuckerman Ravine and they swept into eternity with it." Private Doyle and his fellow observer were increasingly confident in this unpromising forecast, so they wrapped themselves in blankets and quilts secured with ropes and then they tied on iron crowbars lengthwise as further strengthening against the long fall that seemed inevitable. Thus encumbered, they attended to their duties until the storm abated.

The Signal Service recorded temperatures down to −59° and wind as high as 186 mph and they occupied the summit year-round until the fall of 1887 and summers-only until 1892, when the government closed the observatory.

The warm-weather population remained strong, but year-round occupants did not return until the International Polar Year was announced for 1933.

Joe Dodge led the campaign for a new weather observatory on the summit and four observers moved up in the fall of 1932, getting along as well as they could in what was known as the stage office, a building remaining from the carriage trade. It had been built for summer use, but the thick accumulations of rime ice on the outside walls helped keep out the wintry blasts. A good thing, too, because these observers recorded the all-time record for surface winds on the earth at 231 mph. A new facility was built in 1937, it was framed with 9 x 10-inch timber bolted a minimum of four feet into bedrock, and it was reported to be the strongest wooden building in the world. Borrowing an old trick from coastal fisheries in Maine, it was insulated with seaweed.

This new building was equipped with thick plate-glass windows covered with heavy steel grates, and it had a full kitchen and a chemical toilet adjacent to the kitchen. All plumbers know about the need for vents built into their pipes and the summit contractors did not neglect this duty. They also knew about the summit winds and they inquired as to the least likely direction for severe storms, then they placed the plumbing vents so they would have maximum protection from all the other directions. The direction they left with the least vent protection was southeast.

The great Thanksgiving hurricane of 1950 was one of the worst sustained storms ever to strike the summit, and it came out of the southeast. The observatory records wind speed on a revolving circular chart; the wind averaged 120 for an hour and then the pen went off the chart at 162. This wind was blowing straight into the plumbing vents, which argued for caution when using the chemical toilet.

It also suggested an experiment. One of the observers noticed a bottle of child's soap bubble mix on a shelf; nobody knew how it got there, but there it was. So the next time there was a lull in the wind he poured the whole bottle into the sink drain and washed it down with a hearty dose of hot water. When the wind speed went back into three digits there was a demonstration of bubble-making power that set an entirely new standard for this once-gentle art.

Given Joe Dodge's inclinations, radio loomed large in the lives of summit personnel. Electronics made a major move to the summit in 1940 when a transmitter, tower, and domestic facilities for experimental FM broadcasting were built there. This forced the issue of water. Ever since the cog railway trestle reached the summit, water was pumped up from the base station for summer use. The new observatory had an open-top wooden cistern in the cellar and just before the railway closed in the fall the cistern was pumped full, then replenished with ice when the original supply dwindled. This was sufficient, and the observers learned not to think about it too much—when the cistern was drained in the spring a startling variety of drowned rodents would usually appear on the bottom.

A new age dawned with the FM building. When the concrete floor was finished, an artesian well rig was driven up the road and parked on the concrete. Then it started to drill. Water was finally hit 1,112 feet down, just slightly above the surface level of the Lakes of the Clouds, and when the drill was removed the water rose to about 240 feet below the cellar floor. Full happiness was not realized, however. Some time afterward, one of the crew was pumping fuel oil from the storage tank to the cellar tank and he forgot to shut the valve when the cellar tank was full. This oversight was not discovered before a considerable amount of oil ran out onto the floor and down the artesian well. Every theory and effort was applied to ridding the well of the noxious slime, but a distinctive taste remained in the water for as long as the well stayed in use.

World War II accelerated scientific research, as wars always do, and Mount Washington contributed its weather to the cause. The benchmark research for cloud seeding was done by the observatory crew, aircraft wing sections were tested up there, and when jet engines were being developed for military use a prototype of each model was hauled up the road in the fall. This was a joint project by the navy and air force, and at first a whole navy Phantom carrier fighter, minus the folding part of its wings, was mounted in the building, so it was called the "hanger." Then only the engine was mounted, freeing so much space that a second mount was built in the hanger. At first it was anti-icing tests, then production engines were being tested to see if they met their specified performance. The hanger was an immense block-like building at the end of a former parking lot and there was an even more conspicuous dormitory building on the level section of road called Homestretch which is just below the summit, the place where Dr. Ball wandered to such poor effect 100 years earlier.

The dormitory had beds for sixty and this new age brought flood tide in summit population. Previously there were two men in the electronics transmission building and three or four in the observatory, but the military and engineering presence of the 1950s and 1960s put as many as sixty-five men in winter residence, boom times that brought amenities never dreamed of by the pioneers as they braced against the wintry blast in their blankets and crowbars. For instance, two of the engineers set up a bar and imported liquor and beer from the valley which they sold at a favorable rate, though not neglecting their own profits. They also brought up several slot machines to extract pocket change from their summit mates, but it must be said that the slots were set to pay off at a generous rate.

The jet testing program also brought an adaptive response by the summit cat. This was Felony, a beast of such remarkable dimension that his tail could be brought forward over his head and tucked under his chin. Felony began life at John Howe's house down in Jackson, where he liked to spend the night outdoors. Winters were cold down in the valley, and year by year the frost chewed away at Felony's ears until there were hardly more than stubs. Then Felony moved to the summit, where he liked to sleep in the jet building. The grease made it difficult for Felony to keep his coat in good order, but he slept in the hanger and hardly seemed to notice when the engines ran up to full throttle. The effect of Felony's blighted ears on his acoustic defenses was never adequately studied.

Nome also spent most of those years on the summit. He was a malamute dog and, like Felony, he adapted. He lived in the observatory, he was a well-brought-up fellow, and he made his visits outside as required and regardless of the prevailing conditions. One of Nome's most admired achievements was the technique he developed for dealing with the winds of winter and the accumulation of rime ice during these outings, but it was lonely up there and, unlike the other men, he had no scheduled days off. So Nome carried on a long-running romance with Joe Dodge's faithful and very attractive dog Tanana and, when the spirit moved, Nome would go down to visit her. The observatory would know when he left and Joe would note the moment when he arrived, and on the next radio contact they'd calculate Nome's elapsed time. The ardent canine would regularly achieve all-weather descents in times that approached free-fall.

In the pioneering days of winter residency, the summit crew understood that they were on the frontier and it was only natural that they endure hardships whether they were indoors or out. They took it for granted that they'd hike up and down the mountain as needed and meet the hazards as they found them.

These assumptions could not be made in the later days of winter occupancy, these residents were scientists, not adventurers, and their regular jobs were often in the aircraft industry of southern California where the temperature on a chilly winter day was usually warmer than mid-summer on Mount Washington. This situation promised trouble, so a series of refuge shacks was built along the upper half of the auto road. The first ones were built in the 1940s and more were added as the summit traffic increased until there were shacks at five and a half mile, six mile, six and a half, seven, seven and a third, seven and two-thirds mile. These shelters were about ten feet square inside, with a heater and a telephone and army surplus K rations. These accommodations would be barely sufficient by most standards, but under the circumstances, barely sufficient was good enough.

One early test came on February 19, 1946. Vernon Humphreys was in the last stages of his military service and the army loaned him to the observatory to finish an intensive study of rime ice. There had been two days of remarkably fine weather and he started to hike up the road for what promised to be an enjoyable outing. Marshall Smith was a member of the regular observatory staff and he started down the road to meet Vernon.

The weather held fine, but there was a brutal cold front closing in and it hit the two men just before 4:00 P.M. when they were half a mile above the 6-Mile refuge. They realized that the day had turned against them, so they retreated to the refuge hut, chopped away the ice on the door without difficulty, and closed it behind them. They started the heater and called the summit and the valley to report their situation, but all the emergency food was gone except for a can of grapefruit juice. They set up an hourly phone schedule with the outside world and then, attuned to thermal physics as they were, the observers rigged heat shields to absorb the energy of the heater for later release.

The cold front proved violent indeed and the two men stayed in the shelter through the night, all the next day, and through the next night. The storm eventually blew itself out, and at about noon on the third day two men from the observatory arrived with hot tea and soup, then they escorted Vernon and Marshall the rest of the way to the summit and set a meal before them that was entirely adequate to their great need. That is to say, both the observers and the emergency shelters worked exactly as they were meant to.

Lacking bad news from Mount Washington, New Hampshire editors looked for other sources of excitement. *The Berlin Reporter* was the nearest newspaper and it ignored the saving features of the auto road huts, but it did report that the 4-H Wide Awake Club was meeting on schedule and that the stock market had taken its biggest drop in six years, with losses ranging from one to nine points before closing at 76. The plunge continued the next day and the Dow fell to 74.6.

The next-nearest newspaper was *The Littleton Courier*, and the editors ignored the Mount Washington story, too, although they did provide a lemon recipe that should help with rheumatism. *The Manchester Leader*, the state's flagship paper, took a pass on the story in favor of stronger stuff: Jack Dempsey was in town to referee an evening of boxing, Russian spies were causing worry, and children were told to find amusements for themselves.

The winter population of the summit peaked before the perfection of winter transport, but mountaineering enthusiasm could not be assumed among the engineers arriving from Los Angeles and San Diego. Veterans of Mount Washington work worried about this. There was the day, for instance, when the chief of the permanent testing group started up the road with ten or twelve new arrivals from the sunny shores of southern California, and as far as anyone knew the most difficult hiking they'd done was from their desk to the water cooler. So they got to the bottom of Mount Washington and fitted out with clumsy cold-weather gear from the military stockpiles, then they started up, a long line of them. The weather turned bad above timberline and the chief was in the lead group, so he kept going until he hit such strong winds on Cow Pasture that the only way he could move was to lie down on his back and kick himself along toward the summit with his crampons. All of the rest of the new engineers had holed up in twos and threes in the refuge huts behind him. They spent the night in these minimalist accommodations and were rounded up the next day, not much the worse for wear.

By now it was obvious that some way had to be found to manage winter-time shift changes that was less punishing and less dangerous than muscles and crampons. The first serious attempt at mechanization involved Weasels, the tracked vehicle developed during World War II by the American army's Tenth Mountain Division. Passenger comfort was not a priority in wartime; in fact, Weasel design made almost no provision for passengers at all. The troopers wanted something like a snow-qualified jeep and Weasels had no significant heat and only a flimsy canvas top, and the ride they provided on the wind-chopped road up Mount Washington was about like a rowboat in an ocean storm. More to the point, Weasels had very little sideways traction and threatened to slide away downhill on the drifted side-hills of the auto road.

The first mechanical snow traveler of the postwar era clanked out of the back room of the Tucker household in Medford, Oregon. That was in 1945 and one of the continuously improved editions of the Tucker Sno-Cat reached Mount Washington by the early 1950s. It had a roomy interior and it was well heated by mountain standards, but the center of gravity was so high that one of them actually capsized. Furthermore, the drive train was fragile and when it broke the vehicle was in free-wheeling. Nevertheless, the orange Sno-Cats worked the summit schedule for many winters.

One persistent problem was the sidehill drifts on the out-and-back traverse pivoting on Cragway Turn. It was a mile and a half long and no track-driven vehicle could hold the sidehill slope of the drift, so a sort of notch had to be bulldozed to make a negotiable surface. Visibility is always a problem above timberline, fog and wind-whipped snow reduce visibility to almost nothing and erase all contrasts in the light, and the bravest traveler becomes almost helpless. Phil Labbe was the full-time summit driver for three decades and even he was frequently blinded by these white-outs. One early and memorable entry came in the winter of 1953 when he was bulldozing along the Cragway drift to make a level surface when the light went flat. He tried to keep going, but it was bulldozing by memory and by Braille and eventually he simply abandoned the tractor. For a long time after that, the record of his effort was visible from the valley, an increasingly wayward trace punctuated by the abandoned bulldozer at the end. Finally they got a Sno-Cat up to the end of his bulldozed stretch, then something broke and it stayed there for the rest of the winter.

The Tuckers were not the only internal combustion vehicles on the winter road. The first Polaris "Sno-Traveler" was made in 1954, a spidery little

In the 1950s, bodies were brought down from the region of Tuckerman Ravine by Weasels, which were World War II–era military vehicles. Joe Dodge is sitting astride the right headlight and George Hamilton is driving. This is at the beginning of the trail to Tuckerman Ravine, where signs warn hikers of avalanche danger.

Tucker Sno-Cats descend the summit cone on Mount Washington toward the flats known as "Homestretch" in 1960. Dr. Ball mistook this area for the summit and nearly perished before heading down toward two more days of peril.

device with a track on the ground, an engine in the rear, steering skis in front, and a seat for the driver—the prototype snowmobile. Six Polaris Sno-Travelers made a successful ascent of Mount Washington in February 1962 and hope surged, the snowmobile might be the key to quick personnel travel on the winter road. It turned out that the drifts and ice were too tough and the one-man one-machine format was too risky, and the age of the snowmobile for summit workers ended almost before it began. Finally the Thiokol aerospace company in Utah developed their line of snow tractors and these became the standard winter transit for summit personnel. The summit road, however, still wasn't main street.

At least one group thought it could be. This was the Mercedes motor works of Germany, and they were bringing out a new line of rotary snowplows. Someone in their U.S. marketing company wanted something spectacular to launch the new line, and what could be better than clearing the road up Mount Washington? So early in April they brought three models to New Hampshire, the medium-sized one, the big one, and the huge one.

The man in charge was from Germany and he looked the job over. It had been a good snow year on Mount Washington and there had also been a considerable amount of rain, so the snowpack was both deep and solid. The head plowman said they'd take a day to clear the road to halfway and the next day they should be able to get to the summit. The summit regulars thought the Mercedes people had bitten off more than they could chew, and maybe more than they could bite.

On the third or fourth day a veteran of the summit crew went down to see how they were getting along. The surface was the kind of very hard boilerplate that summit people know so well, but he was using crampons and an ice axe and he got along all right. The Germans were not doing quite that well. They'd gotten as far as the five-mile grade and the long sidehill drift that Phil Labbe learned was impossible terrain even for a bulldozer to notch. This is the reason the Cut-off was made, a winter-only tractor route from 4.5-Mile to 6-Mile that does not suffer from too much drifting.

The Germans meant to clear right down to the surface of the road and it was heavy going. They had four or five people out in front driving stakes into the snow to show where the road was, though this had to be mostly guesswork because all they had to look at was a sidehill drift. Not only that, but they had no crampons and their work was punctuated by many quick and desperate scrambles. If the scramble failed, a man would not slow very much until he hit timberline far below.

So the scouts would set their stakes and the huge rotary would back up about twenty feet from the frozen wall that marked its farthest advance. Then the driver would gun the engine, gather speed, and hit the wall with a mighty crash. The work advanced about six inches per crash. The hours were passing, the wind was picking up, and snow was coming on, so the observer found the German's crew boss and told him that neither the weather nor their progress was very promising. The Mercedes marketing campaign looked elsewhere for their triumph.

Phil Labbe survived every imaginable winter situation. One memorable entry came on the Cow Pasture in 1983. This is a sort of summertime oasis, an acre or more of smooth and level green in the rocky desert above timberline, there's even a small fresh-water spring conveniently placed in the middle of it. Samuel Spaulding's herd of cows was presumably happy here during their days of service with the Tip-Top House kitchen, but the cows are many generations gone. Now there are two roadside parking lots near Cow Pasture and it remains a popular place for summertime road passengers to take a fair-weather stroll.

The weather was not fair on a winter day when Willy Harris and Marty Engstrom were due for their shift change. They were waiting on top to ride down with Phil Labbe, but Phil did not arrive at the summit at his usual time, which was rare enough. He didn't arrive later than his usual time, either. In fact, he was lost.

The problem was on Cow Pasture. There were guide stakes all along the road, but they weren't working as planned. The stakes were set on both sides of the road so the driver would go between them, but when the weather was very thick it was difficult to tell the difference between two stakes on one side of the road and a stake on one side and another stake on the other side. This meant that if the driver got ninety-degrees off line he could pass through the expected pair of poles and not realize he was headed for the trackless wastes. Phil had more experience with bad-weather winter transits on the road than any person who ever lived, but he did make that mistake; he got ninety-degrees off line and soon realized that he couldn't see any stakes at all, he was lost.

A Thiokol is a very large piece of equipment, so rather than drive it blindly into an even worse situation, Phil got out to see if he could find any stakes nearby. He couldn't find any stakes. Then he couldn't find his cottage-size orange tractor. Phil did the difficult thing, he kept his head, and he was able to find his way back to one landmark, then to another, and then to his tractor. After this close call, all the stakes were put on the same side of the road and a tether was rigged for anyone who went out looking for the route.

John Howe took a job with the observatory in the fall of 1950 and, with a few absences for other meteorological duties, he worked on the summit until 1988. He was an observer of the old school, he preferred hiking to mechanized convenience under almost any circumstances, and his standards for hiking weather were considerably beyond those of most men.

The large postwar military presence on Mount Washington included another visit from what was now called the U.S. Army Signal Corps, but they were not on the summit. They were working on designs for automated weather stations and they built their research facility on what is known as Cape Horn, a rocky spur of the mountain known by earlier generations as the Ledge. It's just above timberline and the auto road loops around this promontory above 4-Mile.

One shift-change day in March 1952, John started down the road with full winter clothing and his crampons and ice axe, and he also had his skis and poles lashed to a packboard for days-off skiing in the valley. The wind was blowing so hard that he had to crawl across the Homestretch flats, then the situation eased a bit and he was able to get along with his crampons and ice axe. Then just below 6-Mile it suddenly worsened a lot. The wind grew violent—lull and gust, lull and gust. John was getting along by keeping his back to the wind and sitting down into it when a gust hit, then the strongest gust yet hit him and he couldn't sit down into it quickly enough. It tipped him over the edge of the road and he started sliding on the boiler-plate surface of the snow. He was immediately going too fast to catch himself with his ice axe or crampons, and he knew that the only way to stop was to hit something. There was one rock sticking up above the ice below him, and he hit it.

He took the force of the blow under his left arm and his shoulder dislocated, but he did stop. His goggles were broken and he'd lost his mitts, but he managed to get out of his pack harness and chop and push and scrabble back up to the road and he kept going down to the Signal Corps station on

Cape Horn. The men there were due to make a trip down in their Sno-Cat, but the weather was so bad they decided against it—their wind recorder showed that the gust that tipped John over registered 125 mph on Cape Horn, which was 1,200 feet lower than his knock-down. The army crew was not very sympathetic until the sergeant in charge found John squirming around on the floor of one of the back rooms, trying to find a position where he could stand the pain. After that, they started up the Sno-Cat and took him down to the valley. I was working for the AMC at Pinkham Notch and I got to the bottom of the road just as he was brought in. John is my brother and all he said was, "Don't tell mother about this."

I didn't, nor did I tell her about the time the Sno-Cat left him behind in a whiteout near Cow Pasture. It took a lot to stop a shift-change trip to the valley and this one was right at the limit: the summit wind hit 180 that afternoon. Phil Labbe started the Sno-Cat down in the morning when the wind was within travel tolerances at about 80 mph. The air was a fury of blowing snow and visibility was almost nil, so when Phil got to Homestretch he asked John to get out and walk ahead to guide him. John was familiar with the territory and the surface was fairly good for crampons, so he kept Phil on course until the end of Homestretch, then he got back in. They pushed on through the storm until they reached the drift that forms just above Cow Pasture and Phil drove out onto the drift by feeling his way through the steering gear, and suddenly the Sno-Cat slipped sideways six or eight feet. Phil didn't know if he was still on the road, so he asked John to get out again and see where they were.

"Which I did," says John. "I determined where we were and then I turned around to go back to the machine and I couldn't see it. Then the blowing snow cleared and I saw it and at the same moment I fell, a gust of wind toppled me. I must have gotten disoriented or something, because I was watching the machine—I could still see it—and it drove off. There was no question in my mind, it drove off, heading down. So I thought, Well, Phil must have seen where I was and he just wants to get off that little sidehill. So I walked on down across Cow Pasture cross-lots and found the road down at the other end and came back up the road. No machine. I got to where I thought I'd last seen it—no machine. So I did it again, I made three trips down Cow Pasture and on the last trip I missed the road. It was getting worse, the wind was probably getting close to a hundred. I ended up over at the beginning of Nelson

Crag and I thought, Well, I better get out of here before it gets worse—we knew it was going to get worse. So I just walked down.

"I was just getting to the flats down in the valley by the Glen House and here came Phil with the Sno-Cat. They'd been worried to death and finally they'd given up and called my wife to say that I was missing, and Phil stopped beside me and said, 'Never, *never* leave the machine like that!' And I said, 'Phil, you left ME!' Actually, they hadn't moved, it was a visual illusion."

As Private Doyle and his embattled companions learned a hundred years earlier, life on the summit of Mount Washington is never certain.

Chapter Fifteen

FROM HOMESPUN TO HIGH TECH

O N NOVEMBER 30, 1954, A NORTHEAST AIRLINES PLANE crashed while approaching the airport near Berlin, New Hampshire. It was a DC-3 and it hit the crest of the Mahoosuc Range on Mount Success, just south of the city. Hugh Gregg was the governor, he was energetic, and if there was trouble anywhere in the state, he liked to go there to see if he could help. Now he was standing with a group of men at the airport as they were discussing plans for a rescue, and as they talked he learned that the pilot was Peter Carey, who'd been a classmate at Yale. The topography of the Mahoosucs is complex and although the wreckage had been spotted by a search plane, no one seemed sure exactly where it was on the map or how to get there. More to the immediate point, there was no official state organization to attend to the work of search and rescue.

Paul Doherty was there, too. He was the district game warden with the New Hampshire Department of Fish and Game and he was an activist; he was always pushing into distant reaches of his territory and learning the ways of the woods. Paul was standing near a man with a radio who was talking to the search plane and trying to get a ground location for the plane. A friend of Paul's was there too, a man named Claude who was an old woods boss for the Brown Company, the largest timber operator in the area. Claude said he thought the plane was right near the Labonville cutting, up in Leadmine Brook country. Several others in the group said they didn't agree, but Paul told them that if Claude thought it was near the Labonville job, that's where it was. Not only that, but Paul had already organized a group of woodsmen and the necessary equipment and they were ready to go. So Paul and his crew followed Claude's advice and found the plane right where the old woods boss said it would be.

The whole episode was reviewed at a meeting in Pinkham Notch that evening and Governor Gregg was there. He was impressed by the young game warden's initiative and personally grateful for the result, and when he was back in his office in the capital he signed an executive order that put the field force of the Department of Fish and Game in charge of search and rescue. Then the governor promoted legislation that gave Fish and Game the primary and permanent responsibility for people lost in the woods, for drownings, for ground searches in air crashes, and similar emergencies.

The Forest Service was widely seen as the active agent in the New Hampshire mountains, but it was dependent on a federal budget that was under increasing pressure from Cold War concerns, and cutbacks in its White Mountain operations started in 1950. Fish and Game was a state organization that raised its own money from fishing and hunting licenses, a source so abundant that it usually ended the fiscal year with a large surplus. Furthermore, this thrifty reward was not turned back into the state's general fund, Fish and Game kept it.

One other force was at work. In those days, almost every one of the officers in both Fish and Game and the Forest Service was a combat veteran of World War II: of six wardens in the North Country, two had been paratroopers, one was a marine in the Pacific campaign, one was an air corps armorer in the Pacific, another was a B-24 bomber pilot, and Paul Doherty was a marine doing underwater demolition in the Pacific.

This combat experience meant that they were accustomed to taking orders and giving orders and when the orders wouldn't suffice they knew how to improvise. That was a major factor in World War II; the organization of both German and Japanese forces was rigidly vertical and the lower ranks could not make a move without the proper orders. American forces were accustomed to fighting by the book, but when the book ran out they did whatever worked. These habits paid large postwar dividends in the mountains.

So as the century moved into its second half, the emergency format was perfected in the White Mountains and in many ways the sequence reveals the evolution of mountain sensibilities in New England. In the earliest days, no one venturing onto the heights expected any help; this was the frontier, it was wild country, and if they got into trouble they expected to get out of it by themselves or not at all. As improving highways and railroads brought the mountains closer to the population centers to the south, a sense of collective responsibility grew among the keepers of hotels and boarding-houses and the guides and woodsmen who sustained the new age of tourism. News of trouble would call out any number of willing hands, but they were only organized by word of mouth and equipped with their heavy clothes and what equipment they could find in the barn, and their expertise was limited to the best they could do.

These homespun efforts changed forever when Joe Dodge took over the AMC encampment in Pinkham Notch. This provided a communications center and a cadre of devoted young men working for Joe, and when he passed the word they'd drop their hammers and cookbooks and hit the trail. In winter, the Mount Washington Volunteer Ski Patrol was the first line of response to difficulties in Tuckerman Ravine. The MWVSP was a noble organization in the long tradition of amateur rescue and it stood as a bridge between the old and the new on the Presidential Range, something like the passage from the colonial to the federal in our country's organization.

Tuckerman Ravine, like the rest of the White Mountains, had been in the national forest since the earliest days of organized woodland care, but as the number of hikers and skiers increased, the governmental presence did not. As far as hikers were concerned, the White Mountains were a sort of AMC protectorate and Joe Dodge was the territorial governor. Skiing was taking hold in the ravine by the end of the 1920s, but there was no source of emergency help other than skiers themselves.

The Forest Service shelter was built on the outer floor of the ravine in 1937, but to call it by that name does not carry quite the right force. It was built at flood tide of the architectural period that might be known as Federal Rustic, and that original building compared to a shelter as the Sphinx

Mount Washington looms over AMC's Pinkham Notch Visitor Center and Joe Dodge Lodge.

compares to a sand castle at the beach. Those were the days of President Roosevelt's New Deal, and make-work projects spread across the land; it was a time of starvation glory in the halls of Congress, when the whole point of building something was to use as much material as could be found and put as many men and women to work for as long as possible. Timberline Lodge on Mount Hood, Oregon, was built in the same spirit but not the same shape. Timberline was in the style of a French chateau, but the low outline and broad sloping roof of the new building in Tuckerman Ravine bore a strong resemblance to another refuge springing up in unexpected places, and the shelter in the ravine was known forever after as Howard Johnson's.

It was not manned during the early winter, because the weather was too fierce and the snow in the ravine was too unstable for any human purposes. Skiing in the ravine began to get good when most other ski areas were closing down, the high season began in March and usually ran into mid-June, but skiers don't seem to have been at the center of Forest Service concern when they built their outpost in the ravine. The reason for its construction might be found in nomenclature. The tractor route which led from the highway up to the shelter was known to habitues as the Fire Trail, so historians may postulate that the name came from a Forest Service desire to have a base of operations at this midway point on Mount Washington, operations which would not have a winter component. Skiers, presumably, could take care of themselves.

As spring skiers reoccupied the ravine after World War II, they'd fill up the spaces in the Hermit Lake shelters at the top of the Fire Trail and then they'd spread out in the woods and pitch their tents, sometimes a hundred or more camps on a favored spring weekend. Joe Dodge came up now and then, and if he thought the campers were too numerous or too careless he'd cut the guy lines on their tents, and that was about as much organization as most people thought the ravine would ever need.

The numbers kept growing, though, and in 1947 Bill Putnam and Henry Paris thought, separately but simultaneously, that skiers in the ravine might need more help than a random distribution of emergency skills might provide. They pitched the idea to Cliff Graham, the National Forest supervisor, and he said they should raise a volunteer army, so the Mount Washington Volunteer Ski Patrol began with a core of men whose dedication and longevity were remarkable.

Henry "Swampy" Paris was one of the stalwart leaders and the moniker did not denote vagueness of purpose, he earned it when he went to work for a florist and got his truck stuck in a wet place in the gardens. He was almost never seen on Mount Washington without Clinton Glover at his side, but no one knew Mr. Glover by that name. He was, to one and all, "Kibbe." Nelson Gildersleeve and Sam Goodhue were two more regulars, and most weekends would find eight or ten of the MWVSP on duty.

Sam was an engineering student at the University of New Hampshire and he took the lead in setting up telephones for the ski trail descending from the Gulf of Slides, adjacent to Tuckerman Ravine, for the Sherburne Ski Trail from the ravine down to the highway, and for the Wildcat Trail across the notch. The MWVSP didn't really have a budget, so Joe Dodge scrounged wire from the Army Signal Corps test station above 4-Mile on the Auto Road, but it didn't work very well; rodents found the insulation tasty and there were windfalls on the wire and shrinkage breaks in times of deep cold. Then Bruce Sloat, Joe's hutmaster at Pinkham Notch, bargained for another batch of wire from engineering interests on the summit. It proved to be less nutritional and more durable, and it served for many years.

Kibbe Glover had been a ravine habitue since 1932, a tenure only inter-rupted by the war, and his stories define the era. He reached the front lines at the beginning of the Pacific campaign and went in with the invasions of Guadalcanal and Bougainville, and he was under enemy fire for thirty-six months; on Guadalcanal his unit was bombed for ninety-six nights in a row and it took them six tries to get all the way through a showing of *It Happened One Night*, the classic comedy with Clark Gable and Claudette Colbert.

It was difficult to get Kibbe's combat presence into focus. He was a small, almost gnome-like fellow of boundless energy and unflinching good cheer, and a typical moment lives in memory. When the war was over, Kibbe and many other veterans of service with the military and with Joe Dodge came back to unwind for a season or two in the mountains. One fellow's mother came up to Pinkham to see her son and one afternoon she was sitting on his bunk and mending his socks, as mothers are wont to do. Suddenly Kibbe tumbled in through the window from the porch roof outside. Surprised to find an unknown middle-aged woman in his bedroom, he reached into his rucksack and gave her an apple.

Kibbe was an avid storyteller, and one evening in his old age he was perched on top of a laundry dryer in the cellar at Pinkham, tapping his thumbs against his finger tips and remembering how service in the MWVSP worked.

There weren't any interstate highways in those days, or even any firm assurance of winter traction. Route 16 was the main line from eastern Massa-chusetts to Pinkham Notch and, as far as skiers were concerned, the southern anchor was Colby's Restaurant near the railroad station in Rochester, New Hampshire. The Eastern Ski League counted more than twenty-five clubs, and throngs of the faithful would meet at Colby's on their way north. The manager seemed to know where they all lived, and if one group or another didn't show up at their usual time he'd call the state police and tell them that there must be trouble on the road at such and such a place, so get the plows and sand trucks over there.

"We'd collect at Colby's," Kibbe said, "sometimes Friday evening, some-times Saturday morning, and sometimes after early Mass on Sunday. No matter if it was raining or hot or whatever, we'd get over the top of that big hill in Rochester and see Mount Washington seventy-five miles away and say, 'Oh yeah—a little foggy,' but we'd go."

"We used to drive up in a phaeton, big four-door convertible with no heat, fur coats on and sometimes a red setter for extra warmth. Sometimes there'd be about one-hundred-fifty cars at the bottom of Wakefield Hill waiting for a sand truck and then we'd slide that big car off the road in the pines by Chocorua and somebody'd stop and pull us back onto the road—keep going—keep going. On the way home we'd stop at the Eastern Slope Pharmacy in North Conway for a frappe, get down to UNH and stop for a frosted root beer, stop at Colby's again and write all that stuff in a big book, and, Boom—we'd be in Haverhill."

At the beginning of a new winter, MWVSP regulars would each claim a piece of floor space in the attic of Howard Johnson's, a stoop-way place known among initiates as "Chamonix." They'd keep their gear up there and crawl in to sleep, and during the day they'd do whatever had to be done in the ravine. "You've got to take care of each other," Kibbe said, "you got to take care of each other."

Other sources of help were gathering nearby. The navy and air force and the signal corps were all busy on Mount Washington, and the Army Quartermaster Corps set up camp in the old CCC buildings a mile and a half north of the AMC headquarters in Pinkham Notch. They were developing cold-weather equipment and passers-by on Route 16 could watch in wonder as awkwardly clad fellows made their way across the Glen House meadow to the frozen Peabody River, chopped a big hole in the ice, and jumped in.

Perhaps most important for the future, they had Weasels. We have always lived in cold places and we've always tried to find a way to travel over snow that is less punishing than foot and boot. Military forces needed more than that, and in the early 1940s the army developed their doughty little tracked vehicle. When World War II ended, several surplus Weasels were used by the Mount Washington summit interests, Joe Dodge had one, and the quartermasters at their camp in Pinkham Notch had a small fleet of them.

Other dawns were breaking, too. Gentlefolk of the down-country precincts had generally considered winter in the mountains to be a desperate time best left to fur-bearing trappers and hibernating bears. But the spur of wartime necessity drove a postwar surplus bonanza of warm clothing and improved camping equipment not known by earlier generations; for instance, sleeping bags were rarely seen before the war. This led Americans to the snowbound mountains as never before, and this migration was especially strong among veterans taking some time to unwind and among forward-looking enthusiasts in college outing clubs. Most recently, the urge to the difficult mountains had been reinforced by a series of widely publicized mountaineering triumphs. In 1953 an American expedition almost reached the summit of K2, the world's second-highest mountain, the British made the first ascent of Mount Everest the same year, and in 1954 an Italian expedition conquered K2.

I have personal markers on this epochal passage. When I was a teenager my mother made me a heavy shirt from an old woolen blanket. I thought it was splendid and that, with Levis and long underwear, seemed enough armor for any imaginable winter activities. By 1951 I was on the AMC's winter crew in Tuckerman Ravine and I'd added an army-surplus windbreaker, army-surplus mukluks, and a new sense of possiblity—all the winter-proofing I'd ever need.

In the fall of 1952 I went west to seek my fortune. Gabardine ski pants replaced Levis, the army windbreaker gave way to a single-layer nylon parka, and I wound up with a dream job on the ski patrol at Sun Valley, Idaho. That winter also brought the first quilted parkas I'd ever seen; the ski school instructors at Sun Valley had them, and in my second year at the Valley I had one, too. Wearing it brought one of the most startling experiences of my outdoor life: after just a few minutes outside in the cold Idaho air I began to feel feverish and thought I must be coming down with something.

I wasn't coming down with something, I was *warm*! It had never occurred to me that such a thing was possible.

All of these streams converged at the end of 1954, when Philip and Polly Longnecker and Jacques Parysko left Cambridge, Massachusetts, for a winter weekend on Mount Washington.

PHILIP LONGNECKER AND JACQUES PARYSKO
JANUARY 1954

Saturday night dinner was a major event in Pinkham Notch. Fred Armstrong was the cook and he'd learned his trade in the old-time lumber camps, where just one of a woodsman's meals might fuel an ordinary citizen for a week. Saturday was roast beef night in Pinkham, and George Hamilton usually found himself in the area at just that time.

George spent his childhood with oceanic enthusiasms around his home in Marblehead, Massachusetts, and he started hiking on the high ranges of New Hampshire when he was in summer camp before the war. He was mustered out of the air corps in 1946 and, remembering the mountains, he went to work for Joe Dodge. George though he'd like to do as many things as possible in his life, so he joined the New Hampshire Department of Fish and Game in 1950 and was assigned to the White Mountain region. On the evening of January 30, George was doing his best to finish Fred Armstrong's roast beef dinner and three young women were sitting near him at the table, they seemed to be college students from Boston.

One was a notably lively person and she was telling her companions about how she and her brother and a friend climbed up to Tuckerman Ravine on Friday and made camp and spent the night there. She said it seemed like a bad idea, she'd been frightened so her brother came down with her this morning and then he went back up. He and the other fellow were going to spend the weekend up there, it seemed as if they were trying to prove something.

George listened to all this and it alarmed him. A west wind had been blowing all day on Mount Washington and it was rising sharply as evening came on. It had been snowing steadily all week and it snowed all this day and the temperature was moving down through the single digits. Anyone who was familiar with Mount Washington knew that this combination maximized the snow-fence effect in the east-facing ravine and there'd be a great deal of new snow hanging on the headwall. George was in his Fish and Game uniform and he leaned toward the young woman and said, "Let me be sure I understand this—they're up in the ravine in a little igloo or hole and they're going to sleep there?" She said, "It's something like that."

Joe Dodge was sitting at the end of the table near the kitchen; he always sat there when he was having a meal with the guests. When dinner was over George told him about the ravine campers and said that he didn't like the sound of it. Joe didn't either, and he said, "Well, Jesus, at this time of night there's not a hell of a lot we can do about it." George was living down the road in Jackson and he told Joe that he wouldn't be doing anything tomorrow that he couldn't postpone, so if there was a search he'd be available, give him a call. Joe said he'd have to find out more about this and he'd let him know.

The summit observatory recorded −5° at midnight and the temperature sank all through Sunday morning. That afternoon Wallace Barnes came into Pinkham with an unsettling story: he'd been climbing the Sherburne Trail on skis and he found a figure of some kind half buried in the drifting snow up near Windy Corner. He poked at it with his ski pole and saw that it was only partly clothed and stony hard. It seemed like the kind of mannequin you'd see in a store window, and he couldn't imagine how it had gotten there.

The Sherburne ski trail runs from the ravine down to the AMC camp, and Windy Corner is about a mile and a half from the bowl. A party was sent up to investigate and they found that the "mannequin" was the body of a young man who looked as if he'd just gotten out of bed: he was wearing a light shirt and pants and nothing else. His ankles were heavily scratched and there were footprints leading back up the trail toward the ravine.

The track staggered and wandered, suggesting that the man who made them was *in extremis*. The search party followed the trace up to the foot of the Little Headwall, where it disappeared in the snow, then they brought the frozen body down to Pinkham and the arrival caused a stir. The young woman George had talked to was named Polly Longnecker and when she saw the body she screamed; it was her brother's friend.

Philip Longnecker and Jacques Parysko were in the Harvard graduate school, but they were not members of the mountaineering club. Phil had gone to Colorado College and he'd done some climbing and camping in the mountains out there, but Jacques had no climbing experience at all.

This impulse put them in abundant company, it was flood tide of unrestricted camping and on a good weekend of spring skiing in the ravine there'd be throngs staying in the two lean-tos near Hermit Lake and in campsites in the woods around Howard Johnson's. It was a frozen Elysium, tinctured with the fragrant smoke of evening campfires and the tang of balsam boughs fresh-cut to make mattresses for the night. The weekend Philip, Jacques and Polly climbed to the ravine was not a time for rusticated idylls. January brings such extraordinarily harsh weather on Mount Washington that few people venture into the ravine for any purposes at all.

Phil's group did not stop in the woods where everyone would be camping three months later; they kept going up into the bowl of the ravine. Every

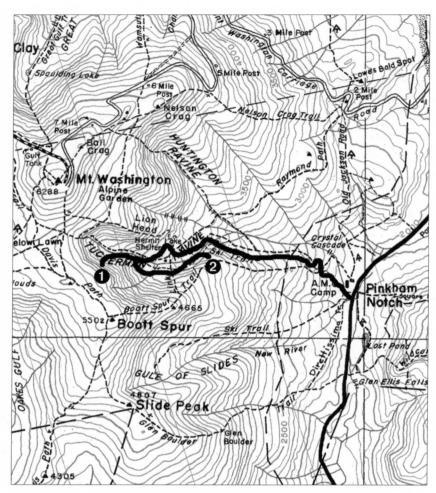

1. Philip Longnecker died in dugout near base of Tuckerman Headwall
2. Jacques Parysko died near Windy Corner on Sherburne Ski Trail

canon of physics, mountain wisdom, and common sense would argue against this plan, and signs at the base of the trail warned hikers of avalanche danger in Tuckerman Ravine. There were more signs up near Howard Johnson's and at least one person and maybe two advised Phil not to camp up there and not to try to climb on the headwall because of the unstable snow, but no one knew their plans in any detail and no one knew where they made their camp.

As it happened, they could hardly have chosen a worse place for it. They made their way over the floor of the ravine to the beginning of the headwall, where they dug a hole and built a sort of roof out of crusted snow and ice. They were in the left center of the headwall, below the section that skiers call the Chute, and there was deep snow everywhere. In this situation, avalanches are not just probable, or even likely, they are inevitable.

Sunday afternoon was partly gone when Jacques' body was identified. The early season, bitter conditions and high avalanche danger in the ravine meant that no skiers were up there, but the men of the Mount Washington Volunteer Ski Patrol were keeping watch at Howard Johnson's. As soon as Jacques Parysko's body was identified down at Pinkham, Joe Dodge said, "I'll call the goddamn fish cop."

Fishing was Joe's one great release from his 24-hour days in service of the mountains, and he regarded it as an art form of such noble lineage and exquisitely difficult practice that it should not be encumbered by very much in the way of statutory restraint. This meant that Paul Doherty was Joe's natural enemy on warm-weather waters, but in every other respect he held the game warden in the very highest regard and they worked shoulder-to-shoulder on more rescues than either of them could count.

Soon Joe and Paul and some other experienced men started up the Fire Trail to look for Phil Longnecker. They joined the MWVSP men at Howard Johnson's and headed up into the bowl of the ravine.

The conditions were brutal, the high winds and the snowstorm were still on the mountain and new snow was accumulating rapidly. The afternoon is still vivid in Paul's memory: "It was so frigging cold and windy and snow blowing up there that you couldn't do a goddamn thing." They did find a bundle of the slender green sticks used for slope marking. This was a lead, and they probed on that site but found nothing except four feet of new snow. Even this hard work was not enough to keep the men warm; the temperature was down to −10° and the wind was up to 60 mph and they realized that the cold was biting too deep. Joe said they'd better get out while they still could, so as the early darkness of January came on they called off the search and went back down to Pinkham.

That evening Joe Dodge called Mack Beal, who first worked for him before the war and was very familiar with the mountain and AMC practices. Now Mack was living ten miles down the road in Jackson and he, too, had joined Fish and Game and was serving as a communications officer. Mack called a cadre of rescue workers and Joe called Major Peterson, commander of the quartermaster camp in the notch.

On Monday morning the snow had stopped and a crew was assembled: Joe and a team of AMC hutmen working at Pinkham were reinforced by Mack Beal, George Hamilton, Paul Doherty, Major Peterson, and seven quartermaster troopers. This kind of interdepartmental effort was new in itself, and it was accompanied by another new arrival. These woods had known the rhythmic crunch of snowshoes for many years, but now they resounded with the roar and clank of two army Weasels and a third that Joe Dodge had. Joe was not a primitivist, he'd be the first one to recognize any advance in equipment and this was the first mechanized search party. Polly Longnecker rode up with Major Peterson so she could help find the dugout.

Snow travel in Weasels was not all the army hoped it would be. Besides the problems of lateral traction, they tended to chew into snowdrifts rather than climb over them, so the combined forces on the Fire Trail had to do considerable digging to clear the way. When the group reached Howard Johnson's they parked the Weasels and put on snowshoes and skis to climb the Little Headwall to the bowl of the ravine. Progress slowed here. So much snow had drifted onto the slope that snowshoes wouldn't hold and the men's progress was often more like upward floundering than a steady ascent.

Paul Doherty loved backwoods tales and as he struggled up the Little Headwall he thought of the days almost 100 years earlier when gold-rushers climbed up the endless, heartbreaking pass outside Juneau, Alaska, heading for the Klondike. Those men wore whatever they found in their closets at home or in the outfitters' stores in Juneau. Now some of the men around Paul were wearing outfits better suited to skiing, Joe Dodge had a cold-weather navy jacket and Alaskan mukluks on his feet, the soldiers had the cold-weather gear they'd been developing at the quartermasters' base, and George

Hamilton had an arctic outfit developed for the navy. Mack Beal's turnout was particularly notable. He was in the Pacific submarine fleet during the war and when hostilities were over he mustered out and joined a weather bureau mission to Thule, Greenland, where he'd acquired a pair of Eskimo boots made in the traditional way with chewed leather and finished with beautiful sewing and insulation made of arctic grass. Mack's father was a textile broker with special interests in long-staple fibers, so Mack gave him a very fine parka made of Egyptian cotton that was virtually windproof. Mack eventually got it back and he paired it with his Eskimo boots for this day's work.

Paul Doherty was well equipped, too. The quartermaster men had an advanced base in the old Halfway House, four miles up the auto road, and they accumulated a considerable store of experimental clothing there. Paul understood the hardships that army rations can inflict, so he'd bring venison steaks up to the men and in return they'd provide him with the best in new cold-weather gear, sort of an inter-service relief program.

Monday was still bitterly cold, but the clouds had lifted to the upper reaches of Mount Washington and the ravine was clear. The combined forces totaled twenty-five and when they reached the ravine they saw that the whole headwall had avalanched. There was a deep fracture line about two-thirds of the way up the headwall and Joe knew that more snow could break loose at any moment, so the first thing he did was station a man farther out on the floor of the ravine to watch for more slides. The search party realized that the new slide reduced their chances of success and new snow was still drifting in, so any kind of low shelter would be buried under a smooth surface that gave no hint of what was underneath.

Polly Longnecker had never been in the ravine before this week and she'd only seen it through a disorienting blur of blowing snow when she was up there with her brother and Jacques. George Hamilton felt a sort of brotherly sympathy for her; she seemed like a genteel young woman and totally out of her element in the winter mountains, and now her brother was probably dead. She was obviously apprehensive, but George thought she seemed reassured by having Joe Dodge and his AMC crew and the game wardens and the army on her side—this was the varsity team. Polly tried to get a sense of where they'd made the dugout and pointed the search party to that spot. It was on the first rise of the headwall, the kind of place that would suggest itself to novice winter campers who wanted a snow shelter without all the

In January of 1954, Philip and Polly Longnecker and Jacques Parysko climbed up to Tuckerman Ravine and fashioned a dugout at the base of the headwall. Polly returned to the valley, while Philip and Jacques stayed in the ravine. Here Polly watches from the foreground while the recovery team digs trenches in the avalanche debris while searching for the body of her brother Philip.

work of building an igloo; here, they could dig into the slope and geometry would do part of the work for them.

The men of the rescue party started at the left side of the likely area and dug four long trenches, each about four feet deep. This effort did not uncover the shelter or any camping debris, so they probed the spaces in between with aluminum rods. This is subtle work; the probers have to interpret the feel of the push to know if resistance means a change in snow texture or a scrub spruce or a rock or campsite debris or a body. This is the first part of the ravine to lose the afternoon sun, and as the shadow slid down the headwall to cover them a cutting wind sprang up. Soon after 1:00 P.M. they struck the wrecked campsite. In that same hour Durban Longnecker, Phil's father, reached Pinkham after flying from Toledo, Ohio. Major Peterson had driven a fourth Weasel up to Howard Johnson's and Polly rode back down the mountain to join her father.

Up in the ravine, the men found an orange, then an ice axe and then a pair of crampons, then boots, a small gas stove, a hunting knife, a pair of pants and some food—all scattered through the packed snow like the relics of some lost civilization. Finally they came to the body of Philip Longnecker, and at 1:30 P.M. word was radioed down from the ravine and Durban Longnecker learned that his son was dead. The roof of the dugout had collapsed and Jacques Parysko's empty sleeping bag was next to Phil, and his boots and his socks and his mittens and his warm pants and his jacket were next to his sleeping bag.

Four feet of densely-packed snow rested on top of the camp. The men dug straight down through this burden to clear the campsite, and as they worked they noticed that the snow face they cut did not show the mixing pattern that would be expected in the remains of an avalanche. It was evenly stratified all the way down to the broken snow of the camp preparations. The first and most obvious assumption was that the dugout had been swamped by an avalanche of new snow hanging on the slopes above them, but the stratification was typical of an undisturbed snowfall and suggested that this had not happened.

Thirty feet farther down the slope, the rescue party found more of the marker sticks the MWVSP men had seen the previous afternoon; in fact, they were probably from the same bundle. It was important to learn the cause of the young men's death, so the rescuers dug sample holes near the sticks. They cut down through almost six feet of new snow before they hit the old crust and the upper levels were stratified but the lower part, more than half of the total, was not. This bottom layer also held irregular pieces of ice and frozen snow, and these could have been torn loose from some place higher up the slope or they could have been part of the roof the campers built over their dugout.

The men of the rescue party studied the contradictory clues and worked out a sequence of events that made sense. Joe Dodge thought that a rather small slide of new snow had come down during the night and swept past the camp but not directly over it. There was enough mass in the slide to knock loose the roof of the dugout, but it was at the edge of the slide and the volume of snow wasn't a large enough to bury the camp. Then a larger slide came down later and buried the site.

Published accounts of the accident reported that there was a heavy block of ice on Phil's head and he died from the impact. Those who were most closely involved in freeing his body do not remember any block of ice or any sign of trauma on his head. On the contrary, they were struck by how peaceful and composed he looked, as if he was in an undisturbed sleep.

This suggested a different cause of death. The snow on the headwall was very cold and powdery. When a slide of this type comes down there's a pressure blowout on the sides, and if the slide brushed the camp as Joe supposed, a dense mist of snow would fill the dugout and Phil would breathe it in, but he would not breathe it out. One of the officers involved in the rescue remembers that the coroner found water in Phil's lungs; from a medical point of view, he drowned.

Opinion was divided on what happened to Jacques. Some thought he'd gotten up to answer a call of nature just before the slide and he was out of the way when it hit. Then, terrified beyond reason, he ran for help without pulling on any clothes or looking to see what had happened to Phil. There was a problem here. He might answer the call without getting into his heavy clothes, but he'd probably pull on his boots. This suggested a different scenario. According to this theory, Jacques woke up in the midst of the slide and his only thought was to get away as fast as he could, so he jumped out of his sleeping bag and ran away downslope in a panic.

In either case, dawn was far enough along so he could see and he ran out across the floor of the ravine and on down over the Little Headwall and down the Sherburne Trail to Windy Corner before he collapsed. This desperate flight took him past three emergency telephones that connected to the AMC base camp, and he died within shouting distance of ten more people staying in the Harvard Cabin just off the Sherburne Trail.

Jacques had seen all these sources of help during the previous days, but they did not register with him in that awful dawn. The rescuers also realized that if the two campers had made the extra effort of digging a cave into the slope instead of covering over a hole with loose debris, they would have been protected by a roof of smooth compacted snow, and the small slide would have passed them without any damage. There was another alternative: they could have listened to the advice of the people they met and heeded the signs warning them not to go into the ravine.

The afternoon was almost gone when the men finished their work at the campsite, so they lashed Phil's body to a toboggan and headed for the Little Headwall. They could sit on their snowshoes and slide down the headwall much faster than they'd climbed up that morning, but the slope was too steep to manage the toboggan very well, so they wrapped a rope around an ice axe driven into the snow and snubbed their burden down to easier terrain.

The Weasels were loaded with the searchers and their sad discovery, and the machines made heavy work of it on the way down to the highway. True to their reputation, one of them slid over the edge of the trail on a sharp turn and seemed certain to capsize, but the army driver kept the momentum going and the Weasel scrabbled back onto the trail. Another quartermaster Weasel went over the edge, too, and it hit a tree and caught one of the soldier's boots. The man pulled his foot free, but the Weasel proved to be more intractable and it had to be retrieved the next day.

Phil owned a jeep and he'd driven his sister Polly and his friend Jacques up to Pinkham to start their days on Mount Washington. Before Durban and Polly Longnecker left for Toledo they gave the jeep to Joe Dodge and it served many useful years at Pinkham.

Chapter Sixteen

A QUESTION OF LIFE OR DEATH

*W*E TRY TO MAKE OUR LIVES SAFE. FOR EVERY HAZARD there are warnings and barriers, for every bold assertion there are fallback positions, for every fallible device there are back-up systems and redundancies. Children go forth to play girded with armor for their head, face, teeth, elbows, knees, and any other part that may suffer assault. I've seen a step ladder with eighteen warning labels pasted to it, another with a six-part lesson on how to avoid falling off, with attendant diagrams. If all else fails, we go to court; when a piece of bridge masonry fell through the top of a convertible, the driver sued the car company for making a cloth top that wouldn't keep out falling masonry. So when we talk about questions of life or death, we usually don't mean it.

There do come times, though, perhaps only once in a lifetime, when we're really up against it, when there's no manual or guide or precedent, when we really do have to answer a question of life or death. The crew at Madison Spring Hut had to do that one evening just as they were serving dinner to a full house; they were all college age and they were up against it.

Madison Springs Hut is one of the great rallying points on the Presidential Range; few places can match its spectacular location and none can be reached by so many trails—there are eleven direct routes to the hut. On August 24, however, MacDonald Barr was primarily interested in climbing to the summit of Mount Madison, which rises 556 feet above the hut.

Don Barr was serious about this kind of thing, and as he started up the trail in Randolph that day he was a candidate for his Ph.D. in geography from Boston University. Beyond that, he loved it. As his wife Yvonne said, "He was the kind who would go the extra steps for a big view or to just see the stars. The mountains were an extra dimension in his life."

The gentlefolk of Randolph's classic age would understand. As Don Barr started up the Valley Way, he was directly across a broad meadow from the site of the Ravine House, which was the home away from home for the generations of vacationing Boston academics who spent their summers in Randolph and built that extraordinary network of trails on Madison and its adjoining peaks on the Presidential Range. They'd go anywhere for a pleasing outlook and a pretty waterfall, which is why they built so many trails.

Don came from a long line of military men. He'd grown up on a number of military posts in far-off climes, but his home base was in Pueblo, Colorado, and he learned the vigorous life there; in fact, he had a reconstructed kneecap as a reminder of an early rock-climbing fall. He settled in Brookline, Massachusetts, to make his own life and after his first college degrees he worked as a civil engineer and city planner for about fifteen years. He continued to believe in the active life, and as a member of the Brookline Town Meeting during the 1970s and as a city planner he pushed for the development of bike paths around Boston. He also went whitewater canoeing and hiking and rock climbing in the nearby Quincy quarries when he could. He and his wife had a daughter, Heather, and a son, Tavis, and as the children grew up these outings were an important part of their family life.

But on this late August day they hadn't made their big summer climb yet. Don had been busy that summer finishing his PhD. in geography and looking for work in the new field of geographic information systems, and he'd be taking another job soon. The Barrs had already taken a combined business and family trip to the West, and the Madison trip was probably their only chance for a New England hike this year.

Don was acquainted with the White Mountains and their upland lodgings. He'd taken Tavis on a hike up the Southern Peaks and they'd stayed at Mizpah and Lakes of the Clouds Huts, he'd taken Heather on a different Mount Washington trip, and planning for family hikes was careful and enjoyable, it was actually the beginning of the trip. They began thinking about this year's White Mountain hike before they went west, and while plans were afoot Don called the AMC to see which one of their huts would have room for a party of three on the night of August twenty-fourth. Madison Spring Hut would, and he made the reservations.

Heather Barr was in Germany that summer, so the three would be Don and Tavis Barr and Christian Steiber, a German exchange student living with friends of the Barrs. Don and Tavis didn't know him very well, but he was added to the roster so he could see another part of American life before he went home. Don was fifty-two, Tavis was thirteen, and Christian was sixteen. They got an early start from Brookline on the twenty-fourth and reached the parking lot at the beginning of the Valley Way Trail at about noon. Don knew that the weather report was not promising, and he and the boys got their gear organized under lowering clouds.

Up on the heights, the weather was treacherous. On the twenty-third, the Mount Washington Observatory recorded mild southwest winds in the teens and 20s rising to a peak gust of 53 a little after 6:30 P.M., but the temperature ranged from 47° down to 39°. This is the kind of summer weather that can presage trouble for hikers who confuse August in the valleys with August on the Presidential Range. In fact, it was on August 24, 1938, that Joe Caggiano died near Madison Spring Hut, and on August 23, 1952, Raymond Davis hiked across the range to his death above Tuckerman Ravine.

On the twenty-fourth, the summit observatory recorded a wind moving steadily into the northwest with a morning average in the 50 mph range. This is a veering wind and it's a good sign; an old sailor's adage promises, "Veering is clearing." My father always called it a northwest clear-off, a promise so eagerly awaited that my generation saved time by calling it an NWCO. This was not the pattern that was developing this day.

The usual plan for an overnight climb to the summit of Madison is to hike up one of the many trails to the hut, spend the night there, and then go to the summit and down to the valley the next day. Don knew the weather report was not promising. Thinking back to that day, Tavis says, "He felt that if we didn't see the summit that day, we wouldn't see the summit. I think maybe he wanted to leave in the morning for somewhere else." So Don decided to climb to the summit of Madison in these marginal conditions before they got worse, then descend to the hut for a good dinner and a cozy night and see what the next day would bring.

Only two trails lead directly from Randolph to the summit of Madison. One is Howker Ridge, which starts almost a mile east of the Valley Way and follows the high arc of the ridge to the summit. It's a spectacular trail, but it's four and a half miles long and would take about that long in hours, too. The only other direct route is a combination of three trails: the Valley Way, the Brookside, and the Watson Path. This route is three-quarters of a mile shorter to the summit of Madison and, like the Howker Ridge Trail, the last mile would be along rough terrain above timberline, with no protection at all from the weather. And, again like the Howker Ridge, there would be another rough and fully-exposed half-mile down to the hut.

Given the late start and the poor weather, the prudent approach would be to stay on the Valley Way, which provides the shortest, easiest and most sheltered route to the hut; in fact, it stays below the crest of the ridge and also below timberline until about 100 yards from the door. Then Don and the boys could see what the next day brought; and even if the weather went against them, they'd have a wide choice of trails back to the parking lot where their car was. They wouldn't get to the summit of Madison, but it would still be a fine and memorable hike. The three of them talked this over and Don decided to stick with the Watson Path.

The Watson Path turns off the Brookside, which turns off the Valley Way. The beginning of the Valley Way is enchanting. It leads over very moderate grades through a cathedral grove of ancient evergreen trees, with the many pools and cascades of Snyder Brook just a few steps away on the left. Remembering the day, Tavis says, "It wasn't raining, but just kind of humid, but in almost a nice way, a blanketing kind of humidity. It wasn't very steep and it was very pretty."

After almost a mile they came to a seven-way junction of trails, an eloquent testimonial to the enthusiasms of those nineteenth-century academics in their summer pursuits. The Brookside is one of the choices. True to its name, the trail runs along the brook up Snyder Ravine and the AMC *White Mountain Guide* mentions its "views of many cascades and pools" and calls it "wild and beautiful, with cascades, mossy rocks and fine forest." It's a mile and a half long and the early going is right beside the brook; then the trail joins an ancient logging road relicked from the original forest cutting early in the century. It follows this easy grade for more than half a mile through a beautiful mature birch forest, the usual succession after a timber clear cut.

The Snyder Ravine finally pinches in, the logging road ends, and the Brookside runs close to the brook and becomes more of a scramble. Soon the trail turns away from the brook at Salmacis Rock and becomes steep and rough. The Watson Path enters from the right on a short and almost flat connection from the Valley Way, and Don Barr's group could have made this quick change to a sheltered trail better suited to the day, but they didn't. Typical of the Randolph Mountain Club's affection for natural curiosities, the Brookside soon comes to Bruin Rock and then Duck Fall, and after a few more strides the Lower Bruin departs on the right for another chance to join the Valley Way, and the Watson Path bears away left. Don Barr turned left.

So far, the hike was a damp but enjoyable riparian reverie, but then everything changed. The Watson Path is a misleading choice. The contour lines on the AMC trail map do show that it's the steepest of the alternatives to the Valley Way, but the 100-foot contour interval is necessarily an average calculation and it does not show that the steepness comes in clumps and the footing is much rougher than any of the neighboring trails. The climb out of Snyder Ravine is the price hikers pay for the gentle walk along the old logging road down below; it's an exhausting and frustrating grind, and not often chosen for a repeat visit.

By now it was mid-afternoon and on Mount Washington the wind was in the 70 mph range; the summit temperature dropped from 49° early in the morning to 32° at noon, it held steady at freezing all afternoon, and the heights were in the clouds with intermittent rain. Madison Spring Hut is above timberline in the col between Adams and Madison, four miles across Great Gulf from the summit of Mount Washington, and conditions at the hut were not much better: afternoon temperature sank into the 30s, the wind was in the 50–60 range, and there was a harsh driving rain. Hikers arriving at the hut were severely chilled and their numbers climbed into the forties as prudent people caught above timberline on the range made for shelter. The numbers rose to the hut's capacity of fifty and the hut crew kept busy warming them and watching for hypothermia.

The Watson Path climbs out of Snyder Ravine on the north shoulder of Mount Madison, and Don Barr and the two boys kept scrambling upward over the steep terrain with its loose stones and root traps, a tough piece of work under the best of circumstances and a severe test in the rain and cold of this afternoon. About three miles after leaving the parking lot they reached timberline and a stretch of peculiarly discouraging terrain; there's a hump that looks like the summit, then three more crests and then another hump, each of which brings false hope. By now, hikers are wondering if there's ever going to be an end to it. Tavis says, "I don't think the map showed where timberline was. So we looked at the map and saw one major topographical bulge before the summit and then the summit and then the hut on the other side. So we looked and we figured, Okay, this is the first bulge and the next one will be the summit." To make matters worse, the trail leads over large angular rocks that tend to shift and tilt underfoot.

Madison Spring Hut is open from early June to early September with a crew of five, but there's always one person on days-off, so in practical terms it's a crew of four. The line-up had changed on this late-summer day. Liz Keuffel had been the hutmaster, but she left just the day before to return to her teaching job for the academic season; Emily Thayer had been assistant hutmaster, so this was her first day in charge.

Emily was no shrinking violet. She'd grown up in a large and enthusiastic family of hikers; her grandparents and parents and aunts and uncles and cousins and two brothers all gathered at their summer place in Whitefield, just west of the Presidential Range, and her memories of childhood were filled with heroic outings on the heights. Now Emily had finished her junior year at Middlebury College in Vermont, this was her fourth summer working for the AMC, and she'd reached her full strength at 5'8".

Lars Jorrens, Alexei Rubenstein, and Dan Arons had been on the Madison crew all summer with Emily, but Dan was on days-off this weekend. It was a good day not to be at Madison Spring Hut and for those who were there to stay indoors, and Emily kept looking out the windows at the dark swirling mist on every side and wondering about people who were out on the range.

Emily knew about bad weather on the range. During one of her childhood summers a throng of relatives set out from Whitefield to climb Mount Jefferson. They started up the Caps Ridge Trail, which is the express route of the Northern Peaks; it starts at the 3,000-foot high point on the Jefferson Notch road and runs straight up the ridge 2.4 miles to the 5,715-foot summit of Jefferson, a delightful climb, but one that's studded with the steep rocks of the "caps" and runs above timberline for most of its length.

The weather went bad when they were near the top of Mount Jefferson and the grown-ups decided that rather than go back down through the weather on the difficult trail they'd come up, it would be better to march the family troop down the summit cone of Jefferson, across the ridge of Mount Clay, around the headwall of Great Gulf, and on up to the summit of Mount Washington so they could take the cog railway down. A family photo album preserves the image of Emily sitting in the summit hotel, twelve years old, soaking wet, and glumly reflecting that the celebrated wisdom of grown-ups might not be all it's cracked up to be. In fairness to the senior Thayers, it must be said that agile children enjoy steep rocks a lot more than grown-ups do, and they also have an instinctive faith that their skin is waterproof.

Now, eight years after that stormy day on the range, Emily turned on the radio to hear the regular 2:00 P.M. call from AMC headquarters in Pinkham Notch. Hut crews take turns cooking on a daily rotation and this was Emily's turn; all huts have a reservation list so they can plan their meals, and the 2:00 P.M. call provides news of late cancellations or late additions that will require adjustments in the kitchen. This day the call did not include any cancellations and Emily had an immediate thought, almost a reflex: "We're going to be going out—we're going to be going out." That is, they'd have to answer a call from distressed hikers.

It seemed to Emily that there had been an unusual number of emergency calls that summer. Twisted ankles and tired hikers are a matter of course and crews take them in stride, but extra dimensions had been added this summer. There was, for instance, the German shepherd dog. One day a man came in and said that his dog needed help out on the Parapet Trail, that he couldn't walk anymore.

The Parapet is a nasty piece of work. It was cut in 1951 to provide a foul-weather route around the summit cone of Mount Madison and the 0.7-mile length leads over large angular boulders and through dense dwarf spruce growth. When the 1951 trail crew got through, it was so difficult to negotiate that the Madison Spring Hut crew thought it must be a rough draft, a sketch to be refined and finished later. It was never refined, and Emily's crew loaded the dog into a litter and spent a very unpleasant time hauling it back to the hut. The owner called for a helicopter lift to the valley; he said he'd pay for it, but this was not arranged and the hut crew had to take care of the dog for three days while the owner went to the valley to look into other arrangements. Finally the dog got a ride down in the cargo net slung below a regularly scheduled supply helicopter.

So 1986 rescue demands on the Madison crew had been heavy, unusual, and not necessarily rewarding. Now, on the afternoon of August twenty-fourth, the people who'd been hiking across the range from the Lakes of the Clouds Hut began coming in. The wind was gaining in strength and they were cold and wet and almost everything they had with them was soaked, so the crew kept busy getting them supplied with warm drinks and putting them into whatever dry clothes could be found; the crew dug into their own reserves of clothing and Emily even contributed her favorite original Chuck Roast fleece jacket, which she never got back.

August twenty-fourth also brought a new crew member to Madison. Kari Geick belonged to an active family in Kent, Connecticut, and she was an equestrienne of very considerable achievement. After college Kari spent four years with the biology department at Tufts University working in animal behavior; then she decided it was time for a career change and planned to relocate in Colorado. She'd hiked on the Franconia and Presidential Ranges and she had a little time before leaving for Colorado, so after she left Tufts she went to the AMC headquarters in Pinkham and asked if they had any openings for end-of-season fill-ins. Liz Keuffel had just left the Madison crew so Kari was hired on the spot and she went right on around to Randolph and hiked up the Valley Way.

Late in the same afternoon, Stephanie Arenalas showed up at the hut. She'd worked for the AMC the previous two summers in several connections, she'd been on the trail crew and on the storehouse crew managing supplies

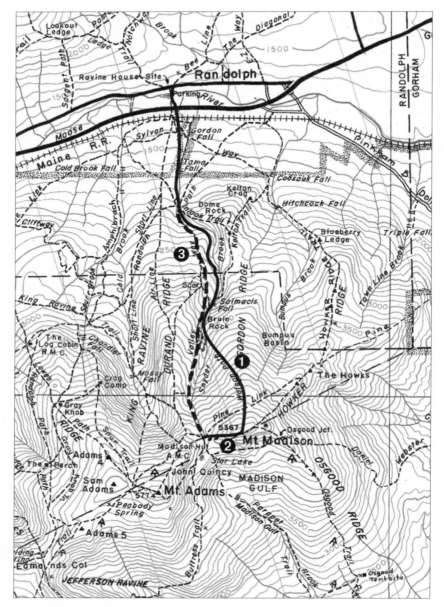

1. MacDonald Barr went up via Valley Way, Brookside, and Watson Path
2. Died on summit of Mount Madison
3. Evacuation via Valley Way

for the huts, but she was not on the roster this summer, so she'd come to the mountains to pay a surprise visit to her friend Liz Keuffel at Madison.

Stephanie hiked up the Madison Gulf Trail, which rises from the bottom of Great Gulf south of the hut and provides the most difficult of all direct approaches to the hut. It's a strenuous but wonderful climb in good weather, but this day the trail was more like a brook bed and the top section was steep water-soaked ledges, so Stephanie reached the hut exhausted, wet to the skin, and severely chilled. Then she learned that Liz had just left. Stephanie knew the ropes, so, in the time-honored tradition of the huts, she stayed to lend a hand.

Don Barr and the boys were still pushing up the Watson Path. Timberline is about 4,000 feet here, with another 1,363 feet to the summit of Madison. The northwest wind was blowing straight onto the ridge and its violence was heightened by the topography: they were climbing the northernmost ridge of the Presidential Range, the terrain turns a corner here, and a northwest wind starts into the long accelerating venturi of Pinkham Notch. Tavis says, "At that point it might have dropped thirty degrees and the winds became a lot faster. It was a little breezy as we were getting up to the timberline but all of a sudden there were the fastest winds I've ever been in. I was out in a hurricane in Boston and the winds on Mount Madison were faster than that." Don's group was not prepared for this; they had long pants, hats, sweaters and light jackets, but no real protection against heavy weather, and the bare rocks gave them no protection at all.

"We were in the clouds and we kept pushing on," says Tavis, "because we thought we were almost there the whole time, we kept seeing these bulges and, 'Okay, maybe that's it.' You get this series and each one you think, 'Well, that's it, we know the hut's right on the other side.' So that's why we didn't turn back."

There was still a chance for an escape. A little more than halfway up this discouraging summit climb, the Pine Link Trail crosses the Watson Path at a right angle. The Pine Link is almost level here and it continues level and then descends slightly to the hut. Tavis says, "We debated taking that and then decided we were probably close enough anyway that we should just go over the summit and get to the hut, that that would be faster. At that point we were basically guessing where we were based on the topographical markers, and we were wrong about where we were."

Tavis remembered that his father had said where the timberline would be. Don Barr would be interested in that kind of thing, it's something that geographers think about. But it turned out that his calculation was about 300 feet too high, and this is revealing. Timberline averages 4,000 feet all around the range, but it varies with several factors. One factor is exposure, and timberline on the northwest shoulder of Madison is lower than Don expected because the weather is harsher here than in most places, and harsher than he expected.

Don and the boys kept pushing on toward the top, but they were going slower and slower and stopping more and more often. Tavis says, "We didn't have any backup clothing, we had T-shirts and sweaters and windbreakers. I didn't carry along a hat and dad actually gave me his hat and then it blew right off my head."

Tavis was only thirteen, but he was already taller than his father and notably slender, a physiotype well-known among teenage boys in their growing years. Christian had a hood on his jacket, he had a solid athletic frame, and he seemed to be managing the conditions fairly well, so he told Don and Tavis that he was going on ahead and he disappeared in the fog. Now the cold rain was in their faces and Tavis tried to wrap his hands in a bandanna, but it didn't work very well. He also realized that his father had changed, he was panting in a way that he'd never seen before.

Tavis also remembered a video his grammar school class was shown before they went on a hiking trip. "It was on hypothermia and I remembered that at a certain point you stop realizing that you're cold. And I think that's just about when my dad got to that point. I wasn't at that point yet. I had started to go numb, but I was quite aware of my condition. At that point he had difficulty walking or moving. I was kind of the unsteady you are when you're drunk. I could maybe not run in the straightest line, but I could run." Finally Tavis saw a cluster of trail signs—he'd reached the top. His father was about twenty feet behind him so he went back to tell him. All his father said was, "Oh, good."

"We got past the summit together, my dad was at the summit, but not for much after that. By that time we realized that it was really too late. We both knew we were hypothermic, by the time we were at the summit it really was the fastest way to go straight to the hut, but it was just too late. He was still lucid enough to know. I think we stopped for just a second to look around and that's just about when his lips were going white. That was the sign that he was really in bad shape. I knew I was in bad shape, I could feel it, but I was still—I would say drunk, but lucid."

There was no lingering on the summit of Madison. "My dad was pushing on. If I reminded him that he was hypothermic and needed to keep pushing on, he would say, 'Oh, yeah, I need to do this.' And I just kept saying, 'We need to keep going—we need to keep going.' He kept trying, and there was a point at which he just visibly couldn't walk anymore. He found a crevice and covered himself up as best he could, and at that point I just started running."

The summit of Madison is not a sharp peak like neighboring Adams, it's more of a short narrow ridge with the trail running just below the crest. Tavis sensed that the storm would get worse before it got better, "but it was so painfully obvious that there was nothing that I could do. He was trying very hard to walk and he couldn't. My choices were either to stay there with him or move on and I didn't really see any benefit in staying there with him. There wasn't—I couldn't really—I didn't have anything to give him."

Down at the hut, dinner was almost ready and yet another group of hikers straggled in. They were soaking wet and they were beyond cold, they had the slurred speech and muddled thinking of hypothermia, so the crew put them into their own bunks in the crew room and made them drink fresh-brewed liquid Jello—the sugar and heat of the dessert is a favorite restorative with hut crews.

It was now 6:00 P.M. and the crew turned their attentions to serving dinner to a full house of hikers; actually, a bit more than a full house. They got everyone seated and just as the soup was going out to the dining room the kitchen door burst open and Christian Steiber lurched in.

Kari Geick was surprised, the weather was so nasty that she couldn't get over how anyone would think it was a good day for a hike. Christian was very much reduced and he tried to tell them urgent news, but it was difficult to learn much about the situation because he had a heavy German accent and imperfect English, and he was further choked by fatigue and cold. The crew did understand that there were two people behind him and going slowly, but they didn't learn how far away they were, how bad their condition was, or even what trail they were on. Trails approach Madison Spring Hut like spokes aimed at a hub and the crew guessed the people were on the Osgood Ridge because that's the only major trail that approaches on the kitchen-door side of the hut. So they got Christian out of his wet clothes and into a crewroom bunk to warm up, and then they waited for a little while.

Here, too, there were complicating factors. The need for help is subjective and it's liable to misreading. For instance, earlier that summer a woman came in to one of the other huts and reported that her mother was out on the range and having chest pains. This is an automatic danger signal and the crew started up the trail at a fast clip. When they reached the afflicted woman, it turned out that the shoulder straps on her pack were too tight.

The crew waited for a few minutes to see if anyone would come in after the German boy, but no one did. Emily was thinking, "Oh God, we've got dinner all underway here . . ." Then she told Lars to make up a pack of useful gear and see if he could find anyone on the Osgood Trail. Lars pulled on as much wool and polypropylene as he had, then a hat and rain jacket with a drawstring hood, and he put his mittens in his pack along with a blanket and extra clothes. He took the small high-band radio and Thermos bottles filled with hot Jello, and at 6:15 P.M. he started up the Osgood Trail toward the summit of Madison.

Lars was a good person for the job. He was twenty-two years old, he'd been hiking in the New Hampshire mountains since he was seven, he was six feet tall and 155 pounds, and after a summer of packing loads up to Madison Spring Hut he was exceptionally fit and strong. Now he found Tavis Barr on the Osgood Trail about 500 feet from the hut.

Topography is important here. Timberline is not a precise location, it's more like a zone, and Madison Spring Hut sits in an open field of rock and grass and moss that's inside a ring of scrub growth that protects the lowest part of the trail for about 350 feet above the hut. Tavis was sitting on a rock just above the top of the scrub growth.

The boy was completely exposed to the wind and driving sleet. He was cold but he was coherent, and he told Lars that his father was farther up the trail. Lars asked him how his father was getting along and Tavis said he didn't exactly know. Tavis remembers that Lars had quite a number of things with him, and when the hutman tried to give him some warmer gear, he said, "No, my dad's going to need them more than I do." He did take some hot Jello and a pair of gloves, but Lars couldn't learn much more about Don except that he'd been going slower and slower and Tavis thought his father was dying up there and he came on ahead to find help.

Lars judged that Tavis was certainly uncomfortable but not in serious trouble at the moment, and he asked the boy if he could hang in there for a while longer. Then he tried to tuck him into a bit more sheltered position in the rocks and started up the trail. Lars judged the wind to be about 60 mph and the fog had cut visibility to seventy-five feet. Tavis hadn't said how far up his father was, but Lars was familiar with the terrain, it was his summer backyard, so he made a fast climb even though the gusty tailwind knocked him down several times. It got noticeably colder as he came closer to the summit and the rain turned to sleet and added a sandblast effect to the misery.

Don Barr was lying in the middle of the trail on the near end of that short summit ridge; he was in a level place in the trail that gave no protection at all from the wind and he was in very poor condition. Lars couldn't tell if he'd fallen or if he simply lay down, but he was only semi-conscious and mumbling incoherently and he didn't seem to understand what Lars said to him. Don's condition had put him beyond reason and he resisted Lars' efforts to help him; he'd stiffen up and try to protect his body, and he wouldn't take the hot Jello and he wouldn't let Lars put any clothes on him. Lars tried to drag him and he tried to roll him, but he couldn't move Don at all. Lars tried to get through to him, he put his face right down with him and tried to talk to him, but Don barely registered the presence of his Samaritan, he'd just groan.

In fact, Lars could hardly manage the extra clothes himself. Don was wearing jeans and a light jacket and they were soaked, so Lars immediately started to pull extra gear out of his pack. The first thing was a hat. The wind tore it out of his hands and sent it spinning away toward the valley.

Lars did not have a large supply of emergency equipment: "I didn't have a tent or anything, no sleeping bag. I brought a blanket to warm somebody if they were moving—I didn't anticipate that the guy would be lying down and not able to do anything. What we understood was that they were coming along and I was just bringing up a Thermos of hot Jello, which is always a good thing. I had a flashlight and a blanket and some extra clothes—I just ran out the door hoping I could get these folks in, so I wasn't equipped to deal with somebody that couldn't move."

This is always the difficult choice: to wait for a while in hopes of getting more information and making a better-informed rescue, or to go out as quickly as possible and see what can be done. Reports of trouble are often

MacDonald Barr collapsed on the summit of Mount Madison in the great storm of
August 24, 1986. His son Tavis was able to reach the patch of dwarf spruce just above
Madison Spring Hut. It took two crew members 40 minutes of hard work to bring him in
from there, but they could not help his father.

fragmentary and vague, the trouble might be a twisted ankle or a heart attack,
and Christian had given the hut crew very little to go on.

By now it was 6:45 P.M. and the situation was critical and moving quickly
to lethal. The wind was rising into the 70–80 range and sleet was mixing
with the driving rain; the sun was still shining somewhere, but the Northern
Peaks were smothered in dense storm clouds. Then more bad luck joined the
emergency: the radio Lars had with him was not on the same wavelength as
the radio at the hut.

Joe Dodge was an expert and enthusiastic promoter of radio since his
childhood. He retired from AMC duty at Pinkham Notch in 1959, and, following his lead, the Pinkham office and all the huts were equipped with
two-way radios in 1964. In accordance with the standards of the day, this was
low-band equipment in rather large cases containing eleven batteries, and

there was a solar charging unit. And, since there was only one radio at each hut, they could not be used as base and remote in emergencies.

Twenty years later, the goal was to provide each AMC facility with two new high-band radios of light hand-held design. These, with a repeater on Cannon Mountain, would put all the AMC huts in contact with headquarters in Pinkham and with each other, and they were suitable for base-remote operations. These radios are expensive and the system was being completed piece by piece with money raised through donations and the sale of various small items such as bandannas. In 1986, Madison had one of the new radios and one of the old low-band models, which meant that both their radios could talk to Pinkham but they couldn't talk to each other.

When Lars left the hut he took the high-band radio, and after he'd done everything he could for Don Barr he pulled it out of his pack to call Pinkham and heard an urgent conversation already going on. Two hikers had been overtaken by the storm on the flanks of Mount Washington, they were above timberline and somewhere between Oakes Gulf and Boott Spur, but they were well-equipped and they did the smart thing, they pitched their small mountaineering tent in a sheltered spot, battened down the hatches, and settled themselves to wait for better weather.

These hikers were overdue on their planned arrival and this had been noted, so search parties were deployed and Lars could hear them talking to each other. In fact, the whole hut system was listening. The eight AMC huts are spaced about a day's hike apart and Peter Benson was listening from Zealand, three huts away at the edge of the Pemigewasset Wilderness. Jennifer Botzo was hutmaster at Lonesome Lake at the far end of the chain and she could hear the exchanges clearly. Suddenly she heard someone break into the talk on Mount Washington. "This is Lars on top of Madison," he said, "this is an emergency." Jennifer could also hear the wind roaring around him.

Peter Crane heard him down at headquarters in Pinkham Notch. It was 6:55 P.M. and the main building was filled with the hubbub of a full house at dinner. Peter was carrying a high-band radio and he heard the call from Lars, but the message was indistinct. The problem was not in the electronics, it was in the air; his words were masked by the blast of the wind, but Peter understood that there was trouble on Madison. In keeping with his careful nature, he began a log on the evening.

Peter was one of the ranking veterans on the Presidential Range. In the fall of 1977 he took the caretaker job at the Harvard Mountaineering Club cabin below Huntington Ravine and the following spring he began work with the AMC. He spent three summers in different huts, three off-seasons in remote caretaker positions, two winters at the shelter in Tuckerman Ravine, and in the spring of 1984 he was appointed assistant manager at the AMC headquarters in Pinkham Notch. By the summer of 1986 he was on the "Notch Watch," one of two people detailed in 24-hour shifts to deal with problems that might arise in the valley operation or emergencies on the heights.

Peter brought more than wide experience to the job; he was also a person of remarkable calm. Now Lars said that he'd done all he could for Don Barr, he said he couldn't move him, that he'd tried to drag him and even roll him, but the man just stiffened up and it wasn't working at all.

Hut crews are housekeepers, not ambulance personnel, and Lars was not feeling very confident, but after just a few exchanges on the radio he felt stronger. "Peter was great. I remember his voice being very calm and that was Peter—he was very good for this kind of situation. I summarized the situation and said there was nothing more here, but there's this kid down below and he is still able to move, from what I can see, and I think we need to get him in, and then maybe we can come back up and try to get this guy down the hill, but I can't do it myself. Peter said, 'You make the call. We don't want to lose you up there—you do what you can.' He asked if I could move him and I said I could not." Peter told him to shelter Don as well as he could and get back down to the hut for reinforcements.

Then Peter asked Lars if the low-band radio at the hut was switched on so he could speak to the crew there, and Lars said that he didn't think it was. This was not a mistake; those old units were in semi-retirement and it was not standard practice to leave them on. At this point Emily and her crew had only the sketchy news brought by Christian Steiber and the situation might be relatively easy—a man was a little way back on the trail and Lars could take care of him with hot Jello, a blanket, a helping hand, and an encouraging presence.

When Peter finished his talk with Lars on Mount Madison he called the weather observatory on the summit of Mount Washington and asked them to try to raise the Madison crew on the observatory's low-band radio, but the summit could not establish contact. Immediately after this, at 7:00 P.M.,

Lars called Peter again and said that he could not find any place nearby that offered more shelter than the one Don was in, and that he hadn't been able to move him anyway. He emphasized that Don was shaking and convulsive.

Peter understood that they had a dangerous emergency on their hands and the moment Lars' call ended he called the Androscoggin Valley Hospital, eighteen miles from the Valley Way parking lot. The AVH staff is familiar with mountain emergencies, so Peter brought them up to date on the Madison situation and asked them to stand by, and they advised him on treating Don.

That call was at 7:10 and at 7:15 Peter called Frank Hubbell at SOLO, an organization thirty miles south of Pinkham Notch that specializes in training emergency personnel. No live voice answered at SOLO and Peter left a message on their machine. Then he called the Mountain Rescue Service in North Conway; he didn't know how many AMC staff would be available for emergency duty and he wanted to put MRS on standby.

Peter also called Troop F of the state police and asked them to engage the Fish and Game unit responsible for the area. Carl Carlson of Fish and Game called back at 7:25 and said that he was putting additional necessary people in the loop. Then Peter called Bill Arnold of the very active Randolph Mountain Club. Bill was one of the Forest Service men at the Dolly Copp campground on the northern flank of Mount Madison and Bill said he'd call Gary Carr about further Forest Service involvement. Then Peter called Mike Pelchat, the state of New Hampshire's manager of its interests on the summit of Mount Washington. All that was done by 7:35.

Meanwhile, Janet Morgan was organizing a team of AMC staff in Pinkham Notch. They had warm clothing, rain gear, heat packs, Thermoses, and headlamps with extra batteries, and they also had oxygen to be administered by Brad Ray, the Forest Service ranger in Tuckerman Ravine and a veteran of thirty years of mountain emergencies. Finally, Peter impressed the nature of the situation on the AMC crew, he reminded them of the first rule of search and rescue: that they could not help the victim of a life-threatening emergency if they became victims themselves.

Up at Madison Spring Hut, Lars didn't come back and he didn't come back and Emily was thinking, "Oh man—what is going on?" The Osgood Path rises directly from the hut to the summit, Lars was young and strong and he had good clothes, but as night came on the conditions were so severe on top of Mount Madison that he was barely able to get back down himself. The wind was in the 70s and gusting into the 80s and it was right in his face. His body did not obey thought, it obeyed cold and wind, and Lars staggered and lurched down the summertime trail he knew so well until he found Tavis.

"He hadn't moved, obviously he was stuck and he was getting pretty incoherent. I thought, 'Alright, I've got to try get him in. It isn't that far to the hut, so give it a try.' I stood him up and I tried to move him but we were getting pushed over, flattened, and we'd be flopping around and I'd try to get him up again. He was very stiff, he was not helping much at all at that point, kind of a dead weight or even worse than that, he was a sort of resisting weight." Lars wasn't sure of Tavis' mental state, "His speech was slurred and I guess he recognized that I came back down alone and he asked 'How's my dad?' and I said we're going to go back up and get him."

Lars got back to the hut at 7:40. He went in through the kitchen door and found Emily and said, "We've got to talk—there's something serious going on out there." The kitchen and the dining room and the crew room were all crowded with people and Emily didn't want everyone in the hut overhearing what Lars had to say, so she hustled him and Alexei down the aisle between the dining room tables and out the dining room door and into the dingle that serves as a wind break, a dank shelter with the space of two telephone booths. Lars said, "There's a guy dying up there." He used a strong intensifier and this all happened so fast that Emily hadn't pulled the door shut behind them. She shot him a warning glance as she latched the dining room door and at the same time she said to herself, "Oh my God—we've got a major thing going on here."

The dingle didn't provide much shelter, so Emily had a hurried conference out there. Alexei was hopeful; he hadn't been out in the storm and he didn't quite believe it could be that bad. The crew had been out in some pretty bad weather that summer and his feeling was, "Come on, are you sure we can't go out there?" Lars was pessimistic about Don Barr's chances and he hadn't been able to move Tavis along either, but the boy was much nearer the hut and in better condition, so that was the priority. By now the guests knew something was going wrong and several of them said they were ready to go out and help, but Emily didn't think she could put any of the guests at peril out in the storm.

Lars called Pinkham from the hut and the connection was still poor, but Peter Crane got more information about the situation on the summit. He learned that there was another person about a tenth of a mile from the hut who was also hypothermic, but could probably walk if he was strengthened against the high winds and slippery footing. Peter backed up Emily's plan that two or three people should help this second person down to the hut. Lars was used up and Emily was needed to keep things moving in the hut and to oversee the developing situation out in the storm, so Alexei and Kari were the ones to go. They'd take chocolate bars, more clothes, and hot Jello, and do everything they could to bring Tavis in.

Alexei had just graduated from high school, he was 6'1" and after a summer at Madison his lean and rangy frame was almost a twin to Lars. Kari was 5'3" and slender, but her many years of riding and the requirements of handling powerful thoroughbreds made her much stronger than her small presence might suggest.

Kari and Alexei left the pots and pans for other hands to finish and got ready for the storm. Kari put on all the pile clothing she had, then wind gear, a hat and gloves, and an extra jacket; then she and Alexei made up a pack with reinforcements for Tavis and took their turn in the storm. There was still enough daylight in the clouds for them to see, but the air was a maelstrom of stinging sleet and the battering wind was still gaining strength. About 500 feet from the hut they spotted Tavis sitting on the rock. He was not on the trail as Lars said he would be, he was a ways off to one side and they were lucky to spot him.

Tavis was so badly chilled that he had difficulty talking, his speech was slow and slurred and Kari remembers that all he said clearly was, "My dad's up there—my dad needs help." Kari felt it was important to stay positive and she said, "We came to help you. You need help now and we came to help you." They got extra clothes and mittens on him, and even though he was having difficulty swallowing they got some warm Jello into him.

Looking back on that night, Kari says, "He had pretty much seized up by that time and he was very, very cold. The winds were very high, it was right around dusk, it was right around freezing and it was raining. The rain was beginning to freeze on the rocks.

"Tavis couldn't walk. Alexei and I could sometimes get on either side of him and haul him along and we did a lot of pushing and pulling and hauling. We kept saying, 'We've got to keep moving, Tavis, we've got to keep moving.' Up on the rocks he would literally get blown over, so we tried to keep a low profile. He didn't have the strength to stand up, anyway."

At first they were out on large, rough and exposed rocks, then the trail entered the scrub. "It was better down out of the wind. We could be on either side of him as much as possible and we tried to get him to walk, but he had extreme cramps in his legs."

As Alexei remembers, "It's not the kind of thing where you hold his hand and walk him down the path, it's a scramble. It was difficult to figure out a method of bringing him down, aside from picking him up and putting him on our backs, because he wasn't able to move very well. His legs seemed almost paralyzed, almost like cerebral palsy.

"So we were trying to encourage him. It was kind of sliding and it was very messy, me pulling on his legs and Kari pushing him from the back, skidding him along." They bumped and scraped on the rocks and tried not to get lost themselves because they had to go where the rocks and wind would let them go rather than where they thought the trail was. Then the terrain finally eased a bit and they got Tavis up on his feet, but he could not stay steady.

It was almost dark, and in the ruthless conditions even the best intentions and surest orientation might not be enough to avoid moving with the pressure of the wind, which would take them across the slope and away from the hut, but the light from the windows was a lighthouse in the fog. The Osgood Trail leads north of the hut, so they cut across the clearing and headed for the kitchen door. Alexei was new to this. "It's August and I didn't maybe think it was a life or death thing, you have this concept that it's summer and he's pretty close to the hut, it's no big deal, but you have this winter storm . . ."

Lars was worried; he knew what it was like out there and it seemed to him that they were taking a long time for the short distance they had to go. "After a while I was beginning to wonder when they were going to show up. I was full of adrenaline when I came in, and when I finally stopped and rested I was pretty cold and shivery and soaked to the bone, and I wasn't in any shape to go right back out again."

Alexei and Kari spent forty minutes moving Tavis that tenth of a mile back to the hut. Inside, conditions were at full stretch. The two hikers who came in without reservations could not be turned away, so the accommodations were two over capacity at fifty-two and a full dinner had to be served, cleared away, all the pots and pans and table settings washed up, and makings for the next day's breakfast started. There was wet clothing hanging from every projection and nothing dry to put on, there was no heat beyond the stray

BTUs that slipped out of the kitchen while the crew was preparing dinner, and the hut had been buried in supersaturated clouds all day. The arrival of Christian and Tavis, both in dire need of restoration, called on an account that had already been fully spent.

Then Stephanie Arenalas took hold. Tavis was hypothermic and barely able to speak, he was soaking wet, his muscles were going into spasm, and he'd been considerably battered as Kari and Alexei hauled him down over the rocks. Beyond that, his father was alone in the storm up above the hut and there was no way of helping him.

The Madison crew room opens off the kitchen and it used to be claustrophobic, with just enough space for two double bunks and a window. Then it was rebuilt and made into a much larger and more comfortable space, with a three-tiered bunk immediately to the left of the door, a double bunk on the adjoining wall, two windows and a table on the third wall, and then a hinged arrangement that's wider than the other bunks and can be used for extra sleeping space or as a daytime settee or folded up out of the way.

Christian was already in one of the bunks, so Stephanie and another crew member got Tavis out of his wet clothes, dried him off as well as they could and gave him warm Jello to drink, and put him into a sleeping bag with blankets over it in that wide folding daybed. Stephanie knew that Tavis wouldn't get any colder, but he wouldn't warm up very fast either. She knew that the 98 degrees of heat she could contribute were all they had, so she stripped down and got into the sleeping bag with him.

While the hut crew was struggling with the storm, Walter Wintturi of the U.S. Forest Service called Peter Crane and said that he was in contact with Brad Ray and three or four USFS people would probably be available to go up to the heights of Madison. Ten minutes later Dick Dufour of Fish and Game called Peter and said he was in touch with Carl Carlson. Five minutes after that, at 7:50, a radio call came from the hut telling Peter that Alexei and Kari were tending to Tavis.

Up at the hut, Emily and whatever other crew member who wasn't out on the mountain working on behalf of Don and Tavis were keeping things going for the guests. They'd set out the usual bountiful dinner, attended to refills and the other table needs, cleared off, and set out the next course. The hut was not very comfortable. There used to be a wood stove in the dining room, but that was gone now and there was no heat except the propane rings in the kitchen and the natural furnace of the hikers' bodies, but the metabolic fires were running at a very reduced setting and the hut was dank and clammy.

At 8:00 P.M., a team of eighteen people left Pinkham in two vans to drive around to the Valley Way parking lot and start up to the hut. Forty-five minutes later Emily called Peter to report that Tavis was in the hut and being tended to, but he was very groggy and debilitated.

That left Don Barr alone in the night and the storm. Emily was in her first day as hutmaster and she was in a tough spot. The weather was still getting worse at the hut and she knew by way of the Pinkham radio relay that the Mount Washington observatory could not promise any relief that night.

On paper, the crew's main responsibility was the hut, but this night's responsibilities were already off the paper. One consideration was the carry itself. There were only four people on the hut crew, which is not enough for a litter carry. Emily knew about that. There's something about a rescue that fixes the imagination on heroic carries to safety, so when a call came to Pinkham during Emily's rookie summer there, she thought "Whoo . . . !" and she was quick to volunteer. It was an easy case; someone went lame on the Tuckerman Ravine Trail a short way above Pinkham and that trail is almost as wide and smooth as a country lane. Emily took her first turn at the carry, stumbling along without seeing her feet and trying to stay in step and keep the litter steady and match the level of her grip to the other carriers and it wasn't very long before she was thinking, "Oh man—this really sucks!"

The situation facing her Madison crew was much more difficult. The guests knew there was a tough situation in their midst and several of them came up to Emily with offers of help. They could help with after-dinner housekeeping, but Emily knew she couldn't ask them to go outside. She was thinking of the chaos that could overtake the evening, how there could be people with all degrees of strength and skill out on the rocks of the summit cone and no effective way of keeping track of them or coordinating their work. Even more to the immediate point, there was hardly a stitch of dry clothing anywhere in the hut. The storm was still gaining strength and the hut crew and volunteers alike would be wet and tired and more prone to hypothermia at the start of the rescue than anyone should be at the end of it.

At this point, Emily was the only one among the guests and the crew who hadn't been out in the storm and she was also the most experienced among them, which would make her the best candidate for a rescue team.

But at the same time, she was the hutmaster and she was wondering where her responsibility really lay. Should she lend her strength and experience to a rescue effort, or should she stay in the hut to hold things together there?

By now, Christian had gotten up and he was in the kitchen having something to eat. Tavis was in bed in the crew room and he was beginning to recover from his own hypothermia, he was saying, "Where's my father—where's my father?" Stephanie was still with him; she told him that they were doing everything they could to help his father, but at the same time she didn't want to give him false hopes, because his father was still out there on top of the mountain and alone in the lashing storm.

The hut crew was finally all indoors and they knew they were up against it, they knew they had to talk it over, they had to decide about MacDonald Barr. This led to another problem. There were people everywhere in the hut, they were finishing dinner and milling around in the dining room and the bunk rooms and some were lending a hand cleaning up in the kitchen. Christian Steiber was in the kitchen, too, and Tavis was in the crew's bunk room. So where could Emily gather her crew for a serious talk?

Madison Spring Hut is T-shaped: The kitchen and crew bunkroom are at the base of the T, the dining room is the rest of the leg, two big bunkrooms are the left and right arms of the T, and there's a bathroom at the back of each of the bunkrooms, women on the left, men on the right. It was after-dinner hot drink time, so Emily asked a couple of the helpful guests if they could keep the fixings coming in from the kitchen; then she called for attention and said that the crew would be busy for a while and could everyone take turns using the men's bathroom.

Then the crew gathered in the women's bathroom to talk things over. They knew the Mount Washington weather observatory had reported no signs of relief on their charts. On the contrary, the observatory crew said the storm would probably intensify through the night.

Emily and Lars and Alexei and Kari tried to think the situation through. Emily thought most about the wind; she knew it can be raining hard or snowing like crazy and hikers can still be all right; it fact, they can enjoy it. But it was the wind—above timberline the wind simply tears away every defense.

The Madison crew knew that Don Barr was in mortal danger, but mortal danger was everywhere on the mountain that night; once out there, everyone would be equally exposed. Lars remembers, "There was a little bit of

An AMC group at the original Madison Spring Hut, January 1906.

A group of hikers resting outside Madison Spring Hut in 1987. The original hut accommodated 12 hikers. Today, 52 people can sleep there.

bravado—'Oh, we can try it—it's our job, we're able to do these things, so let's give it a shot.' We'd all been out, though, and I think we quickly realized that all of us except Emily had just been out in the weather and we probably wouldn't be in such great shape to try again."

There was also the matter of numbers. Even in the best circumstances imaginable, even on a walking path in the valley with fair skies and sweet breezes, the four members of the Madison crew would have difficulty managing a half-mile litter carry by themselves. In the cold and dark and rain and rocks and wind, they would have no chance at all. There was no shortage of willing help among the guests in the hut, but they were there to take shelter, not to risk their lives. Beyond that, taking an unknown and untrained group out on a rescue brings its own hazards, both physical and ethical. The first members of the AMC group from Pinkham were already arriving and the Madison crew had seen them. Lars says, "We started seeing these folks coming in from Pinkham in various states of hypothermia themselves and certainly not prepared to go up on the mountain beyond the hut."

All these thoughts were in the women's bathroom and even though not all of them were said out loud, the hut crew knew that they'd decided. It was not a debate. Lars remembers, "We realized at that point we were making decisions to forget any hope of trying to rescue him or bringing him back alive. We knew that was weighing over us. But we also knew that it was ridiculous to try to go up there to get him. The choice had been made before us." No one asked for a vote or tried to persuade anyone else, but they knew that the risk to a rescue group outweighed the benefit to Don Barr, and Emily summed it up for them: The danger is too great, our resources are too small, and we're not going to go out tonight.

The valley forces were on their way, so at 8:55 Peter Crane called Emily for another report from the hut. Peter was in a position to launch the rescue on his own authority, but, as he says now, "Recognizing that there could be more than one answer to the question, I asked if a party would be going out from the hut. It's very easy for someone in a warm building ten miles away to ask other people to go out, and names like Albert Dow come to mind." Albert was a member of the volunteer mountain rescue squad based in North Conway, and four years earlier he'd been killed while trying to help two teenagers whose inexperience had led them into difficulty.

Peter finishes the thought: "But if those people can actually feel the buffeting of the wind and the stinging ice pellets and have to stare out into the dark fog—if they make the decision that that's excessive risk for them, then I think we in our warm places have to respect that decision, even though it could have grave consequences." Emily told him the difficult news of her decision, and he backed her up completely; he said she should not risk anyone beyond the immediate shelter of the hut.

Right after this exchange Peter called the AMC personnel regrouping on the Valley Way. He told them that twelve should continue up to the hut, stay overnight, and go to work at first light if conditions allowed. The other six in the mobile group should return to Pinkham to keep normal operations going, though that number was considerably below the usual complement. The group should be divided so the strongest members would go up to the hut and those with necessary duties at Pinkham should return. After this conversation, he called Don Dercole of the Forest Service and brought him up to date, adding that his personnel might want to stay in the valley overnight and be ready for an early-morning departure rather than squeeze into the overcrowded hut. He also called Carl Carlson at Fish and Game asking for a call-back on the telephone.

Then Peter called Emily again. The contrast between his strong experience and his mild presence can be disconcerting, and he tells of that dreadful night in a voice that is hardly more than a whisper: "There had been more time to reconsider, or perhaps to wind down a little bit on what had happened thus far. After that decision was made, that initial decision, they had the opportunity to rethink, to reconsider, perhaps to have either more worries go through their head that this was the right decision or to gain confidence within that decision, so I asked again if this was something that they still wanted to follow through with. I indicated that this was a very serious decision they were making and asked if they wanted to re-evaluate their situation and the weather conditions." Emily told him that the situation at the hut had not changed, and they would stay with their decision.

Alexei was still cold and worn from his struggle with Tavis, but it was time for his other duties. The next day was his turn to cook, so he was busy with the small things of hut life; he was laying out the bacon and mixing the dry ingredients for the biscuits he'd make in the morning, and thinking ahead to what he'd make for dinner. He decided on the entrée and he'd probably make cheese bread. Emily taught him how to make cheese bread on the first day he cooked that summer, and he liked it so well that it was practically the only kind of bread he ever made.

Meanwhile, the crew was trying to keep Tavis in the picture, but they were being careful not to give him unrealistic hopes or unrealistic fears. He understood what they were doing. "At that point I knew that he was going to die. They made it sound like, 'We'll see if he's okay,' but you know, as a thirteen-year-old kid I thought they were just kind of delusioned. Now I know they were trying to put a good note on it, but . . ."

At 9:30 P.M. Peter called the Mount Washington Observatory again. They told him that the temperature remained steady at 32° with fog, rain, sleet, snow showers, and maximum visibility of fifty feet; the wind was averaging 79 mph, gusting regularly to the mid-80s and occasionally into the 90s. They expected no change over the next twelve hours except in the temperature, which might go lower. Peter knew that conditions would be only slightly less extreme where Don Barr was on the summit of Mount Madison.

Peter tried to raise the group of AMC staff on the trail at 9:30, but he couldn't get them directly, nor could he reach them through the RMC relay. The upper sections of the Valley Way run through a deep cleft in the mountain and the topography blocks most transmission angles into it. He kept trying and he finally got through to Charlie McCrave on the trail and brought him up to date; Charlie said that his leading group was pretty well up by now and they'd keep going to the hut and regroup there. Peter had been keeping track of the numbers and he realized that Madison Spring Hut was two over capacity before any emergency crews arrived. Now it would be getting critically short of space.

Just then a call came from Troop F of the state police; they had more powerful radio equipment and mobile units on the road, and through them Peter arranged for four Forest Service men and three of his AMC contingent to turn around on the Valley Way and spend the night in Randolph. Ten minutes later he called Carl Carlson, the veteran at Fish and Game, and brought him up to date on the situation.

The regular 10:30 weather transmission from the summit observatory reported no change in wind or temperature, with intermittent snow and heavy icing. Ten minutes later, more members of the Pinkham crew arrived at the hut with their radio and fifteen minutes after that the three Pinkham crew who had turned around on the trail called from the parking lot at the base of the Valley Way and said they'd stand by to see if any more people would be coming down the trail. At 11:30 the last two members of the Pinkham group reached the hut and the five waiting in the parking lot were cleared to return to Pinkham.

Five minutes later Peter went to bed, but he did not rest. "You know there's someone up on the mountain and half a mile from the hut who most likely will not survive the night. It weighs on you." Up at the hut, everyone managed to find a bit of space to lie down and see if they could sleep. The crew room was full, the two big bunkrooms were full, there were people sleeping upstairs in the storage attic, there were people sleeping on the dining room tables and on the floor in places where they hoped no one would step on them. During the night the summit observatory recorded winds of 121 mph.

Emily went to bed in her crewroom bunk, but she did not sleep. She kept getting up, she'd go out to look at the night, she'd sit in the kitchen and think, "Could we do it?" There was wet clothing hanging everywhere and draped on every possible spot and she'd feel to see if it was getting dry. She even thought about how many for-sale AMC T-shirts there were—she could hand those around for dry clothes. She listened to the sleeping sounds of the people all around her in the hut, and most of all she kept listening to the constant roaring and rushing of the wind and she thought that sometimes storms just suddenly blow themselves out and she'd stretch to see if she could hear the slightest lessening that might bring hope, but she never heard it.

Stephanie was still with Tavis. "It was hard for me to know what he was thinking. I don't remember much sleep. I was staring out the window into the darkness and holding him and trying to reassure him that he was okay. People were coming in and out and there was the darkness and he was sleeping some. I was whispering to him and murmuring to him in the night, trying to be quiet."

First light came and at 5:55 A.M. Emily radioed Pinkham with a weather report: 42° and wind-driven rain at the hut, and the rescue group up there would be ready to start for the summit in five minutes. On consultation it was decided to send a carry party of nine to the summit and keep a relief group of five at the hut. Peter reminded the hut contingent that Don should be treated as any person in severe hypothermia: his wet clothes should be removed and replaced with dry insulation, he should be protected from wind and further wetting, and any possible heat loss should be eliminated as far as possible.

Then Peter again made sure that Emily and everyone in her crew remembered the first rule of search and rescue: No member of the rescue group should risk becoming a victim. The litter group left the hut at 7:05 and they found Don Barr thirty minutes later. He was in the trail just below the summit of Mount Madison and the EMT people determined that he was unresponsive.

It was the second time up there for Lars: "The wind was still blowing pretty good, certainly not as high as the night before, the clouds had lifted and the angle of wind had changed just enough so when we got to the flat place where he was lying it was almost calm. He was just lying there with his hands crossed on his chest." Lars stood off to one side in that small island of quiet air, out of the way of the people tending to Don. It was his first death and he kept thinking that he was the last one to see Don alive, and now this. Then he saw Emily go over and kneel down beside him.

Emily was struck by the way Don lay there on his back with his hands crossed on his chest and she thought that he looked very peaceful and composed; this was such a contrast to what she expected that she almost spoke to him. She saw that his eyes were wide open and looking up into the endless sky, and she thought it was time for his eyes to close. Emily remembered all those death scenes in the movies where someone reaches out with a small gesture and brushes a person's eyelids down as a sort of final benediction, but now she learned that unseeing eyes don't close as easily as that.

The guideline among emergency teams is "Not dead until warm and dead," so this was still a rescue, not a recovery. They put Don Barr in a sleeping bag and added blankets and the weatherproof hypowrap, and they were careful to handle him as gently as they could, because when a person is in extreme hypothermia even a slight interruption can push the heart into crisis. They started down toward the hut with the litter, they were thinking, "Maybe there's a chance." The carry required everything they had—at one point the entire team was knocked down by the wind and they struggled to keep the litter from hitting anything.

Earlier in the morning Emily had sent a radio request for someone to start up the trail with dry clothing for Tavis and Christian, and a speedy volunteer was found for that mission. Tavis was in the kitchen while the crew was getting ready to go up to the summit and Lars was watching him, "I could see in his eyes that he kind of recognized what had happened. But maybe there's still some hope, 'Okay, the rescue crew is going up and they're going to see what's going on.' We explained that hypothermia is one of those things where you can recover. We were injecting a little bit of hope into ourselves, that there is a possibility that he could make it. So I'm sure he was still holding out some hope, but he kind of knew that if his dad had been lying up there all night, things weren't very good."

When Kari Geick was back in the hut after she helped rescue Tavis, she decided that her best part was tending to the domestic routine. Everyone else on the crew was between eighteen and twenty-two years old and they'd been together all summer; she was five years older than the oldest of them, but she was still only a few hours into her career with the AMC. She did understand housekeeping, though, and the hut was still in full operation, so she decided to concentrate her efforts on the dishes and pots and pans and other domestic necessities, and free the regular crew for the difficult tasks rising on every side.

The next morning she was struck by what she saw. The crew was tending to routine tasks but there was a stunned quality everywhere. Alexei was the cook for this day and he'd finished his part of breakfast some time ago, so he began the usual business of checking out the guests. "It was kind of surreal, taking their Visas and MasterCards at the same time as all these other things were going on." The guests were very quiet as they packed up and most of them changed whatever other hiking plans they had and went down the Valley Way, where they'd be sure of quick shelter.

Traffic was moving up the Valley Way at the same time. There were men from New Hampshire Fish and Game and from the Forest Service and still more from the AMC. Stephanie was devoting all her time to Tavis, but she heard members of the crew saying, "Rich Crowley is coming up—Rich Crowley will be here soon," as if that would change everything and they'd be all right.

Kari heard this, too, and she was impressed and puzzled. Then she learned that Rich was the long-time manager of the storehouse down at Pinkham; he took the hut crew orders and did the food shopping to meet their cooking needs and then packed it into cartons and delivered it to the base of the pack trail, and this day he was coming up with extra clothes for Christian and

Tavis. Then he reached the hut and nothing changed. Kari decided that Rich was the person who took care of the hut crews—that's what the storehouse man does, he gets what the hut crews need. So, in the awful strangeness of that morning, it seemed natural that he'd be the one who could set things right.

The crew was amazed to learn that Tavis was only thirteen; seeing his size, they thought he was probably seventeen. They were worried about his day; they imagined the ways he could meet his father being carried in a litter with his face covered, and they worked out a timing to avoid that.

At 8:43 further reserves were alerted in an AMC group staying at Camp Dodge, the old CCC station four and a half miles from the Pinkham Notch headquarters. The litter party from the summit of Madison reached the hut at 9:00, and an hour later Emily called Pinkham and learned that further reinforcements of eleven people from the Forest Service, Fish and Game, and the AMC had started up the Valley Way at 9:15. At 11:15, the litter team started down the Valley Way with MacDonald Barr.

Stephanie Arenalas stayed with Tavis through the night and through the early hours in the kitchen when everyone was up and around and she stayed with him through breakfast. She cooked some things to eat for the various people coming up the Valley Way to help and she kept Tavis occupied while the litter party came past the hut with his father. Finally she and Rich Crowley started down the Valley Way with Tavis and Christian.

Tavis hadn't been saying much during the morning; the crew thought he seemed a bit distant and disengaged, and they tried not to crowd him. Then on the hike down he seemed to be bothered by the clothes that had been brought up for him. There wasn't any underwear and the pants were much too big, so the crew had made a belt for him out of a piece of the rope they use to tie loads on when they're packing supplies up to the hut. He kept talking about the pants as they made their way down the Valley Way and Stephanie realized that she really didn't know what a seventh-grader should say at a time like this.

That trail was originally built as a bridle path with easy grades all the way from the valley to the hut, but that was ninety years ago and now it was severely eroded by the many generations of hikers and the rains and meltwater of all the years. The footway was filled with loose rocks and roots and wet places, and a very severe test for a litter carry.

An hour after the litter party started down, a call went to the valley contingent to start up with relief carriers, and another hour after that three more AMC crew members headed for the Valley Way to help. The combined litter crew reached the Valley Way parking lot at 3:40 P.M. and they were met by an emergency response vehicle from the Androscoggin Valley Hospital. Every resuscitation effort failed and MacDonald Barr was pronounced dead later that afternoon.

Rich Crowley drove Stephanie and Tavis and Christian back to Pinkham Notch in his car and Stephanie went into the AMC building with Tavis. There was a telephone booth near the door and he insisted on calling his mother; then he told her abruptly that his father was dead. Yvonne Barr already knew; she'd had a call from an official source.

Stephanie and Rich thought it was time for Tavis to be alone for a while, so they showed him to a bunk upstairs in the crew quarters. Later that morning Mrs. Barr arrived at Pinkham and she met Peter Crane and Stephanie out near the kitchen. Stephanie tried to explain what had happened and what they tried to do up at Madison, but then she had to walk away from Mrs. Barr. She'd done all she could do.

The Madison crew was in the habit of making a little talk to the guests at suppertime. That evening Lars made a larger talk than usual. He talked about his love for the mountains and his respect for them and he said that people are not infallible, they're fragile up in the mountains and there are times when things go wrong, not as a sacrifice but as a reminder of what can happen. He talked about the cold fronts that come through at the end of August and how people start at the bottom and when they get to the top it's a different world. He told them that they'd come to our nice cozy hut expecting all sorts of amenities and we provide that to you, but you have to get here first. Then he said that one of those times came just the night before . . .

When he finished, Lars said later, "They were all looking at me." Kari Geick was looking at him, too. It seemed to her that the talk was partly for the guests and partly for himself, that it was his way of finishing up the terrible night of MacDonald Barr.

Three days later Emily was back at Middlebury College; she was on the women's field hockey team and they had a pre-season training camp. Everywhere she turned there was laughter and cries of greeting and hugs of reunion and, "How was your summer?" and, "My summer was really great!" Emily gave them her greetings and her hugs, but she didn't go into much detail about being in charge at Madison Spring Hut.

THE TWO CLIMBERS WHO WERE MAROONED ON MOUNT WASH-
ington were exposed to the full force of the storm on August 24, but when the weather moderated they emerged from their tent and hiked down the mountain without any adverse effects.

About ten years after the death of MacDonald Barr, two women hit heavy weather while crossing the range toward Madison Spring Hut. They were ex-hausted and felt unable to continue, so they took shelter under a plastic sheet they had with them. The crew at Madison Spring Hut heard about them and, remembering the story of MacDonald Barr, they went out along the range until they found the women a mile from the hut, and then the Madison crew insisted that the women get up and hike on to the hut.

Peter Crane stayed with the mountains. The weather observatory on Mount Washington has expanded its work and now runs extensive educa-tional programs on the summit and in its valley station in North Conway. Peter is Director of Programs for the observatory.

Emily Thayer suffered a severe knee injury two days after the start of the Middlebury field hockey camp and she missed the whole semester. She continued with seasonal work for the AMC for three more years as summer hutmaster or winter caretaker. At this writing her brother Chris is the White Mountain Facilities Director for the AMC and lives in Sugar Hill with his wife and two children. Emily married Peter Benson, who followed the Barr emergency on the radio at Zealand Hut, and they have two children. Peter is the New Hampshire Preserves Manager for the Nature Conservancy. Emily has not forgotten MacDonald Barr; "It's always hovering, it's always there." Since then, she has run many guided hikes for mountain visitors.

Alexei Rubenstein worked at the AMC's Greenleaf Hut in the summer of 1987 and had to deal with a fatal heart attack there. Lars Jorrens took ad-vanced EMT training and went on to teach those skills at Keeping Track, in Richmond, Vermont. He married Jennifer Botzo, who followed the Barr emergency on the radio from Lonesome Lake Hut.

Kari Geick stayed with the AMC longer than she expected. The next summer she worked at Carter Notch Hut with Emily and Lars, she worked as a winter caretaker at Zealand Hut, and she guided hikes for two summers. After that she worked in Alaska and spent three years in Antarctica, including two winters at the South Pole. Her first day of AMC work is still with her. "It shaped my life. With my mountaineering life, or life in general, I look at what can happen."

There was, for instance, the day in May 1999 when she hiked up the Zugspitz, Germany's highest peak. It's a popular tourist climb, and she and her friend took a return path that led over a snow slope lingering from the winter. It was late in the afternoon, the sidehill fell away steeply, and Kari knew the soft snow of the day would be glazing over and she didn't have the right equipment. She took a long look, weighed the consequences of a slip, and turned back to find another way down.

Tavis Barr has not done much hiking since his father's death. Then in April 1999 he was on a trip to California and spent a day in Yosemite, where he and some friends hiked up the path to the top of the park's signature waterfall. "There were people there who were casually out on their day hike," he said later. "I don't think they'd thought twice about it, they were going up in the same jeans and T-shirts that we were wearing. You can see the top of the falls from the bottom, you can see it's not cold. But I could see that they're not cautious enough. I brought along a down coat and a sweater and a hat and gloves. There was no reason I needed a winter hat and gloves up there at the top, but I still remembered."

Chapter Seventeen

THE DEADLIEST SEASON

*T*HE LAST FIFTY YEARS HAVE SEEN LARGE CHANGES IN THE popular view of winter. Cold weather used to be like the mountains themselves; it was something to be avoided, and winter visits to the heights of the Presidential Range were only undertaken by necessity or by impulses that were viewed as borderline eccentricity.

Frederick Strickland reached the summit of Mount Washington in the course of his snow-racked outing in 1849, but he'd been advised not to do it and he did not survive. The old records do not tell of much high-elevation activity until mention of a forward-looking party that tried to climb the Tuckerman Ravine headwall in 1884. They failed.

Two men did reach the summit on December 7, 1885, and they made the climb in the service of a legal dispute of the highest order: ownership of the summit. One of the proprietors of the Tip-Top House disputed the real estate title and a deputy sheriff climbed the mountain to serve papers announcing that the property was under attachment by court order. The summit hotels were unoccupied, but custom dictated that a copy of the papers be physically attached to the property. The sheriff was accompanied on the climb by

In January 1984, Hugh Herr and Jeffrey Batzer climbed a gully in Huntington Ravine, then pushed on for the summit of Mount Washington in the face of rapidly worsening weather and lost their way. A large-scale search was set in motion. This group from the all-volunteer Mountain Rescue Service is huddling at the 7-Mile marker on the summer auto road. These men could go no farther and they made their way down safely. Albert Dow was with another team and was killed in an avalanche this same afternoon. Herr and Batzer were found in Great Gulf and survived.

Benjamin Osgood, the keeper of the Glen House who made the trail to the summit of Mount Madison that still bears his name.

Necessity was the mother of that climb, many years would pass before the idea of winter climbing as sport took hold, and when Joe Dodge kept the AMC cabins in Pinkham Notch open for the winter of 1927, the centers of civilization in southern New England still regarded them as an outpost on a distant horizon. Nevertheless, Joe accommodated 512 guests that winter and served 1,096 meals, and the sale of supplies and sundries totaled $67.15. Wheeled traffic was infrequent and a summertime picture from 1928 shows why: the highway grade up the south side of the notch looked as if it was paved with boulders. It was not plowed for the first several years of his winter occupancy and it was still a lonely place when plows did come to the notch;

Joe's son Brooks remembers that in the 1930s and even in the '40s, whole evenings would pass when he wouldn't hear a single car go by.

Useful winter seasons really arrived after World War II, when the civilian market was flooded with cold-weather equipment developed for the military. Since then, winter equipment has advanced with exponential strides and now there are stores near the Presidential Range where an enthusiast can walk out with $4,000 worth of clothing in addition to a wealth of hardware. Parking lots take the story from there.

On New Year's Day of 1998 I drove "around the mountains"—up through Pinkham Notch, around the north end of the range through Randolph, down the west side to Twin Mountain, around the south end through Crawford Notch, and back up to Pinkham. I stopped at every parking lot that served trails giving access to 4,000-foot peaks and counted cars. The weather had been brutal and the previous night brought temperatures below zero in the valleys and equally threatening conditions on the heights. A generation earlier I would have been surprised to find any cars at all in these parking lots, but on this day I counted 231 vehicles.

I did it again in 1999. The weather was the same, below zero every night for a week in the valleys with several sieges of very high wind, and this New Year's Day the upper elevations were buried in storm clouds. I made the same stops and counted 289 cars. As in the 1998 inventory, I did not include vehicles with the kind of trailer used for off-road vehicles, but I did count a dog sled with 28-paw drive.

Another new age had already arrived. One summer day in 1988 an accident report was brought down from the Carter-Moriah Range on the eastern side of Pinkham Notch. The terrain up there can be difficult and the day was raw and wet, so a full-scale rescue was laid on. The trouble was discovered to be a hiker who was very much reduced by alcohol, and the evacuation took most of the night. Accidents are accidents, the rescue team was thinking, and a bad fall can happen to the best of us, that's why we always answer the call. But this fellow could not have gotten drunk by accident and his rescue put many people at hazard themselves. So he was cited for reckless conduct and ordered to pay a considerable fine.

This kind of situation is now covered by two statutes. The first one was New Hampshire RSA 576:3 Reckless Conduct, which provides that, "A person is guilty of a misdemeanor if he recklessly engages in conduct which places or may place another in danger of serious bodily injury." This was enacted in the early 1970s, and the commentary attached to the statute explained, "In dealing with conduct that endangers but does not harm others (this) fills an undesirable gap in New Hampshire statutes. If actual harm occurs, then a criminal assault will have taken place. Since, when a person acts recklessly, he disregards a risk he knows of and acts with an indifference to the injury he may cause to others, he is just as culpable when the risk does not eventuate in the injury as when it does. Without a statute of this sort, however, a person whose behavior menaces in this way could be prosecuted only if the harm actually occurs."

RSA 576:3 was later amplified by RSA 631:3, which included the addition proviso that, "If you engage in reckless activity, you may face criminal prosecution. If you fail to heed warnings of authorized personnel, in addition to being criminally prosecuted, you may be required to pay the entire cost of your search or rescue."

The rapidly increasing number of hikers in the mountains combined with increasingly sophisticated rescue equipment, and costs became a serious factor: the New Hampshire Department of Fish and Game alone goes on more than 150 rescue missions a year and spends about $150,000 in their support. The matter of cost recovery came up again and again, but the provisions included in those RSA statutes were rarely invoked in mountain emergencies. Then in December 1999, New Hampshire Fish and Game officials announced that they would take a stricter attitude in billing hikers who required aid.

Several questions arose. Who would define reckless behavior and what standards would be applied? If insurance against such claims was available, as is widely done in Europe, would this become a variant of the cell-phone effect? Would it embolden hikers to take more risks than they usually would?

Few seasons provided as many landmarks on this cultural map as the winter of 1994, when four lethal emergencies developed on the Presidential Range. Just one of them enlisted the help of 204 search and rescue personnel including 32 from the Forest Service, 32 from the AMC, 120 from Fish and Game and other organizations, and 20 volunteers, with the services of Thiokol snow tractors, an ambulance, and a helicopter. The father of one of the victims brought suit against the United States of America for failing to protect visitors in the national forest against hazard.

DEREK TINKHAM
JANUARY 1994

Joe Dodge's legacy is a cluster of buildings at the Appalachian Mountain Club headquarters in Pinkham Notch. The "pack room" is a popular spot, the place climbers gather when they're about to start on a climb, or just returning from one. Thursday evening, January 15, 1994, a young man was holding forth at considerable length on his plans, a four-day traverse along the skyline ridge of the Presidential Range. Another hiker was forcibly struck by how easily he dominated the room and the people there, and how his companion sat by, silent and enthralled.

The speaker was Jeremy Haas, the listener was Derek Tinkham; both were college students. Derek had plans. He loved the mountains, he went climbing up here whenever he could, he meant to go on to work as a guide, and he'd gotten a job with the rescue team in Yosemite for the coming summer. His long-time friend Jennifer Taylor often drove him up to the mountains to start a trip and picked him up when it was done.

Their route usually took them through North Conway, twenty miles south of Mount Washington, and Derek would always stop at International Mountain Equipment, a major source of serious gear, advice, and companionship. Jennifer noticed that Derek would let only one person wait on him; no matter how small the transaction or how many unoccupied people were behind the counter, he always waited until a short, compact fellow was free. Finally Jennifer asked her friend why he always waited for that person. Derek explained that the person he waited for was Rick Wilcox, that he was a great mountaineer, that he'd climbed Mount Everest. Derek admired him tremendously and wanted the kind of life Rick had. Jennifer understood.

What they could learn from Rick Wilcox should also be understood, because it's the key to everything that followed. Rick started with the neighborhood mountains of New England and worked his way up. Now he's made eleven trips to the Himalayas and he knows how very small are the margins which determine not just whether a summit is reached, but whether a climber returns at all.

A Himalayan summit day begins years earlier, when the leader applies for permission to make the try. The planning, the money-raising, the risk to business and family relations, the long trek to base camp, the push higher and higher up the flanks, all increase the pressure to make those last few hundred yards to the summit. That's what we're taught to do; our culture is obsessed with success and climbers are our surrogates, they're the ones who keep pushing upwards.

For Rick Wilcox and his climbing mates, the weather had gone bad just a few hundred yards below the summit of Makalu, fifth highest in the world. They turned around without hesitation. Six days of dizzyingly steep snow climbing protect the summit ridge of Cho Oyo, then there's a very long knife edge and, just below the summit, a small rock wall with a drop of 10,000 feet at the climber's heels. Rick's partner was Mark Richey and he led the first move onto that wall and when he began to drive in the first piton he sensed the brittle quality of the rock. He looked at Rick and, with hardly a word, they turned around. The summit was right there, and they turned around and headed for home, half a world away.

On his fifth Himalayan expedition, the summit of Everest was so still that Rick sat there for an hour. From the beginning, he'd had the feeling that finally, on this trip, it was his turn. The clouds came in that afternoon and Rick's partner kept track of his own descent by noting the curious markers at the top of the world. There are frozen bodies on the summit pitches of Everest, climbers who did not plan as well or who kept pushing when the signs were bad. It's too difficult to take dead climbers down, so they stay there forever and wiser climbers use them as guides.

The hike Jeremy had planned for himself and Derek began Friday afternoon, but, like a Himalayan expedition, the important decisions had been made much earlier. Jennifer had urged Derek to take along a small mountaineering tent, but Jeremy wanted to travel light, so they took bivy bags instead, weather-resistant coverings for their sleeping bags. Jeremy also left his over-mitts at home; he wanted the added dexterity of gloves.

Something else had already been decided, probably years earlier: Jeremy had a tendency to keep pushing. He'd led a climb for the University of New Hampshire Outing Club, and when they returned many of the group complained that he'd kept charging ahead and was not sensitive to their needs. He was told he could not be a trip leader anymore and he resigned from the club. Over the Christmas break he took Chris Rose on a Presidential Range traverse and Chris got so cold that his toes were frozen. The trip Jeremy planned for himself and Derek was the same route as the one that had claimed his friend's toes two years earlier.

The pack-up room where Jeremy held forth at Pinkham Notch was built many years after we set out to rescue Raymond Davis, but other elements have not changed. The weather observatory on Mount Washington is 4,288 feet upslope from the AMC buildings, detailed reports and predictions for the upper elevations are always posted by the AMC, and climbers check them as a reflex before starting up. High winds and extreme cold were predicted for that weekend. Jeremy and Derek started for the base of the Air Line Trail, a popular route departing from Randolph and rising to skyline on the northern end of the Presidential Range.

The trees grew smaller and more dense as they neared timberline. There are openings here, certified as overnight campsites by years of native wisdom. The two climbers stopped in one and settled into their bivy bags; "bivy" means bivouac. As they slept, the weather above timberline, severe enough when they started, grew worse.

The summit observatory recorded −6° at midnight and −23° at 8:00 A.M.; the wind moved into the west and at 8:00 A.M. it was steady in the 40 mph range, not high by local standards, but a west wind rakes straight across the skyline teeth of the 6.5-mile ridge Jeremy and Derek would traverse. They climbed to the top of Madison, then Adams, second-highest peak in the Northeast. It was close to noon now, and they'd been making quite good time.

This section of trail leads down to Edmands Col, a mile of easy going. Derek was having trouble, but Jeremy would go on ahead, wait for him to catch up, then go ahead again. Derek was going slower and slower and he was becoming unsteady on his feet, signs that betray the onset of hypothermia. Edmands Col lies between Adams and Jefferson and the mild descent took many times longer than it would in summer. Hypothermia is not just cold hands and feet; it comes when the cold has bitten right through and the core temperature begins to drop. The body circles up the metabolic wagons to make a last stand against death, blood is concentrated in the viscera, the mind becomes sluggish and the limbs erratic.

At this point, there were three refuges nearby, all below timberline: The Perch is a three-sided shelter, the old cabin at Crag Camp had just been replaced with a snug and completely weatherproof building, and Gray Knob

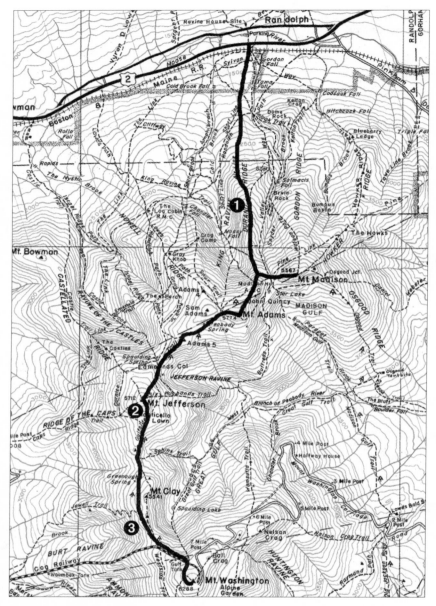

1. Derek Tinkham climbed with Jeremy Haas up Air Line Trail and spent night in Spruce Shelter
2. Up on Air Line to climb Mount Madison, then across Gulfside Trail to Mount Jefferson; Tinkham died on the summit of Jefferson
3. Haas crossed Gulfside Trail to summit of Mount Washington

had also been rebuilt and had a caretaker, heat, lights, and radio contact to the valley. The two hikers discussed a retreat to one of them, but decided to continue upward toward the summit of Jefferson. Jeremy's original plan was to go on to Clay Col, a mile and a half away up Jefferson and down the other side; he remembered an ice cave there during a previous trip and his idea was to use it for the second night of this trip.

In the prevailing weather conditions, this was a plan of breath-taking stupidity. Ice caves are ephemeral, what Jeremy had seen two years earlier might not be there at all this year. Even if it was, Clay Col would be a furious torrent of arctic wind and an ice cave was not what they needed. As bad as it was in Edmands Col, it could only be worse in Clay Col, higher and nearer the Mount Washington weather vortex. The two climbers were getting weaker, the storm was getting stronger.

Afterward, Jeremy said the decision to push on was a mutual one. But veteran climbers know that, since Jeremy was the stronger and more experienced of the two, his job was to get Derek down to shelter, any shelter. As Rick Wilcox puts it, "When you climb solo, you only have to worry about yourself, but when you climb with another person, it's your responsibility to look out for him." In fairness to Jeremy, he was suffering from the same extreme conditions and that might have affected his judgment.

When they got to the summit of Jefferson, Derek collapsed. Having left a tent at home, Jeremy tried to get him into a sleeping bag, then left for the summit of Mount Washington more than three miles away. It was 4:30 P.M., darkness would soon overtake him, the summit temperature had dropped to −27°, and the wind was in the 80s with a peak gust of 96 mph. Jeremy lost his gloves and, having left his heavy over-mitts at home, his hands were too cold to let him get at the food and the flashlight he had in his pack. He kept his hands under his armpits as he staggered and crawled along the ridge toward Mount Washington.

Conditions like this do not match normal experience. One year I went up to the summit for Thanksgiving dinner with the observatory crew; the weather was moderate and the climb enjoyable, but the day after the feast the wind rose to 150 mph; the day after that the recording pen went off the chart at 162. In lulls, the observers would climb the inside of the tower to the instrument deck to clear ice from the sensors. I'd go up to help and found a curious situation: Facing the wind made it difficult to exhale, back to the wind made it difficult to get a breath in. Strictly speaking, it was physics, but it felt like drowning in an ocean of air. Purposive effort hardly worked at all, and years later when I saw news footage of people getting hit by police water cannons I thought of that storm on Mount Washington.

Supper on the Saturday of Jeremy and Derek's trip was a noisy meal in the observatory. There was the hammer of an 80-mph wind and cracking sounds from the building itself: the concrete and the embedded steel reinforcing rods contract at different rates. Ken Rancourt and Ralph Patterson were on duty and they were used to this, but now Ken suddenly looked intent; he'd heard a different, more rhythmic banging in the midst of the uproar. He and Ralph traced the sound to a door on the north side of the building: Someone was out there.

A few minutes later Jeremy Haas was inside. He was barely able to talk, but as Ralph checked for the most obvious signs of damage he asked Jeremy if he was alone. Jeremy indicated that he'd left his partner near the summit of Jefferson. The wind peaked at 103 that night and between midnight and 4:00 A.M. the temperature held steady at −40°.

Some newspaper reports described Jeremy's fierce traverse as "heroic." Others had worked out a different calculus of risk and they did not share that view. Prominent in the latter group are the ones who tried to rescue Derek Tinkham.

By 9:00 P.M. the observatory crew had called the valley to report the on-rushing emergency, and the message reached the Mountain Rescue Service. Joe Lentini answered, then he and co-leader Nick Yardley put the "A Team" on standby. The first decision had already been made: The combination of darkness and brutal conditions made a rescue attempt that night impossible. It's a difficult but accepted calculation; at a certain point, many lives cannot be risked in a try to save one. At 5:00 A.M., the team left for the base of Caps Ridge Trail, the shortest route up Jefferson.

Conditions were extraordinarily harsh as the eleven team members started up. "We looked," one thought, "like an advertisement for every high-tech equipment company you ever heard of." Even so, Joe Lentini was keeping a sharp eye out for signs of frostbite or falter among his crew. Caps Ridge takes its name from a line of three rocky outbursts heaping up above timberline like the bony spines on the back of some prehistoric monster. Summertime hikers have to hold on up here, and in winter it's immeasurably tougher: The caps are clad in ice, with wind-blown snow in the sheltered parts of the jagged skyline. There's dwarf spruce under the drifts and impossible to see, and when the climbers stepped in the wrong place they'd fall through up to their ribs.

Up past the last cap, Tiger Burns advised Joe Lentini that his feet were getting cold. Knowing that it would only get worse and that a disabled team member higher up would vastly increase their problems, he descended to a sheltered place to wait for the others to return. He was still above timberline, but he was ready.

Tiger's outfit was typical of the MRS team that day: He had many layers of specialized clothing under his weatherproof outer shell. He had insulated bib-pants and parka with a heat-reflective Mylar lining, a balaclava helmet, a pile-lined Gore-Tex hat under the hood, and a scarf and flaps snugging up the spaces around his face. He had polypropylene liner gloves, expedition-weight wool gloves, extra-heavy expedition mitts with overshells, and chemical heaters for hands and feet. In his pack, Tiger had two sets of back-ups for his gloves and mitts, two more hats, another scarf, extra chemical heat packs, and a bivy bag. Unlike most of the climbers, he was not wearing goggles. Instead, as his exhaled breath froze in his balaclava he pinched the woolen fabric into narrow slits over his eyes.

Tiger's big problem was his cocoa. He zipped himself inside the bivy bag, loosened his boots, set the chemical heaters to work on his feet, and reached for his Thermos. Hot as it was, though, and nestled under all the other insulating gear in his pack, the stopper had frozen tight.

Up above, the trail led onto an alpine zone of ice and rough broken rock, with the 1,000-foot summit pyramid of Jefferson rising above it. It was just here that the wind hit the MRS team, a blast so severe that they could communicate only by putting their heads right together and yelling. At 10:00 A.M., Al Comeau spotted a bit of color up near the peak of the mountain.

It was Derek's bivy bag. It was just below the summit and Derek was lying there half out of his sleeping bag. He was wearing a medium-weight parka and it was only partly zipped; his other clothes were barely sufficient for a good-weather winter climb, and his hands were up at his face as if trying to keep away the calamity that fell on him at dusk the day before. There were two packs with sleeping bags nearby, on top of an insulated sleeping pad. Troubling things had happened here, but there was no time for reflection now.

As the team started down, the wind hit them straight in the face. It was −32°, the wind was peaking in the high 80s, and they were barely keeping ahead of it in clothing like the outfit Rick Wilcox had on the top of Everest. In conditions like this, you don't go where you want to go, you go where the wind and terrain let you go, whether your feet and burden like it or not.

Suddenly Maury McKinney pulled up lame. He understood life in high places; in Nepal he'd turned back short of the summit in a winter attempt on 26,504-foot Annapurna. Here on Jefferson he broke through into a hole and the whole of his weight drove his heel down. At first he thought the Achilles tendon had torn, but a brief test showed that the damage was higher up in his calf. In this moment, the rescue party's situation became critical. This kind of injury worsens quickly and in these conditions they could neither leave him behind nor slow to his pace, so they'd have to carry him and leave Derek's body behind.

Then Andy Orsini's eyes froze shut. He and Maury had planned a climb that day, but when they saw the weather they decided to watch the NFL play-offs instead. As it turned out, they made a climb anyway. So Bob Parrot helped Andy cover up completely and Maury leaned against his other side, partly to guide him, partly to relieve his own bad leg. This battered troika made its way down through the ice and rock for several hundred yards until Maury was able to reach in through Andy's wrappings to rub his eyes and melt the ice.

Down below, Tiger Burns was still trying to get at his cocoa. He bashed the top against a rock to loosen it, but only dented the cup. He burrowed into his bivy bag for awhile, then reached out to bang on the Thermos again, but he only succeeded in tearing the handle off. The exercise did warm up his hands so he took off his gloves for a better grip but still no luck; it only made his hands cold again.

When the team reached him, they took their first rest in eight hours of continuous maximum effort. Several times they'd considered leaving the body and saving themselves, but then they thought of Derek's family and how they'd feel if their son was still up there, alone with the storm, and they kept going. Once in the woods, they talked amongst themselves about what had happened. "Bottom line," said Mike Pelchat, "I would never ditch a partner like that."

Later, there was time for reflection. Like many members of the recovery groups, Andy Orsini had instinctively shut out the human qualities of the job in order to get on with it. By Tuesday, this insulation had turned to anger. He had the newspaper account and read that, when asked if he had any regrets, Jeremy had said, "Yes, I wish I'd brought mittens instead of gloves." Andy was so appalled that he called the newspaper reporter to verify the remark. "It's something I have to live with," said Al Comeau, "seeing Derek there . . . He was a victim of Jeremy's state of mind and over-ambitiousness. That one really bothered me."

MONROE COUPER AND ERIK LATTEY
FEBRUARY 1994

That winter, Jim Dowd had also been bothered. He was caretaker of the Harvard cabin below Mount Washington's Huntington Ravine and about two miles up from the highway in Pinkham Notch, and it seemed as if practically every climber who came through said he'd read an article about ice climbing in Pinnacle Gully up in the ravine. It was in *Climbing* magazine and it was written by an eager but inexperienced teenager who'd gotten into trouble up there with his friend. The two boys thought the experience was kind of neat and people kept telling Jim they thought it was a great story.

Talk like this made Jim feel a little sick and he'd made a point not to read the article; when he was eleven years old, his father had died while climbing the next ridge. One of the reasons Jim was working up here was a sense that he'd like to give something back, and he didn't like to hear about people rushing into ill-advised risks.

While that issue of *Climbing* was current, Monroe Couper and Erik Lattey were planning their own climb in Huntington Ravine. They were friends in New Jersey, both had young families, and both were just getting started in winter climbing. Now they headed for New Hampshire and signed in at the AMC headquarters at 1:30 on Friday afternoon, February 25. The weather forecast for the next day was favorable: high temperatures in the teens, winds on the summit increasing to 40–60 mph. They wouldn't be going to the summit, so it looked good.

Huntington Ravine has always been place of risk. Monroe and Erik planned to climb Pinnacle Gully, which is just to the right of Odell's Gully, the site of Jessie Whitehead's troubles sixty-one years earlier. They left the Harvard cabin in good season, then they returned—they'd forgotten their climbing rope. Having retrieved their rope, Monroe and Erik started back up toward Pinnacle at about noon. The weather forecast, however, had been wrong; conditions higher up were deteriorating rapidly. Bill Aughton was the director of Search and Rescue at the AMC camp in Pinkham Notch and he was guiding a trip across the Presidentials that day. He was so struck by the unexpectedly bad weather that he took a picture looking ahead to Mount Washington, then turned his group around.

A climber at the bottom of Huntington Ravine spotted Monroe and Erik in upper Pinnacle Gully at 5:00 P.M. They were not moving well. Guides allow three hours for Pinnacle; Monroe and Erik had been up there for five. The usual turn-around time is 2:30 or 3:00, they were two and a half hours past that and still going up, toward the approaching night.

Going up in ice climbing must be understood conditionally: while one climber is moving, the other stays in a fixed position to tend the rope and belays, the safety margin. Thus, either Monroe or Erik had been almost motionless for half of their time in Pinnacle, absorbing the cold. The overnight lodgers at the Harvard cabin were settling in, tending to their gear and making their various preparations for supper, when someone noticed two packs in a corner which didn't belong to anyone there.

The top of Pinnacle eases over onto the Alpine Garden, well above timberline. This place is a summer delight, table-flat and almost a mile wide, and spread with tiny flowers, dense moss, and delicate sedges. One of the several unique plants that lives here has its growth cells at the base of its stalk instead of the tip, the better to withstand the brutal winter.

This was brutal winter, and as Monroe and Erik felt their way out of the top of Pinnacle, they found only wind-scoured ice and rock. Just above them on the summit, the wind averaged 90-mph between nine and eleven that evening, gusting to 108 at 9:50; by midnight, the temperature had fallen to −24°. A maximum rescue effort was being organized in the valley.

The Alpine Garden spreads just below the summit ridge of Mount Washington. In the fair weather of summer enthusiasts come from all over the world to study the tiny flowering plants that have found a way to survive there. Winter conditions are often beyond the endurance of the strongest person and many have died in the vicinity.

At 6:00 A.M., thirty-three climbers gathered at the AMC headquarters; the plan was to send teams up several climbing gullies of Huntington Ravine and also comb the adjacent area, the most likely places to find the missing pair.

The plan was quickly modified. The climbers were getting into their routes soon after 9:00 A.M., it was –16° at the observatory on the ridge above them, and the wind averaged over 100 mph from 7:00A.M. until noon with a peak gust of 127 at 9:45. Tiger Burns was working his way up Escape Gully with two partners and he suddenly found himself in midair, blown out like a heavily dressed pennant in the arctic wind, with only one elbow looped through a webbing strap to keep him from a very long fall. Nick Yardley and his partners were the only ones to get above timberline, and that only briefly—they had to crawl down.

After all the teams were back down on the wooded plateau near the Harvard cabin, it occurred to Jim Dowd that Monroe and Erik might have gotten into Raymond Cataract. It's a broad basin between Huntington Ravine and Tuckerman Ravine with a remarkably even contour, no steeper than a hiking trail, and funneling into an outlet nearby. Jim was thinking that Monroe and Erik might have made a snow cave in Raymond Cataract. They might still be there, probably unhappy, but safe.

Jim and Chad Lewis started up into the Cataract. Snow drifts in heavily here and it almost avalanched on them. Jim had a grim sort of chuckle: Al Dow had died in an avalanche near here during another winter search mission and there's a plaque honoring him on a rescue cache in Huntington Ravine. Jim was thinking that if this slope let go they could just add "d" to the name on the plaque to remember himself.

Their hopes lifted when they found boot tracks, but they turned out to be from Nick Yardley and his partner, descending. Other than that, there was only a fuel bottle and a pot lid, found in the floor of the ravine. They were on top of the snow, so they couldn't have been there long; they'd probably been blown loose from someone higher up. Jim and Chad made a last visual check up Pinnacle and saw nothing. Then they looked at each other and said, at almost the same moment, "They're still on the climb." Privately Jim thought, "Damn, we missed the boat. We were looking in the escape routes." He imagined the climbers thinking, "We need to get out of here and the direction we're going is up." First lessons in climbing teach people to climb, not escape. Monroe and Erik had kept pushing upward.

When Jim got back to the cabin that evening, there were the usual number of recreational climbers in for the night, but the usual banter was missing. "Everyone was looking at me with these big eyes, like, 'What happened to

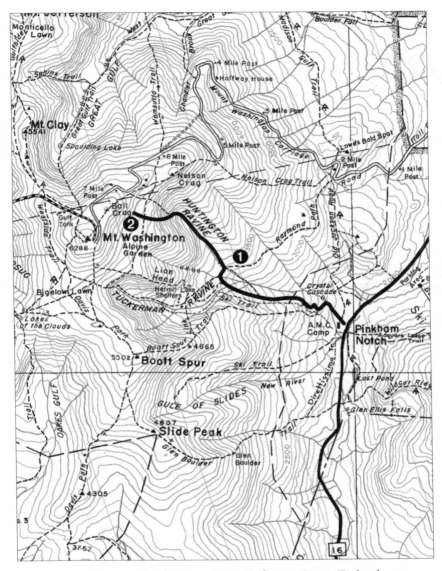

1. Monroe Couper and Erik Lattey went up Tuckerman Ravine Trail and across Huntington Ravine cut-off to spend the night in Harvard Cabin

2. Up Odell Gulley, they collapse and die on Alpine Garden

those guys?'" Jim had gone through their packs earlier to see if he could get an idea of what they had with them by seeing what they'd left behind. He'd also found two steaks, so now, after the long day of work trying to find the missing climbers, he cooked their steaks for his own supper.

Early Monday morning the teams started up again. The summit temperature was steady between −13° and −15° at 5:00 A.M. the wind peaked at 128 mph, just after 8:00 A.M. it touched 124. Ben Miller was with a group climbing Odell Gully. Ben had the longest association with Mount Washington: his father worked up there for thirty-nine years. Himself a climber of long experience, Ben knew the mountain and its habits as if it were his backyard.

Ben's group reached the intersection of Odell with Alpine Garden and found a cleavage plane—lying flat, Ben felt that if he put his head up, the wind would simply peel him off the snow. Working his way up over the crest, he saw others on the Garden fighting through the wind, their ropes bowed out into taut arcs. Rick Wilcox and Doug Madera went up the ridge above the right wall of the ravine. This place has no difficulties for a summer hiker, but when Rick wasn't totally braced against his crampons and ice axe the wind would send him sprawling along the ground. There was a 2,000-foot drop thirty feet away.

As soon as Al Comeau came over the crest of South Gully he saw someone there in the sun. As with Derek Tinkham, Al was the first one to reach the victim, but now he faced the moment all rescue climbers dread—it was someone he knew. Al recognized Monroe Couper, a climbing student he'd had the winter before, a musician of unusual talent and sensitivity, a person Al remembered with great affection. Not seeing Erik Lattey, Al went back down the top section of Pinnacle to see if he'd gotten stuck there.

A few minutes later, Brian Abrams saw a huddled knot of color in the lee of some rocks and, thinking it was another member of the rescue team, he made his way over through the fierce blast of weather and lay down close beside a man in a blue outfit; it's a mountaineer's way of getting a bit of shelter in extreme conditions above timberline. The man was leaning toward an open pack and his gloves were off; apparently he was getting something to eat. He didn't seem aware of Brian's presence, then the rescuer realized that the man providing his shelter was dead.

Al Comeau did not find any sign of Erik Lattey near the top of Pinnacle Gully and when he got back to the plateau he found Brian Abrams and some other members of the rescue team and they took stock of the situation. They realized that Monroe had died in the act of trying to make something hot for himself and his friend. Erik was nearby, lying face down in the rocks with his arms outstretched, heading toward Monroe. It looked as if he'd tried to find an escape route Saturday evening, then gone back for his partner.

This was a tough one. Members of the climbing community had little sympathy for Jeremy Haas, but Monroe and Erik had tried to do things right, they'd taken climbing lessons from the best in the business, and in their last moments they were trying to take care of each other.

The bodies were finally recovered on Tuesday. Then, after three days of almost continuous effort, the teams gathered for a debriefing down at AMC headquarters. An official from the Forest Service offered to arrange psychological counseling for anyone who felt the need, but there were no takers. The consensus was that they'd rather have the Forest Service arrange steaks and beer. This was, after all, volunteer work.

CHERYL WEINGARTEN
MAY 1994

Tuckerman Ravine is a sort of twin to Huntington Ravine, a left-hand punch into the side of Mount Washington by the same primordial giant that made Huntington with his right. The surrounding topography is a little different, though; it has the effect of an immense snow fence, and the drifts pile into Tuckerman all winter long. By spring, snow has banked up against the headwall 150 feet deep, and skiers come from all over America to hike up from the highway and test nerve and technique on some of the steepest skiing anywhere on the planet. "Going over the Lip," making the vertiginous plunge from the higher snowfields down into the bowl, is a major rite of passage. In fact, going up over The Lip can be as scary as most people would want. It's not like climbing a slope in any familiar sense—it's more like climbing a thousand-foot ladder. There's always a line of steps kicked into the snow at the right side of the headwall, and as the slope steepens the surface of the snow gets closer and closer to the front of the bended knees. Darwin is in charge of safety here; skiers usually stop climbing up at the point dictated by thoughts of skiing down.

Darwin was not with me the first time I skied down over the Lip. I'd climbed an alternate route to take the mail to the crew at the summit observatory; not only that, but fog came in on the way down. There are several major choices of route: Gulf of Slides and Raymond Cataract both end at the same place in the valley and are far more accommodating to nerve and technique. I planned to ski down with someone from the observatory, trusting him to navigate on my youthful and somewhat tremulous behalf.

Being above timberline, on snow, in fog, is like being inside a milk bottle: It's a whiteout with no visual references at all. At best you're lost; at worst you totter with vertigo and nausea. As we skied down, my increasing speed told me the slope was steepening, and even though years of hiking had taught me the terrain in mapmaker's detail, it was fair-weather mapmaking. I asked where we were and heard, "The Lip is right down there." In this case, the whiteout was my friend, and I made my rite of passage over the Lip mainly because I couldn't see well enough to be scared.

Not everyone skis, and a good spring day will also bring out hikers who enjoy the cushiony surface underfoot, the bright sun, and the spectacle. On May 1, 1994, Cheryl Weingarten and her friends Julie Parsons, Anna Shapiro, and Nick Nardi, arrived at the foot of the trail in Pinkham Notch and started up toward the ravine. They were all students at Tufts University near Boston and the plan had taken shape at a concert, and there was not very much experience in the group; Nick had the most, he'd climbed Mount Washington twice before and he'd done some other hikes in the White Mountains and some in the Alleghenies. This day they were wearing clothes suitable for an unthreatening spring day on Mount Washington, but they had no crampons or any other equipment that would help them on high-angle climbing.

Matthew Swartz and a friend were starting up, too. They were good skiers and well-versed in ravine days, and they'd come over from the University of Vermont. The next day Matthew posted a report on the Internet. It began, "Tuckerman's 5/1 We hiked thru some rain to get to HoJo's in 1 hour 15 minutes. Trail in decent shape, some snow etc but no creeks opening yet. Rain stopped at HoJo's and we went on, many people turned back. . . . Maybe 30–50 people in the bowl all day. We climbed the Lip and up into the snowfields, there was still quite a bit (of snow) up there. The connector over the Lip into the bowl was pretty solid with crevasses opening on both sides. Water is running pretty good over the rocks now. Saw two people lose it in the Connector and do endos over the falls and cartwheel over the crevasses all the way to the bottom of the bowl. They were extremely shaken and a bit bruised but very lucky to be alive. The Connector (the Lip) should be carefully navigated, unless it loosens up a bit." That is, the top of the headwall was not corn snow, it was frozen snow.

Nick Nardi and his three friends were right in Matthew Swartz's tracks coming up from Pinkham, then Anna Shapiro stayed in the ravine to ski and the others headed for the summit. The weather was not enjoyable; fog was right down on the ground and they could see only fifty or one hundred feet and, as Matthew Swartz noted, this is why so few skiers had decided to come up from Howard Johnson's. Nick and Cheryl and Julie kept going up the ladder of steps that skiers had kicked into the snow at the right side of the ravine.

Trouble was already with them, though; fog had come in, and they couldn't see the larger picture. Caution is largely determined by vision—out of sight, out of mind. They reached the summit and Nick signed the register at what he called "the mall," and then they started down the same way they'd come up.

Conditions were dreary. At 3:00 P.M. the summit weather observatory recorded fog with light to moderate rain and intermittent ice pellets in the air. Nevertheless, the three friends had fun sliding down in the soft snow of the upper, milder terrain. They were on my youthful track exactly, but they didn't have my guide; with no horizon and no shadows, slope and detail disappeared in a wash of gray. They paused near the signs marking a trail junction above the ravine and briefly debated which way to go. Nick had one idea, Cheryl and Julie had another. There wasn't much difference—a little more to the left or a little more to the right—and they decided to take the women's inclination.

As the season advances, the snowpack in Tuckerman Ravine turns to ice and behaves exactly like a glacier; it pulls away from the rocks on the headwall and crevasses open up in the surface, and the ice becomes slightly plastic and follows gravity downhill. Robert Underhill was a notable AMC activist and this glacial effect had always interested him, so late in the snow season of 1939 he surveyed a line straight across the floor of the ravine and set a line of stakes there. He surveyed the stakes again in July and found that in the twenty days of his experiment the center of the snowpack moved thirteen feet farther downslope than the edges, true glacial behavior.

As the springs days grow warmer a tremendous amount of snow melts above the ravine and runs out over a flat rock at one side of the Lip, then plunges down the headwall behind the icy snow that's pulling away from the rocky headwall.

Julie was in the lead as the three friends hopped and slid, then she and Cheryl dropped onto their backsides and began to slide down the slope feet first. The angle gets so steep so fast here that it passes beyond reason and suddenly Julie slid onto the beginning of the waterfall. With a lunge, she got hold of a bit of dwarf spruce and stopped herself. Then Cheryl slid past her and out of sight.

With extraordinary courage and presence of mind, Julie held onto her tiny bit of safety. Nick had not been sliding and he was thirty or forty feet higher up the slope when he heard her screaming. He got down to where he could see her and realized that she was unable to move, she was frozen with fear. He called down and tried to reassure her; he told her to give him one step and it was a long time before she was able to do that. Then he coaxed her again, he told her to give him another step, then another step. This way, Julie pushed and crawled her way back up the dizzying slope to where he was.

Neither of them knew where they were on the headwall and they didn't know where Cheryl was, only that she was farther down. Nick thought that if they went to their left, looking uphill, they could meet up with her by going "around the cliff," as he put it later. As they tried to collect their wits they heard voices off to one side. They called, made contact, and crossed the fog-shrouded slope toward the voices. They found skiers who said they were heading down themselves, and the skiers led the way through the fog.

Not really knowing where they were, Julie and Nick probably hadn't realized that the footstep ladder they'd come up was right beside them when Julie pulled herself off the ledge. It was right there, just a few steps away on the other side of the Lip. Though forbiddingly steep, it was still the easiest way down. The skiers they now joined were heading for the Chute, so scary, so vertiginous a run that many veteran ravine skiers have never attempted it and have no plans to do so. Incredibly, Julie and Nick got themselves down this drop of ice and rock and snow that many climbers would hesitate to attempt without full equipment.

They didn't find Cheryl when they got to the floor of the ravine, and they didn't know where she was. Cheryl had grown up as the kind of girl who was

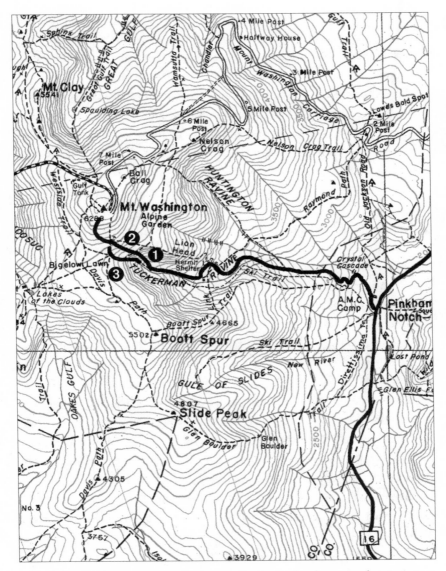

1. Cheryl Weingarten goes up Tuckerman Ravine Trail and up snow slope in ravine to summit
2. Slides over Lip into crevasse and on the headwall
3. Julie Parsons and Nick Nardi descend headwall by the Chute

ready for anything. She was bright and active and very popular, and she had an endless zest for life; she'd been studying in France and only recently she'd survived a head-on crash in Morocco. Knowing Cheryl's eager enthusiasms, her parents sometimes worried about her.

Now they got a call from the White Mountains. Brad Ray was the veteran forest service supervisor for Tuckerman Ravine and by Sunday evening he'd pieced together the sometimes contradictory details and realized what had happened: Cheryl had gone over the waterfall below the flat rock and been carried down behind the snowpack.

After Nick and Julie had made their way down The Chute, they'd gone to the Forest Service shelter and found Chris Joosen, who was posted there as the Forest Service technician, more popularly known as the snow ranger. He didn't remember seeing them earlier in the day and this struck him as unusual; he always tried to remember the faces of people who talked to him. There were only a few people in the ravine that day because of the weather, and he didn't remember seeing this party. It occurred to him that if he had, he would have advised them not to go on up into the ravine with the summer hiking gear they had. Now Nick Nardi told him that one of their friends was missing—she'd slid down the slope above the bowl and they couldn't find her.

Chris got as much information as he could from Nick and Julie, and he realized that they did not have a clear idea of where they'd been on the slope, only that Cheryl Weingarten had slid down out of sight. Brad Ray was the senior snow ranger in the ravine, a man with thirty years experience there, and he'd already gone down the trail to Pinkham and on to his home in Gorham. Chris called him and Brad directed him to begin a search-and-rescue mission with Lewis Baldwin, the other member of the crew at the AMC Hermit Lake Shelter.

The two of them started up toward the headwall, checking the holes and crevasses as they went, and it was almost dark by the time they had climbed up to the crevasse below the waterfall. They rigged their ropes there and Lewis belayed Chris over to the edge of the crevasse. The day had been warm and rainy and there was a tremendous volume of water coming down, so Chris was already soaked by the spray when he was still twenty feet from the edge. Even more troublesome, the roaring was so loud that he and Lewis could barely hear each other when they shouted. Chris shouted down into the crevasse and he got no response.

Then they climbed up above the waterfall and Lewis put Chris on belay again and he worked his way down toward the crevasse. Then he saw sliding marks in the icy snow and they looked as if they'd been made by a person sliding feet first on their backside. Still on belay, Chris worked his way down beside the tracks to about eight feet from the point where they disappeared over the edge into the waterfall. Their line would carry the person who made them straight into the edge of the crevasse.

They couldn't do anything more, so they went back down the headwall, checking other crevasses as they went. Back at the Forest Service shelter, they called Brad Ray again and talked the situation over. Brad told them that the volume of water was too large for any useful work, they'd have to wait until early morning, when the volume would be much smaller and someone with immersion gear could be lowered into the crevasse. Then Brad called the Weingartens and told them that the situation was very serious.

By now a call had also gone to Rick Wilcox in North Conway. He talked the situation over with other lead people in the rescue network and they agreed with Brad Ray's decision, they knew that by the time a group was in position to do anything up in the ravine it would be very late in the evening, extremely dangerous for the rescuers, and almost certainly too late for Cheryl Weingarten.

By 6:00 A.M. the next day, a combined team of Forest Service, Fish and Game, AMC crew, Mountain Rescue Service, and Androscoggin Valley Search and Rescue had gathered at Pinkham. They had a wetsuit and scuba equipment in addition to their more usual ropes and security devices, and when they reached the top of the headwall they found the situation they expected: the temperature on the upper slopes of Mount Washington had fallen to 17° overnight and the chill had slowed the melting and greatly reduced the volume of water. They rigged 300 feet of ropes and anchors, then Jeff Gray of Fish and Game put on immersion gear and was lowered into the crevasse. When he was about sixty feet down he found Cheryl Weingarten.

They brought her to the surface and carefully wrapped her in thermal barriers and secured her in a Stokes litter and belayed her down the headwall. Even though it was clear that she'd suffered terrible injuries and was partly frozen, they took the million-to-one chance and Mike Pelchat began cardio-vascular resuscitation with oxygen. They continued with this as they carried her out of the ravine, put her onto a snow tractor at the Forest Service shelter, and went on down to the highway. The combined rescue forces devoted 204 man hours in their attempt to help Cheryl and more than fifty radio and telephone calls had gone through the communication center at AMC headquarters, but when Dr. Sterns met them in the valley he determined that Cheryl's neck was broken and she was dead.

That waterfall forms every spring and a trace of it usually remains in summer, just to the left of the hiking trail as it rounds up over the top of the headwall. Habitues of the ravine call that place Schiller's Rock to remember Dr. Paul Schiller, a skier who died after sliding over the waterfall and into the crevasse forty-five years earlier to the month, week, day, and hour.

IN APRIL OF 1997, LEONARD WEINGARTEN FILED *WEINGARTEN v. United States of America*. He claimed damages for the wrongful death of his daughter and for the loss of her society and comfort.

There were sixteen charges in the first claim, among them that the "Forest Service by and through its employees was charged with the duty to preserve and protect the area of the White Mountain National Forest and the safety of persons lawfully on the property under its management." And "the defendant breached its duty to the plaintiff's decedent by failing to warn through posting of signs, orally, or in some other manner of inherent dangers on its property which (it) knew or should have known existed; in failing to post warning signs, barriers and/or fences around an eroded area of said property which was dangerous and which reasonably could be foreseen to be a site where injury or death could occur." And "The defendant's failure to warn of the existence of or to barricade the entrance to said chasm was a substantial factor in causing plaintiff's decedent to fall into said chasm." And "the foregoing resulted solely through the culpable conduct of defendant and with no negligence on the part of plaintiff's decedent contributing thereto."

The federal government based its defense on several grounds. One was found in the doctrine of sovereign immunity, a position that descends from the elder days of royal rule: "The United States, as sovereign, is immune from suit unless it has expressly consented to be sued." This led into questions of the court's subject matter jurisdiction.

The defense also argued matters of liability found in New Hampshire's recreational-use statutes. "An owner, occupant, or lessee of land, including the state or any political subdivision, who without charge permits any person to use land for recreational purposes or as a spectator of recreational activity, shall not be liable for personal injury or property damage in the absence of intentionally caused injury or damage." And "An owner, lessee or occupant of premises owes no duty of care to keep such premises safe for entry or use by others for hunting, fishing, trapping, camping, water sports, winter sports or OHRV—hiking, sightseeing, or removal of fuelwood, or to give any warning of hazardous conditions, uses of, structures, or activities on such premises to persons entering for such purposes."

More specific entries are found in the sixteen-page declaration of Brad Ray, who at that time had served as a snow ranger in the ravine for more than thirty-eight years. "As lead Snow Ranger, I have responsibility for managing Tuckerman Ravine consistent with the policy goals of the U.S. Forest Service. As Lead Snow Ranger, the Forest Service leaves me with authority to accomplish that responsibility by using my professional judgement and discretion. Nothing in the statutes, regulations, or Forest Service policies dictate particular actions that I must follow in the handling of hazards, warning the public of those hazards, or managing public safety issues in the Ravine. The *Forest Service Handbook* . . . provides more detailed guidance on things that I, or any other Forest Service official, should take into consideration in managing the Forest's trails. It does not set forth specific steps or actions that I am mandated to take. . . . Nothing in the Trail Management Handbook mandates specific actions that I, or any other Forest Service official, was required to take in the handling of a safety hazard such as the waterfall crevasse.

"In particular, the Forest Plan establishes that the Pinkham Notch Scenic Area is to be managed as a semi-primitive, non-motorized recreational opportunity spectrum class area—a predominantly natural environment—to be managed with minimum on-site controls. For such an area, although restrictions on the use of the area may exist, they are to be subtle restrictions.

"With regard to the Backcountry Undeveloped Areas, which would include Tuckerman Ravine, the management emphasis generally will be placed on protecting the natural resources first and the quality of the human experience second. Thus, in managing the Pinkham Notch Scenic Area as a semi-primitive, non-motorized area, we are to emphasize protection of resources in a manner such that this protection takes priority over the quality of the human experience in using the area.

"Thus, in managing Tuckerman Ravine, I and other Forest Service personnel are to balance issues of public safety associated with the use of the Ravine against the policy goals of protecting or maintaining the Ravine in its natural condition, maintaining a recreational opportunity that has minimum on-site controls, and making the Ravine available for multiple public uses.

"Over the years, and long before Ms. Weingarten slid into the crevasse, I have been concerned about the dangers presented by the waterfall cravasse when it opens up each Spring. For that reason, even prior to 1994, once the waterfall crevasse opens, the Snow Rangers have listed the presence of crevasses on the Avalanche Bulletin and have specifically noted its existence in other literature. But in addition to providing such warnings, prior to 1994, we considered whether we should take steps regarding the waterfall crevasse. In the end, however, for a variety of reasons, I concluded that the best approach to safeguarding the public in a manner consistent with the Forest Service's policy goal for the Pinkham Notch Scenic Area and Tuckerman Ravine has been to continue to provide warnings about the crevasse through the Avalanche Bulletin and other literature, as well as through personal contact with the public. These decisions were ones that, in accordance with Forest Service policies, were within my discretion and exercise of judgement.

"Among the options that we considered, and rejected, prior to Ms. Weingarten's death, was to provide some warning at the site of the waterfall by erecting crossed bamboo poles. Crossed bamboo poles are a well-established means of signaling trail closure or danger to skiers. However, I ultimately concluded that taking such a step would not be effective, would be dangerous, and would lead to a situation potentially contrary to the policy goals of the Forest Service. For example, at that time of the year, snow often melts in the Ravine at a rate of three to four feet every one to two days. Bamboo poles are eight feet long and usually are planted with at least four feet sticking out above the snow. With snow melting at the rate it does, the bamboo poles usually would fall down at least every other day. To maintain the warning, I would have to direct a team of two individuals, diverting them from other responsibilities, to reset the bamboo poles at least every other day. I determined that, in view of the limited benefit likely to be gained from the poles, I could not afford to divert those other snow rangers from their other tasks.

"Moreover, another consideration in my judgement was that it would be dangerous to send those rangers repeatedly to that location to reset the poles. Because of the snow melt and the river, one of the risks in that area is of undermined snow. As one team member belayed down to reset the poles, that individual would be at risk of falling through the snow and over the Headwall. I determined that I was unwilling to expose the rangers to this risk in view of the very limited benefit I expected from the poles. A significant factor in my decision against using poles to mark the crevasse was that I was convinced that it would not be effective. On those rare occasions that I have tried crossed bamboo poles in the area above the waterfall, I have seen individuals go right up to the poles, putting themselves at great risk because of the undermined snow. When questioned, it became clear that they did not know what crossed bamboo poles meant, instead indicating that they thought the poles marked the trail location.

"In addition, although we have considered erecting a fence above the waterfall, any fence would be directly contrary to the policy goal of maintaining the Ravine in its natural state. For example, during late April and early May, the snowpack above the waterfall is often 20 feet deep. For a fence to remain standing, especially given the pressures and movements of the snowpack, it would have to be drilled into rockface. That means, to be visible and effective, any fence would have to be at least 24 feet tall, so that it would stick out above the snow. Moreover, to withstand the pressures of the snowpack and the winds found at the top of the Ravine, the fence would have to be constructed of essentially girder-like material. In the Summer and Fall, that would mean that the Ravine would be marred with a 24-foot tall girder-like fence. Because the existence of such a structure would obviously contravene the Forest Service's stated policy goals for the Ravine, I rejected it.

"For similar reasons, I rejected the idea of placing signs above the waterfall, warning of the crevasse's presence below. For example, to be readable from a safe distance, a sign would have to be quite large, again marring the pristine landscape with its presence. Placing a reasonably sized sign itself at a safe distance from the edge of the Headwall would mean that it would be very easy to miss the sign in the large expanse above the Headwall. As a result, to be effective, I considered that we would have to place multiple signs around the perimeter of the Headwall-waterfall area. Again, I considered that this would be contrary to the goal of maintaining the Ravine in its natural condition.

"Finally, in considering any of these means of marking the crevasse site, I considered the fact that there are many other locations within the Ravine that are equally dangerous to users of the Ravine. I concluded that, if I marked or barricaded this particular location, I would start the Forest Service down the road of needing to mark or barricade those other dangerous locations as well. If the Forest Service marked or barricaded all those locations, Tuckerman Ravine would be a sea of signs and fences, giving its multiple dangers and risks. Because the policy goal for the Ravine is to maintain it in its natural state, I concluded against marking or barricading the crevasse.

"Another available option was to close the areas above the Headwall to any use once the crevasses open. In 1994, and now, there comes a time each Spring when I close the Lip and the Tuckerman Ravine Trail in the Lip area to all use. I use my professional judgement and discretion to determine when to close the Lip and that section of the Tuckerman Ravine Tail, taking into consideration the historic uses of the Ravine, the feasibility of enforcing the enclosure, and the policy goal of promoting self-reliance by users, providing recreational opportunities, and using minimal on-site controls. As a result, I do not close the Lip until, in my professional judgement, I conclude that a good skier or hiker can no longer safely negotiate the Lip, going up or down. At this time, the hiking trail, which traverses above and close to the Lip, is considered too dangerous, as a fall on the steep snow will result in a slide into rocks or crevasses. . . . Because, in my judgment, a good skier or hiker could still safely negotiate the Lip, I had not closed the Lip on May 1, 1994.

"As a result, to further the Forest Service's policy goal of minimizing man-made intrusions or changes to the natural environment of Tuckerman Ravine, I developed a general policy of not marking natural hazards that routinely exist or appeared annually, especially in the upper areas of the Ravine. Thus we do not mark the waterfall crevasse, protruding rocks, or high-water trail crossings. These hazards are obvious, and readily apparent to the users of the Ravine. In addition, in determining what, if anything, we should mark, we take into consideration the location of the hazards and, therefore, the users most likely to encounter them. Users who go over the Headwall into the Lip area tend to be more experienced individuals who try to be prepared and knowledgeable about the risks they will encounter."

Judge Paul Barbadoro heard the case in February 1999, and several points in his twenty-page ruling bear on the larger question of the public in the wilderness. One of the clauses chosen to support his motion mandates that the Forest Service, "conduct all management activities with full recognition of the appearance of the forest, realizing the importance to society of a natural landscape distinct from the man-made environment otherwise dominant in the East." The judge also noted that "the Forest Service is free to engage in a balancing of competing policy interests," and cited a ruling that the "Park Service is not obliged to put public safety concerns above the policy of preserving the historic accuracy of a landmark."

Noting Brad Ray's decision not to erect crossed poles because of the danger to his staff and the limited effectiveness and the risk to visitors who often approach the poles, the judge wrote that, "It is precisely this type of policy balancing that Congress intended to protect. That Plaintiff disagrees with the Forest Service's ultimate decision is of no import to the discretionary function analysis."

Citing a precedent in a Park Service judgment, the judge wrote that, "Faced with limited resources and unlimited natural hazards, the [National Park Service] must make public policy determination of which dangers are obvious and which dangers merit the special focus of a warning brochure or pamphlet. The Forest Service cannot possibly warn the public of every danger associated with skiing and hiking in the Ravine. To do so would not only cut into limited financial resources, but could also have a limited public safety benefit—too many warning brochures and pamphlets would invariably reduce the impact of the individual warnings to the public."

In concluding, Judge Barbadoro wrote, "I find that the defendant's decision not to barricade or post warnings of the waterfall crevasse was a discretionary act susceptible to policy judgements and, therefore, was the type of discretionary government action Congress intended to protect. Accordingly, I find that this court lacks jurisdiction to hear Plaintiff's claims as they are based on acts or omissions of the government which fall within the discretionary function exception to the Federal Tort Claims Act. Thus, I grant Defendant's motion to dismiss and dismiss Plaintiff's claims for lack of subject matter jurisdiction."

SARAH NICHOLSON
JUNE 1994

The last Mount Washington death of the 1994 winter was in June. As the sun climbs toward summer it loosens the ice that forms on the ledges lining the ravine at the level of Schiller's Rock. It's on just such lovely days that the greatest number of skiers come up, and long practice has endowed a citizen's early warning system: when the telltale crack is heard, the cry "ICE!" goes up. Sound carries well in this vast acoustic focus, everyone hears the call, and everyone looks up the slope.

On June 4, Sarah Nicholson looked up and saw a car-sized block of ice sliding and bounding down toward her. Gravity is also on the side of the skier, and a quick escape left or right downslope almost always avoids the danger of falling ice. But this block was breaking into fragments, and it wasn't clear which way led most quickly to safety. It's a familiar sidewalk dilemma: step left or right to avoid the collision? Sarah's moment of hesitation broke the heart of her friends, and brought the list of mortality on the Presidential Range to 115.

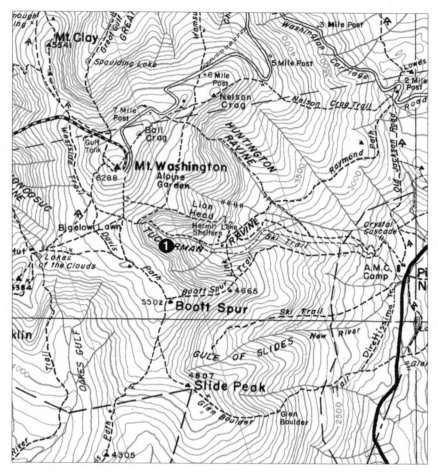

1. Sarah Nicholson was killed by falling ice on the south side of Tuckerman Ravine

Afterword

From the first day of this book's life ten years ago, people have been asking if I ever encountered my own perils on the Presidential Range. In general, my hikes were not marked by misadventure, because I knew what the sky looked like when bad weather was on the way, and there was no hiking on those days. But that is not the whole story.

I'd always known about these mountains because when the summer gathering of cousins played on the lawn of our house in Jackson in the 1930s and 1940s, we'd look up and see Mount Washington filling the northern horizon. On rainy days we stayed indoors and studied the big black photo albums that showed our forebears making heroic hikes on those heights. We knew the stories those pictures told.

Later on, my father took me ten miles up the road to the headquarters of the Appalachian Mountain Club in Pinkham Notch and showed me the big plaster model of the range with all the trails marked on it. He'd show me the list of people who lost their lives up there and we'd find the places on the model where they came to grief. Now I think that those days must have been the real beginning of this book.

My older brother, John, worked at Madison Spring Hut on the Presidential Range in the summers of 1943 and 1944, and I followed in his footsteps and worked at Madison in the summers of 1950 and 1951. We did what we had to do regardless of the weather, and when I returned a year later for a social event I learned that a dead person feels different than other people do, as I had to recover the body of a man who had succumbed to the harsh conditions above Tuckerman Ravine. There was also a day in the fall of 1950 when real danger was just outside the windows.

When I was 17 and a student at Deerfield Academy in Massachusetts, my brother John had taken a job in the weather observatory on the summit of

Mount Washington. Thanksgiving was a holiday of particular importance because, by an unlikely but verifiable coincidence, both sides of my family had been at the first Thanksgiving held by the settlers of the Plymouth Bay Colony. So, by a sort of double imperative, it seemed sensible to hike up to the summit and have the festive dinner with my brother and the crew of the observatory.

I took the train to Gorham and a member of the crew at the AMC headquarters in Pinkham Notch picked me up. The next morning I set out for the summit.

I was equipped with my maximum winter gear. My boots were what all the AMC hutmen used, a pair of single-layer work boots whose original soles were replaced with triple-layer leather. We would hammer in hobnails in patterns of highly-evolved complexity. In addition to those boots, I wore Levis over red Duofold long underwear, a cotton work shirt, a woolen sweater my mother knit for me, and an army surplus 10th Mountain Division parka with a fur-trimmed hood. Feeling ready, I set out on the Tuckerman Ravine trail with Bill Hastings.

Bill also had worked summers in the AMC huts. He was two or three years older and massive, and he was going up to start a job in the observatory. There had been weather observers on the summit since well back in the 19th century. The current observatory dated to 1932 and was a stout wooden structure that was bolted into bedrock. Beyond that, it was not much different from any other place for a small group doing a specialized line of work. The building included a bunkroom, a bathroom, a kitchen, a living room, an instrument room, and an unadorned room that summer visitors could use for a variety of purposes, from resting with other hikers to placing a bandage over a blister.

To keep the interior warm, the observatory had a furnace in the cellar. A certain type of seaweed was packed into the walls, a provision that had been learned from fishermen on the coast of Maine who knew that the small air sacs in the seaweed would provide insulation for their dockside shanties.

On November 26, 1950, the observatory sheltered a crew of Dick Learned, Bill Hastings, Willy Harris, and my brother John. Crew member Gordon Miller was on his down-mountain days off. This Thanksgiving Day started with less hospitable conditions than those my forebears found at their seaside refuge. The observatory's 24-hour data sheet shows that the summit was in the clouds with a midnight temperature of 25 degrees and a southeast wind of 99 miles per hour, and rime ice was forming on the windward side of every outdoor surface. At 3 A.M. the temperature had gone up one degree and the wind had reached 120 mph. Thirty-five minutes later it hit 160.

I was still awake. The observatory had a good lounge and I'd been reading a book by one of the 19th-century observers who told of a day of high wind when the crew was wondering if their building would be blown apart. As a precaution, one of them wrapped himself in a mattress and stiffened the package by attaching crowbars to it.

The violent weather did not worry me. While the tempest outside was tearing at the building, I was sitting on an upholstered sofa in the well-heated lounge and watching television. The medium was not yet widespread and no one I knew at home had a set, but the antenna for this one was 6,288 feet above sea level and I marveled at the choice and quality of entertainment at the touch of my hand.

I also marveled at the contrast between the cozy inside and the ferocious outside that night. The storm was battering the small observatory building and the combination of warming temperature and increasing wind was causing pieces of ice to break off the radio transmitter tower just a few yards away and slam into the observatory. I didn't think I was in danger, because the walls of the observatory had withstood every previous storm and the thick plate glass windows were protected by heavy steel grating, but it was an unusual situation for me.

There was also an unusual effect inside the building. The observatory's plumbing vents opened to the southeast, which was the direction least likely to bring high winds that would blow back up the pipe. That made sense. Now, however, the wind was coming from the southeast, and this argued for caution when using the toilet.

The wind was also blowing up the drain for the kitchen sink. Willy Harris knew an opportunity when he saw one, so the next time there was a lull in the wind he poured a whole bottle of soap bubble mix down the drain and turned the hot water on full. The next gust produced an upward-bound torrent of bubbles that would have brought joy to the heart of the most jaded child who ever lived.

There was more serious work at hand. Ice was forming too fast for the de-icers that were protecting a set of instruments at the top of the observatory's tower. Bill went up the inside of the tower to knock off the worst of the ice. He'd take a full swing with a crowbar, but sometimes he would miss the ice. The wind was that strong even in the lulls.

I went up with him, wearing an experimental facemask that the observatory was testing. It was like a military gas mask except there was a round opening in front that was held by a latch and could be opened for eating or spitting. The makers had not anticipated weather like this. When I opened the latch and faced the wind it seemed as if the air rushing in would inflate me; when I turned around, the wind seemed to be pulling away so fast I wasn't sure I could draw a breath from it. I seemed to be drowning in an ocean of air.

The storm had moderated by the next day and I was due back at school in Massachusetts, so my brother and I started down the eight-mile auto road. It was meant for summertime vehicles and it was closed now, but the road was the most easily followed way down the mountain and recommended for times like this. My brother turned back to the summit at the halfway point where the road entered the woods, and two miles later I turned off on the trail that led two and a half miles to the Appalachian Mountain Club headquarters by the highway in Pinkham Notch.

Now I was worried. I realized that I could be in real and immediate peril for the first time in all my years of hiking on the Presidential Range. The fabric of my parka and its fur-trimmed hood had a color and texture that could be mistaken for the hide of a deer and it was hunting season. There were hunters all through the woods.

Since the season ended in a few days, I was worried that some hunter determined to go home with a trophy strapped to the fender of his car would shoot at any noise that might be a deer. From time to time I yelled "I AM NOT A DEER!" and that took me safely to the end of my Thanksgiving holiday.

To some it may seem odd that my greatest fear of danger in the mountains came from other people, especially the morning after such a terrible storm. But by that age I had learned how to take good care of myself in the wilderness. Researching this book made me even more grateful for the early exposure I had to people who knew how to climb mountains, and return, without misadventures.

Jackson, N.H.
June 2009

Acknowledgments to the First Edition

This book began in the mind of Mel Allen, the long-time features editor at *Yankee Magazine*. I'd written a number of pieces for Mel, all in the manner of pleasant reveries. Then he asked for an article on the terrible winter of 1994 on the Presidential Range. I wrote it and Mel said, "That's a good job of reporting." I understood that he was damning with faint praise. Then he said, "I want to hear voices, I want to hear your voice." I rewrote the piece and it ran in the February 1995 issue.

It drew a large and often touching response from the readers, and some rang unexpected bells. There was, for instance, the letter from Richard Moran, of Port Ludlow, Washington. He'd grown up in Whitefield, New Hampshire, and his father delivered dairy goods to the Tip-Top House, and sometimes young Richard rode up with him. Mr. Moran went on to tell about a winter episode when four hikers were trying to reach the summit by way of the cog railway track; the weather went against them and three of them died. The bodies were brought to an undertaker in Whitefield and the survivor married the nurse who attended him in the Whitefield hospital, thus launching the favorite story of the winter in that remote mountain town.

Mr. Moran said he remembered that vividly, but he wondered why it was never listed in the roster of fatalities on the Presidential Range. I wrote back and told him of childhood days when we'd go into the AMC building at Pinkham Notch and head straight for the death list posted on the wall. Father would stab the list with his finger and say, "There's something missing here—three fellows froze to death on the cog railway trestle. That must have been around nineteen-hundred and thirty." More than fifty years would pass before Mr. Moran confirmed my father's sense of history.

Darby Field's 1640 ascents of Mount Washington had always puzzled me; that was almost 200 years before an American would have thought to climb a mountain for exercise or enjoyment. This long-running riddle was solved by my friend Michael Callis, who is a ferocious researcher and found Mr. Field's curious connections while making his own studies of colonial deeds.

Most of this book was found in ancient texts. The library in Gorham, New Hampshire, has one of the very few collections of *Among the Clouds* known to exist and I'm most grateful to Ida Bagley, Valerie LaPointe, and Judy Blais for putting up with my interruptions; the cabinet holding the bound issues of the old summit newspaper is right behind their desk. The town libraries in Berlin and Jackson, the state library in Concord, and the Dartmouth College library in Hanover were valuable sources; other documents were found in the federal court records and the state supreme court library in Concord. The archives of the summit and valley stations of the Mount Washington Observatory were both abundant and essential, and I owe a very large debt to the staff members who abided my many interruptions and, especially, to Sean Doucette, the staff computer specialist who rescued many photographs from their faded old age.

I must also thank Howie Wemyss and Brian Bennett, managers of the Mount Washington auto road, for their kindness, Adelina Azevedo Axelrod for her research help in Providence, Rhode Island, and my brother John for his tales of life on the summit.

Living memories of the accidents began with Brad Washburn, man for all seasons and all ages on Mount Washington and a principal in the rescue of Jessie Whitehead in 1933. Sixty-six years later he was a tireless help to me and made many minute corrections to the text. Nancy Fielder and Hartie Beardsely and his sister Mary Fenn helped with the story of Jerome Pierce. Fred Stott was on the crew at Madison Spring Hut when Joe Caggiano died in 1938 and Fred is still doing yeoman service with the AMC. Paul Turner also contributed memories of that ill-fated hike.

Sam Goodhue provided details of the elder days on the Mount Washington Volunteer Ski Patrol, and my own inability to throw anything away preserved the stories Kibbe Glover gave me twenty years ago. He embodied an entire chapter in the long story of Tuckerman Ravine, he retired to live at Pinkham in his old age, and now he is sorely missed by everyone who knew him.

The account of Philip Longnecker and Jacques Parysko drew on the memories of Paul Doherty, George Hamilton, and Mack Beal. The story of the terrible night that took the life of MacDonald Barr could not have been told without the very generous help of Peter Crane, Emily Thayer Benson, Kari Geick, Lars Jorrens, Alexei Rubenstein, Stephanie Aranalas, and Yvonne and Tavis Barr. None of their memories were easy.

The original *Yankee Magazine* article appears with some additions as the last section in this book. It was written with the help of Rebecca Oreskes and Brad Ray of the Forest Service, Ralph Patterson of the observatory, Bill Aughten, Jim Dowd, Brian Abrams of Fish and Game, and Rick Wilcox, Nick Yardley, Joe Lentini, Maury McKinney, Mike Pelchat, Al Comeau, Tiger Burns, and Ben Miller of the local rescue teams.

Finally, I must thank Brooks Dodge for his memories of growing up at the AMC camp in Pinkham Notch, for the use of his irreplaceable collection of Joe Dodge's papers and photographs, and for no end of help in a variety of writing projects over the years.

Appendix

DEATHS ON MOUNT WASHINGTON
1849–2009

*Dates from the Mount Washington
Observatory*

October 19, 1849
1 Frederick Strickland, 29, Bridlington,
   England, died after losing his way in
   an early storm.

September 14, 1855
2 Lizzie Bourne, 23, Kennebunk,
   Maine, died of exhaustion and exposure in stormy weather.

August 7, 1856
3 Benjamin Chander, 75, Wilmington,
   Del., died of exhaustion and exposure near the summit.

October 4, 1869
4 J. M. Thompson, proprietor of the
   Glen House, drowned in the flooded
   Peabody River.

February 26, 1872
5 Pvt. William Stevens, U.S. Signal
   Service, died of natural causes on the
   summit

June 28, 1873
6 Pvt. William Sealey, U.S. Signal
   Service, died in Littleton July 2 of
   injuries received in a slideboard accident on the Cog Railway

September 3, 1874
7 Harry Hunter, 21, Pittsburgh, Pa.,
   died of exhaustion and exposure.
   His remains were found six years
   later.

July 3, 1880
8 Mrs. Ira Chichester, Allegan, Mich.,
   was killed when a coach overturned
   on the Carriage Road.

July 24, 1886
9 Sewall Faunce, 15, Dorchester, Mass.,
   was killed by the falling of a snow
   arch in Tuckerman Ravine.

August 24, 1890
10 Ewald Weiss, 24, Berlin, Germany,
    left the Summit House to walk to
    Mount Adams. He was never found.

June 30, 1900
11 William Curtis, 63, New York, N.Y.,
    died of exhaustion and exposure in a
    sudden storm near the Lakes of the
    Clouds Hut.

12 Allan Ormsby, 28, Brooklyn, N.Y.,
    hiking with Curtis, died 300 feet
    from the summit.

August 23, 1900
13 Alexander Cusick, employee of

the Cog Railway, was killed while descending on a slideboard.

September 18, 1912

14 John Keenan, 18, Charlestown, Mass., a surveyor, wandered off the cone of Mount Washington; he was never found.

August 5, 1919

15 Harry Clauson, 19, Boston, Mass., was killed descending the Cog Railway on an improvised slideboard.

16 Jack Lonigan, 21, Boston, Mass., killed with Clauson.

November 1927

17 A woodsman named Harriman drowned in Jefferson Brook while following his traplines.

April 1928

18 Elmer Lyman, Berlin, N.H., froze to death while attempting to walk through the unplowed Pinkham Notch Road.

December 1, 1928

19 Herbert Young, 18, Salem, Mo., died of exhaustion and exposure on the Ammonoosuc Ravine Trail.

July 20, 1929

20 Daniel Rossiter, Boston photographer, was killed when the renovated old engine Pepperpass was destroyed on the Cog Railway.

July 30, 1929

21 Oysten Kaldstad, Brooklyn, N.Y., was drowned in Dry River, Oakes Gulf, on a fishing trip.

September 18, 1931

22 Henry Bigelow, 19, Cambridge, Mass., killed by a falling stone while rock climbing in Huntington Ravine.

January 31, 1932

23 Ernest McAdams, 22, Stoneham, Mass., froze to death while making a winter ascent.

24 Joseph Chadwick, 22, Woburn, Mass., died with McAdams.

June 18, 1933

25 Simon Joseph, 19, Brookline, Mass., died of exhaustion and exposure near the Lakes of the Clouds Hut.

November 11, 1933

26 Rupert Marden, 21, Brookline, Mass., died of exhaustion and exposure in Tuckerman Ravine.

September 9, 1934

27 Jerome Pierce, 17, Springfield, Vt., drowned in Peabody River.

April 1, 1936

28 John Fowler, 19, New York, N.Y., died of injuries after a 900-foot slide down the east side of Mount Washington.

May 23, 1936

29 Grace Sturgess, 24, Williamstown, Mass., died of injuries from falling ice in Tuckerman Ravine.

July 4, 1937

30 Harry Wheeler, 55, Salem, Mass., died of a heart attack on the Cape Ridge Trail on Mount Jefferson.

August 24, 1938

31 Joseph Caggiano, 22, Astoria, N.Y., died of exhaustion and exposure on the Gulfside Trail near Madison Spring Hut.

June 9, 1940

32 Edwin McIntire, 19, Short Hills, N.J., was killed by a fall into a crevasse in Tuckerman Ravine.

October 13, 1941

33 Louis Haberland, 27, Roslindale, Mass., died from exhaustion and exposure on the Caps Ridge Trail on Mount Jefferson.

April 7, 1943

34 John Neal, Springfield, Mass., suffered a fatal injury while skiing the Little Headwall of Tuckerman Ravine.

May 31, 1948

35 Phyllis Wilbur, 16, Kingfield, Maine, was injured while skiing in Tuckerman Ravine; died on June 3.

May 1, 1949

36 Paul Schiller, Cambridge, Mass., died while skiing on the headwall of Tuckerman Ravine.

February 2, 1952

37 Tor Staver was injured in a skiing accident on the Sherburne Trail; died in Boston on February 5 of a fractured skull.

August 23, 1952

38 Raymond Davis, 50, Sharon, Mass., died of exposure after collapsing above the headwall of Tuckerman Ravine, from a heart condition.

January 31, 1954

39 Phillip Longnecker, 25, Toledo, Ohio, was buried in an avalanche during a Tuckerman Ravine camping trip.

40 Jacques Parysko, 23, Cambridge, Mass., died with Longnecker.

February 19, 1956

41 A. Aaron Leve, 28, Boston, Mass., was killed by avalanche in Tuckerman Ravine.

June 7, 1956

42 Thomas Flint, 21, Concord, Mass., was killed from a fall and exposure on Mount Madison.

September 1, 1956

43 John Ochab, 27, Newark, N.J., died from a fall on Mount Clay.

May 17, 1958

44 William Brigham, 28, Montreal, Canada, was killed by icefall in Tuckerman Ravine.

July 19, 1958

45 Paul Zanet, 24, Dorchester, Mass., died of exposure on Crawford Path.

46 Judy March, 17, Dorchester, Mass., died with Zanet.

August 22, 1959

47 Anthony Amico, 44, Springfield, Mass., died of a heart attack near the top of Tuckerman Ravine.

June 2, 1962

48 Armand Falardeau, 42, Danielson, Conn., died of exposure near the summit of Mount Clay.

September 12, 1962
49 Alfred Dickinson, 67, Melrose, Mass.,
died of exposure near the summit of
Nelson Crag.

April 4, 1964
50 Hugo Stadtmueller, 28, Cambridge,
Mass. Killed in an avalanche while
climbing in Huntington Ravine.

51 John Griffin, 39, Hanover, Mass., died
with Stadtmueller.

May 3, 1964
52 Remi Bourdages, 38, Spencer, Mass.,
suffered a heart attack in Tuckerman
Ravine.

March 14, 1965
53 Daniel Doody, 31, North Branford,
Conn., killed in a fall in Huntington
Ravine.

54 Craig Merrihue, 31, Cambridge,
Mass., killed with Doody.

September 6, 1967
The following people died in an
accident on the Cog Railway:

55 Eric Davies, 7, Hampton, N.H.

56 Mary Frank, 38, Warren, Mich.

57 Monica Gross, 2, Brookline, Mass.

58 Shirley Zorzy, 22, Lynn, Mass.

59 Beverly Richmond, 15, Putnam, Conn.

60 Kent Woodard, 9, New London, N.H.

61 Charles Usher, 55, Dover, N.H.

62 Mrs. Charles Usher, 56, Dover, N.H.

January 26, 1969
63 Scott Stevens, 19, Cucamonga, Calif.,
killed in a climbing accident in Yale
Gully, Huntington Ravine.

64 Robert Ellenberg, 19, New York, N.Y.,
died with Stevens and Charles Yoder.

65 Charles Yoder, 24, Hartford, Wisc.,
died with Stevens and Ellenberg.

February 9, 1969
66 Mark Larner, 16, Albany, N.Y., died of
injuries sustained in a slide on Mount
Adams.

Summer 1969
67 Albert R. Tenney, 62, died of a heart
attack on the Crawford Path between
Mount Webster and Mount Jackson.

October 12, 1969
68 Richard Fitzgerald, 26, Framingham,
Mass., died of head injuries sustained
in Huntington Ravine fall.

November 29, 1969
69 Paul Ross, 26, South Portland,
Maine, died in a light-plane crash on
the southwest slope of Boott Spur.

70 Kenneth Ward, 20, Augusta, Maine,
died with Ross and Cliff Phillips.

71 Cliff Phillips, 25, Island Pond, Vt.,
died with Ross and Ward.

March 21, 1971
72 Irene Hennessey, 47, died in a
light-plane crash above Huntington
Ravine.

73 Thomas Hennessey, 54, died in the same crash.

April 24, 1971
74 Barbara Palmer, 46, West Acton, Mass., died of exposure near the Cog Railway base station.

August 28, 1971
75 Betsy Roberts, 16, Newton, Mass., drowned in the Dry River.

October 1971
76 Geoff Bowdoin, Wayland, Mass., drowned in the Dry River.

May 17, 1972
77 Christopher Coyne, 21, Greenwich, Conn., died in a fall in Tuckerman Ravine.

September 23, 1972
78 Richard Thaler, 49, Brookline, Mass., succumbed to a heart attack while hiking Mount Adams.

April 21, 1973
79 Peter Winn, 16, Bedford, N.H., died of head injuries while skiing in Tuckerman Ravine.

August 22, 1974
80 Vernon Titcomb, 56, Santa Fe, Calif., died in a plane crash above Gray Knob during a thunderstorm.

81 Jean Titcomb, 53, died in the same crash.

December 24, 1974
82 Karl Brushaber, 37, Ann Arbor, Mich., died of a skull fracture in Tuckerman Ravine.

October 23, 1975
83 Clayton Rock, 80, Massachusetts, died of a heart attack near the Lakes of the Clouds Hut.

March 26, 1976
84 Margaret Cassidy, 24, Wolfeboro, N.H., died from injuries suffered in a fall in Huntington Ravine.

May 8, 1976
85 Scott Whinnery, 25, Speigeltown, N.Y., died of injuries sustained in a fall in Hillman's Highway.

July 12, 1976
86 Robert Evans, 22, Kalamazoo, Mich., died of injuries sustained in a fall in Tuckerman Ravine.

February 14, 1979
87 David Shoemaker, 21, Lexington, Mass., died of exposure after a fall in Huntington Ravine.

88 Paul Flanigan, 26, Melrose, Mass., died of injuries after falling with Shoemaker.

August 21, 1980
89 Patrick Kelley, 24, Hartford, Conn., died in a fall in Tuckerman Ravine.

October 12, 1980
90 Charles LaBonte, 16, Newbury, Mass., died after a fall into a brook near the Ammonoosuc Trail.

October 13, 1980
91 James Dowd, 43, Boston, Mass., died of a heart attack on the Tuckerman Ravine Trail.

December 31, 1980
92 Peter Friedman, 18, Thomaston,
Conn., died while ice climbing in
Huntington Ravine.

August 8, 1981
93 Myles Coleman, 73, Wellsville, N.Y.,
died of a stroke on the summit of
Mount Washington.

January 25, 1982
94 Albert Dow, 29, Tuftonboro, N.H.,
died in an avalanche while searching
for two lost climbers.

March 28, 1982
95 Kathy Hamann, 25, Sandy Hook,
Conn., died of head injuries in a
fall while climbing in Tuckerman
Ravine.

May 25, 1982
96 John Fox, 47, Shelburne, Vt., died of
a stroke in Tuckerman Ravine.

January 1, 1983
97 Edwin Aalbue, 21, Westbury, N.Y.,
died after a fall in Huntington
Ravine.

March 24, 1983
98 Kenneth Hokenson, 23, Scotia, N.Y.,
died after a fall down the icy cone of
Mount Washington.

March 27, 1983
99 Mark Brockman, 19, Boston,
Mass., died after a fall on Mount
Washington.

July 30, 1984
100 Paul Silva, 22, Cambridge, Mass.,
died in an auto crash at the base of
the Mount Washington road.

August 22, 1984
101 Ernst Heinsoth, 88, Burlington Vt.,
succumbed to a heart attack on the
summit of Mount Washington.

July 21, 1985
102 Marjorie E. Frank, 25, Randolph,
Mass., committed suicide by asphyxi-
ation near the Valley Way Trail to
Mount Madison. Her remains were
found nine years later.

March 15, 1986
103 Basil Goodridge, 56, Burlington, Vt.,
died of a heart attack on the Tuckerman Ravine Trail.

April 5, 1986
104 Robert Jones, 53, Bridgton, Maine,
died of a heart attack on the Tuckerman Ravine Trail.

August 24, 1986
105 MacDonald Barr, 52, Brookline,
Mass., succumbed to hypothermia
in a summer snowstorm on Mount
Madison.

June 30, 1990
106 Edwin Costa, 40, Manchester, N.H.,
died while skiing in Great Gulf.

October 2, 1990
107 Jimmy Jones, 34, Texas, died in a
plane crash.

108 Russell Diedrick, 24, died in the
same crash.

109 Stewart Eames, 27, died in the same
crash.

February 24, 1991
110 Thomas Smith, 41, Montpelier, Vt.,

died while ice climbing in Huntington Ravine.

January 27, 1992
111 Louis Nichols, 47, Rochester, N.H., died of hypothermia on Cog Railway Trestle.

August 12, 1992
112 George Remini, 65, Efland, N.C., died of a heart attack in the Alpine Garden.

January 15, 1994
113 Derek Tinkham, 20, Sunderstown, R.I., died of hypothermia on the summit of Mount Jefferson.

February 26, 1994
114 Monroe Couper, 27, New Jersey, died of hypothermia while ice climbing on Huntington Ravine.

115 Erick Lattery, 40, New Jersey, died with Couper.

May 1, 1994
116 Cheryl Weingarten, 22, Somerville, Mass., was killed by a fall into a crevasse in Tuckerman Ravine.

June 4, 1994
117 Sarah Nicholson, 25, Portland, Maine, died of injuries from falling ice in Tuckerman Ravine.

October 8, 1994
118 Ronald Hastings, 63, Grantham, N.H., died of a heart attack on the summit of Mount Washington.

March 28, 1995
119 Chris Schneider, 32, Pittsfield, Vt., fell while skiing in Hillman's Highway, off Tuckerman Ravine.

January 5, 1996
120 Alexandre Cassan, 19, Becancour, Quebec, died in an avalanche on Lion's Head.

February 3, 1996
121 Donald Cote, 48, Haverhill, Mass., died after a fall on Lion's Head Trail while hiking.

February 25, 1996
122 Nicholas Halpern, 50, Lincoln, Mass., died of hypothermia while hiking near Mount Pleasant Brook on Mount Eisenhower.

March 2, 1996
123 Robert Vandel, 50, Vienna, Maine, died in a fall while climbing in Pinnacle Gully, Huntington Ravine.

March 24, 1996
124 Todd Crumbaker, 35, Billerica, Mass., died in an avalanche on the Gulf of Slides.

125 John Wald, 35, Cambridge, Mass., died in the same avalanche.

September 27, 1997
126 Steve Carmody, 29, Danbury, Conn., died in a fall while hiking on the Tuckerman Ravine Trail.

May 29, 1999
127 John Gringas, 44, Meriden, Conn., died of natural causes.

October 30, 1999
128 Douglas Thompson, 66, Hanover, N.H., died after suffering a heart attack near the summit of Mount Madison.

February 20, 2000
129 David McPhedran, 42, Kents Hill, Maine, died in an avalanche on the Gulf of Slides.

February 18, 2001
130 Ned Green, 26, North Conway, N.H., died in a fall after an ice dam in Huntington Ravine gave way.

June 3, 2001
131 Hillary Manion, 22, Ottawa, Canada, died in a fall while skiing in Tuckerman Ravine.

September 11, 2002
132 Peter Busher, 71, Chester Gap, Va., died of hypothermia near Madison Spring Hut.

September 29, 2002
133 William Callahan, 57, Meansville, Ga., died of natural causes.

November 29, 2002
134 Thomas Burke, 46, West Springfield, N.H., died in an avalanche in Tuckerman Ravine.

135 Scott Sandburg, 32, Arlington, Mass., died in the same avalanche.

January 27, 2004
136 Jason Gaumond, 28, Southbridge, Mass., died in a fall in Huntington Ravine.

March 7, 2004
137 Rob Douglas, 39, Vershire, Vt., died in a fall while skiing on Mount Clay.

August 4, 2006
138 Jean Moreau, 50, Becancour, Canada, died after suffering a heart attack near Tuckerman Ravine.

September 9, 2007
139 Kevin Race, 46, Woolwich, Maine, last seen near Hermit Lake, his body was never found.

January 18, 2008
140 Peter Roux, Bartlett, Tenn., died in an avalanche in Huntington Ravine.

Image Credits

CHAPTER NINE

Jessie Whitehead. Courtesy of George Cleveland, photo by Jean Smith.

Injured woman. Dodge family collection.

Injured hiker. AMC Library and Archives.

The Stokes litter. AMC Library and Archives.

CHAPTER TEN

Simon Joseph. AMC Library and Archives.

Lakes of the Clouds Hut. Nicholas Howe.

Patch of grass. Nicholas Howe.

CHAPTER ELEVEN

Great Gulf Shelter. Guy Shorey photo, Mount Washington Observatory collection.

CHAPTER TWELVE

Fog. AMC Library and Archives.

CHAPTER FOURTEEN

Weasel. Dodge family collection.

Sno-Cat. Mount Washington Observatory collection.

CHAPTER FIFTEEN

Pinkham Notch Visitors Center. AMC Library and Archives.

Polly Longnecker. George Hamilton collection.

CHAPTER SIXTEEN

Dwarf spruce above Madison Spring Hut. Dodge family collection.

Madison Spring Hut, 1890. AMC Library and Archives.

Madison Spring Hut, 1987. AMC Library and Archives.

CHAPTER SEVENTEEN

All-volunteer Mountain Rescue Service. David Stone photograph.

Alpine Garden. David Stone photograph.

About the Author

Nicholas Howe's family first went to the White Mountains as "summer people" in the mid-1880s. As a youth he spent long summers in the mountains and later worked for the Appalachian Mountain Club for four years, serving mainly on the crew at Madison Spring Hut on the Presidential Range and as a muleskinner. After graduating from college he moved to Jackson, New Hampshire, where he lived for many years.

A journalist since 1977, Nick spent twenty years as a contributing editor and feature writer for *Skiing Magazine*. He was a feature writer for *Yankee Magazine* since 1983, and his 1995 feature "Fatal Attraction" was a runner-up for a National Magazine Award. His work also appeared in *The Old Farmer's Almanac*, *Backpacker Magazine*, *Outside*, and several anthologies.

Nick began playing jigs and reels for traditional dancing in 1961 and he continued to hike in the White Mountains until his death in 2019.

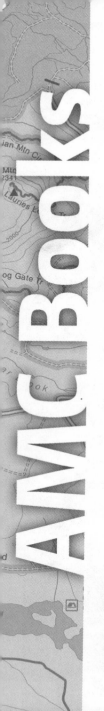